Praise for Whitley Strieber and

THE LAST VAMPIRE

"Whitley Strieber has done more than recapture the magic that made him a modern master of horror literature—he has surpassed himself. This is a wonderfully imaginative book, one that defies the reader to put it down."

—Peter Straub

"With a sensual ascent to an erotic crescendo, this vigorous sequel restores the vampire's power and mystique. Strieber's luxuriously soulless realm of the undead is disturbingly plausible."

—Katherine Ramsland

"Bloodkisses *supreme*. A deliriously meaty cultural anthropology, sickening and delicious."

—*Kirkus Reviews* (starred review)

"Offers a tour de force of mythmaking and emotionally intense action. . . . There's much here to admire, not least Strieber's expert modulation of tone and dialogue."

—*Publishers Weekly*

THE HUNGER

"Vivid, skillfully written."

—*The Washington Post*

"Fast paced . . . intriguing."

—*Publishers Weekly*

"Read this one with all the lights on."

—*Hudson Sun* (MA)

Also by Whitley Strieber

FICTION

The Forbidden Zone
Unholy Fire
Billy
Majestic
Catmagic
The Wild
Nature's End
Warday
Wolf of Shadows
The Night Church
Black Magic
The Hunger
The Wolfen

SHORT STORIES (PRIVATE PUBLICATION)

Evenings with Demons: Stories from Thirty Years

NONFICTION

Confirmation
The Secret School
Breakthrough
The Communion Letters
Transformation
Communion
The Coming Global Superstorm

The Last Vampire

Whitley Strieber

POCKET STAR BOOKS

New York London Toronto Sydney Singapore

A Pocket Star Book published by
POCKET BOOKS, a division of Simon & Schuster, Inc.
1230 Avenue of the Americas, New York, NY 10020

ISBN: 0-7434-1721-6

First Pocket Books paperback printing October 2002

10 9 8 7 6 5 4 3 2 1

POCKET STAR BOOKS and colophon are registered trademarks
of Simon & Schuster, Inc.

For information regarding special discounts for bulk purchases,
please contact Simon & Schuster Special Sales at 1-800-456-6798 or
business@simonandschuster.com

Cover art by Tom Hallman

Printed in the U.S.A.

To Michael Talbot,
of sacred memory,
author of
The Delicate Dependency and
The Holographic Universe

Acknowledgments

I would like to acknowledge the help of my editor, Mitchell Ivers; my agent, Sandra Martin; and my wife, Anne Strieber; all of whom have made essential contributions to the creation of this book.

And what rough beast, its hour come round at last,
Slouches toward Bethlehem to be born?

—*The Second Coming*, William Butler Yeats

"I am part of the justice of the earth."

—Miriam Blaylock, *The Hunger*

centuries, their lives had become. They had once bea

ONE

The Conclave

Everyone knew the sins of Miriam Blaylock.

Her crime, and it was an unforgivable one, was to enjoy human beings as friends and lovers, rather than to simply exploit them. She could kiss them and find it sweet, have sex with them and afterward sleep like a contented tiger. To her own kind, this was perversion, like a man with a sheep.

The fact that this prejudice was nonsense did not make what she was doing now any easier. She pressed herself back against the seat of the pedicab, instinctively keeping her face hidden, not only from man, but from her own kind. The *samlor* moved swiftly down the wet street, spattering through puddles left by the last storm. From the shadows of the passenger compartment, she watched a concealing fog rising from the moat that surrounded the ancient Thai city of Chiang Mai.

How could she ever do this impossible thing? How could she ever face her own kind?

Some theorized that she must have human blood in her family. The idea that there could be interbreeding was absurd, of course—nothing but an old husband's tale. She despised the narrowness of her kind, hated what, in recent centuries, their lives had become. They had once been princes, but now they lived behind walls, kept to the shadows, appeared in the human world only to hunt. They had opted out of man's technological society. They knew human breeding, but human technology was simply too intimidating for them.

Miriam owned a thriving nightclub in New York and had bookkeepers and assistants and bartenders, all humans. She had computers to run her accounts. She could access her stock portfolios using her PalmPilot, and she made money on the markets, plenty of it. She had a cell phone and GPS in her car. *They* didn't even have cars. Once the buggy no longer bounced along behind the horse, they had simply stopped riding. The same with sails. When ships lost their sails, her kind stopped traveling the world. And airplanes—well, some of them probably weren't yet aware that they existed.

The other rulers of the world were now just shadows hiding in dens, their numbers slowly declining due to accidents. They called themselves the Keepers, but what did that mean nowadays? Gone was the time when they were the secret masters of humankind, keeping man as man keeps cattle.

Truth be told, the Keepers were in general decline, but they were far too proud to realize it. Conclaves were held every hundred years, and at the last ones Miriam had seen a change—Keepers she had known a thousand years had followed her mother and father into death. Nobody had brought a child, nobody had courted.

Despite their failure, Miriam valued her kind. She valued herself. The Keepers were essential to the justice and meaning of the world. That was why she had come here, why she had tempted the humiliation and even the possible danger involved: she wanted to continue her species. Miriam wanted a baby.

The last of the four eggs that nature gave a Keeper woman would soon leave her body unless she found a man to fertilize it. For all that she had—riches, honor, power, and beauty—her essential meaning was unfulfilled without a baby. She was here for her last-chance child.

She gazed across the gleaming back of the *samlor* driver at the busy night streets of the bustling little city. How the world was changing. She had chosen a *samlor* out of love for the past, which she most certainly shared with the rest of her kind. She remembered Chiang Mai as a small community of wooden houses with *theps* carved on the pediments of their soaring, peaked roofs, and golden temple spires rising above lush stands of trees. Now, the narrow old streets resounded with the shrill clatter of *tuk-tuks*, which were so rapidly replacing the pedal-driven *samlor*. The traffic wasn't quite yet the hell on earth of Bangkok, but it was certainly going in that direction.

She longed to be home, in her beautiful house, surrounded by her beloved people, faithful Sarah and sweet young Leonore, just now learning her ways.

Just like the black, miserable dens of the other Keepers, her house was full of beautiful things. But hers were treasures of the heart, not the jade and silver and gold pieces her peers collected with total indifference, selling them later just because they'd become "antiques" among the humans. They didn't enjoy their priceless jade Buddhas or their Rembrandt drawings or their Egyptian gold. They just used them. She had a gold Buddha a thousand years old, before which she meditated, and twin Rembrandts of herself and her beloved mother. He had captured the sure gleam of their essence, she thought. She gazed often at her mother's wide, almost innocent eyes, at the subtle humor in her lips.

Over the millennia, Miriam had lost both parents and her husband. Her keepsakes of them were at the center of her life.

Rembrandt had known that there was something unusual about the two women who had commissioned him, a sense of independence and self-possession that human women in those days did not have. He had captured it in the proud, yet easy stance of the figures he had drawn, humming to himself as he made tiny pen strokes and smoked a long clay pipe. He had kissed Miriam's hand and said, "You are cold . . . so cold."

Not only did she enjoy human beings, she took pleasure in human things—painting and sculpture, writing and music. She had been an opera buff from the beginning of the genre. She had been at the opening night of a dozen great operas, had been transported by everyone from Adelina Patti to Maria Callas to Kiri Te Kanawa. She remembered the haunting voices of the *castrati* echoing in the palaces of the Old World.

The other Keepers looked upon humans as animals. Miriam thought that they had souls, that you could feel something leaving their bodies just as they died. It happened while you were all curled up around them, while you were comfortably absorbing their life. A sort of electric charge would seem to come out of them. Only after that would their eyes be totally empty.

They said it was the nervous system shorting out because of the fluid loss. Miriam hoped so. But what if the reality was that men had the souls, not us? If we were the brilliant animals, they the dim angels? That would be an irony, that an animal had created an angel.

When she meditated before her Buddha, she asked these questions: Why do we live so long? Is it because we have been denied a soul? If so, could I trade? And why, O God, if you are there, why are we cold . . . so cold?

The rest of her kind lived to eat. She ate to live. She spent heavily, just as her family always had. She consumed money without thought, like so much candy or caviar. Her club, the Veils, was the most exclusive in New York. In a strong month, and most of its months were very strong, drugs and liquor would bring in a half-million-dollar profit. There was no cover charge, of course. If you were important enough to enter the Veils at all, you certainly weren't the sort of person who would be expected to pay a cover.

Miriam had been the friend of kings for two thousand years. She had seen their generations rise and fall. She loved them in their pride and momentary lives. She loved their finest things, the jewels and whispering silks, the attention paid to the very rich.

When the wallets of her peers opened, you could practically hear creaking. She had fun; they had their careful customs and their dreary, conservative habits. She wanted meaning from life, they wanted only to keep breathing.

But now, for all their rejecting ways, she needed them. Her plan was to travel to all of the current conclaves, at once charming and, hopefully, seducing a man.

Deep in memory's mist, she'd had a baby. She still remembered the moment of conception as if it were yesterday. For women of her kind, conception was the most exquisite pleasure they could know. At the moment a man's semen fertilized one of your eggs, your whole body reacted with an unforgettable explosion of nerve-tingling delight. Even after all this time, part of her being remained focused on that stunning moment.

They always knew the sex of the baby within them, and she and Eumenes named their boy and fell in love with him from that first, joy-filled night. Then had come the pregnancy, a year of gestation . . . and the pain and the loss she'd felt as the silent, blue form of her dead infant was laid on her belly. Soon after, her beloved husband also died. Practically nothing could kill them—they never got sick, they couldn't. But he had weakened and wasted, and no one knew why. All her love, all her care, was not enough to save her dear Eumenes, not after he stopped eating.

He had grown as narrow and cold as a mummy, but his eyes had continued to glow . . . as if death had some special meaning, as if hunger had become for him a state of transcendence. She had begged him to eat, had tempted him, had tried, at the last, to force her own blood into his veins.

Was it grief that had killed him, or some greater despair? Like her, he respected the mind of man. Like her, he was unsure about whether or not humankind had ascended to a point that made it evil to prey on them.

Was it evil to be a Keeper? Was taking conscious prey murder? She thought that her husband had starved himself over these questions . . . and over the blue, hopeless baby he had so gently deposited upon her breast.

The dead may die to the world, but they do not die in the heart. Miriam's side of their love affair had continued on for whole cycles of years. But eventually his memory faded like the encaustic of his face that she'd had painted by Eratosthenes, that hurried little genius, in Alexandria.

Old Alexandria . . . redolent with the scents of myrrh and cardamom, whispering by night, singing by day. She remembered Cleopatra's hollow palace, and the Academia with its great library. She read all 123 of Sophocles' plays there, and she saw thirty of them performed. How many had survived? Seven, she thought, only seven.

Over all the intervening years, she had not been able to

find a man of her own kind to replace Eumenes. Part of the reason was that conclaves only happened once in a hundred years, and *they* did not court except during conclave. For somebody who lived for the moment, that kind of planning just did not work.

Now she was at the end of her choices. Either she would find someone or she would never, ever give another Keeper to the world.

Keeper children learned in school that humans were bred to appear similar to us on the surface so that Keepers could go among them more freely. In the beginning, they did not look at all similar and were not at all smart. They were little apes with lots of hair and huge teeth. We Keepers have always been as we are, beautiful beyond compare.

Miriam had drifted into the habit of taking human lovers because she was lonely and they were satisfying and the emotional commitment was not great. You found a cute male or a sweet, sensual female—the sex mattered not to Miriam, both had their charms—and you seduced, softly, gently, with the caressing eye and the slow hand. Then you put them to sleep with hypnosis and opened their veins and filled them full of your blood, and magic happened: They stayed young for years and years. You told them you'd made them immortal, and they followed you like foolish little puppies. Like the dear creature who now kept her home and business in New York, who warmed her bed and hunted with her . . . the dear creature, so lovely and brilliant and torn by her silly human conflicts. She had almost lost Sarah a few years ago, but had brought her back. The girl should be grateful and compliant, but that was not always the case. Sarah made mistakes. Sarah lived much too dangerously. She was haunted by what she had endured, and Miriam could not blame her. Indeed, she could hardly imagine what it would be like to lie in a coffin like that, slowly deteriorating but unable to die.

Sarah knew that one day the torment would certainly come again. She strove to save herself, using all of her considerable knowledge of medicine to attempt to defeat the process of aging that must slowly consume her, despite the fact that Miriam's blood now flowed in her veins.

To live, Sarah had to prey on man. She was even more tormented by this than Miriam's other lovers had been. Her Hippocratic oath haunted her, poor creature.

Miriam stopped herself. Best not go down that path again. She was always troubled by the tormented lives and horrible deaths of her lovers. The delicious little things were her guilt, her pain.

But not now, not on this nervous, excited night, the opening night of the Asian conclave. At least a proper lover would never die as the human ones did, pleading for deliverance even as their flesh became dust. But she would have to submit to him, obey him, live in his cold cell . . . at least, for a time.

Her body was her life—its rich senses, its wild desires, the way it felt when strong hands or sweet hands traveled her shivery skin.

There would be none of that in her future, not when she was part of one of *their* households, as she would be expected to be, at least for the duration of her pregnancy. Long, silent days, careful, creeping nights—that would be her life behind the walls of their world.

But that was how it had to be. She could almost feel that little body in her belly, could imagine hugging it after it came out, while it was still flushed and coal-hot. Only a newborn or a freshly fed Keeper was ever that warm.

The *samlor* glided along Moon Muang Road, heading for the Tapae Gate and the temple district beyond, moving through the murky, soaked night. How did the Asians stand this wretched climate? And yet, the heat was also nice. She enjoyed sweaty beds and long, druggy nights doing every decadent thing she could imagine.

The others shunned drugs. *They* said that they would rather die than become addicted for the thousands of years of their lives. She hadn't had that experience at all. Your blood protected you from all disease and weakness. *They* were just prejudiced against drugs, which were a human pleasure and therefore assumed to be trivial. But they had never done hash in ginger-scented Tangiers, or opium here in pillow-soft Chiang Mai, the last place in Asia where a good pipe of well-aged opium could be found. They had never smoked lying on silk beneath a hypnotic fan. When the nights were hot and the air was still, she was drawn back to the brilliant oblivion of the pipe. Drugs were less dangerous to enjoy here than in the States. No blustery, narrow-eyed policemen were apt to show up, waving guns and yelling. She'd had to race up too many walls to escape from those annoying creatures.

Well, all that was going to change. She was going to become a proper wife, and she certainly didn't need drugs for that. She wasn't addicted, so it wouldn't be a problem.

She could imagine her man, tall and silent, his face narrow, his skin as pale as a shadow. She could feel him, muscles like mean springs, long, curving fingers that could crush a human's bones or caress her plump breasts. She took a deep breath. These thoughts made her feel as if she were drowning and being rescued at the same time.

The wind rose, sweeping through the dark trees, sending

ripples shivering across the puddles that were like lakes in the street. Much lower now, the clouds raced and tumbled. Voices rose from a little market, two girls singing some popular song, oblivious to the *samlor* that whispered past and to the being within, who was carefully listening to the patter of their heartbeats from a thousand feet away.

Her interest in them told her that the hunger was rising within her. She felt it now, a faint gnawing in her belly, a hint of ice in her veins.

This was bad news. Most of her kind could detect their hunger coming for days, and they could prepare carefully to do a hunt. She'd never been able to prepare. One second she was fine, the next it was starting.

Buddha said it was good to live in the moment. In the Vedas, she'd read that there was only the moment. Her species had no holy books, just records of their possessions. Her mother had told her, "Humans have holy books because they've journeyed closer to God than we have."

She noticed that the smell of the *samlor* driver was washing over her, blown back by the breeze. She took a deep drag on her strong Thai cigarette, attempting to blot out the delicious scent.

It did not work. Okay, she thought, I'll go with it. She looked at the driver's sweating back. A thirty-second struggle and she'd be fed for another couple of weeks. The thing was, the hotel had written down her destination in Thai for him. He would not deviate from the route. She needed to get him to go down some darker side street. "Speak English?"

He did not respond. So she'd have to jump him right out here if she wanted him, and that would never do. You did your kills in private, and you destroyed all trace of the corpse. Even Miriam Blaylock followed those two essential rules.

The driver's skin rippled, his muscles surged. Mentally, she stripped him of his black shorts and T-shirt. She imagined laying him down upon a wonderful big bed, his penis like a cute little tree branch. She would kiss him all over and hold him closer and tighter, filling her mouth with his salt sweat and her nose with his every intimate smell. Her mouth would anesthetize his skin as the feeding began and in a few delightful moments, his blood would be sweeping down her throat.

She closed her eyes, arching her back and stretching, forcing his smell out of her nose with a rush of air. Think about opium, she told herself, not blood. Later, she would smoke to relieve this damned hunger. She needed to get back to familiar territory before she fed. It wasn't safe to do it in an unknown place.

Too bad her flight to Paris, where the European conclave was held, didn't leave until tomorrow evening.

This Asian conclave would end with dawn, and she'd have liked to have gone straight on to Europe. She could feed easily in Paris; she knew the city well. She'd hunted there recently—no more than fifty or so years ago, when it was swarming with Germans.

Of course, she might meet a man here in Chiang Mai. If she did, her new husband would attend to her need for prey during the pregnancy. If she wasn't leaving tomorrow, she'd be staying in Asia a long time.

If she was still alone after this conclave, she'd make her way along Samian Road, then cut into the welter of little streets that concealed a hole-in-the-wall she'd discovered called the Moonlight Bar. Down in the cellar a tiny old woman waited with pipes. Once, there had been thousands of opium dens in Asia. Now only Chiang Mai was left, with two or three small establishments.

At home, she kept her two-hundred-year-old opium in clay pots sealed with beeswax. Her ancient pipes delivered the vapor cool and easy, and Sarah was beautifully trained in the art of preparation and lighting.

She gazed up at the racing moon, thought of New York. It was about noon at home, so the cleaning crew would be at work in the club. Sarah and Leo would be asleep at home, probably in one another's arms ... probably in Miriam's own bed, a curtained, canopied heaven made for Nellie Salter, cane-mistress to Sir Francis Bacon, and William Shakespeare's Dark Lady. She'd drunk too much before she died, had Nellie. She'd made Miriam positively giddy.

Maybe the thing to do would be to convince her husband to come back with her. Or, if that proved to be impossible, maybe she would break even that taboo, and bear the child without a male's protection.

Suddenly, a positively sumptuous girl appeared on the sidewalk, her features carved as if by a master, her skin as soft as mist.

"Speak English?" Miriam called to her. No answer. "*Parlez-vous français?*"

The girl hurried off, disappearing into a doorway. Miriam knew that she appeared enormous and intimidating to these people, an improbable apparition with ash-gray eyes and improbably elegant clothes.

Chanel sent her a *couturier* and staff each year, and she bought a new ensemble. Still, she was told it was all much too conservative.

It was true enough that her kind had trouble with fashion. Fifty years would pass in a blink, and suddenly you would find yourself wearing the last bustle in the world or the last top hat. That's why the few even slightly accurate stories about them so often portrayed them in antique clothes. Bram Stoker, she thought, must have known a little something about the real thing. How else could he have known to portray his Dracula as such a stodgy dresser?

An odor struck Miriam with the force of a slap. Involuntarily, she hissed. The driver's head snapped around, his eyes wide and white. The scent of human blood had invaded her nostrils, raw and still very much alive. Then she saw why: there was an accident ahead.

A powerful instinct urged her to leap out of the cab and suck the bodies dry while the life force was still there to consume. But this was another instinct that had to be stifled.

As they passed the site, she held her breath. She could not trust herself with the scent of raw blood, not when the hunger was spreading through her body. Her skin was already cooling, making her feel heavy and slow. She'd be as pale as ashes when she got to the conclave. They'd all think, *Look at her, she can't even feed herself.*

The moon burst out from behind furious clouds. Lightning flickered on the spire of Wat Chedi Luang. The temple spires here in Chiang Mai were so lovely and exotic. She was used to the canyons of Manhattan.

Again the smell of the driver reached her nostrils. This time her body started to prepare to eat, her muscles growing tight for the assault, her mouth swimming in the mucus that would anesthetize her prey.

She took a long, last drag on the cigarette. If you pulled their blood into your gut with sufficient strength, your feed ended with delicious dregs.

"Be sure and get the organ juice, dear," her mother would admonish her. "It makes for strong bones."

Mother Lamia was hard to remember and hard to forget.

When Miriam needed to fall out of love with a human, she would use her memory of what humans had done to her mother to help her along. It had come as a great surprise, the capture. When Keepers slept, their bodies reached a state near death. They were entirely helpless. So sleep was carried out in deep hiding, or—in those days—in great and protected palaces.

A man they had thought a friend had betrayed Lamia. He had been a faithful partner at cards, had been the Graf von Holbein. But it evolved that he was not a petty count but a powerful priest, and his name was not Holbein but Muenster, Father Deitrich Muenster.

Miriam had escaped across the roofs of the little town where they were living. She had not been able to take her comatose mother, nor to hide her. Miriam had expected to remove her from their prison either by bribery or by brute force.

But they had not tried her. They had not even imprisoned her. They had wasted no time. Mother Lamia had awakened already chained to her stake. She realized instantly what was happening. But all of her struggles and strength did not break the chains or topple the stake.

Mother Lamia had stood proud on the pyre they had made for her, her hair flaring sparks into the night. She had stood there for a long, long time, because Keepers could only die when their blood stopped completely.

They had laughed when she screamed, and when they realized that she was dying so unusually slowly, they were even more delighted. Mother had been burned for a witch in 1761, in a village near Dresden. She had been the most alive, the best person Miriam had ever known. She had a fabulous sense of humor. She loved to have adventures, and she loved to dance.

Mother introduced Miriam to music—sackbuts, violas . . . her beloved viola da gamba. Miriam had been taught to sing, to read and speak many human languages, so many that she'd lost count. The languages of the ancient world had been works of art, Sumerian and Egyptian and Zolor, among many others. They had been supplanted by Greek, with its sublime verbs, and Latin, which was too rigidly constructed—somehow crude. English was a practical tongue. Of the modern languages, Miriam thought that French and Mandarin Chinese stood out as being the most satisfying to speak.

Unfortunately, she had never learned Thai, so she was at a disadvantage here. "Will you hurry, you stupid creature," she growled at the driver in English. He sped up. Her tone needed no common language to make itself understood.

The spires of the temple district rose all around her now. The district bore an ancient enchantment, for it was sacred to her kind, too. Here in the deep eons they had met, ten thousand years ago, fifteen thousand . . . when the world had been their toy and man a mute race of cattle. Look at the pavements left by her kind, still perfect after all this time. Look at the foundations of Wat Phra Singh and Wat Chedi Chet Yot—no human engineer could fashion such precision in stone. Stars curse what had happened among her kind, to make them vagrants in their own world. Give me opium, let me smoke. Let me forget.

She touched the golden key that lay at the bottom of her new purse, the key that would let her into the sanctum in the cellar of the Moonlight Bar. The purse was a Gucci bought at the local night market for 2500 baht. It was a luxurious item and finely made. She didn't need another purse, but she loved to shop and she'd been unable to resist. Every Keeper loved exquisite leather, and calfskin was deliciously close to human . . . which was *very* taboo to wear outside the home. The prey might notice something—the remains of a tattoo or a human birthmark on your gloves or your pocketbook. Personally, she never wore leather from human skin. They might be prey, but they were sensitive, conscious beings and that had to be respected. But their skins tanned *très* softly, the flay off a smooth back or buttock.

The *samlor* driver hunched forward as if some deep instinct was drawing him away from her. The thought again crossed her mind to just jump him. She'd ride him like a little bullock. He would shriek and buck, and it would be a thrill.

His living scent stung the flower-sweet air. Then he turned the *samlor,* going down a narrow street. It was little more than a passageway, very quiet.

She shoved another cigarette into her mouth and lit it. Closer they came to the ancient temple of Wat Chiang Man, the *chedi* within it buttressed to the four corners of the world by four gilded elephants.

The *samlor* stopped. Beneath the *chedi,* in a cellar no human being had ever entered, was the ancient *ho trai* of the Asian clans, a place founded before Siddhārtha was Buddha, indeed before Siddhārtha was born. "Stay," Miriam said. "Wait."

An eye took her in. The slightest of nods. She knew that this temple had a reputation among the ghost-conscious Thai. He sat with his head bowed and his feet clicking his pedals.

Her heels clattering on the wet paving stones, she crossed the short distance to the temple, then entered the *chedi.* Here, it was suddenly quiet. There was a scent of sandalwood and smoke from the single guttering lantern that hung from a rafter, shining on the great Buddha that reclined in the center of the ornate chamber.

She paid respect to the Buddha, drawing her hands together and bowing. Had any of her peers seen her, they would have scorned her utterly.

She ran her fingers along the cunning mortise work, then tapped softly three times, causing the concealed mechanism to give way with a soft click. It was a little surprising, the way the mechanism felt. It was almost as if the lock were sprung. She thought she might have been able to open it just with a push. You'd never find this kind of carelessness in Europe or America.

She went down the steep, curving steps. She didn't need illumination, of course. Theirs was a nocturnal species . . . miserably enough in this electric era. How her father had moped when the humans had discovered electricity. "We should have kept it from them," he'd said.

Keeper men and women did not live together except during pregnancy and, to some extent, child-rearing. But the love between them could be great, and he had never recovered from the loss of his Lamia. "I find myself searching the world for her," he would say. He'd persisted in doing dangerous things—climbing mountains, dueling, and traveling, endlessly traveling. It was death he sought, when he sought the far hills.

Her father had died in the explosion of the Hindenburg in 1937—taken like his Lamia by fire. He saved human beings from the flames, and those he helped can be seen in the newsreel film scrambling from the windows as the ship descends. He comes out last, and his form disappears in the fire.

Over and over and over again, she watched that film,

longing for one more rolling murmur of his voice, one more touch from his kindly hand.

She stopped on the fourth step. There was sound down below, definitely. Good, the conclave was in session. For most of the Keepers down there, this would be the first contact in a century with any of their own kind. Lovers met in sweet battle, and mothers lived with their children. But for the most part, they were a species as solitary as the spider.

A little farther along, she stopped again. Something she was hearing below did not seem quite right. Her people didn't laugh. She'd never heard anybody laugh except her mother and herself. Not even her dad had done it.

She went a little farther—and then she saw something incredible. On the dark wall there was a figure drawn. Or no, it was painted—spray-painted. She had to raise her head to see the whole of it. When she did, she saw that it was a crudely sprayed painting of a human penis in full erection.

Graffiti?

Farther along yet, there were paper cartons from a restaurant, still smelling of pepper and garlic. Nobody ate human food. They had no way to digest it. Inside, they were not made like humans at all. Liquor, however, was a different story. They could get drunk, fortunately. The others disdained alcohol, of course, but Miriam enjoyed fine wines and adored every form of distilled liquor from Armagnac to Jim Beam.

She moved a few more steps down, getting past the odor of the cartons. Her nostrils sought scent ahead.

Then she stopped. Fear did not come easily to her kind, so she was not frightened by what she smelled, only confused. She smelled humans—the dense odor of men, the sweet-sharp scent of boys.

A shock went through her as powerful as one of the lightning bolts that had been tearing through the clouds. She saw, suddenly and with absolute clarity, that the reason for all the odd signs was that there were human beings in this secret place. She was so surprised that she uttered an involuntary cry. The sound shuddered the walls, the moaning, forsaken howl of a tiger at bay.

From below there came a rush of voices, then the wild flicker of flashlights. Footsteps pummeled the stairs, and suddenly two Occidental men and three Thai boys came racing past her, cursing and pulling on their clothes.

Behind them they left a greasy silence, interrupted after a few moments by the scuttle of roaches and the stealthy sniffing of rats. Treading as if her feet were touching sewage, Miriam descended into the sanctum. She growled low, striding about in the filth and ruins.

They must have moved the sanctuary. But why hadn't they told anybody? Keepers might be a solitary lot, but ancient custom dictated that everybody be informed of something so basic as this. Unless—was she really *that* shunned, that they would move a place of conclave and keep only her in the dark?

Surely not. They were far too conservative to alter an ancient convention. So maybe there had been an emergency. Maybe the sanctuary had been discovered and they'd had to move it suddenly.

That must be it. She hadn't gotten the message because there'd been no time.

But then she saw, lying in a corner beneath the ruins of a shattered bookcase, a familiar red shape. She caught her breath, because what she was seeing was impossible. Her skin grew taut, her muscles stirred—the predator sensed danger.

She picked up the red-leather book cover and held it in reverent, shaking hands. From the time their eyes came open, Keepers were taught that the Books of Names were sacred. By these books, a whole species knew itself, all who lived and had died, and all its works and days.

That red leather was unmistakable, as was the inscription in the beloved glyphs of their own tongue, glyphs that no human knew. *The Names of the Keepers and the Keepings.*

They called themselves Keepers because they kept herds. If the rest of the book had been here, there would have been descriptions of the various territories that belonged to the different Asian Keepers and who had the right to use which human herd.

She ran her fingers over the heavy leather. It had been cured from the skin of a human when they were still coarse, primitive creatures. These books were begun thirty thousand years ago—a long time, even in the world of the Keepers. But not all *that* long. Her great-great-grandfather, for example, had been able to imitate the cries of the Neanderthals. Buried in the Prime Keep in Egypt were careful wax paintings of the human figure going back to the beginning.

She crouched to the crumbled mass of paper, tried to smooth it, to somehow make it right. When she touched the pages, roaches sped away. She spread a crumpled page to see if any useful information remained.

The roaches had eaten the ink, what hadn't been smeared by the vile uses to which the paper had apparently been put. She laid the page down on the dirty floor, laid it down as she might lay to rest the body of a beloved friend.

She made another circuit of the chamber, looking into its recesses and crannies, but not a page remained.

She was face-to-face with what was without a doubt the

greatest astonishment of her life. Some of the richest and most ancient Keepers were Asian. There had been—oh, easily a hundred of them.

She slumped against a wall. Had man somehow done this, simple, weak little *man*?

Keepers could be hurt by man—witness her mother and father—but they couldn't be destroyed by man, not this way. They *owned* man!

She looked from empty wall to empty wall and fully grasped the fact that the Asian Keepers must have been destroyed. If even one was left alive, this book would be safe.

When she grasped this enormous reality, something so rare happened to Miriam that she lifted her long, tapering fingers to her cheeks in amazement.

Far below the crazy streets, in the fetid ruin of this holy place, a vampire wept.

TWO

Blood Nocturne

The *samlor* moved with what now felt like maddening slowness through the sighing showers of rain, down the empty streets, while Miriam listened to the tremble of her own heart and smelled the air for danger.

What odor did she seek? The acid stink of a dead Keeper, perhaps, or the oil of a policeman's gun?

How could a human policeman kill one of them? The idea was absurd.

Yet the book had been destroyed. No battle among the Keepers, no matter how violent, would have resulted in the destruction of a Book of Names. Keepers fought for love and herds, but only occasionally, and never *that* hard. Not even in their days in the sun.

Miriam longed now to spend the night beneath the whirling fan, sucking deeply on her pipe, but thousands of years of hunting brilliant and dangerous prey made her too wary now even to consider such repose.

"Airport," she'd told the *samlor* driver. She'd pulled the plastic curtain across the front of the cabin and sat in the stuffy interior smoking and watching the rain pelt the driver's back, trying not to dwell on the scent of his blood.

The ride to the airport was a long one, and toward the

end the creature had slowed to a slumped, struggling walk. If this had been another time, she would have whipped him.

She might be a rebel, but just now she felt an absolute, burning loyalty to her own kind. They had a right to life, just like any other creature. More of a right—this whole earth and every single creature living on it was their property, and much of it—including man—was their creation.

They had given man everything—his form, his mind, his life itself. It was the Keepers who had originally bred the crops that man had been taught to cultivate, the grains and the fruits of the land, and the dumb beasts that he had been given to eat.

Her own great-granduncle had given the northern herds the apple, breeding the plants carefully through a hundred generations, then planting them where human tribes would discover the apparently wild orchards. This had been done as a solution to a nutritional problem. Humans needed fruit or they became constipated. It was most unpleasant to feed on a constipated human.

The *samlor* came to a stop before the shambling Chiang Mai airport, which proved to be empty in the predawn. Flights, it seemed, did not begin early here. She certainly couldn't sit alone in the lobby, not and invite the curiosity of security guards by being the only passenger present.

Nearby there was an area of warehouses, lit only by a few overhead lights. As the driver walked down a ramp to an area where others of his kind slept beneath plastic sheets, she slipped into the shadows at the edge of the main terminal building. A few yards away there was a chain-link fence with a locked gate. She twisted the lock off and moved toward the nearest warehouse, slipping in through a side door.

The black interior smelled of cotton and turned out to be full of T-shirts intended for the western market. "Grateful Dead," "Adolf Hitler, European Tour 1939–1945," "I Am a Teenage Werewolf."

She knew a great deal about fear, as something that her prey experienced. It was interesting to watch, in an abstract sort of way. She never felt it herself unless she got careless or unlucky. After all, humans couldn't do anything to a Keeper. Being killed by man was regarded as a freak accident, about as likely as being caught in an avalanche. Or, that used to be the case. Since about the time of her mother's death, things had been changing. The Keepers had responded by becoming more and more wary and reclusive.

Keepers were ten times as strong; they could climb sheer walls and leap long distances. They were far more intelligent. But were they faster than a bullet or a warning cell-phone call? Had they the skill to outwit investigators armed with the tools of forensic science?

She had been surprised to see the shadow of man in that ruined holy place. But she realized, now, that she should not have been.

Given the destruction of the Asian Book of Names, she had to assume that there were human beings who knew of their Keepers and were efficient enough to have destroyed a whole conclave.

The question was, how much had they actually understood of that book? If man had learned to read Prime, the ancient Keeper language, then a terrible doom might be upon all the Keepers. That book not only contained records of the locations and property of all the Keepers in Asia, but also all of their familial and fiscal relationships to every other Keeper in the world. It told the locations and times of the other centennial conclaves that would be held this month.

Miriam had to warn her kind.

An hour after dawn, workers were coming to open the warehouse, and the airport was slowly returning to life. As Miriam went among the crowd in the terminal, she found herself coping with strange urges, ferocious urges. She wanted to grab a few of them and tear their heads off and drink their spouting necks with the savagery of the ancients.

Perhaps she *was* afraid. A predator experiences fear as an urge to attack. It was why her mother had roared and gnashed her teeth back when—but she didn't want to brood on that again, not now.

Her hunger was starting to actually make her bones ache, and her skin was turning whiter and whiter. The dry, corpse-like coldness that marked a hungry Keeper's skin was stealing her usual girlish flush.

"Bangkok," she said to the ticket clerk, producing a Visa card in the name of the traveling alias Sarah had set up for this trip. A French national called "Marie Tallman" had entered Thailand from the U.S. and would leave for Paris. Miriam Blaylock, a U.S. citizen, would return to New York.

She went to the surprisingly ornate first-class lounge. A hostess came up. Miriam ordered sour lemonade, then sat down and lit a cigarette. She contemplated what had become the problem of her hunger.

She'd ignored it for too long, and now she was going to have to feed before she left Thailand. Why hadn't she noticed this back in New York? She could have sent Sarah down to the Veils to bring back some wanderer. At home, she had reduced the hunt to a simple, safe procedure that delivered her prey right into her arms. Sarah found appropriate victims and lured them to the Veils. Miriam consumed them in a basement room built for the purpose, or she took them home and dined there.

She gave them a lovely time. They died in ecstasy.

She sucked a cigarette hard, blasted the smoke out of her nose. If she didn't feed soon, she would slow down, she would lose her edge. Then she'd have to find some weak human and do a thin feed. This would only stave the hunger off for a few days, no more. So there would be a second hunt in Paris, and more danger.

She ought to race straight back to New York and the hell with the rest of the Keepers. They probably wouldn't appreciate her efforts anyway.

But she couldn't, not when the greatest disaster she had ever known had befallen an entire continent. Of all the Keepers, how could it ever have been the Asians who would be attacked by man? Many of them were true ancients, more than ten thousand years old. Immensely wise, extraordinarily careful, not moving so much as an inch except to feed, they would stay in their black lairs, shadows with gleaming eyes and slow, slow breath, amusing themselves for months by gazing at a bit of intricately woven cloth or some subtly reflective gem.

When these Keepers walked among their herds, the humans would stir in their sleep, sighing with the sighing wind, clinging to one another without knowing why.

They had seen vast ages of man pass, empires rise and fall and be forgotten, thousands of human generations go to dust. More effectively than any other group in the world, the Asians had managed their herds, inducing migrations in order to evoke new strains, breeding their stock for beauty and intelligence and succulence. Humans called it famine and war and migration. Keepers called it stock management.

The more she thought about it, the more uneasy she

became. How much of the secret of their Keepers had the humans involved understood, and who were these creatures? How could cattle enjoying the riches and ease of the feedlot ever realize the truth about their lives? Especially when not one in a hundred thousand of them would ever come into contact with a Keeper. But human beings were not cattle, and it was a mistake to think so.

Somehow, they had used their clever little brains to discover a secret that was larger than they were. They had used their damned science. They never should have been given the wheel, let alone electricity and—God forbid—flight.

But they had been. They were fun to watch, damned things. Also, as their population had risen out of control, they themselves had taken their science to greater and greater heights, seeking to make more food, to move faster, to create room for more and more of themselves on the groaning planet.

She'd had a brush with human science herself back twenty or so years ago. It was hard to believe, now, just how much trouble dear Dr. Sarah Roberts had caused her back then. She'd taken samples of her own blood into a laboratory. She'd damned well discovered the secret of the Keepers, that smart little vixen.

Miriam had eaten her cohort and seduced her. She'd flooded Sarah's body with her own blood, but Sarah had fought the transformation. She had refused to eat, claiming that her medical oath was stronger than her love of life. So she had spent a little time among the undead, her soul trapped in her slowly decaying body.

Meanwhile, Miriam had read Sarah's scientific papers and gained new insights from them about the synergy between Keeper blood and human blood. She had managed to resuscitate Sarah.

In doing so, she had gained a complex and fascinating companion. Sarah had honor, and so could be trusted. But she did not like to feed. She considered it murder.

Miriam had lured Sarah into finding buried parts of herself that loved the soft skin and the considered touch of another woman. When they lay together, Miriam would draw her to climax again and again, with the pressure of the finger or the exploratory flutter of the tongue.

"Passengers for Thai Airways Flight Two-Twenty-three to Bangkok may now board through Gate Eleven."

She began to file toward the gate that led to the plane. Normally, she minded travel far less than other Keepers. For a woman of their kind, travel was limited to courtship during her four fertilities and, of course, attending the centennial conclaves.

Defying convention, Miriam had traveled all over the world. She had tasted it and enjoyed it and watched it change across time, had walked in the grand alleys of ancient Rome and the perfumed halls of the Sun King.

She had lived a long time in the cellars of the House of the Caesars on the Quirinal Hill, had heard mad Caligula screeching and fed on the blood of his slaves, who were fat from their constant stealing of his peacock breasts and zebra haunches, and were too numerous to be missed.

Despite all her journeying, she detested small spaces. During the eastern European crisis of the nineteenth century, when local humans had briefly learned to recognize their masters, Keepers in the Balkans had been forced to hide in graves. Miriam had gone there to see firsthand what had gone wrong. She ended up spending a week hiding in a coffin, an experience that still haunted her dreams. It had taken almost all of her strength to dig herself out of the grave.

Their use of this particular hiding place was how the legend that Keepers were somehow undead had begun.

It was some time before anybody understood why simple Transylvanian peasants had come to understand that they were property. Not until the publication of *Dracula* did the Keepers realize that out-of-date clothing could give you away in a world where fashions had begun to change more than once in a human generation. The Romans had worn togas for a thousand years. In the Middle Ages, fashion had changed perhaps twice in a century.

In the nineteenth century, it began to change every fifteen years or so. Isolated in the Carpathians, the Keepers who lived there had failed to notice that powdered wigs and buckle shoes had ceased to be worn by humans. The peasants soon realized that every time one of these bewigged oddities was seen in the night streets, somebody disappeared. Twenty-six Keepers died during the Balkan troubles, the largest number by far ever to be destroyed at one time by man.

But there had been sixty or more here in Asia. *Sixty*. What if they were captured, starving in prison, or being tracked like foxes? Or worse, already dead.

They *were* dead. She sensed this. There was something missing in the air . . . a sort of silence where there had been music.

She strode toward the far back of the fetid tube full of seats. The only place she would sit on most flights was the very last row. If something went wrong, her great strength might give her an edge, for she would be perfectly capable of ripping a hole in the fuselage in order to escape, if escape was possible. The impact of a jet slamming into the ground at four hundred miles an hour would reduce even a Keeper to pulp.

The damn plane was going to be full, she realized. The wretched creatures were just piling on, and her belly was churning. She had to feed, and soon. She had to do it in Bangkok, and never mind the urgency of the situation or the danger of just being in Asia.

The plane was an A-310 Airbus, a type that particularly troubled her because it was too easy to fly. Pilots got careless in this airplane. Worse, it had only two engines, and she knew from her hobby of reading technical manuals that one of them was not enough to keep it aloft forever.

The Thai were smoking and chattering and eating human fodder: bits of pork and mushroom and pepper wrapped in what looked like edible plastic. Various of her human lovers had tried to introduce her to the pleasures of sweets and such, but she had not been able to digest any of it. She watched human food evolve steadily for thousands of years—until recently, that is, when continued population pressure had caused an increase in quantity and a corresponding decline in quality.

Herd tending was not her specialty, so she wasn't particularly concerned with what the creatures ate. Her parents had been breeders and practiced the art of inducing particular humans to breed with each other, so that babies with preferred characteristics would be born.

Her father and mother had bred a new race among the Egyptians, seeking to make a smarter human. They had eventually caused the birth a brilliant child called Ham-abyra, who is known to history not by his Egyptian name, but by the Hebrew inversion, Abyra-ham. He had been cut out of the Egyptian herd and sent to found a new one in another part of North Africa.

The herd of Abyra-ham were great survivors because they were so clever, but their blood had a bitter aftertaste, unfortunately. You ate a Jew, her father always said, you remembered it for a week.

Originally, there had been good reasons for wanting

humans to be smart. The brighter they were, the better their survival skills, and the cheaper they were to manage. Also, the blood of the brilliant usually offered more complex, interesting bouquets. Keepers bred humans for blood the way humans bred grapes for wine.

The engines of the airplane began to whine. She hated to fly as much as or more than she had hated to sail, but she did it anyway, just as she'd always traveled. Her thirst for knowledge had made her take the spring galley from Rome to Alexandria to read in the library, and the summer galleon from Spain to Mexico to plumb the secrets of the Maya.

There was a problem, though. She'd often ended up eating every single soul on those slow old sailing ships. She never meant to do it, but it was just so tempting, all alone in close quarters with a gaggle of sweet-blooded humans for weeks and weeks. She'd do one and then another of them, starting with the low slaves and working her way up. She'd create the impression that they'd jumped or fallen overboard. Come a storm and she'd do five or six, gobbling them like bonbons.

Ships she took would arrive empty . . . except for one seriously overweight Keeper well hidden in the bilges. One of her most particularly self-indulgent trips had been aboard a Dutch East Indies spice trader. She'd consumed a crew of fifty and all six of their passengers in just two months. She was so packed with blood she feared that she must look like a big blue tick. She'd come into Surabaya at night on the ship's sailing dinghy. As for the ship, it had sailed on alone for years, still a legend among humans, the *Flying Dutchman*.

Shuddering, the jet rose into the air. Fog, touched golden by the sun, hung over the ancient Thai city below. Miriam gazed down at the temple district, at spires just visible through the billowing fog, and wondered.

The hunger was beginning to claw at her belly. Her muscles were tensing, instinctually getting ready for a kill. Her mouth was filling with the sour flavor of need. The scent of people swept through her with every breath.

She turned on the air nozzle above her head to full force, but there was no escaping the succulent odor of her fellow travelers, not packed into this tin can.

You certainly couldn't feed on a jet. If you stuffed the remnant down the toilet, it would be found later in the plane's holding tank. Remnants had to be completely destroyed—ground up and burned, usually. Humans had found just a very few of them over the generations, generally taken for mummies. In fact, she'd once wrapped a news hawker in tape and put him in a mummy case in the basement of the British Museum. That had been when—oh, a few hundred years ago. He was probably still there, her old hawker. It had been the *St. James's Gazette* that he'd been selling. Pretty good paper in its day.

Look at the humans around her, she thought, all happy and fluttery and unconcerned about the thirty-thousand-foot maw of death beneath their feet. How could anybody be as careless of their lives as humans were? They flew all the time; they raced around in automobiles; they went on roller coasters and fought wars. Miriam's theory was that humans did indeed have souls, and inwardly they knew it. That was why they came to her for sex, thrilled by the danger they sensed. They weren't really afraid of death, the humans. For them, it was nothing more than another thrill ride.

For the Keepers, death meant leaving the cosmos forever.

The plane leveled off. Miriam knew by its motion and sound exactly what it was doing at every moment of the flight. Actually, she could have flown it herself. She'd trained herself on her PC with a flight simulator, just in case some pilot died from the airline food or something. If some fool were to attempt to hijack the thing, she'd hypnotize him immediately and simply sit him right back down. They'd have to try to figure it out later.

Two shy children peeked at her over the seat ahead. They gazed steadily at the European, but it wasn't only curiosity in their eyes. She knew that the longer the flight, the more uneasy she would make her seatmates. The presence of a Keeper evoked instincts that humans, being so near the top of the food chain, were as unfamiliar with as she was with fear. What a human felt in the presence of a Keeper was what a mouse felt in the presence of a snake—a sort of horrible question.

They would grow unaccountably suspicious of her, be strangely drawn to her, grow sick in her presence, and if they slept, they would have nightmares about her, every single soul in this airplane.

The stewardess came, her smile fading as she laid eyes on Miriam. She had a cart full of boxed food and piles of plastic chopsticks. She stood close, handing food to the people jammed in the nearby seats.

Her blood had a soft, plain scent, like Beaujolais from an uninteresting year. Even so, it would be smooth and warm and wonderful as it went down. Miriam kept her eyes closed, barely breathing.

Never guessing that Miriam could see through her own eyelids, the stewardess took the opportunity to look long at the tall European in the old suit. Miriam worried that her makeup was too light. By now, her skin would be terrifying to a human. She'd appear as pale as a corpse. But she was also thirsty, so she had to interact with the girl, risk a moment of the creature's attention. "Excuse me."

The stewardess stopped. She organized her face into a carefully professional smile. "Yis," she said, uttering what was probably one of her few English words. *Yis. Nah. Okeh.*

"Water," Miriam said, pointing to a bottle with blue Thai writing on it.

The girl gave her the water and moved off nervously. The plane shuddered, the tone of the engines changing. Miriam fumbled with her water bottle. She knew that the sounds weren't abnormal, but they still made her uneasy.

Again, the plane shuddered. It was heading down, definitely. Surely there wasn't a situation. The engines were fine; she could hear that. But what if they were having control problems?

She took in breath, prepared to tighten the muscles that might be needed if she had to tear her way out of a crumpled fuselage.

But no, the plane *was* landing. Or more accurately, beginning its descent. She fumbled her itinerary out of her purse. Yes, the flight was forty minutes, and running exactly on schedule.

The flaps went down, making a terrific racket. Her startle reflex made her suck her water bottle so hard that it became involved with her teeth, and she accidentally shredded it. Water gushed down her front. Wiping her breast, she stuffed the ruined bottle down into the space between the seats.

She sat facing straight ahead, ignoring her accident. They didn't notice, anyway. They were too preoccupied with their snacks.

The plane was so thick with the smell of human blood that she would have liked to have gone into some sort of feeding frenzy like a shark. Total indulgence.

She'd never been on an airplane while this hungry before,

and she resolved never to do it again. She should have eaten that *samlor* driver. She closed her eyes. Time passed, one minute, then another. She found herself inhaling the smell of her seatmate. He was a plump little thing, just popping with sweet blood. *Délicieux.* The odor of his skin was lively. This was a tasty morsel, sitting here. She sucked in more scent.

She began to imagine how she'd take him. She'd pretend to be one of those European whores who did such a lively trade in Asia. They'd get off the plane together, and then— well, sooner or later the moment always presented itself.

She could get a very nice feed out of this creature. He had noticed her glances and was scanning her. She could smell the spicy scent of his interest.

"Lovely flight," she said.

"Oh, yes," he answered. His English was good, which was a nice convenience.

She gave him a smile, very slight, a bit arch.

He squirmed in his seat, his eyes flickering between her folded hands and her face. Male victims always felt as if the strange woman who had taken notice of them was the most beautiful, most desirable creature on earth. Females found her personable and engaging. They never knew that they'd been bred to react this way to interest from their Keepers.

He crossed and uncrossed his legs, tossed his head, then leaned a little forward. "You spending some time in Bangkok?"

So, he was available for consumption. She considered. She might miss her flight to Paris, and the rest of the world had to be warned about what had happened here, and at all speed. But by the moon and the stars, she was *so hungry!*

"Perhaps," she said softly.

His smile widened to reveal a gold-capped tooth. She glanced down at his fingers, at the shimmering of his wedding ring. There would be a complication right there—a disappearing husband.

He followed her glance, shrugged.

Her gut hummed.

The pitch of the engines changed again. She evaluated the sound, concluded that all was still normal.

She lifted her fingers, poised them above the back of his hand. To touch him now was an ancient act of possession, by which the Keepers had claimed their prey from time immemorial.

She lowered the cool tips of her fingers until they came into contact with his skin. "I'm staying in Bangkok for a few days." She laughed, a musical trill. "At the Royal Orchid," she added, drawing the name of the hotel from somewhere in her memory. She knew only that it was a very fine place.

"As it happens, I'm staying at the Royal Orchid, also, miss." He smiled from ear to ear.

She hoped they had a room. She had no reservation. Doubtless he didn't, either.

A moment later the plane hit the runway, then went jolting along the much-patched tarmac. Despite Miriam's grim worries, it slowed steadily. Still, she was tense, waiting for the damned thing to get off the runway. For an unspeakably long moment, it hesitated. Were the pilots lost? Had the surface traffic controllers made some stupid mistake?

She pictured a 747 landing on top of them, its entire flight crew dead asleep. Years ago, two Keepers had been killed in a catastrophic runway accident in the Canary Islands. But the engines revved up again and the plane moved forward. A few twists and turns and it came to a halt. The seat-belt chime rang.

Immediately, Miriam's mind focused on her victim. Now

she must ignore him a bit, play the coquette, the Occidental woman who was just a little indifferent to the Oriental man.

As they filed out of the plane, she stayed behind him, evaluating moment by moment every subtle change in his manner. A musty smell flowed from between his legs, a sharper odor of sweat billowed off his skin.

There was something just a little odd in these odors. He should have smelled far more of sex and less of . . . well, it seemed that he was afraid. Probably, it was because they'd been in proximity too long. You wanted to move quickly when you hunted, not sit cheek-by-jowl with the prey for an hour before proceeding.

In the airport, they were hit by the wall of filthy air that enclosed and defined life in Bangkok.

No matter his perversion, here the wanderer could find satisfaction. The Thai had originally been bred by luxury-loving Keepers, and they preserved the remarkable zest for pleasure that had been bred into them. But then, every herd in the world bore the mark of its Keepers. You could see the stark love of order and the obsessiveness of the northern Keepers in the Germanic peoples they had created, and the passion and subtlety of the southern Europeans in the French, the Spanish, and the Italians. She loved the wild mix of the Americas, never knowing exactly what to expect from that mongrel herd.

As Miriam and her victim moved out into the main hall of the airport, she laid her hand on his shoulder, the second time she had touched him. Each time she did it, she felt more of a sense of possession.

She felt not the rippling whisper of desire in his muscles, but the tense vibration of fear. This was going to take a great deal of care and attention. This man must be very sensitive indeed to feel as he did now. Perhaps she should turn back.

He plunged into the chaotic cab rank, a mass of bills in his fist, and they were soon in a taxi.

She disliked being driven by others in motorized vehicles, and this driver was typical of these wild folk. In addition, he would certainly remember a run with a Thai man and a European woman.

Her victim sat rigidly, gripping the handhold above his door. When he offered her a cigarette, she did not like what she saw in his eyes. Did not like, did not quite understand. Their instinct was to be drawn to the predator, to be fascinated.

She let him light her cigarette, inhaled deeply. Cigarettes didn't matter to Keepers. Their immune systems swept cancer cells away like crumbs.

An impulse told her to give his cheek a sudden kiss. "Asia," she whispered, "Asia is such a mystery."

"I'm in outsourcing technology. No mystery there."

"Your accent isn't Thai."

"My father was a diplomat. I grew up in London and then Burma."

She remembered the days of the British in Burma, when they used to grow opium poppies on huge Crown estates. They had looked upon their laborers in much the same way that Keepers looked on humans. You could go out into those opium plantations and chew seed and take one picker after another, like an ape gobbling fruit. And then you could engage in the social life of the planters with their whites and their billiard rooms and their gin and tonics. Sometimes, you could even take one of them, for there were still tigers in Burma then and the corpse could be left suitably mauled.

Sweet nostalgia.

They arrived at the Royal Orchid, the cab at sea in an ocean of limousines. She went forward into the broad, echoing lobby. Women stared in open amazement as the fabulous clothes strode toward the check-in desk.

"I'd like a suite please." She presented her—or rather, Marie Tallman's—Visa card. The clerk ran it and gave her a keycard, his polite glance moving toward the next customer in line.

She had made no effort as yet to seduce her victim away from his uneasiness. He needed more subtle handling, and she had to accept that this might not be a successful hunt. She'd be damn mad if it failed, though, and the long journey to Paris would be hell.

She held out her hand to her victim. As sweetly, as innocently as she could, she smiled at him. He looked down at her hand. In it was a keycard. "Twenty-five-oh-seven," she said.

When they were alone in the lift, he finally smiled up at her. His odor had not really changed, though. He was not happy to be here. He was acting.

She kissed him on the forehead. Now that she was committed to what was probably a very foolish kill, she decided that she might as well enjoy herself thoroughly. She would take him slowly and drain him to the very last drop. She gave him a stern look. "How much am I worth to you?"

"How much do you want?"

"A thousand dollars."

His eyes widened, he reared back as if astonished. The lift came to a stop on the twenty-fifth floor. "Two hundred, miss. H.K. dollar."

They got out. She would not bargain all that hard, but also she must not raise his suspicions. "Three hundred, U.S." she said as they walked down the wide hallway.

"Five hundred, H.K."

"It isn't enough to cover my expenses, handsome."

"You'll do twenty men before the night's out."

She slid her keycard into the lock. Here she was, as magnificent a beauty as the earth might know, and this greedy little roach actually believed that she was going to give herself to him for the equivalent of about sixty U.S. dollars. He'd been afraid of her price, that was all. Wretched thing.

Sunlight poured in from the wall of windows that faced the door. There was a couch upholstered in yellow chintz and a huge vase of exotic flowers on the coffee table.

Far below, the wide Chao Phraya River shimmered in sunlight that shafted down between great banks of clouds. Tiny river taxis and long-tails wove the river with their wakes. Up the bank, she could see the spires of distant temples, Wat Phrathukhongka and, just visible along the Klong Phadung, Wat Trimitr, the temple of the Golden Buddha. Farther away, awash in glowing air pollution, were the graceful tile roofs of the Grand Palace and the pencil-narrow spire of Wat Po.

The two of them gazed in silence, both awed for different reasons. He no doubt thought it glorious; she was horrified and fascinated, as always, when she saw how vast were the works of man.

She sat down on the bed, drew her prey down beside her. Too bad she had to eat and run. Normally, she would have gone into the sleep that followed feeding, but this time she'd have to load herself up with amphetamines and do her sleeping on the plane. She'd book a first-class seat for this twelve-hour journey, no matter that the seats were in the most dangerous part of the plane. Still, the idea of entering helpless sleep amid a mass of humans was not pleasant.

She caressed her victim. He stirred, his clothes rustling. A moment passed, another. He had become still in the way human beings did when they were subconsciously aware of danger.

They were sitting on the foot of the bed. She took his chin in her hand and turned his face to hers. She looked into his eyes, looked deep.

What did the gleam in those human eyes mean? She always wondered that, right before she fed.

"Kiss me," she said to the creature. He smiled a drawn smile, then lifted his face to hers, his lips going slack, his eyelids fluttering down. She laid her lips upon his, careful to keep the anatomy of her mouth concealed. Their tongues met, and she felt his muscles stiffen a little as he detected that hers was as rough as a cat's. If he bolted, she would be ready. She was ten times stronger than the strongest human being, ten times faster.

A cat worries its prey because pain flushes muscles with hormones that season the meat. This was true also of her kind, and some of them were casually cruel to their victims.

Stroking his head and purring, she laid him against the pillows and opened up his pants with her deft hands. She took his member out, smiled, then kissed it.

Then she stood before him. She removed her blue silk jacket, twirled, then unbuttoned her blouse. He watched with steady concentration, a slight smile on his face.

Instinct made her sway into the death dance, her arms undulating, her hips moving gracefully. Each time she twirled, her body became tighter and harder, more and more ready. As she danced, she threw off her clothes.

She stood before him naked, like a wound spring, her hands ready to grab him. There was in his eye a sort of curiosity, for she was very pale indeed, as pale as a ghost and as slick as glass, more like a statue than a being of flesh and blood.

He would soon discover that she was also cold, very cold. She sat down beside him and kissed him. But something was not right. As she had kissed him, he had returned himself to his pants.

No matter, she was sexually excited now herself. That was part of her reality and what made her so very different from the others of her kind: humans excited her. She liked their bodies, the way they tasted and smelled, the way they looked, the curves of the females, the pert rods of the men. Perhaps this was because she had discovered that she was capable of taking them to states of pleasure that Keepers could not reach with one another. Sex between species could be a stunning aphrodisiac, if executed with skill.

She lay down upon her little man, snuggled him into her. He seemed to be struggling with himself, fighting an inner battle. She reached into his pants, to see if she could resolve the conflict for him. A few deft strokes, and he was ready.

The human male was not blessed with a large penis, and it probably felt strangely lost in her vagina. He would also be noticing the cold. In fact, she could hear him making little exclamations in his throat. He was becoming aware that something was wrong.

"There, baby," she cooed, "little baby boy, all is well."

He started heaving. He wanted out from under her. She was, of course, far heavier than she had appeared. She tightened her vaginal muscles, over which she had exquisite control. When she began undulating them, he yelped with surprised pleasure. He'd probably never felt anything like it before, not even in Asia.

Her mouth was pressed against his neck, her mucus flooding his skin with anesthetic. Her sharp teeth parted the skin so easily that he probably felt nothing at all. There was a bit of resistance from the wall of the vein. She made love furiously as she exhaled, made herself ready for the ferocious sucking motion that would consume his life.

His muscles worked, he twisted and turned. He would be feeling both the pain of penetration and the pleasure of sex. He grimaced, his eyes shut tight.

She stayed like that for a while, making love at first fast and then slow, bringing him close, letting him relax. She left her mouth wide open to the wound, letting the blood tick past, tasting it just a little, enjoying herself.

When he began to really squirm, trying to reduce what must be by now a quite noticeable pain deep in his throat, she pinned his arms to his sides and enclosed his legs in her own. Her strength was so great that it felt to her human lovers as if they were being encased in iron, or so they had always told her.

The penis, on the other hand, would feel as if it were being massaged by thousands of tiny, careful fingers. One man described it as the most divine sensation he had ever known. He begged her for it, even while he was dying.

She worked him to the edge twice more. His body was a roaring furnace; his blood was singing. She was deep in him, her drinking beginning to kill him. It was now, at this moment, that she was sure that she felt his soul.

She sucked massively and fast, the sound of it roaring through the silent, sunny room. He did not even have a chance to cry out. As he died, the pumping of his loins became disorganized, then stopped.

The blood came into her like living fire, like a flower opening in her gut. Then came the bittersweet flavor that followed the blood, that meant that the organs had also given up their fluids.

She got off him, sat on the bedside and lit one of his cigarettes. Taking a long drag, she enjoyed the sensation of absorbing his life. The males and females felt quite different. After consuming a woman, you had a ferocious sort of an energy in you. You felt as if you could tear the world in half. A man left the flavor of his strength. You got a heady, hard-edged high from testosterone.

She got up and strode to the window. The healthier they were, the more you got from them, and this creature had been very healthy. Her face got hot, her body flushed warm and pink.

She went over to the mirror and touched the reflection of her face. She had been a woman before; now she was a girl, fresh as dew, her eyes sparkling and innocent.

Still enjoying the taste of blood that lingered in her mouth, she rifled through the man's clothing. She'd get his money, then dispose of the remnant and go straight to the airport. She could still make her Paris flight. The European clan was not as big as the Asian, but it was wise and ancient, not like the adventurous Americans. Europe had fixed the Transylvania situation by transforming true vampire lore into myths and stories. Europe would know what to do.

She drew a fat brown wallet out of his hip pocket and tossed it open. Poor wife, smiling so desperately, will you miss this man or feel relief that he has gone? And here were children—damn!

She was furious with herself for looking at the pictures. She never looked at the damn pictures! She held the weathered print of the kids, wondering how old they were, poor little things. She stuffed it back into the wallet, pressing it deep into one of the pockets.

It was then that she noticed a rather strange card. At first, she thought that it might be a Thai driving permit, but when she looked more closely, she found that it was very far from that.

Lying in her hand was an identification card. She stared at it, reading it carefully. It was in French, English, and Chinese, not Thai at all.

The sunken husk lying on that bed over there, now nothing but forty pounds of bones and drum-tight skin lost in a pile of sheets, was no innocent Thai businessman. Lying there were the remains of Kiew Narawat, police inspector with Interpol.

Her breath came short, her skin grew hot and dry. She felt dizzy, her bowels threatened to let go. She threw on her clothes, settled her wig on her head, and applied a smear of lipstick to reduce the glow of her fire-red lips. Going deep into her purse, she pulled out three yellow-and-black bennies and threw them down her gullet. Sleep would drag at her now, but she must not let it come, not until she was in her plane in her seat and covered with a blanket.

Forgetting the remnant lying on the bed in full view, forgetting everything except escape at any and all cost, Miriam Blaylock made a mistake of spectacular proportions, one that she had not made in three thousand years upon the earth. Indeed, it was a mistake so rare that it could bring a Keeper the penalty of confiscation of property.

So distressed was she by the events of the past few hours—the discovery of the disaster in Chiang Mai, and now this horrible discovery, so loaded with dreadful implications—that she left the remnant where it lay.

There was only one thought in her mind: Get out of here. She hurried into her clothes, barely even stopping to see if she had left any of her possessions behind, and took a taxi straight to the airport.

THREE

Hunter of Hunters

When Paul Ward had first realized what the con-fused Interpol e-mail was about, he'd felt as if the entire Petronas Towers complex were about to topple into the streets of Kuala Lumpur. But the towers were fine. Only his program had collapsed.

Jesus God, he screamed silently, they were like roaches. He had cleared them out of the whole continent, sanitized it. And now, instead of cleaning out his office in Kuala, prepar-ing for departure to the States and the start of the endgame against them, he was racing through the streets of Bangkok in this clanking old embassy Caddy.

Paul Ward was dealing with one smart breed of animal. How smart, he had just plain not understood, not until now.

He pressed himself against the seat of the limo, instinc-tively keeping his face in shadow. It was always possible that they knew him, he thought, that they would recognize him. He watched the people thronging the streets and wondered if Bangkok, or any city, would look the same if its inhabitants knew that predators a thousand times more dangerous than the tiger or the shark might be walking just behind them.

The damned thing of it was, he'd even run his traditional victory celebration, with all the traditional goodies, stolen in all the innovative ways that his crew could come up with. There had been a couple of cases of Veuve Clicquot borrowed from the Sûreté outpost in Ho Chi Minh City, a couple of cases of beluga borrowed from the KGB in New Delhi, and a whole bunch of dancing girls who came to the crinkle of the dollar—counterfeits made in Myanmar and borrowed from Pakistani intelligence by the redoubtable Joe P. Lo, who could steal venom from a cobra.

They'd been saying good-bye to the General East Asia Pest Control Company. Good-bye and good riddance to their ironically named front organization. This had been a miserable, exacting, assignment, and an extremely dangerous one. Will Kennert, Addie St. John, Lee Hong Quo, Al Sanchez— these were just a few who'd died fighting the vampires.

If he hadn't needed to be totally and completely centered for the task ahead, he would have told the driver to stop at a bar. He'd go in and suck sacred Stolichnaya like a Russki at the nipple of his still. He'd get a massage that lasted all night. Masseuses in relays. Every sin he could think of and—thanks to being in good old Bang-yer-cock—some he probably couldn't.

"Goddamnit!" he suddenly said aloud.

"Sir!"

The driver didn't know that he talked to himself. Why would he? People didn't know Paul Ward, not even embassy people. They weren't supposed to. "Sorry, son."

The flight from Kuala had exhausted him—just sitting in that damn seat, waiting through what seemed an eternity. He'd tried the phone, but it hadn't worked. The Gulf of Thailand was still an empty corner of the world. He hated empty places, dark places. He hated small places even more. Recurring nightmare: he comes awake, starts to sit up in bed, and *wham,* his forehead hits something with such force that he sees stars. Then he realizes that the air is heavy with his own breath and he can't sit up without braining himself. He knows, then, that he is in a coffin.

He knew a CIA guy called Richie Jones, who'd run afoul of the Khmer Rouge and been buried alive. Somebody who'd been in that prison compound had reported that you could hear him screaming for about half an hour. From Ohio State to a lonely hole in the jungles of Cambo. Had Mr. President ever been told about Richie? Had Mr. Director of Central Intelligence known or cared? Weep a tear for the Buckeye state, for it has lost a son.

To die the way covert ops died in the field, damn hard and damn alone—Jesus God, pass the bottle. And to do what he and his crew were doing, to live the way they were living, chasing these monsters in the sewage and the filth of some of the world's most terrible cities, getting yourself eaten if you weren't careful—Jesus God, pass the bottle again.

He was tired. They were all tired. It had been a hard operation, soaked in the blood of fine men and women. And what a death. It'd be better to be buried alive by a bunch of twelve-year-old Khmers with AK-47s and dead eyes, than to be stung in the neck by one of those filthy things.

Long before he'd been forced to come back, Asia had been a place he wanted to put behind him. Vietnam, Laos, Cambodia, 1971 to 1973. In those days, life had less value than dirt out here, especially American life, and most especially the life of a clean-cut CIA virgin with a buzz haircut and wire-framed glasses. He had made it through the Parrot's Beak massacre when Danny Moore had been pulled apart between two backfiring tractors. He had lived through six weeks in a bamboo cell with nothing but roaches and rats for food, while Betty Chang was methodically raped to death and George Moorhouse starved. He had survived because he was too ugly to rape and so cussed that he could crack rats and drink 'em, blood, guts, and all.

He fumbled in the little cabinet that was supposed to be stocked with booze. "Got any vodka in this thing?"

"No, sir."

Of course not. A CIA officer didn't rate booze in his car. This was the U.S. Government. The foreign service kid driving this thing outranked him by a damn country mile. The kid and the limo had appeared at the airport only because there hadn't been time to find a conveyance shitty enough for a CIA field officer. Had he been from State, there would have been booze and ice both.

"The goddamn bastards."

"Sir?"

"Nothing."

Paul wished they'd sent a girl driver. He wanted the scent of a woman in this car. He wanted, he thought, what all men want. He wanted deliverance.

He closed his eyes. Instantly, he saw an old and hated vision, the prairie grass dancing in the moonlight. He opened them again. He could not go there, no. Better to stay with the wartime memories or the memories of sterilizing those filthy dens with acid. How in hell was it that these things looked so much like people? How had they evolved? Had God gone nuts?

The prairie grass dancing in the moonlight, his curtains billowing with moon wind, and in the distance, the most beautiful voice singing: that was the beginning of a life woven from nightmares.

Paul slapped his breast pocket. Pillbox in position. He'd take two tonight, maybe three. Black sleep, please.

"Shit," he said softly, and then, "Shit!" louder.

"Sir?"

This kid would chatter that he'd had to drive a muttering old crazy man to the Royal Orchid Hotel, and then he'd try to find out just who this VIP third class was.

He would not find out.

The State Department could not tell anyone about Paul Ward because they could not tell anyone about the vampire project. If they did that, they would also have to explain that humans are not at the top of the food chain, that we are prey, legitimate prey, just as nature intended. What is worse, they'd have to explain that the predator is damn clever and has evolved some very remarkable camouflage. The predator, you see, looks just like you. Except that his skin is as pale the light of an October moon, and he will sing to you and dance for you, and comfort you in his arms while he kills you. As far as looks are concerned, you can't tell the difference between a vampire and your postman or your doctor, or your own damn brother.

No involved division of any involved government had questioned the secrecy of this operation.

He stared balefully at the back of a stopped truck. Was it parked, or what?

"Can't you hurry?"

"Sir, this is Bangkok."

"Mind if I drive?"

"You want to drive, sir?"

"I need to get there before dark, for Chrissakes."

"Look at the street!"

"Son, excuse me, but get me there now!"

The car shot forward, slamming up onto the sidewalk. An enraged pedestrian hammered the window as they smashed through a food cart.

"You damn fool! That was that guy's rice bowl!"

"You told me to!"

"I didn't tell you to hurt people." Above all things in the world, Paul hated to hurt. He would put a fly out the window rather than swat it. He would watch quietly as a mosquito gorged on his blood, then brush it off when he thought it was getting greedy.

Ironic, in a man who had killed so much. When he slept at night, his legions of dead would steal near: the kids who'd died in the dark corners of Vietnam, the victims of the vampires, the crew members who had not returned. They would call to him; they would stroke him with their cool hands; they would beg him to return them their lives.

He would wake up awash in sweat and choking with terror and regret. He would go to the brutal light of the bathroom as to an altar afire with candles, and gulp the pills of oblivion. Black sleep.

Asia had made him love certain very bad things, chief among them opium. Better than hash, better than grass, better than coke or any of the new designer drugs, far better than the brute high you got off horse. Opium was a deep pleasure, something wonderful that connected earth and soul. It made you feel at peace with the eternal world. He loved the mechanisms of an opium high: the long pipes, the sweet vapor, even the tickly lice in the greasy old sheets of today's few real opium dens.

Paul Ward had sunk deep and sinned hard. Why not, my friends? Tomorrow we die.

Well, that was what they'd thought back in the seventies, listening to Kissinger on Armed Forces Radio. It had seemed hard then, before he knew about vampires, but it had really been easy.

The Jungle Jamboree. No way could you do opium then. He who tripped died.

Still true now, at least for him and his crew. Killing vampires was horribly dangerous. They were quick, so quick that they could throw a knife at nearly the speed of a bullet.

They could not be killed with normal gunfire. You could empty the biggest, most evil weapon in your arsenal right into one of the damn things and it would just stare at you with its deceptively calm eyes, waiting for your bullets to run out. You had to destroy the head.

If you cut them open after they'd fed, they would gush blood like exploded ticks.

The Book of Names had identified twenty-six vampires in Asia. He and his crew had burned out or poisoned or dismembered twenty-four vampires in Asia, and found the remains of two ruined lairs, creatures that had lost their lives on their own.

Accidents happened even to vampires. They weren't perfect. Statistically, if you live long enough, you will meet with some sort of accident. That was their disease—statistics.

That's why vampires did not travel. They were highly territorial and obsessed with accidents. So the trick was to kill them all in a given area as quickly as you could, then move on before the others realized that they were gone.

Paul's next target was going to be Europe. There were many references to Paris in the Book of Names. He'd been looking forward to working out of Paris. Not that he disliked Kuala, but he could use a little less humidity and a little more familiar beauty around him. The Musée Marmottan with its magnificent collection of Monet water lilies was a favorite. He considered Monet to be one of the most evolved of all human beings, on a par with the D. T. Suzukis and Foucaults of the world. From those paintings, a man could obtain the true balm of peace. The light that shone in from the garden at the Marmottan, that light was holy.

"God help me!" he cried out loud.

"Yessir!"

"Please, son, be quiet. And stop running people down."

"I didn't run anybody down. I just got around that truck."

"You need to go back there later. Give that guy some dough for his cart."

"Sir?"

"Without the cart, he and his wife will starve. Their children become prostitutes. Do you understand that?"

"Sir, I hardly think—"

"*Do you understand that?*"

"Sir, yes, sir!"

Could this be a marine out of uniform? No, look at the hair. Foreign service all the way. He was just yanking Paul's chain with his military lip. He'd be sneering later with his State Department buddies about the old CIA asshole he'd driven around.

With his cart wrecked, that fruit vendor might as well open his veins, and Paul knew this kid would *not* go back, he would not give the guy the twenty bucks it would take to put his life back together again.

Funnily enough, Paul was in his work because he liked people. He'd seen the CIA take such incredible shit over the years and save so many damn lives. The Company could not defend herself, not without giving away secrets she was bound to keep. So she just took it. He'd seen the effects of all the Company bashing in his own life. There'd been a time when the merest hint of a Company connection brought women swarming like darling honeybees. Not anymore.

The car swung around another corner, and the Royal Orchid Hotel finally appeared down the smog-hazed street.

What the hell was he about to find? This would be the first actual victim they had ever had a chance to study. The vampires were obsessive about destroying remains. Except, apparently, this time.

Still, there was something very bad about all this. He could smell it, but he couldn't quite see it. A place is wrapped up, finished. Then, suddenly, it ain't finished.

Okay, think. Think it out, Paul: All of a sudden, they leave evidence in a hotel. The hotel is on a continent that has just been sterilized of their presence.

It was not like them to taunt you. They were too shy, too careful for that. Their lives were incredibly precious to them, because this life was all they had, at least in Paul's opinion. In his opinion, nature had given them immortal lives—potentially, if they were very damn careful—but they had not been given souls. They were damn animals and they knew it.

So if this wasn't a declaration or a taunt, then it must be something else. The thing was, when the National Security Administration had cracked the language in the Book of Names, the whole vampire world had been opened up to Paul and his crew. He returned to the States to become head of a whole new division that would be devoted to eradicating the menace. There were to be units operating on every continent, using the methods that Paul and his group had evolved.

One of the reasons that he was racing back to the States so soon after completing his work in Asia was to deal with a stupid but potentially serious problem: The director of the CIA had been asking legal questions. Specifically, were these creatures to be regarded as animal or human? If they were human, then they were committing crimes, not killing prey.

Declaring that the creatures were human meant that a whole different approach would be necessary. There would have to be due process and trials and prison sentences, and the vampire would like nothing better than this type of leverage. The vampire was powerful and quick and so damn smart. It could get away from prison.

They were almost unkillable. Something about their blood gave them extraordinary powers of recovery. You had to blow that head apart, then burn the creatures to ash, to be absolutely certain they were dead. Then the lair had to be washed in acid.

How could you ever call anything that lived in a filthy hole like a vampire lair human?

But he couldn't stop the wheels of the bureaucracy from turning as they turned. "What is this bunch of agents doing out in Asia killing people?" "Who are these 'vampires,' a terrorist group? A secret society? What in hell is going on here?"

Some Thai were passing the car, banging gongs and chanting. Funerals made Paul physically ill. He had to drown out that sound, and *not* with a Thai radio station because the Asians, God love 'em, had not figured music out yet, not in any way whatsoever. "Are there any CDs in this car?"

"Destiny's Child, Santana, Johnny Mathis. Some kind of opera."

"Put in the opera, turn it up to full volume."

"Yes, sir." The boy sounded crestfallen. Which one would the kid have preferred? Destiny's Child, no doubt.

"Full volume! I want my ears to bleed! You got any cigars?" Paul was a creature of appetites. Fine wines, lots of them. The best vodka in the world, lots of it. The strongest opium, the most exotic, the sweetest, the most delicious of whatever the world had to offer. One of his great regrets was the failure of either the Company to assassinate Castro or, better, of the U.S. to just come to terms with him. The loss of the Cuban cigar had been a blow.

Well, good god damn, that was *Callas!*

"Louder!"

"It's as loud as it gets!"

He reached forward, turned the knob all the way up.

Oh, God, *Lakmé*. Oh, God, the "Bell Song." That she had lived, this goddess Maria Callas, was proof that human beings were of interest to the good Lord. Nothing so fabulous could have come about by accident. "Hey, kid!"

No answer.

"KID!"

"Yessir!"

"That *goddess* is called Maria Callas. You ever worshipped a woman?"

"Sir?"

"It is a very special pleasure, I assure you. To worship something so gentle, so soft, so willing as a good woman."

"Okay."

He'd worshipped at the altar of the female all of his life. Three marriages, six mistresses, and whores enough to populate a small army were testament to that fact. Jesus, but she could sing. "Death, be not proud!"

"Yessir!"

"Do you fear death?"

"Yessir!"

"The goddamn Pathet Lao stuck an electric cattle prod up my ass and left it on so long steam came outa my nose. You know what I told them?"

"Name, rank, and serial number?"

"I told them, if they filled out the forms, they could get

Visa cards from the Thai Farmer's Bank. The deal was, let me go and I would help them fill out those forms. When they got their credit cards, that was the end of that Pathet Lao cell. Who wants to run around in the jungle covered with leeches when you could be sipping a Singapore Sling at the Poontang Hilton, am I right?"

"I guess so, sir."

He could see the kid's eyes rolling in the rearview mirror. Well, let 'em roll.

Let the DCIA and the president whine about whether or not the damn vampires had human rights or whatever. Paul decided that he'd like to *taste* vampire. Probably like—not chicken, no, they'd taste like something else. Snake maybe, except he'd eaten snake in Cambo, and it *did* taste like chicken. They made dynamite snake curry in Kuala backstreets. Little pieces of sour asp meat marinated with asafetida and fried in ghee. Oh, that is good.

They reached the hotel at long living last. It was a pretty place, luxurious. What was a vampire doing in a place like this? Vampires didn't go to hotels. They didn't sleep in beds. They were *animals*, God for damn it! The thing must have been crawling around in the ducts or something.

The problem he was here to solve was twofold: First, he had to get a line on the whereabouts of this animal. Second, he had to contain the curiosity of the local cops, who had a corpse on their hands they could not understand at all. They also wanted to know why an Interpol officer was operating in their country without their knowledge. Of course, the problem there was that he was on CIA's payroll.

Kiew Narawat was a precise, solemn man from Sri Lanka, an excellent operative and a profound friend of the United States. But Narawat wasn't a member of Paul's team, just a garden variety asset who had been detailed to observe any nocturnal comings and goings at a certain temple in Chiang Mai.

Paul went into the hotel.

If they hadn't messed up the corpse somehow, that would be one good outcome from this tragedy. Not only would there be a useful forensic and medical yield, the condition of the body would help him make his case that the vampire killings should not be declared crimes. "This was the act of an animal," he could hear himself saying. "This man was not murdered, he was fed upon."

If they could just get a little more vampire DNA, that would be it. The discovery of the vampires had taken place in 1989, when the Japanese government had asked for help with a very strange murder. They had the attack on videotape from a traffic control point. It was three in the morning and the streets were empty.

An old man was struggling along the sidewalk. He was the only person in the area. Then this strange creature came loping along, and grabbed the man. It had put its mouth on his neck and suddenly the entire body had withered, disappearing into its own clothing. The creature had stuffed it into a satchel and walked off.

The man was unattached, very poor, and normally wouldn't have been missed even in that very careful country. But the police made an effort, because what they had seen was so disturbing. They identified the old man. They went to the spot where the crime had taken place and took careful samples of everything. A hair had appeared in the debris they vacuumed up from the sidewalk that was not human, and not from a known animal.

It had taken years for the mystery to percolate into CIA's

pot. Paul got it because he was an old Asia hand and had his own father's mysterious death in his file. The way the old man looked after his blood had apparently been sucked out of him and the way Paul's dad had looked when he'd been discovered had been strangely similar.

They gave it to him because they thought he'd be interested. Well, he wasn't. And damn them for dredging up his father's memory like that.

Nothing more was done, not until 1998, when a crime reporter, Ellen Wunderling, had disappeared in New York while innocently doing research for a Halloween spoof about vampires. She had delved too deep into the gothic underground, an eerie, subtly murderous subculture that would be an ideal place for real vampires to conceal themselves. He'd begun his own investigation of the disappearance, but then came Tokyo and an opportunity to take immediate and direct action. He had been finding and killing vampires ever since.

Paul got into the elevator. He hated riding elevators. It opened on a wide corridor, with rooms open here and there. The management had cleared the whole floor. In front of one of the open rooms, a small crowd of Thai police, medical personnel, and plainclothes officers came and went.

The instant Paul entered the room, the smell hit him. What was it? A human odor, maybe. But so strange—salty, dry, distressingly organic. He looked down at the yellow flowered sheet with the angular lump under it.

"Thailand will expect extradition of the perpetrator, if he is found elsewhere, Mr. Ward," the colonel inspector said in his heavy, careful English.

Paul grunted, wishing that the man could be made to go away.

Kiew Narawat had been ordered to report if he saw any-body enter the temple. So why had he ended up in this room like this, instead? Paul took the sheet and pulled it back.

He actually had to stifle a scream. This was the most spec-tacularly destroyed human body he had seen in his adult life. But not in his whole life, and that was what made it so terri-ble for him.

He was twelve again. He was awakened by a sound like the last water getting sucked down an eager drain.

The sleepy-eyed boy looked out the window, gazing into the glowing dark. The prairie grass was dancing in the moonlight, and there was a dark figure moving through the field with a burden of some kind on its shoulder.

Paulie stared. Who was that out there? But Big Boy wasn't barking and Big Boy was a hair-trigger watchdog.

The figure disappeared off into the woods. Tomorrow, Paulie would get Dad and go down there, see what had hap-pened.

And then came the terror of the next morning and of the haunted life of Paul Ward: Where's Dad? he had asked his mom. I don't know honey, she had said. When is he coming back? I don't know! I don't know!

Flash forward four years: Paul is walking along the stream beside their pear orchard when he sees something strange down among the roots of a tree. Again, Big Boy notices nothing.

Now, Paul knows why. He knows that they secrete a blocking pheromone that makes it impossible for animals to pick up their scent. The remains of their victims are covered with it.

When he saw the skeleton of his father in a casement of dry and disintegrating skin just like this, he had run back to the house screaming in terrified agony, Big Boy gamboling beside him.

The dental records had been definitive. It was Dad. But Dr. Ford, their local medical examiner, could not figure out what had happened to him. The state police couldn't figure it out. The FBI finally issued a report: death by misadventure unknown.

Little Paulie had become obsessed with secrets. What had killed Daddy? An animal? Space aliens? Nobody knew. Daddy had been strong and big and good, so why had he ended up like that down in the roots of a tree?

Some years later, Paul had awakened to see a woman standing at the foot of his bed, a woman dressed all in black, with golden hair and an angelic face. She looked at him out of sweet eyes, eyes that made the heart melt. But when he sat up, when he called out to her, she faded like a dream.

"The woman in here with him was French," the policeman said, breaking Paul's reverie. "We have determined that her name was Marie Tallman. She took the Air France flight to Paris. She will be detained there when she gets off the plane."

"It was a female?" Paul responded. "You're sure?"

"A woman, yes," the Thai said, his voice gone sharp with surprise at Paul's odd use of the word "it." But Paul couldn't help himself. Paul hated these animals whether God had made them or not, and he was damned if he would dignify them with personal pronouns.

"Under no circumstances is she to be detained."

"Excuse me, but that is a violation of our sovereignty. I am sorry."

Paul really noticed the officer for the first time. "Ask the French to photograph her and follow her. But *not* to detain her."

The Thai smiled. Paul could only hope that they would cooperate. He could not push the matter further, not and risk an inquiry to the embassy about the nature of his activities. The Thai were hair-trigger friends. They did not like CIA operations taking place on their soil without their knowledge.

At high levels in the government, he was golden. But these cops were strictly low-level, and they didn't know one damn thing about Paul's secret brief and his secret powers.

He gazed down at the remains, almost willing them to speak. But they said nothing. The face was stretched so tight against the skull that it looked like something you might buy for Halloween.

"Turn him over," he said. "I want to look at the back."

Two of the cops obliged. Paul knew that the vampires used human skin for articles of clothing—gloves and such—because you found such things in their lairs. He'd thought maybe the back of this man would be as neatly skinned as his own father's had been.

He'd held some of those gloves and purses in his hands for a long, long time. He'd wondered which of the creatures had worn garments made from his dad. Whenever he and his crew found these things, they collected them with reverence and they blessed them and they cremated them and made a little ritual of scattering the ashes.

Melodramatic? You could say so. Sentimental. Sure. But his crew were united on two things: Any human remains they located would be respected, and no vampire would be left alive. Scorched-earth policy. Absolute.

Think if they had to read Miranda warnings. Think if the vampires were allowed legal defense, say, in India, where the prisons leaked and it could take years before a case came to trial? What if they claimed murder as their natural right, and proved that they were created by God to prey upon the human being? Presumably, laws would then have to be written allowing them to take a certain number of humans as prey each year, much as we allow ourselves to take whales.

And what about the endangered-species acts in various countries, most especially Europe and the U.S.? If the vampire was declared an endangered species—and it was conceivable, given their comparative rarity—then Paul and his crew would be out of business altogether. Governments would end up in the business of encouraging the vampire to breed and protecting its habitat—the ghetto, the teeming slum, the homeless shelter.

A man with glasses approached Paul. "We understand that you will be able to inform us of the manner of death."

"Death by misadventure."

"Excuse me?"

"The man had a bad adventure, obviously. So that's the conclusion—death by misadventure."

"You are coming all the way from KL to tell us this—this nothing?"

"The corpse is U.S. property," Paul said. "I'm going to remove it to the States." He needed it. He needed any trace of nonhuman DNA he could find. The hair from Tokyo wasn't enough. But two samples—that would end the human-animal controversy.

"Now, wait," the colonel inspector said, "now—"

"It's a done deal." He pulled the fax he'd gotten from the Thai foreign office before he left KL. He unfolded it. " 'You will deliver the remains to Mr. Paul Ward of the United States Embassy.' That is what it says."

The man nodded, reading the letter. Then his eyes met

Paul's. His eyes pleaded. "Please tell me in confidence what has happened."

"He met with a misadventure."

You rarely saw anger in the Thai. They were a reserved and very polite people. But the inspector's eyes grew hard and small, and Paul knew that there was fury seething within him. Thailand had never been colonized for a reason. The Thai might be polite, but they would fight for their independence quite literally to the last man. No deals. "I would like to know, then, if I may, whether or not we are likely to see any more such murders."

Paul gestured toward the yellow, sticklike corpse. "I'm a scientist. I'm trying to figure it out."

"Is it, then, a disease?"

"No, no, he was killed. You can count on that."

The room was full of police and forensics experts. Bangkok was not happy with this bizarre situation. Interpol was not happy, and asking all sorts of questions about who the hell had been running around with forged ID of that quality in his wallet, while at the same time pretending to Thailand that they knew who the guy was. Lots of secret handshakes being traded all around.

Somebody was going to have to tell the widow and her three kids, too, and Paul suspected that he would be elected.

"I am Dr. Ramanujan," a compact man said, jostling up, gesturing with his sterile gloves. "What has done this? Do you know what has done this, because I do not know?"

Paul hated to lie, and he did not lie now. He kept his secret and revealed it at the same time. "A killer did it, using a very special and unusual method of fluid extraction."

"And where are the body fluids? The blood, for example?"

"The fluids are gone."

"Gone?"

"We will not find the fluids."

Ramanujan grinned, shaking his head. "Riddles, sir, riddles instead of answers."

They bagged the body for him and delivered all their forensic gleanings in a series of plastic pouches, each neatly labeled in Thai and English.

On the way down, the colonel inspector said, "Would you care to have a drink with me?"

Paul would have loved a drink right now. Twenty drinks. But he had an urgent mission halfway around the world. As fast as humanly possible, he and his crew had to follow "Marie Tallman" to Paris. And not on tomorrow's flights, either.

"I'll take a raincheck. I need to get to Paris as quickly as possible."

"There are no more flights from Bangkok to Paris today."

"There's one."

"I know the schedules very well, I am sorry."

"This is off the schedule."

"The American embassy has its own flights?"

Paul thought of the cramped USAF Falcon Jet that would carry them to gay Paree. "Just this one."

"Then that's good for you."

He wondered. He had the sense that Paris was going to be a ferocious confrontation. For the first time, they would be facing vampires who expected them.

The question was stark: Without the advantage of surprise, did he and his people—his brave people—have any chance at all?

FOUR

The Castle of the White Queen

Miriam had been moving effortlessly through human society since before mankind had invented the arch, and she considered herself entirely capable of handling their customs, from the letters testament of the Imperial Roman Curia to the passports of the American Department of State. So she was surprised when the customs officer said, "Please come this way, Madame Tallman."

She stared at him so hard that he blinked and took an involuntary step back. Shaking his head, he glanced again at her passport, then up to her face. "Come, please."

"Is there something wrong?"

"You will talk to the prefect."

The prefect? That sounded ominous. As Miriam followed along behind the customs official, she considered that they must have found the body. They had traced Marie Tallman; it was that simple.

As she walked, she felt somebody fall in behind her. She could smell the gun the man was carrying, just as she could smell the polish on his brass and the wax on his shoes. She knew he was a policeman, in full uniform. His breath was young and steady, powerful. He was also quite close to her, alert for any attempt at escape.

They thought, therefore, that she would be aware of why she was being detained. Ahead of her, the customs officer had hunched his shoulders. He feared that she might attempt to harm him.

These men did not think that they had apprehended some poor soul caught up in a fiasco of identity confusion. They believed that they were escorting a criminal who knew very well that she was in serious trouble.

These thoughts passed through Miriam's mind in a flash. The next instant, she was looking for a means of escape. She was a master of the human being, smarter, stronger, and quicker. It would be nothing for her to overpower both of these men. The gun was a trivial problem. Before his hand had even started to reach for it, both creatures could be knocked senseless.

The problem was the surroundings. There were other people going up and down the hallway. The customs area they had just left teemed with dozens more. The offices, most of which had glass walls, were also full of people.

So Miriam kept walking, hoping that she would be in a private situation for the few seconds she needed, before they locked her away. They would lock her away; she had no doubt of it.

It had been extraordinarily foolish to abandon that remnant. It was drilled into them from childhood: Never let man see the results of your feeding. Humans are cattle, but they are bright cattle and they must not be made aware of their true situation. The entire species could, in effect, stampede.

As appeared to be happening—in effect. There simply wasn't anything left to think. The Asians had already been swept away in the onslaught, and now she had endangered herself in a foolish, heedless moment of panic, and possibly many others of her kind as well. Because of what she had done, she was in the process of being captured by human beings. A Keeper!

They came to a door. The customs officer said, "Enter, please." She could feel the young policeman's breath on her neck. There was no more time. She had to act, and no matter the crowd.

She stepped away from the door and into the center of the corridor. This left the two men facing each other, their eyes widening in surprise at the speed of her movement. To them, she would have seemed to temporarily disappear. Keepers had bred humans to be slow, for convenience. That way they could be outrun, outjumped, and outmaneuvered. Prey should be easy to herd.

Before the two men could turn to face her, she had slipped her hands behind their heads and pressed them together sharply. They dropped like sacks.

A secretary rushed out of an office two doors down. She looked at Miriam. She could not associate a young girl in an elegant suit with two unconscious men. "What has happened?"

"Gas," Miriam cried. "The corridor is full of gas!" She turned and went striding on toward the emergency exit at the far end. A moment later, a horn started hooting. The terrified secretary had pulled the fire alarm and then rushed out into the customs area shouting, "Gas!" as she ran.

Opening the emergency exit, Miriam looked about for a way back into the main part of the terminal. Once out of the customs area, she would be able to go into Paris. She'd have to get Sarah to work up a new identity and FedEx her the passport. She certainly could not use the Tallman identity, and dared not risk her own.

Others were coming out behind her, so she climbed some concrete steps, then went down a long, empty passageway. Behind her, a man shouted that she was going the wrong way. She noticed his American-sounding voice, then glimpsed a narrow, dark figure starting to run toward her. She did not look back again.

She soon found herself in a bustling staging area for the assembly of airline meals. There were shelves full of little trays and plastic cutlery, and a wall lined with institutional refrigerators. Workers stood at tables putting the meals together on trays. Others covered them with plastic wrap. Others still packed them in steel shelves, ready to be wheeled out to the waiting planes.

There were aluminum double doors at the far end of the room. Striding with the confidence of a person who belonged exactly where she was, Miriam went to these doors.

Behind her there was a cry, *"Halte!"*

Miriam ran. She ran as hard and as fast as she could, speeding along the corridor and into a locker room. This was where the various workers changed into their uniforms.

"Halte Halte!"

A new man had burst into the room at the far end. Her throat tightened; she felt a sudden surge of rage. The reason was that this creature had appeared ahead of her. They knew exactly where she was. They must be using radios to surround her. She looked around for doors other than the ones she and the gendarme had entered.

She slipped through one, found herself in a shower room. The door had nothing but a handle lock, which she twisted. At once, he began to shake it violently from the other side.

She threw open a window. There was a drop of about three stories to an area of tarmac crowded with baggage lorries. As the door burst open behind her, she went to the window and jumped.

Her teeth clashed together and her ankles shot pain up her legs from the impact. The palms of her hands burned when they slapped against the pavement. Immediately, she rolled under the overhang of the building, making herself impossible to see from above.

The shock had damaged the heel of one of her shoes. She struggled away, moving among the speeding baggage lorries. Stopping for a moment, she pulled off her shoes. The heel was not usable.

This dim, booming space was extremely alien. She'd never been inside a factory, never seen the raw side of human engineering and architecture. She'd preferred to live her life in an older, more familiar aesthetic. Her home in Manhattan was a hundred and fifteen years old; she stayed almost exclusively in old, familiar hotels when she traveled. She could handle the human world, but she'd never seen a place like this before, never imagined that the hidden parts of the human world were this mechanical.

Ahead of her she saw a passageway. The floor was dark and marked by white and yellow lines. The passage curved up and to the right. This appeared to lead away from the customs enclosure, so she began walking along it. It was lighted by fluorescent tubes, some of them flickering and some completely out. The effect was eerie, and made more so by a high-pitched whining sound coming from ahead. She stopped to listen and tried to place this sound, but she could not.

The farther into the passage she went, the louder it

became. She stopped again. It would rise and fall, then rise again. Then it almost faded entirely. She resumed walking, passing the endless, black-scuffed walls, moving beneath the flickering lights.

The sound screamed out right in her face, and her entire field of vision was filled with glaring lights. A horn began sounding.

There was no room to lie down, the oncoming machine was too low. She looked up—and there, where the lights were, she could grab hold. She leaped, missed by inches. The machine got closer, the lights growing as big as saucers, the glare blinding her and pinning her like the stunned animal that she was. The horn blared and blared. She crouched.

Like most animals', the backs of a Keeper's eyes were reflective. When she looked directly into those lights, the driver would have seen a flare as if from the eyes of a deer or a tiger. Human night vision had been bred away. Better that they sleep at night, giving the Keepers time to tend herd and feed.

There were only seconds left now. The machine would tear her to shreds. She would die from that—actually die. It was an oblivion that had haunted her all her life. She did not think that Keepers persisted in the memory of nature. She did not want to cease to be.

She sprang up from her crouching position and reached toward the light fixtures. She grabbed the edge and drew herself up, hooking one leg along the lip of the long fixture and pressing the rest of her body against the ceiling.

With a hot blast of air the machine went shrieking past, not an inch below her breast. It seemed to take forever, and she soon felt her fingers and toes slipping. She was going to fall onto the roof of the thing.

And then it was gone, and she fell instead to the floor, which she knew now was really a subterranean road. Would another machine come? Of course. Would the driver have radioed her position back to her pursuers? Of course.

She knew, now, that she was in an extremely serious situation. Man had changed. Man was now effective and efficient. She remembered the Paris of fifty years ago, a compact, intricate city traveled by tiny automobiles and herds of bicycles. Only the Métropolitain sped the way this thing had. But it had been on rails.

Ahead, the screaming sound had started again. Another of the machines was coming. She saw, perhaps two hundred yards farther on, a ladder inset into the wall. It led to a service hatch of some kind.

The machine was coming, getting louder. There was a wind blowing in her face, getting steadily harder. This must be a subway system that served just the airport. But how could that be? Paris had a compact airfield, as she recalled, albeit a busy one.

It had grown huge, that was the answer, and she was thinking that maybe her brothers and sisters were at least somewhat right. Maybe she needed to stick closer to home, too, because this situation was getting out of hand, *way* out of hand. She sprinted, moving easily twice as fast as the fastest human runner—but what did that matter in a world where the machines hurtled along at phenomenal velocity? Even the strength of a Keeper was nothing against fifty tons of speeding steel.

As she reached the ladder, the lights of the train appeared. Immediately, the horn started blaring. Worse, a screaming sound began and the train started to slow dramatically. This time, the driver had seen her and put on his brakes. The last thing she needed was a confrontation in this damned tunnel. That would be the end. She'd be trapped then.

She bolted up the ladder, only to find that the steel hatch was battened down tight. Her great strength enabled her to push it until it bent and popped open.

The train came to a stop about ten feet from her. It stood there, invisible behind its lights, its horn honking and honking. Back where she had come from, voices rose, people shouting in French not to move . . . French, and also that one American voice.

She clambered up through the hatch. Now she was in an access tunnel, and not far away there was a door. She didn't think it would make any sense to go along this tunnel, even though it was obviously meant for pedestrians and not trains. Tunnels were damned traps. She went through the door.

Light flared in her face; a roar assailed her. She staggered, and a voice said, "*Pardon.*" She had stumbled into a man in a taxi queue. He reached out, took her waist. "*Madame?*" he said, his voice rising in question.

"Sorry," she babbled in English, then, in French, "*Pardon, je suis confuse.*"

He looked her up and down. The other people in the queue were staring.

"I have broken my shoe," she added, smiling weakly. Then she crept to the back of the line. She had escaped the horrors of the police and the dangers of the maze. Somehow, she had reached the outside world.

She must get a hotel room, she thought, then seek out Martin Soule. He had been a friend of her mother's back in the days of powdered wigs. She'd seen him fifty years ago. Martin was very ancient and wise, very careful. He was also stylish, powerful and daring. Like Miriam, he was a wine enthusiast, and had even desensitized himself to some of their fodder, because it was so difficult to move in French society without eating. Once, he'd made her laugh by drinking the blood of an enormous fish. But then his preparation of it according to human cooking principles had revolted her. She still remembered the ghastly odor of the hot, dense flesh when it came steaming out of the poacher.

She was still well back in the queue when she noticed the policeman with a radio to his lips, staring at her as he talked. Her heart sank. At home, she dealt easily with the police. The police were her friends. She had the Sixth Precinct, where her club was located, well paid off. But she could not pay these cops off.

The policeman came striding toward the queue. He had his hand on the butt of his pistol. She thought to run, but there were two more of them coming from the opposite direction. Her only choice was to leap out into traffic and trust to her speed and dexterity to get through the cars that shot past just beyond the taxi stand. But even that would lead only to a wall.

When she realized that there was no escape, she let out an involuntary growl that made the woman standing ahead of her whip round, her face pale, her eyes practically popping out. Miriam's whole instinct now was to kill. Had she not applied her powerful will, she might have torn the creature's throat out.

Quelling her damned instincts, she forced a smile onto her face. She'd play her last card—give them her emergency Cheryl Blackmore driver's license and claim to have lost her passport. Maybe before they discovered that Cheryl Blackmore was a long-dead resident of Nebraska and most certainly did not rate a passport, she would have found some means of escape.

The three policemen arrived—and began chatting together. They were laughing, completely at their ease, taking no notice whatsoever of her. They'd been talking on their radios merely to arrange their coffee break.

Now, she thought, laughing to herself, there was the old mankind, the gentle, sloppy, genial humanity that the Keepers had so carefully bred.

As she slipped into her taxi, she was filled with a sort of glee. It was delicious to have escaped, delicious and lovely and joyous. And damn, damn lucky.

Her mouth began to dry out, her muscles to relax. The waves of hate stopped crashing in her heart. The taxi moved up a long ramp into the sunlight, and Miriam relaxed back against the seat.

"Votre destination, madame?"

"The Ritz," she said. She'd take a huge suite. The Ritz would mean silk sheets like the ones at home, and a long call to Sarah to say how lonely she was and how far away she felt . . . and to tell her to get that new passport over here fast.

In the cab, she pressed her shoe together as best she could, rearranged her hair, freshened her face, and tried to smooth the wrinkles in her suit. Her suitcase was gone forever, of course, and so she would have to buy new clothes, and there would be no time for proper tailoring at Chanel. That would make Sarah happy. They were both extremely fashionable, of course, but Sarah thought Miriam much too conservative.

So much of the Paris whizzing past was unfamiliar. The huge roads, the endless blocks of buildings that had grown like monstrous cliffs beyond the Périphérique distressed and confused her.

It was remade, entirely remade, and in just these few years! But then the taxi swung off the flying roadway and went down into territory that was, thankfully, more familiar. They were on the Rue de Vaugirard, where Philippe Vendôme had lived. She'd been fascinated by his alchemical studies, had stayed with him a few years while she was recovering from the grief of her mother's destruction. She'd adored him, with his wonderful, sophisticated manner and his passable skill at whist. Miriam loved games, but finding humans who could be effective opponents was not easy.

She had given Philippe of her blood, and turned back the years for him. He had become a searcher after the secrets of the Keepers. Useless, that, in the early eighteenth century. But he had been a pleasant companion, her entire pleasure for a while, until she'd met Lord Hadley's son John.

"Philippe," she murmured, thinking of that lovely house of his. In 1956 it had been something of a ruin. She had walked silent halls where she had laughed and loved with him, and reflected on the brief lives of men. Now she could only glimpse it, the once-proud estate little more than a front on a huge building. The street the taxi bounced along had been laid over part of the elegant park. Here, she and he had come and fed his swans.

Now they went underground, into a roaring tunnel full of autos and lorries, speeding along at a deadly clip. And here, quite suddenly, was the Champs Élysées. They had come by a new high-speed route.

It was all so familiar and all so dear. She remembered it from fifty years ago, even a hundred—the same marvelous width, the same trees, the same grand ambiance. Yes, this was just as it had been since Louis Philippe had commissioned Haussmann to reconstruct the intricate, ancient spaghetti-bowl that had been the Paris of the last age.

They were soon passing along the Rue St. Honoré, lined

with luscious shops, in the windows of which she glimpsed the strangely simple clothing of this era, clothing that increasingly emphasized anything that was male about the female. The ideal form for human women was becoming that of the boy. She preferred elegance.

Then, here was the Place Vendôme. The Ritz was *exact*. Lovely and beloved! She had first come to this place on a rainswept evening back before the motor. What trip had that been? Perhaps 1900, when she and John Blaylock had come here in search of the luxury that was just then gaining the hotel its grand reputation.

Getting down from the taxi—or up, actually, out of this tiny modern sardine tin—she found herself face-to-face with a doorman in the hotel's familiar green livery, even his coat reminiscent of more gentle days.

She went into the lobby, passing across the thick carpet to reception. No face was familiar, of course. Fifty years and all the humans would have changed. They came and went like so much foam on a restless wave. Well, at least she had Sarah free and clear for another century, perhaps two . . . unless, of course, the dear found some clever scientific way to last longer. Sarah knew the ugly secret of her own artificial longevity. Such knowledge would have driven a lesser human mad, but Sarah was often at her test tubes, poor thing.

"I'm afraid I have no reservation," Miriam said to the clerk, who managed to appear affable and also a little concerned at the same time. A blink of his eyes as she approached had told her that he knew exactly how old her suit was. She was travel-weary and hobbling from the broken shoe. Altogether, she could not look to him as if she belonged here. She dared not throw the names of fifty years ago around to impress him, either. Coming from what appeared to be a girl of twenty-five dressed in her grandmother's old clothes, such an attempt to impress would instead seem like the babbling of a madwoman.

"I am so sorry," he began.

"I would like a suite. I prefer the fourth floor front, if you don't mind." These were among the best rooms in the hotel, and the only ones she would even consider using.

He asked for her credit card. She gave him Sarah's Visa. It annoyed Sarah for her to use this card, but there was at present no choice. Using her own card was a serious risk, and Marie Tallman was retired forever. She waited while he made a phone call.

"I'm sorry, madame, this is declined."

Must be crowding its credit limit, she thought. Just like Sarah to have a card like this. Too bad she didn't have a copy of Sarah's American Express card, but the only one of those in her possession was her own.

"Perhaps it's defective, madame. If you have another—"

She turned and faced the doors. She had no desire to push this, even to remain here for another minute. She had to call Sarah. She started to open her cell phone, then hesitated. The call would not be secure.

"Is there a public telephone?"

"But of course, madame." He directed her to a call box. She took out her AT&T card, which was in Sarah's name, and dialed the call straight through to their emergency number. This only rang if it was absolutely urgent, so she could be sure that Sarah would pick up right away.

She did not pick up. It was five hours earlier in New York, making it eight o'clock in the morning. Sarah would be home, surely. She tried the other number, the regular one. Only the answering machine came on.

She tried the club. No answer there, not at this hour. Damn the woman, where was she when she was needed?

Maybe she'd fed. Maybe she was in Sleep. Yes, that was it. Of course, that must be it . . . must be. She put the phone down.

She thought matters over. She was effectively broke. But she was never broke; she'd had scads of money, always.

Perhaps she could try another hotel, some lesser place. There must be some credit left on the Visa card. Then she thought—how could she get into any hotel, this one included, without giving them a passport? The answer was that she couldn't, and the smaller and sleazier the hotel, the more obsessive it would be about identification. The Tallman passport needed to be burned; that's all it was good for.

She saw that she was still in mortal danger. They would have a description of her, and she hadn't even a change of clothes. They'd be searching the hotels, of course. It was logical.

She had to go to the Castle of the White Queen. Fifty years ago, Martin had been there. Maybe he still was, and maybe he could help her. Of course he could. He'd been a more worldly sort than Lamia, or even Miriam herself.

She began walking, soon coming into the Place de l'Opéra. She headed for the Métro. On the way, she stopped at a small *bureau de change* and turned her Thai baht into euros. She got forty of them. As well, she had two hundred U.S. dollars in cash. Not much, not much at all. But she never traveled with cash; she didn't need to. Being limitlessly wealthy made her sudden poverty especially difficult. She didn't know how to function.

She went down the steps into the clanging world of the Métro. She remembered it from her last visit, but she'd only used it once, and that was to get around a traffic accident when she'd been hurrying to the opera. There was difficulty with the change booth, then confusion about which *direction* she wanted. The hurrying crowds made it no easier. But, in the end, she found herself primly seated in a car going in the correct direction.

The Castle of the White Queen had been built on land that the Keepers had reserved for themselves from time immemorial. It was on the Rue des Gobelins, and parts of it had been rented to the Gobelins family and fitted out by them as a tannery. At night, after Gobelins and his people went home; the hides tanned there were not necessarily bovine. The Keepers lived in the upper reaches of the building.

Locally, there were many legends about why it was called the Castle of the White Queen. Some said that Blanche de Castille had built it, others that it had belonged to Blanche de Navarre. The real builder was Miriam's dear mother, who had been known among her peers as the White Queen, for her grandeur, her splendid pallor, and the fact that their family had come out of the white sands of the North African desert.

The scent of man that filled the Métro did not make Miriam's jaws spread, let alone fill. As troubling as all this was, at least she was full, and very satisfactorily so. That had been a healthy little thing she'd eaten. She could easily bear this swim in a sea of food.

An accordionist began to play, and Miriam closed her eyes to listen. Certain things about Paris were almost timeless, it seemed. When she and her mother had been here, the humans had been making similar music, but with different instruments. The music was rougher and wilder then, but they were wilder also, the humans, in times past.

In those days, feeding in a place like Paris had been so easy that some Keepers had overfed, gorging until they bled out through their pores, and their orifices ran with the blood of their victims. The human population had been a seething, helpless, ignorant mass, living in the streets, under the bridges, anywhere there was a bit of shelter. The old cities had been full of nameless, aimless wanderers who could be plucked up like fruits fallen to the ground.

She missed Gobelins and left the Métro at d'Italie instead. Coming up to the street, she looked around her. She experienced a sense of satisfaction: things were really unchanged here.

She quickened her step, eager to get a sight of the castle. If the Keepers had been driven off—well, she'd deal with that problem when she had to.

Ahead was the tiny Rue des Gobelins, hardly an alleyway running off the much wider avenue. She turned into it—and stopped, staring struck with wonder. The Castle of the White Queen was *exact*, just like the Ritz. Worn, but so precisely the same that she thought it must still be in the hands of Keepers.

Until this moment, she had not realized how afraid she had actually been. She needed her kind now. And she needed, also, to warn them. In the hurly-burly of the past few hours, she had all but lost sight of why she was here and not back in New York.

Ironic indeed that the strongest, most intelligent species on the planet, the very pinnacle of the food chain, was in the same predicament as the frog and the gorilla.

It had crept up on them so easily, the result of a long series of what had, at the time, seemed like brilliant breeding maneuvers.

Back thirty thousand years ago, they had almost lost the entire human stock to a plague. They'd rotted where they stood, the poor things. It had been determined that overeager breeding had been the culprit. Generations of them had been bred for their nutritional value, which meant an imbalance of red over white blood cells. The result? They'd become prone to all sorts of diseases.

To ensure that they would survive and still remain the delicious food source that they'd been made to be, the Keepers had decided in conclave to increase the human population. To accomplish this, sexual seasonality had been bred out of the species entirely. This had been done by breeding for high levels of sexual hormones. As a result, the creatures had bloomed into bizarre sexual parodies of normal animals. Their genitals had moved to the front of their bodies, the penises and mammaries becoming huge. Their body hair had disappeared. They had become sexually obsessed, the females much more retiring than other mammals, and the males far more aggressive.

She moved toward the old castle. The last time she had entered this portal, it had been hand-in-hand with her mom. The building had been new then, smelling of beeswax and freshly hewn stone. Inside, the great rooms had glowed with candlelight. Lovely bedchambers had been built high in the structure, behind small windows so that Keepers could linger over their kills, and the cries of pleasure and anguish could not be heard from the streets below.

Just under that garret there, behind the little, arched window was a sumptuous chamber where a Keeper could make sport with his kill for as long as he cared to, flushing it with fear again and again, then calming it and delivering bursts of incapacitating pleasure to it. This would bring the flavor of its blood to an incredibly delicious richness, sweet and sour, reflecting the secret harmonies that sounded between agony and ecstasy.

She had not fed like that in a very long time. Mother Lamia always did. Sometimes her feedings would last for days. But Miriam's human lovers had not cared for it and had felt awful for the victims when she did it.

Sarah, for example, could only bear to see Miriam do the quickest of kills. She herself struggled to live without killing, taking her nourishment from blood bank goop and pleading with Miriam for frequent transfusions that left both of them dizzy and bitchy.

Miriam went to the door. The way she felt now, she'd like to take a big, blood-packed human straight up to that chamber. Full or not, she'd spend a couple of days on it, using all of mother's old techniques.

They were the Keepers, not the kept. No matter how brilliant, how numerous, or how violent, mankind remained first and foremost, their damned *property!*

She pushed at the door. Locked. She shook it three times, making the very precise movements that were designed to dislodge the tumblers, in the event you had no key. Keepers did not have private property. All belonged to all.

It opened. She stepped in, treading softly in the footsteps of her lost past. A profound silence fell, a Keeper silence. Overhead, the great beams that had been so rich a brown in mother's day now were glowing black, as if they had turned into iron. The tanning vats were empty.

She went across the echoing floor of the factory to the narrow stair. Mother had hauled their victims up these very treads, Miriam following along to watch and learn.

How silent it was here, more silent than any human place.

This was still a lair, oh, yes. But where was its inhabitant? Would he not be at least a little curious about the stealthy noises down below, the unmistakable sounds of another Keeper entering the sanctum?

"Hello," she said, her voice uttering the sibilant, infinitely subtle sound of Prime for the first time in many a long year.

He was much smaller than she remembered, and as dirty as a coal-scuttle, a creature that had not bathed since the French court had filled its tubs with milk. His eyes were tiny and narrow, and he had the pinched face of a bat. He came forward wearing the tattered remains of a hundred-year-old frock coat, otherwise as naked as at his ancient birth. He was hungry, hissing hungry, as shadowy and insubstantial as a ghost.

A wound opened in his ghastly face, bright red and dripping. He uttered a sound, horribly eager, and she realized that he thought her human. She was so radically different looking from other Keepers that he believed her one of the kept.

His skeletal hands snatched her wrists, enclosed them in a Keeper's iron grip. Then his eyes met hers. The bright glow of eagerness flickered, faded. He had realized his mistake.

He dropped his hands to his sides, then slumped at her feet. "*M'aidez,*" he whispered, not in Prime but in French.

As she looked down at this filthy, groveling, helpless creature, she stuffed her fist in her mouth. But he was not deceived. He knew that he revolted her. Because he laughed, bitterly, angrily, laughed to cover her screams.

FIVE

The Skylights of Paris

Paul had missed the traveler by ten seconds. He'd glimpsed the creature—tall, wearing normal clothes (an old-fashioned-looking woman's suit), a blond spray of hair, that was all he'd seen.

Rain roared against the skylight; thunder echoed across the roofs of Paris. He shouted into the phone, "Your people lost her. You and the French."

He listened to Sam Mazur's whining, complicated reply. He was CIA station chief at the U.S. embassy. Cupping his hand over the mouthpiece, Paul whispered to Becky Driver, "That's a paper cup. I said *bucket*."

"A paper cup is what we have."

Sam continued whining away about how the French had not cooperated and were not going to cooperate, that unless they knew chapter and verse exactly what the operation was about, it would absolutely not unfold on French soil.

"Tell me this, Sam. I'm curious. Why the hardening of the heart? I mean, the French don't like U.S. intelligence. But we aren't the enemy. They've always recognized that in the past."

"Cold War's over, my friend. Europe is sick of us, and France is sickest of all. They hate the way we and the Brits use the Echelon system to spy on them electronically. U.S.

intelligence has had it here, man. Time to pack up our silencers and go home."

The paper cup into which the entire thunderstorm appeared to be dripping had filled up. "Becky, do you think you could empty this? These are Burmese shoes. I can't risk getting them wet."

She cast her big brown eyes down toward his feet. "You got those in Myanmar?"

"Had them made. I'm suspicious that there's cardboard involved."

"They look like funeral shoes."

"What the hell are 'funeral shoes'?"

"The kind guys wear to funerals. Shiny, black, and from about 1974."

Charlie Frater snickered. Paul glared at them both. He'd brought dumpy, bespeckled Charlie and lithe, lovely Becky because they were the most ferocious close-in workers he had. Charlie was one of those people who just did not stop, not ever. He walked into danger like a priest walking into his church. The wonder of it was he looked like a guy who lived behind a desk deep in some civil service nowhere.

Becky, on the other hand, fancied herself a lady spy from the movies. She cultivated the effect with her dark, flowing hair and her long coats. She was only twenty-three, but she was the most cheerful and fearless warrior he had. And quick. So breathtakingly quick.

Not a man on the team hadn't thought about Becky, probably dreamed about her. Paul had. But she kept to herself emotionally. Paul didn't pry.

The rest of the team would assemble in the States. Paul's highest priority was to eradicate the vampires there, always had been. Asia had been done first because it was available.

Now he had to stop this traveler, lest she get to the U.S. and organize opposition. He had to stop her here.

He returned to Sam. "Bottom line is this: We lost that damn thing and it is now running around Paris telling all of its fuckin' friends that somebody's onto them. I regard that as your fault. I'm sorry."

"May I hang up?"

"You may not."

" 'Cause I have something to do. Important. Secret."

"Tell me, does a ritual chewing out *always* make you need to take a dump?"

"Yes, it does."

Paul carefully replaced the receiver in the cradle.

Becky and Charlie were staring at him.

"What?"

"What do you mean, what? What the hell did he say?"

"He's a CIA bureaucrat. He said nothing."

The skylight was now leaking in five places. As night fell, the immense skyscraper across the street began to light up. Whatever slight sense of privacy the room might have afforded was gone. Worse, there was no way to curtain off the skylight. At least two thousand office workers could look directly down into what was supposed to be a secret CIA safe house.

Paul stared up at the office building. "Let's put together some dance numbers," he said.

Charlie, who was, for some reason, practicing rolling cigarettes with a little machine, responded. "Stick a hat up there and maybe they'll throw change."

"Goddamnit, how are we gonna use this sty? Do either of you have a room that has a little privacy for us to work in, at least?"

"They're way too small, boss," Becky responded.

"Bullshit. We can manage."

"More than one person in my cell and the zipper gets stuck."

Paul thought, *sounds like fun*. He said, "Goddamnit!"

"Is this the cheapest hotel in Paris?" Charlie asked.

"Our employer is not in the habit of billeting its personnel in the cheapest anything. The *Sans Douche* is the cheapest inconveniently located piece-of-shit hotel in Paris. It's conceivable, although just barely, that there exists another hotel with a marginally lower price. But it will not be as bad as the dear ol' S.D. Would you care for some cat hair?" He slapped the bed, which was making him break out. "I've got plenty more than I need."

"What we need is a plan of action," Becky said, stating what was painfully obvious.

"What we need is a way to prevent the minister of the interior from calling in the ambassador and asking him why there are CIA personnel in Paris searching for the goddamn Bride of Dracula!"

"There was no Bride of Dracula, boss."

"There damn well *was* a Bride of Dracula."

"No, I don't believe there was, actually." Becky clicked the keys on her laptop a few times. "Nope. No *Bride of Dracula*, says the Internet Movie Database."

"Take a letter. Steven Spielberg: 'Stevie! Have I got an idea for you. It's Dracula, except she's a woman!' Ladies and gentlemen, I will now retire."

"Thing is, boss, how're we gonna find her?"

"To fuck around with the French or not to fuck around with the French, that is the question."

Charlie began to shuffle along beneath the skylight. "The

problem is, we need to get this done." He started singing, and that was terribly sad. " 'Cause she's spreadin' the news, she's doin' it today, 'cause she wants to be a part of it—"

"Don't they test for people like you anymore, Charles? I mean, when we signed on, the first thing they gave us was a test to see if we were assholes. In my generation."

"Cold War's over, boss. They're putting the old assholes out to pasture, not hiring new ones."

The phone rang. It was Sam, back again for more punishment.

"Hey, bro." They'd been in Cambodia together, in Laos. Paul Ward and Sam Mazur were allies of the blood and soul.

"Tell me something. Where's a good place to get sick on the food in—where are we, again, Beck?"

"Montparnasse."

"Montpissoir."

"There's thousands of restaurants out there."

"Good."

"Very."

"Cheap."

"Not very."

"McDonald's?"

"What're you doing in Montparnasse, anyway?"

"We're billeted in one of the shitty little hotels."

"God, you're low. You're so low that it worries me even talking to you. I have ambition. I want to be a big-timer back at Langley. Got my sights set on the Lesotho/Chad/Botswana desk. Can't swing something like that if people realize I'm tangled up with a liability like you."

"The French said Mrs. Tallman was believed to have taken a taxi into the city. They give you any details?"

"Well, actually, yes."

Paul tried not to hope, but did.

"The taxi is believed to have been French."

Had he not hated the vampires so much and been so obsessed with them, he would have been ready with a comeback. All he could do was plead. "I need French cooperation, Sam. You gotta get it."

"Whatever this is, they think it's some kind of crazy American bullshit, or maybe we're trying to make assholes outa them or whatever. What's that noise, anyway?"

"The rain."

"Really!"

"Really."

" 'Cause it's beautiful here."

"Oh, shut up. Something's bothering me, and lemme tell you what it is."

"I'm all ears."

"Well, this should look to the French like an Interpol operation. So why are they being so damn shirty?"

"Because they know it isn't."

"And why would they know that?"

"Because Interpol told them."

"Clever boys. Okay, Sam—and guys, both of you listen up. Because I do have a suggestion. I think that we ought to detail a fluent French speaker to liaise with the police on the pretext that we have a missing national—"

"All hell will break loose."

"No, listen to me. Tell them it's a matter of the heart. We just need to search around a bit—very discreetly—because this lady has run away from home, and it's politically sensitive. The French will buy this. It's the kind of thing they understand."

"The French will buy. They will not understand. They'll

want the name, rank, and serial number; then they'll tell you whether she's d.o.a. or not. That'll be the extent of their cooperation."

"What we need—look, Charlie, quit fucking with that—what is that?"

"A cigarette maker I bought in Bangyercock. It's neat."

"Bangkok, you sexist bitch," Becky said.

"Put the toy away. What we need—are you still there, Sam?"

"Patiently waiting."

"What we need, and I am talking about right now, the next few minutes, is we need to find the vampires she has come to see. We've lost her. No description except what looked like a Chanel suit circa about 1975 and real blond hair that was probably a damn wig. With no cooperation from the locals, we gotta shift gears. We use the same basic technique we've been using since Tokyo."

"Which is?"

"We cull police records for patterns of disappearance. My guess is that they'll cluster around the lairs, just like everywhere else we've been. Here in Paris, we'll be able to get good maps—sewer lines, wire conduits, building plans, drainage pipes, all of it. It'll be easier than Singapore. A hell of a lot easier than Shanghai."

"Boss?"

"Yeah, Beck?"

"Ask him, who keeps crime records here? Is there a missing persons bureau?"

Paul found a button on the phone next to a grill that was hidden on the side. When he pressed the button, he discovered that he had a decent speakerphone.

"Sam? You're on speaker."

"Hey."

Becky asked her question again.

"Prefecture of Police, Hall of Records," Sam replied. "There are going to be ordinary murders and disappearances mixed in," he continued.

"Meaning?"

"You're gonna have to read the description of each crime to find out if it started as a disappearance. You read French?"

"I read French," Charlie said.

"Sam," Becky asked, "when is a missing person declared dead in this country? If there's no presumption of foul play, say."

"Nine years."

"Are those records held separately?"

"I don't truthfully know. We'll need to ask the French."

"Shit," Becky said carefully.

"What if we tell them it's a historical survey," Paul suggested. "Becky's a student from Harvard. She's got a powerful daddy, and the embassy's been asked to help her do research for her thesis."

"That'll work," Sam said. "I can have her in the Hall of Records within the week."

"Tomorrow, Sam, first thing."

"There's bureaucracy, man. This is France."

"Do it, Sam."

"Is this stuff computerized?" Becky asked.

"You'll be looking at everything from the best databases you ever saw in your life to big black books that weigh forty pounds and make you sneeze."

It was agreed that they'd meet at a bar called Le Lapin Robuste on Rue du Sommerard tomorrow at noon. By then Sam would know exactly how the records were organized.

From there, they'd go to the Prefecture of Police, which was nearby, and see how far they could get.

As soon as the conference call ended, Charlie and Becky began looking through a Paris Zagat's guide for a restaurant for dinner. Paul watched them. He felt once again the awful, frantic feeling that had been coming over him from time to time ever since he'd seen the grotesque remains of poor Kiew Narawat.

For a while, the knowledge that vampires were real had depressed the hell out of him. He'd tried to find some special meaning in the fact that it had happened to his father, but all he'd found was special hate.

There was something ghastly about discovering that you weren't at the top of the food chain. It was like discovering that you had a hidden and fatal disease. You were left feeling horribly out of control. It entered your dreams . . . it was a cancer of the mind.

"Uncle Paul," Becky said, "since there's nothing we can do tonight, could me and Charlie please, oh please, take you out to some cheap-jack hole-in-the-wall for some onion soup and wine?"

That snapped the twig that had been about to snap ever since he'd lost track of the damn vampire. He looked at them—two kids made arrogant by too many easy victories.

"Do you think we've won? Is that why you're so damn smug, with your goddamn toys—" He swept the cigarette making machine out of Charlie's hands. Charlie, who was wound tight by training and had a hair trigger, just barely managed to restrain himself, stopping his flying fist with a sudden jerk of effort. Paul looked at him. "Do it," he said with an easy smile that he did not feel, "and I'll lay you out."

"Paul?"

"And as for you—" He grabbed her purse, which had been on the floor beside a chair. He held it up to the desk lamp. "What the fuck is this made out of?" He knew damn well. They all had this stuff—purses and wallets and belts, God only knew what else. The skin of the vampire was more delicate even than calfskin . . . probably than human, for that matter.

He emptied the purse on the desk and stuffed the damn thing into the trash can. "If they saw this skin, God only knows what they'd do."

"I'm not exactly planning to take it with me into some fucking lair. I'm not *that* stupid."

"Don't you understand? Even yet?" He looked from one surprised face to the other. "No. You don't. So you listen up, children, and you listen close. Something has changed. Big time. We've been dealing with something that's very old and very slow to react, and so far it's been easy. Like killing big bugs. You surprised 'em all, didn't you? Token resistance— gnashing teeth, hissing. It was fun! It got to be, anyway. The professionals. Fuck! Fuck us, we're assholes."

"Not me," Charlie said. His face was burning up. His eyes were beads. He was not trained to take abuse, and he did not take it well.

"Not you, little boy. Little, innocent boy. Lemme see your wallet."

"What the hell for?"

"Lemme see the goddamn thing!"

Charlie held it out. "They use human skin," he muttered.

Paul emptied it and threw it away with the purse. "Belts, shoes, anything?"

"That stuff is valuable!"

"If they see you with their goddamn *skins* in your hands, they're gonna know exactly who you are."

"They are not going to see us."

"Listen to me. One of them has gone up to the fifth floor of a hotel, killed one of your peers, and then flown from Bangkok to Paris on a god-for-damned *airplane!* I've seen it and it looked like some damn lady. *Very* human! So they don't all spend all their time hiding in lairs, do they? We're up against something new! Something we know not one damn thing about! They may be as old as damn Methuselah and they may be slow to respond, but they've taken a blow to the gut, and they are now responding! So you better watch your backs, because they are strong and they are smart and *now they know!*"

In the silence that followed, he became acutely aware of the humming of the little electric clock that stood on the table beside the bed. Charlie went to the window. Becky sat staring at her hands. Then she looked up. He saw tears gleaming in the edges of her eyes. He saw, also, that they were not tears of pain or embarrassment, but tears of rage. That was good. He liked that. Let her burn.

Dad was calling him from the back porch, "Paulie, Paulie let's make ice cream!" Dad smelled of the raw earth that was his livelihood. He smelled of the leaves of summer.

After Dad had disappeared, Paulie had walked on his knees all the way down the pasture road to the river and all the way back. He had done that while begging God that if Dad was found, he would never stop praying forever.

Mom had worked the farm until her bones stuck out, and been scared all the time, because if she did not get her crop in, she said, this family was gonna hit the road. There was no bank in North Carolina, and probably not anywhere, that would give her a crop loan.

"What're we supposed to do?" Becky asked.

"Your jobs!"

"I mean right now, Paul. Right this goddamn *second,* Paul! Because I don't see one damn thing we can do. We got a vague description of a woman who apparently looks nothing—not one thing—like the creatures we've been killing. I mean, I wouldn't make a damn handbag outa some *lady.* I saw little, shriveled monsters coated with dirt. I didn't see anything that looked even remotely like a tall, blond woman."

"We've known about these creatures for just a few years. They've been around for centuries and centuries. They've had a lotta time to think up a lotta things—"

"Not my point. My point is, you're having a goddamn hissy fit because Charlie and I—who happen to have been risking our lives in a filthy, horrible, and completely thankless job for three hellish years—wanted to sneak a couple of hours of downtime when there wasn't another goddamn thing we *could* do!" She folded her arms. "Explain yourself."

"Simple. I'm a field supervisor and you're not."

"So, what do we do, boss? Right now?" Charlie was trying to put his smashed cigarette machine back together.

"Whatever you damn well please. Go to Tour d'Argent and blow a month's pay. Moulin Rouge. The Slow Bar. Paint the goddamn town red, that's what Paris is for."

"I just want a good bouillabaisse."

"I'd like a nice *steak frites.*"

Charlie and Becky went out into the rain. Paul listened to it hammering the damn skylight for about five minutes. And he began to think that maybe he should've gone with them. Maybe he could find a liquor store open somewhere; who the hell knew? He'd buy himself a quart of Stoli and toast himself into a stupor. Do him a world of good to wake up tomorrow with a hangover.

He went down in the tiny elevator, jammed his hat over his head, and set out into what might as well become an all night bar crawl. Maybe he'd even break up the tedium with a few fights. He loved to use his fists, always had. Just loved it. Probably be pretty easy to pick a fight with a frog. Hopefully, he'd find somebody with good enough moves to make it fun. Guys who liked to fight, they could spot each other in a bar. There were signals—some heavyset asshole glares at you for no damn reason, that's an invitation. Practiced bar fighters lived in their own secret world, and he was very much part of it. Nothing like beating the shit out of each other to make a couple of guys friends for life.

He set out along the Boulevard Montparnasse. There were lots of theaters, more than he remembered from when he was last here. Too bad it was night; he could have slipped over to the Orangerie and seen some fuckin' Monets.

Maybe the thing to do was go to a movie and brush up on his French. But there were also lots of bars. He went into one. Fulla damn tourists, wouldn't you know. Nervous Arabs sipping glasses of wine; Americans loudly demanding martinis.

There were a few Frenchies at the bar huddling over drinks or coffee. He slid up and managed, with some effort, to get a Stoli.

It was small and overpriced, but it worked okay, so he ordered another. He wondered if the whores around here were as overpriced as the liquor. He'd been spoiled by the Asians, who worked their asses off for a few bucks, massaging, blowing, sucking, fucking, combing, tickling, licking, and then handing you off to the social director for another round with a fresh face.

He said to nobody in particular, "You know why the predator is always smarter than the prey?"

Nobody answered.

"He has to be. The prey lives by work—crop the grass, till the field, whatever. The predator lives by his wits. That's why the gazelle hardly ever sees the lion. It's why the damn deer doesn't see us." He paused, then raised his glass. The barkeep did him. He knocked it back.

He'd come in here to fight, let's face it. But he was damn forty-eight years old; what was he gonna do? Also, you couldn't insult people who didn't understand your goddamn lingo.

He left. Rain hit him in the face. Striding along, he wished to God he had something to do that mattered. Why hadn't anybody taken a picture of the woman? Why hadn't they confiscated the damn passport? You couldn't even dragnet for her!

He was going so fast that he was practically running. The rain came down in sheets, in torrents. He watched the droplets sailing through the streetlights out of a low, rushing sky. He realized that he was running because he was scared. How must it feel to be eaten alive that way? They were parasites. Big, filthy suckerfish.

How *the fuck* had she eluded them? You don't sneak past customs when they have you caught. You can't! But she had.

Intelligence, of course. She was brilliant, obviously. So what did that mean? How many steps ahead was she? Ten? Fifty? A thousand? "Goddamnit!"

Then he thought, what if she knows about me? He couldn't see how, but he didn't have any two hundred and fifty IQ, either. She could be three feet away right now and he would have no way of knowing.

He found a little shop where they had some wine stuck in the window along with the displays of Orange Crush and Evian water. There was what looked like it might be a nice muscatel for about nine bucks. He shelled out and took it home under his arm.

Back in the hotel, he realized that he had no corkscrew. So he busted the neck and lay back on the bed drinking out of the jagged hole and staring up at the office building. All those dark windows and not a single human figure anywhere.

It wasn't muscatel, not by a long shot, but the wine did him okay, especially on top of the vodka. Maybe toward dawn he slept, and maybe not.

He awoke to gray, sad light and music coming up from the street—some kind of wild Arabic tune. The office building towered like a monster ghost above his skylight. He got up, wanted a cigarette, and went through the goddamn motions with the goddamn gum. He chewed it brutally, stuffed in another piece, and bore down until his jaws hummed.

He'd been rough on the kids last night. But that was nothing new. They'd gotten their frogs' legs anyway. Thing was, he loved his kids. He wanted them to get their fucking frogs' legs whenever they could.

The phone went *brrt-brrt brrt-brrt*. Neat sound, he thought.

"Yeah?"

"We got three places, boss. Three *arrondissements*."

"Beck?"

"Yeah, boss."

"Where are you?"

"Prefecture of Police Department of Records."

"Am I wrong, or is it six-fifteen in the morning?"

"Shit, they're gonna be opening this place up in an hour. We gotta get moving."

"But how the hell did you get in there? That's what I want to know."

"They got a lotta skylights in this town."

SIX

Martin Soule

Miriam had done her screaming and her weeping, and now sat in a little café seeking with increasing urgency for a victim for Martin. She had called Sarah again and again, and still had not gotten an answer. But she could not let this problem, as disturbing as it was becoming, intrude on her urgent mission. She did not know exactly what had happened to Martin, except that he was starving, and it was the most horrible thing she had ever seen.

Patience was essential on the hunt, no matter whether you were in a hurry or not. The trouble was, you could not easily imagine the prey to be dangerous, and in an emergency like this, your instincts screamed at you to just grab one, drag it off by the hair, and give it to the poor sufferer immediately.

She forced herself to sit still, to appear seductive. The waiter was admiring her and so were some of the male customers. But nobody moved, nobody *did* anything.

She sucked in warm smoke from her cigarette, drew it deep into her lungs, then blew it out with a carefully manufactured seductive pout. At least they had reasonably good cigarettes here. This Gitanes reminded her of a Bon-Ton. American cigarettes were awful now.

Why were these stupid men ignoring her? Had customs

changed so much? When she had last taken a victim in Europe, everything had been different. There had been an immediate flirting response, a quick seduction. That had happened on a quiet day in Clichy, in a little bar full of bums and Americans.

She was contacting men's eyes, but they wouldn't take it farther. She did not intend to let Martin starve, or any Keeper she could help, for that matter. As to why this had happened to him, she did not yet know. She could well imagine, though—something awful that had to do with human oppression of the Keeper. She sucked the cigarette hard, blew out a furious stream of smoke.

The temptation was growing ever stronger to just go off down the street and do what instinct urged. To some Keepers, the finest of all meals came from a sudden, spontaneous impulse to just snatch a victim, tear it open, and drink. That was her instinct, always. She'd been drawn to America in the first place by the easy, rambling life it offered her kind. She'd guzzled her way across the wild frontier. You could go a few miles on horseback and pluck your fruit along the trail without the slightest worry. People disappeared out there all the time.

She'd finished her cigarette and was just starting another when she realized that a young male was heading her way. She said in French, "Can you help me? May I have a light?"

He moved past her toward the loo. Could this be a homosexual bar? No. Clearly not. Owning a club in New York as she did, she could tell the sexual orientation of a place at a glance.

From the bar, another man said, "You speak the French of Voltaire, lady. All those 'thees' and 'thous.' " He raised his voice, mocking her, " 'Cans't thou render me assistance? Mays't I take a flame?' We call it a 'match,' now. New word! Where are you from?"

"The past," she snapped. She got to her feet. To hell with the French, if they were no longer interested in a pretty girl.

"Oh, mademoiselle, please, I am just making conversation! Don't be so quick. You must be an American. You learned your French in school. Well, you had an old teacher. Damned old, I'd say! But that can't be held against you."

He was plump. The back of his hands revealed the telltale blue streaks that suggested that the drinking veins would be nice and big. The flow of the carotid would be delightfully powerful.

She gave him a slow, careful smile, the kind that made the males pant. She had practiced smiling for years, and she considered herself an artiste. As soon as she showed her rows of perfectly believable but entirely artificial human teeth, he came to her table.

Finally. She responded with practiced indifference. Smile too eagerly, and he would back off . . . at least, that used to be their way.

"You are not telling me to go?"

She shrugged.

In a lower voice, he asked, "Is this going to cost me?"

"A little." Meaning everything you value the most—your breath, your blood, your very life.

"Then you're for real—a whore staking out the rear table in a café. It's so—I don't know—*charmant*. So 'old Paris!' And that language and the ancient suit. You *are* from the past. Look, I don't mean to spoil the effect, but I have only a couple hundred francs."

"How sad."

"Do you take credit cards?"

How could he ask something so profoundly stupid? A whore who took credit cards, indeed. She sucked in smoke, let it drift slowly out.

"I wish you wouldn't do that."

"Excuse me, my sir?"

"I gave it up. Bad for the chest." He tapped his breast, expanded his lungs, let the breath out. "Bet you couldn't manage that."

She could hold her breath for an hour. Keepers could drown, but it was not an easy death. For them, in fact, there were no easy deaths. The very body, every bone and sinew, was fanatically devoted to life. Man had the immortal soul, not his Keepers. Man could afford to die. Keepers had to stay alive forever, if possible.

Miriam put out her cigarette.

"You have the loveliest hands," he said, watching her.

She lifted a hand, bending her wrist delicately. When he kissed it, somebody over at the bar went, "Oh, my."

"Be quiet, you fucking gorilla!" the victim roared. "Never mind him, he has the manners of an animal."

She lowered her hand, touching his with the tips of her fingers: possession. "Good sir, I cannot stop with you the day long."

"Your French is advancing. Now you sound like somebody from about 1896."

"I have a pleasant room, and two hundred francs will be a good price."

She strolled with him down the Rue de Bobbilo, then crossed the Place d'Italie into the Avenue des Gobelins. It was raining, and she leaned in toward him to be under his umbrella. As they crossed the street, she stumbled against him. He glanced at her out of the corner of his eye, frowning slightly.

It had been a costly slip: he'd noticed her weight. Keepers had dense bones and muscles like rock. Inch for inch, they were twice as heavy as the prey.

The smallest slip would sometimes be all it took to spook a victim. Like most predators, Keepers were successful only about a third of the time. The myth of the vampire as a creeping, unstoppable supernatural force was just that, a myth.

They were passing a small hotel. He started in.

"No, not here."

"Where the hell is it, then? This is the only hotel around here."

"Just a little farther, good sir."

His pace slowed. She could feel him glancing at her again. Archaic language, excessive weight for her shape and size—he was not understanding, and that was making him nervous. She had to brush up on her damn French. Back in 1956, nobody had commented. But then, she hadn't fed here, either, only gone to Chanel for a thorough reoutfitting. She'd spent thousands. They would never have commented on her French.

She gave him a carefully rehearsed look—eyebrows raised, gray eyes gleaming—that was meant to disarm him with a combination of girlish sweetness and womanly experience. This look had worked since she had first developed it, back in the days when one's only mirror was a pond.

He went, "*hmpf,*" like a slightly shocked horse. Then he grew silent. His tread became determined, even dogged.

She had him, by heaven! That was a wonderfully effective look. It had set the hook along the Via Appia and Watling Street, in Ur and Athens, in Venezia and ancient Granada.

"This isn't—oh, Christ—what the hell do you want to go in here for?"

"You'll see."

"Not for two hundred francs I won't. A blanket on the floor of an old wreck like this rates no more than fifty, sweetheart. No way you're gonna cheat Jean-Jacques. No damn way at all."

If she accepted his offer, he'd decide that she was probably diseased and that would be that. She had to waste time bargaining.

"Upstairs is very nice. You must pay a hundred and fifty."

"The hell—"

"But only when I conduct you to the chamber, and if you are pleased." She lowered her eyes.

"If I ain't pleased?"

"Then I am desolate. I will do it for your fifty, and fulfill your pleasure, for one hour of the clock."

"Now we're back to the ancien régime. Your French is fascinating." He looked up at Mother Lamia's old palace, the gray limestone, the sharp peak of the roof, the tiny windows in the tower. She knew what he was thinking: *Dare I go in there with such a strange woman?*

"I have my domicile within. It isn't as it appears."

He smirked, but followed her through the door into the cavernous space. He stopped, looked up into the high shadows. "My God, what a place!"

"Come with me." She moved deeper within, toward the stairs at the back of the enormous, dark room.

"That stairway's a deathtrap!"

She thought, *Don't make it hard, not when I am so frantic!* She said, "But, my sir, this is the way to my chamber." She moved toward the stairs, swinging her hips.

" 'My sir!' 'My chamber!' you're weird, and I'm not going up there with you no matter how pretty you are. Anyway, you probably taste like a damn ashtray, you smoke so much."

Then the damn thing turned and strode toward the door. She sucked in her breath, turned also.

It had moved fast. It put its hand in the ring, started pulling it. She leaped with all her might across the space between them. At the last instant, it saw her, raised a hand. For the split of a second, their eyes met. She fisted the crown of its head, doing it in precisely the right place and with the exact force necessary to knock the thing senseless. It dropped with a sodden thud.

"Martin," she said. "My dear, look what I've brought you."

He'd been watching from behind one of the old tanning vats. He came out, moving with the slow, dragging gait of a very weak Keeper. He smelled like dry, old flesh and rotted blood. His eyes were glimmers inside their sunken sockets.

She watched him lay his long gray form upon the cushioning body of his prey, watched him stretch like a lounging panther. Some of the old Martin could be seen in those easy movements, his grace, even a little of his power.

He laid his jaws on the neck, in the traditional spot. Keepers sometimes took their food from under the leg, or even, if they were particularly hungry and had really strong suction, from the main artery itself, which could be reached by a ferocious penetration of the small of the back.

It was decadent and cruel to take the blood from a small vein, but this was done as well. The victim knew, then, for it would remain conscious for most of the feeding. Awful, mad fun that was. Children did it, and Miriam could remember a few Egyptians she'd tormented that way, when she was still a little slip of a thing. She and that boy Sothis, the son of

Amma, had experimented with all sorts of ghastly and peculiar ways of consuming their prey. Playing the role of child prostitutes in the seedy backstreets of Thebes, they'd often sucked their customers dry right through their erect penises, leaving nothing but a skeleton tented by skin ready for the tanner. Children can be so awful.

Martin's body began to undulate. His esophageal peristalsis was quite strong. The prey woke up and shouted out something, "Oh, shit," or some such thing. He began to toss and turn, and Martin, who was far from a normal weight and strength, started to slip off.

He needed all the nutrition he could get, so she most certainly could not kill the prey to prevent it struggling. Dead blood made a poor meal.

The thing heaved. There was a pop and a gooey, declining hiss. Martin's suction had broken. It heaved again, and this time he slid completely off. The creature sat up. Its neck was red, but there was no blood flowing. Miriam had the awful thought that Martin might be too weak to feed.

"What in the name of God is this?" The creature looked down at Martin, who was sliding across the floor, looking very much like a great beetle. "What in the name of *God!*" It scrambled to its feet.

Martin grabbed an ankle. The creature shrieked, its eyes practically popping out of its head. It kicked him away.

"Jesus in heaven, what's the matter with that guy?"

This creature was surprisingly self-possessed. Miriam did not like this. She stepped forward, grabbed one of its wrists.

It kicked upward with its knee, directing the blow expertly toward her forearm. That was well done; that would have shattered a human bone. She didn't know what she had here. Stars forbid it was another damn cop.

Its free fist came plunging straight toward her face. She caught it, stopping its forward motion so suddenly that the animal's jaws snapped with the shock. She began to squeeze the wrists. It writhed and kicked again, this time getting her right in the midriff. Her muscles were far too hard for the blow to be painful, but it pushed her off her feet, forcing her to let go her grip. Instantly the creature recoiled from her.

"What are you?" it shrieked. "Aliens?"

That again. That was a recent bit of human myth that the Keepers ought to start using. They hadn't been aliens to the earth for fifty thousand years.

Martin had risen to a sitting position, was ineffectually dusting his tattered waistcoat. When she looked back to the human, it was already starting to make once again for the outside door. With a quick leap, she put herself in its way.

"God in heaven! That's three meters!" It showed its teeth, displayed the palms of its hands. "Look, we can work this out. I'm a family man. I can't go to Pluto or whatever it is you want."

Pluto was the human name for Nisu, the farthest of the planets. Beyond that was only Niburu, the wanderer.

"Child, you must give up your life. You cannot escape us."

That would get the mind racing, the blood speeding.

"Don't be absurd. That would be murder! And look at you; why, you're just a baby in your mother's old clothes! You mustn't do something so terrible. You'll regret it forever, *child*."

Behind him, Martin had come to his feet. He began to stagger toward the victim, his shoulders slumped, his jaw gaping. The sound of his shuffling caused the creature to turn around. And now a moment occurred that did not happen often: a human being saw a Keeper naked of disguise, as he really looked.

It drew in its breath. Then silence. Then a burst of wild, panicked shrieking. But it stood rooted, mesmerized for the same reason that the mouse is mesmerized by the snake.

The deepest unconscious of the human being, the depth of the soul, knew the truth. It bore an imprint of that face from the days when Keepers kept them in cages. They had been pure animals then, without any conscious mind. So the terror they had felt had been imprinted on the unconscious and passed from generation to generation as raw instinct.

Too bad that the free-range human had made so much nicer a meal than the caged variety. Inevitably, they'd begun to run them in packs, then in herds, letting them make their own cities, have their own history. Inevitably, the Keepers had taken to living in the cities, and what fun *that* had been. Still would be, if they hadn't all gone into hiding.

It was so unnecessary. Miriam had probably done a thousand kills in New York City since the creation of its police department, and she hadn't had a bit of trouble there. In fact, she'd had almost no trouble at all, not until this last little lapse.

There'd been the Ellen Wunderling affair, when Sarah had panicked and eaten a reporter who had gotten too close to Miriam. But that had blown over.

The truth was, it was not hard to get away with killing humans if you were just a little careful, and the other Keepers should not have become so fearful. Caution was appropriate, of course. But this business of hiding in holes the way they were doing—they were nothing now but parasites. She was the last of her kind, the last true Keeper, the last vampire.

Well, she had to rehabilitate them, starting with Martin. She would feed him and nurse him back to his grandeur, teach him to live in the modern world. She'd teach them all. Then she'd have a beautiful baby, and he would be a prince among them and lead them back into the sunlight.

The creature began to move away, but Miriam was quicker. She embraced it from behind.

It let out a terrific bellow and began to fling its head back and forth, attempting to slam its skull into her forehead. It connected, too. The blow mattered not, wouldn't even leave a bruise.

She tightened her grip. The creature struggled to draw her hands away. She could feel the ribs start to compress. The carefully orchestrated attempt to break her grip degenerated into hammering. Finally, the breath whooshed out.

Martin's jaw opened, and he fell against the prey. It wriggled, flounced, shook its head wildly. Martin fell away, then regained his balance. Miriam crushed out the last of the breath. Martin locked his jaw against the neck once again. The creature's legs, which had been kicking wildly, now began to slow down. Miriam squeezed tighter. She smelled hot urine, heard it sluicing out.

Martin's suction finally took, and the creature's body weight began to decline, slowly at first, then more noticeably. Martin, by contrast, began to flush red through his curtain of dirt. She felt the life go out of the human. The body became limp. A moment later, Martin let go.

"There's more," she said.

He slumped. "I cannot." He found a chair, fell into it. At least he wasn't crawling anymore. That was an improvement.

The blood and fluids that were left had to be taken. The remnant could not be left to rot. She carried it across the room and sat also, on the foot of the stairs. She laid the body out on her lap, bent down and sucked it until there was nothing left to take, just the dry, cream-colored skin tight across the bones.

"Is there acid in any of the vats?"

He shook his head. "That's all finished. No more tannery."

Too bad. It had been a great convenience in the old days, because the remnants could simply be dissolved. It had been Mom's charming idea to let the tanners come in.

"What do you do?"

He looked at her. "Miriam—it is you, isn't it?"

"Yes, Martin."

"I haven't eaten in a year."

Her mouth opened, but she did not speak, could not. She'd heard of Keepers going hungry for six months, even more—but how could he ever have survived this? How could he still live?

"Martin—"

"I begged for death, many times. But it did not come. Would not come." He smiled a little. "I was turning into one of those . . . those things that *you* make."

He was referring to her humans, to what happened to them when her blood in their veins stopped keeping them young. Keepers might not communicate with each other much, but it seemed that everybody knew of Miriam and her humans.

"It's nothing like that. You would have died in the end."

He nodded. "No doubt." He raised his eyes to hers. She looked deep into the burning, black pools. Martin was thousands of years older than she.

"We are coming to our end, Miriam," he said.

"We aren't!"

He nodded slowly, not as if he was agreeing with her, but more as if he was humoring her. "You need to find a way to destroy that," he said. "They'll miss that man soon, and they're bound to come here searching."

"Why here? We've always been safe here. This is my mother's house."

"The City of Paris owns this structure. There are plans to make it part of the Musée des Gobelins, starting next year." He made a dismissive gesture with his hands, a gesture that expressed vast defeat, vast sorrow. "They'll clear all this rubbish out."

"Martin, you were thriving just—well, just a few years ago."

His face, which had filled out and now bore a smeared, filthy resemblance to the narrow-lipped elegance she remembered from the past, opened into a smile. The smile quickly turned bitter and ugly. "During the war, the Resistance built a secret headquarters in the Denfert-Rochereau ossuary. They heard us, deeper down, in the old labyrinth."

This had been the traditional shelter of the Paris vampires, a honeycomb of tunnels that wound beneath the city, from which its stone had been quarried since the time of the Romans.

"They noticed us. They thought that we were spies working for the Germans, and they pursued us."

"But . . . how?"

"With sound! They have those little tins full of carbon black—"

"Microphones."

"Yes, those things. They put them about, and our voices were conducted to their ears through them."

"But they can't hear our speech."

"Ah, Prime is such a trial, isn't it? So complex, so many words needed for the simplest expression." He shook his head. "We spoke French, which requires the central register of tones."

"You're speaking Prime now."

"Am I? Yes, I am. How lovely. I'll try to keep it up. Anyway, they did not really do anything at first. They were perplexed. But you know the French, they are a careful and patient lot. They did not give up on the strange stories collected by the Resistance, of a band of *hommes sauvages* living in the catacombs. When you were last here, we knew nothing of this. But they were working, you see. Always watching, always working. There began to be deputations from the Service Sociale going through the catacombs calling, 'come out, come out, we are here to help you.' Then a stupid fool, that idiot Emeus—"

"He and I grew up together. He was with the Thebes gang, me and Sothis out of Amma, Tayna of Tothen, that crowd."

"Tothen now calls himself Monsieur Gamon. He is here. The others, the wind has taken."

"Tayna was in Shanghai, living as a Mr. Lee." Destroyed, now, Miriam supposed. She did not say it.

"Emeus ate one of the damned Service Sociale people. The hell that resulted has not stopped."

So humans knew, also, here in France. "How much do they understand?"

"I don't know what they know. How they find us. Only that I could not safely feed these years past." He gave her a look that she had never seen from a Keeper before, almost of despair. It made her most uneasy to see such a weak and human expression in the eyes of one of her own kind.

"Why did you have to stop? What exactly did they do?"

"They came! I had just fed—in the Twelfth, coming up out of the labyrinth. The usual method."

"When you say 'They came,' what do you mean?"

"I had chosen a very nice one, smelled great, skin tone

said it was first class all the way. I took it into a—oh, some little covered place, a toilet, as I recall. I ate it and put the remnant in my little case that I carry, and suddenly—there they were, the police! Running after me. Coming in autos. Jumping out of doorways. It was phenomenal. I only escaped by leaping a wall, then to the sewers."

She pulled out her cigarettes, lit one. How tired she suddenly felt. She sensed that more had happened to him than he had as yet said, and she wanted to hear it all.

"Go on, Martin."

"You look so beautiful."

She thought, *I don't want to bear the child of a weak creature like this. I need the strongest blood now.* She said, "But you haven't finished your story."

"Miriam, I have been captured."

The words vibrated into Miriam's shocked silence.

"They examined me, Miriam. They opened my jaw, they weighed me, they extracted fluids!"

"But you escaped?"

"They tried to make me think I had. It was a silly business, though—unlocked doors and such. I knew they had let me go."

She could feel her heat beginning to rise. Her blood was flowing faster. If he had been let go, then there was danger here.

"What happened next?"

"I waited months—a full season of moons. Then I took something—a rat of a thing, half-starved, living under a bridge in the trackless neighborhoods beyond the Périphérique. I had not even opened a vein before they were there, falling on me from the roadway above, rushing up in automobiles—it was horrifying. I ran. All I could do."

"But you must have been terribly hungry."

"I tried again a few days later. This time I took the RER to the outskirts, to an area where live the brown ones that they call *ratons*. Again, I singled one out, cut it out of a little herd in a cinema, then started to have my dinner."

"They appeared again."

"Dozens of them! All around! This time I barely escaped. I came back here. I have remained within these walls ever since."

"But, Martin, how could you have not eaten for—what— at least a year? It's impossible."

" 'Nothing is impossible when you must,' that is the motto of my family. Miriam, I have drunk the feral cats, the mice, the rats. I have eaten the very flies that are spit by the air!"

No wonder he stank so. A Keeper could not live on such blood, or could barely live. She did not want to pity one of her own kind, especially not one she remembered with such respect. He had been a charming lover in his day. She remembered him in the flashing brocades of the last age, a powdered wig upon his head and a gold-knobbed stick in his hand. He knew the fashions of the age; he dallied with duchesses and played cards at the table of the king. Among the Keepers, he was known as an expert on the ways of man.

"You and I have always been kindred souls, Martin."

"I have thought of you often, child. You still live among them?"

"I have a club in New York that is quite *façonnable*. And a human lover called Sarah."

"That business of yours."

"A human to serve you is most useful." Or could be, if only she would answer the damned phone.

"I don't even know the names of those who pursue me."

They had left him alone for these years, interrupting him only when he was—according to their idea—about to "murder" one of their own. There could only be one reason why he had been left like this: He was bait, and the house was a trap.

They must even now be rushing to this place. For they had undoubtedly bugged the entire building. God only knew, maybe there were even cameras. They could make cameras the size of a fingertip, microphones no bigger than specs of dust. Sarah used such things in the club's security system.

"We have to leave here," she said.

"But I—where?"

She stood up. "Is there any fuel?"

"What sort of fuel?"

"To make a fire! Chemicals! Petrol!"

He gestured toward some steel drums.

She went to them, ripped off the soft metal cover. It was some sort of chemical, but it didn't smell flammable. Another was the same stuff.

But a third stank gloriously of the esters of earth-oil. It had been sent through their great retorts until it was a volatile. "This makes the auto go," she said.

"I know what petrol is."

She threw the barrel into the middle of the room. "Is the hidden route the same?" Every Keep had one, usually more than one. There were escapes for fire, escapes for attack, escapes for everything.

"The same."

The petrol had finished gushing out, and now stood in a puddle on the floor. Miriam took the empty drum and rolled it back and forth over the remnant until it was nothing but a sack of powdered bone. Then she tossed it into the petrol, making sure that it was thoroughly soaked.

At that moment, she heard a sound, the creak of pressure being applied against the door. She took Martin's shoulders, leaned against his ear. "They're just outside," she said. "About to burst in the door and all the windows at once."

His lips twisted back in an ugly rictus. He really, really despised them, this hunted creature. Taking his still ice-cold hand, she led him to the far wall, where once the waste from the tannery had poured into the little river Bievre, long since covered over. She counted one, two, three stones up from the floor. Now she pressed the one that was under her hand.

A brutal shaft of sunlight shattered the darkness. The doorway was a white blaze filled with darting shadows. Martin screamed, the shuddering ululation of a Keeper in absolute fury. So rarely had she heard it that Miriam screamed, too, throwing back her head and howling to the rafters.

"Essence!"

The human cry stopped her. They came out across the great room. They had nets, nets and guns. She felt tears of anger streaming down her cheeks. She was almost immobilized, such was her rage at being threatened by them. She did not let herself succumb to these feelings, though. No, she must not. Instead, she drew a book of matches from her pocket.

"Madame, si'l vous plaît!"

Lady, please, indeed! She struck one and lit the others and threw the whole flaming book. Instantly, fire roared up everywhere. The men began to shriek. They leaped and jerked in the flames, as her mother had leaped and twisted in her pyre.

Miriam pressed the stone that would open their route into the sewers of Paris.

Nothing happened.

SEVEN

Deathtrap

Paul called Becky's cell phone for the fifth time in an hour. Her recording came back for the fifth time in an hour. He'd already requested that Communications in Langley track both officers, but their cell phones were off or the signals were blocked, so the GPS system could not find them. Just for the hell of it, he tried Charlie again, also. Same shit.

It was now ten A.M. By his estimation they were two hours overdue, maybe more. He thrust another stick of gum in his mouth and chomped on it. Thank God he hated French cigarettes.

The cell phone rang. He grabbed for it. "Ward here."

"Paul, this is Justin."

What in hell was Justin Turk calling him for now? It was five A.M. in Virginia. "Yeah?"

"I'm getting back to you."

"Look, man, I gotta have more support personnel."

"Shit."

"One of the damn creatures escaped from my net. I've followed it to Paris and lost it. I need more people and more equipment real fast."

"How fast is real fast?"

"Yesterday would've been good. I need at least five more field ops."

"I can't just put people in this thing. You know the kind of problems we're having. The discussions."

"I'm losing a vampire. One that *travels*, for Chrissakes!"

"It takes weeks to clear people for you. A whole new background check, all kinds of shit. Even when I don't have the director on my ass. Which I obviously do."

"At least authorize the people I've still got in Kuala to follow me."

"That's a no-go."

"Come on, man, help me, here."

"This whole operation is under study. Until I have fresh orders, you're all frozen in place."

That sure was shitty news. "I need those people, man. This thing is going south fast."

"I'll work on it."

"Don't sound so convincing."

The conversation ended there, with muttered good-byes. Justin was a sort of a friend. That is to say, he'd be there for Paul as long as Paul wasn't a liability.

One thing was quite clear: There would be no new people, not with international human rights questions beginning to hang over the operation.

He saw somebody getting dropped down a shaft, and that somebody was him.

He hammered Becky's number into his cell phone, then Charlie's. Same results as before. "I'm in trouble," he muttered to himself.

Still, it was possible that the kids were okay. He just wished that they'd followed procedure with this break-in. There would be a hell of a stink if the French found out that

CIA personnel had invaded the records office of their security service. He'd be recalled, of course. He'd have to explain what he was doing in France, and why he'd gotten here by commandeering an Air Force general's private jet.

He sat and stared up at the blank, sunlit wall of the office tower and listened to the water drip in the sink. He looked at his watch. "Ten-fifty," he muttered to himself. "Damn and *god* damn."

And he decided to use the time well. A situation like this could burst into flames at any second. He was as prepared as he could be for the Sûreté and the White House. What he needed to do was to get ready for the really hard ones—the vampires. And there was actually something he could do right now, something damn useful.

Becky had mentioned two areas of Paris: the Ninth and Thirteenth Arrondissements. He opened his laptop and went to the CIA's database. The site didn't offer any magical insights into the workings of the world, just some very good information and lots of detail. You could find practically anybody here, and at his level of clearance, he could input requests for Echelon searches on keywords of concern to any operation approved for the system. Echelon would then look for those keywords amid the billions of phone conversations, e-mails, radio transmissions, and faxes that it monitored.

Problem was, you had to be damn specific to get anything useful. What words might the traveler use on the telephone— what special, unique words? He didn't know who she might call or where she might go, or even if Paris was her final destination.

The CIA database also had a wealth of maps, better ones than could be bought in any store, including maps of Paris that had been drawn by the German military during World

War II. Originally intended to be used in house-to-house warfare, they included detailed floor plans and plans of the sewer system that offered information down to which tunnels and pipes were big enough to admit a man.

The Germans had done this for most of the large cities in Europe. Many of the maps were outmoded, of course, and many like Paul had knowledge that the disastrous bombing of the Chinese embassy during the Kosovo conflict in 1999 had been caused by reliance on an improperly updated Werhmacht street plan of Belgrade. Since then, all maps in the CIA database been clearly marked with the last year of update.

He saw that the Ninth Arrondissement had not been touched since 1944. The map legends and street names were still in German, which wasn't very reassuring. By contrast, the Thirteenth had been revised by the French in 1998, and there were annotations that it had been updated yearly since.

He settled down to stare at the screen. He had to memorize every street, every sewer pipe, every building plan.

The vampire would know its world down to the tiniest corner. It would be able to pick every lock, use every shadow, climb all the walls and cross all the roofs. It would use the sewer system like a railroad. It would be able to navigate the ductwork, the window ledges, the eaves.

Paul hadn't believed how smart and capable the vampire was, at least not at first. He hadn't believed it when he first saw one staring back at him with dark, still eyes, looking small and helpless. There had been a slight smile on its face, a drifting little smile that communicated a sort of casual amusement. Jack Dodge said, "Hey," and stepped toward it—and a knife shot out and sliced Jack's head from his body like a blossom from a stem.

Paul could still hear the sounds: the rip of Jack's skin, the crackle of his bones, then the *shuss* of the fountain of blood that pumped out of the stump.

Those sounds came to Paul in his sleep, in the whine of the jets he took through the night, in the whispering of the wind in the ancient cities where he worked.

The creatures drifted through the cracks and corners of their world, leading him on an infinitely careful chase. They played a kind of chess with him, appearing here and there, slipping away, only to reappear somewhere else.

His pursuit of them had taught him how brilliant they were. They always stayed ahead of him. His only useful weapons were surprise and technology. Brilliance and speed were their tools, but they had no technology. They had been neatly outclassed by a computer database and infrared sight.

The death of the vampire was appalling. It haunted Paul, and he knew it haunted his people. The vampire fought harder for its life than it was possible for a human being to imagine. They hid like rats, because their lives were just so damn precious to them. When you saw their death struggles, you could almost, at moments, sympathize. The vampire died hard. "Real hard," he said aloud.

He sat staring at the map of the Thirteenth Arrondissement's sewer system. There had been structural changes made as recently as a year ago. He tracked his finger along a tunnel that had been blocked up. Probably something to do with containing old waste from the tanneries and dye factories that used to be in the area.

No doubt that was why this map was so carefully kept up. The French had a problem with contaminated water and soils in the area, and they were cleaning it up.

The hotel phone rang. He grabbed it instantly.

"Two of your people were caught in the Department of Records of the Prefecture of Police at six-thirty this morning." It was Sam Mazur at the embassy.

"Oh, Christ."

"The French had them on video from the second they climbed down into the damn room, Paul! Come on, this is amateur night, here!"

"Are they being—"

"They're being released under diplomatic immunity. But the frogs are gonna take 'em straight to the airport and put 'em on the first plane to Washington. They're totally, completely, and thoroughly blown. I'll tell you another thing— the reason that they got to stay so long in that very secure facility was so that the Sûreté could record every damn keystroke they made as they hacked their way into the database. They know how they did it, what they found—everything."

"I'm on my way."

He didn't know the Métro well, but he did know that it was the fastest way around Paris in midday traffic. He got in the train at Montparnasse. It moved off at what seemed to him to be a maddeningly leisurely pace. His mind clicked methodically from possibility to possibility as he tried to devise a new way of saving Becky and Charlie and his whole operation.

In less than fifteen minutes he was trotting up the steps into the Place de la Concorde.

The American embassy was beautiful and very well guarded. It was also quiet, unlike many of its counterparts around the world. The crowds of visa seekers and unhappy citizens reporting lost passports were at the consulate a few blocks away. His own diplomatic passport got him straight past the French guards and the marines.

He entered through a metal detector, declaring and checking the gun that his false Interpol ID allowed him to carry. Well, *false* was maybe too strong a word. The Interpol papers his team used were the result of an accommodation between the CIA and the international police agency.

Sam's office was halfway down a wide corridor that looked as if it belonged in a palace. As indeed, it did. This building had been one before it became the U.S. embassy. He went in, and the atmosphere changed at once. Here there were computer screens and filing cabinets and a dropped ceiling. The outer office blazed with fluorescent light.

"I'm Paul Ward," he said to a receptionist who, to his surprise, turned out to be French. What a local national was doing working in a clearance-required job he did not know. Times had changed.

Sam sat at a steel desk. His venetian blinds were firmly shut on what was probably a view of an air shaft. The rumble of air-conditioning equipment shook the floor, but this office, itself, was not air-conditioned. It was just near the equipment.

"Paul, you old asshole, I thought you'd be arrested on your way here."

"What about my people?"

"Business class on Air France. Not too bad."

Until they reached Langley. This was not over, no way, not for any of them. It was a major screwup, and it was going to take a lot of time to fix it. If that was even possible. The White House had started asking its damn questions at just the wrong time.

"Are they in the air yet?"

"They're being signed out of the hoosegow as we speak.

The Frenchies don't like people getting into their secure areas, *especially* not us."

"Sam, you're gonna hate me for this. But you gotta find a way to keep my people in country. I need them urgently, right now."

He shook his head. "It's over. So over."

"Call in favors. Do anything."

"Nothin' I can do. They're toast."

"Then I need an immediate appointment with the ambassador."

Sam blinked. "You're kidding. You'd bring the politicos in on something like this? A jerk like you couldn't possibly have a congressional sugar daddy."

Paul tried using what he hoped might be a trump card. "It's terrorism, Sam. I'm in the middle of a heavy operation that involves France only because we happened to follow an international terrorist onto French soil. If we lose this woman, innocent people are gonna die."

Sam picked up the phone. "You don't need the ambassador." He spoke in rapid-fire French. Paul couldn't follow it precisely, but he could tell that he was going up the ladder to somebody very senior somewhere, and this senior individual was being asked for urgent and immediate intervention.

Sam hung up. "The chief of the Division of Internal Security of the Sûreté will see us in ten minutes."

This time they had an embassy Citroën with a driver, so it was a lot easier to get around. "You're out there in the middle of nowhere without any support staff, the three of you," Sam said. "Bound to be a problem, an operation that's being run that far outside of guidelines, that thinly staffed."

"We're effective. That's the bottom line."

"I don't want to intrude, Paul. But I gotta tell you, you

look like hell. In fact, I'd give road kill a better rating. Whatever it is you're doing that you're so effective at, it's taking you apart."

He and Sam had learned to strangle people with piano wire and plant microphones under the skin of pet cats together. They'd been in Cambodia together, where none of their training applied and nothing they did worked. They had fought the silent war together when it really was a war.

"It's just another shitty op, my friend. You look great, by the by. Tennised, golfed, and swum."

"Also pokered every Tuesday night with the Brits. It's a good life here, as long as you don't get yourself in the kind of trouble your two goons are in."

If only the French customs agents hadn't made such a mess of things at de Gaulle. If only he hadn't had to screen the operation through Interpol. The way he saw it, they should have disabled the creature with a shot as soon as it reached customs, then dropped it in a vat of sulfuric acid, or cremated it. Instead, they took it to an airport brig. It escaped before they even got it in the cell. Of course it did.

"I wish I could tell you what it is I'm doing," Paul said. "It'd be a lot easier if every damn security officer and cop on the planet knew. But there would be huge problems. It'd be the most unpredictable goddamn thing you could imagine."

"Well, that explains that. You gonna get yourself wasted, old buddy, on this thing. Your politics are all used up, way I hear it."

They pulled up in front of the long, impressively French Victorian building that housed the Sûreté. Paul expected a lot of bureaucracy and a long wait, but they were soon in a very quiet, very ornate office facing an extremely fastidious midget.

"I am Colonel Bocage," he said.

"Where's Henri-Georges?" Sam asked.

"You will interview with me."

Paul said in French, *"J'voudrais mon peuple, monsieur. Tout de suite."*

Colonel Bocage laughed. "Mr. Mazur, this is the man in charge, that you promised us to meet?"

Sam nodded. "I made that promise to Henri-Georges Bordelon."

"And he transmitted it to me."

"I need my people," Paul said. "We're saving lives."

"You speak French. You should think in French. It's more civilized . . ."

"I can't think in French."

". . . because we have so many ways of expressing concepts of good and evil." He smiled again, and Paul thought he looked, for a moment, like a very hard man. "Mr. Mazur, could you step out for a moment? I am sorry."

This wasn't the usual drill when you went to beg to keep your spies in place. But Paul was in no position to ask what was going on. When Sam had left, the colonel went to his window, which looked out over a lovely park. There was a difference between being a high official in the Sûreté and a lowly intelligence officer like Sam.

Colonel Bocage closed a manila folder he'd been appearing to review. It was only a pose, a tension builder. Paul had done it himself a thousand times, to a thousand nervous supplicants in ten different countries. "So," the colonel said at last, "you are here investigating *les sauvages*. Tell me, what do you Americans call them?"

Paul Ward had not had the sensation of his heart skipping a beat since the moment he had looked upon his father's remains. No matter how violent or how dangerous his situation, he always remained icy calm . . . until this second. His heart was skipping a whole lot of beats. He parted his lips, but nothing came out.

The colonel raised an eyebrow and with it one corner of his mouth. "I am your counterpart," he said, "your French counterpart."

Paul wiped his face clean of expression. Tell him nothing.

"You are surprised, I see," Colonel Bocage said. "Genuinely surprised. Tell me, how long have the Americans been working on this?"

Paul reminded himself never to play poker with Colonel Bocage. "A few years," he said dryly.

"My friend, we have been struggling with this problem for fifty years."

"We cleared Asia."

"Cleared?"

"We killed them, all of them."

"Except for Mrs. Tallman."

"Except for her."

"*Elle est une sauvage, aussi?*"

"You call them savages?"

"To keep the record clean. We know what they are. But you come from Asia, where we know you have been working very hard. Why not start in America, where the lives are more important to you?"

"Our first solid lead was in Tokyo."

At that moment, Charlie and Becky were brought in.

"Ah," Colonel Bocage said, "your colleagues. Now, please, we shall all sit together."

"You guys okay?"

"Fine," Becky said. She looked wonderful when she was

angry—her eyes full of sparks, her cheeks flushed, her lips set in a line that was at once grim and somehow suggestive.

Beside her, Charlie played with the damn cigarette machine. His style under this kind of pressure was sullen defiance.

There was a silence. Paul was trying to remember if he had ever felt quite this embarrassed and uncomfortable before. He decided that the answer was no.

"This matter has the very highest level of secrecy attached to it in France," Bocage said. "Government does not care to inform the population of such matters." He paused. "You have concluded the same."

"All governments that we've been to have concluded the same."

"Given that we cannot protect our people, there seems little choice but to hide this until matters are resolved."

Bocage rested his eyes on Becky, so frankly that she looked away. Paul was fascinated. Becky was the very essence of self-possession, and Becky did not look away.

"You obtained what you needed, I trust," he said to her.

"Yes."

He strolled over to his desk. "We used a computer spying program to watch your keystrokes," he said, his voice rippling with self-satisfaction. There were few things more pleasant in the life of an intelligence agent than getting the drop on a colleague from a friendly country. Paul knew, he'd done it. "If you'd like a copy of your work—" He held a file folder toward Becky and Charlie. "In the interest of friendly cooperation."

"It'd be friendlier," Paul said, "if you shared something with us that we didn't already have."

"With pleasure, Mr. Ward," he said. Then his mouth

snapped closed, as if he had caught himself in a moment of indiscretion.

Paul saw that the man's carefully relaxed appearance was concealing a state of extraordinary emotional tension. Paul's experience as a wartime interrogator told him that this man was about to address something that he considered extremely terrible.

"Go ahead, Colonel," Charlie said, no doubt reading the same signs.

"We have had one of these creatures under observation in a house in—"

"Let us tell you that," Becky said. "Thirteenth Arrondissement. Rue des Gobelins."

"Very good. Do you know which house? Or exactly what has happened there?" The colonel was sweating now.

"Tell us," Paul said. He decided that the colonel was a man who habitually exploded in the face of his own staff, but in this situation had to contain the energy.

"We have had *une sauvage* trapped in a house in the Rue des Gobelins for over a year. It hasn't eaten for twelve months, but it still lives."

"So why not go in? If you got the thing trapped, kill it."

"We were hoping that it would attract some response from its peers—curiosity, compassion, something that would draw them to it. But it did not, and now—well, it's too late."

Something had gone terribly wrong, which explained the ominous lowering of the colonel's voice.

"What's the trouble, Colonel?"

"The house is at this moment burning to the ground. In it, there are two vampires that we know of." He stopped again. He rubbed his cheek, as if hunting for stubble. "There are six of my own people."

"God save them," Paul said. He knew, now, why the map of the Thirteenth Arrondissement was so up-to-date, and also why the sewer system had been altered. They had cut off access from the vampire's lair. Exactly the approach Paul would have taken.

"But I do have some good news for you. This 'Mrs. Tallman' of yours was in the house."

"That's goddamn good news, Colonel!" Maybe she hadn't had time to spread her warning. Maybe now she would never have time. "Do you know how long she's been there?"

"She appeared yesterday afternoon at about six. That we know."

"Yesterday afternoon?"

He nodded. "The taxi brought her from a hotel."

"It's possible that she didn't reach any of the others."

"It is. But they are aware that something is wrong, the Paris vampires."

Paul had assumed that there would be resistance if they realized they were under attack.

"Only very recently," the colonel continued, "have we been able to deal with them. Only since we understood the difficulties involved in—the difficulties with the blood—"

"How do you kill 'em?"

"We shoot them to incapacitate them with a gun that has been especially designed for the purpose, then we burn them to ash."

"That'll work."

He bared his teeth, sucked in air with a hiss. Paul thought, *This is one tough bastard. I like this guy.* Bocage stuck out his jaw. "We made many kills over the years. But the numbers, they still went up. Slowly, but always *up!* My God!"

"It's been hard for us, too."

"We would shoot them in the chest, then bury them. They would come out, but carefully, so we would not notice the disturbance to the grave. We thought we were eradicating them, but we were accomplishing nothing. Eventually, even we could see that the pattern of killing went on. But we could not track it because they come up out of mines under the city. All sorts of places. No pattern, you see."

"What about the Ninth and the Thirteenth," Becky asked.

"We eventually tracked one of the creatures back to the Thirteenth. To Nineteen Rue des Gobelins, to be precise. The only one in Paris living aboveground. The rest of them—dear God, those mines are a horrible place." He fell silent for a moment. "We have a seventy percent casualty rate down there."

Paul said nothing. Of the seven people who had started with him, he'd lost four. He and Justin had thought over fifty percent was monstrous.

The telephone rang. Colonel Bocage went around his desk and answered it. He spoke in French at some length, then put it down abruptly. He stood, silent. Paul knew what had happened without even asking.

"Another casualty report. The whole team that entered Nineteen Rue Gobelins was lost. Six men."

"Shit!" Charlie said.

In the distance, a church bell sounded.

"There is good news. Of one *sauvage*, bones were found. They are being taken out to be burned."

"And the other one?"

"Mrs. Tallman was reduced to ash."

"Then we're done," Becky said. "Back home to find out if my fiancé remembers my name."

"We are going to attempt to isolate and sterilize the mines," Bocage said with that carefully practiced mildness of his. "We're short six essential personnel. It'll take us months to find and train replacements." He raised his eyebrows. "I think that our two countries have some secrets to share."

Langley would be as nervous about this as an old maiden aunt about a slumber party. There were protocols to create, careful integration procedures so that the secrecy laws of both countries could be followed during the operation. He ought to go back and make a full report up supervisory channels. On the other hand, he could just stuff the whole damn process straight up Langley's ass, and do it without telling them.

"May I take it that you're on board," Colonel Bocage asked.

He didn't even need to look at Becky and Charlie. Their answer would be the same as his. "You bet."

EIGHT

Flicker of Fire

If she did not have blood immediately—absolutely fresh blood—she would die. Where she lay, trapped, helpless, and in agony, there could be no blood. Here in this dank place, with pain radiating through her body as if an army with burning coals for heels were marching up and down her, Miriam saw that she was coming to the final edge of life.

She had ended up here for one reason only: She had been surprised by the disaster in Chiang Mai and running like a desperate rat ever since. No planning, no forethought, simply a wild race across the world.

The humans had blocked the escape tunnel with concrete and reinforced it with bars of iron. She'd taken to the stairs, running up to the top of the house, to the ancient rooms where Lamia had lived. The old brocades still hung on the walls, rotting and falling though they were. And there was the bed she had used, where Miriam had cuddled with her, and where they had so happily shared kills. But the flames had come, marching like soldiers, and Miriam had been forced to the roof. She'd looked from the edges of the house; the streets had been filled with dozens of police and firemen. She could not climb down the wall into that, not in broad daylight. She could not jump to another building, not quite.

She'd found a way, though. She always found a way. She had climbed down inside the chimney, down into the hearths in the basement, below the level of the fire. As she crawled out, covered with ash, the floor above had begun to cave in. Fire had swept over her, fire and the agony of fire.

There had been a tiny space at the back of the fireplace, where they had pushed the ashes. She'd pulled bricks out and made her way into a brick pipe not more than eighteen inches in diameter, forcing her body into the space until her joints ground.

She lay with her eyes closed, willing herself not to cry out with the agony of it. If she opened her eyes, all she saw was wet, moldering brick a few bare inches above her face. The whole time she was struggling through the crack, she'd heard Martin screaming and screaming. The only thing the food she'd brought him had done was give him enough energy to die slowly.

They were gaining control over the fire, and above her she could now hear human voices. Water cascaded down.

She heard a sound, very distinct, and very different from the water, or the popping of Martin's hot bones. This sound she heard was breathing—*snick snick, snick snick*—quick breathing, very light.

A rat was coming along the tunnel she was in, interested, no doubt, in the scent of raw, bleeding flesh. Or perhaps it was a devotee of cooked food. A French rat might be expected to be a sophisticate.

This rat represented a chance—a small one, admittedly, but its presence changed the odds from nonexistent to . . . well, a little bit better than nothing.

Here, little one, come here, little fruit. "The closer they are genetically to man, the better they are for you. The rats, the apes, the cows, all may be consumed to benefit." So had said the Master Tutomon, her childhood tutor, with his lessons in geometry and languages and survival.

The rat hesitated. She could not see it, but the sound of its breathing and the patter of its feet were clear. It was on her left side, just parallel with her foot. To encourage it to come closer to her hand, she began to wriggle her fingers.

She needed to open her eyes, and she prepared herself as best she could. The space might be entirely dark by now, and that would be better. The light was much less, but she saw the bricks, so close that they were blurred to her vision. An involuntary gasp came out of her. The rat scuttled away.

She raised her head until it was pressed against the top of the pipe, then looked along her arm. The creature came back. She could just see its interested little face as it went *snick-snick, snick-snick* against her fingertips.

She stretched her arm, opening her fingers, letting the rat venture closer to the center of the trap. But it came no closer.

The indifferent trickle of water that had been slipping around her body was becoming a steady stream. If this pipe backed up, they would notice. They would send a crew down to unblock it. They would drag her out, even if it tore her to pieces. There would be no mercy. There was never any mercy; that had become quite apparent.

Now, the rat was returning. The rat, in fact, was very close to her fingers. Her exquisite nerves communicated the sensation as it sniffed their tips. Finally, it decided to stop sniffing and try a bite of the cool, still flesh that had drawn its curiosity. Instantly, it was in Miriam's hand. It was wriggling and screaming its rat screams—*ree-ree-ree*. She sucked in her breath and moved her arm, drawing the creature closer to her mouth. She had to drag it against her naked breast, and as she did its needlelike teeth slashed the pale skin.

Then the creature was at her mouth. She bit off the shrieking head and drank the body dry, crumbling the remains, which were no more substantial than a little leaf.

The blood of the rat tasted surprisingly good. She could feel it spilling through her. It was going to be useful. But would it be enough for the task that lay ahead?

To continue the motion that her exhaustion had stopped, she had to work her arms over her head and press hard against the edges with her feet. In time, her bones would compress a little more, and she would move a few inches. However, if the pipe got any more narrow, she could be trapped.

Now that she was moving again, the water was sluicing around her, bringing with it bits of spent coal and ash. She pushed, felt more pressure, waited. Nothing.

If she was trapped—her heart began going faster. Harder she pushed, harder and harder. Still nothing. She felt her tongue swelling from the effort. Her bones ground and creaked. Her tongue began to push past the rows of cartilage that filled her mouth, that provided the seal when she sucked blood.

Still nothing, nothing, *nothing!* And then—worse— louder voices. Yes, the humans were in the basement, speaking about the slowness of the drain. They must unclog it, of course. They would find within it this strange, distorted being that would slowly return to its previous form, and they would know another secret of the Keepers, that vampires' bones that were not brittle like their own, but pliant.

How would they kill her? Burn her until she was ash, as they had done to her mother? Hammer a stake into her heart until her blood stopped, then let her die over however long it took in a coffin—years, or even whole cycles of years? Or explode her head and dissolve her in acid?

There was a sound, and immediately a dagger of pain shot

straight up her spine. The next instant, she slid along the pipe a substantial distance. She could have howled with the sheer joy of it, the wonderful sensation of release from the terrible compression.

The water she had been stopping came behind her, a gushing torrent that swept her down a wider sluiceway. Where she was now, there was considerably more light. It was coming from slits near the ceiling, that appeared at regular intervals. The space was high enough to stand up in, and she could peer through these slits.

She rose to a sitting position. She was exhausted. A rat was not worth much to her body, and she soon must feed again. She needed a human being.

She drew herself up and up, fighting the great blasts of pain from her tormented body. Finally, she was crouching. To see out, she would have to straighten herself, and she could not until her bones had spread again. She forced herself to try, to hasten the process as much as she could. Agony ran up and down her spine, causing her toes to curl and her lips to twist back. She hissed with it, she stifled the screams that tried to burst out of her throat.

Minutes passed. The water, which had been gushing past her knees, subsided to a milder flow. Its acrid stench was replaced by a surprising odor—the scent of a fresh spring. Her kind needed a lot of water and loved fresh water. She was smelling a clean, limestone spring beneath the streets of Paris, in the very sewer. She turned herself toward it and began slowly placing one foot in front of another, walking toward the source. Now she could see that the arched space widened. To her left and right there were muddy banks. In the water, there swam tiny fish, sweeping along before her like little schools of pale starlight.

This wonderful, entirely unexpected place must be the ancient River Bièvre. The rumbling overhead was a street. And indeed, when she finally managed to peer out one of the slits, she saw passing tires. As she moved along, the water became better and better. No sewage here at all, just the stream still dancing in its ancient bed of stones.

She began to look for a spring. There was certainly one nearby. She could smell its wonderful, stony freshness. Ten steps along, twenty, and she found it, its water bubbling cheerfully out of the ground. Above it, somebody in the long-ago had made a little grotto and set a cross, which now stood encrusted with rust. She lay herself down in the water and let it flow over her, let it kiss her wounds with its clean coldness.

The pain grew somewhat less. The cold was helping to heal the burns, the clean water to reduce the need of her blood to ward off infection. If the process was to speed up to a normal rate, though, she had to have food.

She lay in the pouring spring, twisting and turning slowly, allowing the water to clean every part of her, to sweep away the ashen skin and the burned flesh, and the debris that had collected in the wounds. The thick stink of it all washed away with it, leaving behind only the smell of the water and the smell of her.

Finally, when those two odors had not changed for a long time, she rose from the stream. She began moving along the riverbank, a naked, burned creature, svelte and, she supposed, pale. She was looking for a manhole, some means of getting up into the city again, to the food supply that swarmed in its streets.

What she found instead was a door. It was steel and set high up in the wall, at the top of a series of iron rungs. The door was half the normal height and had a lever rather than a handle.

She climbed the rungs, pulled the lever, which dropped down with a thud. She drew the door open and found herself looking into a dark room full of humming machinery.

She climbed into the room. In contrast with the wet cold that had surrounded her for hours, it was warm and dry. It felt fiercely hot, although she knew that this was only the effect of the sudden change.

Her nostrils had been seared, but her sense of smell seemed unimpaired. She smelled machine oil, the fumes of burning, and the scent of lots of electricity. This was a furnace room. She knew boilers and furnaces well. She had special uses for them. This one reminded her of the Ehler that she had in her house, a good, hot system with an ample firebox.

Beyond the furnace, she saw stairs. She mounted them, stopping at the top to listen and catch her breath. She laid her ear against the door that was there. On the other side, she heard the tap of footsteps. They moved slowly about, *tip-tap, tip-tap,* pausing here and there, then moving on. Suddenly a voice began to speak, using English. It spoke about the manufacture of tapestries.

This work had been going on when she was last here. Across the street from her mother's house there had been a manufactory of tapestry. So it was still in operation, but there were also observers now, people from the English-speaking world being taken on tours of the works.

She turned the handle of the door. Locked. This was of little consequence. They had not learned the art of the lock, the humans. Shaking it a few times, she dislodged the tumblers. She knew exactly what she sought: a female creature of about her own size, preferably alone.

The tour group consisted of about twenty people being led about among the tapestries, which hung on large looms.

She stepped out onto the gloomy area before the door, then slipped behind the nearest loom. On the other side, the weaver worked, stepping on her treadle and sliding thread through her beater.

Beneath the smock, the girl wore dark clothing of some sort; Miriam could not see exactly what it was. The casual dress of the modern age. She peered at the creature. It was intent on its work. She listened to the talk of the guide. The tourists drifted closer. In another moment, they would see this person, observe her working at her loom.

Miriam stepped into the girl's view. She didn't notice, such was her concentration. Miriam moved closer. Now, the girl stopped working and glanced her way, then looked harder. Her mouth dropped open. She looked the naked apparition up and down. An expression of pity crossed her face, mixing with horror as she realized that the woman she was seeing was severely burned.

Miriam stepped toward her. She swayed as if falling, causing the girl to instinctively move forward to help her. Miriam enclosed her in her arms and drew her behind the loom, then opened her mouth against the neck and pulled the fluids in fairly easily, requiring two great gulps to finish the process.

Her whole flesh seemed to leap with joy; it was as if she were going to fly up to the sky. She fought against crying out, such was the pleasure. Her body from the top of her head to the tips of her toes filled with an electric tickling as her newly refreshed blood raced to repair her wounds.

The shuddering, tickling sensations were so overwhelming that she was dropped like a stone to her knees. She pitched forward, gasping, her body deliciously racked with a sensation very like climax. Again it came, again and again, and the voices came closer, and the tip-tapping of the shoes.

She grabbed the remnant, invisible in its heap of clothes, and pulled it behind the loom. As she untangled the dry, emaciated remains from the clothing, she heard a ripple of laughter. The tour guide had said something that amused her audience. The click of other looms went on. Quickly, quickly, Miriam put the clothes on—black jeans, a black turtleneck, shoes that fit her, unfortunately, quite badly. Then the blue smock. No hat, and that was not good because her hair would take time to regrow. She needed a wig, but that could not be had here. She stood up.

"Noelle?"

It was the guide, curious about why she was not at her loom. They would know each other perfectly, of course.

"Noelle, what are you doing? Why are you back there?"

She could not speak. She had no idea what Noelle's voice sounded like. If the woman came around the loom, she would see something impossible—a skeleton covered with skin, and standing over it, a hairless and eyebrowless creature, its skin flushed bright pink. The burns were probably still very much in evidence as well, making her the stars knew only how grotesque. She picked up the remnant and crushed it. The cracking, splintering sounds were appalling.

"Noelle!"

"I'm fixing it!"

"Who is that?"

"It's me, please."

The guide began her spiel again, but her uneasy tone told Miriam that she was not satisfied with what she had heard, just unable to understand what was going on. She'd send a guard around in a moment, almost certainly.

Staying behind the looms, trying to avoid being glimpsed by the workers or the tour group, she went quickly back to

the door. She slipped through and down into the basement.
She went to the furnace and opened the grate, stuffing the
remnant inside. Never again would she be so foolish as to
leave one of these little calling cards behind. In this new
world of aggressive, smart human beings, one more mistake
like that would be her last.

She looked around for a doorway to the outside, saw one
marked *Sortie*, with a red light above it. She went out, finding
herself in an alleyway. In one direction, there was a blank
wall, in the other, an entrance into a rather quiet street. It
was early evening now, and the shadows were growing long.

She immediately noticed a curious flickering effect
against the walls and roofs of the street ahead. Each time the
flickering got brighter, there would be an accompanying roar.

She moved forward cautiously, knowing that she had to go
out into that street in order to escape. The closer she got to
the opening of the alley, the brighter the flickering became,
the louder the roaring. Now she could also hear crackling and
smell a smell of burning petrol. The flickering reflected
against her black clothing. She held out her hands, looking
down at them, at the orange light dancing on them. Then she
stepped forward and immediately looked to the left, toward
the source of the light.

The first thing she saw was the gutted ruin of her
mother's house. The Castle of the White Queen was streaked
with soot, its every window black and dark, its roof collapsed
into the shell of the building.

Before it there were dozens of police and fire vehicles and
milling gendarmes. The light was not coming from their
vehicles, though, it was coming from a bonfire in the middle
of the street, which was being fed by men with flamethrow-
ers. At the mouth of the Rue des Gobelins a high barrier had

been erected. No member of the public could see over it. She did not think that she could easily get around it. In fact, going out into the street would cause an immediate reaction, given all the police and the care with which they were preventing sight of this place.

In the center of the fire, she saw black bones and bones glowing red. It was Martin, of course. Obviously, the humans knew enough about the Keepers to take extreme care that they were really dead. A gendarme glanced at her, made a clear gesture: *stop there, come no closer*. His glance lingered for a moment, then he turned away.

The ring of people around the bones were different from the gendarmes. They were dressed casually; they looked brutal. Nearer, stood a small knot of others whom she took to be the supervisors. These people around the fire, making sure that the very bones of their quarry were reduced to ash, were the killers of the Keepers.

It was possible, if she listened intently, to make out snatches of conversation—a gendarme muttering about overtime, one of the murderers saying something about the temperature of the fire. Then the voice of a tall supervisor boomed out. "Fine ash," it said, "then hose down the street."

That was to be the fate of her kind, then, to be reduced to ash and sent down the sewer.

Silence fell. More orders were given and one of the *pompes* was started up. Soon, water was pouring from its hoses and sluicing along the street. She watched it come toward her feet, watched as it reached the drain. It carried floating bits of burned material and chips of bone. A button came tumbling and bobbing along, and she saw that it was her own button, from the suit she'd had to leave behind in order to squeeze down the pipe that had saved her.

"*Excusez-moi, mademoiselle.*"

One of the gendarmes was coming toward her. He smiled slightly, then took her arm, but quite gently. "I will conduct you out." He drew her forward. He blinked, seeing her bald head.

"What has happened?" she asked, trying to deflect his concern.

"Vagrants set fire to the White Palace. There were deaths."

"Why were they burning the bodies?"

He shook his head. "It's what the authorities said. Who knows why."

She let the gendarme conduct her along. His body was loose, his breathing soft, his expression indifferent. Obviously he knew nothing of the Keepers and only assumed that she was a rather unusual looking woman. Her eyes were on the men who knew.

Closer she came to them, marching beside her policeman. They were engaged in intent conversation. She passed just behind the two supervisors. Then she saw one, a female, suddenly turn and face her. The creature was beautiful, with swaying blond hair. But its eyes, almost black, appeared as hard as chips of obsidian. "Excuse me," it said in American-accented English.

As instinct prepared Miriam to fight, her body became tight beneath the restricting clothes. There were still many burned and injured areas, especially in her limbs, and the pain tormented her like the persistent hacking of slow, dull blades.

The creature followed her a few steps. "*Pardonnez-moi,*" it said, now in French. This creature was concerned and it was curious. It was not sure, though, of what to do. So it could not be certain of what she was.

Then the gendarme was letting her out onto the street. He asked her if she felt well enough to keep on. Instead of answering, she slipped into and quickly through the sparse crowd of onlookers. She did not look back, did not want to delay another moment her escape from the deathtrap.

Now that she had fed, her body wanted to sleep. She knew that it would be the deep, deep sleep of her kind, and that she had to find a place in which to lie safely for the helpless hours it would bring. But she could not afford it. She had an urgent mission to perform. The French Keepers must be warned, their Book of Names protected.

She walked quickly along the busy Avenue des Gobelins. She would go to a hotel somewhere, using the credit cards in this woman's pocketbook. Or no, there was a better idea. She would go to the woman's flat. It was a risk, of course, but she had the keys and the driving license with the address.

A little farther down the street, she saw a taxi at a stand. She hailed it with the same sort of casual gesture she had seen others using. She would also update her language as best she could. Any fool would remember a passenger who spoke like Voltaire.

As she got into the taxi, she opened the pocketbook. Noelle Halff, 13 Rue Léon Maurice de Nordmann. "Treize Rue L. M. Nordmann," she muttered, slurring her words like a modern Parisian.

The driver made a strange sort of a face, then drove on. He rounded the corner into Boulevard Arago, and then they were there. It had been idiotic to take a taxi. The place was barely a quarter of a mile away. "I injured my foot," she said as he stopped in front of a lovely artist's atelier.

"Too bad," he responded as he took her money. She seemed to have done perfectly well. He hadn't noticed anything about her. Perhaps baldness was not unknown among women in Paris. Some *outré* fashion, perhaps.

She went through the bag, looking for keys, soon finding a set. There were four of them, and rather than tumble the lock, she found the correct one. She let herself in, then turned the timer that lit the foyer. As it hummed through its few minutes, she located the next key and entered the atelier itself.

The room was furnished with another Gobelins loom and more tapestries, medieval reproductions that the woman must have been selling in the tourist market.

"Hello," she said. There was no answer. She went across the studio to its small kitchen, and beyond it into an equally tiny *salle de bains* and *toilette*. For sleep, a *couchette* had been installed at one end of the studio.

She searched the *salle de bains,* looking for makeup, but also trying to determine if more than one person lived here. The results were ambiguous. There was a man's razor, also two toothbrushes.

Somebody moved. She glimpsed in the shadows a strange, dark creature. She reeled back out of the tiny room, raising her arms, preparing to defend herself.

But nobody came leaping after her. The only sound was her own breathing, that and a trickle of water from the toilet.

She turned on the light and saw in the mirror a Miriam Blaylock so profoundly changed that she'd thought herself a stranger. The head was bald, the face sunken, the eyes black sockets. She raised a finger to her cheek, felt the skin. It ought to be pink and soft right now, glowing with the life she had just consumed. But it revealed another surprise. She was not sallow, but covered with fine gray ash. The outer layer of her skin seemed to have been carbonized, at least on her face.

She splashed some water on it, then dried it with a serviette. It came up muddy white. The sink was full of gray. She stripped off her clothes and looked down at herself. She had sustained tremendous damage, more than she had realized. There were great rifts in her skin, filled with raw, angry flesh. Her hips were scraped almost to the bone. In one place, she could see actually see some bone.

She drew a bath, watching as the wonderful, steaming water gushed into the big tub. When she sat in it, the ash clinging to her body soon turned the water dark gray, tinged pink with the blood of her wounds.

Soon her whole body was tickling as her blood raced to repair the damage. She closed her eyes. How lovely. How much she needed to sleep. So easy it would be, so warm was the water.

No! No, she had to find stimulants—coffee, pills, anything—and she had to locate the woman's passport, call an airline, and buy a ticket to New York, go to the mines, warn the other Keepers.

She rose from the tub and threw open the medicine chest. There were three bottles of pills—vitamins, an herbal remedy for colds, nothing of any use. The poor young creature had been healthy and clean of even simple drugs. Miriam could not avoid a sense of waste when she destroyed a vital, young life like this. The girl had been not unlike her Sarah.

She had given up telephoning Sarah. All that mattered now was getting home. She was afraid that the disaster had already crossed the Atlantic and that was why Sarah couldn't respond. Would she find her beautiful home in Manhattan a ruin, just like the Castle of the White Queen, and Sarah's very bones burned to ashes? There was no way to know that. It was not given to her.

She peered into the mirror. Actually, her face wasn't so bad. A little makeup here, a little there, a bit of lip gloss, and she would be a girl again. She would be—

She stopped. Like the fall of evening or a black cloak dropping over her, a shroud, a sorrow so great fell upon her heart that it inspired not the usual gnashing anger, but a deep questioning of her own value as a creature, and indeed of the worth of the Keepers as a species upon the earth.

Look around you, she thought, at the complex life that had been unfolding in this atelier, at the wonders in the looms, their colors glowing in the faint light that came in from the street. Look at the book beside the bed, thumbed, earmarked, a book of poems with which Noelle Halff had put herself to sleep at night. *Les Fleurs du Mal*—"The Flowers of Evil." Miriam knew the poems, appreciated them as well.

The girl might not have any pills in her cabinet, but she kept lip gloss and other cosmetics of the very highest quality. Miriam started to make up her face, to return to it an approximation of the endless youth that lay beneath her wounds.

She felt the weight of sleep urging at her brain, at her exhausted muscles, increasing the weight of her bones. She tossed her head, her eyes gleaming with a kind of fury. Even without drugs, she would not sleep. She could not, must not.

For she knew without question, if she lay down in this atelier—if she slept—they would certainly catch her.

NINE

Lady of the Knife

The lower condyles of human femurs lined the walls, joint-end out. Above them were stacked skulls. Paul had known about the Denfert-Rochereau ossuary, but only vaguely, as the sort of grotesque that tourists of a certain kind—fans of horror movies, say—might visit. For ten francs you could spend as much time as you wanted to with the bones of seven million Parisians.

"What's that smell?" Becky asked.

"Maybe there's a fresh corpse."

"Thank you, Charles."

"No bodies were ever buried here. Just skeletons," Colonel Bocage said.

Still, there was a certain smell, and smells were important to this work. Paul inhaled carefully. They all knew the fetors of the vampire—the sour, dry odor of their unwashed skin and the appalling stink of their latrines. Their waste was dead human plasma.

Colonel Bocage and Lieutenants Raynard and Des Roches walked ahead. The two lieutenants had interesting histories. Raynard was not French but Algerian. He had been a Foreign Legionnaire. Des Roches, a solemn-looking man with a quick sense of humor and what looked to Paul like a whole lot of physical power, had been a GIGN officer. The Groupe d'Intervention de la Gendarmerie Nationale was France's elite terrorist intervention unit. These were the guys who stormed planes being held by madmen. These were also the guys who were sent in when the government didn't want prisoners, only bodies.

Because of the catastrophe that had just occurred, these were the last two men Bocage had. Signing people on was just as difficult for him as it was for Paul. They had to be excellent, they had to be clearable to a high level, and it was just damn hard to find people like that.

As they moved forward, everybody was quiet. The French were grieving over the decimation of their team, and everybody was well aware of how this hole had chewed up people in the past. Theirs was brutal, extremely dangerous work. Vampires died, but it cost. God, it cost.

They were passing rows and rows of bones, an incredible sight. They were still in the ossuary itself.

"No teeth," Charlie observed, "no lower jaws."

Des Roches said, "The teeth were sold to button makers to help finance the ossuary."

"Was that legal?"

"Perhaps, at the time," Colonel Bocage replied, "although not politically correct, I am embarrassed to say. But old France—it was not politically correct."

"Madame de Pompadour," Becky said, pointing to a sign.

"Who was?" Charlie asked.

"She was the executive secretary of King Louis XV," Raynard said.

"And the mistress," Bocage added, "of course."

"How'd she end up down here?"

"After the revolution, the bones of aristocrats were no longer held sacred." The tone of Raynard's voice suggested that he did not entirely approve of the revolution. Like many men engaged in extremely difficult military pursuits, he was ultraconservative.

"Stop, please." Des Roches consulted his PalmPilot, which contained a map not only of the ossuary, but of the entire system of mines beneath the streets of Paris. The mines were more extensive even than the legendary Paris sewer system. The map, provided by the Inspectorate General of Quarries, covered the two hundred plus miles of tunnels and shafts that were interconnected. This was estimated to be roughly three-quarters of the total. The rest of it, among the most ancient of the shafts, were either completely detached from the main body, or connected only by openings too small for a human to enter.

Given the danger of entering the tunnels, ground-based radars and sonars had been used to complete the maps, so they were not nearly as accurate as the hunters would have liked. Paul had spent the night with Charlie and Becky studying them. Each had committed a section of the complex to memory. They had quizzed one another on twists and turns, blind alleys and unexpected crossings, until dawn.

They reached a dead end in the ossuary, which was blocked by a gate and marked with a sign, *Entrée Interdite*. Over the past hundred years, the Prefecture of Police had recorded sixty disappearances from the ossuary. It wasn't many, but the points at which these people had last been seen were all closest to this particular connection with the abandoned labyrinth of mines. It was here that Bocage's teams had entered in the past.

"Regard," Bocage said, "beyond this point, we must assume that we are, at all times, in peril of our lives."

Raynard opened an aluminum case that he carried. He distributed lightweight Kevlar body armor. "Remember that they are experts with knives. They can throw a knife almost with the speed of a bullet, because of the arm strength."

Paul remembered the Sinha Vampire. It had killed Len Carter with a knife thrown so hard it went completely through his body and struck Becky, who was standing ten feet behind him. She'd taken thirty stitches in her neck. Had she not been turned slightly away from him at that instant, her carotid artery would have been severed.

Bocage gave out pistols, weapons unlike anything Paul had seen before. "This pistol will fire five of the fifteen special rounds that it carries with a single pull of the trigger. There is no sight because laser sights are useless. They see it and they are too fast. The bullets are designed to fracture into millions of tiny bits of shrapnel. A burst will pulverize everything in a five-meter square. Remember please, to assume that the creature, no matter how badly damaged it appears, is only stunned. Do not get near the mouth, and bind the hands immediately with your plastic cuffs. Is this clear?"

They all knew the drill by heart. But they all listened as if they'd never heard it before in their lives. A professional never ignores a chance to get an edge. Maybe hearing it again just now would speed up reaction time by a hundredth of a second. Maybe that would save a life.

Miriam paid her ten francs and passed through the entrance to the catacombs. She'd spent an hour at the Galeries-Lafayette buying casual clothes and a wig, so the person who came into this place did not appear much like the one who had passed the Castle of the White Queen yesterday evening. All that remained of her ordeal were angry red areas on various parts of her body. Her right hip was still somewhat stiff, as well. But this gum-chewing teenager with black, close-cut hair bore almost no resemblance to the pallid, sunken horror of twelve hours ago. She was soft, her pale eyes sparkling with the eager innocence of eighteen or twenty sheltered years. Any man would want to protect her, even to cherish her. The little gold cross around her neck suggested religiosity. A man, managing somehow to penetrate the mysteries of this sweet child, would not be surprised to hear her murmur, "But I'm a virgin."

Moving as swiftly and carefully as a cat, she descended the spiral stair that led into the crypt. The touristic map she had gotten with her ticket covered only the ossuary itself, but she knew the ancient signs that would indicate the route from the public area to the lairs and, above all, to the Keep where would be stored the Book of Names and whatever other things the French Keepers owned collectively.

Her intention was to warn the other Keepers if she could, but without fail to take their Book of Names with her. She could not risk leaving it here, no matter how they felt about that. If they resisted, she would fight.

There were two sightseers at the foot of the stairs. She shifted her body language, becoming a casual girl, a little nervous. The tourists were German, plump and smelling of their recent lunch of ham. The man had ugly, narrow veins. She loved the woman's carotid. A charming nibble, she would be.

She sniffed the faint wind coming out of the corridor. None of the lovely, infinitely subtle scents of other Keepers. Each Keeper had his own particular scent, mixed of skin and the dust of ages. Miriam longed to smell the skin of a robust male Keeper just after he had fed, when he was warm and moist, his muscles like flowing iron, his odor overlaid by the creamy, intricate scent of fresh human blood.

The rankness of the couple was strong, mixed with the

rather sandy, musty odor of the bones. Again, she inhaled, flaring her nostrils. Yes, there were other human beings within, also, all stinking of their foods and perfumes and the orifices they had secretly neglected. She smelled the damp biscuit odor of little boys, the soft cheese fragrance of girl children, and a bit of an older woman's perfume. A class of mixed sex between the ages of six and ten was a short distance ahead, with their female teacher, who was thirty, no younger, and healthy. Miriam tested the air for new odors, filtering out those she had already identified. Some sort of exotic foodstuff came to her, spices of the East mixed with the odors of skin and spent cigarettes—a couple from Asia.

She entered the corridor. Her glance at the map had left her with a memory of precisely the number of steps she would have to go in every passage in the ossuary. In childhood, every Keeper was trained to use measured gaits, so she knew exactly how many inches she traversed with every step she took, no matter how fast her stride.

The entrance to the ossuary was marked by a group of thick, square columns painted white with black borders. She passed them, entering the earliest of the crypts. The most recent bones, quite naturally, were deepest. By human terms, they were ancient, but she remembered Paris perfectly clearly when there had been no catacomb full of bones and gawking tourists. In those days, the Keepers had the entire system of mines to themselves. One could ascend by an unknown stair into the street, take a victim down, and enjoy it at leisure, then have a nice sleep in the safety of the depths. The Paris Keepers had a pleasant life then.

She moved forward cautiously, seeking a certain spot that led from the ossuary into the deep shafts. There were other entrances, but this one was what you took if you knew what

you were doing. Anyone coming down another tunnel would
be assumed to be human.

The entrance was signaled, she knew, by a great cross. It
would not be difficult to find. But to know its true meaning—
that would be very difficult indeed . . . if you weren't a Keeper.
When she was certain that she was alone, she sprinted along
the galleries. Here was Madame du Pompadour—that hideous old crank who reeked of sour milk and had somehow
captured the heart of one of the later Louises, a prancing
unwise fellow who blew farts and stank horribly himself from
a fungal infection of the skin. Madame de Pompadour,
indeed. Her real name was Jeanne Poisson—Jenny Fish. Well,
so much for that marble tomb of hers. This was far more
appropriate. Philippe Vendôme had made fervid, ratlike love
to her, hadn't he? Miriam recalled watching some sort of
entertainment like that.

She'd been down here in the early eighteenth century
with—which one—was it Lollie? Yes, poor Lollia, she'd been
on her last legs then, frantically trying on powdered wigs and
loading her face with leaded creams. No use, any of it.

Now another turn—and there was the great cross. But
would the entrance still be behind it? Had the French found
it and walled it up, also? She looked at the cross, refocusing
her vision so that the glyphs that were invisible to the human
eye stood out clearly. There was a word to utter in Prime,
according to the instructions, that would open the wall. It
would also alert the Keepers inside that she was there. She
was instructed, as well, to append her name. She drew a deep
breath, expanded her lungs, and released the call. It vibrated
against the stone, its echo fluttering off down the corridors.
Now, the instructions told her, press thrice the upper corner
of the left tine of the cross.

The hidden door swung inward. Beyond was absolute dark. From within there came the odor of many lairs.

"*Halte!*" Everybody froze. "Do not move," Colonel Bocage said. "Listen."

It came again, a sound so deep that it was more a sensation than a noise.

"Could it be the Métro?" Becky asked. "Are we under a tunnel?"

Des Roches laid his arm around her neck, drew her close, uttered a breathy, almost-silent whisper. "That was a vampire."

The French were in some ways far advanced in their knowledge. Becky and Charlie and Paul had been down many a dark tunnel, but they had never had to face anything this elaborate.

The place stank of wet stone and the musk of bats. The group had stopped its march and was clustering together in a low gallery. Becky shone her light on a stone where graffiti had been carved. "*Merci à Dieu, m—*" and there it stopped, as if the carver had run out of strength or light or time. The letters were formed in an old script, perhaps from the last century or the one before.

"Listen—again," Charlie said.

It was eerie, that sound—so deep that you wouldn't notice it unless you were trained to. Paul had heard it echoing off the walls of the night in Beijing, in Osaka, in Bangkok. As a boy, he had heard it mixing with the sullen hoot of the owl and the barking of the fox.

After some moments, there was no sound but their breathing and the busy scuttle of rats. The roar of the great city above them was a bare whisper. Water dripped, echoing as if somewhere deeper there might be a hidden pool or even a small lake.

"Lights out," Paul said. "We go to light-amplification goggles." Their equipment packs rattled as they put the night-vision goggles on.

You could see perhaps fifty feet. Beyond that was the haze of a darkness so deep not even the goggles could gather enough light to be of use.

"Do you wish to go to infrared," Bocage asked his men, his voice, in its softness, sounding curiously as if he'd meant to utter words of love.

"Let's do it," Raynard said. He and Des Roches clicked on the infrared floods.

A hand grabbed Paul's shoulder, the fingers digging in. Becky was staring down the long, sloping corridor.

There had been something there, most certainly. "Vampire," Bocage murmured.

Paul had seen what might have passed for a tall, elegant man, tall and very quick of step. The moment the infrared flood had turned on, it had gone.

The Keepers were calling to one another that human beings had penetrated the barrier. Their voices were calm, which made her throat turn sour and her mind race—*don't you understand, don't you realize even yet?*

She had the map of the ossuary, but there was no map of the labyrinth beyond. She had to go by scent and hearing and what little sight was available.

She had not moved ten steps before the darkness completely enclosed her. Now she had to walk blind, on faith only, trusting in her nose and ears for direction.

Behind her, she could hear the breathing of tourists in the

ossuary and their occasional murmured conversations. There was something about the place that kept them quiet, as if the spirits of the dead demanded it.

Along a low side tunnel that angled sharply down came a faint reddish-purple glow. For a moment she did not know what it was. But then she saw a Keeper, dressed all in black, standing not fifty feet away from her. His back was to her. He was watching the glow, which was bouncing, waxing and waning, as it slid along a far tunnel.

When his odor touched her nostrils—powerful, richly masculine—a thrill trembled through her. He stood tall. His absolute stillness made him seem so very noble.

She murmured low, in Prime, "I, Miriam out of Lamia, greet you." His back did not move. Then, very suddenly, he turned round.

He faced her now, the glow waxing and waning behind him. "I, Uriel from Enoch, now called Henri, greet you." He inclined his head.

She bowed deep at the waist, as was the formality for a Keeper entering from outside a given Keep. He came close to her and laid his long fingers under her chin and raised her.

"I come to present myself before the conclave," she added, still speaking in the measured, formal cadences of Prime.

He switched to French. "You want a kid, Miriam? Or a husband?"

"Both," she replied.

He smiled, then. "You still live in that house, I presume, with your wonderful little pets."

He did not sound too disapproving. Dared she hope? "Yes," she said carefully. She lowered her eyes to him, as manners required.

"How can you bear the smell?" His tone slapped her. He was as contemptuous of her as the rest.

She tried not to reveal her disappointment. But she raised her eyes. Damned if she would show respect to a man who had contempt for her. "What is that glow," she asked. It was getting distinctly brighter, so much so that she could now see the walls of this tunnel clearly, and even Henri's narrow, solemn face.

"It's trivial."

She dropped the manners and looked directly at him. Martin Soule had been in such terrible condition that he had presented no appeal. Henri, by contrast, was not hideous. He was dirty and poorly dressed, but his body was gorgeous. She could sense his strength, and the thought of being held in his arms was not without appeal.

He seemed indifferent to the light. "It's getting brighter."

He was looking at her with the attention a jeweler might pay a gem. "It's true, then," he said.

"What is true?"

"Your beauty is the greatest in the world." He reached toward her, a tentative, caressing touch. As his fingers shivered along the edge of her lips, she tasted of their flat salt. Desire flamed in her. She imagined herself lying beneath him, absolutely, wonderfully helpless as he came roaring into her like an inflamed lion. She would receive him, an open flower, an open wound. She would be a slave to him then, hold his cup and kneel before him. She would let herself be possessed, and in turn she would possess him.

The glow flared, and now she heard a steady tread of—she listened—twelve feet. They sounded to her like human feet. "That light—it's the humans, isn't it?"

"It's nothing. Ignore it."

"Is it human?"

He gazed at her. "You are a forward creature, just as they say."

"Humans are dangerous."

"Don't be absurd."

"You knew Martin Soule, of course."

He nodded. "He went to live in that house your mother so foolishly built."

"He died there."

"Did he?" His voice took on a note of question. "Why would he elect to do that?"

"They burned him! As they intend to burn us all!"

"I remember your mother's misfortune. But that should not—"

The lights appeared like ghostly eyes, six of them, all glaring straight down this tunnel. Henri was trapped in the purple glow. He turned to face it, smiling slightly. "Stop," he said in flawless modern French, "you have no business here."

Paul's breath whooshed out of him when he saw it. He'd never laid eyes on one like this, so large, so strong looking. In Asia, they'd been smaller, and they'd hidden at the back of their lairs.

"There are two," Bocage said laconically.

Then he saw, behind the towering male in its fusty suit from fifty years ago, a female. It drew back into the shadows, but it also had a human appearance . . . just like the traveler. Had he seen blond hair? He couldn't be sure. The creature had moved with the speed and grace of a panther.

"*Mon Dieu*," Des Roches said.

"You saw that female?"

"The face—it was . . . so strange."

Paul had not seen the face. But he didn't care about that now. It wasn't the traveler, the traveler was dead. He raised his gun and fired, and so did all the others.

The noise was shattering; a gust of wind blasted back into his face, as the narrow tunnel compressed the expanding air. The screaming thunder of it was accompanied by a dazzling flare of green light, and followed by hollow, zipping echoes as bullet fragments tore along the walls.

Silence. A distant howl, growing louder. Charlie tore off his night-vision equipment and went for his flashlight. He flicked the switch. The beam shone like a white laser into the murk of dust that now filled the tunnel.

"*Non!*" Bocage screamed.

There was a flicker in the air, no more. Out of the dust had come a knife, thrown with the vampire's bizarre force, moving so fast that it was only a flash of light.

The beam of the flashlight wavered, then went crazy, then dropped to the floor. It rolled toward the vampires, and in a second nothing could be seen but a dim yellow glow in the murk of dust. This glow was pointing straight at them, away from the vampires. So they were visible, but they could not see.

Charlie began to make a sound, one that was almost comically like the whistle of a toy train. It changed to gurgling and splashing and the clatter of a body in seizure. He fell back, his head striking the ground with a crack like a breaking egg.

Des Roches went down beside him. Becky, stifling a scream, pushed close. Her hands touched the knife as if it was blazing hot. She made little, choked sounds in her throat, awful sounds. Her fingers fluttered around the handle. The sounds had a sense of question in them, but it was a question that nobody could answer. There was no answer.

How do you extract a knife that is embedded up to its hilt in a man's face?

There was another blast, this one from Raynard's gun. Then Bocage fired twice more. Paul probably should have been terrified, but he felt the same calm, clear sense of inner control that always came to him at moments like this. His heart was sinking because of Charlie's death. But he did not stop fighting, not for an instant, no matter his breaking heart. He watched that dust, looking for shadowy movement.

Another knife appeared, headed straight for Becky. He saw it gliding as gently as a leaf on the sea, gliding toward her neck. He felt her hair under his hand, and then he pressed with lightning speed and she slammed flat, and the knife went clanging and clattering up the tunnel.

From off in the yellow gloom he heard a faint sound, an unmistakable sound: it could only have been a gasp of surprise.

Wild emotions sped through Miriam—horror to see a Keeper blown to pieces, fear that the next blast would kill her, and then, above all, amazement at what she had seen that man do, and amazement at how she felt about him.

That man—only a human—had moved as fast as a Keeper. She knew the human genome intimately. There was nothing in their makeup that could enable them to do this. Their physical limitations were bred into them. But not into this one, no indeed.

Then there was the way he affected her when he pulled off his ridiculous goggles and she saw his chiseled, complex face. Her body responded to this human as if he were a Keeper. This was not the attraction she felt normally to human prettiness, but powerful, shivering, blood-pounding desire. She wanted him not under her but over her; she sweated and lusted for him; she wanted him to possess her and fill her with a startling, frenetic hardness. Her body was begging her; it was pleading as if he were the strongest, finest male Keeper in the weave of the world.

She backed away, as horrified at these feelings as she was at the power of the weapons that were being raised against her.

She dashed to the end of the corridor, took a turning, another, then flattened herself against the wall. She listened—the ever-present dripping, the scuttle of rats, the deep fluttering of Keeper voices as they called back and forth, in mixtures of French and Prime, inquiring of one another: "What was it?" "Is there reason for concern?"

There were a lot of them here. They had indeed been assembling for their conclave. She knew, after seeing that man, that there would be no conclave. He was going to go through this labyrinth like the red shadow of death, like the hand of an angry god. None would survive him, not with his exploding bullets and his team and his eerie personal speed.

Off behind her, another blast of fire echoed, followed by the awful thudding of another Keeper body being ripped to pieces.

They were going to lose their battle. Therefore, she had to do what was necessary to protect the rest of the Keepers. She had to go to the heart of this Keep and secure their Book of Names. To find it, she must be careful to make certain that every step she took was downward. Turning here, there, she went farther and deeper. Soon the dripping was general, water was running in rivulets, and she was concerned that the center of the Keep might be awash.

Every few minutes, there would be an awful roar behind her, followed by a series of weaker explosions. The humans— led by that eerie, beautiful monster—were clearing out the Keepers, moving with careful method. For their part, the Keepers, who had no call of alarm and no real way to react to an assault like this, were responding piecemeal, although with growing anger and ferocity. One after another, they would attack the human group. Then would come the roaring of the guns, and the distant, liquid thuds of bodies being torn apart.

She was moving fast, head down, when she suddenly sensed a change around her. She was in a much larger space, and not only that, she could see a little.

This was not a manmade tunnel, but something very much more ancient. The precise lines of its walls, the low, graceful arch of its ceiling, suggested that a far more careful hand than human had been at work here. Stalagmites rose from the ground. It looked like a forest on an alien world.

"I am Miriam out of Lamia, come seeking entry to your conclave."

At first, there was silence. Then the light wavered and, with the softest of sounds, a shadow emerged. "I am Julia out of Helene who was Nef-ta-tu."

She had not seen Julia since the days of splendor, when their kind had ruled Egypt, walking as princes among their human herds.

Julia had been as sweet then as a roe, as tender as an apple from the bough. What came to Miriam was a dark creature, so crusted with eons of dirt that only her eyes seemed alive.

Julia had the Book of Names with her, tucked under her arm as casually as some novel. "There is a human band in these caves," she said, her voice mild.

"They are killing us."

She gave Miriam a careful look. "How is that?"

"With guns."

"We are faster than their hands. We can step out of the way before they pull the trigger. I've done it myself now and again."

"These guns leave you no place to go. They spread a mass of tiny bullets. Keepers up there are being torn apart. The humans are coming for that book." She smiled. "Let me take it."

"I will not. You're a pervert, Miriam. You're unclean."

"If they get your book, our whole world will be in danger."

"They will not get our book."

"They will be here in minutes. And they will get it."

"There have been three hundred conclaves in this place. My grandfather built it when the humans were covered with hair."

"May those days live in memory."

"They were sour. The new ones now are much sweeter."

Horribly close, there came the roar of gunfire. It was so close that the flash was faintly visible.

"We have to get out. We cannot waste another minute."

"What is a minute or a hundred years? You have fallen from your nobility, Miriam. Everybody says it. I remember you in linen, how tall you were, your limbs like gold."

"That memory is three thousand years old, Julia! This is now, and the humans are not armed with bronze daggers. Don't you understand that they're tearing the Keepers apart with their guns?"

"They will become lost. The labyrinth is more cunning than their minds can understand."

"That was true a hundred years ago. But now they have

sonar and digital maps and handheld locators. And they're trained to kill us. They have killed all of Asia, and they have their Book of Names."

"Asia is far away."

"It's an airplane flight! I was in Bangkok a few days ago."

"You have the restless soul of a human, always traipsing about."

Miriam heard human voices. They would be here in moments. "Do you not think it strange that you alone are here at the appointed time? Where are the others? Can you explain it?"

"Don't cross-question me. All will unfold in its course."

"Then why hasn't it? What's wrong?"

"What has changed to prevent the conclave? Nothing."

"Everything has changed."

"A few humans cannot change the course of the world."

Miriam saw the humans creeping among the shadows ahead, four of them.

"It's lit," the tall, powerful one said. He walked into the gray glow from the ancient batteries. Humans had found some of the Keepers' batteries in the Valley of the Euphrates some years ago. They were still trying to understand how the ancients could have had electricity.

"Lookit—a power line!"

Discreetly, Miriam drew Julia into a pool of shadow. The humans were now at the far end of the chamber, perhaps a hundred yards away.

"How do you work the lights?" she whispered to Julia.

"They're always on during conclave. That's the rule."

"Julia, there is no conclave. We're all being killed. Turn out the lights."

Julia broke away from her, strode out into the center of the chamber. For a moment, the humans froze. They drew closer together.

"Julia!"

"Miriam, they're only—"

There came clicking noises, ominous, echoing. Only seconds remained. "Julia, run!"

Julia turned to her. Her smile said that she found her friend of old times pitiful.

The tall human raised his weapon, followed by the others. Miriam watched his face, the careful sculpture of it, the hard fury of the eyes.

The guns blasted—and Miriam herself felt a hot slash of pain along her exposed hip. Just a few shots had filled the entire space with bullets—all this huge area!

Then she saw Julia, who still stood, who still held the all-important book. Julia, pouring blood, placed the book beside her on the ground. She sat then, a dark and bloody Venus beside a still-ringing stalagmite. Again the guns rang out, and this time her head went bouncing off her neck. On its face Miriam saw an expression of mild curiosity, nothing more than that.

"There's another one," a voice said. "Over there—that shadow behind the stalagmite. That's a vampire."

Miriam must not waste another instant. But the book—it was lying beside the torn ruins of Julia. It was only a few cubits away, but right in their line of fire.

It was deep brown, its cover an ancient, profoundly aged human skin. On its cover was the Keeper's ancient symbol of balanced nature and balanced rule, known to humans as the ankh. The humans looked toward it, too.

She had to reach it, she had to get it. But first, she must

turn off these damn lights. The copper wires were set on insulators a few feet above her head. She knew that these batteries were very, very different from what the humans had, that they drew their energy from the earth itself, and they were powerful.

To kill the lights, she had to stand up in full view, reach overhead, and yank a wire loose. The electricity would jolt her. If she wasn't fast enough, or could not let go of the power line, she would be burned inside—an injury that would take weeks to mend. In moments they would be upon her, though, and she would end up in their sights.

She was well up behind one of the stalagmites, but they nevertheless fired, all together, the roar of their guns causing the chamber to resound like the interior of a bell. She felt no injury.

The leader said, "Spread out," in a resonant, icy voice.

They came closer to her, led by their monster. His face was so determined, so truly terrible in the hate that was written across it, that she was compelled to think that his emotions were almost full-circle. This human loathed the Keepers so much that he nearly loved them. She would not forget this.

"We need to angle off that wall," he said, "it's pressed itself against the back of the stalagmite."

He spoke with detachment. Well, she also was professional. She reached up to the humming wire. Her fingers paused, hesitating. But this was no act of ritual possession. She curled them, closing them on the wire.

There was a buzzing sound and a choked, sizzling cry, and the lights went out. "Shit," Bocage said.

Paul went down on his hands and knees. "The book," he whispered.

"Forget the damn book; get some light in here," Becky hissed.

"Get the goggles—" Des Roches said.

There was no time, and Paul knew it. "Cover me," he said as he moved off toward the book.

"How?" Bocage asked.

He crawled two, three feet, then five, then ten. He could hear them putting on their goggles. They mustn't use the infrared floods. Vampires could see into the infrared.

Then he felt it. He felt the book's smooth surface and grasped it. But then he knew that other hands also had it, another hand was grasping it, too.

She was there, face-to-face with him, but he could see nothing. He could smell her, though—not the stink of the vampire but a scent unlike any he had ever smelled before, rich and complicated and sexy as hell.

When she growled—as vampires did—he thought that it was the gentlest and yet most lethal sound he had ever heard. She was stronger, he knew that, but he didn't intend to let go of that book. "I know you can understand me," he said.

There was only breathing in reply, breathing like the soft and edgy flutter of a swarm of butterflies. He thought, *She's scared, too—a vampire that knows how to be afraid.*

She yanked the book right out of his hands. Instantly, he dove at her, slammed into her, felt the book clatter to the ground. Again she growled, this time with a mixture of surprise and raw fury that made him think that he would shortly die.

He tried to get his fingers around her neck, to choke her, to try to close off that crucial blood flow.

He sensed somebody coming up from behind. Then

Becky was with him, grabbing at the creature's arms, trying to throw it off balance.

The vampire's neck felt like steel. He couldn't manage to throttle the creature, and his hands were strong. He struggled, getting closer, seeing the face before him, a glowing moon in the darkness, smelling the sweat of a woman and—perfume. Yes, it was perfumed, this one. What in damn hell was going on here.

"Get a light! A light!"

In the split of an instant, the vampire was gone. Des Roches and Bocage appeared. As Paul looked across the empty cave floor, a wave of rage and frustration swept through him. He'd lost the damn book! This meant years more work, hundreds of lives.

Then Becky's hand came into his, her cool hand. A flashlight glowed, and he saw in that glow her shining, triumphant eyes. She gave him the book.

"Goddamn," he said, "good god damn."

She moved toward him, her lips parting, her eyes steady and strong.

There was no time—not here, not now. "We can get it," he said, breaking away.

"It's gone," Bocage said.

Paul could not accept that. He turned; he went a few steps into the deadly blackness.

"Paul! Paul, no!"

He went on.

TEN

The Traveler

As he ran along a low, narrow corridor, he flashed his light from time to time, making sure that he hadn't passed any side entrances and that he wasn't about to hit a wall. He did not think about the fact that he was a man alone penetrating into a lair that was crawling with the creatures. That female—he had never encountered anything like that. It had been clean and perfumed. It had felt soft and smooth, if immensely strong. He had not seen the face, but he knew that there had been beauty, perhaps great beauty. Its scent still lingered: Arpège and womanhood. Its touch had inflamed him even as it had made his flesh crawl. He wanted to bathe, to get its smell off him . . . and he wanted never to bathe again.

Was it the traveler, still alive after all?

He knew that the safety of the book was everything, but he also had to kill this vampire. He had never wanted to kill a vampire so much, not in all the years he'd been at it. This thing could walk the streets without a problem. The idea of vampires that could function in the human world was horrifying.

He came to a T—blank wall ahead, a passage to the right sloping up, another to the left sloping down.

He stopped, shone his flashlight first in one direction and then the other. Far away he heard Becky. "Paul! *Paul!*"

He heard something in her voice that was tender. But she was a professional killer, for God's sake. What man could romance a woman like that?

"*Paaaaul!*"

Her fear for him was heartrending. But he could not answer, dared not. They would have to do their best to follow. Waiting for them to catch up would cost at least two minutes, and there were no minutes available at all just now.

He listened ahead, closing his eyes and cupping his hands behind his ears. The rising passage was silent. But not the descending—down there he heard all sorts of noises—murmurs, scuffling sounds, the low thutter of vampire calls.

He hesitated only long enough to make certain that his gun had a fresh clip and there were still more in the rucksack that Raynard had given him. Three more, to be exact.

It was a lovely gun, the way it tore the things apart. His hand on its comforting butt, he stepped into the downward passage. The descent was steep. Soon, his flashlight was revealing carved inscriptions in Latin here and there on the walls. This tunnel must be very old indeed. The Arénes de Lutèce, where the Romans had held bearbaiting contests, could not be far overhead. Maybe they had quarried the stone for it here. But he did not think so. There was something too perfect about the way these walls were made. As old as it all appeared, every line was dead straight.

He was in a vampire place, something made by them in some uncountably ancient time. When this place was made, mankind must have been—well, maybe still living in caves.

What did it mean?

If they had been advanced enough to make this, they must have ruled the world then, in the deep long ago. The implications for human life were chilling. Anything could be true—they could even have bred us the same way that we breed cattle.

Fear kept rising, and he kept pushing it down. But what if he couldn't win? What if they had reserves of power that he had never imagined?

He tried to be philosophical. If he died here, he died here. At least he'd take some of them with him.

And then—was that somebody breathing?

He stopped, listened. No, it was nothing, just the wind in the halls, or far-off street noise. He started off again.

One of them appeared ahead of him, leaping, screaming, a blur of darkness and fury. He fired, then fired again and again, until it exploded along the corridor with a series of wet splats.

He flicked on his light. He'd expected to see a mass of carnage, a flowing river of blood. But there wasn't all that much blood. And then he saw a bit of fur, gray, and he realized that the light had played a trick on him. He'd shot at the looming shadow of a rat.

"Goddamnit!"

He went on, deeper still, closer to the murmuring, to the whispering movement.

Then he heard a totally unexpected sound. A voice. A child's voice. "Sir?" His heart started hammering—not only because the voice was there, but because it was behind him.

Dare he turn? Dare he?

"Sir?"

Boy or girl, he could not tell. It sounded about ten, perhaps a little older. His finger slipped around the trigger. He felt sick, he did not think he could do this. But he whirled round, dropping to the floor as he did, firing.

There was nobody.

They were tricking him. The rat had also been a trick, he realized. No rat would cast such a big shadow. Somehow, they'd done it. They were tricking him, in order to get him to use up his bullets. They were probably counting his shots.

He looked out into the darkness, could see nothing. He listened, could hear nothing. Only his own breathing disturbed the silence. He was a strong man; he had learned that over the years of his life. But he had also learned that all strength has its limits. He had seen the Khmer Rouge bury a man alive, and listened to that man go mad in his hole. Paul himself had wept with fear, thinking he would be next.

The vampires knew the human mind. They knew his mind. They knew his limits. And that was why, when he heard the creaking, coming slowly closer, it was so very hard not to use his light or fire his gun. It was so hard. But he could not, because he knew that no matter how sure he was, this, also, would be a wasted shot.

As quietly as was possible for a large man, he moved so that his back was pressed against the wall. To give his ears whatever tiny extra edge that might be gained, he closed his eyes. Even though there was no light, doing this would direct his brain a little more toward hearing than sight.

He stuffed the book into his pants and cupped his free hand behind his ear. He listened in one direction. There was the creaking, just over there. But it was not a living sound, and no closer. In the other direction, though, there was another sound, more complex, far harder to hear.

It was, he thought, a living sound. It was the sound of breath being drawn, in his opinion. He would have to lower his hand, grab his light and shine it, then instantly fire if something was there.

But what if it was that child? They had known that he would be unable to fire at a child. They had known that he would take the split of an instant to be certain. That would be *their* time.

It was a duel, and they had rigged it for him to lose the instant he disclosed his position. The only way to win would be to fire into the dark and risk a child . . . theirs, but still a child.

The breathing was close now. He would have to act and instantly. He did not go for his light. Instead, he reached out. He caught a sleeve. It was yanked away but he was fast; he'd always been damned fast. He found himself grasping a large, powerful, cold hand. The fingers closed around his wrist, closed and began to tighten.

There came laughter, soft and entirely relaxed. Foolishly so, he thought. He fired into the sound. In the flash, he saw a male face, powerful, dark, with a long, sharp nose and deep gleaming eyes.

There was a cry, deep, abruptly cut off.

Then he was deaf, as you always were deaf after that blast. When he could hear again, there was a high noise, the most terrible of noises, shaking the walls, echoing as it pealed again and again through the limestone chambers, the screaming of a woman in molten agony.

Now he used his light. It appeared, a female vampire, with beaded hair and a long dress on, dark blue silk, white collar, and the mouth fully open, a broad O filled with teeth. They had awful mouths, filthy and stinking of the blood in their guts, mouths that were made for sucking. They looked okay—a little thin-lipped was all—until they opened those wet, stinking maws of theirs. If you kissed a vampire, he thought, it might suck your insides right out of you.

The agony of grief was great for them, greater even than for a human being, as he had seen in Asia. She came maddened by it, her arms straight out ahead of her, her fingers long, lethal claws. He knew that she wanted to tear him to pieces. He knew that she wanted to feel his gristle break.

He pulled the trigger. In the flash, he saw her dress billow as if lifted by a funhouse blast. Her face folded in on itself, and her cry joined the cry of the gun and was gone.

Her body hit the wall behind her with a slapping thud, and she slid down a slide of her own thick, black blood.

They lay side by side, and he was amazed at what he saw. The male wore slacks and a black sweater, and a leather jacket so supple that Paul hardly dared touch it. The female beside him was equally passable.

These European vampires were not like the Asians, things that moved only in the shadows. These things could go anywhere they pleased, any time they pleased. But how modern were they? Was there anything to prevent them from getting on the phone, calling their friends in the States?

Of course there wasn't. Paul had to admit to himself that he'd been lucky in Asia. But that level of surprise was over now. The only thing he had on his side was speed.

Every single creature in this hole had to be killed, and it had to be done right now, today. Otherwise, there were going to be phone calls, God knew, maybe even e-mails, to vampires in America, in Africa—wherever they were as modern and technologically capable as he had to assume these creatures were.

Either he and his cohorts cleared the place out immediately or they lost any and all chance of surprising others.

A long shape like a gigantic spider came striding toward him from along the corridor, its shadow briefly visible in his light. He turned it out.

He listened to the steps, one, two, coming up the tunnel. He could hear its breathing now, slow, almost soulful, like a man in love. Closer it came, until it seemed as if it were directly before him. But tunnels deceive, and he knew that there was more time yet to wait. It seemed to slide along, as if it wore silken shoes or moved like a snake.

He held his gun straight out. He waited.

The footsteps stopped. The breathing became soft and low. Where was it? He was uncertain.

He turned on the light, and there were eyes glaring at him from three inches away. The face was sallow, gray, not a face from the world of the sun. He fired into the dark crystal hate in those eyes. The body took the whole force of the bullets and went sailing backward fifty feet, bouncing against the walls as it broke up. A leg went tumbling on down the steep incline into the dark.

The head was not severed. The eyes revealed shock, not death. He had to fire again, and he hated it, to waste a shot, but then there would be nothing further to worry about from this vampire.

He aimed, squeezed the trigger, felt the familiar satisfaction that came when they blew apart.

He went on down the passage. He was spattered with vampire blood, and he could smell its rankness. He could feel it in his shoes, slick between his toes. The blood could invade your body. If you had a cut, it could make you damned sick. He'd seen it, they all had—the fevers, the monstrous, weird hungers, the slow recovery.

As he went deeper, he felt his adult personality slipping

into its own past. The love of wine, the love of music, the long days spent in elegant places—all that was going. There remained only a hurt, furious little boy looking for the killer of his father.

On he went, deeper into the secret heart of the ancient nest, deeper still. He was below the meeting hall now, down where no human being would or could ever go, down in narrow corridors painted with glyphs, walls and ceilings and floors forged by the perfect hand of the vampire.

This was the great secret of the world, that places like this existed hidden and embedded in the planet, where terrible minds had orchestrated with terrible cunning the bloody history of mankind.

He knew, suddenly, that he was in a larger space. He knew, also, that there was a new smell here. When he turned on his light, and he would have to do that, he feared that he would find himself face to face with hundreds of them.

He put his thumb on the switch. He pressed.

At first, he did not understand what had appeared in the beam. The place was so large that his light faded before the room ended. There were long brown lines of round objects arrayed in two rows facing a narrow aisle, and it took him a long moment to understand that they were skulls tightly encased in their own skin. Some had hair, and it hung in tufts like something left on totems.

He thought that there might be a million skeletons here. No rat came for them, no maggot, for they were too dry even to attract vermin—only little running things, nameless beetles of some kind, that were slowly turning them to dust.

As he walked slowly along shining his light, he became aware that this place was easily half a mile long. Face after face stared out at him, each with its goggled eyesockets and bucked teeth. They were stacked twenty high.

Here was where lay the *real* dead of Paris, the anonymous, the disappeared, the forgotten. Ironic that this other, more terrible ossuary would lie deep beneath the Denfert-Rochereau, almost as if its human builders had known by some kind of race memory, or the whispered intelligence of the dead, that somewhere beneath their feet, there lay an even greater grave.

How many of these people had left weeping lovers behind, people who never knew whether to mourn them for dying or despise them for running away?

Such an anger filled Paul now that he trod steadily, uncaring of his own life, forgetful even of the vital importance of the book he had with him, marching like a soldier bent only on victory, going step by step toward his next kill.

In all this time, there had not been one more turning, not one place to hide. So all the vampires in this place must be ahead of him.

He had two shots left in his clip. He pulled it out, reached back and dropped it into the rucksack, grabbing a fresh one and jamming it in. If it came down to it, he would use the two shots left in that clip to blast the damn book to bits and then kill himself. He might not get it out of here, but they damned well wouldn't get it back, either.

The idea of being sucked dry like these poor people made a taste rise in his throat so vile that he had to choke back his own vomit. He would never, ever die like that, with the lips of a vampire pressed against his neck.

He had to get out of here. The air was sickening. The place was claustrophobic. The bodies were twisted in a hundred postures of struggle and suffering, the faces still radiating horror, agony, and surprise.

Eventually, he saw a door ahead. He hurried to it, looked for a knob. There was a silver ring. When he pulled it, the door slid smoothly back on perfect hinges.

There had never been any place like this in Asia. At least, they had never uncovered such a place. But they had been on a killing spree, hadn't they, compared to the subtle, expert French? He was good at dealing death, not at the cat-and-mouse game that Bocage was playing with these very much more dangerous vampires of his.

His light played on the walls—and he saw a human face staring at him. He gasped, momentarily disoriented by the eyes that looked back at him . . . from the incredibly distant past. No human being had ever before looked upon what this must be, a vividly lifelike portrait of a Neanderthal, appearing as if it had been painted yesterday.

The picture was painted on what looked like a slab of highly polished stone, maybe using some sort of wax process. But when he looked closer, he realized that this was not a painting at all but an incredibly fine mosaic. It was constructed of bits and slivers of stone so tiny that to his wondering fingers the surface appeared absolutely smooth.

What a very fine hand had made this, and so long, long ago. Beside it there was another mosaic, this one of something he thought must be some sort of genetic map—incredibly intricate, incredibly detailed.

Was he was looking at a Neanderthal with its genetic map beside it? If so, then what was this room? What had been done here? All around the walls were more such images, some of even more ancient creatures, in which the shadow of man was dominated by the staring savagery of the ape. If you looked from first to last, there was a logical succession from a small ape with frightened eyes all the way to modern people.

There were at least fifty of the pictures. They went on until they ended with a woman so beautiful that she seemed to have been born of the angels.

This looked like some sort of record of the evolution of man ... or our creation. Quite frankly, it looked like a record of creation, the way one form followed another in close succession, each with its genetic plan beside it. For years, humankind had been sifting the dirt of Africa and searching the caves of France for its past. But we had never been able to find ourselves, had we? Never quite.

He went to the last figure. Even her green eyes were rendered to the tiniest nuance. Her face was so alive that she might as well have talked to him. She was a girl, maybe twenty, with dusty blond hair and an expression on her face of a sort of delight ... as if she were beholding everything new. Maybe, he thought, he should call her Eve.

The vampires must be very much older than he had imagined. If this place was what it looked like, then they were also very much more important to us. In which case, we had not evolved through the accidents and ideas of God, but rather had been maneuvered out of the apes by another and terrible hand.

He was not a man who often felt like crying. He'd done a lifetime's worth of crying when he'd lost his dad. But tears came now, rolling down his hard, silent face.

Why had they done it? Why not leave us as we must have been—helpless, two-legged cattle? One day, the secrets of the vampires would all be known. Only then, he suspected, would mankind truly come to understand itself.

He had the chilling thought that maybe they were our creators. He'd known that they lived a long time, but this was totally unexpected.

He went on, deeper into this cave of secrets. Now the chambers he found were rough, and here also the hidden past disclosed a story. This was human work, full of gouge marks. In some incredibly distant time, human beings had dug to this very room, to the center of the secret. Had they died here, in some forgotten effort to throw off our slavery?

There were no records of other vampire hunters in history. He and his team had read volumes of old histories, attempting to see if organizations like the Knights Templar or the Egyptian priesthoods might have known something. But they didn't.

He moved through the rubble of the human tunnel—and, very suddenly, he found a lot of vampires. They were moving quickly, just disappearing around a corner ahead of him when he saw them.

They were running. He'd never seen that before. But there were a lot of things about the Paris vampires that were new to him. He sped up, jumped into the corridor they had gone down and fired. He ran, fired again, waited. Scuffling ahead. He fired. Sounds—gabbling, gasping noises. And then a vampire loomed out of the dust. Its chest was open like a cabinet. It came for him, but buckled, its lips working, its mouth sucking air. Another was behind it, and another. He fired. He fired again.

There was one bullet in the clip. He had to reload. He backed up—and tripped, falling onto the one he had just killed. He fell hard, and heard the clips clatter off behind him. As he was scrambling up, a hand grabbed his flashlight . . . and crushed it. The dying vampire's last act had left him completely helpless.

He scrambled to his feet, then kicked into the dark, kicked at the softness of the creature's wrecked body. He heard hissing and bubbling. The damn thing wasn't dead, despite its wounds. He backed away, lest it regain its strength and attack him. Then he squatted, sweeping the floor for his lost clips, finding nothing. And then he heard before him:

"Come here, child."

Was there another of their kids here? He backed up again, trying to get a wall behind him, to gain some kind of defensive advantage.

"Your end has come, child."

He would have turned his last bullet on himself, but that would leave the book. He'd have to destroy it and just suffer the damn sucking death he loathed.

The one that had spoken was coming closer; he could hear it. Should he shoot it? Was it the monster, the queen? Was this her lair? No, he thought not. That voice had been low and musical, but male, very definitely.

He'd lost his gamble, then. He held the book before him and pressed the barrel of the gun up against it.

But before he could shoot, light burst out around him. He saw a crowd of vampires, all watching him with their grave, strangely empty eyes. He saw them in jeans, in tattered clothes from olden times, in dresses and the shorts of tourists. Their faces, though, were filled with hate, and they were not human faces. Down here, they didn't need to bother with makeup and disguise. All the lips were narrow; all the eyes were deep; all the expressions were the same: calm, intractable hate.

Becky was suddenly beside him, her gun flaring. He fired, too, his last bullet.

As he reached around for another clip, a flaming pain shot through his left side. The arm that held the book went limp, and the book thudded to the floor. He saw why—the handle of a knife was protruding from his shoulder.

From the crowd of vampires there came shots. These had some guns—another surprise for Paul. He heard a grunt behind him, saw Des Roches crumple. He and Bocage had come up behind Becky.

The guns fired again, from both sides. Becky moved to protect him with her own body. "Fall back," she snapped as she shot again and again.

Then there was silence. She said, in a quavering, incredibly tender voice, "You're hurt."

That was a lover's tone, and it touched his heart unexpectedly deeply. "I'll be okay."

Her finger quivered along the protruding handle of the knife. "Oh, Paul, oh, God." She kissed his cheek, and his heart seemed to turn over within him. Thrumming through his pain, he felt a kind of contentment. He could see her rich eyes in the dark, full of tender concern. And he had to admit, it felt damn, damn good.

The beam of Bocage's flashlight played across the room. In the smoke and the haze of blood, there were easily a dozen dead or damaged vampires, all heaped against the far wall. "It's good," Bocage muttered. Then he went down to his man. Des Roches was pale, his face frozen. He was in agony and trying hard to suppress it. Paul was in exactly the same situation.

The question wasn't whether they could go out and regroup, then do what needed to be done, which was to get back down here to spray these creatures with acid. The question was whether anybody was going to live long enough to get out in the first place.

"Bocage, are we all hurt?"

He shrugged. "I'll live." His right leg was sheeted with blood.

"Becky?"

"I'm good."

"We must get out," Bocage said. "Des Roches is going into shock."

Becky was playing her light across the broken mass of vampires. "Eight," she said. "That's a total of seventeen in this action."

"We killed a conclave," Paul said. "Half of Europe, maybe."

"The Germans are doing the same in Berlin," Bocage said.

"The Germans! Why don't we Americans get told anything anymore?" Paul asked.

"You have Echelon," Bocage replied. "It's supposed to put the rest of us in a fishbowl."

"Apparently it doesn't."

Bocage smiled a careful smile. "No, it doesn't."

Paul was beginning to feel the shuddering cold that came with shock. He took deep breaths, trying to stave it off.

Becky went over to the vampires. "Bocage," she said, "we need to blow their heads off. In case we can't come back and sterilize."

They rounded up his lost clips, and Bocage and Becky went among them, blasting first one and then the next. Paul wondered what it would be like with a woman who could do that.

The knife was beginning to hurt a great deal. A wound that penetrated a bone into its marrow, which this one certainly did, was exceptionally painful. On his side he had the fact that he was an exceptionally fast healer. But that came later. Now, there was only the pain and danger of the wound.

"We've gotta get moving," he said.

The little band of them ascended slowly, everybody trying to keep their suffering from everybody else.

Despite the waves of searing pain that swept his whole

body every time he took a step, Paul felt like laughing. The damn queen of the vampires, or the traveler, or whatever she was—was somewhere in that pile of broken bodies. No more perfumed innocence walking the streets.

Between this and what the Germans were doing, Europe was likely to be free of the pest. And the book under his arm would soon free the Americas—if they acted fast enough.

He coughed long and hard, experiencing such great agony as he did so that Becky had to hold him up. "There's blood aspirating into the lung," he said as she helped him to the car.

All the way to the hospital, she held him tight to her, so that the bumps would cause him as little pain as possible. It was still a lot. But he didn't mind all that much. This was not a bad place to be, not at all.

ELEVEN

Queen of the Night

I n the hours since she had first looked into the haunted
eyes of Miriam Blaylock, Sarah Roberts had become
more and more afraid. Now she held Miriam's hand; Miriam
lay against her friend's shoulder.

Sarah had never seen her like this and so far had not been
able to find out what was wrong.

Incredibly, they were using the Concorde, a plane Miriam
had vowed she'd never fly again. Groaning and thudding
came from under the floor where the four engines lay
embedded in the wings close to the fuselage. For the first ten
minutes of the flight, the cabin smelled of jet fuel. They'd
taken this plane for years, believing it to be safe. Then had
come the crash and a morbidly careful period of evaluation
on Miriam's part. She'd gone over every detail a thousand
times, imagined herself in the cabin of a plane she took
often, looking out the window at the fire, hearing the awful
roaring, feeling the vibration and then the sickening moment
of free fall.

For the human beings in it, death would have been
instantaneous. Miriam would have lost consciousness only
slowly, as she was inch by inch consumed by the flames.

She'd had Sarah get every document there was about the

refit. Despite all that had been done, she was still in a fright over flying on it. But she had insisted, absolutely.

Sarah thought perhaps the other Keepers had assaulted her. If so, it would be an anecdote for the book she'd been secretly writing about the Keepers for these twenty years of her captivity.

Sarah could tell that Miriam was awake. She was always awake unless she'd fed or done opium in extraordinary quantities. Miriam's hand was soft and cool. Sarah lifted it to her lips, enjoying the heft of it, the taste of the skin, the softness against her lips. She inhaled the sweet smell of her friend's skin. Miriam sighed and laid her lips upon Sarah's neck, sucking until it almost hurt.

Sarah closed her eyes, listening to the howl of the engines, feeling the great soul beside her, loving her deeply and dearly . . . and feeling the evil of her at the same time.

Sarah told herself that a wolf might kill a deer, but never would it be murder. She told herself that. As a doctor, though, she was committed to human welfare, and that certainly did not include killing. The creature beside her had eaten children and fathers and mothers—had *eaten* them. As had she herself . . . in the shame of her secret life.

And yet, this was the agony of it: nature uses predators to ensure balance. One reason that human overpopulation was destroying the world was that the Keepers had failed in their natural mission. There were not enough of them to make a difference.

Miriam called herself part of the justice of the earth. And Sarah could not deny that. She had looked into the teary eyes of victims, seen them fade as she did her own clumsy sucking. She had known what it was to be engorged with human blood. Afterward, you felt as light as air. Any small imperfection disappeared. You became supple. Your skin regained a girl's flush and milk. And your heart—it beat with a happiness that seemed founded in something that was deeply right. You had dared the abyss, to do the bidding of nature. What an addiction it was, the addiction to death.

Sarah knew that she was using her strange new relationship to the laws of nature to justify herself. But she had not been given a choice. Miriam had fallen in love with her and had infused her own blood into Sarah's veins without her permission, putting her to sleep to do it. Sarah had awakened exhausted, aching in every bone, not knowing what had happened.

There had begun an awful struggle. She had tried to live on blood bought from commercial blood banks. She had tried to live on animal blood. Then she had refused to live at all. She had actually died and been put in a coffin and slid in among Miriam's other expended lovers in her attic.

But Miriam had used Sarah's own research to bring her back. Sarah had eaten, then. She had not been strong enough to return to the terror of the coffin. Because, when Keeper blood flowed in human veins, you could live for centuries, but you could never really die.

Sarah had experienced the silent, trapped sensation of being unable to move, to breathe, to so much as flutter an eyelid in that coffin. She had been aware of the dark around her, of the lid above her, of the rustle of insects along her skin and the murmur of street traffic outside.

She'd heard Miriam playing her viola, had heard jets passing overhead, had heard the lapping mutinies of the East River and the hiss of the FDR Drive. She gone mad a hundred times, mad in the locked-up remains of her body. All around her, there had been other such coffins, some of them thousands of years old, that contained other trapped souls.

Then she had heard the tap of heels on the wide attic boards, and light had swept in, and her vague eyes had seen a smooth shadow, and life, *life*, had come marching up her arm like a grand orchestra pounding a grand tarantella.

Miriam had read Sarah's studies and her papers, and devised an experiment that had worked. For the first time in two thousand years of trying, she'd brought a lover back. She'd tried with the others, too, but it had been too late even for the most recent one, John Blaylock.

Alive again, Sarah had wandered the streets of a new world. She could be entranced by the play of sunlight on the edge of a spoon. A child's rude singing sounded the carillons of heaven. Each breath that swept her freshened lungs felt like the caress of an angel. She had learned to live in the cathedral of the moment, for the supple touch of fine leather and the sweet of morning air, for the fluttering of a bird in the birdbath or the drip of water in the kitchen sink. She had given away her doubts and her fears with her lost past (where there had even been a lover and a little apartment and a spreading career). She had given away her terror of the coffins upstairs, to the extent that she would sometimes go and lie in her own and draw the lid down and stay there until the rigors of asphyxiation thrilled her throbbing sex and made her frantic. It was sick, she knew that. Miriam's love had transformed her from a healthy young physician into a decadent, murdering libertine with a sick and sorrowing soul. But it was so beautiful . . . or it had been, until this awful thing happened, whatever it was.

When, just after being resurrected, Sarah had looked upon her savior for the first time, she had spontaneously dropped to her knees. She was Lazarus, was Dr. Sarah Roberts, enslaved by gratitude to she who had returned her to life. To try and find some sense in the servility that she now felt, she had read long and carefully in the literature of sexual enslavement and finally into the lore of zombies. She worked hard to free herself, even going to Haiti to interview a man who had been killed in a zombie ritual and brought back by a witch doctor. He, also, was mysteriously bound to the man who had dug him up and resurrected him by rubbing him with a foam made from the blood of rats. The moment this man's teary, passive eyes had met her own, she had known that they were kin.

Miriam drew back from her, whispered to her, "I ought to really punish you, you devil."

Sarah turned to her, looked into her amazing eyes, with their child's fresh intensity. You would think she was just a girl, to look at those eyes. There was not the slightest trace that this was an ancient being. If you were observant, you would see that the lipstick was painted on a strangely narrow mouth, and you might suspect that some inner thing had been done to fill out the cheeks. But that would take a very acute observer. To most people, Miriam appeared to be a rav-ishing, wonderfully dressed, wonderfully affluent young woman, still dewy from girlhood.

Miriam sighed, her breath's heavy sourness filling Sarah's nostrils. "Bring me vodka," she said.

Sarah got up from her seat, moved down the aisle toward the steward, who was serving meals in the second cabin. "Oui, mademoiselle?"

"Madame in Seven-A wishes vodka, very cold, served without ice."

"Oui, mademoiselle, a moment."

"Immediately, please."

The steward understood her tone and poured the drink, a

large one. Sarah took it to Miriam, who emptied it in an instant.

It was clear that Miriam had been through absolute hell over these past days. Sarah had suspected that her odyssey to the conclaves would be a disappointment, but whatever had happened was far worse than that.

"Another?"

"Perhaps in a few minutes."

"I know how you hate this thing."

"I just wonder if the repairs are satisfactory."

"We have to hope."

"Another vodka. Bring the bottle."

Sarah went back to the steward. "She wants the bottle."

"A service of caviar, perhaps?"

"No, only the vodka."

"Mademoiselle, is madame afraid? Would she like the pilot to come and speak to her?"

"That I cannot ask her."

"I understand," the steward said. He had concluded that Sarah was a personal servant, and that madame would be taking all her service from her, and gave her the vodka on a small tray. "Will you want me to call you for her meal?"

"Madame will not be taking a meal."

"Very well." He returned to his passengers. The service in the three cabins of the Concorde was exactly the same, but by tradition the third cabin was for tourists, the second for business people, and the first for personages. Air France might not know just how distinguished this particular passenger was, but Sarah had made sure, as always, that Miriam was treated with the greatest respect.

The fact that Sarah was not privately reconciled to Miriam's way of life and even doubted her right to her prey did not mean that she did not respect her. Miriam was a creature of God, also, and a triumph of nature. To a scientist, which Sarah most certainly was, her blood was one of nature's truly remarkable organs. It had six different cell types, including one that Sarah had watched under the electron microscope trapping and destroying virus particles, transforming them back into the chemicals out of which they were constructed.

The blood sometimes seemed almost intelligent, the way it laid traps for bacteria. And the cells were remarkable, too. Unlike human cells, they did not scavenge for free radicals with mechanisms that grew stiff and unresponsive with age. Instead, the blood converted them into nutrient components, actually changing their atomic structure.

Sarah had allowed herself to imagine that Miriam *was* her blood, that the body was only a receptacle for this brilliant organ.

She had watched it as it worked in her own veins, how after a period of acclimatization, it had adapted itself to her needs, preserving those parts of her own blood that were essential to her life and adding most of its strengths as well.

It could not change the structure of her cells, though, which continued to try to destroy free radicals. What Miriam's blood did in Sarah's veins was to destroy so many of them that little more was necessary. Still, Sarah aged. Just very, very slowly.

Sometimes, she would go to the attic and whisper to the others, "John, I'm coming, Lollia, I will be here soon." She would tell them of Miriam's doings. She would tell them of her own work, trying to find a way to bring them back to life. How it must be in those coffins, she could scarcely imagine. To have been like that for even a few days had been so extremely awful that she still had nightmares about it. But Lollie had been there for three hundred years. And there were others who were little more than teeth and long strings of hair, who had worshiped at Miriam's feet when she was pharaoh's daughter.

The selfishness of Miriam's making herself gifts of these "lovers" had crossed Sarah's mind. This was an unambiguous evil, and for a time she'd believed that she could find in herself moral ground to sabotage Miriam, on this basis.

But the nights in that bed of theirs, the *nights* . . . and living Miriam's exquisite life with her, playing their violas together and going to the club, and seeing the world through a Keeper's eyes, as if everything were always new-washed with rain—she did not have the strength to say no.

She wanted Miriam right now. To lie naked in her steel-strong arms, to taste of the kisses of a mouth that killed—for her it was an ecstasy more appealing, she suspected, than that of being lifted in the arms of God.

The truth was that she revered this creature, whom she ought to hate. She had not the moral strength to hate the pleasures of being Miriam's possession. Had she been the maid of Hera or Proserpine's sotted girl, it would not have been different. A human being had fallen in love with a terrible god.

When Miriam traveled, Sarah made all the arrangements. Normally, she stayed beside her lady, making certain that everything was perfect, that all was as she desired and deserved. It filled her heart with a deliciously awful joy to serve Miriam. She understood her history and her significance to mankind. Miriam's family had invented Egyptian civilization. Her own father had moved the Israelites into Canaan. As far as he was concerned, he was only expanding his holdings, but the significance to human history was, of course, remarkable. Miriam herself had created and nurtured dozens of different aspects of western civilization. Her image haunted our literature. She was the Shulamite maiden, she was Beatrice, she was Abelard's Heloise and Don Quixote's Dulcinea—or more accurately, she had once sung a song for a hopelessly smitten Miguel de Cervantes, and become the model for his character.

She wasn't Shakespeare's Dark Lady, but she had known the girl. The story of her mother, Lamia, had inspired Greek mythology. It had emerged in the seventeenth-century *Anatomy of Melancholy* and the whispered legends of Lamia had inspired John Keats's *Lamia and Other Poems* in 1820.

There were many Keepers, but Miriam and her parents had been more influential in human affairs than any of the others.

And now she was the friend and lover of a humble doctor from Queens, whose highest ambition should probably be to make her happy and keep her safe. Instead, Sarah was caught in an eerie web, unable to believe that Miriam had the right to kill, but also unable to do anything but serve her.

In a year, a Keeper took perhaps twenty lives. Sarah herself took ten . . . and each squirming, weeping victim consumed part of her heart. After a murder, she would weep for days. She would resolve to quit. She would renew her efforts to find a way of feeding on blood-bank blood.

Sarah returned with the vodka and served Miriam a second drink. "I wish I could comfort you," she murmured. "I know something's wrong, something more than just the flight. Please tell me what it is."

Miriam knocked back the drink. "Five thousand dollars a seat and still I cannot smoke."

"You can in the car." She glanced up at the map that was set into the bulkhead. They were traveling at Mach 2, just passing over the Irish coast. "Just two more hours, madame."

"Why are you calling me that?"

"Because you seem so regal today."

Miriam took her chin and turned her head until they were sitting like two intimate girls, face-to-face, their noses almost touching. "I have been through unbelievable hell. And I am angry, Sarah. I am angry at you."

"I know you are." She'd gone to spend a few days in the Berkshires, away from the club, away from Miriam's demands. She had not taken her cell phone.

"Love, if I can't count on you, who can I count on?"

Sarah felt her cheeks grow hot, as they had in the hotel room when she'd been bathing Miriam and had seen the rough areas and angry blushing of her skin. That was healing trauma. Because Sarah knew the power of Keeper blood to overcome injury, she was aware that Miriam had suffered fearsome damage.

"Tell me what happened, love."

Miriam turned her face to the window.

Sarah touched the black silk arm of her blouse, but Miriam said nothing more.

Very well. Sarah had learned to accept Miriam's moods. "You look so extraordinary in those clothes," she offered, gently flattering her, hoping to win a more full response. There was none.

Whatever had happened in Paris, at least it had brought those archaic Chanels to an end. They had gone to Maria Luisa and gotten some delicious Eric Bergère designs. Miriam had been extremely compliant at the shop, spending twenty thousand dollars without complaint, and revealing truly wonderful taste and an extraordinary awareness of what might flatter her the most.

Sarah gazed at her. She was so splendid that you never got tired of looking at her, and in that fabulous black blouse of sheer silk with a bloodred satin body shirt beneath—well, the effect was almost perfect. The way it held her breasts high and suggested her curves was marvelous. This ensemble had been created by a hand that loved and understood the female form.

"I was nearly killed."

Sarah leaned close to her, kissed her cold cheek, laid her lips there a long time, until she felt her body tickling within itself, lusting for the quick finger, the deep tongue. "Don't say that if it isn't true."

Miriam bridled at the statement. "How dare you!"

"I'm sorry! I—just—please forgive me."

Miriam leaned back, closed her eyes. "Is the passport going to be all right?"

"Perfect."

"Why so?"

She had asked this about the passport ten times. It was a perfect passport because it belonged to a real person. "Leonore is a master of disguise," Sarah said.

"Leonore," she said. "Do you think she would be a good meal?"

"Miriam, you know I don't find that sort of thing funny."

"Maybe she'll replace you, then, and you'll be the meal." She smiled that slight, fetching smile that looked so innocent and concealed such danger. "That might be best."

She was truly a mistress of verbal torture. "I would open my own veins for you," Sarah said.

"I suppose so." Miriam's voice was leached of emotion. "You're certain of the passport?"

"Look at it. It's you."

The instant Sarah had understood that Miriam was without a passport, she'd gone down to the Veils, where Leonore was supervising the cleaning crew, and gotten her to make herself up to resemble Miriam. A slightly fuzzy passport photo had been taken to an expediter with a two-hundred-dollar fee and a thousand-dollar bribe. Miriam's new passport—in the name of Leonore Patton—was in Sarah's hand by five that afternoon. The next morning, Sarah had come over on the Concorde to rescue their distressed lady. That was yesterday.

Word had passed through the upper echelons of New York society that something untoward had happened to Miriam in Paris.

The whole club was in vigil, CEOs, aristocrats, celebrities, the brilliant and the beautiful. There would be a hundred of the most fashionable people in New York waiting to greet the queen when her plane landed.

"Please tell me what happened."

Miriam's eyes met hers. Sarah forced herself not to look away, but Miriam was certainly furious. "In good time," she said.

"I wish you could be at peace."

"I cannot be at peace."

Miriam's hand came into hers. Her eyes became like penetrating needles. "You remember I have spoken of Martin Soule," she said slowly, evaluating Sarah, trying to look into her mind.

"He inspired Baroness Orczy. He was the real Scarlet Pimpernel."

Quick as a flash, Miriam's iron fingers were crushing Sarah's wrist. "You're not sad," she snarled.

"I'm scared! What's happening?"

"I ought to put you back in the attic with the others, you ungrateful *bitch!*"

"Miriam?"

Miriam released her wrist, tossing it away from her with a contemptuous gesture.

"Miriam, please tell me what's wrong!"

"My French has become archaic," she snapped. "I want a teacher standing before me at ten tomorrow morning. Ten exactly."

"Yes," Sarah said, aware that her voice was shaking badly, "a teacher at ten."

There was a silence, during which the jet shuddered slightly. "I needed you, Sarah, and you weren't there for me."

Sarah closed her eyes. Tears swam out beneath the lids.

"You weep for me?"

Sarah nodded. "You're the love of my life."

"And yet you ignore the emergency number. You love me, but you want me dead, Sarah. That's the truth of it."

"I don't want you dead."

"You've hated me ever since I gave you my blood." Her lips curled. "The gift of eternal life!"

"You ought to have asked me."

"You're an idiot, Sarah." Then, unexpectedly, she smiled. "But I do enjoy you. You're such a scientist!"

"You're a murderer, Miriam."

"Don't be ridiculous."

"And I love you, too."

Miriam said, "The vodka's warm."

Sarah got up like a robot and moved down the aisle. The faces of the other passengers seemed vividly alive, their cheeks rich with blood. Sarah knew that this was an early sign of her own hunger. In a week, she would need to feed again. She'd try to stave it off, as she always did, with the blood she bought from the little blood bank on Thirtieth Street.

"I need a colder bottle," she said to the steward.

"Of course, mademoiselle." He drew a new one out of the refrigeration unit in his cart, put the old one in.

She took it back to their seats and poured Miriam another drink, then sat down. "I want to help you," she said.

"You're dangerously incompetent."

"I'm the best you've got!"

"For the while," Miriam said, her voice almost indifferent, as if the subject was no more than dull.

A shock passed through Sarah. "If you'd tell me what I've done—"

"I called you and called you."

"You've told me that fifty times! But you have to tell me what happened. Why did you need me? Why are we running like this? Miriam, for the love of God, what's happening?"

The pitch of the engines changed, followed by the angle of approach. "Finally," Miriam said, "you agree that you've proved yourself hopelessly incompetent."

Sarah nodded.

"So you agree that I can't take the risk of relying on you."

Sarah nodded again, and this time tears sprayed her breast. "Miriam, no matter what you decide—"

"It's decided."

"At a time like this, you need me. Whatever it is, I can help. I can correct my mistakes and do better."

"Yes, indeed."

"You're being chased. We've got to get you out of the house. Hide you."

"Do we?"

The plane roared, made a steep turn into its final approach. "It's all right," Sarah said automatically, "everything's fine."

The steward reminded them to place their seat backs upright and fasten their seat belts. He came past and collected the vodka. "Will Madame be wanting a wheelchair?" he asked.

"Mademoiselle will not," Miriam said.

A short time later, the plane was drawing up to the gate. The moment it stopped, Sarah stepped into the aisle in order to prevent any passengers behind them from pushing past Miriam or impeding her way.

As far as the world knew, two resplendently beautiful young women stepped off the plane, one discreetly attentive to her companion, who walked with her cool gray eyes fixed to the middle distance, emeralds and gold glowing around her neck, a wide-brimmed Philippe Model hat on her head. The other girl might have been a friend, slightly less wealthy, or even an indulged secretary or servant. Indulged, because she was so well kept herself, with her superbly tailored green *peau de soie* suit and her fashionably tousled hair.

They passed through customs with the easy indifference of people so powerful that such things did not matter to them. The officers were quick, discreet. "Welcome home, Dr. Roberts; welcome back, Miss Patton."

When they appeared in the Concorde Lounge, there was a discreet spatter of applause. Miriam slowed, then stopped, then turned. She raised a gloved hand, smiled. Nobody who did not know the truth could possibly have imagined, not for an instant, that she was anything but a girl—a girl with wise eyes, but still a girl.

She stepped forward into the richly dressed crowd.

They surrounded her, kissing her cheeks, touching her as children do a mother they have not seen in a very long time. In each pair of eyes was the same regard, the same awe. Sarah watched this with the dispassion of a captive. Most of them probably thought of her only as the sparkling mistress of the most exclusive club in all of the Americas, a secret, exquisite club, a place where the most powerful of people could express their true selves without shame or restraint, where there were no restrictions . . . once you had passed the door. Some few knew part of the truth, the whispered reality of Miriam.

Only Leonore Patton was entirely certain of the truth. Leonore was being brought along. She was being educated. Sarah knew that Miriam planned to infuse Leo with her blood. Now she wondered if she herself would be killed or set adrift on her own?

People murmured around them, expressing happiness to see Miriam—some familiar faces, others less so—while Sarah anguished inside over what was taking place.

Some were staring with the mixture of fascination and horror that the true insiders shared, the ones who knew to be thrilled but also terrified when she swept them into some dark corner of the Veils, and kissed their necks in a moment of tipsy excess.

Miriam went to a young Latino—a kid she had marked as an upcoming star—and kissed him, brushing his cheek with the rough tip of her tongue. Miriam was never wrong about such things as stars. Carlos Rivera would certainly become one. So, for that matter, would Kirsten Miller who stood beside him, her careful, beautiful face radiating intelligence.

Then Miriam was finished with them, speeding out with Sarah behind her. Luis, their driver, came up to take the bags that others had conducted through customs. Inner New York, secret New York, had been waiting for nothing but her return. Now the delicious terror could continue. Was she going to feed? Would it be some forgotten soul, ready for death? Or someone who deserved it—one she had judged in her correct and careful way? If so, would it be one they knew, perhaps some garish magnate who had tried to lie his way past the Veils? If it was, then who must they carefully fail to notice was missing, who next?

"One of my shorts paid off," Sarah said after Luis had pulled into traffic and Miriam had settled back with a cigarette.

"How much?"

"It was BMC Software. We made thirty-three percent."

"On what?"

"Six hundred thousand."

Miriam smoked, gazed out the window. Sarah had heard the little grunt of approval that the awareness that she had made nearly two hundred thousand dollars had drawn from her.

Suddenly she snatched off the big hat, which she had been wearing since Paris. Then she said, "My head is warm." She inclined it toward Sarah, who set about removing the wig. Even when Sarah had bathed her in the enormous tub at the Crillon, she had not allowed this wig to be taken off.

"Are you ready for this, Luis," Miriam called, her voice tart with angry irony.

The silky blond strands of hair that had waved in the wind like fronds in the sea were gone. The effect was so disturbing that Sarah drew back. Miriam smiled, her face looking utterly false and improbably small on her strange, long head. In Egypt, they had concealed their heads beneath tall headdresses. Raise the crown from Nefertiti, and you would see Miriam's mother with the same long head. She was called Lamia only among her own kind, and in myth. In the nations she had ruled, she had been many queens.

Miriam's eyes were wet. The baldness embarrassed her, even before Sarah, who knew every intimate stroke of her being.

"Oh, my love! My love, what—what—"

"They tried to burn me to death," she said.

"The other Keepers? My dear God!"

Miriam's eyes bored into Sarah's. In that moment, she seemed more profoundly alien than ever before. They were the eyes of a goddess . . . or a predatory insect. Glassy, cruel, and way too quick, the way they flickered about.

Sarah's heart broke for her. Lamia had died by fire, and Miriam had spent many a Sleep with her head in Sarah's lap, crying out as she helplessly relived the horror of that day.

Sarah threw her arms around Miriam. "Miri," she whispered, "Miri, I will never let that happen to you, *never!*"

"We're in terrible trouble, child."

"I know it, oh, God, I know it."

Miriam came close to her, took her hand. They remained like that—both silent, Sarah weeping—on the long, traffic-choked drive home.

TWELVE

Sourball Express

Paul watched Justin Turk fool with his pipe. You weren't supposed to light up inside the building. Langley was a nonsmoking facility. Justin lit up. "You know," he said, "you're a good ten grades away from the use of exclusive air transport."

"What the hell are you talking about?"

"You requisitioned a Falcon Jet assigned to General Ham Ratling and took it from Bangkok to Paris on a noncontracted run. Meaning that we got a forty-eight-thousand-dollar bill from the Air Force, plus a letter from Secretary Leisenring. A very pissed-off letter. The general and his wife and kids all ended up in first class on Thai Airways, and we got a bill for that, too."

"It was a hot pursuit, Justin. For Chrissakes."

"A hot pursuit." He pulled a yellow pad out of his desk. "So how do I write this up? Give me words, buddy."

"Agents were in hot pursuit of a female vampire—"

Justin held up his hand. "Say something else."

"Terrorist."

"A terrorist contact incident has to be written up on one of those—lemme see here—Candy!"

Candy Terrell, his assistant, came in.

"I need a TCI form," he told her.

"What the hell is a TCI form?"

"Terrorist Contact Incident. Every field op who thinks he's encountered a terrorist, whether known or unknown, has to fill one out and file it within six hours. It's been days in this case, of course. But nobody expects less from our boy."

Candy left the room.

"We'll return to the plane issue later. I thought you were injured."

"It healed."

"In two days? The police report said you had a knife wound in your left shoulder that took eighteen stitches. Why isn't your arm in a sling?"

"I heal fast. Always have."

Justin cleared his throat and shuffled some papers. Paul was perplexed. He had healed fast—incredibly fast. He should have been in a sling. He should have had a cast.

Why wasn't Justin curious about that? Paul sure as hell was.

"You also have a body coming back. Was it on the transport with you?"

"The French flew it from Villacoublay to Ramstein. It oughta be in Santa Clara tomorrow. It's being delivered directly to the family."

"You've written a letter?"

Paul had not written a letter. He couldn't do that, as Justin well knew. "It has to come out of the pool." Next of kin were handled out of a central office when agents died or were injured in the course of secret operations.

"You do it. Let the pool send it."

"Okay."

"Because I want you to feel it."

Paul sucked in breath. He really did not want to deck Justin Turk, his only ally at Langley, but Paul's tendency was to go physical when he felt threatened, and an insult like that was damned threatening. He was sitting here, and getting this. "I took a hit, too," he said. "We had a terrible time in there. Just awful."

"You couldn't have stayed out of harm's way? I mean, given the French presence on French soil?"

"We couldn't." What else was there to say? Just let it go. The desks never understood operational issues, never had, never would.

Justin was watching him carefully. Paul realized that the needle had been inserted on purpose. Justin was probably trying to make him feel vulnerable, to throw him off-balance.

This meant only one thing: this was not a conversation. It was not a report. It was an interrogation and he was in trouble. The question was, what the hell kind?

"Well, Paul?"

"Justin, I don't know what to say. I don't like your drift. 'Want me to feel it'—what the hell is that supposed to mean?"

"You lose agents!"

"I'm fighting a war!"

"You and Don Quixote. We're not sure about your war."

"The White House is bothering the director, and you're taking heat. Is that it?"

Justin did not reply, confirming the accuracy of Paul's diagnosis.

"Tell 'em they have no need to know. Like the alien business."

"The alien business! We don't exactly have a directive from

another world enforcing the secrecy in this particular case, Paul. All we have is you."

"Thing is, how did the White House find out in the first place?"

"The French have a program. The Germans have a program. For all I know, everybody has a program. This is a secret that's about to come out. And they are scared, because when that press conference has to be called, they will have to explain you and your killing spree, and they don't know how to do that."

"I've done my job. The French have done theirs. No doubt the others have, too. We've been effective. End of story."

"Yeah, the French have a casualty rate of seventy percent. You've lost four out of eleven people in two years. That's very effective, but not in the way we want, Paulie Paul."

"Everybody loses personnel. I saw the French clean out dozens of vampires when I was there."

"We prefer to call them differently blooded persons. DBPs."

He did not like the drift of that. "Who decided this?"

"The Human Rights Directorate." Justin shuffled more paper. "I printed out their memo for you."

"I didn't know we had a Human Rights Directorate."

"It's attached to the Office of the General Counsel. It was mandated under PD 1482 a year ago."

Presidential Directive 1482 had established humane practices guidelines for the Directorate of Operations. Since Paul was not dealing with human beings, humane practices, he had assumed, were not relevant to his work.

Justin held the paper out to him. "We've been instructed to use these guidelines as the basis for a policy recommendation. We're assembling facts for the Directorate of Intelligence now."

Paul took the sheet of paper. "Who wrote this?"
Justin did not answer directly. "Read it."

We must determine if these alleged vampires are human. These are the questions that should be asked in making this determination: Do they have language? Do they plan? Do they experience emotion? Have they enough basic intelligence to perform human activities? If all of these things, or most of them, are true, then it must be assumed that they are human or humanlike creatures, and should be afforded all the protection of the law.

Further, if indeed they must consume human flesh as a natural condition of their lives, then it is not clear that they can be identified as murderers or terrorists, any more than any predator species can be considered the murderer of its prey.

At the same time, there is nothing that prevents us from warning our citizenry about them and providing, for example, survival guidelines. The right of the prey to attempt to thwart the predator would seem to be as fundamental as the right of the predator to kill. However, their status as conscious creatures would preclude simply destroying them to relieve the threat.

Additionally, their relative rarity may identify them as an endangered species and, on that basis, mandate a level of protection of their habitats and limits on killing them.

In summary, the existence of these creatures should be made public, along with guidelines about how to avoid capture by them. Their lives would be protected under the International Human Rights Convention and possibly by endangered species acts in vari-

*ous countries. Their right to kill to eat must not be
interfered with, except insofar as to aid legitimate
attempts to avoid them.*

Paul continued to stare at the document, not because he
was still reading it, but because he was literally paralyzed with
amazement. Had all of his blood descended into his feet? Is
that why he felt this sense of having totally lost contact with
reality? Or was it the piece of paper in his hand?

"Justin, could you tell me something? Could you tell me if
Franz Kafka is still alive?"

"He's dead. What's the point?"

"Oh, I just thought he might have written this—you
know—as a sort of kafkaesque joke."

"Paul, I'm required to inform you that an investigation of
your activities has been instituted. As there is a possibility
that criminal charges could be levied against you, it is our
official recommendation to you that you retain counsel. If
you don't have a lawyer of your own—"

"I haven't got a damn lawyer!"

"Then you can apply to the Office of General Counsel for
a referral to a legal representative who has an appropriate
clearance match with you, so that you can discuss your situation
with him freely. If you cannot afford to pay your
lawyer, you can be referred to a legal aid lawyer with a clearance."

Paul thought, *Just sit, keep breathing, don't turn white,
don't turn red, don't hit anybody or break anything.*

"Paul?"

"Just a minute. I'm trying to decide if I should laugh or
cry. What's your thought? Tears?"

"I didn't write it, Paul."

"Damnit, Justin, don't you see what this is?"

"It's an attempt to recognize the human rights of an alien species."

"It's a license for the vampires to hunt and kill human beings. Jesus Christ, I lost my father to these things! A little boy waits, and a wife, she waits and waits, and Dad just never comes home. You go on for years wondering, 'Did he die or get killed, or did he walk out on us?' It eats away at your heart and makes you hard, and gradually, it kills your heart. In my case, I found my dad. Most people never find a damn thing."

"The government has decided that the differently blooded are part of nature."

"Justin, pardon my stupidity, but aren't we out there trying to protect people? I mean, isn't that the fundamental promise of government? If a rancher gets his cattle killed by coyotes, you know what happens? He goes out and he damn well shoots the buggers or traps 'em. Nature made the coyote to eat cattle. But that doesn't mean the rancher's just gonna let it happen."

"You're under investigation for suborning your orders, Paul."

Suborning was an ugly word. It meant misusing your orders or intentionally misinterpreting them. It was the kind of word you heard in trials. "That's the criminal route."

"I told you to get a lawyer. This is a serious situation, buddy. You could be looking at a count of murder for every single creature you've killed."

"Justin, for the love of God, help me!"

Justin stared at him like he was something in a damn zoo.

"This is coming from the White House."

"A bunch of college kids with no experience of life. Look, this is about people being killed. You know—mothers and sons, fathers and daughters."

Justin worked at his pipe. "I'm only the messenger."

"Why don't you tell Mr. President something for me—for this stupid grunt nobody who just happens to value human life above all things. A couple of days ago in Paris, I was in a room—deep underground—where I saw maybe half a million dead people stacked in rows . . . long, long rows. Every one of them was a tragedy. Every one of them was a broken family, or a broken heart, or at least a life stolen from somebody to whom it was precious."

"People will have the right to defend themselves."

"From something that can move so fast you can't see it, that's four times as strong as you are and twice as smart? I don't think so."

"The state will protect them."

"Only one way to do that. Kill the vampires."

"Paul, a stupid rancher does the environmentally unsound thing when he traps and poisons the coyotes on his place. A smart one plans so that his herd is never in jeopardy. The state's simply gonna be the smart rancher."

"But they'll get through. They'll find ways!"

"Some people will be killed. But it's been like that for all of history, hasn't it?"

"Let me pose you a hypothetical. You wake up some night, and one of these things is drilling into your neck. What do you do—I mean, personally?"

"This isn't going to happen to me."

"Hypothetically. Do you call Nine-one-one? Come on, be real, here! Christ!"

"The good rancher uses various appropriate and effective

means to chase off the coyotes. We'll be proactive in the same way."

Paul got to his feet. "I'm in the middle of a mopping up operation in Paris. Gotta get back."

"We are not going to continue with this barbaric exercise of yours. It's over, Paul. Totally and completely *over!* Okay? And there are some people you need to meet."

Danger always tapped on Paul's shoulder before most people realized that it had entered the picture. Something about Justin's tone of voice suggested that these people were going to give him a whole lot of trouble.

The U.S. had secret prisons for people who had broken the law in the course of classified activities. The law in those facilities was a strange, surrealistic version of the law on the outside. You had rights—just not the right to leave. Administrative prisons, that was what they called them.

Well, he still had the right to leave at the moment, or at least the ability, so he damn well walked out the door. He went through the outer office and into the corridor. There were two men coming toward the office. He went the other way.

Behind him, he heard their footsteps get quicker and louder. Goddamn, he didn't want this. He'd been part of this organization all of his adult life. He had stood before the Memorial Wall and wept a tear for fallen comrades. He had loved CIA and stood by CIA and been absolutely loyal to CIA, no matter how dumb he thought the latest director was or how misguided the latest policy.

He got the hell out of the building, hurrying out the new entrance to the west lot where he'd parked. As he got into the pretty little Saab that had been waiting in his garage for the past two years, he wondered if he would be fast enough to pass the gate or if Justin had already called them and told them to detain him.

He pulled up to the guardhouse, showed his ID card, waited. The guard looked at it, made a notation, and opened the barrier. He drove out and was soon headed for the freeway. It was a sunny summer afternoon, and once he was out of Reston, the world came to appear innocent again, even sweet. He loved the people in the cars, felt their hopes and loves with the special empathy that only a person who has killed in the line of duty can ever know. There is something about the taking of human life that makes human life seem incredibly precious. Even if killing somebody is necessary, the fact is that your dead remain with you all the rest of your days. Not your dead vampires, though. Only the people.

What if people knew that they were liable to be hunted down and killed, and it wasn't against the law? The very notion was absurd.

On this deceptively peaceful afternoon, he knew that he had to act with the utmost professionalism and speed, or he was going to be hunted down himself. Right this minute, there was an urgent meeting taking place somewhere in the building—probably in Justin's office—covering the issue of Paul Ward. He'd become what was known as a "runner," an agent who, when his actions were challenged, had immediately taken off. To CIA, this response was *prima facie* evidence of guilt. The Company was very skilled at hunting such people down.

What he needed to do was clear: he needed to kill as many vampires as he possibly could between now and the time they did manage to catch up with him.

He took 495 to 95, thinking that he'd go to Baltimore, park the car somewhere, and take mass transit to the Amtrak station.

According to what little he knew about the vampire in America, he needed to go first to New York. The reporter Ellen Wunderling had disappeared there researching the gothic subculture. In Paul's opinion, it was possible that she had stumbled across a real vampire, discovered too much, and been eaten.

So he'd go back to the plan of looking for her. She had disappeared in New York, so that would be his first destination.

He was a man who carried a lot of cash, always, so he'd be able to put some space between himself and his pursuers.

What a hell of a thing that he'd sacrificed lives for the French Book of Names and now he couldn't use it. He couldn't read a word of it himself, and he certainly couldn't stop by NSA and ask them to help him with the translation.

When he reached the exit for Route 32, he decided to make it interesting for whoever would be coming after him. He took 32 up to Columbia, which was a big enough town to have both a bus system and a taxi company.

He went to the Columbia Mall and parked in the covered parking, where his car would be harder to spot. He turned on his cell phone and strolled into the mall. It was so nice, so damn American. He went into the Sears, strolling easily, looking at the washing machines, the clothes. He bought a couple of shirts, a pair of pants, a blue blazer and some black sneakers. When he came out of the men's room, he looked like the same guy in different clothes. He knew that you weren't going to be able to disguise Paul Ward, but every little bit helped.

He dropped his phone in a lady's shopping bag. They'd follow that, for sure, probably track it down in about an hour. There was going to be some excitement in her sweet life.

He went outside and hailed a cab, which he took to the campus of St. John's College in Annapolis. A thousand years ago, he'd been a St. Johnnie for a couple of semesters. The school followed a great-books curriculum, starting with Homer and ending with Freud and Einstein. He'd read the *Iliad* and the *Odyssey* under Professor Klein, who'd had his fingers broken by the Nazis for playing the piano better than an Aryan. Still, as much as it hurt, he had played of an evening, Debussy and Chopin and Satie . . . He hadn't weaned young Paul away from doo-wop, but the playing had been awesome.

Paul had been the only kid in the whole school who'd favored the war in Vietnam, and also been dumb enough to put a statement up on the bulletin board about it. As a result, he'd soon found himself being recruited by CIA, and thus had begun the rest of his life. Old George Hauser, of blessed memory, had sat with him on that bench right over there under the great oak and spoken to him of what it meant to be an operations officer, how hard it really was, and just how disappointing it could be . . . and how much it mattered.

He went up the brick walk toward McDowell Hall, the administration building and meeting hall, where the choir had met. The young voices returned, calling to him from the quiet that he entered when he entered the building. Downstairs was the coffee shop, and there also was the bulletin board where his current life had begun.

There were people here and there, but the campus was quiet in midsummer. He went through the basement of McDowell and out into the little quad. There was Randall Hall, where he had lived—given a single room even though he was only a freshman, largely because they could not imagine anybody who had written an entrance essay like his successfully living in close proximity to another person. He'd written on Saint Thomas Aquinas, the *Summa Theologica*. In those days, he had been a fiercely ardent Catholic. How long ago that was, the days of the skinny kid with the close-cropped hair and the delicate wire glasses.

He wondered why he had come here. Was it because he was dying, and the inner man knew it? He'd seen many an operational death that started with just this kind of official abandonment. *I will not go to prison*, he told himself as his eyes counted windows to his old room. How small Randall Hall looked now. He remembered it as a grand place. But look at it, you could almost jump over the damn thing. A vampire probably could, or come close.

He'd gotten to this place on the back of a hell of a scholarship, the Stephens Piper Award for Scholastic Diligence. Full tuition to the college of his choice.

He thought to himself, *How do I kill vampires, now that I am alone? Dare I assemble my people? No, they'd all be stopped at their ports of entry.*

He'd signal Becky not to come back—stop at the college library, see if they had a public computer. He'd send her an e-mail, using the team's own emergency code. She could share it with the ones still in Kuala. He went over to the library, which was wide open and, typical of St. John's rather tangential approach to organization, totally unmanned.

He booted up the computer behind the librarian's counter. No password needed, of course. St. John's was still St. John's. It wasn't that they were especially trusting. It was details—they avoided them. Was it the best college in the United States? Not by all standards, but by any standard at all, it was the most intellectually healthy.

His opinion. He opened up Outlook Express and logged

onto their server. One code he'd never expected to use was "sourball express." It meant the unthinkable, that CIA had turned against the operation and everybody needed to go to ground immediately, wherever they happened to be.

When she saw it, she would go into meltdown, but she would do her duty. He typed the words. Then he added, "Go to B." There was a guaranteed job, given his recent casualties. Bocage understood American intelligence very well. He'd give her a good home.

He sighed. It was likely that he would never see Becky again, never hear from her, never know how her life played itself out. Well, hell, that was the nature of this game. You worked in total darkness. Sometimes there were other figures beside you, sometimes you were alone. He could have loved that kid, though. He could have loved her.

He sent the e-letter from the name of the person who used the computer, then immediately shut it down. There was no point in encrypting it. All of their encryption was backdoored to CIA. The point was not to write anything that would make an Echelon search possible. He hadn't done that, he was quite sure. Pretty sure. Somewhat sure.

He went out, hurrying down toward the playing field and the bridge with its bus stop. There was the tree under which he had kissed Connie Bell. Even all these years later, he remembered just how sweet she had tasted, Connie Bell. She was the loveliest woman he had ever known, even to this day.

He recognized, abstractly, that he was crying. At least, his eyes were wet. What a damn asshole he could be. Fortunate that he was alone. He was crying for his lost career, for his despised honor, but more for Connie Bell and lost youth . . . and for Becky Driver, whom he had never gotten an opportunity to kiss.

He crossed the playing fields and came to the bridge and the bus stop. He'd take the bus into Baltimore, to Penn Station.

His pursuers would spend their time looking for cell phone usage and credit card usage and ATM usage. Nobody would take to the streets, nobody would try to think as he thought, try to follow him in the old-fashioned way, by following his mind.

He did not intend to stop killing vampires simply because he'd lost his backing. To hell with the CIA; he was going to do this thing. Maybe he'd rid the United States of the creatures before his employers caught him, who knew? Let Justin stuff that in his damn pipe. Endangered species, hell. If he rendered the damn things extinct before they could be protected, what would those White House pantywaists do— apologize to the world for allowing such a terrible thing to happen?

They were totally out of touch with the situation. If the vampires were free to hunt openly—if they had rights and legal status—oh, God, how awful that would be. Inside of a decade, they would rule the world again.

The bus came, and he paid his fare and took a seat. He leaned back, closed his eyes. "Should've graduated from St. John's, asshole," he told himself. He could've become a professor of classical languages, a doctor of philosophy. He could have led a quiet life, tasted of love and marriage. Except if you went through a childhood like his you were— well, you were scarred. He was a strong man. Tough guy.

But why? What motivated him to get so good with a gun, to learn the art of killing, to live in the shadows?

He knew. Hell yes, he did. This particular mystery man had himself figured out. When his dad disappeared, the world changed for him. It became a place where anything could happen and nobody was safe. He was as he was for a very simple reason: he lived in deep inner terror, and it never, ever went away.

What if his kids disappeared? Or his wife, or him? He was too insecure to be able to enjoy real love.

In his lifetime, he'd killed at least fifty men, some of them with his bare hands. He'd tortured people, done it sadly and methodically, but with the same determination that drove him now. He could see beyond the immediate tragedy to the greater reward. He had wired up the gonads of Cambodian kids to get information that would save American lives. Would the mothers and wives whose lovers and sons he'd sent home alive tell him he'd done wrong?

He transferred to another bus line and rode this one to the station. He went to the newsstand and picked up some magazines, then bought a club ticket for the 4:35 Metroliner.

There was always the possibility that the station was being watched, so he went to the men's room and sat in one of the stalls reading. Guys came and went, toilets flushed around him. He read about elk hunting, then paged through the classifieds. *Field and Stream* always reminded him of the last time he had hunted, which had been with his dad. They gone up along the Chattaminimi Ridge, and just at sunrise had seen a buck to stop your heart. That had been about two weeks before Dad was killed. The vampire would have been watching him by then, for sure. It was probably only a few feet away during that walk, pacing them, waiting, doing its research on its victim. "What's that smell?" young Paul had asked. "Bats," Dad had said. "There's a lotta bat caves up this way." It had not been bats.

He waited until four-thirty-two, then left the john and hurried across the station. This would cause a sudden redeployment of officers, if there was anybody there. He knew how to flush a tail.

There was no tail, and he also nearly missed the damn train. But he did not miss it. He got in the club car and found his seat, dropped down and opened another magazine, *Newsweek*. He stared at it, while actually evaluating his surroundings and all the other passengers. There was a woman with two little girls, some businessmen, a couple of tourists, maybe from eastern Europe. Any of these people could be tails preset on the train. He was especially interested in the mom. That'd be a clever twist, the kind of thing they might use when a pro was the target.

Still, he didn't think they were on him, or anywhere near him. He thought he'd have a good week before they decided to put him on wanted posters. Probably call him a serial child killer or something. Be sure to get police attention all over the damn country that way.

He gazed out the window. This was his America he was passing through, this America of rolling hills and tidy suburbs, and rusty old factories clinging to the rail line. He remembered a very long time ago when this was still the New York Central Railroad, and the cars had been painted olive drab. He'd made his first trip to New York on this line, emerging in Penn Station with saucer eyes and fifteen wadded up dollar bills in his pocket. He'd stayed at the Taft Hotel on Seventh Avenue, with three other guys from the college.

It was on that trip that he had seen his first truly great painting, Van Gogh's *Starry Night* in the Museum of Modern Art. It was also on that trip that he had gone to his first opera, *Turandot*, about a cruel princess in a moonlit palace of long ago.

He had been a person, then—a young person, just awakening to the world around him. Fresh as the dew, drinking his first drink, smoking his first cigarette, lying in bed at night with Connie Bell on his mind.

He was a killing machine now, was Paul Ward. He'd lost his ability to love women. He could still have sex, and he did that whenever it was convenient, either with whores or casual pickups. But love? No. That part of his heart had gone out like a spent old coal.

It did not seem as though two and a half hours had passed, but they were entering the Pennsy Tunnel, sure enough.

New York. It probably wouldn't be where matters ended, because he intended to follow this path to the last vampire in the country. He probably should have started here. But nobody they were aware of had ever even seen a vampire in those days, so Tokyo looked like found money. Too bad the Europeans had kept their programs to themselves.

He left the train last, walked up the platform alone. Nobody was watching him. He crossed Penn Station. Nobody here, either. He went out, up the stairs to Eighth Avenue.

Cabs roared past, people swarmed the sidewalks. He was tired, bone tired, and he wanted a major drink. A whole lot of 'em. He'd really love to have found some bar fighters, but he was too deep in cover for that now. First chance he got, he planned to spend some time smashing his fists into a goddamn wall.

You burned down your house, fella. Just jumped up and ran out of there. What the hell did you know? Maybe those two guys were gonna give you a decoration.

He stuffed his hands in his pockets and started up the avenue. He wasn't going anywhere in particular—just away from here. He needed a place to crash, for sure. The flight from Paris to Dulles had been lousy—a middle seat, a kid with massive quantities of popcorn on one side of him, the King of Sweat on the other. Then touchdown and straight to Langley, and the shit spitting through the fan.

He was so fucking tired; he didn't think he'd ever been this tired. Tired or not, though, he was a man obsessed, and his obsession kept him going. He was here to find and kill the parasites that had taken his dad away from him, and he was going to do it. He slogged off down the street—and soon found himself passing the Theater at Madison Square Garden. Lou Reed was giving a concert tonight, which might actually make him feel a little less miserable. Also, dipping into a crowd never hurt. He'd use it to strip tails, then find a room later. He turned the corner and went up to the ticket booth, asked for one on the aisle anywhere in the auditorium.

"Sold out."

"What're they scalping for?"

"Eight hundred up. Guy on the corner, black jacket, he's got a few."

The hell with that. He couldn't afford anything nice, never had been able to. Intelligence work was not a comfortable life, especially not in the field. James Bond was a cruel fantasy.

He decided to hunt up a fleabag that would sell him a few hours sleep for cash. Then he would start his investigation, and he would find the parasites in their holes, and kill them all.

THIRTEEN

All Through the Night

Across the sour reaches of an uneasy day, Sarah had waited and Miriam had remained silent. At the last moment, Miriam decided not to go to Lou's concert, saying that she was too tired. But that wasn't it. Miriam was never tired. The truth was obvious to Sarah: she was too scared.

Whoever she was running from was obviously extremely dangerous. But who could be dangerous to her? The other Keepers might not like her, but they weren't going to terrorize her. Could it be a human being? That seemed impossible.

Miriam's world had gathered her in, shielding her behind its walls of money and power. Only a few of her admirers *really* knew—or, if they had been told, actually believed—how she sustained her life. They preferred to view the *frisson* of danger that clung to her as part of her extraordinary personal style—an intoxicating mixture of sin and savagery and high culture. Had they known for certain that the whispers were true, most of them would have abandoned her to the police. Or so they told themselves.

During the watchful, uneasy night, Sarah's hunger had increased. Miriam did not offer Sarah the comfort and support she was used to getting from her. Instead, Leo was given the responsibility of attending to Sarah's suffering, giving her aspirin, then preparing a pipe for her. Leo's presence, since they had returned from England, had obviously become more important to Miriam, and Sarah found this disturbing. She did not like Leo. She did not want her in their lives.

Sarah smoked in the library while Miriam paced and consulted an old Keeper tome. She seemed to be looking for something in her books, paging carefully through their heavily illuminated pages. Sarah had been unable to crack the incredibly intricate hieroglyphics, and when she asked to be taught the language, Miriam had said, "Your species isn't intelligent enough to learn it. I might possibly be able to teach you to read a list, but who wants to do that?"

Of course, all of the important information about the Keepers was recorded in long lists in the Books of Names. If Sarah was ever to complete her own book, she needed to know that language. But she would need professional linguists and cryptographers to help her, if Miriam would not.

Miriam was now wearing one of her many wigs, a darling bobbed affair, pert and blond, that made her seem even younger. In it, she appeared her usual resplendent self. But she had been *burned*. Who would have done that? Even if it had been Keepers, why was she still afraid? Keepers didn't hunt each other down. They argued and fought, on occasion, but their battles were never to the death.

Could it have been a human being? If so, then what manner of human could have managed it?

Near dawn, Sarah had awakened from a sleep made gaudy by opium. She felt awful, her stomach full of acid, her body aching, her heart hammering. She knew the symptoms perfectly well: Miriam's blood—that strange otherness within her—was literally devouring her in its hunger.

The symptoms were not unlike those of a severe bacterial

infection, as her immune system fought the part of her that was turning against her own flesh. Soon, she would be feverish. Then later, she would grow delirious. In the end would come death. Sarah had to feed. She had to do it now.

She was surprised to hear more than two voices coming from the direction of the kitchen. At this hour—about six in the morning—it was most unusual for there to be a stranger in the house.

Sarah hurried toward the kitchen. She found Miriam and Leo attending to the needs of a shabby, heavy woman who wore a tattered coat and scarf and smelled of ammonia and sweat. Sarah the doctor saw immediately that she ate badly and drank—was, in fact, somewhat drunk right now—had untreated skin cancer, and, from the droopy look of her right eye, an undiagnosed stroke.

Beneath her feet Sarah could feel the rumble of the big furnace, which was used to incinerate remnants.

She continued to look upon her—perhaps sixty, obviously a street person, eating a piece of Leo's rhubarb pie. Leo could bake. She could make fried chicken. Now, her sleeves were rolled up. There were handcuffs in the hip pocket of her jeans.

Sarah was appalled. Leo was being allowed to participate in this. Leo! Had Miriam lost her mind? This sort of business was for the Keepers and the blooded only. Never should Leo have been involved.

"Hi," Leo said brightly. "I got you what you need."

Sarah looked at Miriam, who leaned against the drainboard, watching with those crystal eyes of hers. She murmured, "Do it now."

Leo said to the woman, "More milk?"

She replied, "Sure, lady."

"Miri," Sarah said. She nodded toward Leo. You didn't feed in front of one of those. No way!

Leo went behind her as if to go to the refrigerator. As she pulled open the door, she also drew a sock stuffed with ball bearings out of her tight jeans pocket. She positioned herself behind the busily eating woman.

Miriam had obviously instructed her. She had *instructed* an ordinary human in this terrible secret. What if Leo went to the police, tried blackmail—there would be no way to stop her unless she was imprisoned like Sarah, in the bondage of Keeper blood.

Leo hit the woman. It was a gingerly, inexpert blow. She barked with surprise, pie flying out of her mouth.

"Again," Miriam said. She was completely at her ease.

The woman started to her feet, her eyes bulging with surprise. Leo struck her again, but she was in motion now and the blow was even less effective. She stumbled forward against the table. She said something, perhaps in Russian.

Miriam answered her in a harsh voice, in the same language. The woman shoved the table aside, began to run toward Sarah and the doorway behind her.

"Keep after her, Leo," Miriam barked.

This blow came down right on top of the cranium—not well placed, but there was plenty of travel in it and the woman went down like a bag of lard. Her forehead hit the granite tile floor with a jarring crack.

"Now," Miriam said, "Sarah will prepare her with a little bleeding knife, won't you, Sarah? Get your kit to show Leo."

Sarah looked at the body, the slow rise and fall of the chest, the strange repose on the face.

"It's in my office," she said.

"Then get it. But be quick."

She went up to the bedroom, through it, and up the narrow stairs to the tiny space that was her own. Its window looked out on a wall, but it had a lovely skylight. On fine days, she would sometimes lean back in her chair and let her thoughts wander in the sky that unfolded overhead.

Her desk was stacked with papers, and a frame from a statistical analysis program she'd been using glowed on her computer screen. She had been analyzing the effect of a new plasma solution made from Miriam's blood on the decayed cells of her former lovers' bodies. So far, the results were ambiguous at best.

She knew she shouldn't, but she sat down. Her hunger was calling to her, screaming to her. But she still sat down; she still looked at her figures, thought a little about the deliverance she was working on.

A life was about to be wasted, and this was comfort, because somewhere in these statistics and the cellular structures they reflected, there was a way to eject Miriam's blood from your body . . . maybe even a way to rescue those who had faltered while it still flowed in their veins. Faltered, but not died . . .

She clicked her mouse a few times, and a photo appeared on the screen of somebody who had most certainly died. This picture had been strictly forbidden by Miriam, not allowed anywhere in the house.

She gazed into it, into the smiling face of her beloved Tom. She and Tom Haver had discovered Miriam together. It had been a heady time for them at Riverside Hospital, uncovering together the fact that this was a new species of intelligent creature, sharing the earth with mankind.

In the picture, Tom was smiling. It had been their last

carefree moment together. In fact, the last carefree moment of Sarah Roberts's life.

Behind him was the South Street Seaport Maritime Museum, in the days before all the new restaurants and attractions. They'd just come down off one of the old sailing ships. It had been a sunny autumn afternoon. He was wearing a windbreaker.

She knew every detail of how he had been when she had snapped that picture, remembered even his aftershave. It had been something called Jade East. They had walked hand in hand up South Street, bought some oysters at the Fulton Fish Market, gone home and eaten them on the tiny deck of their apartment. They were so in love.

Eleven days later she had killed him. She had killed Tom, and now his soul rested within her. She never spoke of him, hardly dared think of him because sometimes it seemed as if Miri could read thoughts. But he was part of her, and it was to him she would go, if ever her soul was released from the prison of this life.

Working quickly, she returned the picture to its hidden file. Miriam never touched the computer. But she might, and she was certainly smart enough to understand it. Sarah could not imagine what would happen if she discovered the picture.

If Miriam understood the depth of Sarah's rebellion, she might be returned to the attic.

She looked toward the small door in the side wall. It led up.

She knew that she should get her fleam from the desk drawer and take it down immediately, that she was already overdue, but instead she gazed at that door.

It did her soul good to go up there. But it was hard to do

it, to see them . . . and to see the other thing that was there.

She laid her hand on the knob, twisted it. The dark stairs rose steeply. She mounted them, hesitated, then walked quickly up.

Before her was a room dimly lit by small oval windows. There was something almost noble about the wide space with its sweep of gray floor. The attic ran the length of this large house, and thus was its largest room.

Bats roosted in the upper timbers. Ancient brass lanterns hung from crossbeams. This room had never been electrified.

Here were the coffins and boxes that represented her mistress's incredible greed, her invincible belief in her own rights over the rights of others. Here, also, was a humble coffin made of gray steel, still looking quite new.

Sarah went to it. She drew it open. It was here that Miriam had laid her after she had attempted to destroy herself. She ran her fingers along the white satin facing, touched the little pillow where her head had rested.

Here she had passed through death and here been brought back. This coffin, she felt, was her true home. This was the center of her reality and her being. It was where she must one day return. And she did return, when Miri was deep in the dead sleep that followed her feedings or—as now—otherwise occupied. Sarah would get in and draw down the lid, remaining until the air ran out and she finally had to open it to breathe.

There was a deep, profound satisfaction involved in doing this. When she pulled that lid down, it was as if fresh water was soothing her burning, tortured soul.

She wanted to right now—especially now—so very badly. But she had to get back. She had to take the fleam. Her victim was waiting to be robbed of her life.

Through tearing eyes, she looked along the far wall, to the coffin that Miri so frequently came to see. This was John Blaylock. What Miri did not know was that Sarah would sometimes open this coffin . . . as she was going to do now.

She went to it, unlocked it, raised the lid. A familiar dry, spicy scent came out—the potpourri that Miriam kept there. The corpse was narrow, dressed in a tail suit with a wing collar. The neck had grown thin, and the face was distorted by the profound necrosis of a body dead and from drying out for twenty years.

The lips had slid back from the teeth, and the cartilage in the nose had dried out. The corpse was grimacing. But there was something about the grimace—some, strange living essence that made it hard to look upon for long. For this was no ordinary corpse. This was a living corpse.

She laid her hand lightly in the corpse's delicate hand. Then she leaned into the coffin and touched her lips to the dry, rotted cheek. She whispered, "I'm making progress, John. A little at a time. But it's there, John. It's there."

With the slowness of an hour hand, the fingers of the corpse were closing. If she had an hour or two or three, John Blaylock would gradually grip her hand with an appalling grip. His fingers would feel like corded steel. His nails would dig as if seeking to break through to her blood.

But now, there was only the subtlest of changes—a slight tickling of a bony finger in a soft palm, the sighing pressure of a long, hard nail upon the tender inner edge of one of her fingers.

She drew away from him. In his eyes, she could see fire. See it—but was it there? Then she heard the sound of the corpse—for it made a sound when she came. It was moving—dry muscles, dead skin, every part of it. This created a rustle no more than the whisper of falling leaves, but it was unmistakably a sound of life.

In her clear, gentle voice, as soft as the tender airs of the night, she sang to him a song that was familiar to all of Miriam's people:

> *"Sleep my child and peace attend thee,*
> *All through the night. . . ."*

With that she left him. Miriam would not be pleased with this delay. But Sarah had a relationship with John and the others. One day, she would either bring them back to life or give them the release of true death. One day.

Her research had proceeded much farther than she had told Miriam. In fact, she was probably farther along in understanding the physics of the soul than anybody else in the world. This was because science rejected its existence. But she had *been* a soul, one trapped in its own corpse. So she knew that the soul existed. She had discovered that this rich electromagnetic being was accessible to technology, for it was part of the physical world, not some strange supernatural essence. The soul was a living plasma composed of trillions of electrons, each one cast with a slightly different spin, and each spin expressing a tiny part of the harmony and memory of the whole incredibly detailed being.

There must even be a medicine of the soul, she felt, for it could be sick and it could suffer. Oh, yes, it could suffer.

As she crossed the attic, the rustling grew faint, fading on an unmistakable note of dejection.

She drew her spotless sliver fleam out of its case of human leather and hurried downstairs.

They had cuffed the victim, who was laid out on the white enamel kitchen table.

"Pull up a chair," Miriam said to Leo. "It's quite a spectacle." She glared at Sarah, but made no other comment on her slowness.

Sarah tried to control her shaking hand as she felt the pulse. With her doctor's precise knowledge, she could determine exactly which neck artery would offer the best flow.

"What is that instrument?"

Sarah looked at Leo, who was sitting with her chin in her hands, watching from two feet away. She was going to watch an innocent human being die, and all she could bring to it was this ugly fascination. Sarah went from disliking Leo to despising her. She was actually tempted to go after her with the damned fleam.

When she did not answer Leo's question, Miriam said, "It's an antique surgical instrument, from when they used to let blood. That hooked end nicks into the vein, then the blade opens it. It's very neat."

"You don't use one, though."

With a dry sound, Miriam opened her mouth. Leo gasped at the funneled cavern with the pointed, black tongue at its center. "I don't need one," Miriam said, chuckling.

"Fleams were used by vets to bleed horses," Sarah said. "It's a brutal tool."

"It looks beautiful."

"That's because she keeps her instruments so clean. She's a doctor, remember."

"How does this make you feel?"

"How does it make me *feel*?"

"Hurry up, Sarah," Miriam said quickly.

Her throat was closing, her eyes tearing. But she tried to

be proud, to do well what she must do to survive. She was weak; she should let herself die. But she couldn't stay in that coffin of hers, no more than you can kill yourself by holding your breath.

"Aren't you going to wake her up for it?" Leo asked.

Miriam burst out laughing. "She likes them out cold! She has no taste!"

What Miriam meant was that the blood of a suffering victim tasted better. The adrenaline gave it a delectable piquancy.

Sarah hooked the fleam into the carotid on the right side. Leo came around the table so she could see the sucking process up close. Sarah's cheeks were hot with embarrassment; her soul was wretched with shame. But the blood that dripped out—oh, God, oh, it smelled *so damn good!*

There was a small struggle. The woman shifted on the table, moaning dryly.

"Do I hit her again?" Leo asked Miri.

"Please," Sarah gasped.

Leo hesitated, looking at Miriam.

The woman stirred again.

"Leo, *please!*"

Miriam stayed Leo's hand.

The victim's eyes opened. Sarah glared at Miriam. "Miri!"

"Leo, don't you move!"

The woman said, "What the heck?" She started to sit up. Sarah pushed her down, nicked again with the fleam and locked her lips to the dirt-ringed neck. The woman said, "The *fuck!*" Then she rattled along in her own language, obviously cursing. She squirmed; she tried to free her hands.

Sarah forced every iota of air out of her lungs. She distended her belly. She locked her lips tight to the neck, making the best seal she could. The woman flounced and struggled, but Miri held her head and made Leo lie across her midriff. The woman made rasping sounds—desperate attempts to scream.

Sarah sucked. The artery wall resisted, then gave way, spurting a flood of fresh, hot, salty blood straight down Sarah's gullet. The effect was a thousand times more powerful than a hit of the purest heroin ever made. From her toes to her head, her skin rippled and shivered. An orgasm came, spreading through her until her whole body was a single, pulsing, vibrating dynamo of sexual genius. Somewhere far away, she could hear Leo laughing and crying at the same time, and Miri's voice comforting her, saying soft things that she did not mean.

She sucked and she sucked, and the old voice went down to a growling babble. She sucked and the old heart came to a stop. And then the body went slack, and the flow went down.

Sarah drew back. Blood, very black, dribbled onto the table.

Leo was standing at the far end of the room, her eyes round, her face covered with tears. Miriam said, "Come here to me."

Leo shook her head.

Miri went to her and drew her by the wrist. *"Watch!"*

With one huge drag, Miriam did what no human being could ever do, no matter how evolved their technique. She emptied the woman of every trace of fluid that was in her. The skin sank back against the skull, drew tight, crackling as it turned to dry parchment. The eyeballs withered, the clothes went slack around the body. And then Miriam came up, the corpse still popping and crackling as cartilage snapped and muscles twisted themselves into hard, narrow ropes.

Leo put her hands to her cheeks and screamed. Her eyes wild, she turned to run out the door.

Miriam was on her in an instant. She grabbed her collar, gave her a slap that snapped her head aside. "Shut up! You *watch!*" She glared toward Sarah, who was feeling the gorgeous postprandial levitation that came when you fed really well. Moral guilt had its limits. Now all was right with the world. Like an addict who has ridden the horse and lost, she was content with herself, made so by the charm of the drug that had seduced her.

"Sarah," Miri said, "take Leo down and show her how to do a proper burn. And I expect to see no ash, do you hear me?"

"Yes, Miri."

"I'm sorry, Miri!" Leo babbled, rubbing her cheek. "I panicked." Leo went to the remnant, touched the skin that tented the face. "This is incredible!"

"It's a small penalty to pay for eternal life, my dear. An occasional hobo goes to the Big Rock Candy Mountain."

Leo frowned. "The what?"

"Gets released from the toils of a miserable life," Sarah explained. Slang tended to enter Miriam's vocabulary with a fifty to hundred year lag time.

Leo would not touch the remnant, so Sarah threw it over her shoulder and took it down. In the basement, Sarah said, "Having fun?"

"That's not appropriate," Leo said officiously. "A woman had to give her life."

"For me? Maybe I ought to kill myself."

"No, you have a right! Nature made you this way."

"Miriam Blaylock made me this way. And she's going to do it to you, too."

"Miriam Blaylock *is* nature. And if she bloods me, it's going to be the biggest privilege of my life."

They burned the remnant in a fire kept blue by Sarah's careful attendance at the controls.

As they were starting to ascend the stairs, Miriam said, "Come into the infirmary, please."

Sarah turned, surprised to find her down here. She was even more shocked when she saw that she was naked and all trace of makeup was removed. Her hair was coming back, a blond fuzz on her otherwise bald head.

Leo gasped. Sarah took her hand. "Don't be afraid," she said.

"But she's—"

"She's not a human being, Leo." Sarah was stirred by the long, lean body, the deep, dark eyes. This was a being she loved, who had covered her with wild kisses, who had expressed every shading of passion upon her quivering, delighted body. No matter how much Sarah hated Miriam, she also loved her, and loved the fact that Miriam took pleasure in her. "You're my beautiful one," she would say, and kiss every part of her body, her lips, her eyes, her moist pudenda. "You pretty little angel, you dear, soft baby."

Leo made a terrified sound in her throat as the tall creature with the bright red eyes and wire-thin lips strode into the light. She took Leo's hand. Sarah knew that Leo was now trapped. Nothing the girl could do—no matter how hard she struggled and fought—would release her from that seemingly gentle grasp.

Sarah was horrified at what was happening—at how swiftly Miriam was acting, so that the girl had no time to consider her situation. But she was also fascinated because she had wondered about the scientific issues involved in the transfer process. She welcomed a chance to observe it clinically.

Miriam drew Leo into the infirmary, a superbly equipped laboratory designed by Sarah, who followed obediently along.

She was already being buoyed by the effects of her feeding. In an hour or so, the Sleep would come and she would take to bed, and Miri, as was traditional between them, would sing her a lullaby. The Sleep would take her, and as it did, she would deliver herself body and soul into the protective custody of her beloved and despised mistress.

Miriam had tamed Sarah, after a fashion. But so also, Sarah had tamed Miriam . . . after a fashion. Thus does a love affair between species proceed—wild creatures finding what is universal between them, sensual delight and what abides in the heart, that love can cross any boundary and flourish anywhere.

The blooding instrument—a black hose fitted with a small hand pump and two large silver needles—was already dangling from Miriam's arm, one enormous needle a gray shadow in the flesh above the crook of her elbow.

Leo was staring at it, her eyes practically popping out of her head. Stumbling, she followed Miriam into the small hospital room. Miriam patted the examination table. Leo sat.

"Get the ice packs," Miriam said.

"What ice packs?" Leo asked.

"We use ice packs in the procedure," Miriam said. "Now strip." She clapped her hands. "Chop chop!"

Leo threw off her clothes. She lay down on the table, arms rigidly at her sides. Miriam looked at Leo's arms. "Set it," she said to Sarah.

"I don't like needles," Leo said as Sarah stroked up a vein. How Sarah hated her now, the poor, scared little cow with her drippy nose and her big brown eyes.

Now this kid would get what she wanted. Later today, Sarah would take her to the attic, let her listen to the rustling, introduce her to who lay there.

"You will now be delivered of the blood of your eternal Keepers," she said. "You will become part of me and I of you. Do you understand this?"

Leo said in a tiny voice, "I think so."

"You will be given eternal life."

"Miri!"

Miriam cast a glance at Sarah so terrible that her jaw snapped shut.

"Eternal life! But you will be bonded to me by an unbreakable bond. You will be expected to serve me in every way, without question. There will never be an end to it. Do you understand this?"

Leo turned her tear-streaked face to Sarah, and Sarah saw there a call for rescue from the very depth of this human creature. A soul was being lost, and it knew that it was being lost. But she said nothing.

"Set the needle."

"N-no," Sarah said. "No!"

"You do it!"

"Leo, this is wrong!"

She tried to meet Leo's eyes, but Leo would not look at her. Miriam grabbed the needle and jammed it into Leo's arm. Leo cried out.

Sarah reset it properly, secured it with tape.

"You are free to go, Leo," Miriam said. "I haven't started yet."

"It hurts!"

"Again I say to you, you are free to go."

Leo began to cry.

Sarah was awed at what she was seeing. She had a sudden, electrifying insight into who the Keepers were, into what Miriam was. They were indeed a force of nature, and she thought that they might be killed, but they would never die. No matter who hunted the Keepers, the Keepers would always in one way or another wander the world, seeking the ruin of souls.

Miriam grasped the pump in her long, narrow fingers and crushed the bulb smartly. Leo flounced on the table, giving a loud cry. Again, Miriam pumped, and again. Leo's upper arm turned fiery red. She began to sweat.

"How does it feel?" Sarah asked.

"My arm's on fire!"

"Do you feel faint? Woozy?"

"I see an ancient city!"

Hallucinations. Interesting.

Sarah touched the skin of the neck. Pulse very rapid. She laid her hand on the forehead. Hot, dry. She got the ice packs and laid them along Leo's sides. Leo began to shiver.

Miriam pumped, waited, pumped again. Leo's eyes fluttered back into her head.

"Slow down," Sarah said, "she's seizing."

Leo's bowels let go.

"Clean it up," Miriam snapped, and Sarah went to work with towel, sponges, and bedpan.

Leo cried and moaned. Sarah had to hold her arms so that she wouldn't tear the needle out. She arched her back and writhed; she shook her head from side to side.

Sweat, blushed pink, began to bead on her upper lip and forehead. Her epidermal capillaries were hemorrhaging.

Sarah took her blood pressure—270 over 140. Pulse rate 132. Temperature 106 degrees. She had perhaps half an hour to live, fifteen minutes before brain damage or a stroke. Sarah got more ice, put a pack behind her neck, another between her legs. The temperature dropped to 104 degrees.

Over ten slow minutes, Miriam pumped five more times. Leo came to and looked from one of them to the other out of agonized eyes.

"How do you feel?" Sarah asked.

"Water, please . . ."

Miriam withdrew the needles. Sarah took alcohol and iodine and cleaned Leo's wound and stopped the leakage of blood with a small pressure bandage. She didn't need to do anything for Miriam. Her wound healed itself inside of a minute.

"How did you know when to stop?"

"Her skin told me."

Miriam's people could diagnose practically anything in human beings by merely observing their skin tone. It was quite remarkable.

"What would have happened if you'd kept on?"

"I would have wasted blood. She would have died."

Miriam took Leo in her arms and went out with her, saying nothing to Sarah. She was more alien right now, less human, than Sarah had ever seen her. She realized that Miriam's whole personality was a sort of act. Seeing her like this, you realized that she was light years away from being human.

Sarah followed Miriam up to their bedroom. Miriam laid the girl, whose whole body was now flaming red, in the center of their bed. The Sleep was coming heavily onto Sarah, and she longed to lie down, too. But Miriam went to bed with Leo, enclosing her in her arms.

Sarah was left to the daybed. As she drifted into the dreams she would share with the victim whose life flowed yet within her, she heard her Miri singing to her new captive,

"Sleep my child and peace attend thee,
All through the night.
Guardian angels God will send thee,
All through the night. . . ."

She cried herself to sleep, Sarah did, but when sleep came, it took her into a golden ship that sailed a windswept sea. In the purest blue sky she had ever seen, white seagulls wheeled and dove and cried. They came down and flew among the sails of her ship, and called to her with their harsh, haunting voices.

She knew that they were the birds of God's careless and unquenchable love, calling to her and to Leo, and even to Miri, as indeed they do to all.

FOURTEEN

The Veils

Sarah awoke when the afternoon sun, glaring in the tall bedroom windows, turned the inside of her eyelids bloodred. Leo was there instantly, kissing her, embracing her. "Oh, Sarah, I'm so glad you're awake! I've been missing you like crazy!"

"You—you're not sick?" She should have been hanging between life and death.

"Oh, I was," Leo said. "I was *so sick.*"

"You slept for two days," Miriam said. She came down out of the light like a descending angel. She was dressed in bright white silk. Her hair was nearly grown back, and flowing golden blond across her milky shoulders. She was perfectly made up, looking absolutely ravishing. Her eyes were their usual ashy gray.

"We're going to play this afternoon," she said. "You'll want to call your musical friends."

Sarah took Leo's hands. "Leonore, do you know what's happened to you? Do you understand anything about this at all?"

"Look at my skin!"

How well Sarah remembered that miraculous discovery. A woman loves a pure skin, more than most realize—until she suddenly has something she never dreamed possible.

Leo shook her head. "And my hair!"

It was as pretty as Sarah's, almost as pretty as Miri's.

Perfection had transformed a pretty girl into a shockingly beautiful one. Leo smiled down at her. "I threw up all yesterday, but I'm better."

"I used up all the antinausea stuff," Miriam said. "She took to it more easily than you."

"But now I feel—" Leo shivered her shoulders. "I feel *fabulous!*"

As Sarah went about the duties of her life, showering and washing her hair, Leo chattered away about herself. When should she feed? Should they hunt together or was that wise? On and on. It was utterly grotesque.

"Leo," she finally said when she was dressing, "I usually take this time in my office."

It was a lie and Leo knew it. But she understood and withdrew at last.

When Sarah arrived downstairs, Leo was sitting crosslegged on the floor of the library looking at Keeper books she'd never been allowed to so much as touch. She tossed one of the ancient volumes aside and rushed up to kiss Sarah, chattering about yet more sensations and symptoms.

Sarah picked up the book and replaced it in its box. "These are very fragile," she said.

"Yeah, they're in Egyptian! Are they from Egypt?"

"They aren't in Egyptian. They're in the Keeper language, which is called Prime. The book you were paging through is thirty thousand years old. It is made entirely of human parchment and is also the finest illustrated medical text on the planet. If it had a value, Leo, it would be, very simply, the most costly artifact in the world."

Leo had the hangdog expression of a surprised hound. But then she tossed her coltish hair and asked, "What are the first signs of hunger? I don't actually know."

"You feel cold. Your skin starts to get cold. Then you become a bit less energetic. That's how it begins."

"Should I get my own fleam?"

She sounded very like a bride planning her trousseau, or a pregnant girl deciding the furnishings of the nursery.

"Use a fishhook."

"A *fishhook!*"

"A shark hook works quite well. I used one for years. The fleam be-longed to my predecessor. Miriam just gave it to me recently."

"Your . . . what do you mean, 'predecessor'?"

"Oh, didn't Miri tell you? We last about two hundred years. Unless there's an accident, of course."

"We die?"

"Oh, no. That we cannot do. We end up in the attic." She smiled. "Like cast-off overcoats."

Leo glanced toward the stairs.

"Miri didn't tell you?"

"No, she didn't."

She took Leo's hand and led her upstairs.

Miriam was at the head of the stairs. "I thought you were going to make an arrangement, Sarah."

"An arrangement?"

"Flowers. For our guests."

"I—yes. I was."

"Miri, do we die?"

"You do not die."

"But she said—"

"The contents of the attic are my affair. As are those

books. You girls do not *ever* touch Keeper things without my permission!"

"I thought—"

"You thought you had the run of my house just because you're blooded? You go downstairs and get things ready, both of you. And, Sarah?"

"Yes, Miri?"

"Be careful. Be very careful."

As Sarah was arranging the flowers that would stand on the piano during the musicale, Leo chattered away about the kinds of people she preferred to "do."

Finally Sarah snarled at her, "You've become a serial killer."

Leo went silent.

Sarah turned on her. "You have! During the hundreds of years you now have before you, you'll take thousands of lives! Men, women, children, every one of them wanting life and deserving life, and you will take their lives—steal their lives—because you're a greedy, self-involved little monster!"

"Sa-*rah!*"

"You're not worth the warts on one of their fingers! Not one! But in your arrogance, you think you've gained some natural right to kill them! Miriam has such a right—maybe! But you certainly do not."

"Then neither do you!"

"I had this done to me. I didn't ask for it. You did, Leo. You knew what it meant and yet you asked for it!"

Miriam strode in. "Miri," Leo wailed, "she's—"

"I can hear," Miriam growled. She looked from one to the other. "Two canaries in the same cage," she said. "You'd better learn to get along, because you won't be let out. I'm in trouble and I need you, both of you. Hell, I need ten of you! Fifty!

But I do *not* need any bickering or moralizing or bitching. You'll work together as a team or suffer the consequences." She glared at Sarah. "Severe consequences." She looked at the flowers. "That's quite nice," she said. Then, to Leo, "You are not her equal. You will learn from her and take her advice and, in my absence, her orders. Is that understood?"

"Yes, Miri."

"Miriam to you, child." She went out.

"Wow," Leo said.

As the sun slanted across the floor, Sarah got out their violas da gamba, and she and Leo set the chairs. Among musical circles in New York, Miriam's talent was well known. Far more had heard descriptions of her playing than had actually been privileged to listen, however, for she never gave public concerts. In fact, she didn't perform at all. This would be, as far as she was concerned, merely an hour's casual entertainment.

Leo greeted the guests, watching to see if they noticed how beautiful she looked. They noticed, all right—especially the women, who were always more aware than men of the details of beauty, the grace of the hands, the taper of the neck.

Sarah and Miriam had been working together on LeSieur de Malchy's splendid "Fifth Suite for Two Violas da Gamba" for a few weeks before Miriam went to Thailand.

Maria Sturdevandt came and said hello to Sarah and Miriam. She would sing Madama Butterfly tonight at the Metropolitan Opera. With her was her companion Charlie Gorman. Bootsie Ferguson, the wife of Henry Ferguson, CEO of Goldman, Sachs was there.

Miriam could play most instruments simply by picking them up, but she had practiced on the piano, the viola, and the flute, and on these she was masterful. Sarah had not been much involved in music before meeting her. But her own viola was now one of the loves of her life.

As she played, she gazed from one member of their small audience to another. She watched Falstaff Rosenkrantz, editor of *Vanity Fair*, searching his pockets for what turned out to be a Chap Stick. His powerful shoulders and narrow waist suggested good-sucking veins. She imagined how he would taste, all salt and wine.

As she watched Miriam's long, splendid hands manipulate her bow with the lightness of a breeze, she drew her own notes as best she could.

Sarah felt rotten about feeding and about Leo, and Miriam was distracted by her crisis, but the listeners, by their expressions, obviously felt as if they were in the presence not simply of musicians, but of masters of music. The suite proceeded from its dancing allemande to the saraband and finally the subtle, generous minuet. They sat side by side, Miriam in a summer dress of the lightest blue silk, Sarah in jeans and a black turtleneck.

Standing open on the piano was a bottle of claret, a Latour nearly a hundred years old. There were glasses about and another, identical bottle beside it. A half-filled crystal carafe, shaped for use in ice, stood on an extraordinary little table. This wine was a white, but its color—a pale, rich gold—suggested that it, also, must be very fine. In fact, it was a freezing cold, exquisitely sweet Yquem, just now, at forty years, coming into its maturity. When guests sipped these wines, they would close their eyes.

The furnishings, also, were extraordinary. The chairs upon which the guests sat were Directoire pieces, some of them. It is to be remembered, though, that the designs of that period were inspired by classical models, and some of the other chairs were originals, carried from hearth to hearth in Miriam's baggage for millennia. Their wood, having been lovingly cared for by Sarah and all of her predecessors, was as rich as when it had been cut in the now-vanished forests of Greece and Italy and the Levant.

Miriam remembered when this piece had first been played. It fit the moment so well because it had been composed out of pain, and this was a time of pain.

LeSieur de Malchy had fallen in love with Lamia, and Lamia had amused herself by leading him on, letting him kiss her alabaster limbs and gaze into her proud and laughing eyes. She had drawn him into deep, true love, as she was so very expert at doing, with the intention of then abandoning him to his music. She didn't want a man. She wanted a composition.

Out of his anguish had emerged music fit to satisfy the ancient heart of the Keeper. Among humans, it had never been all that popular, but when Keepers joined to play, LeSieur was inevitably among the choices.

The instruments that Miriam and Sarah used had belonged to LeSieur, made by Barak Norman, of London, for him.

Miriam, as she played, well recalled LeSieur and her mother playing the piece together.

The room had been small and close with candle smoke, but finished in gold, with scenes of forest walks painted on its walls. The music, Miriam remembered, had captured, as if in a living amber, the passion that this man felt for the woman who sat with him in her tall wig and splendid white gown.

Only Miriam had been their audience, as she was audience to every moment of her adored mother's life. As Sarah served her now, she had once served Lamia.

The music came to its end. There was no applause. They had learned long ago, her friends, that such displays were not wanted. She poured herself some wine. It was the least refined alcohol she could tolerate, wine. But the soul of the grape, captured, gave her spirit enough pleasure that she had collected wine through the years. She'd drunk Falernian in Rome, for she had been intimately involved with the lives of the old emperors.

Most of these men had not died by assassination as history recorded, but as vestal sacrifices. Rome had been secretly ruled by a concealed religion. The emperors were only seasonal kings, doomed to serve the state until the priestesses of Vesta decreed that it was time for them to die. They learned of this little condition only after they achieved the purple. It was no wonder that so many of them went mad.

Some had been throat-slit or smothered or strangled, but others had been delivered to certain dark villas, rich, strange places whose graceful inhabitants spoke a tongue like thunder. The Vestas were a conclave of Keepers.

She put the glass down and walked out, never thinking to excuse herself from her guests. This house was run according to very ancient principles. It was an extremely exclusive place but, like an ancient palace, wide open to all who had the right to enter.

Whatever happened in here, they were free to come and watch . . . or at least, so it was meant to appear. They did so, full of nervous excitement over their attendance at what they perceived as extremely private moments—Miriam at her toilette, Miriam making love.

This was the way the aristocrats of history had conducted their lives. Their privacy consisted of being surrounded by their people, and Miriam could be comfortable no other way.

Or so it seemed. Miriam's ancient life was, of course, far more complex than it appeared. There were secrets within secrets. For, as Sarah and now Leo knew, this splendid house was also a place of murder, where innocent blood was guzzled like cheap champagne.

Paul was pushing a cockroach to the edge of the shower stall with his toe when he noticed something very odd about his feet.

He squatted, then got out of the shower and looked more closely.

It was the vampire blood that had made his skin so pale and smooth. Back in the ossuary, his shoes had been flooded with it. He rubbed his shoulder. Had it also sped his healing even more than usual?

He went back into the shower and washed and washed, using the cheap sliver of soap that had come with this cheap sliver of a hotel room. He stood in the small oblivion of the drumming water, watching the suds go down the drain.

It felt as if he were washing off a whole lot of his past in this lousy shower. Down the drain went his loyalty to his agency. Down the drain went his expectations about his own future: the successful end to his career, the honored retirement. He'd been a priest of death, and down the drain went this celibate life. Freud had said that all men want the same things: honor, riches, power, fame, and the love of women.

Well, he'd lost it all, hadn't he?—except maybe the love of a woman. But what woman would want a burned-out guy who couldn't even tell her what his life had been?

Becky, damnit, was the only woman he really wanted to talk to, and he hadn't realized it until too late. Probably all she'd ever felt for him anyway was a little compassion, maybe. Women didn't fall in love with him. They sensed all the damn violence, was his theory. He scared them. Or maybe it was all the traveling, the lack of time in one place.

He'd taken care of sex almost clinically, using whores like toys . . . or machines. Soon he wouldn't even be able to afford to do that.

Lying on the bed in his tiny room, he concentrated on his immediate course of action. He had eight grand. That would last a couple of months. But he didn't intend to spend anything like that much time here.

He lay paging through his well-thumbed copy of *New York by Night*, looking for the names of clubs, then calling information and asking for the numbers. Things in the world of Goths and Vampyres changed fast, and what had been au courant six months ago was way past its time now. None of the clubs mentioned had numbers. Probably they were all closed or transformed into more trendy incarnations.

So maybe the thing to do was to go downtown and just walk the streets. He'd pass the locations of the old clubs. Who knew what he'd find.

On the other hand, maybe this approach was total bullshit, just an excuse for a bar crawl. In his heart of hearts, what he wanted to do was to get seriously fucked up, then find some whore to suck him off. That would put a decent end, at least, to a real bad few of days. He'd arrived in the Big Apple almost hallucinatory with lack of sleep and jet lag and the spiritual exhaustion that comes after you've been doing a lot of killing. And he'd arrived on the run. He'd holed up here, phoning a sandwich shop for food and newspapers. The room had no TV, so he'd slept a lot. At least one thing: the shoulder was doing lots better. Still hurt, but hell, by all rights he probably ought to still be in the hospital.

He had to get a gun. If he was going to blow the shit out of vampires, he sure as hell was going to need one. Too bad he couldn't get hold of one of those fancy French jobs. Now, that had been a weapon. Hadn't that baby *worked!* He'd settle for a good old .357, though. It had done good service for him in Asia, and it'd work fine here. You got close, aimed at the head. It was effective. Blew their noggins into meat and ketchup.

Problem was, where did you get a gun in Nueva York without triggering some stoolie network? Guys in the illegal gun trade made money two ways—off their customers and off the cops they tipped. Of course, they wouldn't tip on a real customer, but some jerk coming off the street, he'd get fingered for sure. His full description would arrive at the nearest precinct in ten minutes tops. Gun raps were a good collar in this town. Looked nice in a cop's paper.

First things first. Locate the vampires. If the club scene didn't do it, then go to public records, work the pattern-of-disappearances angle. What worried him about that was that a whole lot of people evaporated in this town. It wasn't like Beijing or Singapore or Tokyo, where a disappearance was news. Hell, most missing persons didn't even make the back pages in this wild old burg. So okay, he'd work the club angle to death.

They were on their way to the club, the Bentley rolling down Fifty-seventh Street toward Fifth Avenue. Miriam and Sarah sat side by side. Leo was on one of the tiny jump seats facing them.

Miriam said, "A man may show up tonight asking after Ellen Wunderling. It's about time for him to find us. I want to be informed the moment it happens."

The bottom dropped out of Sarah's gut.

Leo asked, "Who's Ellen Wunderling?"

"One of our dear princess's little follies," Miriam said, playfully kissing Sarah's cheek.

Ellen Wunderling had been Sarah's worst mistake until the Paris emergency debacle. But why would anybody still be investigating that case? The police had closed it.

Sarah wasn't like a Keeper. She would not be able to escape from prison. If she went, she would die there, horribly, of hunger. What would happen to somebody like her, buried in a prison graveyard?

"What man?" she asked carefully, worried that Miriam would say no more. Since Paris, Miriam had obviously lost a great deal of trust in her.

Miriam reached up and opened the car's sunroof. They were now speeding down Fifth Avenue. The spires of St. Patrick's Cathedral swept past one side of the Bentley, Rockefeller Center the other.

Sarah curled up to her. "Miri, I'm so sorry I did her!"

"Don't start apologizing again. We're past that. Anyway, it turns out to be useful." She stroked Sarah's head. "Ellen is our little tar baby." She smiled softly.

Sarah didn't quite understand. She knew, however, that questioning would do no good.

"I hope Rudi's there early," Leo said. "I want to do all kinds of stuff tonight! I want to see how it feels now. Does it feel different, Sarah?"

"No crashes, no hangovers," Sarah said. She gave her a false smile. "But the only drug that really matters—" She glanced toward the intercom button. It was off. "—is blood."

"You're hungry, dear," Miriam said to Leo. "You just don't realize it. We'll need to find you a victim."

Leo kissed Miriam's neck. "Give me more of your blood. I want to be more like you."

"You're as much like me as you'll ever be."

"You're a fool, Leo," Sarah said.

Miriam gave her a shy sort of a smile. "Twenty years of love, and that's all the loyalty you can offer."

Sarah smiled right back. " 'Into whatever houses I enter, I will go into them for the benefit of the sick, and will abstain from every voluntary act of mischief and corruption.' I violate my Hippocratic Oath by the very nature of my life."

"Take off your clothes," Miriam said.

"What?"

They were crossing Thirty-fourth Street. The Empire State Building swept past above, visible through the open sunroof.

"Do it."

Sarah didn't want to, not here, not in front of Leo.

Leo said, "I'll help you."

"Sarah." There was a clear warning in the tone.

A few contortions between her and Leo, and Sarah was naked. She felt herself blushing. She covered her breasts with her arm.

Pushing her arm aside, Miriam took one of her nipples between her fingers and pinched it, watching Sarah's face. At first, Sarah tried to conceal her agony, but she finally cried out; she couldn't help it, the pain was so intense.

Leo watched, her eyes going nervously from Sarah's contorted face to Miriam's impassive one. "What's going on? Why are you hurting her?"

Miriam turned on the intercom. "Luis, take us on a tour. Fourteenth, down Broadway, give us half an hour." She released Sarah, who clutched her agonized breast.

Miriam took Sarah's face in her hands, gazed into her eyes. After a moment, she kissed her, pressing her tongue against Sarah's lips until she opened her mouth.

No matter how often they kissed, Sarah was always shocked by the sensation of those narrow teeth and that rough tiger's tongue. Miriam's mouth had a faint, meaty sourness that was at once sickening and delicious. Then Miriam broke away, spread Sarah's legs, and slipped to the floor.

Sarah could not have been more amazed. She looked at Leo and shook her head, to communicate her total confusion.

While Manhattan slid by above them and the Broadway crowds shuffled up and down outside the tinted windows, Miriam buried her face in Sarah's lap.

Never had Miriam taken such a posture. This was Sarah's place with Miri, not the other way around.

But—oh, my. Oh, *my!* Sarah thrust herself at Miri's face, her hands moving to guide her head, to press her mouth more tightly against her.

Miriam knew how to restore the bondage of a rebellious slave; she had done it thousands of times over the eons. She injected her tongue deep into Sarah's vagina. The powerful organ stretched the membranes as tight as drumskins. When there was resistance, Miriam pressed harder. Sarah writhed. Miriam moved her head back and forth, but slowly, pumping carefully. Sarah held Miriam's temples with shaking hands and glared down at her, crying and laughing, then threw her head back and grimaced through a fusillade of explosive climaxes. When they finally stopped, Miriam slowly withdrew, dragging her roughness along Sarah's clitoris. When she raised herself, Sarah embraced her, clung to her, kissing her face and neck, then knelt on the floor of the limousine and kissed her hands and feet.

THE LAST VAMPIRE 259

Sarah lay at Miriam's feet, her head in her lap, weeping softly. *And so,* Miriam thought, *the little creature has come back to me.*

"Hey," Luis said over the intercom, "you're drivin' me crazy up here. I'm gonna come in my pants."

"Leonore'll do you at the club," Miriam said to him as she lit a cigarette. She drew Sarah up beside her, took her head down to her shoulder. "You're my girl?" she said, her tone kindly.

"Yes."

She looked at Leo. "Hot?"

"Oh, my."

"Take it out on Luis."

"I don't want to make love to Luis."

"I'll expect him to report that you were sensational. Incidentally, you're going to feed tonight, so what do you want?"

Leo barely whispered the words. "A man like my father."

"Ah. And your father was?"

"Powerful."

Miriam smiled slightly, parting her lips just a little.

"When you do that," Sarah said, "you look ten and ten thousand at the same time."

Miriam burst out laughing. "It's one of my *best* smiles!" The laughter was brittle and harsh, and Sarah was glad when it ended. "Stand up," Miriam said suddenly. They had never closed the sunroof.

"I'm naked!"

Miriam gave her a familiar look out of the corner of her eye. Immed-iately, Sarah rose to her feet.

Miriam thought, *Good. She does not think, she obeys. She's come back at last.*

The slipstream roared in her face, sending her hair flying

back. They were going down Houston Street toward the
Hudson. Crowds on both sides of the street started cheering
and applauding.

Sarah threw back her head and raised her arms high and
screamed and screamed and screamed.

New York wasn't exactly the most dangerous city in the
world, but the screams that Paul was hearing made him
think that a woman was being killed. He looked up West
Broadway toward the sound—and saw a black Bentley pass,
going west on Houston Street. Some idiot girl was standing
up in the open sunroof bellowing her head off, that was all.

She'd scared the hell out of him, damned rich bitch.
He'd've liked to have given her a piece of his mind. Probably
some damn tripper, that was why the screams were so bloodcurdling.

New York was one giant drugstore. Everybody was young,
everybody had money, and every damn thing was definitely
for sale. Ecstasy, crystal meth, crack, coke, hash, grass, horse,
even old-fashioned shit like his beloved opium. God knew,
you could probably buy laudanum somewhere. You could get
ten percent absinthe, for sure, *hecho en Mexico*. He liked getting drunk on absinthe. There was a poet in him, and the
wormwood brought him out. Last time he'd done a bottle of
good absinthe, it had been on the terrace at Las Brisas in
Acapulco, one of the most beautiful places in the world to do
serious drinking. The mountains, the city lights below, the sun
setting over the Pacific—the view was unequalled. He'd gone
back to his room afterward and written a thirty-page epic
poem about the death of Nebuchadnezzar. Next morning,
he'd had to go on the Internet to find out who the hell
Nebuchanezzar was. Some ancient king.

A couple came toward him, dressed all in black. The girl's long, loose dress suggested possible gothic overtones. "Excuse me, I'm looking for a club called Shadowcat. Is there a place called Shadowcat around here?"

The couple stopped. The girl was a heartbreaker, round face, merry brown eyes, and one of those smiles that says *I know what you want.* She had a cute rack, too, a couple of sweet little apples. She said, "The things you're staring at are called breasts," and the two of them walked off laughing.

Was he losing his touch, or what? Then he saw a bookstore. Maybe they had some kind of SoHo guide that was more up-to-date than his copy of *New York by Night.*

He loved to read, and he hadn't been in an English language bookstore this big in years. Hundreds of titles, everything very colorful and appealing, all sorts of stuff. A dozen SoHo guidebooks, all brand-new. He opened one, *SoHo Unbound.* Under the heading, "Deep Dark Deadly," was a list of spots with appropriately strange names—The Marrow Room, Bottomley Topps, Dragged to Death.

He sure as hell felt dragged to death, but he decided to try The Marrow Room instead, because it had a more vampirish sort of a ring to it. Actually, none of them sounded much like they had anything to do with gothic play-acting. But one could always hope.

The Marrow Room turned out to be a lavish nightclub full of what looked to him like little kids. There was music blasting, strobes and lasers flashing. Wonderful little bubblegum girls kept dancing up to him and waving their mermaid locks. He smiled and nodded, forcing himself not to so much as glance down. It wouldn't have mattered, anyway—the whole damn place was full of jailbait.

He went to the bar. "Stoli on the rocks," he said.

The bartender looked at him. "Parents room in the back, mister. But it's BYOB."

He didn't really know what the hell kind of place he'd blundered into, but there was no damn point in finding out, that was for sure. When had rock clubs for children come in?

He left. A clutch of what looked like eight-year-olds clustered under a nearby stoop smoking and muttering together. This was different from Asia? How?

Then he saw a storefront with a black cat discreetly painted in one corner as the only indication that it wasn't altogether abandoned. A black cat was promising. He pushed the door open.

There were skulls. His stomach gave a turn. He never wanted to be in an ossuary again. But the skulls contained candles. There was music, very bad rock of some indeterminate kind, and here and there a few people in vaguely gothic costume sitting at tables. A couple danced mechanically under purple light on a small dance floor. The place smelled like cigarettes and sour beer. The bar had a rack on it with bags of potato chips.

"Stoli on the rocks," Paul said.

The bartender, a listless woman of about sixty wearing a black dress, poured something clear out of a bottle with no label into a glass with a whole lot of ice. She brought it over. Her face was painted white, her lips dark, dark red. She was wearing plastic teeth.

"I'm looking for Ellen Wunderling," Paul said.

"You a cop?"

"Not."

"Wanna bj? Fifteen bucks."

Paul was beginning to think of a whole lot of reasons to throw up. He was homesick. He wanted to go to one of those

Bangkok barbershops where a cloud of comely maidens massaged you, cut your hair, did your nails, *and* gave you a blow job for fifteen damn bucks.

"I'm doing research on Ellen Wunderling."

"Never came in here." She turned away, busied herself pulling a beer—for whom it wasn't clear.

"Any other place I could go? I'm new here, and I don't know the scene."

"Well, the first thing to do is not dress like a bus driver trying to pawn himself off as another bus driver. That horror show isn't gonna get you in anywhere."

"These are new clothes."

"Go over to Shambles on Prince Street. You can get all kinds of stuff there. Get a hat, some blacks, some fingernails." She cackled. "Get pierced, officer, then we'll all just *love* you!"

"I'll pierce you," a voice called.

"Oh, shit," another voice murmured.

Paul went over to the table. He wasn't absolutely sure if he was talking to a man and a woman, two women, or two men. But he sat down anyway. He wasn't planning to get in bed with them. Or get pierced. "I'm looking for Ellen Wunderling," he said.

"Mistah Wunderling, he dead," the most likely to be male said. His mouth was full of potato chips.

"Miss Wunderling."

"You gotta go deep into the jungle, man—real deep. Try Hexion or the Hellfire Club—"

The girl—and Paul was now sure she was a for-real female and that underneath all that Vampirella makeup, she was your basic Queens chick—shook her head. "Hexion is a cannibal place," the girl said. "They serve brain soup."

"It's not *real* brains."

"What's the Hellfire Club?"

"A Catholic hangout. Run by former nuns."

"Any Ellen Wunderling connection?"

"He should go to the Veils."

"Him and the Count of Monte Cristo."

"What's the Veils?"

"Just the most exclusive club in Manhattan."

"The world."

"Same difference. But it was the last place Ellen was seen alive."

FIFTEEN

Scorpion Dance

Normally Leo was not much interested in the lesbian stuff that went on between Miriam and Sarah, but watching them this close, with Sarah going wild like that right in her face, was thrilling. When Miriam had kissed her before, she'd been polite about it and pretended, but it hadn't really been a turn-on. This had been the most amazingly intimate, beautiful thing.

She'd been a lonely little rich girl before she came to the Veils, her main claim to fame being that she was the daughter of, like, the second cousin once removed of General Patton. She had a co-op loft in SoHo in an artist building that was full of lawyers. She had a Maserati and a little pocket yacht called the *Y'All Come*, but Y'all generally didn't.

At, like, four o'clock one morning when she was so fabulously wasted, Miriam had said to her, "Come and follow me." They'd laughed. But she'd been totally in wonder because she was not exactly the kind of super cool person who'd be invited into Miriam's *house*.

Next thing she knew, she'd been given a little bedroom with cute curtains and a high brass bed. She'd had pretty much the run of this, like, amazing house. Gradually, she'd realized what Miriam did, Miriam and Sarah. They were lovers, but they also—well, wow, she was one of them now.

She squeezed her toes in her shoes. It was totally incredible to suddenly have this ultimate power. She'd never had any power at all. But now she sure did. She could point to somebody and say, "I want that one," and that person would undergo the most important experience of his or her life.

She wanted to feed for the first time. Even if she didn't have all that much hunger. She wanted this to happen.

It was unimaginable that she would live a really long time. But Miriam had stuff that was, like, Egyptian that was still in use. They had some three-thousand-year-old chairs in there. Leo had researched it. She'd priced it. A chair like the one Miriam had been sitting on during their viola drag would go on at Sotheby's easily for one million bucks.

She was going to see, like, the future. Spaceships. Aliens. Whatever the hell. Unless the world ended. Global warming, was that for real? Miriam said, "What happens happens." That was the way to approach it.

They were coming up to the club. Great. She was already high. She'd been awful sick at first, but since this morning, she'd started to feel better and better and better, and now she felt completely damn wonderful. She didn't have any aches or pains at all.

The Bentley stopped. "Okay," Leo said, popping the door.

But Sarah grabbed Miriam's wrist. "Don't do this!"

"It's safe enough."

"You can't be certain."

Leo watched them bicker. They'd both been real scared lately. For sure; Leo was no fool—she could see it. This guy was bad news.

Miriam started to get out again.

"The front of the club's too public. Go in the back."

Miriam stroked Sarah's head. "There's going to be a confrontation, child. And the club is where it's going to happen."

Leo watched her go in. Then she helped Sarah dress. "That was so cool. I feel like I really know you now, Sarah." Nervously, she kissed her cheek. Maybe Sarah would do something sexy with her. She'd love to find out how it felt. Or Miriam—but that was too, too awesome.

"You know me," Sarah said. She followed Miriam, and Leo hurried after her. As usual, the club was dark, entirely invisible from the street. There was never a crowd outside the Veils. Ordinary people couldn't find the place. They weren't supposed to—only those who knew. And now Leo was, like, at the top of the food chain. She knew the truth behind all the rumors about Miriam Blaylock and Sarah Roberts. Sarah'd had a lover whom Miriam had killed, that was the main rumor. Another doctor. *That* they never talked about.

Miriam intended to capture the monster that was tracking her and feed off him, maybe even feed him to Leo; she wasn't sure. That depended on Leo. She was a tiresome little thing, truth to tell, but pleasant to have around and very eager.

Sarah, by contrast, was that most dangerous of slaves—one who did not understand the real meaning of servitude. An evil old Roman emperor, Septimius Severus, had once asked Lamia, "As all the world is my slave, why is it that only I am not free?"

Contained in those words was the ironic essence of the relationship between slaves and masters. Sarah was a poor slave because she thought of herself as a captive. Leo would be a good one because she would always look upon her accession to the blood as an achievement, not an imposition. This was why Miriam had been so careful to let her make a clear choice.

As Luis opened the door to the club, Miriam gave a tweak to the little rod in his pants. "Leonore," she said, "will go to you in the Pump Room."

"Yes, ma'am."

"I really gotta do him?" Leo whispered.

"Leo, I've serviced Luis dozens of times myself. You'll enjoy it."

"But I'm not a whore, Miriam. I'm . . . one of you."

"And we are objective about sex. It's a commodity just like booze and drugs. Sex is part of this business. Leave your emotions out of it, and your ego. Sex isn't the sort of Blue Broadway that the average Jill imagines, my dear."

Sarah laughed. Miriam wondered what she found funny, let it go. She strode across the glittering bar that was the club's first and most public room, calling out, "The front's to be open tonight, Bill."

"You want the sign up, ma'am?"

"I want the sign."

Sarah came hurrying along behind her. It was only ten, so there were few people here. "That's a bad idea," she hissed.

Miriam stopped, turned to her, put her hands on her shoulders. She had not understood the notion of the tar baby. "He's going to find us. But he must do it on his own, and the sooner the better."

She went to Bill, who was digging behind the bar for the small brass sign that said on it only, "Veils." This sign was placed on the door. Beyond that, they never went. "William, love, there's a good chance that a man will come in looking for Ellen Wunderling."

"That again! Don't they ever give up?"

"He's not a cop. I want him drugged a little. Offer him a drink. Lace it with—I don't know—something that'll relax him, make him a little hallucinatory, perhaps. Ask Rudi. But be careful with him."

"Oh, yeah, you bet."

"What's the crash so far?"

"Nobody upstairs. Dungeon's active, though. Seth's on the horse, and that bishop is back. Upstairs is gonna get jammed later. We got DJ Bones tonight."

"Make him a regular." His sound had incredible drive, but there was an elegance to it that fit this club very well.

"Twenty thousand dollars a night."

"Do it."

So that her early guests would see her and be able to tell the later ones that she was indeed here, she went to her customary table at the rear of the bar. Also, she was most interested in watching who might come in that door. He'd had three days to find the place, and he was far from stupid. He'd be here.

At first glance, this room appeared to be the extent of the Veils. But the point of the name of the club was that there were many levels, many layers to pass through. Beyond this room, there were eight others, but many more than eight different ways to sin.

Rudi came up to her. "I got great meth," he said, "plus them new Hi-Los and some dig hash. The hash was cheap."

"Push it hard," she said, looking past him. "I'm probably going to do a pipe later with a friend." She had a room in the basement that was locked using Keeper techniques. Not even Sarah could enter it unless invited. Sometimes, when the club was crowded and some target was available, Miriam might take it down there. Hidden in the room's floor was an entrance to a short tunnel that led into the boiler room of an adjacent building. The boiler there had a very good firebox, where Miriam could dispose of remnants quite easily. She would crush them to jagged bits, and they'd burn with a sparkle and a hiss when she threw them in. If the tunnel was ever found, it would appear to be nothing but an old, disused drainage line.

Miriam liked her room. She enjoyed the absolute privacy, the absolute secrecy. Being that it was entirely hidden, she had done some extremely wicked things there, so wicked that not even Sarah could know.

She intended to be very, very wicked to the hunter, more wicked than she'd been to any human being in hundreds of years. If he brought his little gang of helpers, so much the better. She would take them all, gorging herself in the fashion of old, tormenting them so terribly that the ones who had to watch would be sick all over themselves before their turns came.

"Cigarette me," she said to Leo, who was hovering.

The girl lit a cigarette, handed it to her. "Um, can I go down with Seth after I do Luis? They've got that Presbyterian bishop in the cage."

"Play your heart out, baby."

Sarah leaned close to her, whispered. "Thank you so much for what you did. I'm still singing inside."

Miriam smiled up at her, then watched her carefully as she disappeared into the back of the club. She was watching the way the shoulders were held, and the head. A slave's posture was very subtly different from that of a free man. Not that they were bowed, but there was in the way they moved the aimlessness of somebody who has not planned their own actions. Sarah walked with decision.

Miriam sighed. Sarah was perhaps too much in love to be a good slave. A lover sought constantly to remake the beloved in the image of her dream. A slave accepted mastery.

"Sarah," she said.

Sarah turned back. Miriam noticed that there were tears in the edges of her eyes. "Yes, Miri?"

"Turn on the veils, dear!"

"God, I forgot!"

Sarah turned the doorway on, causing the back of the club to disappear behind what appeared to be a dark mirror.

Doug Henning had designed the doorways for her, using his unique skills with light and mirrors. People seemed to disappear into a shimmering black haze when they left one room of the club, and come into view just as uncannily in the next. Thus the Veils.

She sat smoking and waiting. Miriam could wait well. She could wait for days, weeks.

She wondered if the hunter had as yet done any of his evil work in the United States. At the last conclave, held in January of 1900, there had been nine Keepers in America. Perhaps a few more had come over the past century, but probably not. They were not a migratory people. They had divided the corners of the world when they first arrived here, and nobody had wanted the Americas—there had been no indigenous population to work with there.

Two American Keepers had been killed in the airplane collision at Tenerife Airport in 1977. It was thus possible that there were only seven Americans left, including herself. It was also possible, if the murderers had already been here, that she was alone.

Even alone in all the world. That was possible, too.

She was contemplating this eerie thought when she heard a male voice, pleasantly strong, say, "I wonder if you've ever heard of Ellen Wunderling?"

He stood at the bar, a tall man with penetrating eyes, smiling at Bill with a detective's careful eyes.

Miriam's heart never beat with excitement. At least, it hadn't in so many years that she could not remember the last time. It was humming now.

"That's him," Leo hissed excitedly, "that's *him!*"

"Have you done Luis?"

"Miriam, do I *have* to?"

"Go! Now!"

The girl left. Miriam could now concentrate on the hunter. Look at those eyes, that face, the rippling power of the muscles beneath the cheap clothes. He was damned beautiful, this one. She felt herself getting wet for him . . . which was quite odd, but not entirely surprising. Humans could amuse her, but they did not cause spontaneous sexual arousal. Even as her sex came trembling to life, her mouth filled, for another part of her was threatened and preparing to fight.

Look at him there, in his rumpled clothes, with that fearsome face of his. Did anybody else find him so ferocious looking? They had no idea what he was. They had no idea where he had been or what he had done.

Look at the cast of his jaw, the line of his nose, his darkly glowing skin. And his eyes, look at the way they flicked here and there, like the eyes of a nervous fox.

Almost, it was not a human face. Almost, it was the face of some sort of exotic animal.

The outline of his suit told her that he was carrying, and the gun was big—a magnum, maybe worse.

She was well back in the shadows, but she wondered now if it had been wise to get even so close as this. If he recognized her—but that was absurd. He was, after all, only human. But look at his movements, the grace, the precision—*was* he only human?

Well, of course he was. She was losing her grip, actually panicking. And yet . . . it wasn't panic. It was desire, damnit, real, live desire. She wanted to be with this man.

What had she done to herself, playing around with human beings? This *was* perverse, to want to lie beneath a human male. She'd had a little of this with John Blaylock, which was why she'd switched back to females after he faltered. The females could give you real pleasure, and they were also better servants. Sarah, with all her conflicts, was fun. Interesting. Leo was going to be a hungry little animal. Miriam had all sorts of delicious wickedness planned for that one . . . beginning with Mr. Hunter, here, who was to be her first human meal. The warrior was going to die a lingering, humiliated death at the hands of a rather stupid girl. That would be most fitting.

She watched him sipping a vodka on the rocks. He'd ordered Stoli, then asked Bill a question that she had not heard. Bill had said very little to him, but she knew what it had been: "That's the owner over there. Ask her."

So he was fortifying himself. She watched him throw the drink back. He turned toward her.

This was the moment. If he recognized her, she was going to be blown apart.

He met her eyes and came toward her.

"You're a Stoli man," she said as he approached. "You ought to try Charodei."

Paul was so stunned when he looked at her that he almost lost his balance. In all his nearly fifty years on this earth, he had never beheld a woman who affected him more powerfully. She was a vision, just a damn vision. He loved noses, and she had one of those graceful, sweet noses with a tip that begged to be kissed. He loved complexion, and her skin was like frozen cream, a rich, deep white, perfectly smooth. He loved lips, and hers were exquisite, and they had in them the kind of small, amused smile that suggested a good personality. And eyes—her eyes were so calm, so gentle, so fresh-looking that he thought she couldn't be a day over twenty. She was wearing dark blue silk that looked as if it cost a few bucks. And she owned this fabulous little place. It was small, but it was class.

"Please," she said in a voice that would put the angels to shame, "have a seat." She glanced away from him. "Bring him a Charodei, Billy."

When she met his eyes, he found himself unable to look away. God, her eyes were frank. God, she was confident. He loved that in a woman.

"I want to see if you like it. It's my little test." Her smile—it was incredibly kind. That was the thing; this was a hell of a sexy woman, with those fabulous, beautifully proportioned breasts and that angelic face—but she was *kind*. You could see it in the gentle ease of the smile, hear it in the melody of the voice. In a place like this, he would have thought "pretty, but hard." He knew special when he saw special, and this lady was *real* special.

But Paul was also a very single-minded human being. He was here to kill vampires, not to fuck-talk some kid into bed. He said, "I'm doing research on Ellen Wunderling," but in his mind he was saying, "If I leave here without your phone number, I'll kill myself."

Her smile turned, he thought, a little sad. "I didn't catch your name, mister."

"Ward, Paul Ward. I'm a journalist."

"May I see your press credentials? I'm sorry to ask, but we're almost a tourist attraction because of that story. It's ironic, because we aren't even involved in the Goth scene."

"No, this looks like a very nice place. I wonder if you could tell me—"

"Sir, I really think you should ask at the precinct. Detective Lieutenant Timothy Kennerly. They questioned every employee in this place at least three times."

"Nothing ever came of it?"

"I saw her. We all did. She came in and got a Coke. She was sweaty; she'd been running or something. She seemed totally at ease. Not a problem. That was it."

Paul realized that he was going to have to leave in a minute, as soon as she demanded the press credentials again. He had no credentials. In his wallet were driver's licenses in five names from three different countries, and half a dozen credit cards, some of which might be good, all of which would flash red lights from Langley to Foggy Bottom the instant they were used.

Miriam saw that he was getting ready to stand up, and realized he was about to go. If he did that, she'd have to have him followed, but there was nobody here capable of doing it except Sarah. She did not want use Sarah that way; it was just too dangerous.

Ward himself was her key. He seemed so straight, though, that she didn't know quite how to seduce him, or even if it was possible. She would do it by acting the young, innocent girl. Given the panting-dog expression presently on his face, it was a type he liked.

"Listen," he said, "I'm working real hard on this. I think it's a huge thing. There's something incredible behind it— what happened to her. Almost certainly. And I'd like to enlist your help. What I want to know is, do I have any chance at all?"

"Try me."

He knocked back the drink. Miriam pointed to his glass, and Bill brought another. At that moment, a crowd came in. Among them she saw Jewel and a rather nervous Ben Stiller. Good faces for the club. It would be a good night.

Paul watched the people disappear one after another into the back wall. It told him that there was a lot more to this place than he'd initially thought. He wondered what would happen if he suddenly got up and went through. This little girl sure wouldn't stop him. When he'd first sat down, he put her at about thirty-two. Now he was wondering if she could even damn well legally drink the liquor she sold. Christ, though, she was lovely.

She also knew a little something about Ellen Wunderling that she hadn't disclosed. A flicker in the edges of the eyes had been his tipoff. He wished that he could interrogate her freely. She was an innocent little thing. You wouldn't even need a rubber hose to get her going. A light slap would set this powder puff to babbling.

He wanted to get in her pants, and it was distracting him. This damn town had to be full of vampires, ripe for the killing, and if this bitch was holding back about Ellen, maybe she was also holding back information that would lead him to them.

"Let me ask you this," he said. "In the *New York Times* story—do you know it?"

"Of course."

"It suggests that there are people who think they're vampires. Who actually drink blood. If I said, maybe such people drank Ellen's blood—how do you react to that?"

"The vampire scene is dead."

"Not for these assholes. They think they're getting something from the blood—besides AIDS, I mean. Some kind of life force. The soul, I guess."

As he spoke, she thought of how he looked behind a gun. She remembered the hate in his eyes, the eager spark as he killed. This creature *loved* his work, damn him. When she let Leo feed on him—and she would certainly do that in the end—she would make her go very, very slowly.

"Soul eaters," she said. "Wow, that's heavy."

"I know it's heavy, but it's true—I mean, in the sense that it's what they believe. Of course, it's all bullshit—"

"Of course."

"But they believe it, that's what's important. You look at the stats. A lot of people disappear without trace, don't they?"

"I don't know."

"In the U.S. in a year, over three hundred thousand."

"You're kidding . . . walking out on their debts, or a spouse they don't like, that'd be most of it, I'd think."

"There's plenty of foul play, Miss—what's your name?"

Beautiful, he was. Gracious, not. "Miriam Blaylock."

"Miss Blaylock." He paused. His eyes were searching hers. How hungry he was. She realized that he was an innocent. Incredibly, his sexual curiosity was that of a boy.

She said, "You look like a soldier."

"Is that good?"

She laughed, raised her eyebrows, delivered a slowly developing smile. "Is it?"

His left hand came into view as he brushed his cheek with the tips of his fingers. *For God's sake,* he thought, *let her see there's no ring.* She was talking to him like a person, here. She was being nice to him. He was beginning to think to himself, maybe he should lay off work for a little while. Lie low here in Manhattan. Let some personal life develop for once. He'd been married to the damn Company for too damn long. He was ready for a little real life.

He tried an opening line. "So, how long have you been in the club game?"

She took out another cigarette, offered him one. She lit them both with a lighter that looked as if it belonged on the *Titanic*. It was tiny, gold, and complicated. He wouldn't have been surprised if it had blown up in her face.

"Lemme see that."

She handed it to him.

"How old is this?"

"I bought it in a shop. I thought it was cute."

"Well, it could be dangerous."

She tried to recall how long she'd had the damn thing. Seventy, eighty years, at least. She'd never had occasion to get a new one. She took the lighter back. "It's fine."

"I'm gonna get you a real lighter."

"It's fine!"

"No, I'd like to. I'd really like to." He'd go to Bloomingdale's, spend fifty bucks. This lady had to be impressed. He could not let her slip through his fingers.

She looked at him out of lowered eyelids. There was even a little hint of Asia in her miraculous face. He loved the way Asian women looked; they were just so damn beautiful. She was more beautiful.

He just plain wanted to kiss her. But how did he get there? Maybe she'd drink with him. He said, "Listen, lemme buy you one a these Cordiers—what are they—hey, this is great vodka. And coming from me, that's high praise."

How pathetic he was. For the moment, his attraction to her was pushing his fanaticism aside. If she kissed him, she wondered, would it draw him closer or scare him away?

"What do you actually do for a living?"

What was this, he wondered. Was she evaluating him? What if he told her he was CIA? Sometimes that was a major turn-on; sometimes they hated it. Usually, they thought you were a complete asshole.

"What I really do is—I'm a—well, I'm not a reporter."

"I know you're not a reporter, and I'm getting kind of pissed off, since you won't show me any kind of credentials and I'm still waiting."

"You're waiting, and I'm gonna—well, this is not kosher at all. This is really against regs—"

"You are a cop. I thought you were."

"No, no." He pulled out his wallet, opened it to his ID card.

Miriam took the wallet, looked at the card. She thought that it appeared entirely legitimate, and it was certainly not a good piece of news. Her opposition was apparently governmental.

She memorized the card, and the information on the driver's license, and the number on the one credit card that was visible.

"Are you offended?"

"I'm curious. I mean, this is—it's so weird. What the hell was Ellen Wunderling really up to, that she rates attention from you people?" She motioned to Bill, who gave him a fresh drink—lots of vodka, less ice. "I mean, this vampire thing seems like something pretty stupid for the CIA to take an interest in."

"What if I told you it wasn't stupid at all?"

"I wouldn't know what to say. But I wouldn't be real interested, either."

Paul found that a very unexpected reaction. He sat back and regarded her. Given the past few minutes of conversation, he decided to revise his opinion about little Merry Blaylock. He'd bet thirty years in clandestine service that this kid did not know a single useful thing about Ellen Wunderling or vampires or anything connected with them. But the way she was looking back at him, with that dee-licious little smile—well, her innocence told him that conversation should go in another direction entirely.

The smile widened a little, played very fetchingly in her eyes. He could practically see her deciding that she thought his being CIA was kind of cool. The damn tag had worked for once. Damned amazing.

"Would you like to see my club?"

"They say it's the most exclusive club in New York."

She reached over, touched the back of his hand with the tips of her fingers. Then she laughed, a deliciously suggestive little bell-note, one of her favorites. "Oh, it is. Very, very exclusive. But if I like you, then you can come in. Welcome to the Veils."

SIXTEEN

Demon Lovers

"It looks like a wall—I mean, *just* like a wall." Paul extended a large hand toward the entrance.

"Doug Henning was a master."

"Isn't he the one who died? Kinda young, wasn't he?"

"Yes, he was." He'd been a delicious young man.

She took his hand and stepped through with him.

Techno music hit him like an avalanche—one made of pure sound. The space was dark, milky with smoke. Lasers played in time with the very fast music, revealing random slices of a whole lot of dancers. On a small stage, its floor glistening like a mirror, was a shadow capering behind the most complex set of control panels and turntables he'd ever seen in a club. The dj was faceless, even his head was covered. He appeared to be as thin as his bones, but that was probably some sort of an illusion.

The intensity of the music was completely beyond anything in Paul's experience. For a few seconds, he was virtually unconscious, reeling through a fog of reefer and crack and crys so thick he felt himself getting high on his second gasp for air. The next thing he knew, the music swept him up, seeming to yank his soul right out of his body and levitate him across the floor. He cried out, he knew it, he could feel it. But the music was so loud, the beat so intoxicating, the rhythm so danceable that his consciousness lost control of the primitive parts of the brain and his body began to move of its own accord. He thought voodoo, the shaking of priests, the trance of the gods.

He was dancing, and he could not do anything but dance. He was helpless to stop himself. The lasers showed sweating faces all around him, beautiful faces, goddesses, gods, and he thought he'd gone to some Olympian mountain. He thought he had risen above the ocean of life into the air of life. He was so happy, his heart was exploding with happiness, and it rushed through him as if fire had replaced the blood in his veins.

It was sorcery, he thought, it was magic. Satan's hooves were trampling him, but Satan's soft hands were also stroking him. He saw the girl—Miriam—standing there beside the stage with two other young women—both lovelies as well. Then a guy came out and began racing around the room like he was in some kind of a major seizure. He was wearing a magician's coat, black with red sequins and green sequins in the shape of a pentacle on it, and he ran in a jerky, unnatural way, striking dancers with a sparking wand and making them cry out.

Then Paul saw that most of the dancers were stark naked and there was a girl shooting a huge syringe straight into a guy's mouth, the needle penetrating under his tongue, and his eyes were flickering like a dying sign. There was sweat in the air with the smoke. There were pills rolling on the floor. The drugs were more plentiful here than anything he had seen in Paris or Bangkok.

It was hell, it was heaven, he was happy, he was scared to death, and he felt as if Satan were right there in this god-for-damned room and he was being butt-fucked by that NVR interrogator again in Muang Sing. Jesus wept, why had they done shit like that to him? The music got louder still and tighter still, driving, driving, crushing through his heart, burning through his brain, and then the magus struck him with the wand and the blow felt like an incoming mortar round.

The lights changed from lasers to white slits, and huge shadows swept over the dancers. When he looked up, he saw into a tremendous sky full of cloud towers and in them there was the Hindenburg exploding and burning, and from its belly there fell sparks that were people.

His whole self was torn away and torn out of him—his name went, his sense of being, the presence of and pain over his father, his place where his mom lived in him and said, "You're a good boy, a good boy"—all of his innermost self was torn out of him and swept away in the sea of smoke and the goddamnest best, most exciting, genius-level rock and roll he had ever heard in his life.

Then there was a girl there, one of the lovelies who'd been with Miss Blaylock. She had dark bangs and the kind of shape you wanted to put your hands around. She came dancing up to him and started undressing him, dancing with him and pulling off his clothes. He thought, *You know what I'm doing?—I am letting this happen, because this is the most fun I have ever had or known about.* He helped this exquisite girl with the light brown brush get every stitch of his clothes off and toss them down on the floor.

Nobody gave a shit, nobody stopped, he was dancing in a wonderful ocean of vibrating pricks and sailing boobs, and all the faces of all the gods and goddesses of the dance were smiling on him.

He yelled out, "I'm blown away! I am just plain *blown away!*" Then he remembered that he'd been carrying. The gun—had it been in his pocket or where did it go? Well, it wasn't his lookout anymore, and anyway, who gave a damn? He was not hunting vampires now.

This was not like any kind of damn club he'd ever heard of before. This was some kind of magic shamanic demon hole, this was.

Cool!

The room changed again, and this time he screamed bloody murder because he could not help it, he could not even think about stopping it; he screamed and he stumbled forward because the floor had disappeared and he was standing a thousand feet *above* Manhattan, and down there the traffic was racing as fast as the music, and little puff clouds were shooting past beneath his feet. The illusion was so perfect—man, it was so perfect!—you did not believe that you were standing on anything. That music, that wonderful, driving, animal-perfect, jungle machine music just totally blew out his nerve endings, so he was not a body with weight and age but an eternal light-being flying over the city.

Somebody knelt in front of him and started blowing him, and for the first time in his life, he just enjoyed it without worrying about who was there. He didn't care if it was a girl or a guy or a damn gorilla; he just loved; he loved with all his blood and his hammering, crashing heart, and the little light in the middle that was him.

Then he did look down and he saw the naked woman from the limo on Houston Street. She was giving him a hard-sucking blow job in the middle of the goddamn dance floor, and it was the best damn blow job he'd ever had.

The pleasure was so intense that he could not stand, his knees started to give way. Somebody held him up, somebody strong as shit, so he just let himself go limp. The hands were long and thin and cold against his skin, but the arms were as steady as steel rods. No way was he gonna get dropped. The pleasure swept up and down him, crashing like great waves from the top of his head to the singing tips of his toes.

He closed his eyes, and in his mind he saw not the woman blowing him, but Miriam Blaylock. How could she be that beautiful? How was it possible? With this club, she was some kind of magician, some kind of demon, but God love her, she was so beautiful.

Then he noticed that he wasn't being blown anymore. Hell, that was tough, that was intense to leave him with his gob half down the chute. "Shit!" he yelled aloud.

The music snatched him up like a wave. His balls were aching from him being hard too long with nothing happening but the *music;* the music just did not stop, did it? He was dancing again, they were all dancing again. When he looked over at the stage, he saw six women and six men dancing in front of the consoles, and behind them the dj had his hood off. Paul noticed that his eyes were yellow.

Miriam Blaylock was dancing, too; he saw her. She saw him and her eyes sparkled; then she saw he was naked and she cocked her head and gave him a mock-angry look and wagged her finger at him. Oh, she was just the cutest little girl he had ever seen. God love her for letting him into this wonderful place where he was dancing with the beautiful. She must actually like him. She must be impressed. Actually. He'd tell her he was the damn CIA director, if he had to. He never wanted to leave this place as long as he lived.

Then it was total dark, total silence. He stumbled, almost fell again, but nobody else moved. Everybody else just stayed still. He couldn't hear a damn thing, not after that music.

The lights came on, and all of a sudden the magical

beings were just people. They were boys and girls in their teens, mostly. Some older ones. There were famous faces here and there, not people whose names he knew, but the kind of faces you recognized from TV or the movies but you didn't know exactly who. He'd never been in the same room with famous people before.

A guy came onto the stage. The dj. There was a faint sound like rustling leaves, and Paul applauded, too. Had the music fucked up his hearing or what? He'd listened to plenty of loud rock in his life, but this had been something more. This had been music that blew you so far out of yourself that he now felt as though some sort of internal reset button had been pushed. He felt blank, a deprogrammed soul.

In the light he could see people were getting dressed, and they were still doing drugs, right out in the middle of everything. Some of them were even still making love. Guys were still hard, thinking nothing of it. Some of these kids were not even teens. They were, like, teenyboppers. There were friggin' children in this place, drinking and doing drugs, naked with naked adults. It was total, amazing, awful sin.

"Hell," he said to two of them standing nearby, "this place almost got Bangkok beat!"

Waiters came through two big doors and started laying out food and wine. They brought it in on huge gold trays, in golden bowls and crystal bowls, and the utensils and the plates were all gold, too.

"Christ," he said to another couple, "those pots must be worth a million bucks!"

He hadn't noticed that he was the only one making any noise until a guy held his finger over his lips.

"Be quiet?"

The kid nodded.

Hell, he didn't want to be quiet. He wanted to talk dirty to some frail. He wanted to get finished getting blown. But, hell, he was okay with it; this was what they wanted to do. He was the damn newbie, looked like.

Sarah watched Leo pull Miriam away from the dj's stage and heard her say, "Miri, that *man!* He's utterly dreadful!"

Very quietly, Miriam said, "He's also utterly alone."

Leo seemed not to comprehend. "Well, just get him out of here, please. He's pissing everybody off."

Sarah marched over to her and said, "We don't talk to Miriam like that."

"What? About him? She was an idiot to bring him in. He even had a gun!"

Quickly, Sarah took Leonore out of the room. The hard lights of the kitchen were a better setting for this discussion. "Listen, Leo. Do not *ever* make demands of her. What's been done to you doesn't give you the right. In fact, it does the opposite. Before, you were her friend. Now, you're her possession."

"You know something, Sarah? You're a complete asshole." Leo flounced off through the doors.

Sarah was amazed at how angry she felt, watching those doors swing behind that arrogant little ass. It was a calm, dispassionate sort of anger, a deep anger. The idea that she would have to live years and years with Leo interfering between her and Miri was just plain awful.

Before Leo, she had not been loyal enough. She had been unable to shake the scruples she'd brought from her old life. Miri had stolen her from herself. But because she was not a volunteer but a captive, something else was also true. Miri was responsible for her. Miri, also, belonged to her. She had rights in this relationship. She had her place, and did not intend to be disloged.

She went down to the office and stood at the one-way mirror, where she could see the dance floor. Everybody was eating, gobbling away at the braces of honey-dipped sparrows and other exotic foods that Vincent had prepared at Miriam's instruction. Miriam had little interest in human food, but it wasn't as if she didn't know about it. Her recipes spanned three thousand years. Honey-dipped sparrows had been the hot dogs of Elizabethan England.

Sarah watched the man. He was, in a way, beautiful— huge, muscular, his eyes extremely intelligent. She'd gone out on the floor and sucked him for a little while. She imagined that his ample organ would feel really nice inside her.

"You're drooling," Miri said as she came in. "And get your clothes on, you're the only one still naked except for that big slab of ham you're drooling over. Want to eat him?"

"What's the deal with him?"

Miriam sat down behind her desk. She tossed a small suitcase on it, clapped her hands. "Chop chop."

"The count, already? It's only two, Miri."

"Rudi's bag got too full. You'll have two counts tonight."

"I thought it was gonna be good."

"You want to know what the deal is with him?"

"Yeah." Sarah was sorting, preparing the pile for the count. It was over a hundred grand, though; she could already tell that. Money came to Miriam like metal shavings to a magnet. Ancient Keeper magic, Sarah thought. "So, what is it?"

"I don't know if I should tell you."

"Please trust me, Miri. It's agony for me when you don't."

"It's agony for me when you forget your place, child."

Sarah sorted bills into neat stacks of fifties, hundreds, a few twenties.

"I've been thinking about that. I want to ask your forgiveness. I want you to know that you've got my absolute loyalty."

"Now that there's a replacement threatening, yes. I wish you'd come to me before I blooded her."

"Why did you? We've got to endure her now forever and ever! And she's—oh, Miri, she's tacky and she's quite stupid."

Miriam shrugged. "You want to do pipe later, child?"

"I thought you were mad at me."

"I'm not mad now. In fact, I'm going to do celebration pipe. The two-hundred-year-old opium."

"What possible occasion could there be now?"

"I'm going to take that man downstairs with you and me and Leo, and we are going to spend a very long time with him. We're to feed Leo with him. Her first pabulum. Do you think she can handle it, Doctor?"

She was instantly excited, instantly appalled. A "very long time" would mean hell for the poor man. "Miri, I hate for them to suffer."

"What if I told you that he's the one who assaulted me?"

She stopped counting. In fact, lost the count. "You mean—"

Miri smiled slow. "I snared him, Sarah, in my very fine net. Anticipated his moves correctly. He is, at present, our prisoner."

"He's the one from Paris?"

"Yes."

Sarah looked at him again. "If we kill him, is that it? You're out of danger?"

"They'll be set back, because that man out there is a very powerful weapon. That man is the reason they win."

"Who, Miri?"

"There are people killing the Keepers, Sarah. Making carnage of us all over the world."

"*People?*"

"And that man is their leader."

Sarah found a chair. "And we're going to feed him to Leo?"

"She needs to eat, dear, just like us. She has a right to her food, too."

Paul wanted his clothes. Everybody else was already dressed. This was becoming not fun. "Excuse me," he said again, "I think that's my—" But it wasn't his. Nothing was his. "Look, hey, I'm missing a wallet, here." He really didn't need to lose *that,* for Chrissakes. There was six hundred bucks in there. The rest was safe enough inside the springs of the bed at the Terminal Hotel, except for the three c's he'd spent on the also-gone magnum.

"Hey, ladies!" he called out to no one in particular. "I got no clothes, here! Is there somebody in charge?"

They were purposely ignoring him, all of them. That was obvious. It was some kind of joke, apparently. He was now the only person naked. The lights were so bright they might as well be on a beach. Goddamnit, this was like one of those dreams—you're naked in a department store or something.

He spotted some guy giving him the eye and flopped his dick at him. "Like to look at it, doncha?"

"It's pretty."

Oh, Jesus, and he'd been having so damn much fun. Normally, he had very little fun. Getting blown and then sick drunk in whorehouses was not fun; it was a job, servicing your urges.

The management was undoubtedly back there watching

the New York sophisticates having their vicious fun at his expense. *Lemme put one of you turds in a vampire lair sometime,* he thought, *see if you find that fun.* He glared around him. Female laughter bubbled up from somewhere in the crowd, was instantly extinguished.

He went over to the food table. Little dead eyes stared at him. But there was also caviar, and his guess was that this was the most expensive thing on the menu. So he cupped his hands and got a great big glob of it, causing all the cognoscenti to gasp. Then he threw the caviar at the damn one-way mirror.

"Gimme my damn clothes," he said quietly. "Or I'm gonna tear this place apart." He spoke with the kind of gentle intensity that suggested that immediate compliance was essential.

Leo, who had had enough of this jerk for this evening and the rest of what might be a very long life if things went her way, said, "I'll get your clothes."

"Wise girl."

The delay was because Miriam had decided that she didn't want him to get back into his rags. She wanted him properly dressed, so she had sent Luis up to the house to get some of John's clothes. He had just reappeared with a black silk Donna Karan suit and a bloodred shirt, also of silk. Miriam would not allow John's things to be put into storage, not even yet. Maybe Sarah would come up with some new process someday, that would work for him. His body was still fairly intact, after all. So his things waited for him.

"It's crazy to have this guy here," Leo said.

Sarah, who was counting again and could not interrupt herself, did no more than glare. Now that she shared a secret with Miri that the bitch wasn't party to, she felt better, less threatened.

Miriam put Paul's wallet in the breast pocket of the

superb jacket. The magnum, which was on her desk under some piles of money, stayed there.

"You're to bring him to my room," Miriam told Leo.

Leo knew that people who went in there did not come out. "Am I invited?"

"You are indeed," Sarah said.

A chair hit the one-way mirror, bouncing off with a distant thud. He was getting physical about his nudity.

Miriam shook her head. "My, my."

"He's out there naked in a fully dressed crowd," Sarah said. "I'd be pissed off, too."

Miriam chuckled. "Show him the club, Leo. Let him play with you a little. But don't you dare fuck him dry. Is that a promise?"

Leo came around behind the desk and kissed Miriam's cheek. Sarah couldn't watch it. She stared down at the magnum. She picked it up and pointed it at Leo. "Remember this," she said. "He's dangerous."

Another chair thudded into the window.

"Arrange to be at the door to my room with him in half an hour," Miriam said as Leo hurried out. Then she turned to Sarah, "Don't point guns at her."

"She's rude to you."

"She's as she is. Accept her."

"You want her instead of me!"

Miriam went close to Sarah, cradled her face in her hands. "Control yourself," she said, pressing harder, compressing the jaw and cheeks until the eyes almost popped out of the head. "Will you?"

Sarah nodded. She could not speak.

Miriam could crush a human skull. She pressed harder. "Are you certain?"

Sarah nodded again. Mucus began dribbling from her nose. Her feet stomped and scuffled, her hands came up and fluttered along Miriam's arms.

Miriam let her go. Sarah gagged, sucked air, pitched forward out of her chair. Then she came to her feet. Her cheeks were flaming.

"No jealousy," Miriam said.

Tears pouring from her eyes, Sarah threw herself against Miriam. "Please don't abandon me!"

Miriam had heard that cry from every one of them, and it went straight to her heart. They were tragic beings, her humans. She was ashamed of them. But she enjoyed them a great deal, and that, ultimately, was what mattered to her. Keepers caused human suffering. That was simply the nature of nature.

She kissed Sarah. "Better?"

"I'm sorry, Miri. It's just that you're so precious to me. I can't live without you."

"My love, I have a task of great importance that I need you to do." She held out a brass key. "This is the key to his hotel room." She tossed it onto the desk, told Sarah the address. "Go up there, take Bill or somebody with you. Go through the room, take every trace of him out with you. And especially, if you find a small, black book, very old—"

"He has a Book of Names?"

"If we're lucky."

Sarah was shocked. "What use would it be to him?"

"They can read Prime. Some of it."

Sarah was truly amazed. She had counted a hundred and eighty different symbols in a single glyph. It was the most complex written language by a factor of a thousand. Who could possibly manage to crack a code like that?

"You're sure of this?"

"I imagine they used National Security Agency cryptographers."

Sarah felt a coldness within her, as if her heart had been pierced with a knife of ice. "Your name is there. Your holdings. Oh, Miri!"

The Keepers were in terrible trouble if these people were able to read such records. "Where would he get a Book of Names? How?"

"When you get the book—if you do—bring it straight here."

"And if I don't?"

"Then we'll just have to get him to tell us where it is, won't we, dear?"

Sarah managed a smile. Sometimes Miri made them scream, which Sarah normally hated. She would not hate it if this man screamed.

"We'll make him tell us," she said. She put her arms around Miri. "Thank you for trusting me again."

"Now go, child. Go like the wind."

Paul pulled on the pants, got them sort of closed. "This guy must be thin as a rail," he said. He managed to get into the shoes, too, which were of leather so soft it made his skin crawl. Could these people have somehow gotten something from a vampire? From what he'd seen in Paris, the vampires were much more capable of mixing with humans than he'd believed. His sense of it was that the Asians were more ancient than the Europeans and far less able to be seen on the streets. Maybe the Americans were younger and more humanlike still. Hell, maybe they would even fit into a hip crowd like this.

He looked more carefully at the shoe. Gucci sure as hell didn't make them out of human skin, so that theory was out.

The clothes actually fit pretty well, although they seemed decades out of date. The jacket had a wide collar, and the trousers were subtly flared. They belonged to a man with big shoulders like Paul's, a tall man and a strong man. But a slimmer one.

He regarded himself in the mirror. "Jesus," he said, "I look like a million bucks."

Leo decided that she utterly loathed him. "You look just fabulous," she lied.

"Whose clothes are these, anyway?"

"A friend of ours. Listen, I've got an idea. The next set doesn't come up until after dinner. Want to see the rest of the club?"

A guided tour from this babe? "You better believe it."

She walked through another wall. Expecting to be blasted by music again, he followed her. But he was not blasted. In fact, he wasn't in a room at all. He was in a Japanese garden, outside—at least it seemed like outside. The sky was velvet swarming with stars, a sickle moon just turning yellow as it slid toward the horizon. Bamboo chimes made restful sounds; water hurried over stones. Crickets chirped; a bat whispered past his face. Here and there in the dark, he could see pale bodies. There were at least a dozen people here, all covered by black cloaks, lounging on benches or on the grass. A guy with glasses and an old-fashioned doctor's kit went among them like a waiter, discussing in quiet tones, then ministering to them out of his case.

Paul smelled opium . . . real good opium. He was already contact high and passive-smoke high, and maybe high on something he'd ingested in the food or those damn drinks he'd been given a million years ago. But he really loved opium, and it was one hard drug to come by these days. It took him back to quiet times in the Cambodian jungle, those magical times when they were more-or-less safe, and they could sweetly indulge.

They weren't outside, of course, not really. They were under a deep country "sky," and this was the middle of Manhattan. Leo took his hand, led him around the edge of the garden.

"Hey, wait, I could do some pipe."

"Um, if you stay in here, it's a thousand dollars an hour."

You could probably drop ten grand on this place in a single goddamn night. "Let's see the rest of it."

"This next room is rather unusual. But please remember, our credo is no limits and no restrictions."

"Sounds like fun." Paul followed her through another veil and into a completely mirrored foyer. There was a tunnel entrance. He hesitated. "Where does that go?"

"Just downstairs. And it only looks like a tunnel. There's a stairway when you get past the veil."

It was not easy to walk into what looked exactly like one of the Paris tunnels, but he followed her. He found himself in a stairway, dimly lit with recessed bulbs, its walls and ceiling black. The rubber treads on the steps gave it an institutional feel. He thought that it must be like this in certain prisons.

There was a thick iron door here. "What is this place?"

"We call it Foggy Bottom," she said with a laugh. "It's full of politicians." She drew the door open.

The first thing he saw was a red butt. Leonore went in, giving it a spank as she passed. "Thank you," a male voice said.

Paul followed her. "Should I? A guy?"

"He doesn't care."

Paul gave him a whack, and not a light one.

"Thank you, sir!"

Paul looked down, trying to see the face of the guy who was trussed up there.

"No, honey, we don't pry. Not in here."

But he had seen, and he knew the face. "Um, are these people all from Washington?"

"Washington, the Kremlin, Downing Street, the Vatican. You name it."

Not all the whipees were men. There was a woman hanging naked from the ceiling, with what looked like heavy chains hooked to her nipples. "Ouch!" Paul said to Leonore, who kept walking. Another woman was encased in spectacular bondage, tied up like some kind of a ball, with what looked like a pair of underpants stuffed in her mouth.

"My God, who's that?"

"A publishing executive on a guilt trip."

There was a guy tied to a pole being whipped by two other guys with thick, black paddles.

"More publishers?"

"Two congressmen kissing a senator's ass. They'll be taking their turns on the post later."

"You ever get a president in here?"

"What country?"

"U.S."

"Which one?"

"Well, how about Bush?"

"Which one?"

Okay, that question was answered. "How much for this room?"

"Oh, you can do this room on my nickel. I'll top you."

"In your dreams, sweetie. Not my *schtick*."

She shrugged. "You'd be surprised what it's like, getting topped really well. Your ego is, like, imploded. This whole club is about blowing the ego away. Every room does it, but differently."

"The Japanese garden?"

"The right kind of high, and you'll feel very close to heaven there."

"High is high."

"No way. Our dealer is an MD who not only deals, he designs. He's given all our customers physicals, he knows exactly what makes them tick. He's doing blood tests, prescribing, adjusting, all during the course of the evening. They are being taken so high they're gonna forget even their damn names."

"And then the music blows you wide open."

"You can get very close to God in here, mister. This place is sacred."

Hell called *sacred*—that was something he never thought he'd hear. "Can we go somewhere else?" This was not the part of the club for him. He wanted to do some pipe, or at least get another drink. There wasn't much second-hand smoke down here, and he was crashing.

This time they went up in an elevator so small that they were touching. He sprang up instantly. When the doors opened, he stayed like that, because this was a ballroom full of beautiful beds, and there were people openly making love on them.

A pair of singers, a lovely, tall girl and a young man who was even taller, stood together singing in voices so filled with gentleness that they might have been saints. He recognized "All Through the Night."

"O'er thy spirit gently stealing,
Visions of delight revealing,
Breathes a pure and holy feeling . . ."

There was a solemnity to this place that seemed at odds with what appeared to be an orgy in progress. Paul was a smart man, and he was well able to see the careful thought that had been put into all this. This room, for example, was about disconnecting sex from sin. No more need to hide.

Once in a while, he'd hit a house in Vientiane or Phnom Penh with a bunch of guys, and it would develop into pretty much of an orgy. It was fun but it was ugly, and you felt dirty afterward. In this room the lack of shame brought with it a sense of purity. Thirty or forty human beings were enjoying one another in all kinds of intimate ways, doing everything you could imagine with each other. Their faces glowed with lust, they sweated. But it was all so joyous.

Maybe Leo was right, maybe there was something kind of sacred here.

Seeing all these bodies entwined, he was starting to look at Leo real hard. But she probably outclassed him like everybody else in this place . . . except for the morons in the dungeon. They were pols, and that was sorta his world. But he could not relate to getting whipped. He got punished plenty without any assistance. The knife wound was still healing good, for example, but he sure as hell knew it was there if he tried to raise the arm too high.

Leo was terrific looking—clean as a whistle and sexy as hell. He could get into her in a second, *way* into her. His equipment had been considered pretty sensational by some. Maybe she'd like a little taste.

He decided to give it a try. "Look, I'd like—" She rested her eyes on him, which instantly shut him up. "Let's go downstairs," he said, his voice husky with embarrassment. He couldn't proposition her in here, for Chrissakes. He was no damn angel; he needed his privacy.

She strolled out into the foyer. He wasn't quite sure where she was coming from, and he didn't want to insult anybody. But he had to get it on somehow. He was human. He couldn't just be left to Sally Five himself in his hotel room, not after all he'd seen and felt here tonight. He wanted to be loved, too. But since that didn't seem likely to happen to him, maybe she'd just give him a break, here.

"I think you're really—I mean, I could sure as hell give you a nice time. If you need a tip—if that's the drill—"

"I want to show you a very special space now," she said. She took his hand.

How anything could possibly top what he had seen so far, he could not imagine. This wasn't just a place of pleasure. It was a whole new approach to pleasure, as something that did not need to be hidden and wasn't a sin. Even the ones in the dungeon were learning that lesson, in their own peculiar way.

The people who could come here were immensely privileged. All of his life, he had thought that the social barriers by which we live were a tragedy. Miriam Blaylock, whom he viewed now as something of a young genius, was challenging those barriers here, and he was beginning to decide that she was succeeding.

They went down a back stairway, steel stairs in a fluorescent-lit well. There were doors with Exit signs all over the place and a hose station on every landing. He'd also noticed that the place was sprinklered and smoke-alarmed. "I've never seen so much safety equipment."

"We're very careful. You don't want the least feeling of danger."

"I've never felt so safe in my life."

She squeezed his hand.

"Look," he said, "I'm sorry if I embarrassed you. Or insulted. I just—I find you, you know, really, really attractive."

"I'm flattered."

They came to the bottom of the stairs, where there was a door with a breakaway bar that looked as if it must lead into an alley. A horrible thought crossed his mind. "I'm not getting the boot, here, I hope?"

She opened the door. There was a tiny chamber entirely made of mirrors. When he went in, there were Pauls staring at him from every direction, all of them disappearing into an infinity of repetitions. It was a sort of visual echo. "Hey, this is—"

"Have a fabulous time." She slammed the door, and he found himself alone in the small space. He turned around immediately, but saw only more mirrors and could not find the door.

Above all things, he hated confinement. But this was a place of pleasure. He was getting the ride of a lifetime for a poor bastard like him. He was not going to ruin it by freaking out.

So he wouldn't freak out, but the guy looking back at him out of all these mirrors, he looked like he would. Look at the eyes, look at all that pain. Then he thought he saw another face. He saw—Jesus God, he'd been a fool to come here! It was one of them, watching him through the damn mirror. He went for the gun that wasn't there, then lashed out. His fist smashed into the mirror. The room shook, he felt a blast of pain up his hurt arm . . . but the mirror did not crack.

There was a voice then, very soft, "Turn right and walk toward me."

He turned right. There was nobody to walk toward but his own reflection.

"Come on."

He took a step, feeling ahead—and felt air. This mirror was another one of the veils.

Was he walking into whatever had swallowed Ellen Wunderling? Some kind of damn superexclusive vampire lair? Oh, hell, if he was, he'd at least take a few with him.

He stepped into the most palatial bedroom he had ever seen. On the bed sat Miriam. She was playing the flute, and doing it with exquisite skill. He gaped at her, at the tall bed she was in, at the phenomenal tapestries on the walls.

There was a window, and outside he could see smiling green fields with people working in them, men with brown tunics and caps. A horseman rode along a path, a man dressed in the fabulous clothes of the distant past.

She stopped playing long enough to say, "It's a TV screen."

But it was very well done. The image was so clear that it looked more like a window than a window.

There was a chair across from the bed, big, carved, almost a throne. He sat in it. He watched Miriam Blaylock play, watched and listened. This was one talented lady. What the Veils was about was limitless wealth and the power of human genius. If you had the cash, the Veils could rebuild your soul.

Or if you were a damn dogface on a lucky streak, like yours truly.

Miriam was wearing a white nightgown cinched just under her breasts with a pink ribbon. He thought, *I have never been in such a wonderful place with such a wonderful person before, and I think I'm about to get laid.*

Christ almighty. Now, he had to prepare himself. When she was finished with that sweet prelude, she was going to raise her eyes, and he was going to see once again her angelic and spectacularly sexy face. He was already as hard as iron. The issue was, how did he do it, if indeed he was to be afforded that privilege, without wadding her on stroke two?

The music came to an end. She put down the flute.

When he applauded softly, she laughed. "I was just fooling around."

"You fooled around with the *Prelude to the Afternoon of a Faun* better than anybody I've ever heard. Better than Galway."

"I adore James."

"You know him?"

"We've played together."

"Okay."

Silence fell. He didn't know what to do next, what to say. He was way out of his class; that was the truth of it. He looked up at the ceiling, which was painted with a night sky, dark blue with gold-leaf stars and a moon that looked more like it had a snake in it than a man. The constellations were strangely off, too.

"That's an antique ceiling. Do you like it?"

"Oh, yeah. How old is it?"

She got off the bed and came over and sat on the arm of the chair. "It's from Atlantis."

"Okay," he said again, and instantly felt like a total jerk. What was he, a stroke victim, here? Couldn't he come up with something a little funny at least, in response to a funny remark from her?

"Okay what?"

"Sorry, I'm just—well—I gotta be honest. I'm just totally overwhelmed, here. Your club—I mean, Jesus. I admit to feeling just a little outclassed."

She leaned down and grasped him through the silk pants.

There was no underwear involved in this outfit, so it was a pretty intimate contact. The pleasure was intense.

"You need to cool down a little," she said.

"I need to cool down," he repeated.

She got up and went over to a big chest. It was made of dark wood, carved with writhing snakes. She opened it and he was amazed to see her bring out an opium rig with two of the most magnificent ivory pipes he'd ever seen. "You said you'd like a pipe. I think it'll help a lot." She stopped, though, then cocked her head, as if considering something that was a little new to her. "We're not against drugs, are we, Mr. CIA man?"

"Nah, the Company's a big importer. Anyway, I been doin' shit since 'Nam. I'm in an extreme business. You can't handle it without extreme relaxation. You gotta compensate."

She gave him a pipe, started to prepare it for him.

"There's that antique lighter again. Lady, you gotta ditch that thing; you're gonna burn up."

She glanced at him in a way that kind of shook him up. Was it a cold glance? Or hate? Jesus, if—

But then she smiled, and it was just so sweet that he could not believe that she was anything except very charmed by him.

He took a long pull and in a second was rewarded with good vapor. It seeped through him like blood in a sponge. It was very good vapor.

She lit her own pipe, then went to the bed and lay back, cradling it. He did the same, lying face-to-face with her. As he smoked, he felt his erection calming down. That was good. The opium would make the evening last.

She kissed him on the neck, just a peck, then giggled. He kissed her back, right on the mouth, hard and long.

After that she didn't giggle again.

SEVENTEEN

Blood Child

Miriam was careful with his kiss. She was not sure how much Keeper anatomy he knew, and until she was, she would take no chances touching his tongue with her own. Afterward, he gazed at her with what she thought were the saddest eyes she had ever seen.

Now, they were smoking together. She was handling the pipes.

He was still devouring her with his eyes, and there was in the back of her mind the thought that he might have some level of recognition.

She gave him a smile calculated to seem shy, a little surprised.

He sighed, smoked, closed his eyes.

She removed the pipes after a few more minutes. She wanted him calm, but not in a stupor. Two pipes of this opium would put a human being in one, no matter how strong he was.

"Nobody's interested in opium anymore," he said, lounging back on the bed. "I mean, I picked up on it in the jungles of Cambodia. Primitive place."

"My opium is grown on a Crown estate in Myanmar, processed in a facility built for the CIA in 1952. Some say it's the very best pipe on earth. Did you know Maurice McClellan? He was in charge of that operation for CIA."

"I knew Maurice."

Then he was suddenly watching her with eyes as hard and cold as black diamonds. She was surprised—stunned, in fact—to realize that she'd just now made a mistake. If she were really in her early twenties, Maurice would have died when she was just a child.

"He was a friend of my father's," she said, rolling over on her back and putting her hands behind her head to telegraph how complete was her ease. "He introduced him to Prince Philip."

"Yeah, that'd be Maurice. He traveled in pretty rarefied circles."

"You know what we should do?" she said.

"What?"

"We should get you more comfortable."

"This is a boss suit. I like the way it feels."

"It's club wear. When somebody comes in—"

"Dressed like a bum, like me."

"You were confusing my guests. They thought you were some kind of a cop."

"Do you get cops around here?"

"Sure. The precinct's just around the corner."

"I noticed."

"It's not a problem." Not when fifty thousand dollars a week was being sent over there and half the powerful people in the city were making sure that this particular block just plain was not patrolled.

She slid her hands under his shirt. He blinked his eyes. He got so hard so fast that there was a hissing sound as his organ slid against the silk of his trousers. As she unbuttoned the shirt, she wondered how much blood he could lose without dying. He was very strong. He'd probably last and last.

Once he was well trussed up, her plan was to remove all her makeup, to let him know that he had been captured by a Keeper. Then she would prick a tiny hole in his neck and use him as a teaching tool, letting Leo take him by small sips.

She ran her hands along his shoulders, pushed back the shirt. "You're *so strong*," she breathed.

"I work out."

"What do you press?"

"Oh, two hundred. Two-twenty if I'm healthy."

"You're unhealthy?"

"I tend to get wasted." He nodded toward the pipes. "That, booze, girls. I've lived in Asia too long, done too much—too much work."

"What is your work?"

"Classified."

She laid her head against his chest, drew herself, catlike, close to him. "That's exciting."

"What do you think I do? What's your guess?"

"You—let me see—you're *very* strong. But you're also smart." She whispered. "You're a government assassin."

He chuckled. "You kept my gun."

"You can't bring a gun in here. It's against the law."

"I thought the law didn't apply to you."

"My law."

"How did you get so rich?"

"My great-great-great-great—let's see, five greats—one more—great-grandfather was Lord Baltimore. He owned Maryland."

"That'll do it. But I still want my gun back."

"When you leave."

For a moment, he looked, she thought, kind of like a wild animal. He was hair-trigger; she knew that. Up close like this, he seemed even more dangerous.

She stretched, lying half in his lap and half on the bed. When she stopped, the edge of her hand was lying against his erection. She said, "Uh-oh." Then, "Can I be a bad girl?"

"Be a bad girl."

Very lightly, she touched it. Then she snatched her hand away. "Oh, it's *huge!*"

He swallowed. He was trembling a little.

She felt more intimately. "It can't be as big as it feels."

"Have a look," he whispered.

"Shall I?"

He was too big around the waist for the pants, so they were only three-quarters zipped. She opened them. He came out, bobbing, the glans gleaming in the soft light.

He *was* huge. She pressed into the tender glans with a fingernail, then held the enormous thing in both of her hands. She drew off the pants. He shuffled out of the shirt.

She had not seen a male so beautiful in years. His muscles were fabulous, his skin lustrous. His face was purest masculine poetry, chiseled and hard, but with the complex, haunted eyes of somebody who had led a dangerous and uncertain life.

Whatever, he was a lovely specimen and he was going to make a sumptuous meal. She was actually a little jealous of Leo. What a great first supper!

A few minutes before he was brought in, she had gone down and checked the furnace next door. All was in order. Under the bed was the black overnight case that she would carry his remnant in.

But all that was for later. Until Sarah returned, she would continue to play with him. She needed that book. If Sarah did not find it, then this creature would discover that Foggy Bottom could be used for more than just games. There were some very serious implements there, and she knew just exactly how to apply them.

She stroked his chest, made a ring around one of his nipples with her finger. She touched the puckered wound on his shoulder. "This hurt?"

"A little. It's healing."

She remembered how good it had felt, seeing that knife dig in. If there had been a little more room for her backhand, she would have sliced the arm off.

"What happened?"

"A client became upset."

"Very upset."

"Very."

She kissed the corner of his mouth, but drew aside when he tried to kiss her back.

"You know, Miriam, I have to be honest with you. This is the nicest night of my life." He looked her up and down. She was still wearing her sheer nightgown. "You are—oh, gosh— so much more than you seem. I mean, please don't take this wrong, but you're just a kid, and this place is really deep, here. That girl that took me around—she said it was sacred and I thought she was a complete moron at first. But I started realizing what you were doing. And I want you to know this—I agree with it."

"Thank you."

"You came up with the whole concept?"

"Yes." She took his hands to her bodice, put the ribbons in his fingers. Then she drew his hands slowly apart. As she did so, the ribbon came away and the gown fell down her shoulders like drifting smoke.

"Oh, my," he said. Her breasts were gracefully full, curved just right to fit the cup of the hand. He raised his hands. But he dared not touch. They were like some kind of perfect art, a porcelain dream.

She took his hands to them. When they lay in his rough palms, the nipples became erect. Gooseflesh dusted the pink areolas.

"Oh, Lord," he said, watching this. He bent to her, laid his lips on that sweet skin of hers. Up close it had the texture of a child's, absolutely smooth, as if life had not yet touched it.

Christ, he ought to ask for her driver's license. But he wouldn't, because if this was a minor, then God had made this kid to boogie and he was sorry, but she was gonna boogie tonight.

Her lips hung slack in a way that said she was real interested and real ready. He kissed her, which was awful nice. But he was careful, because he had a thing about him that had not always gone down with women, although the whores pretended to love it, of course. His tongue was kind of—well, rough. No other way to put it. He had a cat tongue. He went deeper, though. Couldn't help it. The kiss itself was luring him, so sweet was her mouth. He just loved kissing this woman. Oh, wasn't she a *woman?* Nice!

He wanted to touch his tongue to hers, but she didn't seem to have one. It was way back in there. 'Course it was. She was probably scared to death.

But then he did, and when he did, she arched her back and cried out so loud it broke the kiss.

"Sorry!"

She threw her arms around him and latched onto him with her legs. She kissed him and kissed him, and he thrust his tongue into her mouth and her groaning and crying made him wild for her. She loved it; she loved the way he was.

She was haunted by how much he reminded her of Eumenes, who had been not only her husband, but her only Keeper lover. Power like this was something she had not tasted in eons. He was like the roaring oceans of the world, the flames of the stars, a tornado, a typhoon.

She locked her lips to his and opened her mouth to him, and he thrust in and rested in the kiss. Even though he had not yet entered her, she came to climax, came again and again beneath his sweating, eager body.

She looked at him, drinking him with her eyes. Never had there been a man so beautiful, never so filled with raging sexuality, never so—so—there were no words to describe it. No words.

They rolled and he was under her. The opium had done perfectly: he was ready, but he wasn't going to explode.

He let her sit on him, felt her take his penis in her two hands. Her cheeks flushed as she stroked it, loved it, kissed it, and licked it. It wasn't human, it couldn't be—because it was going to fit her and they did not fit her. They were wasted, small creatures in their sex, not like a real man, a Keeper man.

He was—but this was impossible. They didn't interbreed. She put that stupid idea right out of her head. He was a lucky accident, is what he was and that was *all* he was.

She wanted to taste of him. She wanted to know his every intimate truth. He excited her, truly, despite the hate that flapped in her heart.

"Hey," he said, lifting his head and kissing her hard. "You've got a tongue like mine. We're two cats."

It was true, and this was getting very strange very fast. "We're made for each other," she said carefully.

He slid to come from beneath her. She knew what he wanted and responded instantly, with delight. She was *never* on the bottom, but with him yes. Yes. She belonged under him. It felt meant to be. She shifted her weight.

His huge form dominated her. Gazing into his eyes, she spread her legs.

"Okay, baby," he said, "this one belongs to *me*." On that word he pushed into her.

The world turned black. Then a dam burst. Thunder rumbled in her head. Thrusting at him, she screamed out his name, *"Paul, Paul, Paul!"* as he pumped deep and withdrew, pumped deeper and harder, lingered then drew back, thrust and pumped, thrust and pumped.

It was as if she had become a single, blazing point of pure pleasure that was racing out through the universe at a million times the speed of light.

Then he rested upon her, and the feel of his surprisingly great weight on her body was the most wonderfully natural feeling in the world. He felt so much like Eumenes it almost broke her heart.

His loins surged, and the pleasure became a fiery comet that went straight through her. He slid himself almost all the way out, then plunged in again. He held her down, and she enjoyed the illusion of being helpless—oh, for the first time in years and years and years—and it was just so damned awfully wonderful. It wasn't scary—or it was, but that was part of the enjoyment. He was slow with her, and precise with her, sliding in and out, in and out while she shook her head from side to side and arched her back and yammered his lovely name.

It was *just* like being under Eumenes, having all her power stripped away by his greater power, and being free in bondage to him at last.

While he thrust, Paul drank her with his eyes. Not only did she look wonderful and taste fabulous and feel great to touch and hold, she had a very special instrument down there. This lady could use those muscles, yes, she could, to kiss the shaft and compress the tip in ways that not even the most skilled whores of Bangkok or Seoul or H.K. could even dream about.

Oh, my stars and bars, thank God for that pipe, he thought, *or I would've come and been done in the middle of stroke one.*

As it was, he went slow and careful while she kissed his chest and bit his hairs and licked his nipples. She cried out, she trembled like a branch in a storm, she pumped while he pumped, faster now, yelling, grasping his buttocks, pulling and pushing him. He was riding this filly, for sure; he was bigger than he'd ever been, and it felt better than it ever had.

Miriam was screaming, her eyes frantic and amazed.

She shrieked; she bellowed.

This was a damned thing, a very damned, damned thing! Because she was feeling a fire blazing inside her, and she knew what that fire was.

No Keeper woman who had felt it ever forgot it, the alarming, painful, delicious heat that told her she was about to conceive. But her egg wouldn't drop for a human! And it mustn't!

No, no that must not—not—

But the process went on, and she went helpless with it, a speck of a woman lost in a restless, living ocean. He was the storms above; he was the lightning striking her tortured waves.

The lightning, it seemed to her, was alive. And if so, then—well, then he was fertile!

Oh, stars, what was happening?

She had never dreamed that any human male would trigger this response in her body. It was her egg, her last egg, and it was moving within her, she could feel the searing delight of its journey.

She had not had a Keeper man in millennia, but she had wanted one always, and now suddenly this enormous body surging above her—that dear, powerful face, those driven eyes—this was a Keeper!

Paul was pouring with sweat, his thighs working, his every muscle singing with the amazing pleasure of this long, long session. Every thrust touched the shivery edge of climax; then as he pulled back, she loosened her muscles and they started again.

He'd never been in a state of pleasure this intense for this long, and things were happening to him that had never happened before. His heart was thundering harder than he could ever remember. Even his skin was tingling with pleasure, especially where it was in contact with her. Electricity—real, humming juice—seemed to be passing between them.

Again he thrust into her. Then he paused, drinking in her perfect flower of a face, her lustrous, joyous eyes.

She screamed. She had screamed a lot for Paul, but she *really* screamed now. She could feel the egg. Definitely. It hung in her, touching the mother lode of nerve endings, and where that egg touched that womb, a million dancing needles of sheer, tickling, joy sent their prickles marching out through her every sizzling nerve.

Paul was on fire with the sweet fire of the angels. Look at her pure, dear face—she *was* an angel! Oh, look at those eyes, those gray pools of innocence—she was the maid of Solomon's fancy. He pressed himself hard against her, thrust harder, and then as if molten gold were speeding in his shaft, he came roaring and yelling and laughing; he came as he had never come before or thought you ever could come. He came in pleasure and in love, in dear *love*, which had caught his soul afire.

She felt his semen speeding into her like a great flaming fire, a sweet sun—and she knew that it washed the egg, and it went screaming through the wall of the egg and sped down to the center, where slept the waiting shadow.

She threw her pelvis forward and arched her back, and they hammered at each other, squeezing the last demanded juice of the pomegranate, the last starry flower.

A burning wave snatched Miriam up and away, filling her with wonderful fire, shocking her more than she had been shocked since the pyramids reflected the sun, since she had opened her eyes to the eyes of her Eumenes and managed to murmur to him, "It feels like a boy."

Paul collapsed onto her chest, and they both burst into tears like two scared schoolkids.

Miriam Blaylock and Paul Ward had just conceived.

She was crying for the little baby that lay now within her, its cells already waking up. She was crying for she had no idea what that baby would *be*—Keeper, human, alive, dead, deformed—only that it was her second and it was her last.

"I love you," he said, "oh, my God in heaven, I love you!"

She looked scared, and he touched her dear eyes to wipe away the tears.

"Miriam," he said. He suddenly felt awful. "Please never make me leave you."

She gazed at him, her eyes slow and contented. "I adore you," she said, and there was such reverence in her tone that he wanted to cry. Maybe somebody would want a broke-down old CIA officer after all. And maybe that somebody would be this wonderful, special girl.

Miriam slid out from under him and drew his head down

into her lap. With loving eyes, she gazed at him. Then she bent closer, kissing the tip of his nose and then his lips, and then the pulsing vein in the curve of his neck. She lay her mouth there for a moment, then withdrew.

Paul felt her sucking his skin a little. It was a nice sensation.

Suddenly he jumped away from her.

There, across the room, stood the woman from the limo, the woman who had blown him on the dance floor.

Miriam got up, went to her, and took her hands. Sarah nodded her head, and Miriam burst out laughing. Her laughter pealed out again and again, and it was so pretty and so full of fun that he started laughing, too.

"How long have you been in here?" Paul asked her.

"Since you started."

"You sure got an eyeful."

Sarah shrugged.

"May I know your name?"

"Sarah." She nodded toward Miriam. "I do her books."

"You let your accountant in here when you're—" He chuckled. "To each his own, I guess."

"It was lovely," Sarah said. "You're a very lovely man."

The look in her eyes, though, did not suggest that she was pleased with what she had seen. In fact, there was something real on edge about this lady.

Then another one came in through the wall.

"Oh, hey," Paul said as the girl who'd shown him the club appeared. He got his pants on. Not that one more naked male would matter to this crew.

Then he saw that she was blushing like a tomato. She had a funny little silver thing in her hand. A strange knife.

"What's that?"

It disappeared into her jeans. "Sorry, Miriam!"

Miriam went to her. "This is Leo. The three of us run this club together. Leo's the granddaughter of General Patton."

"He was my mother's cousin."

He threw on the shirt, started buttoning it. "General Patton, Lord Baltimore, Morrie McClellan, and Prince Philip. Not to mention Ben Stiller, who was in your place earlier. Lotta names to drop."

"Lord who?" Sarah asked.

Miriam smiled at her in a way that told Paul she was being made to shut up. Which meant that Miriam's story about Lord Baltimore was a lie. Which meant that she felt a need to conceal the origin of her wealth. Interesting.

"We're going home," Miriam said, her voice rippling.

"We are?" Leo's eyes flickered toward Paul.

"I'm in love," Miriam shouted. She raced back to the bed, threw herself at Paul, kissed him hard, then flounced back on the bed, pulling him with her. She said, "He's the best lover in the world." Then she was convulsed with laughter, peeking out from beside his big chest at Sarah and Leo. "Am I being naughty?" she chirped.

"Naughty is not the word," Sarah purred.

"What do I do?" Leo asked.

Paul said, "I think we fell in love."

Sarah suddenly smiled. "I'm so glad." Then she said to Miriam, "Miri, it's four. Can I let the staff go?"

"Is the house clear?"

"Ready for the nighthawks."

Miriam lay back in his lap, her hands folded behind her head. "Leo, tell Luis to get the car ready." She gazed up at Paul. "I'm bringin' my baby back home."

The two women went out without a word.

"They seem kind of upset."

"Pets don't like surprises."

"Am I a pet?"

"You, my dear, are a great big beautiful *man!*"

They got dressed and went out of the little room, then through the kitchen to the rear of the club. The Bentley limousine he'd seen on Houston Street stood there gleaming in the predawn glow.

He got in, settling into the plush cushions.

"Want a drink?" Miriam asked brightly.

Sarah and Leo came in.

"You know what I'd like? Have you got a good cigar? After lovemaking like that, nothing in the world would be as nice as a really fine cigar."

Leo grunted with barely concealed disgust.

"We have some Cohiba Piramides in the club," Sarah said in a dull voice. "But it's awfully confined for you to smoke a cigar here."

"Luis," Miriam called, "go back in and get my lover some cigars."

Luis brought them out and held open the humidor.

"I was looking for a Macanudo, maybe," Paul said.

"Cohibas are a bit better," Leo replied, unable to conceal a sneer.

"We'll all smoke," Miriam snapped, handing cigars to Sarah and Leo. "Self-defense, Sarah! Let me get my hand grenade—Paul says my lighter is dangerous, did I tell you? Hadn't that ever occurred to you, Sarah?"

"I'm sorry, Miri, it hadn't."

"Well, he's going to get me a new one. He says we wouldn't want my pretty face to get burned, would we?" She cut and lit a cigar and handed it to Paul.

Paul took a drag of a smoke that was hard but incredibly rich, and he knew that it was true, that this cigar was better than a Macanudo. Way better, in fact.

Miriam offered one to Sarah, who waved it away. She pressed it on her.

"Look," Sarah said, "I don't want to!"

"Smoke!"

Paul was fascinated. What kind of accountant took orders like that? Miriam treated Sarah more like some kind of a slave.

Sarah took the cigar. Leo lit up in a hurry. In the front, Luis lit up. Only Miriam didn't smoke. She sat glaring at Sarah. Whatever was going on between those two, Paul thought, they were absolutely furious with each other.

There was some cognac in the car, and Paul had a snifter with his cigar. It was as soft as a pillow, this brandy, but full of flavor. He didn't bother to ask how old it was. Probably came straight out of Napoleon's hip flask.

He allowed himself to imagine that what had come between him and Miriam might be serious.

"Where is home, by the way?"

"I have a beautiful home. You're going to just love it. And if you *don't*, then we are going to change it so you do. Isn't that right, girls?"

"Yes, Miri," Sarah said, tears in the corners of her eyes. Paul felt sorry for her. Knowing Miriam, she'd been bedding this sweet little thing. They could have been serious lovers. And then all of a sudden, here comes this guy, and bang, Sarah's strictly backseat.

Paul wanted to kiss Miriam again. He wanted to be in her again, to go in there and just live in there. That was his damn wheelhouse from now on, that fabulous twat of hers. What a creature. What a damn night.

It got quiet in the car. Leo and Sarah were staring daggers at Miriam. They looked as if they wanted to beat her up, as a matter of fact.

Well, let 'em try, Paul thought. She was his girl now and nothing anybody could say, nothing they could do, could change that. Except—he was aware that it was a little dangerous to say you'd fallen in love forever because of a single great roll in the hay.

But, hey, there was something *there,* something damned wonderful and serious. It had happened. It damn well *had.*

He watched Sarah puff a little on her cigar, then closed his eyes and sipped some more cognac.

This was the life, despite the fact that all the exercise had made his shoulder start to sing. He'd like a couple of naproxen or something. No more opium. He'd done his share of drugs for the night.

He thought of his seven grand at the Terminal Hotel. If he didn't show up sometime tomorrow, they'd be sure to toss the room. Probably they already had. That would mean the Book of Names was gone. Also the seven grand. Everybody knew to toss the bedsprings if you were tossing a room.

So, what did that mean to him, now that he was on the lam? Loss of the seven grand would be tragic. As for the Book of Names, he wasn't sure if he was going to continue in that line. Maybe he'd done enough killing. He could write a pretty decent report, so maybe he'd interview at *The New York Times.* They hired out of CIA all the time . . . but mostly from the analytical divisions, not from the tough guys.

They arrived on no less than Sutton Place and pulled up—guess where—in front of the prettiest house on the whole block.

"Man," Paul said as he got out. This was way far away

from his side of the tracks. He looked up at the imposing façade. It looked damn old, but it was perfectly kept.

Miriam hurried up the steps and threw the door open. Paul joined her. "I oughta pick you up and carry you across the threshold," he said.

"Welcome to my abode. Girls, he wants some breakfast! Caviar and eggs! Champers!"

Sarah and Leonore marched off into the back of the house.

"I don't think they like me too much."

"They'll get used to you. In fact, I have a prediction. Sarah is going to totally change her opinion of you."

Paul had big plans for bedtime, which came after a breakfast where Miriam picked and drank champagne, and he thought he must have consumed sixteen eggs at least. Sarah served table, and Leonore cooked. Sarah was awful pretty when she was mad.

Paul smoked another of the cigars in the big library. He saw all kinds of amazing books. There were also locked bookcases with really ancient looking black books in them, their spines unmarked. There were even scroll boxes, smelling of beeswax. He drew a scroll partly out, but it was real old and he was afraid to unroll it for fear he'd crack the parchment and cost her a cool million or something.

He would not have been surprised to find a Gutenberg Bible in here. What he did discover was to him equally amazing—a portfolio containing an original collection of opera libretti. These were not simply early printed copies. They were the manuscript scores.

Here was *Rigoletto* in what was apparently Verdi's own hurried scrawl. Reverently, he drew the score out. Miriam came up behind him so quietly that he was startled.

She laid a delicate hand on his shoulder. "You take an interest in opera?"

"A great interest."

She took the score and walked through to another wonderful room. The wide parquet floor was covered with a Persian rug—the real thing, undoubtedly. But Paul's attention was taken by the Steinway, a concert grand set in an alcove all its own. The windows that framed it appeared to be Tiffany stained-glass.

The sun was rising, spreading golden light across the rich mahogany top of the piano. On it stood a vase that was probably an ancient Greek original. Sarah was quietly filling it with flowers from a garden that could be seen beyond the windows, just beginning to glow with the light of morning.

Miriam opened the piano. She toyed with the keys for a moment, then riffled in the score. "Sarah," she said, "would you?"

Sarah sat down at the piano. Suddenly she looked up at Paul. She held out her hands. "These belong to a surgeon," she said.

What was she getting at?

She trilled up and down the scales, shaking her head in the shafts of sunlight, so that her locks shot red-brown sparks.

Miriam set the score before her, and Sarah began to play, and quite well. It took Paul a moment to recognize "Caro Nome," and then Miriam was singing it, one of the greatest homages to the female soul that had ever been written. That she was singing it directly from the hand of its author made the experience all the more haunting.

Leo came in and listened, wiping her hands on her apron and blowing a curl out of her eyes.

When the song came to an end, Paul wanted to hold

Miriam, to let her know again how he felt. They had just had profound sex together, and he was in profound love. It sounded stupid, he knew that, and he couldn't actually *say* it. He'd only known her for a few hours, for the love of Christ.

She threw back her head and sang at the top of her lungs, "I'm in love, I'm in love, I'm in love with a wonderful guy!" She danced him round and round the room.

At noon she was still showing him her collections, her poetry—she had the original folio manuscript of John Keats's "Lamia," and Tennyson's "Tithonus," among many other wonders.

Paul struggled to show interest, but he had been asleep in the chair where he sat for at least a full minute when she shook his shoulder.

"Come on," she whispered in his ear, "you need a cuddle."

She took him upstairs, then, and they stripped in the sumptuous bedroom. She dropped her clothes to the floor for Leo to run around picking up. He was afraid to do the same, and put his on the edge of a little daybed.

Sarah drew them a bath in a huge onyx tub that must have, in itself, cost a million dollars. In fact, it was the damnedest tub he'd ever seen—beautiful, glowing stone embedded with gold nymphs and satyrs and sea creatures.

It reminded him of something you might find in a palace. It had an ancient Roman look to it. The only place he had ever seen anything carved with such perfection, however, was in the King's Chamber of the Great Pyramid. The sarcophagus there looked a little like this tub.

Sarah wore a green dress with a maid's cap and a white apron. Between her soft good looks and Miriam's wondrous, long-legged nudity, Paul was damn well ready to go again. Sarah gave him a playful tweak as he stepped into the tub.

"Don't misfire his cannon." Miriam laughed as she joined him. Sarah washed their hair and their backs with fragrant soap. She washed his face, which was an incredibly intimate experience. Being naked with Miriam would mean being naked with her friends, apparently. Hell, the more the merrier.

Here in this bathtub with these amazing people around him, he definitely decided that his past was no longer his problem. He told himself that this decision was now and forever. The world had survived a long time with vampires hiding in its shadows.

From this moment on, he had a new job: getting Miriam to marry him.

He lounged back, eyes closed, as Sarah's fingers delicately massaged his cheeks and softly caressed his forehead. Miriam's toes appeared between his legs, pressing and touching.

Yeah, it was heaven. The crusty old tough guy had found one hell of a pasture, looked like. He thought—hoped—that he was presently feeling the tiredness and disappointment of a lifetime, and maybe even its many, many sins, slipping away into the past and welcome forgetfulness, being cleansed away by the ministry of angels.

Then he noticed Leo. She had come in quietly. She sat on the john with her legs crossed, smoking and watching him. He saw the strange little knife again. It was outlined in the pocket of her very tight jeans.

Their eyes met. She smiled.

EIGHTEEN

Careless Love

Miriam and Sarah stood hand in hand looking at the magnificent human specimen lying asleep on the bed.

"He's in hog heaven," Sarah said.

"He is."

Leo took out the fleam. She moved toward the bed, then looked to Miriam, her face questioning.

"Leo, we're not going to do him."

"But I feel—" She shuddered. "We have to."

"She's right, Miri. Think what he's seen. Think who he is!"

Paul stirred, throwing a large hand out from under the covers. "Miri . . ."

Miriam went to the bedside and knelt and kissed the hand. "I'm here, my love."

The hand reached out, stroked her cheek. "Mmm . . ."

She slid in beside him.

When Sarah saw the tenderness in Miriam's eyes, she was horrified. What had happened to her? Had she gone insane? This was the most foolhardy thing she had ever done.

"Leo," Sarah said, "do it."

Leo looked at the fleam. "H-how?"

Miriam's head came out of the covers. She raised herself

up. She whispered, her mouth close to Sarah's ear. "I think I'm pregnant."

Sarah stepped back, for a moment too surprised even to respond. She was a scientist and doctor who'd had twenty years to study every aspect of Miri's body. A limitless budget had made the lab in the basement a wonder of science, equipped with every conceivable instrument, including many that Sarah had designed herself and had built by the finest medical engineering establishments in the world.

Sarah knew, therefore, that this "pregnancy" was a tragic fantasy. It must mean—could only mean—that Miri's last egg had dropped. She was not pregnant; she just wanted to be. She could not become pregnant by a human being. All that had really happened was that Miriam Blaylock had lost her last chance to bear a child.

Sarah rushed into her and Miri's sunroom, where they had their private little place together. Miri sewed for a hobby, using the intricate stitches taught her by her mother, producing the exquisite leatherwork of the Keepers. On the floor where Sarah had laid it, beside a couple of ancient half-opened scrolls, was the Book of Names that so much blood, human and Keeper, had been shed over in Paris.

Sarah threw herself down on her daybed and let the bitterness and the sorrow that had built up over the last terrible hours flood out of her in the form of huge, gasping sobs. Sometimes Sarah hated Miri, but mostly she loved her, and especially when she was suffering and vulnerable, as she most certainly was now.

It would fall to Sarah to examine her in the stirrups, as she had done so often, and to give her the news that would break her heart. In the end, Miri would come back to her, turning as always to Sarah's enfolding arms for comfort. Sarah would give her what comfort she could, but how can you relieve the sorrow of a woman who has just learned that she has lost her last chance for a baby?

And worse, by so doing she had exposed herself and her household to mortal danger. She was in there alone with that evil creature—how could she *be* so heedless?

There were tender sounds coming from the bedroom, sounds of lovemaking. Sarah went to the door and signaled Leo, who was standing by helplessly and self-consciously.

"Sarah, I feel dreadful!"

"I know, dear." As much as she detested this foolish girl, she could only sympathize with her now. She had lived this suffering.

"I've got to have blood." She gave Sarah a desperate glance. "I tried to eat some of the omelet I made him, but it was revolting, it tasted like wet paper." She threw her arms around Sarah. "He smells good. He smells like—like—"

"Food."

"What have I done, Sarah, what have I done to myself?"

Sarah could not answer her. There were no words to describe the ruin of a soul. But she held her, she kissed her soft hair. "We'll hunt you up a meal. Like that old woman. A nice meal."

Leo looked at her out of awful, stricken eyes. "I don't want to kill anybody."

"You made a choice."

"I don't want to!"

Sarah moved quickly to close the bedroom door. He mustn't overhear this.

"Leo, I'm going to tell you something about that man in there. I don't want you to be frightened. It's all going to come right. I hope it is."

She went across to the graceful New Kingdom table that stood beneath the wide window. Paul's magnum pistol lay there. The table had been a gift to Miri from Thutmose IV, "in exchange," as she put it, "for some girlish indiscretions that he found very enjoyable."

"This is going to come as a surprise, I know. That man in there is a killer of the Keepers. A professional."

Leo's eyes went to the closed door. "I didn't think anybody knew about them."

"There are people who know. He's one of them. He's murdered hundreds of them." She said nothing of how that made her feel—the combination of relief and cold terror.

"Oh, my God. But why is she—"

"Leo, something happened tonight that I still don't fully understand. She apparently enjoyed that man immoderately. She thinks, for whatever reason, that he fertilized her egg."

"Only another Keeper can. Isn't that true?"

Sarah nodded. "It's a fantasy, nothing more. A tragic fantasy."

"She can make a mistake like that?"

"Miriam—a Keeper woman—has only four eggs in her lifetime. This is her last one."

"Does she have any children?"

"No. Apparently she's lost her last egg, and—well, she seems to have had a bit of a breakdown."

"Can't you give her anything? I mean, you're a doctor and all."

"What we need to do is to give her a pregnancy test. When it comes up negative, my hope is that she'll come to her senses."

"And I'll get—I'll get to . . ." She lowered her eyes. Her face burned with shame. "I hate this!"

"You bought it," Sarah said. "Wear it."

"I don't want to do any more killing! Not ever, Sarah."

"Join the club."

"But I have to, don't I?"

"Join the club."

Leo began to weep. The hopelessness in the small, defeated sobs was familiar from Sarah's own private moments. Sarah embraced her, and Leo held on tight. "It hurts, Sarah. It hurts terribly!"

"Blood will fix that."

Leo grew pale. "I'll kill myself," she said.

Sarah was silent. Leo hadn't yet seen the attic. Better to put that off for a few days.

"What do I do, Sarah?"

"Leo, that man in there is a monster. He's killed hundreds of Keepers, and he'll kill Miri the instant he discovers what she is."

"She won't let him."

"In bed together for hours, exploring each other naked, and him being familiar with Keepers and how they look—it could happen at any moment." She gestured toward the magnum. "That thing is loaded with explosive bullets. They'll blow your brains right out of your head, your heart out of your chest. The only thing that Miriam's body can't survive is the failure of blood flow. Given an intact circulatory system, she'll heal. Always. He knows this. He knows exactly how to kill a Keeper."

"I had a nice life. I had my loft and my little boat and my friends—a few friends—and I was collecting cool artists like the Starn brothers and John Currin . . . but I spent most of my nights at home, or going to clubs by myself, trying to look like the group I wanted to be part of. But nobody wanted me. I was a washout . . . until all of a sudden *Miriam Blaylock* starts taking an interest. In me! I was totally impressed, Sarah." She choked back a sob.

To her credit, she did not break down, which is what Sarah had thought was going to happen. She raised her head, stuck out her chin, and said, "What we have to do is pretty damn simple."

"It is indeed."

She took out the fleam, handed it to Sarah. "You know how to use this; I don't."

Sarah opened it. "You hook the end in behind the vessel, then jerk it toward you. The blood'll come out in a stream. You get your mouth over it and just keep swallowing as fast as you can."

"What if I throw up?"

"You won't. You're carrying around a pint of Miri's blood in your veins. It'll be like taking the most intense drug you've ever known. It makes the most powerful horse ever sold seem like aspirin."

"He'll go nuts when he gets stuck. I mean, he's gonna feel it, Sarah."

"I'll do the incision. All you have to do is cover the wound with your mouth and suck as hard as you possibly can."

"He'll fight."

"It's not like that if you're fast. They lose consciousness in a couple of seconds."

"You better do it."

"You need to eat! If you don't, her blood's going to start destroying yours. You'll go into shock."

"I'll die?" She actually sounded hopeful, as if she thought it might be a welcome release. Sarah thought of what was in the attic.

"Feeding draws the blood right out of the brain. He won't even get a chance to yell."

Leo looked to her with the gaze of a little sister, and Sarah realized that her feelings toward this kid were changing. She squeezed Leo's hand, trying to reassure her. "You're going to be perfect. The hard part is the incision, and I'm doing that."

"It's quiet," Leo said, looking toward the closed door of Miriam's bedroom.

"He's sleeping."

"But she isn't?"

"No."

Miri only slept after she fed. Since she hadn't, she would be completely conscious the whole time.

"You stay at the door, Leo. Come in at my signal."

Sarah went into the bedroom, her fleam concealed in her blouse. Paul was as comatose as a mouse-stuffed snake. Miri was cuddled up to him like a schoolgirl with her first lover.

She looked so happy, eyes closed, face blissful. She was nuzzling his chest hair.

When Miri saw Sarah, she gave her a secret, delighted smile. Sarah went to her and stroked her hair, which was twice as full as it had been even a few hours ago. The Keeper body was astonishing in its ability to regenerate and restore itself. Sarah had been fascinated to find out how it all worked. Some nature somewhere had evolved this wonderfully regenerative organism, but it had not been earthly nature. Miriam had never told Sarah where they had come from, only that it was the stars. Why they had appeared here, as colonists or refugees, or—as Sarah suspected—on some far more exotic mission involving the evolution of species, she would not discuss, and perhaps did not know.

Sarah went around the far side of the bed from Miri. She hated so to hurt her, but this had to be done, and there was no time to waste. Poor Miri could be foolish in love. It was her one failing. Sarah had been the victim of some of that foolishness, but also the beneficiary of its indulgence, for which she was profoundly grateful. Miri's love also lasted. In the past twenty years, she had probably spent ten million dollars on Sarah's scientific efforts, even indulging her struggle to see if she could remove the Keeper blood that Miri herself had put in her veins.

Sarah slipped into the bed. Paul's back was to her, his form concealing her from Miri's vision. She stretched out against him.

"Isn't he wonderful?" Miri whispered.

"He's certainly big."

Sarah brought out the fleam, then drew the narrow silver blade with the hooked end out of its ivory sheath. Using the delicate tips of her surgeon's fingers, she found his jugular.

The pulse was excellent. He was going to be an extraordinary first meal for Leo. In fact, there'd be plenty for Sarah, too. She could top off that weak old woman and maybe get a month more time before she needed to feed again.

This was one kill that she wasn't going to mind. How strange her heart was, to want to kill an enemy of Miri's who had literally stolen her from herself. But she loved Miri at least as much as she hated her. She didn't think of herself as a lesbian—she had no interest in Leo, for example—but what Miri had done for her in the car on the way to the club had been wonderful beyond words, so fulfilling that it seemed to literally feed the soul. Not even with Tom had it been like it was with Miri.

This love across the border of species was deeply awful, yes, but somehow also deeply sacred. For all of her anger and all of her striving to escape her fate, Sarah knew that she would always be here, always in the end choosing her Miri over freedom, over death, over everything.

She rose into a sitting position. Now she could see Miri, whose eyes were closed, whose lips reflected deep happiness—deep and pitiful.

She motioned to Leo, who came quickly to her side. Sarah gestured toward the sleeping man, then toward Leo's mouth. Leo nodded. On her face was a child's expression of fascination.

With the quickness of long practice, Sarah slit the vein. Blood spurted, and she pressed Leo's head against the wound.

She did surprisingly well, sucking with ferocious energy.

"He's out," Sarah said, as Paul's body sagged.

But then a shock like an explosion went through the huge body. Sarah heard air rush into the lungs. Leo was sucking hard, but he was most certainly not out.

On the contrary, he roared out his pain and surprise. Miri screamed, too, and leaped back away from them.

Still roaring, with Leo stuck to him like a stubborn leech, Paul lumbered up off the bed and started pulling at her, trying to rip her off him. She was not going to be pulled off, though. She sucked, he screamed, he staggered, Miri screamed.

Obviously, this man was not like ordinary men. Somehow, this man had remained conscious through a sudden and total loss of intercranial blood pressure. Somehow, this rather easy kill had become a disaster.

He lurched across the room, trying to peel Leo off. Her eyes were wide and she remained stuck tight. It was the blood, Sarah knew, the incredible effect of the blood. Her first taste had driven her almost mad with pleasure, and she would fight off the devil before she would stop sucking it out of him.

Sarah also knew that this monster was not going to be killed. She raced out of the bedroom.

Leo was hardly even aware of what was happening. This blood—it was a miracle, it tasted like sunlight, like heaven. Every gulp of it went gushing into her starved cells, filling her with energy and power and buzzing thrills.

Then strong arms—really strong arms—came around her and yanked her off. Paul dropped to his knees, his neck spurting. He was gasping, he was swaying—and then he reached out and grabbed Leo's wrist and drew her down to him. He tried to speak but nothing came out. But the look of hatred on his face was something phenomenal, something unnatural. He was like some kind of hell creature, this man.

Miri grabbed her away from him and screamed directly in her face, a banshee wail. "He's of my kind," she shrieked. "Of *my* kind!"

A high-voltage shock of total surprise flashed through Sarah, who had returned to the bedside. She was saying that this man . . . was a Keeper? *This* man?

He rose up, his eyes blazing. He tore a newel post off the bed and swung it. It whistled past Leo, nearly hitting her. Then he swung it at Miri, who ducked easily. It shattered instead against the wall with such force that the whole house shook.

He leaped on Miri. His hands tightened like a vise around her neck. Leo grabbed his arms, but he could not be dislodged. No matter the blood he had lost and was still losing, he was as strong as iron.

"He's killing her," she screamed. She beat on his back. Miri's eyes came bulging out of her head. Leo screamed, she cried, she hauled at the iron arms. Miri's face was disintegrating, her mouth returning to its natural shape, the prosthetics that altered her appearance popping out. Then the compression of her throat forced her tongue between her lips. It appeared, black and pointed, gorged with blood. His own blood was still spraying out of his neck, spattering her with a red shower.

Leo hit him and hit him, but he was totally fixed on this; he was like a robot programmed to kill.

Suddenly there was a terrific, blinding blast and he dropped like a stone. Leo threw herself between him and Miri, who went to her feet coughing and rubbing her neck.

Sarah stood quietly, the magnum in her hands.

Miri staggered. Then she threw herself on him; she turned him over, tried to stop his bleeding. "Help us," she screamed.

"Miri, let her feed! Let her take him!"

"You're a doctor! Help us!"

"Miri, he's dangerous! He's got to be killed, come on!"

"Save him, Sarah! *Please!*"

"Miri, no! Leo, take him!"

Miriam leaped up, and before Sarah could stop her, she had tossed Leo across the room like a rag doll. Then she yanked the magnum out of Sarah's hands.

Sarah prepared to die.

But Miriam stuck the gun in her own mouth. She screwed her eyes shut.

This would not kill her, but it would leave her too damaged to recover. In the end, Sarah would have to stop her heart.

"Miri, *no!*"

"Then help him."

Sarah knelt to the unconscious form, stemmed the bleeding from his jugular with a finger. His eyes were fully rolled back, and he was seizing from blood loss and shock. He had probably five minutes, maybe less.

"We've got to get him downstairs," Miri said. She tossed the gun aside.

Miriam carried his shoulders, Sarah his feet. They took him to the lift in the front hall, squeezed in with him while Leo raced ahead on the stairs. She had the examination table dressed with a sheet by the time they reached the surgery.

He was in deep shock now. "This is going to be a problem," Sarah said. She slapped a pressure bandage on his neck. The flow had dropped by two-thirds. His blood pressure must be almost nothing. "I'm losing him."

Miriam burst into tears, threw herself on him.

"Get her off," Sarah said to Leo.

But when Leo touched her, she threw back her head and howled with an agony beyond anything Sarah had heard from her or anybody ever. She'd never seen her like this, crazy with grief, her emotions like an exploding volcano.

"Leo, have you ever assisted in a surgery?"

"God no."

Sarah took Miri's shoulders. "Miri, can you hear me? Miri!"

Slowly, by what looked like tormented inches, a more sane expression returned to her face. "You did not have the right to take him." Her eyes flashed with a ruler's pride. "*You did not have the right!*"

"Please forgive me," Sarah said.

"Then save him! Save him!"

Sarah stabilized the neck wound, then got them to turn him over on his stomach. The entry point of the bullet was below the heart. If the artery was intact, he might have a chance. She couldn't type his blood, there was no time, so she had to go with O+. She told Leo, "Get me six pints of blood from the fridge. Miri, set him up." While they worked, she went to the cupboard and took out her instruments. She had a complete surgery here, even an extractor for bullets. She had once promised Miri, "If I can get you here, I can fix it, no matter what may befall you."

There was an X-ray machine, but there was no way they could move him to the table now. There was no time. "Scalpel," Sarah said as she swabbed the entry wound with Betadine. A glance told her that Miri had set the blood properly.

If he was really a Keeper of some unknown kind, she was flying almost totally blind. In Sarah's own veins, Miriam's blood functioned like a separate organ. It flowed with Sarah's natural blood, but did not mix with it. It could not. Sarah could not even begin to guess what was going on in this man.

She dissected around the entry wound, opening it wider and wider, snapping orders. "Spreaders!" she called when she reached the rib cage. "Clamp!" she said when she found torn blood vessels.

She could not entirely save the lung, but she managed to isolate the bleeding enough to resect. Time disappeared for her. She concentrated totally, remembering her training and her work experience from so many years ago. Her fingers worked sometimes almost by magic, but for the most part it was her careful training that saw her through this terribly challenging procedure without—she hoped—a serious error.

When she could at last close him up, his blood pressure had risen to 80 over 50 and his pulse was 160. A temperature of just 99 suggested that he was tolerating the transfused blood well. She put him on an electrolyte drip, then got her prescription pad. She wrote for some time, then handed it to Leo. "They'll have all this in the drugstore at Riverside Hospital."

"What's the situation?" Miriam asked. Her blood-spattered robe still hung off her naked body. Her face was hollow, her skin gray.

"He's hanging on."

Miriam's face twisted, and she threw herself sobbing into Sarah's arms.

"Oh, baby," Sarah said, "baby, I'm so sorry. I didn't understand. I didn't know . . ."

"There was an attempt to cross the species, recorded in the Books ten conclaves ago. Keepers trying to escape from the need to eat human blood. The result wasn't good. We'd created human beings with the speed and power of Keepers. So we destroyed all the family lines, except one. We found a last survivor about forty years ago. He was destroyed. Apparently he had a son."

"I don't think this is true, Miri. There's no way we could interbreed. We're as different as tigers and cattle, except on the surface."

"You have no idea what our science was capable of—when we had a science."

"What happened to your science?"

Miriam regarded her. She laughed a little, and Sarah sensed a whole hidden history in that laughter, a history of secrets that would never be told. "It was so good to be with him; it was like going back to the one time in all my life that I was truly and deeply happy. Oh, Sarah, I love him so!"

Sarah found herself hoping that the pregnancy was real. Because if this was true, and it was a healthy fetus, then maybe the great hope of Miriam's life was being realized.

But still Sarah saw Paul to be mortal danger, and Leo was stationed to watch his monitors.

"How about your hunger?" Miriam asked her.

"I got some blood," she said. But Leo's hollow expression told them both that it had not been enough.

Sarah took Miriam back upstairs, to their private room. They turned on the video system so she could watch the infirmary every moment.

She lay back on the little sofa where she so often read and worked. Sarah knelt beside it. "Please forgive me, Miri."

Miriam gazed at her. "I forgive you, child," she said. "But you must help me with this."

"Miri, he hates you. And he's a killing machine."

"He has a heart, Sarah, a huge heart. I want my chance to try to reach his heart."

"When he wakes up, Miri, God knows what'll happen."

"I want you to help me. Both of you."

"Of course we will. That goes without saying."

Miriam went over and picked up the encaustic painting of her lost Eumenes. "I left my happiness in another world."

"We have happiness."

She smiled a little. "I'm the last of my kind, you know—the last Keeper."

"There are others."

Miriam looked at her. "Living in holes? That's not being a Keeper—a true ruler of mankind." She gazed at the portrait of the handsome young man in his white toga. "I'm lost in time." She put it down and came back to Sarah. "But I have a baby. I have hope."

Sarah did not know what Miriam had in her belly, and she wasn't sure she wanted to find out. If this much-shattered heart took another blow, it was even possible that Miriam would join her peers in the shadows, living like an animal and waiting—no doubt hoping—to die.

"I want a pregnancy test."

Sarah played for time. "As soon as Paul recovers."

"No, no," Miriam said. "You'll do it immediately."

"I need the resources of the infirmary for him."

Miriam came to her. "You can do the test and we both know it."

Sarah took her in her arms.

"I have to know," Miriam whispered.

Sarah hugged her tight.

They stayed like that, in the declining light of the afternoon.

Leo paced to the wall and back to the door, and she remembered chocolate icebox pie and blinis and blintzes and beluga. She went to the back windows and wiped off her sweat and remembered Mommy's chicken fricasee and Aunt Madeline's molasses cookies. She slapped the wall and hugged herself and sweated rivers and remembered rib eyes at Sparks and smoked salmon at Petrossian.

But all that really mattered was the raw, delicious taste in her mouth and the smell in her nose of blood, blood, blood.

When she'd drunk his blood, she'd drunk his soul, and she was drunk on it and she had to have more of it.

Her jeans were soaked with pee, her underarms and hair were awash, and she felt as if she couldn't breathe and couldn't think because she needed more, she wasn't finished—she wanted a lovely bowl of cherry cobbler, but she needed blood.

She went to the black front door, put her hand on the gleaming brass handle, and she pushed out into the flaring evening.

The city was its ordinary self, humming its indifferent hum, traveling down its million uncaring roads.

She was a hunter now, off to the hills. She ranged down the turning street and to the secret steps that led down to FDR Drive.

A car screamed past three feet away, then another and another. Leo darted out into the roadway. Two more cars came speeding toward her. She leaped forward just as one almost grazed her back. Then she was on the far side of FDR Drive, climbing the iron railing and going along the narrow promenade.

A full moon hung over the surging East River, its glow touching the black, uneasy waves.

She was absolutely frantic; she'd never felt anything remotely like this. By light-years, this clawing, flaming inner agony was the most intense sensation she had ever felt in her life. She ached the way people ache when they can't get enough air.

She dashed along, searching for a derelict like a pig snuffling for truffles. She was strung worse than she'd ever known anybody to be strung. This made you wild; it made you want to run and never stop; it seethed like ants under your skin; it pumped pure desperation straight into your brain.

As she ran, she thought of home, the imposing house in Greenwich, her taffeta-and-lace bedroom, her daddy probably right now watching Monday night football, her mom reading.

Home was lost to her, home and all she had known of the peace of life. Her feet throbbed; her heart raced; her skin felt as if it were being sandpapered. The taste of Paul's blood lingered in her mouth, its scent in her nostrils. All she could think about was blood, the way it tasted, the way it felt going down, the way it had cooled the fire that was consuming her from within.

Then she saw a clump of shadow on a moonlit bench. She went up to it. Just a mass of rags. Good. Man or woman? Man—not so good, they were stronger.

She sat on the end of the bench nearest the head. Her hands almost shook too much, but she managed to get a cigarette lit. She'd quit two months ago, but that was before she met Miriam. Miriam smoked all the time. She didn't care. Why should she? Keepers were immune to cancer.

She dragged hard, wishing that the smoke was stronger. You could get a nice hit smoking horse in a cigarette, but she didn't have any horse. She had to calm down on her own.

She had the fleam and she had the victim. All she needed now was the guts. She looked down at a shock of dark, oily, lice-ridden hair. She knew he was dirty and that he probably stank to high heaven, but all she could smell was the blood, which was so good that she kept sucking in air and leaning closer.

She took the fleam out, fumbled the blade open—giving herself a nasty little nick in the process. Before she had even sucked it, the wound closed.

A damn miracle.

Stealthily, she shuffled the rags aside. There was the neck. Not an old neck. She knew she was supposed to take them back to the house, burn the remnant in the furnace and all. But how could she get some drunk back across FDR Drive and up the narrow steps that led to their property? The business with the lady, whom she'd found on Fifty-fifth Street and First Avenue, had been difficult enough.

She held the fleam close to the neck. She couldn't see any

veins. She dared not touch the guy. She tightened her grip on the instrument. Then she plunged it down. There was resistance; then it went sliding in—way deeper than it should. In fact, she almost plunged it all the way in.

She was snatching for it as he rose screaming through clenched teeth out of his pile of newspapers and rags. He was face-to-face with her, his teeth bared.

He was a kid. Maybe younger than she was. He had long eyelashes, and the moonlight shone in his dark eyes. His hands went to his neck, his head cocked—and a flood of blood came out of his mouth.

Instinct made Leo go for it, but it was all over the ground already, splattering and splashing like spilled milk on the kitchen floor. He went to his feet, still screaming behind his clenched teeth, and began jerking and staggering, his bloody fingers slipping on the bloody hilt of the fleam.

And then, incredibly, she recognized him. Not from the club, not from her present life at all. She recognized him from prep school, from Andover. It was Benno Jones. He'd been a performance artist. His family was wealthy but very conservative. Obviously, there'd been an estrangement.

She was confused. But also now, desperate. She lunged at him; she got her fingers around the fleam and yanked it as hard as she could. It came partially out, dragging red gristle, followed by a gurgling black flow of blood.

She latched on like a starving jungle leech. The blood seemed to flow into her almost automatically, pouring down her throat into her belly. Benno staggered along, his back bent, his hands made into fists, his barely-remembered acquaintance inexplicably sucking the life out of him.

He went down like a staggered bull, to his knees. She pushed him over and dragged his head into her lap, bending the neck to give herself the best possible angle. Then she put her lips around the bubbling gouge and sucked as hard as it was possible for her to suck. She got lots more blood, and from his lips a gentle question, "Leo?"

She did it again and it worked again. A third time and it worked, but less well. The fourth time, it hardly worked at all.

But he wasn't getting any thinner or lighter. He was still normal looking, except he was very dead. She tried again, sucking with all her might.

Nothing happened. She sat back on her haunches. Only Miriam could dry them out. He was way too heavy to carry. He felt like a sack of lead.

Then she saw, some distance down the promenade, a man walking about ten dogs. They were coming toward her and the dogs were going completely berserk. You couldn't hear the man, but you could see him yelling at them. Their voices were a riot of barking and howling, and they were struggling so furiously to reach the kill that their paws were digging dust up off the pavement. They looked as if they had exhaust.

She managed to get Benno to the railing and, with a massive, grunting effort, to roll him over and into the East River. Then she ran like hell, and as she ran, she began also to feel wonderful.

Behind her, the dogs quickly consumed any small trace of Benno that she had left behind. She could hear the dog walker now, still screaming himself hoarse.

Her body seemed almost ready to lift off. She could run and run without even getting tired. Incredibly, it felt as if there were somebody inside her, a living presence that was not her but was friendly to her and part of her. It was a grand way to feel as if you had your own angel in you.

She did not see the solitary figure on the high cliff that separated Miriam's neighborhood from the Drive, who had been watching her from the beginning. She did not see it put a small instrument away, perhaps a set of binoculars, perhaps a camera.

She did not see it as it got into a car, nor did she see the car drive swiftly away.

NINETEEN

Trapped

Miriam raced through the house screaming for Leo, her voice shrill and shattering. Sarah was terrified. She'd never seen her like this. She was crazed with fury; there was no other way to describe her. Then those awful, inhuman eyes were suddenly glaring at Sarah.

"Miri, calm down. Please, Miri!"

Miriam shot across the sitting room and grabbed her and slammed her against the wall. "Where in hell were you?"

"I was with you, Miri!"

"You let her out, goddamn you! You careless, foolish—"

She slapped Sarah so hard she went flying. Then Miriam was on her again, shaking her, screaming and smashing her head again and again into the floor. Sarah saw stars; the world reeled; she screamed, screamed again.

Miriam went to her feet, lithe and quick, glaring down at her. Then she was back again, her eyes glowing, her narrow lips twisted in some expression so alien that Sarah couldn't even begin to interpret it.

She kissed Sarah. Then she lifted her and helped her to a chair. She knelt before her and kissed her hands. "I'm sorry. Sorry. I'm just—" She made a small sound, the snarl of a hurt tiger. "I'm feeling things I've never felt before." She laid her head in Sarah's lap. Now she was weeping. "When I last had a baby in me, I was *so* protected. We owned Egypt! We lived in walled compounds. The wealth, the power—you can't even begin to imagine! But now—I've got my last baby and I need to feel safe and I don't!"

Sarah stroked her hair. She looked down at the lithe, powerful body in the magnificent butterfly robe, a garment made in China six hundred years ago, of thousands of individual bits of silk sewed together with tiny stitches. It was like a cloud of butterflies, this robe. Miri wore it casually, but that did not change the fact that it could easily be the most beautiful garment presently on earth.

Sarah had always been a lonely sort of a soul, but Miriam was *really* alone. Her baby had been her hope—Sarah realized that now—her one hope to relieve the despair that lay concealed behind the elegance and the headlong decadence that filled her time.

When she found out that this baby was a fata morgana, a mirage, she was going to be absolutely devastated.

Paul knew he was alive because of the pain. From his waist to his neck, he was a mass of sheer agony. His breath was coming in light little gulps, but he felt no air hunger, so he knew there was oxygen running.

He inventoried his body, working from training and long experience. He could wiggle his toes and hands, and lift his arms. That was good. He was too weak to lift his legs. That was not good. The left side of his neck ached. That must be a healing wound where that bitch had tried to suck his blood. His chest was gunshot real bad. There was bubbling when he inhaled, which meant that his lung capacity was dangerously low.

He was looking up, at least, into the ceiling of a hospital room. He could hear monitors beeping, and he could see an IV.

How the hell he had ever gotten himself to a hospital, he could not for the life of him imagine, but he damn well had. His self-evaluation told him that he had been shot in the left lung, which had resulted in aspiration pneumonia, caused by blood and debris. There wasn't any fever, so whatever antibiotics were in that drip were clearly doing their job. Also, the pain was diffuse, not concentrating on a certain spot the way it did when you had a bullet in you. Okay, so he'd been operated on. How much of the lung was left in there he had no idea. Maybe none, the way it felt.

Altogether, he had been in worse shape than this and come out of it okay. So, great, he was going to have himself a killing spree as soon as he recuperated . . . unless, of course, his presence in this intensive care ward meant that he was back in the hands of the Company.

After a long five minutes, Miriam came up off Sarah's lap. The red eyes glared up at her. Instinct made Sarah cringe back away from her. Miriam sucked in breath. Sarah realized what was happening: she was hearing something.

"Is it Paul Ward?" But a glance at one of the monitors that had been set up in every room said that he wasn't the issue. He was stirring from the woozy state induced by his Valium drip, but he came in and out of consciousness three or four times a day. His lung capacity was too low to allow him to be fully awake.

Miriam came to her feet, catlike. In an instant, she was at the front door, listening against the thick mahogany. Then she rushed across the foyer into the music room, sat down at the piano, and—of all things—began to play Beethoven's *Moonlight Sonata*. The vision of the cloud of butterflies floating around that narrow, incredibly graceful being was heart-stopping. She played with a touch as soft as a dusting of snow.

Sarah watched the great front door. The lock clicked. The handle moved. Leo's face appeared. From its flush, Sarah knew at once that she had fed. Hearing the music, seeing Sarah sitting with her head back against her chair, Leo's nervous face smoothed. All seemed well to her, all at peace.

Sarah could not imagine the reason for the false tableau. It was as if Miri didn't believe that Leo would come in unless she was lured by an artificial appearance of serenity. Perhaps Miriam overestimated Leo's intelligence, because she was entirely deceived.

She came strolling in, smiling a conspiratorial smile at Sarah. There was blood on her blue T-shirt, more on her jeans.

"Where's the remnant?" Sarah hissed. Leo tried to go around her. Sarah grabbed her collar. "Where is it?"

"Leave me alone!"

"Leo, *where the hell is it?*"

Miriam played on, seemingly oblivious.

"None of your business," Leo sneered.

"Did you leave it on the street—for God's sake, answer me!"

"If you must know, it's in the East River. And so is that stupid toy of yours."

Sarah felt a nervous twinge in her left eye. "What toy?"

"Oh, that thing—that stupid thing went all the way in his neck."

"You left my fleam in your victim?"

"I couldn't get it out!"

"Jesus!"

Leo tried again to go around her.

That damn bunch of vampires had been smart, real smart. They'd played him like a piano. God only knew how many of the parasites infected that filthy club. And the house—this vampire was a rich bitch, wasn't she? She was light-years beyond the others. Kill this one, and you got the queen bee. Just like that really human looking one in Paris. Just like Mrs. Tallman.

Holy Shit—maybe they were one and the same. And maybe, if it was in any way still in his power, he was going to really strike a blow when he destroyed the damn creature. It had fooled him totally. Even making love to it had felt great, better than making love to a real woman. A fucking animal had tricked him into screwing it, and that made him even angrier.

His throat had the metallic taste that you get when you're having electrolytes pumped through your body. He wanted water and food.

"Nurse?" he called.

He listened. Whatever hospital he was in, it was as quiet as a damn tomb. Probably an isolation ward for cases with classified material. He felt around for a call button, found one attached to the headboard.

Thing was, when he pressed it, who was going to come through the door—a sweet little nurse or Justin Turk? His money was on Turk. They'd been on his tail, for sure. Whenever he'd gotten into trouble before, the Company had very kindly rescued him.

So maybe he wouldn't be free to kill the filth. Goddamnit,

maybe he ought to get up and bust out of here before it was too late. Unless it was already too damn late.

He actually started to raise himself, thinking to pull out the IV and take off. He felt pretty strong, except for his breathing. But if he tried this, he'd violate a rule that had kept him alive over his entire career: Never attack into the unknown. If all you knew was who was there, or supposed to be there, that was enough. But if you knew nothing, then you had to wait.

So he'd get the lay of things, build up his strength. Right now, what he wanted was a big rib eye, but a cup of broth would do. He pressed the button again. Nothing happened. Typical, probably meant this was some VA hole. He pressed it again, harder.

Sarah watched the monitor. Faintly, she heard the buzzing as Ward struggled to get some attention. He was more awake now than he'd been since the surgery five days ago. She thought, *He's healing.* She could not help but feel a little professional pride. She'd brought a man back who should be dead.

The music stopped. Miriam got up. She turned and came toward them, the butterfly robe billowing behind her, a cigarette fuming between her narrow lips, her eyes flashing. "Where the hell were you?" she snarled.

"Me?"

Miriam's eyes met Sarah's. "The remnant's exposed," Sarah said. "My fleam was left in the neck."

Miriam went up to Leo. Long fingers grabbed her throat. "This is how you repay me?"

Leo pulled away from her. "I threw the guy in the fucking East River. He's gone."

"A body is never gone unless it's burned," Miriam shouted.

Once or twice, she'd alluded to the fact that she had done away with human companions who hadn't worked out. Sarah thought for a moment that she was going to finish Leo right now, right here on the marble floor of the foyer.

But then Miriam threw back her head and laughed. It was strange laughter, almost silent. "Come with me," she told Leo.

"Come where?"

Miriam grabbed her wrist and dragged her off up the stairs. Sarah got up to follow. Miriam stopped her. "My husband is calling," she said. "Can't you hear him?"

Paul heard a sound beyond the room's closed door. He'd punched the call button about fifty times. He shifted in the bed. "Nurse," he said. The single word ran him out of breath, and he sank back against his pillow sucking oxygen.

When Sarah Roberts's face came into his view, he was so surprised that he delivered a croaking "Oh, shit!"

She was a vision of absolute beauty, her eyes glittering like coals. He tried to lift his arms, to strike out at her, but something stopped him.

He was cuffed to the bed. "Christ!"

"You're healing," Sarah said.

He inventoried his situation. Both wrists were cuffed to a length of chain fastened to the bed, along with both ankles. He had about two feet of travel, which was why he hadn't noticed until he began trying to move.

"Where the hell am I?"

"In my infirmary." She came over to him. He got ready to grab for her. "I'm a doctor, you know."

"Yeah, that's believable."

"You've survived a lung wound from a three-fifty-seven with an exploding tip. I think it oughta be damn believable."

"You kill people for food. How can you be a doctor?"

Sarah came closer to him. "I need to examine the wound," she said. Her tone, which had been carefully neutral, now seemed sullen—or no, sad. It seemed sad.

He prepared to make a grab for her. He didn't know what he'd do next. All he knew was this: he was in the worst situation he'd ever been in, and he had to do whatever he could to get out of it.

She tossed back the sheet, barely glancing at his nakedness. She drew back the dressing that covered the left half of his chest.

As she gazed at the wound, a sound came through the open door. Somebody out there was screaming, and horribly. Even as he lay here, somewhere else in the house, the vampires were killing.

His speed was not up to its usual standard, but he managed to grab Sarah's arm. Bandages flew from her hand as he yanked her to him.

He found himself staring down the barrel of his own damn pistol.

"God damn you," he said.

"God damn you! If it wasn't for her, you'd be dead, you vicious bastard!"

She reached up to his IV, opened the cock. His attention wandered. She seemed to sway, then to float above him like a madonna ascending to heaven.

The screams rose and fell like a terrible wind in a winter tree. Sarah Roberts's eyes bored into him—cold, indifferent, murderous. Despite his pounding, relentless hate, his anguished hunger to rise from the bed, knock that gun aside, and physically rip her head from her body, he sank into sleep. The awful screams wove themselves into a dark and nameless nightmare that the drugs in the IV soon transformed into an empty, aimless void.

Miriam held Leo's wrist and would not let go, not even as the slow, dry hand came and closed around her fingers. Leo felt the strange, dry strength of the corpse; she saw the spark of life in the withered eyes.

She couldn't look at it. She couldn't bear its touch. But she also couldn't understand what this awful place was, and above all, what was the matter here.

"Open your eyes!" Miriam said. "Look at it!"

"I am! But what—why—"

"You stupid little cow—didn't you think there'd be something—some price to pay?"

"Make it let me go! Let me go!"

Miriam dragged her away from John's coffin. His clinging fingers caused the corpse to rise up, then, as its grip failed, to fall back with a dusty thud. Miriam slammed the lid.

"But he's not dead! We have to help him!"

"How compassionate you are." She marched her over to Sarah's coffin. "This is where your friend came from."

"What friend?"

"Sarah. That dreary zombie."

"Zombie?"

"After I blooded her, she cut her own wrists. But she's clever. She left me the knowledge I needed to bring her back." She gazed toward John Blaylock's coffin. "Too bad it was too late for him."

"But they—I don't get it!"

"Now that my blood is in your veins, Leonore, you cannot die. You're not like us. We don't have souls. But you do have one, and my blood has bound it forever to your body." She glanced around the room, tossed her head. "This is your fate."

Leo stood up. She backed away from Miriam. She had to get out of this awful place; she had to find a cure for herself. This was—it was unimaginable. And she had to kill—to stop this from happening to her, she had to kill and kill for the rest of her . . . time.

"Sarah's become servile. She's not an independent soul. She's boring and I hate to be bored. I hate it!"

"Bored?"

"You have no fucking idea! This isn't life, always hiding, creeping in the shadows. I'm a princess, not a damned sneak thief! I want the philosophers, the kings about me, not the sleazy gaggle of decadents I attract now."

Leo had never known a thought this strange, this subtle, but her mind at last grasped the terror of her situation. "You've stolen me from myself," she said. She felt wonder at the evil, the cunning of it. "I'm a slave."

"No! *No!* Not like her, you aren't. When I resurrected her, her will was gone. She knows it, but there's nothing she can do about it. She even went to Haiti, to try to learn about zombies, to understand her predicament." She laughed a little. "By all the stars in heaven, she's *boring!*" She yanked Leo's hand. "You're going to be great. You've got a mind of your own. You went out there and fed, against my specific rule. You did it *your* way. You know how that makes me feel?" She grasped Leo's hand, glanced back toward John's coffin. "Ever since he died, I've been alone. Now I'm not."

"What about Sarah?"

"You are foolish, though. But never mind, you've got excellent basic intelligence. I will educate you. Do you know what you're going to be? Why I've taken you into my home?"

"God that I did."

"You're going to be governess to my son."

"Husband," the vampire said, "you're awake at last. Welcome, welcome back!"

He didn't have any idea how to react to that particular gambit. But you never knew what an animal as smart as these things might come up with.

The vampire took his hand in the same slim fingers that he had kissed. He felt his gut wobbling at the thought that he had ever touched his lips to its skin . . . let alone the other things he had done. It pressed his hand against its belly.

"Do you feel him?"

He looked up at it. It was all aglow, like a real woman asking you to feel a real baby.

"He's kicking, he's *very* strong. And Sarah says he's robust. That's the word she uses—*robust*. We're going to have a son, Paul!"

What bullshit. You couldn't make a baby with a creature that wasn't human. "You're a liar," he said, barely disguising his contempt.

They left, then, all except Leo, who stayed watching him. She had the gun, Paul could see it stuck casually into her belt. This was a tough kid, this Leo. She looked like a cross between a punk rocker and a schoolgirl. She was stationed right in front of the door.

Even if he hadn't been shackled, he was probably too weak to do anything at the moment. But he wasn't real concerned. He'd get his ass out of here soon enough. He looked at Leo, and she looked back at him.

Here was a question: Was this pretty kid, this Leo, a vampire or not? You really could not tell with these creatures.

They were that good. He needed to know because he needed to know what kind of physical abilities he was dealing with. His instinct was that Leo was not a vampire. She was a hanger-on who knew the score. A very sick puppy, this Leo.

Paul tried an indirect approach, an interrogation technique he'd used a thousand times. Let the subject assume you know more than you do.

"So, Leo, what're you in it for? Drugs? Dough?"

Leo looked at him.

"Love."

"Oh, yeah, that. You love the monster. You ever fuck it?"

"Shut up."

"You know, I don't get you people. I mean, you're not a vampire, but you tolerate it. You go along with it."

"Miriam is a beautiful and ancient being. She deserves our support."

"Oh, I *see!* I guess Ellen Wunderling would agree with you. Hell, yes!"

"Sarah took her, not Miriam."

He stopped. He thought about it. Sarah had come after him with some kind of an instrument, not her sucker mouth.

Could it be that she didn't have a sucker mouth, but that she still fed on blood? If so, was there more than one species of vampire? Meaning, more vampires than he thought?

"Ellen wasn't the right kind of food for Miriam's species, or what?"

"We're blooded. Miriam gives us her blood, and—it's a miracle. You stop aging. You get incredibly healthy. You live for—well, a very long time."

Paul stared up at the ceiling. Now it develops that Miriam can make ordinary people into vampires. Jesus *wept!*

Then Paul had another, equally chilling thought. Maybe

this baby bullshit was not bullshit. If this blooding thing was real, maybe the two species were closer than anybody thought. If he'd given a vampire a baby—

He uttered a carefully contrived chuckle. "I can't believe that I knocked her up. Like, I'm human!"

Leo came over to the bed. She had the gun down at her side, hanging there in her hand. One step closer, and he could reach it. "You're not human," she said. "You're a Keeper—or half a Keeper."

It hurt, but he laughed. He really got a good laugh out of it. She was quite a bullshit artist.

"Okay. So, when do I feed on my fellow man? When I'm asleep?"

"You're something that isn't supposed to exist. They were trying to create a line that would live forever like they do, but not have to eat human blood. A better version of themselves."

He remembered them in their lairs, their sneering, contemptuous faces. "They have utter disdain for the human species," he said. "They don't care whether they eat our blood or not."

"They only hate those who kill them!"

"You're a liar."

"They do what they have to, to live. But there's no hate in it. Just hunger."

"You're lying through your teeth! They hate us and they love to kill!"

"You think so? You remember when your dad died? The way he just suddenly disappeared?"

The words seemed to come from a very long way away— echoing, strange words, terrifying words. Because there was no way she could have known about that unless—

Bellowing like a stuck bull, he rose up out of his IVs and his monitoring cuffs and his oxygen line. She backed away, but he lunged at her—and collapsed against the shackles. He was a helpless pile of rags.

She stood over him, the gun expertly braced. Somebody had taught this lady how to make a mag work exactly right.

"Don't you fucking move," she screamed. "Don't you fucking *breathe!*"

He stared up at her. "You lying bitch." But he knew she was not lying. She knew something, all right. He hadn't ever told any of these people about his dad.

"Your father was killed because he was a part of a failed mutant bloodline. We think you must have been overlooked. Unfortunately, because now you've gotten Miri pregnant with God only knows what."

"The baby's okay?"

"The first ultrasound's in two weeks."

During his outburst, she'd obviously tripped a silent alarm, because Miriam and Sarah came blasting in. They all had magnums. This place was hatching guns.

They got him rearranged in the bed.

So, Paul thought, *I guess this is a setback.*

Over the next few days, Dr. Sarah Roberts methodically showed him things about himself that he had never even dreamed. She took his blood and showed it to him under a microscope. He could see the strange cells that had been in the past attributed to a benign deformation. Then she drew blood from Miriam before his eyes and showed him the two samples side by side.

He was not blind, but he still did not want to believe. He clung to the idea—which in his heart he knew to be ridiculous—that this whole thing was a coincidence. Because he could *not*—no damn *way!*—have their blood running in his veins.

Sarah created a chromosomal map and showed him how his own nineteenth chromosome differed from that of a normal human being in the area known as 19a22.1. She showed him smaller differences in sixteen of his twenty-three chromosomes. Then she showed him Miriam's chromosomal map. It was different in every single place that his was different, as well as in three more places.

Those three places represented the need to consume human blood, the great brilliance, and life eternal.

Paul's grandfather had lived to a hundred and eleven. The whole family was like that. Supposedly there had been a Ward back a couple of centuries ago who'd made it to a hundred and nineteen.

She demonstrated to him that, because of the chromosomal differences, he would probably never be able to have a child with a human mother, but that he could indeed fertilize Miriam.

Finally, he had to face it. *He* was one of *them*. He wanted to crawl out of his own skin. If he'd been able, he would have put one of their damn guns in his mouth.

His dreams became nightmares. He hungered for death; he begged God to kill him. But he did not die. Instead, he kept getting stronger and stronger, throwing off the injuries the way he always did. Only now he knew why. It was because of his damned, accursed, evil *blood!*

Often, he would awaken and find Miriam gazing at him. She changed his dressings and cared for his bedpan, brought him his food and asked after his pain. Once in the morning and once at night, Sarah would examine him. Always she was cool and detached. Often, when they were alone, she would threaten him: "If you hurt her, if you break her heart, I will kill you with acid, I will rip your living heart out of your body."

His response was always the same: "Same to you, bitch."

He came to loathe himself. He'd fallen for Miriam because he was *one of them.* As the days passed, he got lots better. He also began to lay precise plans for the destruction of this household. He had to win their trust, first. It would not be easy, but Miriam—dear Miri—was totally smitten by him. That would be his opening.

So when Miriam came to him and sat gazing at him, he started to play little coy games with his eyes.

Miriam would twirl through the house singing "Caro Nome," and laughing, all the while feeling the baby within her. They took a year to gestate, and giving birth was very hard. But the baby—the baby was fine! "No indication of a problem," Sarah kept saying.

She really didn't know. She didn't even know for certain that Miriam was pregnant. She'd given her a urine test, but who knew if chorionic gonadotropin levels in a Keeper would be the same as in a human female. Probably not, in fact. Maybe their placental tissue produced another hormone altogether.

Unspoken in the household was the fact that the date of the first ultrasound was approaching. They would know then for sure, then and only then.

Miriam sang to her baby, she sang to her friends, and when Paul started smiling at her again, she sang to all the world.

Miriam had never before been so happy. Her household

was thriving. Her body was glowing with health. She sensed that the baby was growing beautifully. And her new husband was slowly coming round.

"You know, Paul, I think you need to see it from our viewpoint, morally."

"Try me."

"We didn't make ourselves. Nature made us."

"That's what the CIA says."

She was quite interested in this. He'd never referred to what his employers might think of her before. "How so?"

"You're not murderers; you're predators. You have a right to kill us, and we have a right to defend ourselves. That's the basis of a policy statement they're working on."

"Well, that's exactly my point." She just ached to kiss him, he was so luscious. But he had not so far been willing to do that again.

Tomorrow, she was going to surprise him. He was finished with the infirmary. Her hope was that he would return to the marriage bed. She was going to be as sweet and as tempting as she knew how.

She got Sarah alone and said to her, "It's time to take off his cuffs."

"It'll never be time for that."

"Do it."

"Miri, it's crazy!"

"Do it."

Sarah went to him. She locked the door behind her, then produced her key.

"Hey," he said.

As she unlocked first the ankle cuffs, then the wrists, he watched her. She did not like his eyes, hadn't liked them from the beginning.

"Well," he said as he rubbed his wrists, "that feels a whole lot better."

She backed away from him as she would from a spreading cobra, with care and sick fear.

He smiled.

She had been made what she was by Miriam. She was thus weak and vulnerable, the victim of inevitable imperfections. But he had been made by nature, and there was something she did not trust about nature. Perhaps it was because of something she had seen in her scientific work, that nature did not appear to be blind. The wildness of nature, the ruthlessness, was the outcome of thought.

Because of this, no matter how tame he seemed, how compliant, how much at ease, she would fear him and hate him. She knew a secret about nature, and she sensed that Paul Ward was an outcome of this secret. Nature, she knew, had a great and terrible mind.

TWENTY

The Love Child

The vampire was partial to him, so he would use that. Every hour that passed, he was closer to the moment when he could kill them all.

She loved him, but they were damn careful anyway. They watched him on video cameras, every move he made, and they kept the infirmary locked. His approach was to go along with it. He didn't even try to get out. He sat up in his bed reading *War and Peace* and listening to endless opera CDs.

He ate lots of rare steak, which had always been his comfort food. Sometimes he asked for Thai cuisine. Everything he was given was beautifully cooked. He wondered if it was also drugged. With the steaks would routinely come bottles of wine worth thousands of dollars. Château Lafite-Rothschild 1945, Château Latour 1936.

He smiled at his captors. He was affable. When Miriam came in, shining and beautiful, he let her kiss him, as much as he could bear. When she put his hand on her belly, which she imagined even now to be a little distended, he would smile at her.

* * *

"As much as he hates the Keepers," Sarah said to Miriam, "when he found out what he was, you'd think there would have been more of a reaction."

"Sarah, the man is in love. He's realized that he's one of us. He sees the moral situation. Even his agency sees it. His hate is dying. That's why he's so quiet. It's a very thoughtful time in his life."

"I just think you need to be very damn cautious when you let him out of there."

"Oh, come on. You're too careful."

"I thought you were the one who was too careful, Miri."

"He's my husband and I want him in my bed. I want to have him in me again, Sarah."

"That's unwise. This whole thing is unwise."

"What do you think, Leo?"

"I think he's a really cool looking guy."

On the afternoon of the release, they came down with a cake. They made a party of it with a thirty-year-old Yquem and the Lane cake, made after a sumptuous eighteenth-century recipe, with macerated fruits and cognac. Miriam joked by carrying a cherry to Paul in her mouth. He took it with his teeth and chewed it sensuously.

Miriam gave him the run of the house, all except the attic.

Sarah waited and watched. She tried to enlist Leo, but Leo was little more concerned than Miriam. Leo was a young fool, in Sarah's opinion. Sarah noticed a subtle change in her own personality. A certain realization came upon Sarah that was similar, she thought, to the kind of assumption that comes to dominate a man's mind in a terrible battle. It was the assumption that there would be no escape, that what

Miriam was doing was so foolish that it could not lead to anything but destruction.

How could it be, though, that somebody who had clawed their way through so much life and so much danger to have a baby would, upon becoming pregnant, put at risk both her own life and that of the child?

Miri was a dear and familiar friend. Sarah knew her every mood, the meaning of every expression that flickered in her eyes, had lived with her in deepest intimacy for two decades and more. She knew Miri's fears and her joys, had drawn her to extremes of sexual intensity and observed her with a lover's fascinated dispassion as she lost herself in pleasures. She provided friendship and love and loyalty. But Sarah thought now that they had come to an extreme edge, a strange country of the Keeper mind into which her understanding could not penetrate.

There was only one conclusion to be drawn from her actions: Deeply, profoundly, Miriam wanted to be destroyed as much as the rest of her race did. They had a death wish, otherwise why would beings so brilliant and wise be so easy to kill? The Keepers might not know human science, but they knew the human soul, and that was the key knowledge, what was required to defend yourself.

That they did not defend themselves was, as far as Sarah was concerned, an act of willful self-immolation. They must have recognized this in themselves eons ago, probably as soon as man became intelligent. This was when they began to experiment with melding the two species. They had been trying to escape from their own nature.

Miriam looked forward to feeding, though. She relished her kills, especially the ones that put up an interesting fight.

Every time Miriam stood close to Paul, Sarah waited, her

insides cringing, for the end to come. Didn't she see what he was—a loaded gun, a trap ready to spring?

Eventually, Sarah and Miriam had to feed, and nothing she said could convince Miriam to make her meal of Paul Ward.

So they did it at the Veils. There must be absolutely no chance that Paul would see. At least Miriam agreed to that. So far she had not allowed him back to the club. That, also, meant that she had not yet become a complete fool.

They left Leo with him. Privately, Sarah instructed her to carry the gun, and to never get closer than twenty-five feet to him. If she saw the least sign of his trying to leave the house, or if he tried to come too close to her, or even to use the telephone, she was to blow his brains out.

Sarah hoped that it would happen. They would deal with Miriam's fury. But Miriam threatened Leo—if you kill him, I will kill you. Wound him if you must, but do not kill.

When they came back after taking two Korean businessmen, they had to sleep their deep and helpless sleep.

Sarah told Leo, "If he makes the slightest move toward our bedroom, kill him. No matter what she says."

"But—"

"I'll deal with her! You'll be in no danger."

"Sarah, can you think of any reason *not* to kill him?"

"No."

"What about the fact that Miri loves him?"

"She doesn't know her own mind right now—and her name is Miriam, not Miri."

"You call her Miri."

"And you don't."

Despite the many tensions, life in the household had

returned to something approaching its normal pattern, at least on the surface.

Sarah and Leo managed the Veils. Miriam went occasionally. Paul kept asking to go, and every time he did, Miri was a little more tempted, and Sarah trusted him even less.

She and Miri played their music. Miri began teaching Leo piano, then took her on as a student in a way Sarah had always wanted but had never gotten.

Leo began to receive a classical Keeper education. It began with the Ennead of Ra, the first tier of the Egyptian pantheon of Gods. She started to learn spoken Prime. Sarah doubted Leo's ability to learn the written language, but Miriam was optimistic.

Sarah was surprised that Leo was such a good student. If Miri had wanted a tabula rasa who did not need reeducation because she had nothing to unlearn, she had chosen well. What was amazing to Sarah was that Leo turned out to be a very quick learner. She was actually quite brilliant.

Miriam had picked her out one night at the club with a mere glance. They had been looking for somebody else to blood. They needed more personnel to keep ahead of the burgeoning of their business affairs. Sarah had assumed that they would take a man. But then, almost as an afterthought, Miriam said, "That one." Leo had been in the Japanese garden with some friends, calling on Rudi's skills to get them really, really high.

Slowly, Leo had left her old life behind. Now, all that remained of it was an occasional nervous visit to her parents, and soon even that would end.

Sarah knew that she was being prepared for something, and she came to think that it probably involved her own eventual removal from grace.

So Sarah was waiting for the coming of Leo. She was also waiting for Paul Ward to take whatever action he was planning. She was waiting, in other words, for the end of her world.

When she had been with Eumenes, Miriam had been too young to understand the rarity of happiness. She treasured it now. The overriding reality was that she had a baby in her, her very own baby after all these long years. The trouble was, her husband was turned against himself—a Keeper who had come to hate his own kind. True, he didn't have life eternal and he didn't feed on blood, but he was still a Keeper, and she was still working on him. She longed to draw him into the magic ring of her joy, and she thought that she could. What she was planning was a seduction. Back in the old days, Keeper men had found her hard to resist. She had lost none of her ability to seduce.

But that was all for later. First, there was a door she had to pass through, an essential door. As the days had passed, she had grown steadily more uneasy about it. She'd wanted to roll back the days, to prevent them from dawning. But they did dawn, one and then another, and her baby grew.

Now, Sarah told her, the baby would be sufficiently developed to see. In the way of Keeper mothers, she already knew that she had a son. But what was his condition? It could be that he was deformed. Nobody could be sure what would happen when a Keeper was fertilized by one of these exotics like Paul.

At noon on the appointed day, Sarah came to her. She was in the library teaching Leo. Sarah said, "It's ready." She smiled down at her. These days Sarah was very warm and very grave. There was about her a sadness that Miriam found distressing to be near. Sarah thought that their life together had come to its burnt-out end.

She thought wrong, of course. She must midwife, then become a pediatrician and gynecologist for another species. Sarah thought that Leo was replacing her. She could not understand that Miriam's needs were expanding.

The group of them went down to the infirmary together.

Sarah had bought the very finest new ultrasound machine, so the baby would appear almost as clear as a photograph.

Miriam got up on the examination table. Sarah started the machine, which made a high, whining sound.

"Is it radioactive?" Miriam asked nervously.

"Not at all. It sends out sound waves, then reads the reflections. It's entirely benign, but just to be safe, we'll only use it for a couple of minutes."

Miriam lay waiting, her eyes closed, her body trembling. If it was bad news, she did not think that she had the emotional reserves to bear it. She did not think she could live past the loss of this child, but she didn't know how to die.

She felt the cool instrument sliding on her stomach, which was ever so slightly larger now . . . or was that her imagination?

She put her hand out and Paul took it. They had kissed a few times recently, but he was still being very cool. He wasn't dangerous to her, though, not since he'd understood that he was partly a Keeper. At least, this was her opinion.

"Miri, look."

There on the screen was a ghost. It had a small mouth and tiny, still-unformed hands.

She opened her eyes. She stared at the image on the screen. She always had trouble decoding pictures generated by machines, and at first all she saw were red smears.

"There are the hands," Sarah said, pointing to a slightly less smeary part of the screen.

"Oh, hey," Paul said, "that's my boy."

Miriam still didn't see . . . and then she did. A tiny face swam into focus. "He's—oh, he's *beautiful*."

Paul asked, "Does he have teeth?"

"His mouth is human," Sarah said.

Miriam felt a tingle of concern. "How will he feed, Sarah?"

"Not like you do." Sarah had tested the blood of the fetus. He was ninety percent Keeper.

"Won't he starve?"

"Miri, he has what look like normal human organs and something close to pure Keeper blood. He's going to live— well, maybe forever."

"As a predator," Paul said.

"I don't see any evidence of that," Sarah replied. "This child has an entirely human mouth and organs."

"How can you tell? It's a tiny embryo."

"I can tell because I'm trained to tell."

"You're a gynecologist?"

"I'm a gerontologist. But you're talking basic medicine."

Paul's face went white. He sucked his cheeks in, a sign in a human being of great rage. Miriam watched him, her heart on a shivering edge. She wanted so to love him, but if he threatened her baby, well, she would have to do what she had to do.

When he spoke, his words were knives. "It's important to me, Sarah."

"I see a human embryo."

"Damned, damned *important!*"

Miriam tried to conceal her smile. In that instant, she had understood something new about Paul Ward.

Leo, fearing his tone, dragged her ever-present pistol out of her belt. "Okay," she said, her gum cracking. She didn't like Paul any more than Sarah did. She wasn't afraid for Miriam, though, not like Sarah was. Her concern was that Paul was a rival for Miriam's interest and affection.

Paul looked at the gun. "Thank you," he said.

Sarah, who had been examining the embryo, was the first to see an extraordinary phenomenon. For some moments, she watched, her attention captured by what she was seeing. She moved her hand back and forth in front of the monitor. She found it difficult to believe what she was seeing.

Sarah was a scientist. She didn't believe in the supernatural. She only half believed in the human soul that Miri was always talking about. "You have souls, we don't." Uh-huh. "You humans are the true immortals." Okay.

But this was something very extraordinary. This was a genuine miracle, unfolding before her scientist's eyes. "Look," she said, her voice gone soft with awe.

Miriam immediately saw that the tiny, unformed eyes, little more than blanks to which the art of seeing had not yet come, were somehow looking straight out of the monitor. It was as if the fetus were staring at them.

"Can he see us? Is that possible?"

"Miriam, I don't know."

Then the eyes flickered again, and they were looking at Paul.

"It's an optical illusion," he said.

But the eyes did not look away. Paul said, "My God." Then he, also, fell silent beneath their eerie gaze.

Miriam's heart seemed to her to open in her chest like a flower. "Our baby is a miracle, Paul," she said.

He smiled the way he always smiled, and that made her sad. Why wasn't he the beaming father he should be? He had a magnificent son. He should be so proud that he could hardly bear it.

Sarah brought the ultrasound examination to a close. Then she presented Miri with her first picture of her child. "His face is aware," Sarah said laconically. "It's impossible, but there it is."

They all gathered around. The photo was detailed. The soft, half-formed face with its black eyes and its slight smile was just luminous.

Miriam drank in the picture. She felt the presence in her belly. Her heart beat with love, her blood flowed with love. And he wouldn't be like her, he wouldn't have to suffer the curse of being a predator. Her son would be great, but he would also be free.

She was not a weeper, but she wept now. Sarah noticed the tears and laid her arm around her shoulder. Miriam did not respond. She wanted Paul to hold her. She wanted him to embrace her and cry and laugh with her, and ask for a copy of the picture for his wallet, to treasure just as she would treasure hers.

Still, he made appropriate noises of admiration, and maybe that was a beginning.

"Let's go upstairs," Miriam said. She took Paul's hand. "I think I'd like us to be alone together."

"Me, too," Paul agreed.

She led Paul into the music room, closed the door. "Do you like my playing?"

"I love your playing."

"Then I'd like to play for you. You know this piece?"

"You've been working on it for weeks."

"Sarah's working. I've known it for three hundred years."

He laughed a little. "It sounds so strange when you say something like that."

She shrugged. "I'm just me." She got her viola out of its

case. She set her bow, tuned the instrument for a moment, then began to play.

Miriam was not completely surprised when Paul launched himself at her.

To see that *thing* grinning at him over the health of the monster in its belly was more than Paul could handle. He knew as he flew toward it that he had snapped, that this was wrong, that he was making a huge mistake.

He slammed into the creature, certain only that he had to stop it from making a sound or the others would come in and he would die. Even though they were human, the other two wanted to kill him a lot more than the vampire did; he was certain of that. They would blow him to pieces without hesitation.

It was smaller than he was. But for all its grace and beauty, it had even denser bones. So it was the heavier of the two. It staggered with his weight, but absorbed the blow.

He clapped his hand over its mouth. Its steel-strong arm came up and grabbed his wrist. They fought a silent battle, strength against strength.

He locked his elbow, tightened his muscles. The two of them twisted and turned, falling against the piano, then against the chair where it had been sitting. Its viola crunched and twanged beneath their slow dance. Paul caught the instrument with his shoe, purposely driving his heel into its body, making certain that what the creature loved was destroyed.

Its free hand came between his legs. It got a grip on his balls and began crushing them. They compressed harder and harder, until his deep guts were awash in pain. He used breathing techniques he'd learned in the war to try to control the pain. But he could not control the pain; the pain was astounding.

He started to lose the use of his legs, began to buckle.

Then he got his teeth into the flesh of its neck—its own favorite place. Too bad he couldn't suck its blood. He bit, grinding down with all his might, his incisors ripping into the hard muscles.

Check.

They broke away.

He waited for it to call to its people. He waited to die.

It stared at him. He stared back. It did not call anybody. They began to circle, and while they circled, he wondered why not . . . and because he did not know, he began to get scared.

It turned its head to one side, lowered it, and looked at him out of the side of its eyes. He knew that it was made up, that it didn't really have those perfect lips or those beautiful, soft eyes, but he could not help reacting to it as if it were the most wonderful woman he'd ever known.

Why didn't it call out? Was it here to die, or what?

He leaped at it again. He grabbed its throat, preparing to give it the most fearsome uppercut he could manage. He would stun it; then he would take the shattered neck of the viola and rip out its throat with it.

It stopped the uppercut in the palm of an iron hand. Then, very suddenly, his own hands were trapped at his sides. It was riding him, using its knees to pin his arms. It smashed its fists into his chest, using him like a punching bag. He toppled back, his chest wound making him cough hard.

It lay on him full length. He felt its weight, felt its vagina pressing hard against his penis. He fought to free his arms, but he couldn't. This was a death grip.

Its head came up; its lips contacted his neck. He threw himself from side to side, but it was no use. The creature's mouth locked onto his neck.

He could feel the tongue then, probing against his skin. At the same time, its wriggling, squirming body brought him to sexual life. His erection grew until it felt as though it would rip out of his pants. Faster it rubbed back and forth, harder it drove into his neck.

This was the death they gave their victims—an evil sexual charge and then the penetration—and he felt it—the cold, slim needle that was normally enclosed deep inside the tongue—as it came out and pricked delicately against his skin, seeking the vibration of the humming artery.

As it penetrated, the delicate, persistent pain made him gargle miserably. He was as stiff as a steel rod, its haunches were pumping, but he could also feel his blood sliding out of his neck, leaving him breathless and faint.

This was death by vampire, what his father had known.

And then, suddenly, it was on its feet. The lens was gone from one of its eyes, and it glared at him out of one red eye and one ash-gray one. Its face was smeared, the prosthetics gone from one sunken cheek. Along its lips was a foam of blood—his blood.

He was too exhausted to move a muscle. He could only watch as it opened his pants and sat on him. He felt himself being inserted into its vagina, and he struggled to prevent that, but he could not prevent it.

The creature raped him. There was no other way to describe what was done. What was worse—more humiliating, more angering—was that the sensation was not like the dull, empty horror of a true rape. There was something else there, another emotion, one that he did not want but could not deny.

It wasn't only that she was incredibly beautiful, even without her makeup—maybe more so without it. It was that she just *felt so right*. That was the reality of it. In her makeup or out of her makeup, she was the most wonderful woman he had ever been with.

He realized that he had been tricked into making his move. This was no battle to the death. It was a damn seduction!

And, oh, my, but it was a good one—so smart, so deeply knowledgeable of Paul Ward. It made his very soul ache to see her trying so hard to win him and to love him through his hate, to draw him to her side and the side of their son.

She stopped. He realized that he had climaxed, but also that she had taken a lot of blood out of him, so much that he was surprised that he was still conscious, let alone capable of coitus. But she knew the human body with incredible precision. The borderland between life and death was where she was most comfortable.

"So," she said as she got off him, "what do we call him? I think it ought to be Paul. Paul Ward, Jr." She smiled the smile of a sultry Venus, the most amazing expression in the most amazing face he had ever seen. "Agreed?"

She lifted him to his shuffling feet and led him through the house in triumph. They had to help him, but he went upstairs. He went into her bedroom—their bedroom—and fell upon their bed.

"It's only a quart," she said. He'd tasted lovely. It had been hard to stop. "You're not *that* weak."

His eyes almost twinkled, and he seemed to revive himself. "Okay," he said, "maybe you're right. So let's finish this in bed."

She was heavy, just like him, and lean and strong . . . but

also soft, soft in wonderful ways that seemed to fit him just about perfectly.

She lay in his arms, gazing at him with such adoration that he almost wanted to laugh from the pleasure it gave him. All the love and tenderness that he had been trying to suppress, that were part of his nature and one with their bonded spirits, now blossomed forth in him.

"I never will leave you," he said.

"I never will leave you."

This, he felt, was their marriage vow. "You're my wife," he said.

"My husband."

Leo and Sarah, who had come with them, now withdrew from the room. "I think she made it," Leo said.

Sarah just shook her head.

When they had been in bed together for a little time, however, she felt it her duty to be sure that they were entirely comfortable . . . and that all was indeed well.

Miriam gave her a very large smile, her lovely face almost buried beneath Paul's big, plunging back.

Sarah laid her hand on Paul's shoulder. Then she went softly out and closed the door.

Paul finished, a second time within just a few minutes and with a lot of blood lost. He sank down upon her, then slid into the softness of the bed.

What had he done? He'd capitulated. Maybe it was the damn blood loss, maybe it was the brilliance of her seduction by violence, maybe it was the staring eyes of the baby—but one thing was certain: He was not going to kill this vampire.

She lay beside him as still as still water, her eyes closed, upon her face a narrow smile. He slipped his hand into hers, and she made a startlingly catlike purring sound.

It was while she was purring that he heard another sound, very soft indeed. Curious as to the origin of this very slight thud, he turned his head and looked toward Sarah's office.

As if by magic, the door came slowly open. First he saw a blond head, then a pale face in the gloom of the curtained bedroom. A small figure came in, moving quickly, almost as catlike as Miriam herself.

What the hell? It looked like Peter Pan. As much as his mind wanted to believe that it was part of a dream, he had to face the fact that it was real. He stared. It came, catlike, closer to the bed.

It was small but it seemed extremely dangerous. Paul's struggling heart started to struggle harder. He did not understand. There was nobody else in the house, and they were incredibly careful about that.

When the figure reached the bedside, he almost leaped out of his skin with surprise. It was Becky. Cocking her head, she gave him a look that said, *Naughty boy,* and the slightest of smiles traveled across her face.

In that instant—seeing her so unexpectedly—Paul came back to himself. It was a homecoming to see her. His very soul rejoiced. She reached out and touched his cheek, and he was so incredibly glad that he would have cried if he hadn't been such a tough sonofabitch.

She smiled, then, more broadly. She pointed a finger at the vampire and mouthed, "Bang bang."

Paul nodded.

Miriam burst out of the bed, leaping almost to the ceiling. She came flying across Paul and tackled Becky, who was sent crashing all the way back into the office, where her rope still hung from the open skylight.

Paul wasn't as fast, but Becky recovered herself. She dragged out a pistol—and it wasn't a damned magnum. It was one of the French babies. Good! This thing was going to be decided at last.

Miriam snarled when she saw it. She snarled, and then she backed away. In two lithe steps, she was beside him. "Shoot us," she said. She knew damn well how it worked. It was meant to clear a room. Becky could not kill Miriam without killing Paul.

"Hey, Beck," Paul said aloud.

"I thought we were a thing, you prick!"

The natural goodness of a love like that was fresh water in a desert that Paul had not even realized was dry. "Becky," he said, "oh, Christ—"

"Men. They're all the same," Miriam said. She had that little smile on her face that was always there when she felt in control of a situation.

"She's an ugly cuss, Paul! Jesus, you must be drugged or something, man!"

"Becky, I thought you were with Bocage. I thought—"

"We're here for you, Paul. All of us that are left."

"What about Justin?"

"Screw him. And screw the Company."

"They take an enlightened approach, it would seem," Miriam said.

Why in hell was she so calm? What did she know? "Be careful, Becky."

"Oh, yeah. Look, Mrs. Blaylock, we've got this place surrounded. We've got video of one of your little helpers committing a murder. And we've got you."

"You won't kill Paul."

Becky's face changed. It grew as hard as stone. Nothing

needed to be said. Miriam took Paul by the arm and began to back out of the room.

Becky stalked forward, bracing the gun. "Shoot, girl," Paul said.

Miriam backed them up another step. Becky came forward. "I love you, Paul," she said.

"Me too, baby." And his heart told him—it's true, it's always been true. He wanted her. He wanted normal human love, and that was what she had to offer. By the God in heaven, he wanted her.

She closed her eyes. He saw tears. He knew that he was about to die at the hands of the only normal human woman who had ever loved him, before he had even damn well kissed her.

So he made a move. Why the hell not? Might as well attempt the impossible. What he did was to leap toward Becky, hoping that Miriam wouldn't expect that.

He was free, falling toward her. Becky danced aside. And suddenly he was behind her.

The two women faced each other. Miriam covered her belly with her hands. Miriam screamed. It was the most terrible, bloodcurdling wail of despair Paul had ever heard.

The bedroom door burst open, and Sarah and Leo piled in behind her, both of them bracing Magnums. Paul recognized a standoff. He also recognized a situation that wasn't going to last more than a few seconds.

"We're gonna get 'em all," he murmured to Becky.

In the same instant that she squeezed the trigger, a desperate Miriam used her great speed to leap into her face. Instinct made her raise the weapon—and the blast went crashing into the trompe l'oeil ceiling, which came crashing down in sky-painted chunks, filling the room with dust.

Becky was hurled all the way back against the far wall of the office. She hit the wall with a resounding slap. But she was Becky, she was no ordinary girl, and she came back immediately.

Paul had the gun. Behind Miriam, Sarah and Leo were getting ready to open fire. He started to squeeze off the shot that would reduce them all to pulp.

Then his finger stopped squeezing. He stood, agonizing. "Pull it," Becky shouted, *"pull the damn trigger!"*

The clock ticked. Sarah Roberts began moving slowly to the left, sliding like a shadow. He saw her plan: she was going to throw herself between them, try to absorb the shot.

"Pull it!"

"Please, Paul," Miriam said.

He stood there like a pillar, and pillars cannot move, they cannot pull triggers. He saw not Miriam, but his baby, the little half-made child who had maybe looked at him.

In all his years of killing, he had never killed a baby, and now he found that this was his limit. This was the one murder he could not commit.

His mind searched for a way to let his heart win. And his mind spoke to him in the voice of his father . . . or maybe it was his father's real spirit there, giving his son the guidance that he needed: "If you kill that child," his father's voice said to him, "my life and my death and all the suffering of our family will have been for nothing."

All those thousands of years of struggle on the earth—the slow evolution of the apes, the coming of the Keepers with their breeding and their feeding and their tremendous acceleration of human evolution—all of it had led to this moment, to the burning, unanswerable moral question of the mother, and to the baby.

"Gimme that gun," Becky said.

He did it. He gave it to her. As he did so, Sarah Roberts came forward. Her face was white, her eyes were huge. She loomed up, pointing her own weapon. With the clarity that comes to men at moments of great extreme, Paul saw a tear come out of her left eye and start down her cheek. And then her magnum roared and Becky's pistol roared, and the room was choked with dust and debris.

Silence followed, and in it the improbable bonging of a distant clock. Before them lay the shattered remains of Sarah Roberts.

Becky looked down, then stepped quickly across the blood-soaked corpse.

The other two were nowhere to be seen. Paul and Becky followed them out and downstairs, saw them as they were disappearing into a pantry.

There was a brick tunnel leading deep. "Know where it goes?"

"Nope."

"Shit. And there's no map?"

"No map."

"Then we've lost it."

"Temporarily. It ain't over till it's over, girl."

She dropped her gun to her side. "That one really got to you," she said.

He looked down the dark tunnel where the monster that carried his son had taken him. "Or ever the silver cord be loosed, or the golden bowl be broken . . . then the dust shall return to the earth as it was."

"Okay."

They were silent together. Paul could feel the cord that linked him to his boy, feel it unwinding into the void.

"That's the last one," Becky said.

"The last vampire? Are you sure?"

"They're cleaned out. All of them."

"Even here in the U.S?"

She nodded. "Bocage is almost as good as you."

He felt her hand in his, her strong, good hand. "Becky?"

"Yeah?"

"How the hell did you get in here?"

"They got a lotta skylights in this dump, boss."

He threw his arms around her. When he kissed her at last, he immediately found what he'd lost hope of ever finding, which was his heart's true happiness. This was where he belonged, in the arms of this wonderful, normal, completely human woman.

They left the house, leaving the maggots or the police to deal with the corpse upstairs. As far as the vampire and its helper were concerned, they would be found. Their time would come.

But not until his son was born, no way. Not until then.

"What's your opinion on kids?"

"Kids're okay."

"You could raise a kid?"

She looked at him. "Married to you I could."

"Married to me."

About the Author

WHITLEY STRIEBER is the #1 bestselling author of the landmark horror novels *The Hunger* and *The Wolfen,* and the million-copy bestsellers *Communion, Transformation,* and *Confirmation.* He is the coauthor, with radio talk-show host Art Bell, of the *New York Times* bestseller *The Coming Global Superstorm,* published by Pocket Books. His newest novel is *Lilith's Dream: A Tale of the Vampire Life.* Visit www.unknowncountry.com.

ATRIA BOOKS
PROUDLY PRESENTS

LILITH'S DREAM

Whitley Strieber

Now available in hardcover
from Atria Books

Turn the page for a preview of
Lilith's Dream. . . .

Lilith's eyes focused, then focused again, until the firmament revealed its wonders to her. The reefs of stars became a jeweled host as she began to perceive each individual strand of light. As the rays entered her eyes, each sent its own message to her heart.

She could not keep from singing, and she raised her voice in the long, rich tones of her kind, a shimmering regiment of notes like the deep songs of the whale and the wind. The jackals laughed and yapped, and when she stopped, she heard them rutting again.

Motionless, she waited for them to return to their task of guiding her. Her stillness was as precise as her movement. Indeed, she was so still that a cruising owl used her as a perch, hooted twice, then swept back into the sky, its wings trembling the silent air. She thought nothing of this, she who had slept upon the desert reaches in the company of lions, and, in her youth, swum the crystal waters off the point now called Aden, singing until the whales rose from the dark ocean.

She walked steadily and precisely, as silently as the jackals, a shadow in the shadows of the night. But for her skin glowing pale beneath the hood and her eyes gleaming with a tiger's shine, she revealed nothing of herself to the world around her.

Long before she came upon a Bedouin camp, she knew that it was there. Ten leagues away, she spread her nostrils and drew in the scent of blood and cooked meat and dates, and the scintillating odor of human skin. She lived as much by scent as sight, and it was one of her favorite smells. They liked to be kissed, which was a matter of indifference to her. But she would kiss them to smell them. She knew the different ways each part of the human body smelled, and enjoyed it all.

Romans bathed and slicked themselves with oil. So these were not Romans. She lengthened her stride. The jackals scampered ahead of her, then stationed themselves on a tall outcropping, their forms dark against the sky glow. She moved directly toward them, knowing that the village or camp of the humans would be in their sight.

She caught the sweet, milky scent of young children, and the odor of men with sweat in their hair. Also, now, the musk of the women, of whom there were three young and two old. She went closer, rising to the point on which the jackals stood.

As she approached, they melted away. She looked down into the top of a canyon. There were three pinpricks of light lost down there in the darkness—cook fires.

Then she noticed something odd. On the far horizon, just where the afterglow of the set sun marked the horizon, there were lights moving back and forth. She listened. Below, she heard expected sounds—soft adult voices and the sharper cries of children, the rattle of flames and the hiss of cookpans—human sounds no different from any others. But the horizon offered a different noise. What was it, though? It was extremely faint, perhaps thirty or forty leagues away. Not growling, not a living creature. What, then? She could not place that noise. Almost, the rumbling of wagon wheels. Almost, the running of a waterfall. Almost, but not quite, either of those things.

She could make a nice meal down in the campsite, but her instinct was not to take even the smallest chance. Far better to do it in a back alley, to some social cull, than to cut out a paterfamilias or a valuable slave, and cause the others to rush from the nest barking and waving torches.

What would they do if a noble came walking out of the dark of the night? They would think her a goddess, no doubt of it. That would be well. She would prevail upon their transport, and they would relate to their grandchildren the story of the deity they had conducted to town.

When she started down the mountainside, the male

jackal yapped three times. She stopped, confused and amazed. Why, in a setting that offered absolutely no threat, would it sound warning? Had she missed something?

She drew in scent. Nothing but the peace of the cookfire and the fragrance of the bodies. She listened. The voices were as calm as the night.

She continued on. Again, Anubis sounded warning. Again, she stopped, and again detected nothing. The moon rose above the mountains behind her.

Soon, she was close enough to see the creatures moving about. They were all heavily clothed, and so prosperous enough to afford ample cloth. Could they be Sumerian merchants, then? They had far more linen to weave than Egyptian peasants, and wore long robes to announce their wealth. She might take a Sumerian merchant, who had far to go before he could raise an alarm. Or maybe they were travelers from the land of Punt, far to the south.

The women were covered all over, even their faces. Now, this stopped her. It was strange. But no, when she'd gone to examine the Englishmen, she'd seen such. Yes, they must be Egyptians living in this new fashion. The Egyptians were thriving, to have this much cloth. Even the children wore blue leggings and white shirts imprinted with letters and designs.

She came to the edge of their firelight. They were playing on an instrument and singing, watching their fire with sleepy eyes. She could wait until they were in their hutches, then creep in and take one by stealth. Or she could simply rush in and grab one so quickly that the others would be unable to follow. Still, it would be best to do it the safe way.

She walked into the camp. For a moment, they did nothing. Then the one with the musical instrument stopped playing it. The children became quiet. She stood before their fire and said, in Egyptian, "Carry me to Thebes."

One looked to the other. A smooth boy went against its father's hip. She repeated her demand. It was obvious, though, that they did not understand her. She switched to English. "Take me to your city."

Still no reaction. She could speak many human languages from many different times: Prakrit, Ogham, Vitelieu, Akkadian, Egyptian, Greek, Latin, French, Russian, Chinese, Farsi, and Deutsch were just a few. In each, she had a few hundred words and could easily absorb more. She tried the next logical choice, which was Arabic. "Please convey me to your city. God is good."

"We are wanderers, by the mercy of God."

"Then to the Romans. Take me to the Romans."

They glanced at one another, muttering. Finally, the oldest one spoke, a creature with a white twist of beard and a dirty cloth turban. "Do you mean those ruins in the Abu Ma'mmal? Are you a tourist?"

Some of the words passed her by. "I am a traveler," she said. She drew back her hood. The men all gasped. Their eyes opened wide. Behind their veils, the women did the same. The children went into defensive postures, clinging to the adults. Two of the men began backing on their haunches, slipping away from the firelight.

A sour whiff of fear told her that she had only seconds to deal with this unexpected situation. She had bred man not to fear her, but these certainly did. She opened her hands, palms out. "I am in need of your help."

A woman said, "It's a djin. A djin of the night."

The elder man raised his own hand in a gesture of dismissal toward the woman who had spoken. "God willing, would you take some tea?"

She came closer to them, then went down on her own haunches, her superb clothing whispering around her as she dropped. "It would be my pleasure, sir."

It had been a long time since she had done this, but she found herself enjoying the company of her creatures more than she had expected. Really, now that she thought of it, she'd been tucked away in her cave much too long. Here, beside an open fire, beneath the crystal of the moon, surrounded by the jackals and the sailing nightbirds, this was the life.

The old one came close to her, his eyes down, his poor hands trembling so much that he almost spilled the tea. She watched the veins of his neck throb. They were a little caked inside, and would offer a hesitant draw. With this one, she'd go straight to the main artery and with a single heave of her belly dry him to dust.

Laughing easily, she took the tea. "Thank you."

"May God be with you."

As she sipped her tea, the tension among them continue to rise. The children and women had repaired to their tent, and could be heard speaking softly together. A little boy was whispering, "It is a rich djin, look at the gold!" A female replied, "It is an American."

That was a word she did not know. She made a note to discover its meaning.

Taking tea with her were four males. From their eyes, she could see that they found her beauty hypnotic. Her spell was coming down upon them as swiftly as the dew that falls before dawn.

She noticed, however, that they were moving themselves about, maneuvering so that her way was blocked except directly behind her, which would take her into their tent. Within, there was rustling. An ambush? She said, "How may I get to Thebes?"

The old man nodded toward the west. "The road is there. You can get the bus to Cairo. There's tours to Thebes." There was another unknown word for her list, 'bus.' "A few kilometers."

There was no road off in that direction, she knew quite well. If she walked west, she would go many leagues before she reached the Nile, a journey that would kill a human. Perhaps they were trying to trick her to go off into the desert, with the intention of following her and attacking her.

If they did, she would take them all. She'd bloat like a tick, but she wouldn't need to eat again for quite a time. Her tongue was stiffening with eagerness when she heard a distant and very surprising noise: a clanking sound, followed in a moment by clattering that quickly became continuous.

"My cousin comes," the elder said. "He will take you

in his car as far as el Maadi. There you can take an East Delta bus into Cairo. Is your hotel there?"

She had understood some of it. His "cousin" would be a blood relative. But the rest-whatever did he mean? How was it that there were so many new words in the language of Arabic, in just—what—oh, it couldn't have been more than a hundred years or so.

Of a sudden, the clanking sound became louder. There was a rhythm to it, and seemed to be moving faster than was natural.

All the animals that had been lingering about her in the shadows hustled away. To the west, she saw a glow. She had no idea even how to ask a question about it, so she remained silent. In what seemed like just a moment, it became enormous and burst over the edge of a nearby hill. The light was accompanied by a terrific roar and an odor of some sort of bizarre fire.

Forgetting all of her careful poise, Lilith jumped up, cried out, and scrambled into the tent. She tripped over a child and went sprawling, her cloak settling around her as the great light swept across the thin fabric walls.

Then it went out. A moment later, the noise faded, and with it, but more slowly, the odor.

"God be with you," a male cried cheerfully. "You have a lost American! What beautiful good fortune for us, my brothers!"

"She speaks Arabic," one of the young men murmured.

"Well, all the better, may God be pleased! My dear lady, come forth, would it please you."

She stepped from the tent. There was a carriage visible in the light of the fire. It had obviously come far, for it was covered with dust. It was also the source of the odor of fire. There was not the faintest scent of a horse, or sound of one, or sight of one.

Very well. It was a puzzle that would be solved.

"Look, I can take you for twenty pounds. Do you have a cell? Is there somebody to call? What hotel are you in?"

None of the questions were sensible. In fact, only the inflection told her that they *were* questions. "All is well," she said. "May I go now into the carriage?"

"She talks like an old movie," the cousin said. "What kind of Arabic is that?"

"It's her way. But look at that costume. She must be a rich one."

The cousin gave her a long, frank stare. "You are pale," he said, after his appraisal was over.

"I have not been much in the sun, in these past years."

"Hey, Abi, I have to get that line up tonight or the boss'll be on my ass. The fatties don't get their air conditioners at the monastery until I do."

"How many fatties?"

"A bunch. Big busload. First-class extra and a bit."

"Tips if we go to be pictured?"

The cousin nodded. "Borrow that camel from Duli. You'll get nice money. But be late. They'll not be up with the sun." He laughed, then, through gaps in his teeth.

"Lady, we go now."

How interesting this would be, to go in a carriage without a horse. Did he pull it himself? Roman boys played at war, making their slaves pull their baby chariots about in the peristyles of their houses. But a human being was not strong enough to pull a heavy conveyance like this carriage. It had two rows of seats within, and four doors, and seemed at once dirty and beautiful. It also had wide, small wheels that would make it quite impossible in the sand, even for somebody much stronger than a human being.

She got into the thing, seating herself behind a circular rail, placing her hands firmly around it. She detested the bouncing of carriages, and there was always the threat of the ditch.

"She can't drive," the cousin said.

"The American thinks the Arab cannot drive, my cousin. She is afraid of your foolish ways."

She heard this. How dare they consider her a drover. "I'll not drive," she said.

There was a silence from without. The men grouped together at the back of the machine. As low as they whispered, she could hear them with ease.

"I tell you, it's a djin."

"There are no djin, no more than your foolish god who never—"

"No, no, Allah be praised, go with God. Look at her! Look, she looks like some kind of a—what is it? Marble. A woman made of marble. It's horrifying."

"I see money. Twenty pounds for ten kilometers, and she says not a word! I'm going."

"Cousin, I would not go out into the night with that thing."

But he went.

• • •

Leonore Patterson looked down at the steak that her servant set on the coffee table before her. She cut into it and watched the blood come out in runnels, then spread in intricate rivers across the bright white china plate. She touched one of them, then brought the tips of her fingers to her lips. Memory.

She wanted to get high and drunk both, anything but feel what she was feeling right now. Compared to this addiction, alcoholism was baby stuff and drug problems were child's play. No, no, this was what you could safely call the big time.

She didn't want to, but she left the room. She left the apartment without eating. There was only one food that would work now, no matter how little she wanted to consume it. But there was no choice, and she went out into the streets, out along the blowing, shadowy side streets and into the broader reaches of Third Avenue.

It was not long before she came to what she expected, a lonely man looking for some kind of love. When she smiled at him, he nodded sharply, telegraphing that he wasn't to be taken for granted. He was a man to be bargained with.

His eyes met hers, flickered away. So he wanted a kink. He was out looking for something odd. Fine, she'd done it all five times over. Guys looking for anonymous sex weren't generally interested in the missionary position. He offered her a weak smile.

"Look, honey, you want a date or not?"

"What're you—uh—"

"It's a date. Whatever you want."

"Uh, I, you know, it's just ordinary."

"C'mere." She put her arms on his shoulders, smiled up at him. "Now nobody can hear us but us." She met his eyes. "Honey, you look like you lost your mommy."

"Maybe that's what happened. I did. You know, what about the, sort of, that I'm—I have a big job. A lot of people work for me. I spend my life giving orders and my wife, she's not—she can't . . . she just can't."

She took his hand. "You just forget it, okay. Okay? 'Cause I know what we're gonna do."

"You do?"

"Baby, don't you worry. You found the right girl. It's lucky. I'm looking for it. I love it. So just—here, come on, don't you pull away now, honey." She took him by the wrist and led him toward the old house, the place where she had found her miracle and lost her humanity. She didn't actually enter it often, not unless she had to.

When he entered, she immediately pushed the door closed. He could not know that there was now no way for him to get out, not through that or any door or any window, not without her keys and her knowledge of these intricate locks. No matter who he was or what he was, a dead man now stood before her.

He smiled, revealing neatly kept teeth. "Well, wow," he said. "Wow."

"It's very old."

"This is—I don't know, you're just a little girl and this place—is this your folks' house? I don't know."

"What's the game, honey? We can't do it if you don't say it."

He remained silent.

She sat down on the bed, drew him down beside her. Then she saw that his face had changed, that he was not a sweating, nervous fool anymore, that there was something acute in his eyes. His hands, which had seemed as soft and loathsome as the rest of this bloated maggot, came around her throat, and proved to be not at all maggoty. No, the pudgy fingers concealed iron.

"Fuckin' cunt," he snarled.

"You're killing me!"

"So. The fuck. What?"

She writhed. He was strong, damnit, real strong. "You're a—"

He smiled, thrust against her. "You're number twenty-one, filth! You goddamn fuckin' piece o' shit, in this nice house, how dare you. How dare you!"

As his fingers jabbed deeper and her windpipe threatened to collapse, her mind registered the truth: she had picked up a serial killer. He was strong, too. He was very strong. He was humping her, not entering her but thrusting against her as he killed her.

Incredibly, she was actually in trouble with this guy.

She lay still, and in his eagerness he shifted just a bit. This gave her the chance to use her hidden strength, and she exploded out from under him. He flew up and back and landed with a thud that shook the house.

The vampire blood made you strong. It made you much stronger than anybody thought you would be.

Snarling with surprise, shaking his head in confusion, he leaped at her. Her hands shot up as quick as the flicker of a falcon's wing and took his wrists in a grip that he would not be able to break.

His eyes bulged with the effort. He growled and shook and struggled until purple veins throbbed in his delicious neck. She watched, waiting until he bent down, preparing to throw himself back away from her. Then her knee came up and connected with his face. Howling, his teeth bared, he flew back ten feet into the wall, which his head hit with a sound like an egg cracking. As he sank down, she took handcuffs out from under the bed and snapped them around his wrists.

She marched the astonished, spent man straight down to the basement and hooked the cuffs to an eye in the wall.

ACCLAIM FOR KELLY IRVIN

"Kelly Irvin's *Through the Autumn Air* is a poignant journey of friendship and second chances that will illustrate for readers that God blesses us with a true love for all seasons."

—AMY CLIPSTON, BESTSELLING AUTHOR
OF *ROOM ON THE PORCH SWING*

"Irvin's fun story is simple (like Mary Katherine, who finds 'every day is a blessing and an adventure') but very satisfying."

—*PUBLISHERS WEEKLY* ON
THROUGH THE AUTUMN AIR

"This second entry (after *Upon a Spring Breeze*) in Irvin's seasonal series diverges from the typical Amish coming-of-age tale with its focus on more mature protagonists who acutely feel their sense of loss. Fans of the genre seeking a broader variety of stories may find this new offering from a Carol Award winner more relatable than the usual fare."

—*LIBRARY JOURNAL* ON *BENEATH
THE SUMMER SUN*

"Jennie's story will speak to any woman who has dealt with the horror of abuse and the emotional aftermath it carries, as well as readers who have questioned how God can allow such terrible things to happen. The choice Jennie makes to take a chance on love again and to open her heart to God after all she has suffered is brave and hopeful, leaving readers on an uplifting note."

—*RT BOOK REVIEWS*, 4-STAR REVIEW
OF *BENEATH THE SUMMER SUN*

No doubt, what Jesse felt is often what modern-day Amish men and women must feel when they are at a crossroads in their faith. The story was brilliantly told and the struggle felt very real."

—DESTINATION AMISH

"Something new and delightful in the Amish fiction genre, this story is set in the barren, dusty landscape of Bee County, TX . . . Irvin writes with great insight into the range and depth of human emotion. Her characters are believable and well developed, and her storytelling skills are superb. Recommend to readers who are looking for something a little different in Amish fiction."

—CBA RETAILERS + RESOURCES
FOR *THE BEEKEEPER'S SON*

"*The Beekeeper's Son* is so well crafted. Each character is richly layered. I found myself deeply invested in the lives of both the King and Lantz families. I struggled as they struggled, laughed as they laughed—and even cried as they cried . . . This is one of the best novels I have read in the last six months. It's a refreshing read and worth every penny. *The Beekeeper's Son* is a keeper for your bookshelf!"

—DESTINATION AMISH

"Kelly Irvin's *The Beekeeper's Son* is a beautiful story of faith, hope, and second chances. Her characters are so real that they feel like old friends. Once you open the book, you won't put it down until you've reached the last page."

—AMY CLIPSTON, BESTSELLING
AUTHOR OF *A GIFT OF GRACE*

"*The Beekeeper's Son* is a perfect depiction of how God makes all things beautiful in His way. Rich with vivid descriptions and characters you can immediately relate to, Kelly Irvin's book is a must-read for Amish fans."

—RUTH REID, BESTSELLING AUTHOR
OF *A MIRACLE OF HOPE*

"Kelly Irvin writes a moving tale that is sure to delight all fans of Amish fiction. Highly recommended."

—KATHLEEN FULLER, AUTHOR OF THE HEARTS OF
MIDDLEFIELD AND MIDDLEFIELD FAMILY NOVELS

THE BISHOP'S SON

OTHER BOOKS BY KELLY IRVIN

AN AMISH OF BIG SKY COUNTRY NOVEL

Mountains of Grace (available August 2019)

AN EVERY AMISH SEASON NOVELS

Upon a Spring Breeze
Beneath the Summer Sun
Through the Autumn Air
With Winter's First Frost

THE AMISH OF BEE COUNTY NOVELS

The Beekeeper's Son
The Bishop's Son
The Saddle Maker's Son

STORIES

A Christmas Visitor in *An Amish Christmas Gift*
Sweeter than Honey in *An Amish Market*
One Sweet Kiss in *An Amish Summer*
Snow Angels in *An Amish Christmas Love*
The Midwife's Dream in *An Amish Heirloom*
Mended Hearts in *An Amish Reunion*

ROMANTIC SUSPENSE

Tell Her No Lies
Over the Line

THE BISHOP'S SON

Kelly Irvin

ZONDERVAN

The Bishop's Son

Copyright © 2015 by Kelly Irvin

This title is also available as a Zondervan e-book. Visit www.zondervan.com.

Requests for information should be addressed to:
Zondervan, *3900 Sparks Dr. SE, Grand Rapids, Michigan 49546*

ISBN 978-0-7852-1709-1 (repack)
ISBN 978-0-310-35449-9 (mass market)
ISBN 978-0-310-33966-3 (e-book)
ISBN 978-0-310-33954-0 (trade paper)

Library of Congress Cataloging-in-Publication Data

CIP data is available upon request.

Printed in the United States of America

19 20 21 22 23 24 / QG / 20 19 18 17 16 15 14 13 12 11 10 9 8 7 6 5 4 3 2 1

To my family, love always.

You, then, why do you judge your brother or sister? Or why do you treat them with contempt? For we will all stand before God's judgment seat. It is written:

> *"'As surely as I live,' says the Lord,*
> *'every knee will bow before me;*
> *every tongue will acknowledge God.'"*

So then, each of us will give an account of ourselves to God.

Therefore let us stop passing judgment on one another. Instead, make up your mind not to put any stumbling block or obstacle in the way of a brother or sister.

ROMANS 14:10–13 NIV

For there is one body and one Spirit, just as you have been called to one glorious hope for the future. There is one Lord, one faith, one baptism, and one God and Father of all, who is over all, in all, and living through all.

EPHESIANS 4:4–6 NLT

DEUTSCH VOCABULARY*

aenti: aunt
bopli: baby
bruder: brother
daed: father
danki: thank you
dawdy haus: grandparents' house
dochder: daughter
doplisch: clumsy
eck: "corner table" where bridal party, including
     groom and bride, sits during wedding celebrations
Englischer: English or non-Amish
fraa: wife
gmay: church district meeting
Gott: God
groossdaadi: grandpa
groossmammi: grandma
guder mariye: good morning
gut: good
hund: dog
jah: yes
kaffi: coffee
kapp: prayer cap
kinner: children
lieb: love

mann: husband
meidnung: shunning
mudder: mother
nee: no
onkel: uncle
Ordnung: written and unwritten rules in an Amish
    district
rumspringa: period of running around
schtinkich: stink, stinky
schweschder: sister
wunderbarr: wonderful

*The German dialect spoken by the Amish is not a written language and varies depending on the location and origin of the settlement. These spellings are approximations. Most Amish children learn English after they start school. They also learn high German, which is used in their Sunday services.

Featured Bee County Amish Families

Mordecai and Abigail (Lantz) King
Leila
Rebekah
Caleb
Hazel
Esther
Samuel
Jacob
Susan King (Mordecai's sister)

Abram and Theresa King

Deborah and Phineas King

Stephen and Ruth Anne Stetler

Leroy (bishop) and Naomi Glick
Adam
Jesse
Joseph
Simon
Sally
Mary
Elizabeth
Solomon Glick (grandfather)

Andrew and Sadie Glick
Will
Patty
Henry
Catherine
Nehemiah

CHAPTER 1

Goose bumps prickled up Leila Lantz's arms. Her mother, wearing a blue cotton dress she'd finished sewing earlier in the week and black tights, marched with a determined air past their entire community of family and friends. The pink blush on her cheeks told the story of a woman who didn't welcome being the center of attention from so many folks, some who'd traveled from as far away as Missouri and Tennessee to share in this wedding. The rubber soles of her black shoes squeaked on the linoleum of her future son-in-law's front room, loud in a silence replete with anticipation. Her witnesses scampered after her, their cheeks equally pink, smiles irrepressible.

It seemed like a dream, watching *Mudder* marry another man. This man, Mordecai King, who stood tall, a broad smile on his craggy face, his witnesses at his side.

A man not Leila's father, now dead for more than three years.

Leila inhaled the scent of fresh-baked bread, rolls, cakes, and cookies that wafted from the kitchen. The aroma of shared happiness and celebration floated around them, reminding them that today two hearts would join as one in a sacred ritual that could not, should not, be torn asunder.

Mudder should marry again. Leila, her sisters, and her brother needed a father. Back aching, Leila wiggled on the hard pine bench. Still, how strange to think of Mordecai sitting at the head of the supper table each evening, from now on, in that place that had once been reserved for *Daed*.

A new daed. *Nee*. Mordecai could never fill those work boots.

Nor would he try. Mordecai had proven himself to be a wise man in the year and a half since Leila's mother had moved her family from Tennessee to south Texas. Kind and funny, he'd tried to be helpful in the year since he began to court Mudder in that strange way older folks did who were too grown up to shine flashlights in windows late at night and go for rides, laughing and whispering secrets in the pitch-black countryside.

At least that's what Leila supposed happened on those buggy rides. She'd not experienced one—yet. Her glance slid across the room to the men's side. Jesse sat between his older brother, Adam, and his cousin Will. They seemed as entranced as everyone else by the spectacle of this widow and widower, each on the north side of forty, becoming *mann* and *fraa*.

Jesse coughed, a harsh, grating sound in the still quiet of this time-honored tradition, and slapped a hand to his mouth. His gaze shifted for a second and landed on her. The tanned skin on his smooth face reddened. He ducked his head covered with dark brown, thick curls usually hidden by his straw hat.

Her own face burning, Leila whipped her head toward the front. He should look embarrassed. The man talked a good talk, but not once had he followed through with a flashlight shining in her window. No buggy rides, much as his gaze seemed to promise something. Nothing had materialized.

What did she lack that made him hesitate? Leila asked herself that question over and over.

She rubbed her sweaty hands together, then forced them to lie still in her lap. The bench creaked and skirts rustled. She hazarded a glance at her sisters. Deborah, Rebekah, Hazel, and her soon-to-be stepsister, Esther, sat in a row in their gray dresses, their expressions serene for this most solemn yet joyous occasion. If they felt any of this welter of warring emotions, it didn't show.

Leila forced her gaze back to the front of the room. Leroy Glick posed each of the questions in that no-nonsense tone he employed during the nearly three-hour sermon that had preceded the vows. Would they remain together until death? Would they be loyal and care for each other during adversity, affliction, sickness, and weakness? Each time, Mudder's soft *jah* followed Mordecai's gruff, firm response. Each jah brought them closer to that moment in which the act of marriage would become irrevocable. Every muscle in Leila's body tensed. Her bones ached. Her jaw pulsed with the pressure of her gritted teeth.

Gott, Thy will be done. Thy will be done.

A sharp elbow jabbed her ribs.

"Ouch." She covered her mouth with her hand and glared at Deborah.

Her sister leaned so close her warm breath brushed Leila's ear. "Sit still. You're rocking."

"I wasn't—"

Deborah, hands now resting on a swollen belly no apron could hide, shook her head so hard the strings of her white *kapp* flopped and wisps of her blonde hair escaped. Her frown turned her into a replica of their mother when the cornmeal mush burned or the clothesline fell down under the weight of the men's wet pants. "Not now."

Not now indeed. Mudder's moment should not be marred. Leila swallowed back hot tears of joy for her mudder's happiness. For Mudder's happiness, but also for Daed. He would've wanted this. He would've said that his days on earth had numbered less. They were complete. Mudder's were not. Nor were Mordecai's. Gott's plan, however unfathomable to Leila, was His plan.

Leroy took Mudder's hand and placed it in Mordecai's. His own calloused hands, big as catcher's mitts, covered theirs.

"So then I may say with Raguel the Gott of Abraham, the Gott of Isaac, and the Gott of Jacob be with you and help you together and fulfill His blessing abundantly upon you, through Jesus Christ. Go forward as mann and fraa."

The now-married couple turned and faced their friends and family, Mordecai's tall, muscle-bound frame dwarfing Mudder's smaller, slighter figure. Her wide, tremulous smile made her cheeks dimple. She glowed. No other word could describe the transformation. She looked no less radiant than any first-time bride Leila had ever seen. Years fell away. Time and heartache disappeared in that rare moment of happiness that stood between what had been and what would come in her new life as Mordecai King's fraa. Whatever new obstacles, whatever new tragedy or pain, whatever came, she would share it with her new husband.

Praise God. Leila rose on trembling legs and heaved a breath. God willing, one day soon she, too, would look like that. *Please, Gott.*

Deborah dabbed at her face with a handkerchief. Hazel whooped. Rebekah grinned and hoisted the younger girl to her hip. "Hallelujah."

Hallelujah indeed.

"What is wrong with you?" Deborah whispered in her ear as she pinched Leila's arm. "You look like you just ate a slice of armadillo. This is Mudder's day. Don't be spoiling it for her."

Leila rubbed her arm. "I'm not. I just . . . I'm . . . I'll go help with the serving."

Deborah's expression softened. "We're all thinking of him too. He'd be happy for Mudder."

"Jah." Leila swallowed against the tears yet again. "He *would* be happy for her."

"Because that is the kind of man he was."

"Jah."

Deborah patted a comforting, circular pattern on Leila's back, her hand warm and soft. "Get a breath of fresh air. You're white as a sheet. Go for a little walk."

"I don't need air."

"The others will understand. Phineas understands. He's thinking of his mudder today too. It's not like Mordecai isn't thinking of his first fraa. Or Mudder of Daed. It's only natural."

The knot in Leila's throat threatened to explode. Why couldn't she be more like her older sister? Somehow marriage to Phineas had changed Deborah. Impending motherhood had changed her. Each day, she sprouted new wisdom like a baby bird growing its first feathers. Leila managed a quick jerk of a nod. "Just a few minutes. I'll be back to help."

Deborah gave her shoulder a last, quick squeeze and moved away, enveloped in the flow of folks surging forward to congratulate the newlyweds. Leila pressed herself along the wall, edging her way toward the door, out onto the porch and into the muggy air of late September in south Texas. Butch, Mordecai's dog—or maybe he was Deborah's, Leila couldn't tell anymore—raised his head, stood, and stretched. The black patches on the *hund's* white face made him look like a pirate, an old, mangy pirate.

"Stay, hund." Leila didn't need a companion, not even the four-legged kind. She longed for solitude. Fat chance in this place. "I'll be back soon."

Butch yawned and flopped back on the cement porch. He surely looked as if he were smiling at her with that grizzled snout of his.

Shaking her head at her own flight of fancy, Leila skirted the dozens of buggies and vans parked across the yard and made a beeline for the barn. Beyond it stood a thicket of mesquite, live oak, and hackberry trees interspersed with clusters of nopales, pale green against the faded blue sky. She could walk a few minutes out of sight of the house and all the visitors crammed into Phineas's home, spilling out into the backyard where picnic tables had been set up to serve the overflow.

Her head down against a dank southeasterly wind, she rounded the corner of the barn, intent on finding peace in the stark landscape she'd grown to love in the last year. No one would call it pretty, but she found it easy to turn to Gott for direction in such a barren place.

"You said you wouldn't tell." A barely contained river of anger coursed through the low, hoarse statement.

"Tell what?" Leila stepped into the shadows of an old live oak just in time to realize the words hadn't been directed at her. The acrid *schtinkich* of burning tobacco filled her nostrils. As she rubbed her hand across the rough bark of the broad trunk and peeked beyond it, she realized her words had been lost in the wind and the rustling of the leaves.

Will Glick stood in the shadows cast by the barn in the late-afternoon sun, a glowing cigarette raised to his lips, the smoke curling and wafting over the wide brim of his Sunday-service black hat. Jesse Glick had his back to her. Will took a puff on the cigarette and let his hand drop, his fingers cupping it. "I didn't tell." He coughed and sneezed. "Do you think *Onkel* Leroy needs this on top of everything else? The drought. The Planks leaving? Even my daed is talking about whether we should stay or go. The district is fading away, and you're thinking of making it worse."

Leila slapped a hand to her mouth to muffle her soft cry of denial. Mudder had uprooted her family and moved them here from Tennessee less than two years earlier. She hadn't said a word. Did she know of this? If she did, she'd done well at keeping such a big secret.

"Onkel Andrew moved here when he was a boy." Jesse's scoffing tone grated on Leila's ears. "Your daed grew up here. He'll never leave."

"Daed says we have to go where Gott leads us."

"If he goes, will you go?" Jesse's tone softened. He sounded like a kid missing his friend already. "You're old enough to stay here on your own."

"Without my family?" Will's tone matched his cousin's. "I don't know. Would you miss me?"

They were so different in every way—Will, tall and wiry and blond, Jesse, shorter and sturdy and built like a barrel, with dark, almost black hair—yet they sounded like brothers when they talked, brothers knit together by time and circumstance.

"Jah, I would miss all of you—"

"All I know is worry is a sin. Gott has a plan." Will took another pull on the cigarette, the fiery red end throbbing in the shadows. "Do you think carrying on the way you are is part of His plan?"

Jesse whirled and stomped toward the tree without answering. Pain etched his chiseled features. Why? What was he thinking of doing? Whatever the topic, it wasn't intended for Leila's ears. She shouldn't be acting like a small child playing a game of hide-and-seek. She stepped from behind the tree.

Jesse slammed to a halt. "What are you doing here?"

"I'm stretching my legs." To her chagrin, her voice quavered. She couldn't tell them how bittersweet the day had been, seeing Mudder marry Mordecai. "I needed a breath of fresh air before the celebration begins."

Stop rambling. She picked her way through the weeds, intent on resuming her walk before she embarrassed herself more.

"It's not what you think." Jesse stepped into her path, forcing her to stop again. "We were just talking."

"You can argue all you want. You can smoke if you want. It doesn't make me no never-mind." Leila pretended to misunderstand. They needn't worry. She wouldn't repeat their conversation about the district's future. It would only sow seeds of worry and division with the others. "You can smoke if you want. It's your *rumspringa.*"

"Like Will said, we were just talking . . . about stuff."

Will flicked the lit cigarette to the ground with his thumb and forefinger, then dug the heel of his boot into it until it disappeared into the muddy soil underfoot. "Yeah, we're just talking."

"About what?" Leila couldn't help herself. They looked as guilty as the coyote caught eating cantaloupe in the garden over the summer. That they shouldn't have been talking about the future of the district was a given. Or smoking. "How to burn up hard-earned cash with a match?"

"Nee. We were talking about getting jobs in town."

Jobs in town. To earn money. To help their families make it through another winter in Bee County so they could stay, so they could keep their community together. Leroy hadn't allowed but a few of the young men to take jobs with *Englischers*. The men had met to talk about it after the drought had decimated crops this year and orders for buggies had dropped off at the same time. "Have you asked Leroy—your father?"

Jesse shrugged. "Not yet. I'm thinking I'll ride into town and see what I can find first. If I have something to offer, it will be harder to say no. Bird in the hand and all."

A man like Leroy would not make his decision based on anything other than the dictates of his conscience and the *Ordnung*. "How can you spend money on cigarettes when we can hardly put food on the table?"

"We didn't." The cellophane of the package crackled between Will's fingers. "One of the guys in town asked me to hold them when we were playing pool last week. He left before I could give them back, that's all." He handed the cigarettes to Jesse. "Here, you keep them or do whatever you want with them."

Jesse accepted his offering. "I'm throwing them away."

"They cost like seven dollars a package."

"What's going on here?"

Leila closed her eyes, hoping the gruff voice that rumbled behind her didn't belong to the last person who should see her standing behind the barn in broad daylight with two men and a package of cigarettes.

"Well, someone answer me."

She opened her eyes.

Leroy cupped one mammoth hand to his forehead to shelter his eyes from the sun. "Are you deaf? I said what's going on here?"

CHAPTER 2

Simply at the wrong place at the wrong time. That's how Leila wanted to answer Leroy's question. But she didn't. It wasn't her place. She waited for Jesse or Will to answer him. Jesse was his son, Will, his nephew. They should do the explaining, not her. She had no idea what they were doing out behind the barn. Other than smoking. And arguing.

A dog barked. Crickets sang. A mourning dove cooed.

"I don't like to repeat myself." Leroy's voice boomed. His silver beard bobbed and swayed as he shook his head, his eyes sharp behind wire-rimmed glasses perched low on his long nose. "Has the hearing gone bad on all three of you? What's going on here?"

"Nothing, Daed." The fingers of one hand wrapped around his suspenders, Jesse back-stepped until he stood next to Leila. "We were talking."

Something about Jesse's tone suggested the conversation had been between Leila and him. She opened her mouth, then shut it.

"I reckon Leila should be up at the house helping her sisters with the wedding meal." Leroy's gruff voice boomed again. "You boys can water the horses."

Jesse's boots made squelching sounds in the mud and scraggly grass. Leila didn't move, thinking Will would tell the bishop the cigarettes didn't belong to his son, but instead to his nephew. Will stood as if frozen. "I'm sorry, Onkel, I—"

"Your cousins came all the way from Missouri and Tennessee. You should be visiting with them." The edge in Leroy's voice could've cut stone. "I hope all three of you start to think about baptism classes soon. Spring will be here before you know it, Easter, and the *gmay*."

He turned, back stiff, and stalked away.

Leila exhaled, realizing for the first time that she'd been holding her breath. Leroy had said as much as he could say, truth be told. All of them were still in their rumspringas. The parents might not like what they did, but mostly they didn't interfere as long as no one rubbed their noses in their activities.

Which didn't amount to much out here in the middle of nowhere, south Texas. They had neither the money nor the means to do much more than ride into town now and then to listen to music and play pool at the bar and grill that served truckers passing through Beeville to and from Mexico.

She couldn't imagine how it must be to have a bishop as a father. If it were her, she might feel pressure to always do the right thing. Not that she didn't feel that now. Every day.

Mudder's favorite admonition fluttered in her ears. *Gott is watching.*

"Go on, Leila. It's okay." Will seemed a lot calmer

than she would be under the circumstances. "Lots of mouths to feed up at the house."

"If she wants a walk, she should take a walk." Jesse jerked his head toward the path that meandered through the brown weeds that passed for grass. "What with the folks from Tennessee and Missouri, there's more women up there than fit in the kitchen. They're elbow to elbow and nose to nose."

"Will's right, they'll be wondering where I am—"

"Let them wonder for a few minutes." Jesse started walking. "I'll go with you."

"But your daed—"

"He did his duty. He won't interfere with my rumspringa. Or yours."

Was this rumspringa? Or was it courting? Both? The thought made Leila's head swim. She hesitated. Leroy had spoken, but Jesse knew his father better than she did.

Will stepped in front of her. His blue eyes were dark in his tanned face, his expression troubled. "It's nasty and muggy today. Wouldn't you rather be inside?" He swiveled and glanced toward Jesse, who continued to walk as if confident she followed. "With the women."

"Why didn't you tell Leroy the cigarettes were yours?" Her tone was more accusing than she intended, but she couldn't help it. What kind of friend was he? "You let Jesse take the blame."

"He doesn't care." Will's face reddened. "But you're right. I'll fix it. Don't worry."

"You coming?"

It might have been a question, but Jesse said it as if he already knew the answer.

"I have to go."

Will's mouth worked. "Be careful."

"Of what?"

Will gave her a halfhearted smile, then brushed past her. "Sometimes things aren't what they seem."

With that cryptic statement, he disappeared around the corner of the barn, leaving Leila exasperated but no less determined. "Wait, Jesse."

A litter of kittens doing belly flops in her stomach, she tromped through the knee-high grass and weeds to catch up with Jesse. Her chance had finally arrived, one she'd hoped to have months ago. Here it stood, within her grasp. She waited to speak until they reached the gully that passed as a creek bed beyond the clusters of nopales bigger than some of the mesquite trees. "Why didn't Will tell your daed the cigarettes belonged to him?"

"Because he knew I didn't want him to get on Daed's bad side."

"But it's okay for you to get in trouble?"

Jesse snatched up a straggly blade of grass and twisted it. "I won't get in trouble. I haven't done much of anything that would shame him during four years of rumspringa. A cigarette behind the barn is slim pickings."

"But you weren't smoking."

"Will is my cousin and he's my friend."

"A good friend doesn't let his friend take the blame for something he did."

"I owe him."

"Owe him what?"

"That's between him and me." Jesse pulled back the

low-hanging branches of a live oak and waved Leila toward a downed trunk graying with decay. "Sit. You look like you're about to heave."

"I won't heave. I'm fine." The wind whipped through the tree branches, lifting the ribbons on her kapp. She shivered. "I feel like stretching my legs, that's all."

"Your legs are awful short. They could use some stretching."

His tone had a teasing quality that surprised her after the scene with his father. "My legs are fine."

"Jah, they are."

He couldn't actually see her legs under her long skirt. Still, heat mixed with a chill that ran up her arms, goose bumps popping up in its wake. "I'm-I'm," she stuttered, making the heat burn white hot. "That's not—"

"I'm just teasing you." He held out his hand, his fingers wiggling. "Sit. You need to smile more. You have a fine smile too."

"My smile's been around here for a while now." Mesmerized by Jesse's sudden grin that brought out dimples in his tanned face, she took his hand. He had calluses. His fingers gripped hers in a warm, sure hold. "So far you haven't seemed to take particular notice of it."

He led her to the trunk, his face so close she could see the curls of his black hair under the back of his hat. She inhaled. He smelled like burning mesquite. He plopped down next to her and leaned close, eyes the color of burnt caramel, intent and amused. "Well, I'm noticing now, aren't I?"

Leila ducked her head, her thoughts jumbled by

his closeness. After a few seconds, he leaned away and plucked blades of grass. He began to braid them together, his blunt fingers nimble. She cast about for a subject—any subject—that didn't involve her legs and him noticing them. "Do you think the district will fail?"

"Gott's plan."

Leila had heard that response her entire life. How did a person know? "That's what your father says. What do you say?"

He added more blades of grass to his braid. Soon it would be a rope. "I say Gott's plan could be that we are meant to go somewhere else or be somewhere else. Some of us, anyway."

"My family just moved here over a year ago." To her horror, tears pricked at her eyes. She blinked them away. The move from Tennessee had been hard for all of them so soon after her father's death, but they'd adjusted. They'd made friends. And now, Mudder had married again. Deborah had married. They had put down roots. "Can you imagine Phineas or Mordecai living anywhere else?"

Jesse's chuckle sounded hard and dry. "You can raise bees anywhere." He shrugged. "But I see your point. Mordecai might thrive up north or even back in Tennessee, but take Phineas away from this place, he'd wither."

"You sound like you don't think leaving would be a bad idea for you."

"I never said that." He handed her the braid as if giving her a gift. She took it. Their fingers touched, his calluses rough against her skin. "I do think we can plop this district down anywhere and our folks will worship the same way they do here. Only living will be easier."

"So what were you and Will arguing about?"

Jesse studied his empty hands. Something in his expression flickered. A sadness mixed with fear or anger, she couldn't be sure. "We weren't arguing, just talking."

Leila had imagined riding in a buggy next to Jesse many times. It had never been like this. They'd have light conversation. They'd laugh. He'd smile that smile. Instead, here she sat next to him in broad daylight a stone's throw from her brother-in-law's house, the sunshine breaking through clouds that scudded across the sky as if driven by God's breath, and Jesse looking like he'd just lost his best friend. Maybe he had. *Let it be. Let Gott's plan unfold.*

Maybe he'd only offered to walk with her to escape his father's wrath. Maybe he had no intention of courting her, or he would have asked under better circumstances.

"I haven't seen you leave the singings with anyone." He dusted his hands on his pants as if ridding them of dirt she couldn't see. "I mean, leastwise, not with one of the fellows."

"Nee."

"Me neither." He chuckled, a halfhearted, embarrassed sound. "I mean, with a girl, me, I mean."

He sounded as nervous as she felt. She folded the grass braid and made a knot, forming a crooked cross. "I know what you mean."

"Have you ever been to a movie in a real movie theater, you know, with the big screen and the sound system and all that?"

Of course not. "Nee."

"You know, it takes two to have a conversation, and you're not making this any easier."

Now he sounded like a little boy much aggrieved that he didn't get that one thing he longed for on Christmas Day. "I don't know what to say." She had no experience being alone with a man, making conversation with him. She cleared her throat. "I've never been to a movie—any movie."

"I've been a few times. It's fun, if it's a good movie. Loud and silly, if it's not. I have an Englisch friend who wants me to go to the movies. In George West."

Leila mulled over his words, trying to interpret the unspoken message woven into those she'd actually heard. "Are you asking me to go with you?"

"Would you?"

"Why me?"

"Because I'm asking you."

"You walked out here with me to get out of talking to your daed."

"In part."

"What's the other part?"

"I always wanted to ask you to take a buggy ride with me. I didn't for reasons you won't understand. But neither did I ask another girl."

What reasons couldn't she understand? She hadn't been a great scholar in school, but she had some book-learning smarts. Jesse wanted to ask her to the movies, but he wasn't doing a very good job. Did she want to go to the movies? So far, her rumspringa had been a series of gentle forays into the Englisch world. Letting her hair down in town. Wearing a thin necklace of fake pearls when she, Sally, and Patty ate tacos at the taquería on the highway and then watched friends play pool, a game she couldn't seem to master.

"If it takes you that long to figure it out, I'm thinking the answer is no." Jesse didn't sound surprised or even disappointed. "It's only a movie."

"It's not the movie."

"Ah. It's me."

Leila chewed her lip, seeking a response that wouldn't offend.

"My daed is the bishop, but that doesn't make me any different than you."

"He doesn't watch you closer?"

"Nee. He worries same as any other parent, but he's determined not to interfere."

"Still, being the bishop's son must weigh on you sometimes."

He wrinkled his nose as if assailed by a bad odor. "You have such a sweet, innocent face."

So he didn't want to think about the truth of the matter. Everyone was equal in their faith. All were to be humble and obedient, even the bishop. Yet how could it not weigh on him, son of the bishop and grandson of the founder of this district? Jesse had been the anchor of the group of young men who attended the singings. Always listening to the younger ones. Showing up when surely he had tired of their silliness and shenanigans. He and Will were the oldest. "What's that supposed to mean?"

"You surprise me, that's all."

Did men like to be surprised? Leila couldn't wait

to ask Deborah. Her sister had more experience with men. At least with men like Phineas, and it appeared God had broken the mold when He made that man.

"You think I'm addled or stupid? You talked to me a couple of times at a singing, said you were going to take me for a ride sometime, and then decided I wasn't worth knowing and moved on."

"It wasn't like that."

"What was it like?"

"Other stuff happened. Stuff you wouldn't understand."

"See there, you think I'm not smart because I'm a little . . . *doplisch*."

"A little? You knocked into the table and broke three glasses at the singing last month."

"Once. That happened once. You've seen me play volleyball and baseball. I'm just fine doing that." How could she explain to this man how she felt every day, like a chubby goat stumbling around in a meadow filled with a herd of sleek horses? "It's social stuff that . . . Anyway, if you hadn't been teasing me about the burn on my apron, I wouldn't have done that."

"I like teasing you. It makes your cheeks turn pink and you giggle. Since that first time I saw you in the store, I've always thought you were sweet."

Leila remembered that day too. The memory made her cheeks heat even in the fall air. He'd been working for his father, unloading baskets of fresh squash, beets, and okra, sweat beading on his forehead, his tanned face flushed, biceps bulging under the rolled-up sleeves of a shirt washed so many times the cobalt had faded to a pale blue. "I liked you too."

More heat. Should a girl say such a thing aloud to a man?

Jesse snorted but said nothing for a long moment. Maybe she had said too much. How did a girl know? Would it always be this hard?

His breathing sounded harsh. "So go to the movies with me."

Maybe she'd done it right. But a movie? The goose bumps reappeared. Mudder wouldn't like it. But wasn't that the point of rumspringa? To find a special friend? It might be her only chance to know Jesse and for him to want to know her. "If we go in a buggy, it'll take half the night to get to George West."

His smile flashed. He did indeed have a nice smile, all white teeth and full lips. "Who said anything about a buggy? Just be ready when I shine a light in your window."

"When?"

"I don't know exactly when. We have company now and next week, the auction. Maybe the weekend after that. Saturday night in a week's time before we get too close to Thanksgiving." He slapped a hand on hers, clasped in her lap. His fingers were icy now. "Don't look so worried. How much trouble can you get into with the bishop's son?"

Indeed. Exactly how much?

CHAPTER 3

The creak of the rickety lawn chair on the front porch gave his daed away. Jesse ducked his head against a night breeze just cool enough to suggest fall might be about to show its face in Bee County. He strode across the yard and up the three steps that led to the porch and front door of his family's home. The brash light of the full moon had disappeared behind a cluster of clouds thick as a pile of winter quilts. Which meant he couldn't read the bishop's expression.

He often thought of his daed that way. As the bishop. His daed drew the lot when Jesse was twelve, and everything changed. His mudder said it wouldn't, but it had. Sermons and gmays and weddings and funerals and disciplinary actions. How could it not?

Not that Jesse begrudged the district its bishop. Daed made a good bishop. Fair, even-keeled to the point of cool under pressure. He had a keen mind and a methodical nature. Which gave Jesse hope that this exchange would be a peaceful one.

"You're back."

"I am."

The clouds drifted and the light of the moon spilled

over them, giving an odd shine to Daed's glasses, masking his expression. "Sit a spell with an old man."

It wasn't an invitation, as quietly as it was delivered, but an order. Daed had a way about him. He rarely had to ask twice, a quality that served him well as bishop and as head of his family. Only Mudder dared argue with him, and then only for a minute or two before she gave in. Jesse endeavored to see his father's face as he eased into the nearby hickory rocker that squeaked worse than the lawn chair. Heat and humidity had warped it, making the rockers off kilter.

Daed held a flashlight resting on his thigh. With his other hand he stroked his beard. Dark circles hung like bruises under his eyes. Officiating a wedding and all that went with that important role had taken its toll. His wire-rimmed glasses sat low on his long nose, meaning he'd been deep in thought, too deep to remember to slide them up with the flick of a finger as he so often did while making a point during a sermon. He'd been ruminating on something important.

Jesse leaned back and waited.

"Talked to Will." An innocent enough beginning, but Daed's tone left no doubt that there was more to come. "Saw him at the house with the others."

With the other unmarried men, sitting at a table across from the unmarried girls. This long-standing tradition offered a chance to pair off after the singing and games. A chance Jesse had missed. "Jah."

"He told me the cigarettes were his. Is that true?"

"Will doesn't lie."

"You didn't say anything."

The wind kicked up and a fine mist dampened Jesse's face. They would have rain before dawn. Coupled with the downpour of the previous day, it heralded at least a start to the end of a painful summer drought. Maybe the fall and winter vegetables would do better. Maybe hard times would ease up a bit. "Nothing to say."

"I don't care about the cigarettes." Daed drummed his thick fingers on a stack of upside-down bushel baskets that sat between them. "I do care. They're a waste of money we can ill afford and bad for you, but what I mean to say is, don't flaunt your rumspringa in my face."

"Didn't mean to do that."

"See that you don't."

"I will."

Daed started to rise. Then he sank back in the chair and leaned forward, his elbows on his knees, the flashlight rolling from one big hand to the other and back. His suspenders strained against his broad, barrel chest. "I know there's been talk."

The ever-present band of guilt and worry tightened around Jesse's chest, causing a hitch in his breathing. "Talk?"

"About whether we'll survive another year here."

"Jah."

"What are your thoughts?"

Daed wanted his thoughts. A year ago that idea would've brought Jesse a certain measure of satisfaction. Daed valued his opinion, not son to father, but man to man. Now, he stumbled, trying to order his thoughts in a way that wouldn't reveal his turmoil. "This district's been here going on twenty-five years. It's survived this long."

"Andrew's considering moving back to Tennessee. His mudder is ailing and his daed wants to retire to the *dawdy haus*."

Will had been right. Two families had moved to Missouri the previous year. Scholars at the school had dwindled to fifteen. Church fit easily into their house now. Moreover, his Onkel Andrew had been chosen by God to lead as minister. "He drew the lot. He'd ignore that?"

"He's praying on it."

"What does *groossdaadi* say?"

"You know him."

Jesse did. His grandfather Solomon had ridden through Texas on the way to Mexico to pick up cheap materials. He'd decided he liked the wide-open spaces. Tennessee was too crowded for his taste. He liked the humidity. He didn't mind the isolation. He never batted an eye in the face of year after year of drought that turned green fields into brown dust that caked a man's face and left grit to grind on his teeth. "No turning back."

"No turning back. Every man must put his shoulders into the work here. The crops. The greenhouse. The store. Breaking the horses. Selling honey and the milk from Abram's cattle."

As if Jesse hadn't done that his whole life. "Understood."

"Sometimes I'm not so sure."

A chill crept up Jesse's arms and curled around his

neck. Thankful the dark hid his face, he leaned forward and rested his hands on his knees to hide sudden trembling. "I don't work hard enough?"

"You got something stuck in your craw, something you want to say?"

"Nee."

"You ain't been yourself of late."

"Did Will say something?"

"Does Will know something?"

Not a question Jesse dared answer. "Is my work around here and at the store not pleasing to you?"

"Your work is fine. It's . . . your face . . . I see it in your face at Sunday service when I'm up front. You look . . . disagreeable."

"Mostly I'm tired on Sunday morning."

"Get yourself home earlier on Saturday night and that will take care of itself."

"Jah."

Daed fiddled with the button on the flashlight. It flickered, casting a weak light over the mesquite, hackberry, and live oak trees in the front yard. "When you didn't partake of the baptism classes this summer . . . again . . . your mudder and I didn't say anything."

As well they shouldn't. The point was for a man or woman to be ready to take that next step without cajoling or coercion. A decision for a lifetime. No going back. No second thoughts. Jesse couldn't do that.

Not yet. Maybe not ever.

"I appreciate that."

"You're twenty. Now you're stepping out with Leila . . ."

Jesse's walk with Leila was a private matter. "It's the first time. Nothing may come of it."

He shouldn't have asked her to the movies. He'd thought for a fleeting second that he might find what he was looking for in her. Sweet Leila. The very first time he'd laid eyes on her in the Combination Store more than a year ago, he'd known she was something special with those bright, inquiring blue eyes, wheat-colored hair, dimples, a figure that filled out her faded cotton dress, and full lips made to be kissed. She might be a bit awkward and not much interested in baking and sewing, but he liked the way she looked at him—as if she suspected he could make her happy. She didn't deserve to be hurt.

What had he been thinking when he asked her to the movies?

He hadn't been thinking with his head, but rather with his heart.

Which more often than not led to trouble.

"I thought it had been longer." Daed turned the flashlight on and off again as if making sure it still worked. "You've been gone a lot of evenings, coming home late and all. We figured, your mudder and I, well, you were . . . courting."

Again, not something to be discussed. "Out and about."

"Be that as it may, we'll start classes in January to be done in time for baptism before the gmay and Easter services."

" . . . n aware."

Daed stood. This time he didn't hesitate. He clomped

past Jesse, his boots making squelching sounds on the wet wood, and pulled open the screen door. "Dawn comes early."

Indeed it did. Jesse thanked Gott that he could count on that, if nothing else.

Daed let the screen door shut with a gentleness that spoke of a houseful of sleeping people accustomed to rising early. "Get some sleep. Tomorrow's another day."

Jesse didn't bother to argue. He followed his daed into the house, knowing his knees were in for another long night on his bedroom rug.

CHAPTER 4

A piece of pie was good for what ailed a person, no matter what it might be. Leila swiped at piecrust crumbs on the table with a damp washrag, then arranged the paper plates with slices of pecan pie, apple pie, and lemon meringue pie in what she hoped served as a pleasing, appetizing array. She slapped away flies determined to make the slices their home. She'd been helping with auction fund-raisers her whole life, but she'd never been more aware of how important this auction, this year, was to everyone.

Mordecai and Mudder talked about it, their voices lowered, faces somber, after evening prayers. Mudder, with her darning in her lap, her glasses perched on her nose, Mordecai, *The Budget* newspaper spread across his knees, matching glasses slid down his nose. They needed a good turnout, and they needed good sales.

If cars were any indication, the turnout couldn't have been better this first Friday of November. It seemed all of Bee County congregated in this little strip of land for a few hours. Monster pickup trucks, vans, and cars as far as Leila's eyes could see along the road. The sight made her itch for a ride somewhere. Anywhere. This wanderlust confounded her. Did it have something to do with Jesse and his promise to take her to the movies next Saturday night? In a car. What kind would it be? A big pickup truck or one of those little cars that looked like a ladybug?

No, to take them and the Englischers, it would have to be a regular-sized car. Maybe a minivan. Did Englisch teenagers drive minivans? Her cousin Frannie claimed to have driven a station wagon on a dirt road outside of Jamesport, Missouri, where she lived now with Onkel John and *Aenti* Eve. Leila would've liked to have seen that.

"Stop daydreaming, child. Here comes another customer." Mudder nudged Leila with a gentle elbow. "When the line slows down, you can wipe off the tables and pick up trash."

"I'm not daydreaming."

Nor was she a child. Leila clamped her mouth shut as Mudder offered an Englisch lady dressed in a neon-orange T-shirt and blue jeans the menu of a meatloaf plate, hamburger, or barbecue sandwich. Fighting the urge to argue with her elder, Leila wiped the vinyl tablecloth a second time with more elbow grease.

The lady made the smart choice of the meatloaf plate. The entire day before had been spent making meatloaf, green beans, baked potatoes, and coleslaw for the plates. A veritable feast that made Leila's mouth water. If there were leftovers, they'd all get to share in them. She hadn't eaten meatloaf in a month of Sundays. Ground beef was expensive these days.

"Wheat bread or white?" Rebekah sounded so timid

it made Leila want to giggle. Her sister acted like a kernel of popcorn in a skillet of hot oil most days, but she didn't have much experience with Englischers. "It comes with the meal."

The Englisch lady balanced the plate in one hand and adjusted her leather bag's strap on her shoulder, her gaze fixed on the pie, which Leila agreed was much more interesting than bread. "Wheat. Does the pie come with it too?"

"It does." Leila's department. "What kind would you like?"

"Leila, Leila, there you are!"

The high voice with its Texas twang sounded familiar, but it took Leila a second to register the source. Rory Beale, now Rory Chapman, their neighbor from down the road. Before she'd had her baby, Rory often rode her horse to the Combination Store. She bought honey and teased the Glick boys and stopped to chat with Leila every chance she could. Now that she balanced a baby with finishing high school, her visits were sparse.

Leila slid a plate of apple pie toward the lady, who smiled and moved on. She squeezed toward the end of the table, hoping Mudder would be too busy making plates to notice the interruption. Rory zigzagged through the crowd, little Trevor bouncing on her hip.

"Hey, Leila, just the person I wanted to see!"

"Trevor is getting so big." Leila smoothed her hand over the baby's silky brown tufts of fine hair. He cooed and smiled a toothless smile in response, slobber sliding down his chin into a strategically placed bib. "He's as sweet as ever."

"Yeah, except when he's keeping me up half the night fussing because he's teething on the night before I have a biology test." Rory's wide smile said she really didn't mind all that much. She'd made it perfectly clear to Leila that she stayed in school because her father insisted. "I have a proposition I've been dying to make to you. Just dying. How I wish you had a phone, girl. There's an opening at the day care where I work after school. Little Angels. I immediately thought of you. You're so good with babies and you said you wanted to get a paying job."

Leila ducked her head, not wanting to see what curious glances like darts her mudder might be hurling her way. She'd been in a *wunderbaar* mood since the wedding, but that didn't mean she wouldn't be on guard as she always was at these auctions. Her girls were not to draw attention to themselves. Or they stayed home.

Furthermore, Leila had talked to an outsider about their hardships. Mudder wouldn't like that either. The conversation about jobs had been an idle one, the idea she hadn't shared with anyone else but Rebekah, who thought she had a better chance of being allowed to drive a car than get a job in town. Leila returned to the other side of the table and began cutting another pie. "I don't know." She kept her voice low, forcing Rory to bend toward her. "I'd have to get permission from the bishop."

"Ask!" Rory shifted Trevor to her other hip and held out a five-dollar bill. "I have to have some of that pecan pie. It looks yummy. The job pays nine dollars an hour.

It's full-time. We could pick you up every morning. We have to drop Trevor at the day care anyway. Then I come over to work after school and we leave together at six thirty. It's perfect. I told my boss all about you. She says Amish girls are great workers. She used to live in Pennsylvania."

Rory did talk up a storm. Mudder moved their direction, the wrinkles on her forehead deepening. Leila shoveled another piece of apple pie onto a paper plate and wiped the spatula against the pan. "We're different from the Lancaster County Amish."

"You work just as hard, right? And you take care of lots and lots of babies and little kids because your families are *muy* big."

Muy big. Rory was studying Spanish in school, a fine skill to have so close to the Mexican border. Leila had been to the border a couple of times but was not yet allowed to cross since she had no photo ID. How did Rory define *muy* big? Leila couldn't help but giggle. She caught sight of Mudder's concerned expression and wiped the smile from her face. "I'll have to let you know."

"No *problema*. The lady who's retiring still has another two weeks to go." Rory scooped up her piece of pie, ignoring Leila's attempt to give her change for the five-dollar bill. "I have to find Dad. He's looking at some rototiller thingamajiggy. As if his job at the prison doesn't keep him busy enough, he wants to plant a big vegetable garden next spring."

Trying to keep busy so he wouldn't think about the passing of Rory's mother. Leila had watched her own mother do that when Daed died. "Good for him. You and your little brother could use some fresh vegetables on the supper table."

"I'd rather buy them at the Combination Store—then I'd get to see you more." Rory wrinkled a nose covered with a smattering of freckles. "Gotta go. A certain little boy has a dirty diaper. I can smell it. Call me—I mean, come find me when you know when you can start. We're gonna have so much fun."

She slipped past a knot of people putting ketchup and mustard on their hamburgers at the condiment table before Leila could contradict her. Not that she wanted to disagree. Working at the day care would be perfect until she could have her own children. They needed the money and she loved taking care of babies. It was a perfect fit. Getting Mudder and now Mordecai to see it that way and convince Leroy—that would be a challenge the size of the state of Texas.

"We keep ourselves apart."

Startled, she turned to see Mudder frowning as she brushed piecrust crumbs from the table. "What do you mean?"

"We keep ourselves apart. Especially from folks who aren't living according to Scripture."

"Rory's married to Trevor's father."

"Now."

Mudder didn't need to elaborate. Trevor's daddy still lived at home with his own parents. He was a senior at the high school in town and worked at an auto parts store on weekends. Nobody seemed too happy about the arrangement. Rory didn't seem to know how lost she was, and Leila longed to tell her friend about God's grace and provision, but it wasn't the Plain way. Besides, Rory seemed determined to make the best of her choices. She said she loved Dwayne and one of these days, when they both finished school, they'd get a house together and live happily ever after. "Sometimes folks get things out of order, I reckon."

"Not if you stay on the straight and narrow path. That's why you have Andrew to guide you in the baptism classes."

Unless Andrew decided to take his family and move back to Tennessee.

Maybe Mudder didn't know about that possibility. This was simply her way of asking when Leila would begin taking instruction. "I know. I'm looking forward to going."

"Why don't you take a plate to Caleb?" Mudder knew better than to push on this topic. Leila had to make up her own mind. "Knowing him, he's starving or thinks he is."

"I thought you wanted me to wipe down the tables and pick up the trash." Leila followed Mudder's gaze. Rory had found her father, and they seemed to be arguing over something near the entrance to the shed that doubled as a restaurant today. "Caleb can wait a little longer."

"I'll have Rebekah do it. See that you come right back." Mudder's frown eased as she handed Leila a plate of green beans, coleslaw, baked potato, and corn. No one got to eat meatloaf until customers bought their fill. "Try not to dally in the barn. I know it's all very exciting, but you'll be in the way of the customers actually trying to buy something."

It was nice to know Mudder hadn't forgotten how exciting auction day could be—even at her age. Holding the plate close to her body, Leila dodged customers wandering about, deep in conversation about doohickeys they wanted to buy, mostly not watching where they walked. In the few dozen yards from the shed to the barn, she almost collided with four people. Flies buzzed around her face. The smell of the chickens, ducks, and pigs in the livestock section nearly knocked her back a step. She held the plate up, hoping to breathe in the enticing scent of food instead, and walked faster.

Looking much older than his ten years, Caleb manned the soda table at one of the side entrances to the barn. Business was brisk given the dank air and lack of the slightest breeze. The tip of his tongue poised in one corner of his mouth, her brother counted out change for a ten-dollar bill and then counted it again, much to the amusement of a tall man in a white cowboy hat, red plaid Western shirt, and jeans so worn they had a round, white circle on the back pocket. When he smiled, he showed off teeth brown from chewing tobacco.

Caleb handed him a Dr Pepper dripping with condensation and nodded at the man's thanks. He turned and grinned at Leila. "It's about time. I was ready to chew off my arm up to my shoulder."

"Don't be so dramatic." She slid in behind the table and plopped the plate on the crate behind him. "It's barely noon."

"I've sold three cases of water." Caleb slapped the metal box shut, a satisfied expression on his face that made him the spitting image of Daed. That face gave Leila a chance to remember what her father looked like. He'd loved auction day. "The Englischers really like their water."

"Eat your lunch. I'll man the booth." That wasn't what Mudder had in mind, but Leila wanted to extend her stay a little longer—until Leroy or Andrew noticed—then she'd hustle back to the food shed. "I can handle it just fine."

"Leroy will see." A mouth full of green beans muffled Caleb's words. "Or worse, Stephen. You know how he's always picking at us, now that Mudder chose Mordecai instead of him."

"I don't know why. Everyone knows he and Ruth Anne are courting. Let me do this just for a minute."

She had to yell to be heard over Leroy's voice and the shout of the spotters who were keeping track of bidders on one side while the Englisch auctioneer kept up a steady patter on the other side, simultaneous auctions that no one seemed to have trouble following. On Leroy's side, they were bidding on a nice cedar chest. It would be handy for storing quilts in the summer. Englisch folks milled about everywhere. If Leroy let her take the job at the day care, she'd surely see some of these people on a regular basis. On their territory, not hers. What a different life she would lead—at least for a little while.

She grabbed a bottled water and handed it to a lady who used her free hand to mop her face with a huge flowered handkerchief. "That's a dollar."

"Worth every penny." The lady tucked her handkerchief in a canvas bag covered with fancy embroidered flowers in purples and reds. "At this rate they won't get to the livestock until midnight."

"They move along pretty fast—"

"Hey."

Jesse stalked up to the table as the lady rushed past him, her gaze intent on some item on the other side of the barn.

That's all he had to say after not speaking to her since the day of the wedding? *Hey?*

He glanced at Caleb, who grinned and kept shoveling food into his already-full mouth. "Help me with the horses?"

Leila shook her head. Mordecai would notice for sure. He never missed a thing and he stood not ten feet away, jawing with a man about a double rocking chair he'd built special for the auction.

"I have to check on them." Jesse glanced at the platform where Leroy never missed a beat, calling out numbers and pointing at folks as the bids for a hand-carved leather saddle shot up. "Come with me."

"I thought you were helping Leroy spot the bidders and showing off the items."

He shrugged. "Daed gave me twenty minutes to get something to eat."

"Then go eat."

"I will." He glanced at Caleb, whose spoon hovered between his plate and his mouth, cheeks bulging like a chipmunk storing his acorns. "In a minute."

He slipped through the open double doors without

looking back. So sure of himself. Leila chewed on her lip. Maybe he'd changed his mind. Maybe he wasn't coming for her after all. She needed to know. "I'll be back for your plate."

"Leila has a special friend," Caleb sang, grinning as if he'd just opened a birthday present. He still had food in his mouth. "Leila's in *lieb*!"

"Don't talk with your mouth full." She squeezed from behind the table. "And just you never mind."

"I won't tell."

He wouldn't tell, but he would tease her about it every chance he got. Sighing, she dodged a lady with a double stroller filled with roly-poly twins dressed in matching pink-checkered dresses and two men carrying dented milk cans as if they were priceless. She made her way around to the back of the barn where the horses were lined up waiting their turns. Jesse patted a butterscotch-colored filly and whispered something in her ear.

"Do you always talk to the horses?"

"They're good listeners."

What would Jesse think of her working in town? She wanted to ask, but the matter of their impending date took precedence. If he didn't want to go out with her, what she did with her time would be of no interest to him. "They look fine to me. They don't know they're about to be sold."

"I know." He slid his fingers through the horse's mane, untangling the hair. She shook her head and whinnied, apparently not happy with his ministrations. "I don't think we should go to the movies after all. For your sake."

He added the last three words in a stammered mess. Leila had been right. He'd had time to think about it, time enough to realize asking her had been a big mistake. She swallowed a sudden knot in her throat as big as a Texas Ruby Red grapefruit. Her eyes stung. Just the dirt and hay dust in the air from all these folks traipsing around, nothing more. "That's fine. It's fine."

She lifted her hand to her mouth to hide the painful red burn that scurried up her neck and across her face. She whirled and headed toward the food shed.

"Wait, wait, it's not you, it's me." Jesse's voice had turned hoarse. Somehow Leila doubted that. She should've known better than to think a man like Jesse, so sure of himself, so good at doing what men do, would be interested in a girl so doplisch. She would not make a good fraa, surely he saw that. His hand clamped on her shoulder. "I said wait."

The heat of his fingers permeated the thin cotton of her dress. The burn wrapped itself around her throat, spread to her chest, then to the pit of her stomach. Her breath caught. His fingers were strong. *Stop it.* She forced herself to tug free of his grip. "It's fine. I have to get back to the food tables. Mudder will miss me. She'll make me go to the back and stay with the little ones."

"I don't want to . . . lead you down the wrong road."

She turned to face him, planting her black sneakers so hard in the dirt that puffs of dust floated around them. "I'm not a horse to be led anywhere. I have a mind of my own." Not necessarily a quality Plain men looked for in a fraa. "I mean I know what's wrong and what's right."

He stood so close she could see tiny beads of sweat on his nose and flecks of green in his dark brown eyes. His hand came up as if to touch her again. She fought the urge to lean in. His hand dropped. "I know you do, but you haven't been exposed to some of the things I have."

Her breathing came in short, painful spurts. "Like what?"

"Like . . . I don't know . . . you wouldn't understand."

What she didn't understand was this. Him. The on and off again. "I'm not stupid."

He ducked his head so she stared at the top of his straw hat. "I know that."

"What is it that you don't want to tell me?"

"If I tell you, you'll have to tell someone and I can't have that."

"So I'm stupid *and* you don't trust me."

"I want to. I want . . . I need . . ." He lifted his hat from his head and smacked it against the hitching post. The horses tossed their heads and whinnied, jostling each other in their anxiety. "Sorry, sorry, sorry."

Leila couldn't be sure if he directed the refrain at her or the horses. "Tell me, please tell me. You're scaring me. What is it?"

His Adam's apple bobbed. "I'm—"

"Hey, y'all, what's going on?" Will's voice, normally a soft drawl, had turned to a growl. He stalked across the yard, his arms straining under the weight of a huge box of Ball quart canning jars. "Leroy is looking for you, Jesse, and he isn't happy."

CHAPTER 5

Only the weight of the box of canning jars in his arms kept Will from surging forward. He was supposed to be delivering them to Molly Carter's minivan. The sight of Leila and Jesse out here in public arguing, Jesse's hand on her shoulder, had sent him spiraling off course. He swallowed, his anger tight in his gut. He'd always thought of Jesse as the smarter one among his many cousins. Not anymore. He seemed intent on dragging Leila down with him as well. He knew better than to put his hands on her, especially at such a public event. Everyone in the county milled around at this auction, whether to buy something or simply because they wanted to socialize with their neighbors and take home a bit of gossip, along with a jar of Mordecai's honey.

Every member of the district knew best behavior was expected, and punishment for stepping out of line would be quick and severe. He and his brothers had made only one trip to the woodshed for a whupping to understand that. He was nine at the time. Jesse was old enough to know better.

Will took a breath and tried to smooth his expression.

"Leila, you should get back to the food shed. Your mudder is looking for you too."

Leila's already pink cheeks darkened to a radish red. She looked as guilty as he had felt that day in the woodshed when his daed asked him why he'd been playing shoot the trash cans using BB rifles with the Englisch boys instead of manning the water table. "Did you tell her where I was?"

"Nee. I didn't know until I saw you here . . . with Jesse." He shifted the heavy box again and shot Jesse a meaningful glance. His cousin's whiskerless face reddened. He turned his back and smoothed the mane of the closest horse. Will had to remind himself that Plain men didn't resort to physical violence. "Guess I should've known."

"What's that supposed to mean?" Jesse whirled and muscled his way past Will, forcing him to take a step back. "Isn't none of your business, for one."

Jesse was right, except Will knew too much to let him go without a struggle. Too much was at stake. Drawing Leila into it would only make matters worse. "I know. I just don't want there to be a scene here in front of all the folks from town."

"Nobody's making a scene except you." Jesse ducked his head. "Besides, I was just leaving."

"Don't go." Leila squeezed past Will. He could smell her scent of soap and vanilla, so light and sweet after the smells of livestock and sweaty men. She didn't even look at him. "What were you going to tell me?"

Jesse shook his head. "I'm—"

"Not here. Not now." Will shoved forward into the

small space that separated his cousin from a girl Will wanted to protect from something he didn't understand. "Think about what you're doing to her."

"Doing to me—"

Jesse shoved forward as if to close the gap between Leila and him. His arm swung out and smacked the box between them. Will lost his grip and it tumbled to the ground, jars clanking against each other, the sound of breaking glass ominous in his ears.

"Now look what you did." Will squatted and righted the box. At least three jars were broken and two cracked. "Molly Carter already paid for these."

"I'm sorry. I'm really sorry." Jesse backed away, both hands in the air. He shook his head, the pain on his face so acute it hurt Will to look at him. "I didn't mean to do that."

Consequences were consequences, regardless of the intent. Will would suffer the consequences for his actions, coming out here instead of delivering the box to its new owner. "That's the problem. Sorry isn't enough, not for this and not for the other thing."

Jesse stared down at Will, his chest heaving. He backed up, whirled, and stomped away.

"Jesse, Jesse! Now look what you did." Leila shook a finger at Will, the picture of righteous anger. "He was going to tell me why . . ."

The pique in her face faded. She sighed, dropped her hand, and knelt next to him. "Never mind." She picked up a jar and set it upright in the box. "It's not your fault, I reckon."

"I'm sorry. I didn't mean to interrupt something

important." Could she be more oblivious to his feelings? Not that it was her fault. He'd never stepped up and said anything. Everyone knew he'd been interested in her sister Deborah, who'd also ignored him, such was her preoccupation with Phineas. No one wanted to be second choice—especially to a sister. He didn't think of Leila that way, but she surely would. "I just don't want y'all to get in trouble."

"That's sweet of you, but I reckon we can both take care of ourselves."

Sweet? His emotions, normally so even-keeled, seemed to billow like smoke from a raging grass fire on a windy day every time he encountered Leila. He'd never felt that way with Deborah. "Not really. It's no fun for anyone if things go wrong at the auction. It's supposed to be a good day."

She stared at the empty space where Jesse had stood. Probably not even hearing Will's voice. Jesse had been going to tell her his big plan, the plan that would break his mother's and father's hearts. Making her privy to it would only put Leila in a precarious position as well. She was such a pretty girl with a sweet nature—how could Jesse do that to her? He was being selfish, that's how. On the other hand, Leila might be the one person who could hold Jesse, keep him here. Will couldn't stand in the way of that. "I'm sorry, but you know how Leroy is. Everyone is to be on their best behavior."

"Stop saying you're sorry. Jesse talking to me isn't good behavior?"

"Don't be dense. He had his hand on you. I saw it. If

I could see it, others could too." Will wanted to brush a bit of straw from her cheek and run his fingers down the small patch of white skin exposed on her neck. How could he judge Jesse when all he could think about was touching the very same girl? *Think about something else. Anything else.* "That kind of behavior is frowned upon at any time, but especially in the middle of the auction with all the folks from town here."

"It wasn't what you think." Her voice quavered. "He was . . . unasking me out."

Her expression bereft, she wiped at her nose with the back of her sleeve. The girl never had a hankie when she needed one. So Jesse had managed to hurt her already. Will needed to do something. Something physical. A long evening chopping firewood loomed in his future. "I'm sorry."

Her forehead wrinkled and she shook her head. "Why do you care?"

Will studied the horses beyond her. "I don't like to see you sad."

More than that, he wanted to be the one asking her out. He would never unask her.

She sniffed and smiled a determined, if watery, smile. "That's nice of you."

He took a jar from her hand and settled it into the box. "I don't ever want to see you . . . hurt."

The sadness faded, replaced by bewilderment. "What are you saying?"

What was he saying? He had no right to horn in on his cousin's intended. But how could Jesse pursue Leila knowing what his attentions might cost her? The dilemma tightened around Will's throat in a strangle-hold. He coughed and sucked in air. "I'm saying there's something you should know—"

"Will, what are you doing?" His daed marched across the yard, Molly Carter behind him. "Molly is looking for her box of jars. She said you were to carry them to her van."

"I was. I stopped . . ." How to explain this to his daed? "I mean, I . . ."

"I got in his way and the box fell," Leila jumped in. "I'm sorry, Molly, some of the jars are broken."

The Englisch lady frowned, her pudgy face full of disappointment. "I already paid for a full box. I plan to can pickles next summer. I paid a fair price."

Daed's expression scorched Will. "We'll refund your money, and you can keep whatever jars can be salvaged. Will, take the box to her van while I settle up with her."

"I'm sorry."

The woman nodded, but the pique didn't fade from her face. "Just see that you don't break any more in the two hundred yards between here and the van. I don't see how you ended up back here with my jars when the van is out there on the road."

"I don't either." The growl in Daed's voice didn't bode well. "Be sure I'll have a word with him about learning his directions."

They started back toward the barn just as Leila's mother flounced across the yard, her usual smile turned down in a worried frown.

Leila ducked past Will. "Mudder—"

"Go." Mudder's gaze flicked over Will. "Now."

"I'm sorry, I was just talking to Will."

Funny how she didn't mention Jesse. Will moved out of Abigail King's way. She was a woman on a mission. She slapped both hands on her hips and bore down on him with a withering glance. "You know better. I'm sure you have a duty assigned to you. Get to it and stop keeping Leila from her duties. You both know better."

"Yes, ma'am."

Leila rushed away, head down, her mother marching behind her, skirt swishing in a determined rustling sound. Will picked up the box with its broken contents. An all-around fiasco. His daed would not soon forget this incident. Leroy would surely hear about it. Abigail King would tell Mordecai. It would be the talk of the district.

About Leila and Will. Not Jesse. Jesse came out smelling like one of Mordecai's beeswax candles. All Will had wanted to do was help. Instead he'd caused a major incident. How had that happened? He shook his head and started walking. The road to hell was paved with good intentions, that's how.

CHAPTER 6

Now or after supper? Leila mulled the question as she deposited a basket of hot cornbread on the table next to the enormous cast-iron pot of venison chili. The mingled aromas of onion and garlic made her mouth water. She inhaled and brushed crumbs from her apron, trying to ignore the stains where the chili had dripped in her haste to carry the steamy concoction from the kitchen on the previous trip.

She stole a glance at her mother. Mudder busied herself correcting Hazel's enthusiastic, if haphazard, attempts to lay out the spoons and butter knives. Mudder had been wordless during most of the preparations for supper. In fact, she'd said little to Leila in the three days that had passed since the auction. No mention of Will. Which was good, because Leila had no idea what he was trying to accomplish. Leila wanted to tell Mudder her assumptions were incorrect, but to do so would involve explaining about Jesse. She had no desire to explain him, even if she could.

If Jesse wasn't interested in her, the job at the day care became all the more important. She wanted to broach the subject, but nothing in Mudder's silence suggested she would be open to that idea either. No other woman in the district had done such a thing—thus far. If she couldn't convince Mudder, she'd never have the opportunity to try to convince the bishop. If Leila waited much longer, surely the position would be filled and the opportunity lost. She straightened the silverware next to her soup bowl. Then she began to pour water into the glasses at each place. *Gott, give me the words. Soften her heart.*

Now. Say something. Go on.

"Whatever's on your mind, spit it out." An amused smile on her face, Mudder added a jar of pickled jalapeños to the table. Mordecai liked some extra heat in his chili. "You've been wiggling around all afternoon like you have a splinter in your behind. You've got something to say, best say it."

"Rory, you know the Englisch girl—"

"The one with the *bopli*?" Mordecai clomped into the room, drying his hands on a dish towel as he went. He tugged his chair from the table and plopped down. "I talked to her daed at the auction. He bought a rototiller. He mentioned he's interested in the mare Andrew's selling."

"Poor man, he hasn't gotten over his fraa's death yet." Susan set a pitcher of water on the table and wiped her hands on her apron. The concern on her face made her look the spitting image of her brother Mordecai. They were two peas in a pod when it came to feeling deeply for others. "He needs to work the earth. It'll do him good."

"Rory says he's planting a big garden this spring."

Not the opening Leila was looking for, but she'd take what she could get. She helped Hazel climb into her chair and picked up the ladle to start serving. Caleb dodged his stepbrothers, Samuel and Jacob, racing to beat them to the table. She raised her voice to be heard over their good-natured squabbling. "Anyway, she says there's an opening at the day care where she works after school. A full-time job. She asked the director if she would consider me. The director said she would. She said Amish girls are good workers."

She said it all in a rush, then stopped, dropped into her chair, and stared at her bowl, afraid to look at Mudder's face. The scent of chili, so tantalizing a few seconds earlier, turned her stomach now. Mordecai was the deacon. He could have a word with Leroy. He would have a say in the decision. And he was the head of the household now. Mudder would have to listen to him and acquiesce to his decision.

"What has gotten into you, *dochder*?"

Leila looked up to see a forlorn expression on Mudder's face. Not the disapproval she'd expected. Mudder looked disappointed in her. Why? "I want to help. It's a chance to earn some money to help us make ends meet, that's all." Leila kneaded her napkin in trembling fingers. "I'd be taking care of babies. Little *kinner*. All the workers there are women. What harm could there be in that? Rory's daed would give me a ride. It's during the day only, weekdays only. It pays nine dollars an hour."

That last fact drew a collective *aah* from the other young folks in the room. Susan, Mordecai, and Mudder didn't share in their enthusiasm.

"You would be taking care of Englisch folks' kinner all day." Esther passed the cornbread to her brother Samuel, who extracted a huge chunk and plunked it on top of his chili. "Wouldn't that make you nervous? I know it would me. They raise their kinner differently."

The banns for Esther and her special friend Adam Glick had been announced at the service on Sunday. She need not worry about what her future held. Soon she would be married. She would have her own babies to raise. Unlike Leila, who'd been dumped by Jesse before they even had their first date.

Leila gripped the ladle and filled her bowl. "I love boplin. I know I can do it. I take care of them around here all the time."

"I know you could do it." Her shoulders hunched, Mudder sat across from Mordecai, her gaze fixed on him. "The question is, should you do it?"

"A question that will need to be answered by Leroy." Mordecai smiled at his fraa as if giving her reassurance. "This is a conversation best had with him."

Mudder's returning smile faltered. "You would go to Leroy with this?"

"Leila's desire to help us and the district is good." He gripped the edge of the table with long, calloused fingers, his gaze bouncing from one family member to the next. "Gott will provide for us. He always has. When an opportunity is placed in the road right in front of us, do we take it or do we try to find a detour?"

"But she's just a girl."

"Nee, she's a young woman in her rumspringa." Mordecai lifted one hand as if to silence Mudder. "This is the time for her to learn what's out there and what's important to her, don't you think?"

The look that passed between the newlyweds left Leila wondering how she would learn to be an obedient fraa. She was glad Mordecai saw her request as a good thing, but a rush of guilt rolled over her, guilt for putting her mother in this position. She would accept Mordecai's decision even if it wasn't to her liking.

"If Mudder doesn't—"

Mordecai bowed his head. "Food's getting cold."

Leila bowed her head, but she couldn't keep her mind on praying for the food. Thoughts milled about like cattle waiting for slaughter. Chagrin at causing a rift between her mother and Mordecai. A kernel of delight that Mordecai saw her side of the situation. Nerves at the thought of talking to Leroy about the job. Even more nerves when it occurred to her she might see Jesse when she visited Leroy. She sighed and scrunched her eyes tighter. If ever she needed to pray, now would be the time.

CHAPTER 7

Leroy's house. Jesse's house. Leila smoothed her apron with damp hands. She wrapped her fingers around the soft cotton material to still their shaking. Her first visit with Leroy in his capacity as bishop, and the possibility existed her supper might end up on his boots. It didn't help that she might encounter Jesse here. Jesse with his on-again, off-again approach to courting.

She sideswiped Mordecai with a glance. He nodded, his expression somber but his eyes kind. He seemed certain Leila could be trusted to comport herself well in the Englisch world, a vote of confidence that surprised her. That Mudder had chosen not to accompany her on this trip did not surprise her, however. She'd stood at the kitchen sink, back to the door, when Mordecai announced they were leaving. She hadn't turned around.

"Go on." Mordecai tugged open the Glicks' screen door and stood back to let her pass. "Leroy won't bite you. Leastways, not as long as you don't irritate him too much."

He chuckled and Leila felt the nerves that whirled in her stomach settle, at least temporarily. So far, so good. No Jesse in sight. Before she could pass through the door, Will Glick strode out. A toothy grin stretched from ear to ear on his smooth, whiskerless face. "Hey, Mordecai." His gaze dropped to Leila and the grin disappeared. "Leila."

His voice held a wary note. Maybe because of Mordecai. As far as Leila knew, Mudder had said nothing to her new husband about seeing her with Will. She nodded and inched back on the porch to let Andrew and him pass.

His daed clomped down the steps as if in a hurry to get on with things. Will paused, then turned back, his grin reappearing. "Leroy said yes. I can work at the nursery."

"He said yes." She forgot to whisper. A momentary sense of hope coursed through her. Nee. Men were different. Leroy would surely see it that way. "Good for you."

Will's gaze went to Mordecai, who had one hand on the screen door as he looked back, his expression benign, then back to her. "I hope you get what you want too."

Was he talking about the job or something else? With men, who knew? She settled for a quick wave, but Will had already jumped the steps and headed for the buggy.

Gott's will. Gott's plan. The men in their district worked with the Englisch all the time. Building buggies for those who had a hankering to stick one in their front yard like an ornament. Making their saddles, harvesting their crops, breaking their horses. Women, that was another cup of *kaffi*. At least, that's what Mudder said. Still, it was Leila's rumspringa. She could push a little harder. She wanted this. She needed it, now that Jesse had rescinded his offer to take her to the movies.

Will kept giving her those strange looks and leaving things half said or unsaid, but he had yet to speak up and he probably wouldn't, given that he thought Jesse was interested.

He was wrong about that.

After taking a deep breath, she slipped through the door, inhaling the scent of fried potatoes and onions that hung in the air in Leroy's front room. He sat in a hickory rocker, his big hands still in his lap. Without so much as a howdy, he nodded toward two straight-back chairs, arranged side by side across from the rocker.

Leila sank onto the closest one, thankful her legs hadn't betrayed her. She glanced around. No Jesse. Naturally, Leroy would want privacy for these meetings. Jesse likely was doing chores outside. *Please, Gott, let him stay outside.*

Mordecai removed his hat and settled it on his knees. His thick, curly black hair stood up all over his head, giving him a wild mountain-man look that would've been funny if Leila didn't feel as if she'd contracted a sudden case of the flu. "Leila came to Abigail and me with an idea that bears looking at. Requires your approval."

Leroy plucked at his long gray beard. "It's getting late. Let's not belabor this."

Leila held her breath. Did he mean her or Mordecai?

"We think it's a good idea." Mordecai picked up his hat and planted his elbows on his thighs. "She wants to try her hand at taking care of boplin at Little Angels Day Care, there in Beeville. They've said they'll take her. Forty hours a week. Nine dollars an hour. Nolan Beale is willing to give her a ride to and fro."

He leaned back and gave the hat an expert twirl on one finger. Leroy's eyebrows rose and fell like thick strands of gray yarn escaped from their skein. "You and Abigail think this is good." He grunted and sniffed. "In what way is it good for our girls to be exposed to the shenanigans of those folks?"

"She's in her rumspringa. Better she get this itch taken care of now, so she can be baptized and get on with business here." Mordecai didn't flinch at Leroy's perturbed expression. "You know as well as I do we're going into the winter low on provisions and funds."

"Gott will provide."

"Indeed. Maybe this job is one way He's doing that. She didn't seek it out. It came to her. Makes me think Gott's hand might be moving in it."

Leroy pursed his lips. His gaze whipped from Mordecai to Leila. She fought the urge to shoot from the chair and flee. Leroy stared at her, wordless, for seconds that seemed to stretch into months. He sniffed. "Cat got your tongue? What do you have to say for yourself?"

She swallowed and glanced at Mordecai. Leroy shook his head. "Mordecai said his piece. I want to know how you think you're going to do this."

"It's taking care of little ones. That's all." Her voice quavered. She sucked in air and let it out, steadying herself. She wanted this. She wanted to feel those babies, warm and sweet smelling in her arms. She might not have her own, but she could do the next best thing. "I'm good at that. There's not much chance of problems. They're just boplin."

"Who have mudders and daeds." Leroy crossed his

arms over his rotund belly. "You'd be talking to them every day. I imagine they have all manner of fancy appliances and such there at the day care. Piles of stuff for those babies."

"I'll only talk to the Englisch folks about their boplin. I'll change diapers and fix bottles and play with them, rock them to sleep when they fuss." She could see it now, their tiny little bodies snug against her chest. "You don't need fancy appliances for that."

"What if something happens to one of those boplin? Something they blame you for. Then what?"

"I would take care of them just like I take care of the little ones around here. Like they were my own."

"Only they won't be."

Leroy couldn't know his words were like vinegar poured on an open wound. "Boplin are boplin. Not much to it."

Leroy tapped his work boot on the faded linoleum, still tugging at his beard. The hard lines around his mouth didn't dissipate. Leila steeled herself for the inevitable no. Why had they wasted their time on this? He would never allow it.

"We've had no trouble from you in the time you've been in Bee County."

"Nee." Not much trouble a girl could find in a place so barren and so sparse of people.

"We best pray on it." He rose. Mordecai did the same. Leila scrambled to her feet. Did he mean now? She peered at Mordecai. He didn't bow his head. Leroy headed to the door. "Andrew, Mordecai, and I will pray on it."

So the answer wasn't no. Relief made Leila's legs and arms feel like wet towels. She scurried to keep up with Mordecai, who paused at the door. "Time with the Lord on this will make things clear."

Leroy nodded. "Gott's will."

"Gott's plan."

Leila took one last look around. No sign of Jesse. She couldn't be sure, truth be told, if she was happy or sad about that. She wished she knew just exactly how these wise men figured out what God's plan was. She didn't have a clue.

CHAPTER 8

"Whatcha doin'?"

Leila jumped, shrieked, and dropped the tiny mirror she'd been attempting to use to see her face. It clunked with a thud on the wooden floor. She didn't believe in luck, but breaking a mirror didn't bode well, especially when it belonged to her new stepsister Esther. "Rebekah! Don't you know you shouldn't sneak up on a person like that? You'll give me a heart attack."

"Mudder sees you preening in front of a mirror, she'll give you a heart attack herself." Rebekah giggled and flounced on the quilt-covered bed Leila shared with Hazel and her. It was squeezed up against the wall in the tiny bedroom the sisters occupied in Mordecai's house—their new home. After living in three different houses during their first year in Bee County, it was good to have a permanent home. "'Course she's probably doing a little preening herself, seeing how she spends every waking minute thinking about what new shirt to sew for Mordecai, what Mordecai wants for breakfast, dinner, and supper, when he'll be back from working the apiaries, and when he'll be leaving her again."

"I'm not preening, and stop talking about Mudder and Mordecai. She's his fraa. She's only doing what's expected of her because she loves him." The word *love* stuck in her throat. What girl wanted to think about her mother loving a man besides her father? Even a man as kind and funny as Mordecai. Leila veered away from that thought, instead focusing on trying to smooth the wrinkles in her dress. No good. The dress was a hand-me-down, also from Esther.

Leila didn't know why she bothered to look at herself in the mirror. Obviously, Jesse didn't see what he was looking for in her. She didn't look ugly, but then again, she wasn't as pretty as Deborah or Rebekah. The plain middle sister. She scooped up the mirror, which had survived intact, and stuck it facedown next to the kerosene lamp on the crate that served as a table of sorts. "Don't you have cookies to bake for the service tomorrow?"

Rebekah rolled from the bed and pulled back the curtain hanging on the room's only window. No breeze wafted through it. For November, it was downright warm. "Cookies are done. Kitchen's clean. We've swept, mopped, and dusted. Everything's ready for us to move the furniture and set up the benches in the morning."

Leila chewed her lip. She should've been helping her sisters and not mooning around in the bedroom. Leila didn't want to be selfish, but she'd been listless since the meeting with Leroy. No trip to the movies, and so far, no permission to work in town. She wanted . . . something . . . something to which she could look forward. Mudder would say she should be looking forward to baptism. And she did, but first she wanted . . . an adventure. She wanted her rumspringa to be something she'd remember when she was married and the mother of her own children.

If that ever happened.

She turned her back on her sister and picked up a dress of Hazel's that needed the hem let out. The four-year-old was growing like a weed. "I thought Mudder said you should finish cutting down the hand-me-down dresses for Hazel that Sadie gave us. And the hems in Caleb's pants. He can't keep going to school in pants that are two inches too short."

"Well, if it ever decides to really rain and fill up the pond, he'll be able to go wading without getting his pants wet." Rebekah logic. Sewing was not one of her favorite chores. "Besides, Mudder said you were supposed to help."

"Only one sewing machine."

"You're just trying to get rid of me. Why are you mooning around in our room all the time? There'll be a singing again next week. Maybe you'll get an offer for a buggy ride then."

Rebekah had already experienced her first ride, and she was a year younger. But then, she was prettier than Leila, with her blue eyes and dark hair and fair skin. Plus she was taller and had a slim build. Not a roly-poly bug like Leila.

"Pretty is as pretty does." That's what Mudder would say. Men needed fraas who could cook and sew and take care of babies. They didn't care about looks. Which must be true. Look at Deborah. She'd married a man

with a disfigured face and she doted on him. So why didn't anyone look at Leila the way Phineas looked at Deborah?

"Leroy Glick just pulled up in front of the house." Rebekah pulled her head back from the window and whirled. "What do you think he wants? Do you think it's about you working in town? Do you think they made a decision? Mordecai didn't say anything about it at supper. You know he talked to Leroy and Andrew about it. They decide everything—"

"Rebekah. Rebekah! Enough already." Leila clutched her hands to her stomach and swallowed against sudden nausea. A bitter bile swelled in her throat. "There's no point in getting all worked up. Whatever he wants, we'll know when we're supposed to know."

"Let's go downstairs and see what they're doing." Rebekah scurried to the door, her face a study in curiosity. "I could serve some cookies and sweet tea."

"If they want us around, Mudder will let us know."

"Since you started courting, you've been no fun at all."

"Who said I was courting?"

"Sally says Patty saw you walking with Jesse at the wedding, and then you were talking to him at the auction and Caleb said—"

"Caleb doesn't know what he's talking about." How she wished he did.

"Jesse is easy on the eyes and everyone likes him. But still, it's strange that he hasn't asked anyone to go for a ride in a long time. He's getting old; he must be at least twenty. Esther says if he doesn't settle down soon, he may never do it. All the girls will be married off. There won't be a soul left."

Only Leila and he wasn't interested in her. Leila slipped past her sister and headed out the bedroom door. She inhaled and exhaled, willing the frolicking kitties in her stomach to take a nap. Wiping her damp hands on her skirt, she proceeded down the stairs at a steady pace. No need to look in a hurry.

Mudder came into view. She stood in the front room, a pitcher of tea in one hand. Leroy and Mordecai were seated in the two oak rocking chairs Mordecai had made himself.

The other kinner were nowhere in sight. Maybe Susan and Esther had taken Hazel for a walk to wear her out before bedtime.

Leroy set his glass of tea on the table and looked up, his gray eyes stern behind his glasses. He nodded without speaking.

Leila breathed.

Her mother turned. She looked flustered. "Leroy wants to talk to you about the job at the day care."

Leila sucked in a breath. "Jah." She managed to stutter that one syllable.

Leroy gazed up at her, his dark eyes piercing over his glasses. "Sit."

She sank onto the one remaining chair in the room.

"I was just telling your mother we'll start the baptism classes in January." Leroy picked up his glass, sipped, and returned it to the table. "That will allow us to finish them before Easter."

"Jah." Nothing more to be said. She would begin the

classes. Gott called her to commit to her faith. Her life would be barren without Him to give it meaning. She had no doubt about that. Other things, but not about her faith.

"Mordecai, Andrew, and I have thought about this. We've prayed. We've talked."

"Jah."

Leroy eased back in his chair, the rockers squeaking on the linoleum. He folded his beefy arms over his chest. "I don't make this decision lightly, is what I'm telling you."

"I understand." Her voice failed her, instead the barest of whispers. Her anxiety had stolen it. "If I can't work—"

"You may work at the day care. For now. Until you are baptized, whenever you decide that will be."

Leila's mouth dropped open. After a few seconds, she managed to shut it.

Leroy stroked his beard. "It's up to you to make good decisions. You know how to behave in a way pleasing to Gott. That won't change because you work with Englischers' kinner. This is a part of your rumspringa. It will help you make your decision. I pray it will be the right one. And that it will come sooner rather than later."

Leila managed a nod. "I won't disappoint you."

"Don't worry about disappointing me. It's Gott's judgment you need to be concerned with."

She nodded.

"Never forget you are the first young woman from our district to be allowed to do this. How you behave will affect the others who might also want to help their families by earning money in town."

"I understand." The weight of the responsibility made her neck hurt. "I won't let them down."

"I wouldn't say no to a refill of that sweet tea now, Abigail." He leaned back in his chair, making it clear the women had been dismissed. His gaze encompassed Mordecai only. "The Millers over by George West came by today. Asked me to break another horse for them."

"Good news." Mordecai's voice was a vague rumble in Leila's ears as she eased toward the stairs. Business accomplished, they would settle in for a long, rambling conversation about horses and honey and the drought. "Are you headed there Monday then?"

"Jah. Jesse will run the store for a few days."

"Let me know if you need me to take a turn. I'm happy to do it. We're done with the hives until spring."

"I will do that."

Leila made a beeline for the stairs. She could rest now, knowing what her future held. Knowing Jesse wouldn't be in it. She would be like Susan, who taught at school and seemed content with her lot as a single woman. She had her scholars. Leila would have her Englisch boplin to love. Best get some sleep and begin again tomorrow.

Leila was almost to the stairs.

"Don't let Gott down."

She'd almost made it. She glanced back at Leroy. The flickering lamplight glinted on his glasses, making his expression hard to read. "I won't."

"See that you don't."

. . .

Jesse felt warm and cold at the same time. He leaned back against the headrest and let the cool air from the open window rush over him. Why had he let Tiffany and Colton talk him into this? He'd had the guts to tell Leila he couldn't take her out and now here he was, changing his mind again. The poor girl would think he was an idiot.

"There's nothing to be nervous about." Colton craned his neck from the front seat of the Impala, then snapped his attention back to the dirt road. The tiny evergreen-tree air freshener hanging from the rear-view mirror bounced, along with a cross on a chain of beads. "It's just a movie. It's not like you're getting married or something."

Tiffany snorted, not a ladylike sound, but one that she often employed when her boyfriend said something she found silly. "Jesse will never get married if he doesn't start doing something about his love life. Like dating for example."

"I'm not looking to have a wedding." Leila's sweet face the afternoon of her mother's wedding presented itself front and center. He hadn't told Colton and Tiffany about the discussion behind the barn that day or the encounter at the auction. The way he changed his mind and hurt Leila. The look on her face. The look on Will's face. His cousin had reeked with disapproval. Will need not sit in judgment. Jesse knew he'd caused that pain, that disappointment. His friends would want to stop and pray about it, and he'd already covered the topic thoroughly. *Gott, are You listening?* "I shouldn't be asking out any Plain girl right now."

Tiffany wiggled in her seat until she faced him, her chin resting on the rust-colored seat cover. "Why? This isn't wrong. We're not wrong. There's nothing different about what we believe and what you believe."

She was right. But a world of difference existed between how the Amish lived and how his Englisch friends lived. He would never judge. It wasn't his community's way. But one look at Tiffany's getup, the tight jeans, the glittering green goop on her eyelids, the pink lipstick, and the dangling earrings, proved that. "It's not that simple."

"I know that." She blessed him with a smile that let her true self shine through all the goop. "Which is why you're in my prayers every single day."

Much as it embarrassed him to think of her praying about him, it also touched him. "Appreciate that."

"It'll all work out in the end." She gave him a thumbs-up that featured a long bubble-gum-pink nail and turned back toward the front. "That's what my dad says. If it isn't working out, it isn't the end yet."

Jesse swallowed the lump in his throat, glad she couldn't see the morass of emotion that battered him. Tiffany might be the daughter of an Englisch minister, but she couldn't really understand his situation. She couldn't understand the consequences of choosing not to be baptized. Of not joining his church. Eventually he would have to leave his family and his friends and his life. His community's faith encompassed a way of life.

Leila would understand. Not only the consequences

for him, but for her, should she do more than just go to the movies with him. If, by God's grace, something came of their courting, she would lose her family and friends. Which made this whole thing unfair to her.

Which brought him back to the original question. What was he doing in this car headed toward her house?

Her innocence. Her eagerness. The pink of her cheeks and the simple, plain beauty of her round face. No goop. No jewelry. No painted-on jeans. Something told him Leila had a beauty inside her of which he'd seen only the merest of glimpses.

He wanted to see more. Jesse didn't understand it. He didn't even want to think about it. His desire to see Leila kept growing, no matter how he tried to stifle it. He simply hadn't found a way.

Or he'd lacked courage. Nee, he had courage. The courage not to ask her, knowing she would end up hurt. It took a man to do that. He would have this date and maybe that would get this hankering out of his system. They'd both realize they weren't right for each other and it would be done. A person so often wanted what he couldn't have. Having it took the mystery and suspense from it. He'd be able to move on and so would she.

Tiffany smacked her hand against Colton's arm. "Hey, watch out. Buggy alert."

The car slowed and Colton eased farther to his right. Sure enough, a buggy kept a steady pace toward them, its battery-operated lights bobbing in the deepening dusk. Who would be leaving Mordecai's this late in the evening? On a Saturday night with services tomorrow.

Jesse leaned his head through the window, squinting against the lights, trying to see.

The clouds parted and the moon beamed down on them. His father's disgruntled face, his hollow cheeks sculpted in the moonlight, stared at him behind wire-rimmed glasses as they passed. Jesse's stomach lurched. He sucked in air, afraid the butter noodles and fried chicken his mudder had prepared for supper would end up on the floor of Colton's newly vacuumed car. "Ach."

"Who is it? Someone you know? Will they tattle on you to your dad?" Tiffany knew all about Jesse's conflicted feelings about Leroy Glick. "You're not doing anything wrong. We're just going to the movies. Even if whoever that was says something, it's no big deal, right?"

"That was Leroy Glick." He kept his tone light. "My father."

Colton pulled the car to the side of the road. "We can talk about this."

"There's nothing to talk about."

"Pray then."

Prayer seemed the only option left these days, and Jesse's knees ached from spending so much time on that bedroom rug. "Sure, prayer would be good."

. . .

Leila stood at the window, letting the cool night air waft over her warm skin and listening to Rebekah snore, a soft, gentle rumble that seemed to have lulled Hazel to sleep. The little girl had her chubby hands clasped around her big sister's right arm. The two looked so peaceful. Leila longed for such sweet repose. She'd tried to sleep after her conversation with Leroy, but she was too keyed up. She wanted to grab the buggy and race to Rory's house to share her good news, but Mudder had said no, not until after services tomorrow. Time ticked by so slowly. Everyone had to have gone to bed now that Leroy's buggy had pulled away from the front steps. If she could just sleep, tomorrow would come sooner.

She turned from the window. Time for her nightgown and her pillow. Dawn would creep into the bedroom before she knew it. Lights flickered on the road, casting beams against the dark night. She hesitated, then leaned on the windowsill, trying to make out the bearer of that light. A car. A car coming up the drive to Mordecai's house after dark on a Saturday night.

It could only be one person.

Nee. Jesse had uninvited her. He'd been clear about that.

She waited, her heart a hiccup in her chest. The car stopped and the engine died, leaving the same silence as before, yet different in the knowledge that someone sat in the car, someone who would get out any moment and everything could change for Leila.

A car door opened. Butch began to bark. Nee. He would wake Mordecai and Mudder. Leila flew down the stairs and out the door. The dog stood at attention on the narrow front porch, a low growl emanating from his throat. "Hush, Butch, hush." She grabbed his collar and tugged. "Settle down."

The growl died to a soft whimper in the back of his throat. He was simply doing what he did. "Good dog, it's okay, it's okay." Leila strained to see in the darkness. A new light appeared, quivering against the black night. A flashlight held by a nervous hand. She swallowed and breathed. The light approached, dancing and bobbing. She put her hand to her forehead to shield her eyes as she strained to see. The light hit her in the eyes. "Hey, hey, stop it. Who is that?"

"Leila, it's me."

The loud whisper filled up the night. A distinct male voice. Jesse. "Shh, you'll wake everyone. It's the middle of the night."

"It's nine thirty. Come on, let's go."

"Go where?" She dropped her shoes on the porch. "What are you doing here?"

"Taking you to the movies."

She straightened and crossed her arms. "Are you telling me you didn't pull me aside at the auction to tell me you were uninviting me to the movies?"

"I had a . . . what my friends call a . . . momentary lapse in judgment."

"Those are some awful big words for saying you acted like an idiot."

"Agreed."

"So I'm just supposed to forget that and jump in some strange car with you?"

"It's not a strange car. It's an Impala."

"You know what I mean."

"I do. I don't know that I think this is a good idea." He flipped off the flashlight. "I'm pretty sure it's not. But nothing ventured, nothing gained. That's another thing my friends say."

"They're sure full of lots of sayings."

"They're full of other things, too, but I think you'll like them. Get in the car and you'll find out."

"I'm just supposed to trust you now."

"Come on, get in the car."

"You sound more like an Englischer than you did before."

"So will you when you start working at the day care."

"How do you know about that?"

"My daed was here this evening, wasn't he?"

"Jah."

"He saw me coming up here."

The hiccup was back in her heart. It twisted, all out of whack. "And you still came."

"He knows what we do during rumspringa is not for him to judge. This is our time, so come out with me."

As much as her head said no, her heart said yes louder. "Are you sure you want me to come?"

"Let's go."

Ignoring the naysayer in her head, she shoved her feet in the shoes. "What took you so long?"

CHAPTER 9

Leila sat still, sunk into the plush padded seat that
felt like velvet under her fingers, her gaze glued
to the enormous screen that lit up the dark theater
with bigger-than-life images. She inhaled the mouthwatering scents of buttery popcorn and chocolate. She
couldn't contain a small sigh. The movie told a beautiful story. So beautiful. What could be so bad about
a movie like this? The lion protected the children
and stood strong against evil forces and taught his
followers the difference between right and wrong. A
parable. That's what it was. A story with a meaning.
She liked that. If all movies were like this, what could
be the harm?

Jesse leaned close to her and scooped a handful
of popcorn from the enormous bucket he'd handed
to her before the movie began. His fresh scent of
soap mixed with the peppermint on his breath. He
smelled good. Leila tucked a handful in her mouth
and chewed, trying not to think about how close he
sat. Trying to think about the popcorn and the movie
and the cool air that brushed her face from vents
overhead. Not the way the muscles in his arms bulged

against the sleeves of his shirt and his teeth shone in the flickering light.

It was almost too much to take in. This movie probably cost a pretty penny. Jesse refused to let her pay for anything. It was a rerun, he said, showing at the all-night dollar theater. A bargain in her book, but one she gladly would've paid for herself.

The salt burned her chapped lips. She longed for a sip from the large soda Jesse had nestled in a cup holder in the chair arm between them. Was it meant to be hers too? He hadn't offered any to her. The enormous cup held more than one person could drink, surely. But did a boy and a girl share a cup? Germs didn't scare her. Overstepping and sharing something more did.

The music thundered from the speakers, pummeling her from all sides. The figures on the screen seemed poised to leap on top of her. She jumped. Why did it have to be so loud?

She sneaked a glance at Jesse, who tossed the popcorn in his mouth and wiped his hands on his pants, his expression unperturbed. He had more experience with movies than she did. He looked almost morose for a man in the middle of courting. The Jesse who'd stood outside her house, flashlight in hand, had disappeared somewhere along the highway into George West.

She looked beyond him. Colton and Tiffany were snuggled together, her head resting on his shoulder. Colton leaned down and landed a kiss on Tiffany's forehead. She responded with a kiss on his cheek. She giggled and he shushed her.

Her cheeks burning, Leila jerked her head back

toward the screen. Plain folks didn't go for that sort of thing. Kissing in public. She hunched her shoulders and tried to delve back into the movie.

"What's the matter?" Jesse leaned into her, his deep bass a whisper in her ear. He picked up the cup, slick with condensation, and offered it to her. "Don't you like the movie?"

She shrugged and took a long pull from the soda—root beer, icy cold, bubbly, and sweet. The liquid helped her swallow the lump in her throat. Grateful, she took another sip to give herself time to form a response. The couple next to him acted in a shameful manner. How could it not bother Jesse? He sat right next to them.

Or maybe he wished he could kiss her too. Did Plain folks kiss on the first date? Surely not. Despite the chilled rush of air from the overhead vents, Leila felt flushed and sweaty. If Jesse did like her, would he want to kiss her? Did she want him to kiss her?

If her heart and lungs had a vote, it would be yes, because both seemed to be off kilter at the thought. Nee. Nee. A girl didn't do that, especially with a man so on again, off again.

She should've asked Deborah. Deborah would know and she wouldn't laugh at Leila for asking.

"Well?"

Jesse was waiting for an answer.

"It's . . . good . . . nice," she whispered. Her voice quavered. "I like it."

"Good." He slumped back in his chair, one hand on the chair arm between them.

Leila took another sip of the soda, trying to swallow

her anxiety. Enough. She didn't want to hog Jesse's drink. She slid the cup back in the holder. Jesse's hand caught hers before she could return it to her lap. His long, calloused fingers grasped hers, warm and strong. They enveloped hers as he pulled her hand toward him. Leila jerked back. "What are you trying to do?"

"Shush, shush!" He let go and sat forward, head ducked toward her. "I just wanted to—"

"You know better." Was this what Will had been talking about? Was Jesse falling into the Englisch ways? She didn't know what those ways were. Or if they were bad. "This is our first . . . time."

"I'm not trying to kiss you or anything." His hoarse whisper carried embarrassment and the same uncertainty she felt. "I didn't want you to think I didn't . . ."

She stood, aware the people in the row behind them were fidgeting. "Let me out."

"Where are you going?"

"Hey, some of us are trying to watch the movie," a group of girls chorused almost in unison. "Come on, we can't see."

Jesse stood and squeezed past Colton and Tiffany, who patted Leila's arm, her perplexed expression clear in the flickering images on the screen. "Hey, you guys, come back. It's just getting to the good part."

Leila doubted Tiffany had been paying enough attention to know. Her stomach rocking with nausea born of embarrassment and shame, she tromped past them. Jesse waited at the end of the row and then led her down the dark aisle to the exit. She pushed through the door and into a hallway empty except for a man in a theater uniform sweeping popcorn into a dustpan with a long handle.

"What's wrong? Where are you going?" Jesse caught her elbow with an iron grip. "What are you so mad about? I only thought I would . . . hold your hand. Is that bad?"

"It's just that I've never done this before. Never been someplace with an Englisch couple who thinks it's okay to . . . do that kind of thing in public."

"What thing? You mean kiss?"

Heat drenched Leila from head to toe. She glanced at the man with the broom. His shaggy eyebrows lifted over black-rimmed glasses, his cheeks covered with painful-looking, swollen acne. He pivoted and scooted down the hallway, leaving them to their argument. He probably thought it was a lovers' quarrel. Another wave of heat washed over her. She planted her hands on her hips and looked Jesse in the eye. "Jah, kiss."

"I had no plans to kiss you, if that's what you're worried about." The scorn had turned to a rough whisper as if someone might still hear the conversation in the now-deserted hallway. "Not in public or anywhere else."

"*Gut.* Because I don't want to kiss you either. I don't know why you asked me out in the first place if I'm so . . . so . . . unlikable."

"That's not what I mean." His voice rose. Pretty soon the people watching the movie would be able to hear them over the booming dialogue and thunderous music. "I mean not yet. I know that's not what you would want."

"Why did you ask me to come with you?"

"I told you before. I like you."

"Then why are you acting like this?"

"Like what?"

He couldn't be that dense. He'd been like an irritable bear late for hibernation all evening. "From the minute I got in the car, you've acted like I did something wrong. Like you wish you hadn't asked me. Then you try to hold my hand. Why would you do that?"

"It doesn't have anything to do with you." The words were almost a growl. "I'm just . . . You wouldn't understand. Maybe after working at the day care, maybe then you'll be able to understand."

"Understand what? The only reason Leroy said yes is he wants us to be able to stay here. To stay in our homes. We're not making enough to keep food on the table."

"He said that? We might have to leave Bee County?"

Jesse's expression puzzled Leila. He didn't look so much concerned as . . . excited. Maybe *excited* was too strong a word, but he didn't seem to mind the idea. "Not in so many words, but that's what he meant. I heard Mordecai and my mudder talking about it."

Jesse stared at a point somewhere beyond her shoulder. "My daed told me we're staying. Groossdaadi told him we have to stay the course."

"I hope so. We uprooted ourselves once to come here. I don't want to do it again."

"Right." He chewed on a nail already bitten to the quick. "We should go back into the movie. I promise to keep my hands to myself."

She stared at his face. The words said one thing, but his expression said another. He looked . . . sad. She wanted to wipe that look off his face. How? By letting him kiss her? Courting was harder than she'd ever imagined. "I really want to go home." Surely they'd seen enough of the movie that the two dollars wasn't a total waste. "The story was a book first. Couldn't we just read the book instead?"

His dimples appeared even when he frowned. More a scowl than a frown, really. "Colton's driving. It's his car. And Tiffany loves this movie. She's seen it at least twenty times."

Twenty times. Twenty dollars. Forty if she saw it with Colton, which, of course, she had. Now *that* seemed a waste of money. "Then she knows how it ends."

"I suppose you're right, but I don't think it's fair for us to ask them to leave early because I did something to get you all worked up."

"I'm not worked up." She wanted to stamp her foot and shake her fist, but she wasn't worked up. "Not much, anyway."

For the first time, the corners of his mouth turned up. If she didn't know better, she'd think Jesse was laughing at her predicament. She felt a tiny tickle of a giggle burble up in her. She slapped her hand to her mouth to keep it prisoner. He couldn't know how much looking at his lips made her wonder what they would feel like touching hers.

"I promise I won't try to hold your hand again." He took a step toward her, despite the studied intent of his words. "Ever, if that's what you want. I promise to never, ever kiss you."

She took a step back and felt the wall nudge her shoulders. "That's not what I want." That sounded all wrong. "I mean, I want to do things the right way. Don't you?"

"I do. I think." He rubbed his forehead with two fingers and grimaced. "Jah. Most of the time."

"Most of the time?"

"Don't you ever wonder if there's a different way to do things?" Something in his eyes begged her to contemplate the question with care. He cocked his head and shook it as if doing that very thing himself. The sadness deepened and carved lines around his mouth and eyes, making him seem older than she knew him to be. "A way that isn't bad, just different?"

Leila had a terrible but fleeting urge to give Jesse what he wanted, anything and everything he wanted, anything to wipe that forlorn, pleading look from his face. But she couldn't lie. She was Leila Lantz, a Plain girl who believed Gott to be good. He provided. His will be done. "I like the way we do things. I like the rules. I like knowing what I'm supposed to do. Don't you?"

"You like knowing what to do. Good for you. I wish I knew what to do." He tucked a curl of her hair back under her kapp with one calloused finger. She swallowed, sure she would sink to the floor and dissolve into a puddle. His gaze traced her features. "Sometimes the rules don't feel right. Sometimes the rules only tell us what not to do. Not what we should do. What would be so wrong about holding my hand?"

"I would like to hold your hand . . . someday." The words whispered themselves over her insistence they stay quiet. She wanted to reel them back in. Her body quivered with embarrassment. Perspiration trickled down her temples, and she shivered in the refrigerated air. "When the time is right."

"What about kiss me? Would you like to do that too?"

Let the ground open up and swallow me now. Please, Gott.

Again her heart fought with her mind and all she knew to be right. Her heart had survived the death of her father and the move from Tennessee to barren south Texas. It was strong, far stronger than her head. "Someday. Jah."

A smile broke across his face like dry lightning, sudden and jagged, then gone from the dusty, flat south Texas horizon. "Let someday come soon then."

He started down the hallway.

"Where are you going?"

"To tell Colton you need to get home. You have a service at your house in the morning—later today."

"You do too."

"We'll see."

The sadness returned. His gaze enveloped her. She couldn't help herself. She reached for his hand and caught it before he could move away. "Don't be so sad. The Sunday services aren't that bad. Your daed is a good preacher."

His Adam's apple bobbed. "I like the shape of your lips."

She had to lean in to hear his whisper. He leaned closer yet. His lips brushed hers. Soft and warm. A kiss so fleeting she didn't have time to close her eyes or protest or kiss him back.

"Sorry." The painful smile came and went again. "I

didn't mean to do that. I guess someday came sooner than you expected."

"It was . . ." She couldn't find a word. Her pulse pounded in the hollow of her throat. Her breathing sounded loud in her own ears. She licked her lips, wishing she had balm. "I'm . . . it's . . ."

"Leila Lantz is speechless." He smiled for real then, the dimples appearing, making him look younger and somehow, for a second, carefree. "Maybe I should help you find the words."

He kissed her again, this time letting his lips linger on hers. His hands settled on her shoulders. His lips trailed across her cheeks and then her forehead, leaving behind a strange sensation like floating on a lake, the only sound the water dashing against the shore. "Now?"

"Nice. It's . . . nice." She couldn't seem to control her breathing. Her words fluttered between them. Whether they should kiss no longer presented itself as the question. When would they kiss again—that question planted itself foremost in her mind and refused to budge. "Maybe . . . maybe we should stay for the rest of the movie."

Jesse wrapped his long fingers around hers and held on tight, his grip grounding her, comforting her. "Maybe it would be better to take you home before you get into any more trouble."

Leila closed her eyes for a second and concentrated on drawing one breath, then another, then another. How much trouble could she handle? If tonight were any indication, she had set a course right into the heart of that very question. "I want to see how the story ends."

CHAPTER 10

They'd stayed out too late. Jesse put his hand on the car door, ready to open it the second Colton stopped in front of Mordecai's house. Leila would likely meet her mudder or one of her sisters as they rose to begin preparing for church. They should've come back sooner, but Tiffany had insisted on donuts and hot chocolate after the movie, and then a drive along the back roads and a stop to count the stars. He was too enthralled with Leila's hand in his to protest. Next time, he would take her out on his own where he had control over the situation.

Next time? He shouldn't be thinking of a next time.

Leila shifted, her body warm against his shoulder, making it hard for him to concentrate on what he should and shouldn't do. She'd drifted off to sleep somewhere between the highway and the dirt road that led to Mordecai's. Her eyelids fluttered. A second later, she straightened. Her hand went to her mouth, her eyes wide, cheeks stained cherry red. Their gazes met. Her uncertain smile quivered.

She didn't need to be embarrassed. They hadn't done

anything wrong. At least, not in his book. His father's book? That was a different story. "It's okay—"

"Here we are." Colton braked and brought the car to a stop in the yard in front of the house where buggies would soon be parked. Hay stanchions were already in place for the horses. "I hope we didn't keep you out too late."

"It was fun." Leila rubbed at her face with both hands as if trying to rub away the sleep. "It was nice to meet you."

"Wait, wait." Tiffany, who'd been half asleep in the front seat, popped up and swiveled so she faced Leila and Jesse. Most of the goop had migrated from her eyelids and eyelashes to the area under her eyes, creating dark circles, and her hair fuzzed up around her face. "We have to pray."

"Pray?" Leila's gaze skipped to Jesse, her eyebrows raised over bloodshot eyes. "Now?"

She wouldn't understand. It was too soon to explain. Jesse didn't want to scare her away, even though far away would be the best place for her. "It's been a long night, and Leila has to get inside. We're having church service at her house today."

"Oh, come on, we need to give thanks for the great time we had and we got home safe and sound and you had a great time with your new girl—"

Not his girl. Leila couldn't be his girl. Tiffany would never understand the sacrifice a Plain woman would be required to make if she chose to follow him down the road Tiffany represented. "Don't you have to get to church too?"

"We go to the late service. We've got lots of time—"

"Leila needs to get inside. Her mother will be up soon, if she's not already."

"So we'll pray she doesn't get in trouble. Come on. Hold hands. Leila, you can go first if you want."

Leila's hand hovered in the air. Her look beseeched him. He knew exactly what she was thinking. They didn't recite their own public prayers. The Lord's Prayer was best. Jesus' own words were best. Otherwise they prayed silently. "Why don't you pray, Tiffany." He made it a statement, not a request. "We'd rather pray silently."

Tiffany's eyebrows popped up and down. "Whatever. He'll hear either way."

Nothing could stop Tiffany when it came to praying. It was one of the things Jesse admired about her from the first time he met Colton and her when they came into the tavern where he and Will and a few others were playing pool and watching TV, the big rumspringa activities available to them in such a small town. She'd handed each of them a flyer for a youth group at her church. The others had chuckled over it, finding it funny that this Englisch girl would try to convince Plain men of the gospel, something of which they had more than a passing knowledge.

Something about the couple had stuck with Jesse. So much so, he'd taken them up on their offer. Just once, he'd told himself, just out of curiosity. No one had to know.

No one could know.

One time had turned into two and three and four.

Now he counted Colton and Tiffany as friends who'd shown him another way to worship.

Jesse bowed his head and prayed his real, true community would never find out.

CHAPTER 11

"Coming or going?"

Leila dropped her sneakers. Taking a quick breath, she forced herself to turn back from the foot of the stairs. Deborah stood in the kitchen doorway, a dish towel in her hands. She looked crisp and clean and wide awake. Which only made Leila more aware of her rumpled clothes, disheveled hair hanging out from her kapp, and a face that felt greasy from buttered popcorn and a stop at an all-night donut shop. "You're here early."

"So are you." Deborah draped the towel over her shoulder and smoothed her apron. "We came to help get ready. What's your excuse?"

The question made heat race along Leila's neck and scorch her cheeks. She rubbed eyes gritty with fatigue. The first rule of rumspringa: A person didn't let it interfere with carrying her weight at home. Parents might turn a blind eye to late-night activities, but they still expected their kinner to contribute, same as always.

"Just let me freshen up and I'll come help you with the bread."

"At least get a cup of kaffi first." Deborah turned,

her hand still rubbing her belly as if it hurt. "Come on, *schweschder*, I don't go anywhere anymore. Share."

"Kaffi sounds wunderbarr."

How much could she tell Deborah? Leila chewed her lower lip and followed her sister into the kitchen. The fragrance of baking bread wafted around her. It smelled so fresh and sweet and so . . . like home. She breathed it in. She belonged here. Not at a noisy movie theater in George West. How could she get so turned around in a foreign place like that?

She felt as if she'd awakened from a long, troubled dream in which no familiar landmarks existed.

Deborah handed her a chipped blue mug filled with coffee that looked strong enough to take the enamel off her teeth. That her sister didn't drink coffee was apparent in the way she prepared it for others. "Who was that in the car?"

"You saw it?"

"Phineas did, from the front window. He said Jesse got out, but he couldn't see who was driving."

"Friends of Jesse's."

"Don't worry. Phineas keeps things to himself. He's a big believer in folks learning from their own mistakes."

"It's not a mistake."

"I imagine it's too soon to tell. Don't you?" Deborah waddled to the wood-burning stove and opened the oven door. The heat made her cheeks rosy. She pulled out a pan of bread and set it on the top of the stove. When she turned, her forehead was creased, her mouth down in a frown that made her look like Mudder, with their matching wisps of blonde hair always peeking from below their kapps. "I've heard some things about Jesse."

"Like what?"

"Not to gossip."

"Nee, of course not."

Deborah slapped pot holders creased with age onto the counter. "It's his rumspringa. Has been for an awful long time."

"Better he wait and be sure."

"I know." Deborah's hands flew up in the air, signaling her concern. The more agitated she got, the more her hands moved. "He spends a lot of time with Englisch kids."

This was not news to Leila. "Like you said, his rumspringa."

"I'd hoped you might take a shine to his cousin, actually."

"You mean Mudder hoped."

"We all hoped."

"He hasn't asked and Jesse did." She sank into a chair at the pine prep table and spooned four tablespoons of sugar into the coffee. "Will tried to warn me off Jesse."

"Will's a good man."

"So is Jesse."

Deborah shook a finger at Leila as she sank into a chair across the table. "Then tell me why did he take you courting into town with his Englisch friends instead of a proper ride in a buggy?"

"Maybe he thought that would impress me."

"Did it?"

Maybe it did. Maybe she wanted to know what it felt

like to be someone else for a few scant hours. Maybe Deborah, with her happy marriage and impending motherhood, couldn't remember that feeling.

"I'm still in my rumspringa too." The memory of Jesse's lips on hers sent another wave of heat cascading through her. Followed by the memory of Tiffany's bent head as she prayed with an openness and abandon that Leila had never heard before. Like she was talking to a close friend. Leila could use a friend she could talk to like that. "I'm trying to figure things out too."

Frowning, Deborah stood and lumbered across the room. She manhandled a huge cast-iron skillet onto the stove and began cracking eggs into it. Maybe it would be easier to talk to her with her back turned. Leila opened her mouth. Deborah turned. "You sound . . . like you're feeling guilty about something."

"Can I ask you a question?"

"Anything." Deborah picked up a fork and began to whip the eggs in a frenzied motion. Her scrambled eggs were always the lightest and fluffiest. "Except how babies are made. You'll have to figure that one out on your own."

"Deborah!"

"Shush, you'll wake everyone in the house. What is the question?"

"Did you and Phineas kiss?" It was easier, somehow, to ask about the physical part than the praying. "I mean, not to get in your business or anything."

"Jah, we kiss." Deborah's cheeks, already red from the heat of the stove, turned a beet color. "Married folks do that now and then."

"Nee. Before. When you first started . . ."

"Things were different for me and Phineas. He's different." Deborah ladled pancake batter in small beige puddles in a second cast-iron skillet. It sizzled and the aroma made Leila's mouth water. All the same, her stomach clenched. Deborah turned and faced Leila, her expression thoughtful. "He never thought anyone would want him, because of his scars, the silly goose. So he never let me get close. Not until . . . not for a long time."

"Do you think it's wrong to kiss someone the first time you go out with him?"

"Jesse kissed you?" Deborah's hands batted the air again. "Already?"

"Is that bad?"

Her head bent, Deborah wrapped the bread in a towel and laid it in a basket. "Sometimes we get ahead of ourselves. Phineas wasn't the first man to kiss me."

"Nee?"

"Nee. Remember, I courted before we moved here."

Leila searched her memory. "Aaron. Aaron, right?"

"Right."

"You kissed Aaron?"

The blush spread across Deborah's face, blotches decorating her neck. "I've always regretted that I didn't save that for Phineas."

"Does he know?"

"Nee, he never asked." She picked up a spatula and flipped the pancakes with an expert flick of her wrist. "I just hope you don't experience the same regret."

Leila tugged the spatula from her sister's hand and

waved it toward a chair. "Take a load off your feet. I think I already do. Jesse is so . . . He runs hot and cold. He can't seem to make up his mind."

"He's probably as new at this as you are. It's not like we get a lot of advice on how to treat men. Men don't get much in the way of advice either." Deborah waddled back to the chair and sank into it, her hands rubbing her hips. "You're a good girl. Daed raised us all to be good girls. If something doesn't feel right, most likely it isn't right. You'll know it in your heart and you'll step away."

Only Leila hadn't stepped away. She'd stepped into that kiss. "It's hard to think about what's right in the middle of it all."

"I know." Deborah sighed, her light blue eyes somber. "My advice? Don't go places in cars with Englisch folks. Makes it hard to walk home."

A day late and a dollar short, as Mudder was wont to say.

Still, good advice. Deborah might have good advice about praying with Englisch folks too. How could praying ever be wrong? Leila couldn't put her finger on it. Her district didn't have Bible study or Sunday school. They got their needs filled through Sunday services and private prayer. They didn't judge how anyone else worshipped, but their Ordnung was clear on how the Bee County district would do these things. Worship as a district kept them together as one big family.

Still, at the childlike enthusiasm of Tiffany's prayer, the abandon with which she shared her feelings with the Lord, and the joy in her face as she prayed, Leila felt something precariously close to jealousy. How could it be jealousy? She walked a righteous road, a road carved by Mudder and Mordecai and the bishop and all those Plain folks who came before her.

She needed to talk to Jesse about all this. His palms had gone clammy when they held hands with Colton and Tiffany during the prayer. He'd barely said good-bye before he slid back into the car and slammed the door, leaving her standing there waving.

He'd be back for church soon. She slid the pancakes in a stack onto a nearby platter and dropped the spatula on the counter. "I should get cleaned up."

"Was there something else?"

"Nee. Why?"

"You looked like you were mulling over something. Is it about the job? I heard Leroy said you could go to work at the day care."

The events of the long night had overshadowed this astonishing development. "I'm so excited. If I can't have my own bopli, I can take care of others."

"You will have your own." Deborah rose and went back to the stove. She sniffed a huge pot of corn mush, picked up a ladle, and stirred. "Especially if you keep going like you did last night. Schweschder, do take care."

"I'll be back down to help with the cookies."

"Are you sure you couldn't see your way to spending time with Will?"

"He hasn't asked."

"Maybe because you haven't shown an interest."

"He's Jesse's cousin."

Deborah dropped the ladle on the counter with a bang. "You can tell a lot about people by the company they keep."

Was she talking about Jesse or Leila? "It was one date."

"Kisses lead to more. Think with your head and not just your heart."

Her heart shouted, drowning out her head. "I know."

"Hurry up." Deborah made shooing motions. "If the boys get down here before you, there won't be anything left except a *schmier* of peanut butter on yesterday's bread."

Leila trudged from the room, Deborah's words chasing her. *"Kisses lead to more. Think with your head."*

Kisses couldn't be taken back, any more than words could.

CHAPTER 12

The belligerent *a-oo-gah* of the horn sent Leila racing out the front door, a slice of bread, peanut butter, and honey clutched in one hand and the cooler containing her lunch in the other. She did a two-step and narrowly avoided stumbling over Butch, who sat in front of the door keeping guard. She would have to learn to manage her morning rituals better. She'd spent too much time helping with breakfast, doing dishes, and getting the younger ones ready for school.

Her fourth day of work at the day care. Her stomach clenched as she remembered the look in Mordecai's eyes at the breakfast table on Monday. *"Take care,"* he'd said. *"Remember where you come from."* So far, she hadn't seen or heard anything that made her feel any more than a simple Plain girl. No one beckoning her to a life of sinful easiness. No one luring her into any dens of iniquity. What exactly was a den of iniquity, and where did a person find one?

Not at a day care, obviously.

Or little Beeville, Texas, at the corner of Back Road and Nowhere.

"Leila."

Mudder's voice stopped her in her tracks. She turned. "I don't want to keep Nolan waiting."

Mudder pushed open the screen door and stuck her head out. She had patches under her dark blue eyes, smudges of deep purple. Red spots deepened under her high cheekbones. "I know. I just want to tell you I'm praying for you."

Her mother had never said that to her in her whole life. Plain folks didn't talk about such things. "I know."

"Keep your eyes lifted to Gott."

"I will."

"He sees and He knows."

"And I know." Mudder should trust her. "I have to go."

"Have a good day and . . . be careful."

"I will."

Sighing, Leila tripped on the steps and caught herself just as Rory pushed open the door on her father's enormous diesel pickup truck and scooped up the cooler so Leila had a free hand to pull herself up and into the double cab. *"Danki. Guder mariye."*

Nolan nodded and smiled, but his gaze traveled to the silver watch on his wrist. He couldn't be late for his shift at the prison. His consent to provide her with transportation had been contingent on her not making him late for work.

"Sorry, I'm here, I'm here." Leila squeezed into the tight space next to Trevor's car seat and struggled with the seat belt stuck down in the cracks of the seat. With Rory's little brother, Sawyer, on the other side with his backpack and lunch box, they were like a family of birds snug in a nest. The baby cooed, bubbles of drool posed for liftoff on his pursed rosebud lips. "He's chipper this morning." She tickled his cheek and planted a kiss on his silky brown hair. "No fussing?"

"Only all night." Rory turned sideways in the front seat. "Kept me up. I'm going to bomb on my history test for sure."

"Keeps me up at night too," Sawyer, a miniature Rory with freckles and dark-rimmed glasses, grumbled. "I can hear you singing and carrying on."

"Just trying to get him down so I get two minutes of sleep." The dark smudges under Rory's eyes revealed she hadn't been successful. "I don't know how I'm supposed to keep up at school on three hours of sleep a night."

"No excuses." Nolan's frown revealed itself in the rearview mirror. "You and Dwayne went out last night on a school night. It's wrong of you to expect your Aunt Cheryl to watch the baby, especially when he's in day care all day long."

"We were studying, Daddy. Most of the time." Rory's smile disappeared. She wiggled in her seat, her expression suggesting this wasn't a new argument. "Besides, we hardly see each other at all. If you would let Dwayne live with us, we'd see more of each other during the week. He could spend more time with Trevor too."

Sawyer snorted. Leila glanced his way. The boy's hat was on backward and his coat buttoned wrong. He stared out the window, his expression sour. Poor child, he must feel like he'd heard these squabbles a thousand times and he had no one he could tell. No mother. "Did you get your homework done, Sawyer?" She squeezed the question in quick, hoping to end the battle in the front seat. "You have a test in math today, too, don't you?"

Nolan hit the horn in a long, angry *a-oo-gah*, drowning out his son's response. He hit the brakes and the truck fishtailed and then righted itself. "Deer in the road again." His fingers drummed the wheel. "I'm not supporting that boy."

Inhaling the scent of pine air freshener and Nolan's spicy aftershave, Leila tried to make herself small in the corner of the backseat. Sawyer continued to look out the window, the back of his head a silent barrier. Trevor whimpered. She hushed him. She didn't want to be privy to this argument between father and daughter any more than Sawyer or Trevor did.

She didn't understand why Englisch kids went to school so long, especially if they were going to have jobs like working in a hardware store or a day care. Book learning wasn't much use when it came to diapering a baby or loading a truck with baling wire.

On the other hand, she didn't understand having a baby before becoming mann and fraa either. Her district frowned on that, as did Scripture. Nolan didn't look too happy about it either. Yet she saw no sign he'd turned to the Lord for help. There had been a time the Beale family had attended church. Without Lois Beale to guide them, they seemed to have lost their way. She longed to remind them Gott was still there.

Was it her place to do that? Leroy would say to hush up and lead by example, not to judge, and not to be so prideful as to think she knew the way.

The sound of sniffles wafting from the front seat told

her Rory was crying. Her friend's head swiveled toward her father. "You wouldn't have to support him. Dwayne works." She sounded as if she were begging him for something. "He wants to be a good husband and father."

"Twenty hours a week, minimum wage isn't going to support a wife and baby."

"If you'd let us quit school—"

"No one quits school." Nolan's face turned brick red. His gaze met Leila's in the rearview mirror. "That was the deal when you got married. This argument's done been had."

"You started it." Rory sounded like Leila's sisters, picking at each other while washing dishes and cleaning the kitchen after supper. "Not me."

"You could be studying for that test right now."

"I'm ready for it." Rory scooted around in the seat to look at Leila, her tone suggesting the argument had indeed come to an end. Tears stained her red cheeks. "So tell me, have you heard any more from Jesse since your big date?"

Ever since Rory had first met Leila at the Combination Store, she'd been on a mission to help Leila find true love—just as she claimed to have done at the age of sixteen. She'd been suitably impressed with Leila's story of her first outing with Jesse and pooh-poohed Leila's concern about the kiss. Everyone kissed on the first date, according to Rory. Leila suspected that attitude had been the one that sent Rory on the road that had her juggling motherhood with history tests.

"Come on, give. What's up on the Jesse front? Give it up!"

Leila took a bite of her bread and chewed, trying to ignore the sudden heat that bloomed on her cheeks when she thought of that first date.

"You're blushing!" Rory chortled so loud Trevor's lower lip curled down and his chubby face scrunched up in that look that often preceded loud squalls. "Spill it. Come on!"

"You're okay, you're okay." Leila rubbed Trevor's tiny chest. She glanced at the back of Nolan's salt-and-pepper hair cropped short on his head. He seemed consumed with the market reports on something called hog futures and milo and wheat recounted by an announcer with a gruff voice. "No, not a word. I think he decided I wasn't worth the trouble. After all, we argued on the first . . . date."

"Men! They're such pigs." Rory's short brown curls bounced as she wiggled in her seat. "Not Dwayne. He's the best. He took me to a nice restaurant last night in George West for our first anniversary."

"What he spent on you yesterday should've been spent on diapers." Nolan, like Mudder, seemed to have the ability to do five things at once and still follow three conversations. "That's how it works when a man becomes a father. Whatever money you have goes into putting food on the table and clothes on your children's backs."

Here we go again, Leila wanted to say. But she didn't. Not her place. Besides, Nolan should know. He was supporting his daughter and his grandson.

"You never liked Dwayne. You could at least give him a chance."

"I should never have let you go out with him. I knew he was nothing but trouble the first time I saw him."

"Don't you love Trevor?"

Nolan's hand slammed against the wheel. "Don't make it about the baby. I'm no monster. I'm disappointed. That's what it is. Disappointed."

"You've told me that a million times. No way to change it now."

Silence ensued, broken only by the drone of the announcer on the radio talking about the chances of rain—slim and none.

Rory swiped at her face with the back of her hand and turned toward the window. Leila stroked Trevor's rosy cheek. She worked hard at not envying her friend, but when she held Trevor the day Rory introduced her to the day-care director, his warm body snug against her chest, his sighs like music in her ears, she caught herself imagining he was her bopli.

She was nineteen and ready to be baptized, ready to be a fraa, ready to be a mother. Far more than this Englisch girl with her high school classes and her dreamy plans for going to dances with her husband who went to high school, practiced for wrestling matches, and worked in a hardware store. She tried to imagine her mudder's reaction, should she come home one day and announce a bopli on the way.

Unimaginable.

But not unforgivable. Her community believed in forgiveness for all sin.

But actions had consequences. What would they be?

She never wanted to find out.

Should it be this hard? Mudder would say the answer to that question was yes. Things that came easy weren't appreciated. Hardship honed character and developed faith.

Hers should be honed by now. Daed's death. Leaving Tennessee to come to this dirty, windswept place. Trailing after Mudder from house to house while she tried to figure out God's plan for herself. It had not been an easy time.

"For someone who went on her first real date, you don't look happy." Rory had turned in her seat so she faced Leila again. She had a smile pasted to her face despite red eyes and a red nose. "Is Jesse not the one?"

"That remains to be seen, I reckon." Love at first sight didn't exist, only a love that grew and blossomed over time. That's what Mudder said. Leila never argued, but she couldn't help but look at Deborah and Phineas and wonder if there could be more than one kind of love. They'd known each other six months when they married, and now they had a bopli on the way. Not that either one of them had mentioned that precious little fact. "He's nice, but I don't really know him yet."

Other than kissing him and holding his hand. Her cheeks burned at the memory. She wiggled in her seat, her palms sweaty. She knew of Jesse. She knew what she saw, but she didn't know what he thought about, what he dreamed about, what he cared about. Knowing those things about a man made him a husband and not just another friend. Until she did, no more kissing and holding hands.

"Mind your ways, dochder. Gott is watching." Her mother's voice reverberated in her ears.

Gott had received an eyeful at the movie theater.

Nolan maneuvered the truck into the circle drive and under the portico that sheltered the day care's double-door entryway from the blazing sun and hot south Texas wind in the summer and rain in the winter, saving Leila from trying to explain all this to the man's wayward daughter.

Rory made quick work of removing Trevor's car seat while Leila climbed down on the other side. She adjusted the blue crocheted blanket around his roly-poly body and gave him a quick smack of a kiss on his forehead. "Be good for Miss Leila, little one. I want a good report this afternoon."

Tears welled in Rory's eyes as they had every day so far. "See you this afternoon. They have my cell phone number—"

"She knows, she knows," Nolan growled just as he had every day so far. "I'm gonna be late."

"All right, all right. Here's his bag. There's five bags of my frozen milk in there, and a new bag of diapers."

"She knows." Nolan tapped on the gas, making the engine rev. "Let's go."

"Be sure they put the bags in warm water until the milk is warm. He doesn't like my milk cold."

"I know." Leila tugged the diaper bag from her friend's hand as she had every day so far. She could only imagine having to leave her bopli in the care of others all day. As a Plain woman, she would never have to know how that felt. If she ever had a baby. "Go on before your daddy leaves you in a cloud of fumes. Have a blessed day. Trevor will be fine. I'll take good care of him."

Rory sniffed and swiped at her face with the back of her hand. "I don't know why I'll ever need to know about Texas history—"

"Rory Anne Beale."

Nolan still called his daughter by her maiden name, which spoke volumes about his acceptance of the path his daughter had chosen—or had been thrust upon by her own actions.

"It's Rory Chapman, Daddy, and you know it."

"Rory Anne."

"Yes, sir. Aye, aye, Captain!" She scurried back to the truck, pulled herself in, and slammed the door. A hairbreadth of a second later, the truck took off, leaving Leila standing in a cloud of nasty diesel fumes.

Coughing, she turned and lugged the car seat, diaper bag, and her lunch toward the door. Trevor was getting heavier by the day.

"Guder mariye."

Leila halted.

Will Glick pushed away from the red brick wall and straightened. With his blue shirt, black hat, and black pants and suspenders, he stood out like a turnip stuck in the middle of a basket of tomatoes. Parents pushed past him—women in suits, women in medical scrubs, women in prison guard uniforms, women in all manner of dress, rushing to drop off their children and get to their jobs. "I need to talk to you."

CHAPTER 13

Timing was everything. Contemplating the man who towered over her, the brim of his hat hiding his eyes, Leila let the car seat rest on the sidewalk in front of the day care, her lunch box next to it. She took her time rubbing the muscle in her forearm. She needed a moment to gather her wits. What possessed Will to show up at the place where she worked simply because he needed to talk to her? Could they not talk at her house? In the evening? "What are you doing here? Shouldn't you be at the plant nursery by now?"

"I had Bob drop me off here with enough time to walk to the nursery."

Will took a step back to let Janine Martin pass, her one-year-old on her ample hip and her four-year-old trotting behind her, a tattered teddy bear clutched in her arms. The mother who ran a local real estate office nodded and Leila nodded back. Janine had forgotten to wipe toothpaste from her upper lip, her skirt appeared to be on backward, and she wore only one earring. Such was the life of a working mom in the Englisch world. "I have to get inside. The parents are dropping off. I can't be late my first week—or ever for that matter."

"Can we talk over there?" Will pointed to a cluster of spindly live oaks that shaded a fenced playscape, all bright reds, greens, and blues in the dreariness of the cloudy morning. He picked up the cooler and the diaper bag, having the good sense to know that Leila was in charge of Trevor. "I promise to make it short."

"What's this about?" She followed him as far as the cedar wood fence. "I have to clock in by six fifteen."

"I know." He settled her things on the dewy grass and took off his hat. He rubbed his fingers along the brim. "I just wanted to tell you . . . I mean . . . warn you . . . just be careful."

"Careful? Of what?"

"Of Jesse."

Jesse. What did Will know about her date with Jesse? Had the cousins talked? Had Jesse shared the intimate details of that first evening? Of the kiss? Heat blasted through her. He wouldn't. Jesse wouldn't do that to her. "What are you talking about?"

"I'm saying there's no stopping the grapevine in Bee County. I'm saying I know he took you into George West to the movies and all . . . with those *Englischers*." His Adam's apple bobbed and the cords in his neck stood out as if he gritted his teeth. "Just be careful."

And all? "Jesse is your cousin. And your friend."

"He is both."

"And yet here you are warning me off him." Anger replaced the embarrassment, equally warm on her face despite the early-morning chill in the air. "It's wrong to talk behind a person's back. I'm surprised you would do it and call yourself his friend."

A loud squawk emanated from the car seat. Apparently Trevor agreed. Or he was getting hungry already. "I have to get Trevor inside. He's likely hungry."

Will squatted and tickled the baby's cheek with his long fingers. "He's so little."

"He is and he's hungry." Trevor cooed and gurgled. Traitor. Men stuck together, at any age. "I have to go."

"I got dropped off five miles from my job to do this." Will straightened and stood, once again towering over her. "I will do it and you will hear me out. For your own good."

Will spoke like a Plain man who had a right to tell a Plain woman what to do. He wasn't her father or her husband. Or even a brother. Yet his tone commanded. She opened her mouth, then shut it.

"Jesse has strayed."

So had she. "None of us is perfect. It isn't right to judge."

"I'm not judging." Red stained Will's whiskerless cheeks like beet juice on a white towel.

"I'm warning. I don't want to see you, I mean, I don't want you, it's just that . . ."

He sounded an awful lot like she did whenever she tried to talk to Jesse about something. Tongue-tied. Words twisted. He sounded nervous, like a boy who liked a girl.

Leila stared up at him. Surely Will didn't want to step on his own cousin's territory. He couldn't have Deborah, so he settled for the middle sister? If she said no, would he try out Rebekah for size? The idea stung like a drove of bees. "Have you no shame? I have to go in. Now."

. . .

Will fumbled for words. He was messing this up. Just like he always did. He'd planned to simply say his piece and go about his business. He didn't expect Leila to look so much like a mother sparrow in her beige dress, black tights, and black kapp. Even with peanut butter on her face and what appeared to be a splotch of honey on her apron, she looked as if she knew what she was doing. Put her out on the field for a game of baseball or a volleyball match and she was in her element. But singings and such? She tripped over the bench leg or hit a high note whenever everyone else sang low. She always had a stain on her dress or a wrinkled kapp. Not like her sisters, Deborah and Rebekah, who always looked so pretty and neatly put together. Leila might not be the most social girl, but she knew the important stuff. How to hush a baby.

Maybe she didn't need his advice or his warning. Maybe he had the wrong idea about her.

She undid the straps on the car seat and lifted Trevor into her arms. Will had never seen a woman look more . . . motherly as she cooed and shushed the fussy baby. Instead of searching for words, he found himself mesmerized by the dimples that appeared when she smiled at Trevor and the soft timbre of her voice as she uttered the silly baby language all women seemed to know instinctively. She might not be the fairest of the girls who came to the singings, but there was something about her. Something about her nature. He couldn't quite put his finger on it. She made him want to do . . . something.

She glanced up at him, the fact that she'd caught him staring obvious in her startled expression. "I said I'm going in."

"You have peanut butter on your cheek." The words came out in a stutter. He raised his hand and dabbed at the spot. The rosy red of her cheeks deepened. Her skin was soft and warm. "Got it."

"I was in a big hurry." She swiped at her face with the back of her hand. Now she looked downright miserable. He hadn't meant to embarrass her. She wouldn't meet his gaze. "I didn't want to keep Rory's dad waiting."

"It was just a smidgen. If you're planning to spend more time with Jesse, be careful." He jumped in, wanting to save her any more explanation. "He's a little . . . lost right now and it would be easy to get lost with him."

"He wasn't the one smoking behind Leroy's barn after the wedding." She tucked the blanket around Trevor's tiny feet clad in apple-red socks. "He's not the one who kept silent when the bishop asked what was going on."

"I know, I was there." She didn't know the whole story and Will couldn't tell her, not without betraying the confidence of his best friend. "I've said my piece. Just be careful."

"Jesse's nice." She laid Trevor back in the car seat and picked it up. "Careful of what?"

Jah, Jesse was nice. But he trod on a dangerous path. One that could take him away from his family and his community, and that included Leila. "Just what I said. Be careful."

"Of what?" She was back to being peeved at him. "Come out and say what's on your mind instead of hippity hopping around it like a jackrabbit on a bed of coals."

She had a way with words. "I can't tell you anything more. Just be careful."

"Will Glick, you've said that about five times now. You're not making any sense." She slipped past him, her shoulders slumped against the weight of the car seat. "If I didn't know any better, I'd think you were jealous. What kind of man tries to wave a girl away from his best friend?"

"That's not what I'm doing."

"Sure looks that way. Why do you feel the need to warn me about a man you went to school with all the way through eighth grade?"

"I can't explain. I promised." Stupid promise.

"Promised what?"

"Not to tell."

Without another word, she tugged the diaper bag from his hand, looped the strap over her shoulder, and relieved him of her lunch cooler.

"Leila."

"I have to get this baby inside and I have to get to work. You should do the same."

"Just do me one favor."

"What?"

"I may not be able to tell you why I'm so . . . worried, but Jesse can. Ask him one question."

"Ask him what?"

"Ask him where he goes every Wednesday night. Ask him if he plans to be baptized this spring."

"That's two questions."

"They're part and parcel of the same thing."

She chewed her lip. "Where does he go on Wednesday night?"

Will shoved his hat down to shade his eyes from the sun. "Just ask him."

"Maybe I will. Or maybe I'll mind my own business. Like people should." She shoved through the door with her shoulder and disappeared from sight.

Will glared at the door. A skinny man dressed in a prison guard uniform with redheaded, toddler-sized girls dangling under both long arms jostled past him, forcing Will to move from the busy sidewalk.

He'd done what he could, but it didn't feel like enough. Leila wouldn't want anything to do with him anytime soon, and if she told Jesse about it, his cousin most likely would feel the same.

Sighing, he started the long walk to the nursery. His daed would call this a fool's errand and Will had played the role of fool. A Plain man who took a Plain woman aside in broad daylight outside an Englisch day care didn't have his head on straight.

This thing with Jesse had him off kilter. He had to do whatever it took to get Jesse back on track. He wasn't just his cousin; he was his friend. That was more important than his feelings for Leila. Jesse liked Leila. That made her out-of-bounds.

Period.

It couldn't be allowed to matter that Will had a picture of Leila in his head, the likes of which he couldn't shake.

Leila Lantz with a baby in her arms and peanut butter on her cheek.

CHAPTER 14

No fuss, no muss. Leila grabbed baby Kaitlin's kicking feet with one hand, tucked the diaper under her, and quickly fitted it around her rotund belly. These disposable diapers had a knack to them. They were easy to use. But they cost a pretty penny. More than a Plain woman would spend when she could wash diapers and reuse them again and again.

"You're too cute for words." Inhaling the scent of baby wipes and diaper-rash cream, she blew raspberries on the white patch of belly above the diaper. "Did you know that, pumpkin?"

The baby crowed with laughter, her tiny hands flailing.

"You have a way with her."

Leila turned at the low voice. Kaitlin's father stood a few feet from the changing table, one hand on a Bee County EMS cap with the bill twisted to the back. His words held a hint of something she couldn't fathom. Like the sudden, unexpected pain of accidentally touching a hot stove. She forced a smile. "All babies love to have their tummies tickled."

He didn't return the smile. "I suppose."

"She's fed and changed. Is she headed home early today?"

He lifted the hat from his head. Tufts of his dark brown hair stood at attention. "Yep. I had a thing at the courthouse. No sense in going back to the station this late in my shift."

Tom Fletcher was an emergency medical technician, according to Rory, who felt it necessary to give Leila the life story of every parent and every child every chance she got. Tom's wife had skipped town when Kaitlin was a newborn. Rory claimed she suffered from a bad case of postpartum depression, which made her leaving a good thing for Kaitlin. Leila couldn't imagine how a mother leaving her baby could be classified as a good thing, ever.

"Kaitlin's very happy to see you."

She held the little girl out to her father. Kaitlin immediately began to wail.

"Funny, that's mostly what she does at home. Cry." His frown belied the word *funny*. His fisted hands slipped into the pockets of jeans washed enough times to be a pale blue. He took a step back, leaving the baby dangling in Leila's hands. "I keep hoping I'll get better at it, but I guess that's wishful thinking."

His crestfallen look hurt Leila's heart. "Don't you worry. All babies fuss. It doesn't matter who takes care of them, mother or father—"

"We'll never know, I guess. Kaitlin doesn't have a mother, but I guess you probably already knew that. The grapevine is lightning fast in this town."

"She still has a mother even if she's not—"

"She's never coming back and it doesn't matter if she does. A judge just gave me sole custody." His voice broke on the last word. He shook his head, his almond eyes dark with emotion over the black stubble of a five o'clock shadow. "I'm it and I don't have a clue."

Leila held Kaitlin to her chest, pressing her close to her heart, feeling for the baby and for the man in front of her. What did a woman say to something so heart-breaking? This job taking care of babies appeared to require more of her than she'd thought. "I don't know, Mr. Fletcher—"

"Tom. Mr. Fletcher is my father."

He swiped at his face with the back of his sleeve. He seemed to be waiting for her to explain to him how he would do this. How would he do this? "Babies just want to be loved. They want their diapers changed, they want to be fed and warm, but mostly they just want to be loved." She held up Kaitlin. "From the looks of this little roly-poly pumpkin, she's getting everything she needs."

He cocked his head. "She does look healthy, doesn't she?"

"And happy." Leila held her out again. "Go on, take her. She wants to do some loving on her daddy."

Kaitlin cooed this time, right on cue. Leila breathed a sigh of relief when Tom took the baby, her head resting in the crook of his arm. She giggled and burrowed into his shoulder, trying to pull herself up. "She acts like she has ants in her pants."

"She's six months old. She's ready to explore the world."

He nodded. "Thank you."

"For what?"

"For listening. And for taking care of my baby girl."

"It's my job."

"Yeah, but you seem to take extra joy in it." He rubbed Kaitlin's Onesie with a hand almost as big as her back. "Maybe you could help me out."

"Help you out?"

"Yeah, it seems like she always gets a rash on her bottom. I wonder if I'm doing something wrong, you know, and she spits up a lot after her bottle, and should I be giving her cereal right now? I've heard the mothers at the park talking about giving their babies cereal at night so they sleep longer. The good Lord knows I could use more uninterrupted sleep—"

Leila held up a tube of diaper-rash ointment and her hand at the same time, hoping to stem the rush of his words. "Be sure to change her before bed, and every time you feed her, check to see if the diaper is wet. It's about prevention, that's what I always say." A squawk from behind her told her one of her other babies was waking up. "As far as spitting up, all babies do that and my mother always said wait until the baby can sit up on his own to feed him cereal, but you folks usually ask your doctor that kind of question."

"Good, yeah, that's good, true."

He started toward the door, Kaitlin on one hip. Leila leaned over to pick up Joshua, who had creases on one side of his face from the sheet and smelled like he needed his diaper changed.

"Do you do house calls?"

Startled, she scooped the fussy baby up and turned. Tom had padded back across the room, his sneakers soundless on the tile. He stood within arm's reach. She took a step back and settled Joshua against her chest. "Sorry, what?"

He shifted Kaitlin to his other hip and tucked the strap of her diaper bag on his shoulder. "I could use someone to watch her at the house while I get some things done. It seems like I never get the dishes clean or the laundry and I haven't had a decent night's sleep since Diane—that's Kaitlin's mother—left."

His hangdog expression ate at her heart. "I'm sorry, Mr. Fletcher—"

"Tom, please."

"Tom, I can't. This is a full-time job and my mother needs me at home when I'm not working. I reckon Miss Sally could refer someone to you—"

"Kaitlin already knows you."

"That's nice of you to say—"

"Leila?"

She looked beyond Tom to Sally, the center's director. She looked none too pleased. "Yes, ma'am?"

"Just checking in. Tom, is there something I can do for you?"

"No, no, Leila was just giving me some advice about Kaitlin's diaper rash."

Sally pursed thin lips, her expression sharp behind blue-rimmed glasses with lenses so thick, her eyes seemed to bulge. "Leila is new and she still has a lot to learn, but she does seem to have a knack with the babies."

"Kaitlin sure likes her."

Sally wrinkled her nose in disapproval. She did that a lot. How could being good with babies be a bad thing for a day-care worker? Sally gave Tom a bright smile. "Did you need anything else?"

"No, no, just headed out."

He smiled at Leila and strode past Sally without looking back.

Sally waited, arms crossed, head cocked, until he was gone. "Keeping a professional distance from our parents is an important skill to learn." She straightened and picked her way through jumpers and Bumbo seats to where Leila stood. "Do you understand what that means?"

Leila tugged Joshua's pants down and unbuttoned his Onesie. "Yes, ma'am."

"That means when one of the children's fathers comes on to you, you back off and let him know you're not interested."

"Comes on to me?" Heat toasted her cheeks. "Tom just wanted some advice, that's all."

"*Mr. Fletcher* is a lonely man in a stressful situation. He's drowning and he's looking for a life preserver."

"I don't even know how to swim." Leila kept her tone firm but polite as she made quick work of removing Joshua's sodden diaper. She glanced up at her new boss. "Changing diapers and burping babies, that's what I know how to do."

"Good." Sally tapped the lever on the diaper pail with one white sneaker-clad foot. Her nose wrinkled. "Your pail needs emptying. And make sure you sanitize it after."

"Yes, ma'am."

She waited until Sally marched from the room to take a deep breath and let it out. Tom Fletcher hadn't been "coming on to her" as her boss put it. He'd been sweet and sad and he needed her advice. He needed a friend and he loved his baby. They had that in common. She wouldn't be rude to a man so sad. She would pray for him, for Kaitlin, and for Kaitlin's mom.

Any woman who could run away and leave behind a baby needed lots of prayers.

CHAPTER 15

A trailer park was the last place Jesse expected to be on a Wednesday night. He leaned through the open window of Colton's Impala and stared at the rusty double-wide resting on cinder blocks. It had a set of spindly wooden steps pressed up against the edge under a dinted door, with a gap between them big enough for a toddler to fall through. A naked overhead bulb did little to throw light on the narrow gravel drive where a gray van sat, its windshield cracked and paint bubbling.

He pulled his head in and swiveled in his seat to look at Colton. His friend had a fox-ate-the-chicken look on his thin, acne-scarred face that warned Jesse. Colton, who had said he needed to make a stop on the way to church, was up to something no good. "What are we doing here? I thought we were headed to youth group. Are we picking up Tiffany here?"

Colton shoved the gear in Park and turned the key. The engine ceased to rumble, leaving behind a soft *tick, tick* sound. He leaned back in his seat and tossed the keys in one hand, *jingle-jingle* joining the *tick, tick* in an annoying melody. The scent of his cologne mixed with burnt oil and exhaust fumes. "We'll meet Tiffany at youth group later. We have a meeting here first."

"Here where?" They usually met at Tiffany's or Colton's house and then went to the Dairy Queen to give pamphlets to the other teenagers who were busy gobbling down ice cream so fast they always whined about brain freezes. The youth group meetings were fun, but he hadn't gone any further than that. He hadn't attended a service. Not yet. "One of the guys lives here?"

"Not exactly. This is Matthew Plank's place. His father, Levi, is one of you folks—"

"I know who he is." Jesse smacked his fist against the door frame. "I can't."

"He and his family have been coming to services. Not regular, but now and again. Y'all need to talk."

"No. I can't."

"Just because the rest of your folks aren't talking to him and his brother doesn't mean you can't. Hear his side of the story."

"I can't. It's not permitted. He's shunned."

Meidnung was an act of love. An intentional act designed to bring a wayward child back into the fold. That's what his daed said. It wasn't punishment, even if it felt like it. It was also meant to protect the other members of the community from being led astray by that wayward child.

Colton picked up his Bible from the dash and smoothed one hand over the leather cover. "He loves Jesus enough to leave his father and his mother and his other brothers to follow Him. Luke 14:26–27." He offered the book to Jesse. "See for yourself."

Blood pounding in his ears, Jesse hunched down in his seat. Colton loved to do this. Pin him against the wall, challenging him, knowing he didn't have the knowledge of Scripture his friend did. He had his own Bible, with its English and German translations, but he didn't need to study it. He'd been attending church services his whole life. His daed shared the Word, along with Andrew, when it was his turn. "I don't need to see."

"'If anyone comes to me and does not hate father and mother, wife and children, brothers and sisters— yes, even their own life—such a person cannot be my disciple.'" Colton recited the verse without opening the book. "Look it up."

The unspoken question hung in the air.

Did Jesse love Jesus enough? That's the way Tiffany and Colton looked at it. Jesse's Plain district didn't have Sunday school. They did things differently. Who was right? Did God care about their human-made rules? Jesse inhaled and caught the acrid scent of trash burning in a barrel somewhere nearby. "I don't hate my mother and father. I thought we weren't supposed to hate anyone."

"I asked Pastor Dave about it, and he said that was Jesus' way of saying you have to put God first above everything else." Colton laid the Bible on the console between them. "Be willing to give up everything, even family."

"We put God above everything. Joy—Jesus first, others second, you third. It's one of the first things children learn in our community." As usual, Jesse found himself grappling for words. Why couldn't he be more like his father, who never faltered in those endless three-hour sermons? "Look at the way we live. Just so we don't slide into the evil ways of the world."

"And what about being fishers of men? Winning the lost and making disciples?"

Sometimes it seemed as if Colton spoke a foreign language. English was hard enough, but this stuff, Jesse couldn't fathom. "What?"

"Your people don't evangelize."

This Jesse knew how to answer. He listened—most of the time—to his daed's sermons. "We set an example by our ways. We are light to His feet and a lamp unto the world."

"And that's very good. I respect that." Colton touched the Bible again as if looking for words there. "But sometimes it's not enough. Sometimes people need to be invited in. They need someone to reach out and say, 'Hey, come on in.' That's what we do. Jesus calls us to be fishers of men."

Just as Colton and Tiffany had done for Jesse. They'd invited him in. Jesse didn't want to argue with Colton. Colton would win. He had years of practice and a way with words far greater than Jesse, who'd never had to defend his faith or his way of life in what felt like a physical fight. "I know you're trying to help, but you're putting too much pressure—"

"It's a big deal. There are people out there who need saving. It's the most important work you will ever do."

"I need time."

"Just listen to what Matthew has to say. He really wants to see you. Talk to you."

"He could come home. Then we could talk whenever he wants. The community will take him and his family back anytime. He knows that."

"He just has to repent of his sin and promise never to do it again?"

"Something like that."

"He hasn't sinned. He's closer to God than he's ever been."

"When he was baptized, he committed himself to our way of life, our rules. He drives a van and uses electricity and sends his kids to public school. His fraa—wife—doesn't even cover her head anymore."

"And that's sinful? You think we're sinful—me and Tiffany and Greg and Sophie and Louis and the other guys in youth group?"

Jesse struggled with the question. He was no bishop. He'd read more Bible and talked more Scripture since walking into the first youth group meeting two months ago than he had in his entire life. He'd always relied on his daed and Mordecai and Andrew to steer him in the right direction, to steer all of them toward a godly life. They had the Ordnung. If they followed the rules and kept God at the center of their lives, they would be fine. They were obedient and humble and hardworking, asking nothing of others, doing no harm to others. "Electricity and cars are not sinful themselves." He could say that much. "But the more we're connected with the world, the more we become like it. That leads to sin."

According to Daed.

"Do you know that for sure, or did someone tell you it did?"

Colton liked asking questions to which he already knew the answers. Jesse breathed in and out, in and out. Maybe this was his chance to talk Matthew into coming home. Maybe this was God's way of sending him into the fray. "Fine. We talk for a few minutes and then you give me a ride home or I'll hitchhike."

"I would never let you do that." Colton grinned, his face alight with the thought that he'd won this particular scrimmage. "What kind of friend do you think I am? Besides, we still have youth group after."

The kind of friend who had the best of intentions but didn't know how to let up.

Colton shoved his door open and loped around the car as if he had known all along Jesse would capitulate. He hated to think he was that predictable. With much greater hesitation, he opened his door and slid out. He marched up steps so wobbly he put out his hand to steady himself. Colton already had the door open.

Little Sarah, Matthew's youngest girl, peeked out, her eyes wide, curly blonde hair snarled in a rat's nest, face smeared with what looked like blueberry jam. She waved with both hands and then stuck a thumb in her mouth.

"Sarah, get back! You know better. Scoot, girl." Matthew scooped her up with one arm and held her football style, legs dangling, as he waved them in. "Welcome. Jesse, it's good to see you."

Feet planted on a welcome mat crowded with an assortment of work boots, Jesse said nothing. The darkness of the trailer, lit by only one electric lamp and a bulb over the kitchen sink, was at odds with the smell of chili and fresh-baked bread. It still smelled like home.

His father wouldn't agree. It couldn't be their true home. Daed's disapproving face hovered in his mind's eye. Not following the Ordnung cost them a great deal. It cost them their community.

It had to be that way, Daed had told him on more than one occasion. The terrible possibility existed that others would be infected by this rebellion, by these worldly ways. Then they would all succumb.

That was the word Daed had used. *Succumb. Wither and die.*

"It's okay. Come in. Have a seat." Matthew waved his hand toward a sofa covered by an orange and red crocheted comforter. His four boys, stepping-stones a year apart from five to nine, scooted down, their freckled faces bright with anticipation and curiosity. They wore T-shirts and faded jeans and assorted colors of dirty sneakers. Jesse sank onto the edge of the couch, not leaning back.

"Are you our cousin?" the oldest asked, his face turning candy-apple red at his own impertinence. "Are you a Plank?"

They didn't know. It had been so long since their parents left the community, they didn't know their own family's members. The Planks had since moved back to Ohio, only returning to Bee County once to try to talk some sense into their two sons. To no avail. Their stoic faces as they loaded into the van that would take them to the bus station in George West were still burned on Jesse's brain.

"No, he's not a Plank. This here's Jesse Glick." Matthew rescued Jesse. He plopped into a plastic lawn chair, leaving Colton to squeeze into a rocker, the only other chair in the long, narrow living room that ended in a kitchenette on one side and a dark hallway on the other. His boys might dress Englisch, but Matthew still wore a blue work shirt, suspenders, and black pants. The exterior hadn't changed, but the interior of the man had. "He's family, all the same."

Jesse cleared his throat. Words clogged it. And an emotion that surprised him. He had liked Matthew. They'd played together as kids. His absence had been keenly felt by all of them. He nodded at the boys, then ducked his head to study the matted carpet of no particular color under his scuffed boots.

"Colton wanted me to talk to you." Matthew didn't sound any fonder of the idea than Jesse felt. "I told him you can't push a person into this. A person has to come willingly. He has to be willing to pay the price."

Jesse forced himself to meet Matthew's gaze. He sucked in air and nodded. "On that, we agree."

"I know you think we must be suffering something awful." Matthew tugged at his ragged beard with a big, calloused hand. "But we're not. We have Jesus. He's all we need. We've gotten used to the other."

Used to the other. The not having family anymore. How did a person get used to that, exactly?

And what did it mean to have Jesus? Didn't they all have Jesus? They had the Bible. They had Sunday services. They prayed. What made Matthew and Ruth special? Jesse gritted his teeth and studied the carpet. It had a rip right at the spot where the sofa leg punished it under his weight.

"You're not going to hell for looking at me."

The amusement in Matthew's voice did nothing to improve Jesse's mood. He jerked his head up and let his friend—ex-friend—see his scowl.

Matthew smiled, but the sadness in his eyes relayed another message.

"It's not something I can explain. It's not knowledge." He touched his chest with two fingers in the vicinity of his heart. "It's something I experienced. I'm at peace now. Me and Ruth, we're at peace with our decision."

Peace. That sounded good. Jesse tried to remember the last time he felt at peace. The memory came to him with quick, painful clarity. The darkness, the rush of the wind through the cracked window in Colton's Impala. Leila's hand in his, her eyes closed, her head against his shoulder, her expression peaceful and trusting in sleep. His throat ached at the thought. He stood. "I shouldn't be here."

"I know you're torn." Matthew rose as well, Sarah still dangling from one arm. She wiggled so she could bury her face in her daddy's shoulder. He nuzzled the top of her head with his beard. "But you haven't been baptized yet. It's different for you. You won't be shunned."

"No, but if I choose not to be baptized, my family will be shamed. My father is the bishop."

"It's a hard road, but it's worth it to be able to think freely and worship freely."

"I do that now."

"You think you do, but you don't. They tell you what

to think. They tell you to be quiet. They tell you not to think on your own."

His daed did say it was better to listen more and talk less. Nothing wrong with that. "That's not the way I see it."

"Angus and I are doing good with our carpentry work. We have more houses to fix up than we can handle. We can always use another set of hands and a strong back."

"I have a job at the store."

"That pays you nothing. How will you raise a family?"

The same way his father and grandfather did. Sharing in the work and in the profit. He shook his head at Colton, hoping his friend could read his thoughts. He never should have come here. He put his hand on the doorknob.

"Don't go yet!" Ruth hustled from the hall at the other end of the narrow room. She carried a baby in each arm. "I was just changing Esther and Mary, our newest additions."

Ruth looked the same. She still wore a long gray dress and an apron, but her hair hung down her back in one thick braid. If they were going to drive cars and use microwaves, why not dress like the Englischers? She smiled up at him, still a pretty woman despite the dark smudges under her eyes and a roundness that spoke of giving birth recently.

"Congratulations." His tone sounded churlish, even to him. "They're healthy?"

"Almost five pounds apiece. And their lungs work real good." Matthew laughed. "Keep us up half the night with their caterwauling."

Ruth chuckled. One of the babies began to fuss. She handed one bundle to the oldest boy, pulled the other one up on her shoulder, and began to pat her back. "I just wanted to say hey. Tell your mama I miss her pecan pie. No one makes it like her." Her caramel-colored eyes seemed to beseech him. "I make it all the time, but it's just not the same."

Did her words hold a hidden message? Jesse couldn't be sure. He did know he couldn't tell his mudder about this visit. She would have to tell Daed. The bishop. He'd have to explain why he'd come here and talked to these folks who were shunned. He nodded and touched the brim of his hat.

Ruth's smile faltered. "She's well? Everyone's good?"

He nodded.

Her features dimmed into something he did recognize. He'd seen it on his own face reflected in the mirror behind the bar at Carl's Grill, where Colton and Tiffany liked to go for burgers, fries, and pool on Saturday night. Resignation. The baby in her arms yawned, her pink rosebud lips opening wide. "It was good to see you, Jesse. Real good. Come on, boys. Time to get ready for bed. Ten minutes till prayer time."

The boys popped off the couch in quick succession without so much as a murmur. They traipsed past Jesse, grinning, the two younger ones pushing and shoving while the older one sang "Jesus Loves the Little Children" off-key to the baby. The youngest boy plowed to a stop. "Do you ride a horse to work?"

He shook his head. "I drive a buggy."

"I like horses."

"To bed." Matthew set Sarah down on her feet, gave the boy's bottom a playful slap, and sent both on their way. "They like horses. No place to have one around here."

They would never be close to horses, not as long as they lived in a trailer park. Most likely they would never be farmers. Matthew must've followed his train of thought. "I figure they'll make up their own minds about what to do with their lives once they're older."

"You'd let them come home, then, if they wanted?"

"They are home." Matthew held the door open and nodded at Colton as he passed through first. "But I am for people making up their own minds about how they live their lives and about how they worship."

"Even if they decide to worship as Plain folks?"

"As long as they get a chance to make that decision for themselves."

"Isn't that what rumspringa is for?"

"That's what they say. But if you make the so-called wrong decision, look what happens." He waved his hand around the trailer. "I ain't heard from my parents in three years. I sent them a card to tell them about the twins. They never answered."

"They can't." Jesse clomped down the stairs, hoping they didn't collapse under his weight, and turned to look up. "It's not because they don't love you. It's because they do."

"My point exactly." Matthew put one hand on the door frame and leaned against it. "It doesn't make sense. I believe all the same things you do. I live by the gospel. I believe Jesus is my Lord and Savior. Why shun me?"

Jesse stared up at the other man. Why? A reason existed, surely it did. At this moment, with only a naked lightbulb illuminating the soft mist that had begun to fall, wetting his face, he couldn't think what it was. "Good-bye."

He folded his legs into the car and locked the door as if whatever pursued him would try to squeeze in next to him.

No locks could keep his thoughts out.

CHAPTER 16

Of all the holidays, Thanksgiving had the best smells. Leila eased the pumpkin pie from the oven, the heat singeing her eyebrows and toasting the tip of her nose. The aroma of turkey fresh from the second oven mixed with the pumpkin spices. Her mouth watered. She turned and displayed the pie with the golden, fluted crust to the dozen or more women crowded into the kitchen her mudder and Susan now shared in Mordecai's house.

This was the first year Mudder had let her be in charge of the pies. Deborah had the potatoes and gravy, and Rebekah helped with the breads. The cranberry sauce belonged to the younger girls who took turns cranking the hand grinder attached to the table. For some reason they found the sight and sounds of squishing cranberries, apples, and oranges hilarious. Mudder had them washing the prep pots and pans now to keep them out of trouble.

"That looks beautiful." Aenti Alma leaned over and sniffed, her long nose dangerously close to the hot pie tin. "Smells delicious too. Are we making whipped cream?"

"Already on it," Susan volunteered. "Can't have pumpkin pie without whipped cream."

"I need more flour for the gravy." Deborah stood at the stove, a wooden ladle in one outstretched hand. The size of her baby bump kept her from getting any closer. "We had plenty of drippings. It should have a nice flavor."

Leila set the pie on the pot holders Hazel had made and given to Mudder for Christmas the previous year. It looked lovely sitting next to the two turkeys shot by the men earlier in the week, now baked to a golden brown and ready to be carved. She reached for the canister filled with flour, opened it, and slid it toward her sister. Something smacked her in the back of the head and thudded on the floor behind her.

"Hey! Ouch!" She whirled, rubbing the spot just below her kapp. Hazel and her little cousin Emma shrieked with laughter as Hazel scrambled across the room and scooped up an apple that rolled around on the floor at Leila's feet. "Did you do that?"

Giggling, Hazel and Emma slapped their hands over their mouths, eyes wide, looking like twins. Muffled nees emanated from behind their plump fingers.

Leila grabbed an orange from the basket on the table and tossed it in the air. "Playing catch with our food?"

"Juggling," Emma piped up. She grabbed two oranges from the basket and tossed them in the air, her hands flailing. One piece of fruit stayed aloft, while the other plummeted to the floor.

Hazel grabbed it and tossed it to Leila. "Think quick."

Laughing, Leila snatched it up midair and still managed to catch her own orange. "You girls are silly willies."

"Catch, catch!" The other little girls joined in, grinning as they grabbed fruit and tossed apples and oranges around the room. "First one to let it drop loses."

"This isn't a game!" Mudder didn't sound at all cross as she caught an orange just before it hit the floor and tossed it to Esther, who neatly forwarded it in the same motion to Aenti Alma. "We have a lot of food to serve. The men are getting hungry."

"A little game of catch will help us women work up an appetite." Susan caught the toss from Alma and whirled to throw it to Deborah. "Seeing as we haven't done any work today."

Leila ducked in the same direction. Her sister had her back turned. She was busy with the gravy—and hot oil on the stove. Leila stuck out her hand and deflected the orange. The fruit slammed into the open container of flour. It plopped on its side and spilled its contents, flour blooming in a white fog that coated the counter. And Leila.

She breathed in flour and coughed.

"Let me help you!" Deborah dropped her ladle and grabbed a towel. She dabbed at the mess, spreading it down the front of the apron and adding to the layer on Leila's shoes. "Oops, maybe you should go outside and dust yourself off."

"We could hang you from the clothesline and beat you like a rug." Rebekah offered this suggestion, her face contorted with mock concern. "We'll have you cleaned up in a jiffy."

The women's giggles turned to gales of laughter. Leila looked to her mother for help. Mudder's cheeks were red and tears of laughter trickled down her face. "It's not that funny."

"Dochder, you should see yourself. You look like a ghost or a snowman or a giant marshmallow."

Leila looked down at her dress and apron—all covered with flour. "Ach!" She grabbed her apron and shook it. Flour puffed into her face. More coughing. "What a—"

"I've been sent to see what all the commotion is about." Will strolled into the kitchen. He halted, mouth open for a few seconds. "I've heard of pancake makeup, but I've never seen a Plain woman going in for it."

"We were just . . ." Leila searched for words to explain such a mess. "Cooking."

"So that's the secret. The more flour on the cook, the better the food?" His gaze slid around the room to the other women. He grinned. "How come you're the only one with flour all over you?"

"The orange was about to hit Deborah so I batted it away." The words sounded ridiculous in her ears. Emma and Hazel tittered. Even *Mudder* grinned. "I mean, we were—the girls were having some fun, that's all."

"Nothing wrong with that." Will scooped up an apple from the table and tossed it in the air. It fell neatly in his enormous palm. "I just hope you made the gravy before you used all that flour on your face. I really like gravy." He turned and strode from the room, still grinning.

"Someone is in lieb." Esther nudged Susan, a grin as big as Will's on her face. "Don't you think?"

"He's not!" Leila turned her back on the other women

and began sloshing water from the tub in the sink on her face and hands. It did little to cool the burn that roared across her face. He couldn't be, or she had an even bigger problem than the insurmountable one presented by Jesse. "You're imagining that."

"Nope, and from the way you're hiding your face, so are you." Susan joined in the chorus. "You've been doing a real good job of keeping it private. I didn't know y'all were courting."

"We're not." She and Will had been too busy waiting for Jesse to make up his mind. At least that's the way it looked from her perspective. "He hasn't asked me. Maybe he's never gotten over losing out to Phineas for Deborah."

Deborah laughed so hard she snorted, which made the rest of the women laugh. "It's not funny." Leila flapped a dish towel at her sister. "You have your husband."

"Will never even asked me out."

"He didn't get a chance."

"Or he wasn't all that interested. He can't ask you because he thinks his cousin is interested, that's what it is."

"Nobody is courting anybody at the moment."

"I think that's about to change." Susan, a short, round version of her brother Mordecai, swept the floor with short, hard strokes. "A man who has lost out once is not going to want to do it again, that's for sure."

Leila turned to study her. "From a one-minute conversation, you could tell all that?"

"That boy has it bad." Susan whipped the dustpan into position and swept up the flour that surrounded Leila's feet. "I suspect he'll be visiting a whole lot more."

"How can you tell?" Leila blurted the words before she could think about how they would sound. She'd let Jesse kiss her in the movie theater. How could she be thinking of Will? It was too confusing. "How do you know which person is right for you?"

"There's no hurry." Mudder smiled as she poured a quart mason jar of bread-and-butter pickles into a bowl, the pungent smell of vinegar and pickling spices adding to the piquant bouquet already floating in the air. "Just remember that. Don't let teasing from these girls sway you. You'll know when you know."

"How did you know with Mordecai?" Leila would rather know how her mother had known with *Daed*, but she didn't want to cause her pain. "I mean, how did you know it was . . . Mordecai and not Stephen."

Mudder shrugged. "I felt it in my heart. As much as I'd like to advise you differently, it doesn't matter what makes the most sense. I wish it did. It would be so much easier. It's what you feel in your heart. Like this is the person you want to commit to for the rest of your life. In fact, you couldn't do anything else."

Deborah waved her hands in front of her face, damp with a sheen of sweat, as if to cool herself. "Believe me, schweschder, you'll know. Maybe not at first, but it grows on you until you can't ignore it. You think about the person more than you want to. You look for him when you should be doing something else. He'll irritate you to no end, but you still can't get enough of his company."

Leila thought about Jesse because he'd plowed his way into her life, planted the seed with that kiss, and then bailed out on her. That wasn't love. That was meanness. Will, on the other hand, had shown up at the day care to warn her about Jesse. He wanted to protect her heart.

Or he wanted it for himself. Maybe Will acted as if he wanted to say something, but he didn't because he was too honorable to horn in on Jesse.

Which left her alone at the singings. Caught between cousins, neither of whom had made his intentions clear.

"Doesn't sound like much fun," Alma observed, saving Leila from having to speak. "I'm thinking I'll do like Susan and become a schoolteacher."

Susan, with her book-learning smarts and keen sense of humor, seemed perfectly happy never to have married. She taught her scholars and took care of her brother, Mordecai, and his kinner after his first fraa died. Then Mudder came along and took her place. Leila examined Susan's face for signs she regretted her life. Not an iota. "It's not up to you." Susan emptied the flour into the trash can and balanced the broom against the wall next to it. "Gott's will, Gott's plan."

Leila tried to find it in her rebellious heart to accept this fact. She gritted her teeth until her jaw ached.

"Amen." Esther smoothed back black hair that had escaped her kapp, a dreamy look on her face as if she were seeing something none of the rest of the women could share in. Another shorter, rounder version of Mordecai. "I can't wait to become Adam's fraa."

She only had a few weeks to go. Without moving, Leila swatted away the ugly green bugs of jealousy that bombarded her at the thought. *Praise Gott for Esther and Adam's happiness.*

Praise Gott. Through hardship and suffering and pain. *Praise Gott.*

"Fun is making Leila dump flour on herself." Hazel took a bite of her apple, her nose crinkling, chewed with a crunch, and swallowed. "That's the most fun."

Everyone laughed. Except Leila. She wasn't having much fun at all. This love thing was a thorn in her side. She longed to pluck it out.

Gott wasn't known for plucking thorns from sides.

Give me a sign, Gott—please give me a small sign.

CHAPTER 17

Oh, for a wheelbarrow and someone to push her to her bed. Leila patted her full stomach and eased onto the front step. *Thank You, Gott, for such bounty.* A puff of flour settled around her, reminding her of the fun they'd had preparing the food. *Thank You, Gott, for family. Every day, not only today.* Even with the painful turn in the conversation, she was blessed to have family and friends. The rest of her problems would have to wait. Today was a day for enjoying family and counting blessings.

By the time they had the food on the table, she'd been hungry enough to eat a cow by herself. Or maybe she ate to console herself. Mashed potatoes and gravy were called comfort food, after all. Fresh air might help her overcome the desire to nap. Otherwise, she'd lay her head down on the prep table in the kitchen and go to sleep in half a second. Turkey, two servings of cornbread stuffing, mashed potatoes, gravy, corn, green beans, beets, a roll, and a gigantic piece of pie would see to that.

"You have flour on your kapp."

Leila slapped her hand on the back of her head. She

raised her other hand to her forehead to shield her eyes from a gorgeous afternoon sun that took the November chill from the air. Will Glick towered over her. She dropped her hand and switched her gaze to the corral. "What are you doing out here? How come you're not playing kickball with the others out back?"

"Twisted my ankle the other day." He plopped down on the step next to her, a little too close for her liking as a matter of fact. She leaned away. He grinned. "Besides, if I run around after eating all the food, I'll probably hurl."

"Nice."

He shrugged. "It's a day for being lazy."

"A day for being thankful."

"I am thankful." He dug at his front teeth with a toothpick, his expression thoughtful. "Thankful my daed accepted the invitation to have Thanksgiving with the Mordecai Kings."

Leila hadn't been so keen on the idea after her strange encounter with him at the day care not so long ago. After Susan's observations in the kitchen, Leila couldn't help but feel even more awkward. Was Mordecai's sister right? Did Will have intentions toward her? How she wished she could come right out and ask him. Life would be so much simpler. "It's nice to share a meal, isn't it?"

"Especially when the Mordecai Kings include you."

The tiniest bit of hope fluttered through her. Maybe Susan was right. Will hovered around the edges at the singings. Sometimes she caught him staring at her with a look she couldn't decipher. Almost like worry. He was worried for her.

Jesse, on the other hand, hadn't been to a singing

since their trip to George West to the movies. He hadn't made a single appearance at her door either. Not a word after church services. Not even a note. Heat scorched her cheeks. She'd given Jesse her first kiss. She should've saved it for someone who thought she was special. Someone she considered special.

Maybe that man was Will.

Will's shoulder touched hers. "Are you cold?"

She leaned away. "What?"

He cocked his head, his forehead wrinkled, eyebrows lifted. "Your face is all red. It's not that cold out. Cold for south Texas, but that's not saying much."

"Nee. I just ate too much."

"Me too. Want to take a ride?"

"What?"

"Is your hearing going?" His face was the one red now. "It's hard enough to ask once. Don't make me ask twice."

"You're asking me to take a buggy ride with you?"

"Actually, I brought the two-seater. I came on my own today. If you don't want to, that's—"

He'd planned to ask her out. He brought his own ride just so he could ask her to step out with him. If her face had been red before, it surely was the color of an overly ripe tomato now. "I do, I do, I'm just surprised. What about Jesse?"

Again with the blurting out of words. When would she learn to hold her tongue?

Will looked around with exaggerated care. "I don't see him here. I ain't seen him anywhere near you in two weeks."

"You've been watching?"

He ducked his head and picked up a stray twig, which he proceeded to worry with both hands. "Not trying to mind the business of others or anything."

"Nee, why were you watching? Why don't you just ask him? Did you ask him?"

She wanted to know what Jesse was thinking. More than anything, she wanted to know.

"We're not talking much right now."

"Why?"

"It's—"

"Personal, I know."

Leila swiped a side glance at him. His pulse pumped in his temple as his jaw jutted. He had a nice, strong jaw and white, even teeth. And he was here, now, and asking her to take a ride with him. "Jah."

He tossed the twig on the ground and swiveled his head so their gazes met. "Jah what?"

"I'd like to take a ride with you."

"Jah?" The consternation fell away, replaced by a genuine smile. "Are you certain?"

"Better hurry before my mudder notices I'm not in the kitchen cleaning up."

"There's at least a dozen women in there. You won't be missed." He stood and swept a hand toward the row of buggies on the other side of the dirt and gravel road that cut in front of the house. "I'm ready to roll."

• • •

The *clip-clop* of the mule's hooves on the pavement ringing in his ears, Will contemplated the endless farm-to-market road that stretched before them, brown fields of stubble on either side, sun low in the western sky. A wispy cloud huffed and puffed across the sky as if in a rush to escape the sun. He had Leila Lantz in the seat next to him, a dwindling autumn day before him, and a blank mind. Absolutely, utterly blank. He had a dark void where thought should be. He'd been planning this moment for days, since he'd come to the realization that he couldn't wait for Jesse to make up his mind. If Jesse continued down his current path, Leila would get hurt, and Will couldn't have that.

Even if it cost him his friendship with his cousin.

If Jesse chose to leave the community, Will would lose him anyway. He didn't want to lose Leila too.

As if he had her. Which of course he didn't. Not yet.

And he never would, if he didn't open his mouth and say something interesting or funny. What did girls think was interesting or funny?

"Beautiful day. Mite warm for so late in the year. Hard to believe Christmas is only a month away."

Resorting to weather. He sounded like an old man making conversation with another old man at his uncle's store.

Leila nodded and brushed back a tendril of hair that had escaped her flour-caked prayer kapp. She was such a funny girl, not caring at all about her appearance. That flour would still be there at the end of the day. He found that appealing. And her hair was the color of corn silk. He'd like to see the rest of it. Down around her shoulders.

Mortified at where his thoughts had taken him,

he clamped down on his tongue until he drew blood. "Ouch."

She swiveled and gave him a look of grave concern. "What happened? Did a bee get you?"

"Nee. Bit my tongue, that's all." A feeling akin to the panic he'd felt one time when the tide almost carried him out to the Gulf from the beach at Port Aransas burbled up inside him. *Think. Think.* "I like to hunt. Deer mostly. But dove and quail too. No alligator though. Too big. And the license is expensive. What's a man gonna do with all that alligator meat and skin? Some folks make belts and boots, I reckon, but me, I . . ."

He stopped, certain the heat of embarrassment would cause his skin to burst into flames and his whole body would burn to a crisp.

Leila giggled. She slapped a hand to her mouth, but the giggles came louder. Her blue eyes widened and tears formed in the corners. "I'm sorry," she gasped. "I'm sorry. That just sounded . . ."

"Funny, I know." Will laughed too. He couldn't help it. Her laugh was contagious. So all he had to do was say stupid stuff to make her laugh. "I'm no good at this."

"Me neither."

"You do fine with Jesse."

Her smile disappeared, taking the warm, balmy sun with it.

"Sorry." Will kicked himself with an extra-large work boot. "That was a . . . stupid thing to say."

"Nee." She leaned back against the seat, staring straight ahead. "Will Glick, what are we doing?"

"Taking a ride." Determined to salvage the moment,

he stuck his hand under the seat without taking his gaze from the road. He fumbled around until his fingers found the handle and he was able to produce the prize he sought. "With music."

She took the old-fashioned boom box in both hands as if it might shatter in her grasp. "Where'd you get this?"

"At the secondhand shop next to the feed store. I had my first paycheck in my hands and I thought, why not just look around a minute or two?"

"So you bought a radio?" She slid her fingers across the row of black buttons on the top with a soft, almost loving touch. Will couldn't rip his gaze from her fingers. She looked up, frowning. "Something you know you can't keep?"

He had wanted to do something a little reckless during his rumspringa, but he'd never found that thing. He didn't feel comfortable around the Englisch teenagers the way Jesse did, and he had no desire to tag along to the youth group meetings. The words *slippery slope* kept buzzing in his ears every time he thought about it. "I can keep it in the barn until I'm baptized."

"As long as your daed doesn't find it and throw it away."

"He'll do worse than throw it away; he'll stomp on it real good."

They both laughed, an uneasy sound in his ears. She nestled the radio in her lap and studied it, the tip of her tongue slipping from the corner of her mouth. "How does it run? Do you have to plug it in?"

"Nee." Delighted at the obvious interest on her face, he pointed to the Play button. "Just push that button. I already put new batteries in it. You can't get a lot of stations out here. But there's one that plays country music. The others are mostly in Spanish."

She did as he said, and sure enough, a song in Spanish blared, accompanied by the brassy sound of trumpets and accordions so loud they both jumped and laughed. The singer sounded as if he had a bellyache with all those *ay-ay-ays*. Will had heard this music before, blasting from the stores on the strip that led to the border crossing when they had to go to the doctor or the dentist. It sounded like a raucous party to him. Even though he couldn't understand the words, the songs sounded happy.

Leila grinned at him and twisted the knob until a country music song wafted from the radio, a little staticky but definitely a fine bit of music for a sunny afternoon. "Better?"

He nodded and turned left onto a dirt road that led to property belonging to one of their Englisch neighbors. He pulled the wagon into the first shady spot near a stand of gnarly mesquite trees that provided almost no shade with their fine, feathery leaves.

"What are you doing?"

"I thought we could sit and talk a little bit."

Leila tilted her head, the sparse leaves of the tree making a dappled pattern on her face as the sun played hide-and-seek in the branches overhead. Before he could get down, she hopped from her side and spun around. "What do you want to talk about?"

He hauled himself down and wrapped the reins around a branch, his back to her as he tried to think of a topic of conversation. He was awful at this. He squeezed his eyes shut and concentrated. Nothing. A fierce void.

"We have music." Her voice held a note of something . . . giddiness. He'd never thought of her as giddy. She tugged the boom box from the wagon and set it on the bedraggled grass between them. "We could dance."

Dance. He'd never danced. He had no idea how to do it. Why that? Why did she want that? He turned and faced her. "I'm not like Jesse."

Her smile disappeared once again. "Didn't say you were. If you don't want to dance with me, fine. Let's go."

Will stepped between her and the two-seater. Maybe he needed to offer her something exciting, something a little bad, like Jesse had with the movies. "I just mean, I'm not looking to experiment or anything. I just want to get to know you."

She nodded, but her eyes were bright with tears.

"What's the matter?"

"Nothing."

"You're crying."

"Am not!"

No doubt about it. A tear trickled down her cheek. She brushed it away, her lips twisted in a defiant smile.

"It's not that I don't want to dance with you—I don't know how."

"Me neither." She wrapped her arms around her middle. "Does it ever make you sad to think of all the things we won't do?"

"Nee. I'm happy thinking of the things we will do." He grasped her hands in his and placed them on his shoulders. Her eyes widened and she sniffed. She had to stand on her tiptoes to reach. "I think about getting married and having . . . kinner."

She nodded, her gaze fixed on his. Swallowing hard, he laid one hand on her waist with the same care he used when asked to hold a bopli. Her startled intake of breath forced him back a step.

"Nee." She took a quick step forward. "I think that's right."

It felt right. The curve of her hips. Her warmth. "I think so too."

The song on the radio died away, but still they swayed to the sound of the wind rustling in the trees, their gazes locked. "We're dancing," she whispered. "I think we're dancing."

"I think you're right."

She stared up at him, then slid her hand down his chest and inclined her head until it nestled against him. No doubt she could hear the hammering of his heart. It might burst through his rib cage any second. He couldn't breathe. They were dancing. He and Leila.

He moved one foot, then the other.

"Ouch!" She jerked back. "That was my foot."

"Sorry, sorry!"

"It's okay." She hopped on one foot for a second. "I don't think my toes are broken."

He let go and backed away. "Sorry. I'm a big oaf."

"No, don't stop!" She caught at his hands, placed one on her waist, and wound her fingers in the other. "Another song is starting. We're dancing."

So they danced, one, two, three songs. Mostly, they swayed. He was afraid to move his feet for fear of doing more damage. They didn't talk. After a while she let her forehead rest on his chest again. He memorized the top of her head dusted with flour and the curve of her cheek and savored her scent of vanilla and soap.

"What are you thinking about?" Her voice was soft, barely a whisper. "You're so quiet."

"I'm thinking about you."

She raised her head. "What about me?"

"I like the way you smell." If he could melt into the earth, he would. "I mean—"

"Thank you. It's just soap."

"You smell clean and sweet."

She leaned her head against his chest again. "I can hear your heart."

"I wish you could feel what it feels."

"What does that mean?" She kept her head down now, for which Will was eternally grateful. "What does it feel?"

"Content. Like this is how it's supposed to be."

"Dancing?"

"Nee, you and me, together."

"How do you know for sure? How does anyone know?"

"It feels good, like we could just do this forever, go on and on."

"Except we can't."

"Nee. We can't."

"Danki for this. It's nice." She tilted her head back to look at him, her face glowing in the dwindling light. "We should go back. Mudder will be looking for me."

He swallowed. He didn't want it to end, but he didn't want to spoil the moment either. Step by step. That's how these things were done. Forging a bond a little at a time. *Gott, give me enough time. Please.* "Maybe we can do it again sometime."

"Jah, I'd like that." Her cheeks turned pink again. The poor girl couldn't hide her feelings—her face gave her away every time. Her gaze drifted over his shoulder to the horizon. "I like slow. Let's just go slow. Can we go slow?"

"Slow is good." Especially when it came to dancing. He didn't want to break her foot. And he didn't want to get his own heart broken. He grabbed her hand and squeezed. He didn't want the contact to be lost. He didn't want to be far from her for any length of time. This was bad. He had it bad. Someone needed to tell his heart to go slow. "That's not a problem."

She nodded, but her gaze slipped beyond him. The soft contentment in her face fled. "Someone's coming."

Will shifted to follow her gaze. They weren't doing anything wrong. So why did his throat constrict and his lungs stop working? He leaned down, reaching for the volume knob on the boom box. They weren't doing anything wrong. He flicked the Off switch. The music died, leaving behind an odd, hollow silence broken only by the rustling of leaves in the wind. "Who is it?"

Her hand went to her forehead. She squinted against the setting sun. A deeper pink bloomed on her cheeks. She took a step back, then another. "It's Jesse."

Will's mind contemplated the words, but his body continued to think about the space that had opened up between them. So much space. He forced his gaze to the road.

Sure enough. Jesse.

CHAPTER 18

Leila smoothed her apron, sure it somehow held evidence that she'd been pressed against Will's body only seconds earlier. She would not turn a fiery red. She hadn't been doing anything wrong. Jesse never came calling a second time. Weeks had passed. He had no hold on her. She lifted her chin and waited until the buggy drew near, then graced him with a wide smile and quick wave. A normal, everyday greeting for someone she'd known for a long time now. A friend.

Jesse reined in his horse and buggy and stopped. He didn't return her greeting. He studied Will first, then her. His hands remained wrapped around the buggy reins. "What are you two doing out here?"

"None of your business." The words barreled from her mouth before she could stop them. So much for the high road. "I mean, we're stretching our legs. We both ate too much."

Will picked up the boom box and tucked it under the seat. "We were just headed back."

"Stretching your legs?" A doubtful tone mixed with a painful attempt at nonchalance in his gruff voice. "It's funny. From down the road, it looked like dancing."

"What do you care?" Again with the ugly, spiteful tone. Heat rushed through Leila. How could she be so angry with Jesse when a moment ago she'd been dancing a lovely, sweet, swaying dance with Will? Was she that shallow? Nee. She wouldn't have thought so, not until this moment. She breathed, unable to meet Will's gaze. "We were enjoying the afternoon and getting some fresh air, that's all."

Will's hand squeezed her elbow, then dropped. "Like Leila said, we were—"

"I know, stretching your legs." Jesse jerked his head toward the road. "Where everyone can see you."

"Rumspringa—"

"Doesn't mean you rub people's noses in it."

"What are you doing out here?" Will's tone was even, but the red blotches on his neck and chin crept across his face. "Just riding around on Thanksgiving Day or headed into town to see your Englisch friends?"

Jesse's face darkened to the color of an overripe tomato. "You said you wouldn't say anything."

"I haven't." Will jerked his head toward Leila. "Not a word. But I won't stand by—"

"I'm not asking you to—"

"Then go about your business and leave her out of it. Otherwise, she'll pay the price."

Leila felt like a spectator, watching two men spar. Plain men didn't spar. Not even with words. Will's words sank in. "Leave me out of what?"

Neither man looked at her, but Jesse's shoulders sagged. He ducked his head and stared at the ground. "You're right, but there's no need to rub my nose in it."

"I didn't think you'd be out here gallivanting across the countryside on Thanksgiving Day." Will didn't look at Leila either. He sounded ashamed. Ashamed of what? "It wasn't my intent to cause you . . . discomfort."

Jesse's head bobbed. "I know. It's pure happenstance."

"Or Gott's way of pointing us in a certain direction."

Jesse's face contorted in a painful grin. "Gott's will, Gott's plan."

"Right about what? What plan?" Leila studied Jesse's face, then Will's. They didn't sound angry anymore. Will looked as if he'd just lost his best horse, and Jesse grimaced as if he had a pain in his chest. They were staring at each other like they were saying good-bye forever. "Somebody tell me what's going on, please!"

Without another word, Jesse jerked the reins and guided his buggy back onto the road.

"You don't want to know." Will untied the reins from the mesquite. "Get in. It's time to go."

She climbed into the two-seater, feeling as if she no longer stood on solid ground. "I don't understand. What just happened?"

Will hopped in next to her and snapped the reins. "Some things aren't meant to be understood. Let it go."

"I can't."

"Why?"

"He kissed me." Why had she said this to Will, of all people? Because she couldn't hide her feelings from this tall, thin bundle of muscles whose hands were strong and who would never take her to a movie theater and then kiss her in an empty hallway that smelled of stale popcorn and hot dogs. He would do things in the right order and show her how to do the same. She'd never felt more sure of a fact. "I'm sorry."

Will halted the two-seater in the middle of the road. He stared at Jesse's buggy disappearing into the distance. "He shouldn't have done that."

"We shouldn't have done it. I didn't mean for it to happen. It was wrong."

"Nee." Will leaned closer. So close she thought he might touch her. "I've wanted to do nothing else all day."

Leila shrank back on the seat. She'd made this mistake once, not again. "I can't. I'm sorry."

"I wouldn't. Just because a man wants to do such a thing doesn't mean he should." He straightened and snapped the reins again. "Don't be sorry. You're right. Everything in its time."

And this wasn't the time. Not with Jesse still visible in the distance, a tiny shrinking speck on the horizon. Not with the sound of his name still on her lips.

"Our time will come."

Will whispered the words so softly she almost didn't hear them. Yet they sounded as if they were a promise.

CHAPTER 19

Jesse gritted his teeth and tugged on the reins. If he didn't slow the buggy down, he'd end up on his head on the side of the road. He wasn't a child, to throw a tantrum because he didn't get his way. He wanted as far away from Will and Leila and the two-seater as possible. But no amount of distance would relieve him of the image of the two of them, arms entwined, swaying in broad daylight in the thin shade of a mesquite tree in an empty cornfield along a country road. What was Will thinking?

The same thing Jesse had been thinking in that movie theater hallway or out behind the barn at the auction. Not thinking. That was the problem. A man didn't find it easy to think in certain situations. He was finding that out. Feelings drowned out thoughts. It was dangerous. The green snake slithering across his shoulders and down his back belonged to a man who wanted something he couldn't have. To a man who didn't want to see his friends happy if he couldn't be happy too.

Gott, forgive me.

He had no claim on Leila Lantz. One trip to the movies. A kiss. He hadn't even taken her for a ride after that. What must she think of him? Her first kiss stolen by a man who didn't appear to care about how important it was.

His stomach roiled. He pulled off onto the dirt road that led to Phineas's place. They'd all be at Mordecai's for Thanksgiving. He needed wide-open space to burn off the ugliness that enveloped him the second he saw Leila with one hand on his cousin's shoulder, the other clasped in his.

Forcing himself to inhale a deep breath of cool November air, Jesse eased up on the reins and let the buggy slow some more. Had he really expected Leila to sit at home and wait for him to come to his senses?

Nee. Not courting her was the right thing to do. He had to stand firm on that decision. And stop acting like a boy denied the opportunity to hunt on the opening day of deer season.

He eased around a bend in the road, contemplating the future as he did a hundred times a day. Time to concede the truth. Time to give in. He couldn't live a Plain life, not when every fiber of his being ached with a sense of being called. Called to what he wasn't exactly sure. Not yet. But called to something more. Something bigger than himself or his feelings for a woman.

A harsh screech filled the air, deepened, and became a scream. Jesse jerked the reins and stopped. He stood, searching the surrounding area. What was it? The angry sound, much like that of an unhappy, hungry baby, emanated from the other side of a stand of live oaks and nopales. "Who's there?"

Nothing. No one could hear him over that ruckus.

He eased back on the seat, pulled to the side of the road, and stood, craning his head to see over mesquite and scrub brush.

There. Phineas.

Phineas?

Leila's brother-in-law bent over a mesh of netting attached to an old, abandoned chicken coop. Despite the cool air of a fading fall day, he'd shed his jacket on the ground. Exertion and sun had made the thick, ropy scars that marred his face stand out in stark relief against red skin. He didn't look up at the sound of Jesse calling his name. "Phineas! What are you doing?"

"Hang on! I'm rescuing this bird." Phineas made it sound like the most common thing in the world. While his brethren hunted birds, he spent a good part of his free time watching them. For him, this most likely wasn't an unusual occurrence. "He's stuck in this netting and he's not happy about it."

The bird was unlike any Jesse had noticed before, but he wasn't one to notice a bird unless he planned to shoot it and eat it.

Phineas worked at the netting, which apparently had the bird gripped around its neck. The more it struggled, the tighter the noose. "There you go," Phineas cooed, as if singing to a baby in a hoarse voice that had never been the same after his accident. "You're fine. You're fine. Almost there. Got it. Go on, get out of here."

The bird did just that, gone, leaving an impression of a flash of red on its head and a golden-yellow patch on its forehead that stood out against its black-and-white-barred back.

Jesse watched its headlong flight. He longed to join the bird, to get untangled from his predicament. To escape. Not thoughts he could share with a man like Phineas. "Different-looking bird. Kind of pretty like."

Phineas slid a pocketknife into the green canvas knapsack lying on the ground next to his tattered black coat. "Golden-fronted Woodpecker."

Huh. "The ones that make such a racket smacking the chimney in the spring?"

"That would be the one." Phineas raised a hand to his forehead, squinting in the glare of the setting sun. "Only two kinds of woodpeckers in this part of south Texas. The Red-bellied Woodpecker and the Golden-fronted Woodpecker."

That would be Phineas, a fountain of interesting if useless information to Jesse's way of thinking, just like his daed, Mordecai, who knew something about everything, it seemed. "Why are you out here instead of visiting with family?"

"I visited."

That was Phineas, a man of few words. He would do his duty with family, but he preferred the solitude of tending his bees and watching the birds.

"Yeah, me too."

"I don't reckon you're out here bird-watching."

"Nee."

Phineas squatted and picked up his jacket. He frowned and swatted leaves and twigs from the wool. "You know why I started bird-watching?"

It had something to do with the accident that claimed

Phineas's mother's life and left him disfigured. "I reckon it gave you something to do when you were . . ."

"Healing."

"Jah."

"I used to wish I could fly away with the birds. Grow wings and take off. Downright fanciful, ain't it?"

The hard knot in Jesse's chest loosened. "Not so much."

"You learn there's no easy way to escape." He threw his arms out in a flourish, north and south, the coat plopping on the ground. He retrieved it yet again. "You have to decide to walk away."

What did Phineas know? Had Will said something to him? Phineas had never been a rabble-rouser. He'd kept his own counsel, married a woman any one of them would've been glad to call his fraa, and now seemed an example of the obedient contentment every Plain man strived to attain and maintain. "It's a long walk."

"Too far to come back?"

What were they talking about? Jesse chewed the inside of his cheek. "Did someone say something to you?"

"A man has eyes in his head."

"I'm trying to figure some things out, that's all."

Phineas shrugged on his coat and picked up the knapsack. "I wouldn't say no to a ride up to the house."

"You walked all the way down here?"

"Don't see a lot of birds on horseback."

"You're welcome to ride."

Phineas climbed in. Jesse waited for him to settle, then took off. The man next to him whistled in a soft, tuneless way for a few seconds, his hands laced and relaxed in his lap. "So what are you really doing out here?"

Running away from home. Getting his heart broken. Deserved though it might have been, it still hurt worse than having an arm chopped off. "Fresh air."

Phineas chuckled, a hoarse sound more like a cough. "You've never struck me as the fresh-air type."

He liked the outdoors as much as the next farmer. "I intended to see about . . . a girl."

"Ahh."

"Jah."

"Didn't turn out like you expected?"

Jesse snorted.

They rode in silence for a while, the *clip-clop* of the horse's hooves thudding against the dirt. Jesse contemplated the streaks of gold and pink in the clouds, bright against the darkening sky. Phineas had stepped up to be baptized right after his eighteenth birthday. He hadn't hesitated, even after what had happened to him.

The house came into sight. A small, compact structure, newer than the wind-and-sun-battered homes that dotted the land owned by the Plain folks of this settlement for almost twenty-five years. Jesse pulled on the reins and stopped short. Phineas straightened. "I don't mind walking." He put a hand on the running board. "Happy Thanksgiving."

"Wait."

Phineas leaned back, his thick eyebrows raised, the beard he'd started growing a scant year ago bobbing.

He looked so much like Mordecai. "You got something on your mind?"

"Before you were baptized, did you have any . . . thoughts about . . . not doing it?"

Phineas rubbed his hands together and then stuck them under his arms as if to warm them. "Can't say that I did."

"Even after what happened to you?"

"Maybe because of what happened." He stared at the horizon, not meeting Jesse's gaze. He'd never been one to talk about the accident. "I survived."

"Jah, but . . ."

His gaze swung around and met Jesse's head-on. "Maybe a merciful Gott would've let me die?"

"Nee, I didn't mean that."

"I've had a lot of years to come to terms. I'm the man I am because of what happened. Honed by the fire. The thorn in my side will never go away, but Scripture says Gott's power will be made great in my weakness."

"I know."

"You got doubts, you should talk to your daed."

"I can't."

"He's the bishop."

"Exactly."

Phineas cocked his head and pulled the bill of his hat down so the brim shaded his eyes. "What about my daed?"

"I think . . . I've walked down a road and there's no going back."

"There's always a way back."

"I'm not sure I want to come back."

"What is this road?"

"I'm trying to understand some things. Scripture that says we should win the lost and make disciples."

"Evangelism. So this is about the way we practice our faith?"

"I've made some friends."

A look of comprehension spread across Phineas's mangled face. "Englisch friends."

"Jah. They have Bible studies and they meet at the Dairy Queen and talk to people about what they believe. They pray a lot. Aloud. Prayers they make up in their own words."

Phineas studied the horizon, quiet for so long Jesse feared he'd gone too far, revealed too much. The other man hopped from the wagon in a quick motion, turned, and looked up. "Come in. Deborah's still at my daed's. I have a few minutes before I go for her."

"Forget I said anything."

"I'll not forget. Neither will you. What you're talking about is complicated. We believe in the same Gott as your Englisch friends. We take our beliefs from the same Bible. But we live our lives differently and they don't understand why. You don't have to justify our beliefs to them. We're held accountable by Gott, no one else. Come in."

Jesse blew out air. His chest felt tight and his ears rang with Phineas's stern lecture.

For a man of few words, he'd exhausted an enormous supply on Jesse. He slid from the wagon and walked next to the taller man, feeling small and chastised. His feet didn't seem to want to cooperate. He didn't want to choose. He wanted to live in both worlds.

Every Plain man and woman had to make this decision. Why was he any different? Irritated at his own inability to navigate the prickly thicket, all thorns and burrs, that was his mind, he stomped up the steps and held the door for Phineas, who entered without comment.

In a neat, clean kitchen that still harbored the tantalizing aroma of fresh bread and pumpkin pie, Phineas filled a kettle with water and set it on the wood-burning stove. He took two green ceramic mugs from cabinets that had no doors and added a tea bag to each one. "Milk?"

"Nee."

Phineas settled into the chair closest to the stove and rubbed his hands to warm them. "I'm not the thinker my daed is."

"But you understand my . . . situation."

"I'd be lying if I said I don't understand how a person can get turned around, a little cattywampus, when it comes to trying to understand the whys and wherefores of our faith. But don't let those folks keep you from making up your own mind about what you believe."

"We believe the same things, but we don't do things the way they say the Bible says we should."

"It's not for them to interpret Gott's Word for you. Any interpretation should come from our entire congregation, our community, our district. That's why we have the Ordnung and the gmay every year to discuss any possible changes."

"Why don't we pray like they do?"

"We don't try to improve on Gott's Word. Jesus

remained mute in the face of mocking taunts. Silent prayer models His behavior. And He taught us how to pray, gave us the very words we are to use when we pray."

For a guy who wasn't much of a thinker, Phineas knew what he thought.

The words of the Lord's Prayer echoed in the silence around them. Jesse had heard them every morning and every night of his entire life. He'd heard them at Sunday services, weddings, and funerals. The same words over and over. He slapped his hat on the table and ran both hands through his hair. "I've been going to Bible study."

Phineas didn't flinch. He held his hands close to the stove, his expression serene. "And look how divisive it's been for you already. You're questioning your beliefs. You're losing your sense of community, your family. People are giving you their own interpretation and trying to convince you to see it their way. You're being torn apart, not unified with other believers."

That was exactly how Jesse felt. Ripped apart. Torn in two directions.

Phineas stood and poured the hot water into the mugs, covering the tea bags. He handed one to Jesse and nodded toward the table. "Honey's there."

Jesse took his time doctoring the tea, waiting, hoping for words that would knit together what had been ripped asunder. Phineas stirred his tea and stared at the flames leaping behind the open door. "What it comes down to is that our faith is focused more on how we live our lives than on what we believe. We live by example.

We surrender to Gott's will. We believe in discipline and obedience and humility. We don't judge others on how they worship. We hope they'll give us the same leeway."

"I know." Jesse did know, so why was this so hard? "You know what to say, how to answer people's questions. Maybe someday you'll draw the lot."

That he might also draw that lot was not lost on Jesse. Gott's will, Gott's plan. Could he wait until that day? It would only come when his daed or the other men who served as deacon and minister were too old and weak to perform their responsibilities—not a time that Jesse wanted to see come anytime soon.

Colton would say the better question would be, should he wait?

And could he live with the limitations that came with that responsibility?

Phineas's face reddened around the ropy, white scars. He ducked his head. The thought of standing in front of his family and friends and speaking surely terrified him. It would Jesse, and he didn't have a bent nose and dangling ear and scars that split his face forehead to chin. Phineas raised his head and shrugged. "Gott's will be done."

Jesse had heard those words every day of his life as well. He still didn't know how a man knew what God's will was. "This girl . . ."

Phineas's face deepened into a frown. "You steer clear. Until you get yourself straight, you have to steer clear."

"I know."

"It's not right to lead her astray."

"I know."

"Gott's will."

"Gott's plan."

Phineas stood. "I need to fetch my fraa."

Fetch my fraa.

Jesse stood as well, every bone in his body aching with the knowledge that he might never say those words.

CHAPTER 20

Hunting had never been so much fun. Will fought the urge to hum under his breath as he stepped over a fallen mesquite and slogged through underbrush and brown cornstalk stubble. The tune wouldn't scare off the deer, but his father wouldn't cotton to the noise. Especially since the tune sounded a lot like one of the songs to which he and Leila had been dancing on Thanksgiving Day. Definitely not a hymn. In his head, Will still felt as if he were dancing. He'd been dancing for two days now. What an odd thing for a Plain man to think, yet he couldn't help himself. He could still feel the sway of her body and the way one of her small hands gripped his while the other pressed into his shoulder. The look on her face. Delight married to guilty pleasure.

He ducked behind a huge snarl of nopales, sure the grin on his face would give him away. "Straighten up," he muttered.

"You say something?" Daed stalked between the trees, his shotgun at the ready in his hands. "Did you see something?"

"Just talking to myself." Will surveyed the open

field. Not a deer in sight. They'd been tromping across pastures and through stands of straggly trees since dawn and had seen nary a one. "The deer sure are making themselves scarce."

"Yep. With the drought, a lot of them have moved on to look for water."

"We need a deer blind."

"We need to keep moving."

The early-morning chill of a late November day had given way to a bleary sun that hid itself behind dull gray clouds every chance it got. Sweat dampened Will's shirt. His boots felt heavy as bushel baskets of potatoes. "Mind if I take a load off for a minute?" Will tugged his water jug from the strap that held it over his shoulder. "I'm parched."

"You coming down with something?" Daed rubbed at his face with his sleeve, his expression sour. "Your heart doesn't seem to be in this. We need to stock up on venison. Your mudder's waiting to start canning."

Will could've asked Daed the same question. His expression reminded Will of a child who thought he was about to eat vanilla ice cream and instead found himself with a mouthful of sour cream. "I'm fine. Just thirsty." He held the jug out. "You could probably use a swallow yourself."

Daed took the jug and settled himself on the stump that Will had been eyeing upon which to rest his own weary bones. Keeping his grumble to himself, he squatted instead. Daed's gulps were loud in the silence. He wiped his mouth with his sleeve again, then handed the jug back.

"As good a time as any to give you the news." He burped, a prolonged affair that made Will smile at the ground. "I've made a decision. We're moving back to Tennessee."

Will's smile slid into the pit that had just opened in front of him. "When?"

"We're headed home after the new year."

Will had been to Tennessee a dozen times or more to visit family. Usually for a week at a time. He always enjoyed it, but he was always glad to come home. "Home isn't in Tennessee for me. I was born here."

"We can't make ends meet here anymore. We never really have."

"We don't need much." A piece of dirt to farm. A woman to call his fraa. Leila. "We have what we need."

"We have family there, too, folks who will be glad to see us. It won't be much different than it is here, except the ground is meant to be farmed. You'll feel at home." Daed's color darkened under a fading tan. "It's time you settled down. There's more young women there ready to do the same. Slim pickin's here."

"Not so slim." Will straightened and stood. He let the sun, now shining full-on overhead, warm his face. He closed his eyes, but he could still see the light burning through his eyelids. Tennessee might be more fertile and the climate more forgiving, but south Texas had Leila. He couldn't tell Daed about her. "I'm grown now, though, and I reckon this is my home. I'll make my own way."

Daed stood as well. "And I reckoned you might say that, but your family needs you."

"I'm ready to farm my piece of dirt here." He had

roots here. Deep ones. "Sell it to me and I'll make my way on my own."

"If that were the plan, I'd give it to you. You're my son. But your mudder wants her family together in one place."

"Kinner grow up and move on. It's part of life. She'll get used to it."

Daed put a finger to his lips and jerked his head. Will swiveled at the hips, slowly, without moving his feet, just enough to look behind him. A buck meandered through the tall, brown grass on the other side of the dirt road that separated their property from the Planks'. He stopped, lowered his long neck, and munched on a clump of weeds. Will eased into a crouch. His daed lifted the shotgun.

The boom of the gun shattered the silence. The buck jerked, stumbled, went down.

Will knew exactly how the animal felt.

CHAPTER 21

Sometimes babies simply needed a distraction. Leila plopped Duncan into the closest jumper and pushed the button so the animal sounds of monkeys and elephants would play and lights flash yellow and green. The toddler reached both chubby hands for the red parrot dangling in front of him. He crowed and giggled. A second before, he'd been inconsolable over his empty bottle. Leila couldn't help giggling with him. "You are such a cutie, little chunky cheeks."

"Hey, you'll scar him for life if you tell him he's fat." Rory strolled into the room, Trevor on one hip, toddler Sophia Cramer on the other. "You'll give him a complex."

"What are you talking about?" Leila picked up Alyssa, who had a smell wafting from her behind that overpowered. A diaper change was in order. "His chunky cheeks are adorable, and I love Alyssa's thunder thighs."

"You do now. But just wait, she's not going to want thunder thighs when she's in high school and headed to cheerleader tryouts."

Having seen the skimpy cheerleader outfits worn by the high school girls, Leila hoped Alyssa chose choir or the school newspaper instead for her extracurricular activities. "She'll run off the baby fat when she starts walking."

"I can't wait until Trevor starts walking."

"You'll have to race to keep up." Leila laid Alyssa on the changing table and tugged a diaper from the basket with the baby's name on it. Alyssa cooed and grabbed her foot, tugging it to her mouth. "You'll chew on anything, won't you, bopli?"

She glanced back at Rory, who bounced the two babies on her hips as adept as any older woman. "Why aren't you in Miss Rachel's room, helping her?"

"I just came to tell you that Daddy called. He picked up a second shift, filling in for some guy who went home sick, so he can't pick us up."

"How are we getting home?"

"I called Dwayne. He's headed this way as soon as wrestling practice is over."

Leila mulled over this information. Mudder wouldn't be happy to see her show up in Dwayne's rust-decorated pickup truck with its big rumbling engine, but what could she do? Spend the night at the day care? "Okay, but we have to go straight home."

"Sure, sure. No problem." Rory adjusted Trevor on her hip, her tone airy. "Sawyer is taking the bus home from school and Daddy doesn't want him at the house by himself too long."

The day care didn't close until six thirty. Sawyer got out of school at three and the bus ride took at least an hour. He was at the house alone every day for a couple of hours. But he was ten, plenty old enough in the Plain way of thinking. "See you out front in half an hour."

By the time she cleaned the room and handed off her charges to their parents, Leila felt as frazzled as they looked. She loved taking care of babies, but it was a nonstop proposition. Her arms ached and the muscles in her shoulders were tied up in knots. The late fall sky had turned dark. Another day and she'd missed the sunshine.

She pushed through the front door and sure enough, Dwayne's primer-gray, fumes-spewing pickup rumbled at the curb. Rory had beat her to the punch. She sat in the front seat, close enough to be in her husband's lap. Trevor's car seat was wedged into the backseat of the extended cab. Suppressing a sigh, Leila squeezed in next to it, the other side being taken up with a gym bag, a pile of books, half a dozen greasy, stinky fast-food bags, and a variety of mismatched sneakers that reeked of boy feet.

"Hey, Leila." Dwayne gave her a half salute under hair still wet from a shower, his usual semi-amused stare greeting her in the rearview mirror. "What's shaking?"

"Not much."

He pulled away from the curb with a jerk, tires squealing. The driver of a minivan laid on his horn, the sound adding to Leila's throbbing headache. Dwayne saluted the man with a different finger than the one he'd used with Leila. She swiveled and glued her gaze to the passing scenery, trying not to inhale the odor of stale French fries and old hamburger.

A couple of turns later and she knew one thing for certain—two things—Dwayne drove with reckless abandon despite having his baby son in the truck, and they weren't headed out of town on Highway 59. "Where are we going?"

"Just a little detour. Don't you worry, it'll be fun."

She didn't want fun. She wanted supper and bed. "I have to get home and help clean up after supper."

"All work and no play makes a girl a sad sack."

He grinned at her in the rearview mirror, his teeth white and his cheeks dimpled. She could see the resemblance to Trevor, even though the baby had Rory's curly brown hair and eyes the color of milk chocolate, whereas his daddy had sandy-blond hair and green eyes. "I like work."

He chuckled and swerved to avoid a pothole. The force sent Leila against Trevor's car seat. He began to fuss.

"Hush, little guy," Dwayne hollered. "We're almost there."

Trevor's fuss turned to an outright cry. "Shhh, shush, shush." Leila patted his cheek and dangled a pacifier over him. Trevor's fat little hands grasped at it and a second later he quieted, except for the *thwack-thwack* of the pacifier in his mouth.

"There" turned out to be a park. Leila liked parks just fine, when it wasn't cold and dark and her stomach growling for its supper. "Rory—"

"Just for a few minutes, Leila, please. I never get to spend time with Dwayne during the week." Rory already had her door open. "Please, pretty please with sugar on top of it."

She didn't wait for Leila's answer. She popped from the truck and ran across the dried, brown grass to the lone swing set illuminated by tall streetlights, leaving Leila to deal with getting Trevor from his car seat. With the truck door open, a gust of cool, damp night air wafted through the car, making Leila shiver.

"Let's go, sweet pea." She unsnapped the straps and tugged his chubby arms out. Rory hadn't thought to put his jacket on him before taking him from the day care. Leila rummaged in the diaper bag stuck on top of the pile of books until she found his coat. "Just for a little bit, and then I'll convince your mommy to go home. I'll steal her cell phone if I have to. Your granddaddy will set her straight."

Hopefully it wouldn't come to that. She lugged Trevor across the grass and settled into a swing. The baby crowed with laughter when she pushed off and sent them sailing through the air. She liked to swing too. Except when she was cold and tired and hungry.

Rory and Dwayne seemed to be engaged in a game of hide-and-seek. Rory ran from tree to tree, pretending to hide behind fat trunks while Dwayne danced around on the other side. When he pulled her out into the open, she collapsed to the ground and he followed suit. They rolled around, giggling and snuggling as if they weren't in the middle of a city park on a cool autumn day that had already turned to night in the middle of Beeville, Texas.

"Your parents are a little strange," she told Trevor as she tightened her grip on his roly-poly body and pushed back from the ground to reach new heights. Then again, she was a grown woman enjoying herself—she could admit that—by swinging. "I reckon they're allowed to act silly now and again."

Most folks did. Like her and Will with their dancing in broad daylight. Or her and Jesse, kissing in a movie theater hallway.

Will or Jesse. Will or Jesse. The refrain echoed in her head in time to the squeak of the swing's long chains. *Up and down. Up and down. Squeak, squeak. Will or Jesse. Will or Jesse.* Will with his blond hair and blue eyes and broad shoulders and his simple, straightforward approach to life. Or Jesse with his stocky body and barrel-shaped chest and curly black hair and brown eyes. Jesse with his strange disappearing acts and his sad face when he thought she wasn't looking. So different.

How could she like them both? Will tried so hard to do the right thing, while Jesse couldn't seem to make up his mind what the right thing was. Something about his ferocious gaze had embedded itself in her heart. It wasn't the kiss. The intensity of his questioning gaze held her pinned to a wall of emotion. He wanted something from her, but she had no idea what it was. Will might give her what she needed, but Jesse might give her what she wanted.

Stop. Stop. Stop. The squeaking of the swing chains kept time to the refrain in her head. *Stop. Stop. Stop.*

She needed to do the right thing, even if Jesse couldn't. *Gott, forgive me. Gott, help me keep my eyes on You. Gott, Thy will be done.*

So easy to pray. So hard to do.

Mordecai said once during evening prayers that sometimes faith was an act of will. She hadn't understood then. She did now.

Will could help her do the right thing. Maybe Gott had planted this man in her path to help her do what was right. He wanted to help her. He'd made that obvious.

Doing the right thing surely didn't involve hanging out in the park instead of getting herself home. She didn't need anyone's help to know that. She slowed the swing, digging her heels in the dirt where the grass had worn away under the sneakers of a steady stream of carefree children.

"Time to go," she yelled as she strode toward the couple. Now they were involved in a kiss the likes of which she'd never seen. Right there in front of her. "Rory, time to go. Sawyer's home all by himself and it's way past dark."

Dwayne threw himself back on the grass, gasping for air. "Can't go yet."

"Why not?"

"Friends coming."

His long arm wrapped around Rory and pulled her against his chest. She giggled harder and buried her head in his jean jacket.

"Rory!"

A car painted the color of pickled beets pulled in behind Dwayne's truck. The doors flew open before the engine died and a jumble of people exited. All boys with leather jackets that featured big fuzzy *B*s on the back and little medals pinned to the front.

"They're here. They're here." Dwayne sat up, bringing Rory with him. "Dude, did you bring the stuff?"

Apparently *dude* referred to a specific guy in the group of half a dozen boys. The one with red hair and pale skin covered with freckles produced a brown paper sack with a bottle neck sticking out the top. "Straight from my daddy's liquor cabinet."

"Yee-haw."

Rory slapped her husband's arm hard, then added a second whack for emphasis. "Dwayne Chapman, you know better. You can't drink and drive. Not with our precious little bundle of joy in the car."

Dwayne scowled. "I suppose you're right. You could drive and then I could—"

"Daddy will have my hide if I drive after that last accident. He took my license."

"How 'bout you, Amish girl?" Dwayne dangled the keys on a bottle opener key chain in the air. "Wanna drive us home after we have some fun?"

His idea of fun didn't jibe with Leila's. "Amish folks don't drive cars."

"Right. I knew that." Dwayne flopped his base-ball cap on the ground. "This being a daddy is no fun sometimes."

"Well, excuse me, you think it's so much fun for me, changing diapers and getting up to feed him every three hours?" Rory hauled herself to her feet and dusted leaves from her jeans. "And then getting up to go to school and then to work and then do homework. Guys have got it easy."

"No fair. If we lived together, I'd get up with him."

Leila didn't bother to try to get a word in edgewise. At least Rory had the good sense to know better than to let Dwayne drink and drive. Rory took off, Dwayne in close pursuit. His friends invaded the swings and the monkey bars, hooting and hollering like a bunch of first graders. She chewed her lip, eyeing them. *What now?* She shivered. The night air had taken on a sharp chill.

"Hey, who are you?"

Leila forced her gaze from the teenage boys acting like children loose at a rodeo carnival. A tall, thin guy wearing a cowboy hat, skintight, faded jeans, and well-worn, scuffed cowboy boots plopped down on the merry-go-round. He had dark, kaffi-colored eyes and the wispy beginnings of a beard. She forced a smile. "A friend of Rory's."

"I'm Shawn. A friend of Dwayne's. And Rory's. We have that in common, I reckon." He shoved his cowboy hat back, revealing dark brown curls that dangled just above his eyebrows. "How do you know Rory?"

"She buys honey at our store sometimes, and now we work at the day care together."

He tickled Trevor's cheek and smiled at the baby's gurgling attempt at conversation. "I can't imagine having a baby right now." His gaze traveled to Rory, still jawing at Dwayne, hands flailing to make her point. "I mean, I still have geography tests and book reports, you know?"

"I know."

"Could I hold him for a second?"

Leila contemplated Shawn's face. He reminded her of Caleb, even though he was much older. "Have you ever held a baby?"

"Sure, I got cousins and a nephew." He held out his hands and wiggled his fingers. "I know what I'm doing."

She handed Trevor over. "Support his back—"

"I know, I know." He held Trevor up to eye level. "What's up, dude?"

Trevor spit up, liquid running down his chin and onto the front of his jacket and Shawn's hand.

"Dude!"

Leila wanted to laugh at the horrified look on his face. "It's just milk."

"Warm, regurgitated milk!" He held the baby up, legs and arms dangling. "All yours."

She pulled a burp rag from Trevor's diaper bag and wiped him down. "You said you were an expert."

"No, I didn't." He laughed, a deep chortle that made Leila want to laugh too. He plopped Trevor into her lap. "All I know about babies is they poop, eat, sleep, and cry."

"Yep."

"You have any babies?"

"I'm not married."

"Well that doesn't mean anything these days."

"It does to me."

"Good for you." He tugged a red bandanna from his hip pocket and applied diligent elbow grease to the thick puddle of spit-up white against his jeans. "Can I give you a ride somewhere? You look cold and it's getting dark."

She was cold, it was getting dark, and the way Trevor kept rubbing his eyes and fussing told Leila he was as tired as she was. "That would be nice, but I can't leave Trevor."

"His momma's right over there."

They turned in unison to look at Trevor's parents. Dwayne had Rory pinned against the bright-yellow plastic slide, his long legs covering hers. Apparently the apology had been accepted and followed by the usual kiss-and-make-up routine. "I think they're gonna be awhile." A few bars of a country music song wafted in the air. Shawn tugged a slim cell phone from his front pocket, frowned at something, and shoved it back in his jeans. "My mom's looking for me. She's got supper on the table. Let me take you home. I have to go anyway."

By the time he drove all the way out to Mordecai's, his supper would be cold and his momma mad. Trevor's whiny fuss turned into an outright cry. Leila snuggled him to her chest and began to rock. "Sorry, little one, sorry." She shook her head. "You go on. Your supper's waiting and I'm not leaving Trevor."

"You're a good friend to watch out for Rory's baby." Shawn cocked his head, studying her with a surprisingly serious expression. Leila was reminded that a person should never judge another by appearance. "I reckon having a baby doesn't make a person a grown-up."

Leila glanced back at Rory and Dwayne. The lip-lock continued. How did they breathe? "Making babies has nothing to do with being a good parent."

"At least get in my car. It has a good heater. You and Trevor can keep warm until they cool off. I also have an excellent sound system. What kind of music do you like?"

Shawn didn't know much about Plain folks, that was obvious. "I like . . . church music and country music some. But it doesn't matter. I don't want your supper to get cold."

"I'll warm it up in the microwave. I like country music. I've got Lee Brice and Blake Shelton and Jason Aldean on my iPod. Come on, I promise to be a gentleman—"

A horn cut the air in a long, fierce blare. Leila whirled. Colton's silver Impala pulled up to the curb, Jesse hanging out the window. "Leila! What are you doing here?"

"I have to go." She stumbled away from Shawn, her heart hammering in her chest. "It was . . . nice to meet you."

"I thought y'all drove buggies." Shawn followed after her, his long legs eating up the ground. "You'll take a ride from somebody who just randomly pulls up?"

"Friend of a friend," she hollered without looking back. "Thanks for the offer, but I'm fine now. I promise."

He halted, his expression confused, hands on his hips. "Take care then."

"You too." Trevor clasped tight to her side, she scurried across the grass to Colton's car. "What are you doing here?"

"That's the question I asked you." Jesse's jaw worked. His face had that same expression it had on Thanksgiving Day when he'd driven up on Will and her. How dare he look hurt? "Who's that guy you were talking to?"

Once again, what right did he have to ask? "A friend of Rory's. Why are you here?"

"We were on our way to . . . Colton happened to notice you. We were just driving by."

A dull shade of red crept across his face. "We'll take you home, okay?"

Colton revved the engine, then let up. "We don't have time to go out to her farm and still get back in time for—"

"She shouldn't be here with these guys," Jesse cut in, his tone brusque. "I'm not leaving her here."

She didn't want to stay, but she didn't need Jesse to tell her right from wrong. He hardly knew himself. Who was he to judge her? Trevor's warm weight against her hip and side reminded her that she wasn't the only one stuck. "I can't leave the baby."

"He's not your baby." Jesse blew out air, inhaled. The fierce emotion etched across his face seemed to abate. "His mother should take responsibility. Take the baby to her."

He was as bad as Will about telling her what to do. They didn't have a right. Neither one of them. Not yet. Maybe never.

Colton shoved open his door. "I'll help."

He took Trevor from her arms and together they trudged to the slide. Dwayne and Rory stood on the top step. She waved, hooted, and together they whipped down it on their behinds, a single unit. "Wahoo!" she screamed and laughed. "You gotta do this, Leila, it's fun. Hey, Colton, what are you doing here?"

So they knew each other. Of course, from school. "I have to go now. Colton will give me a ride. You should get Trevor home. It's time for his bath and bed. And Sawyer's waiting."

Rory wrinkled her nose, her gaze on Colton. "How do you two know each other?"

"Colton's the one who took Jesse and me to the movies that time I told you about."

Rory picked herself up from where she'd landed at the bottom of the slide and brushed off her hands. "I wish you'd told me, girl. Colton is famous."

"Not famous." Colton didn't seem fazed by her teasing tone. "Committed to standing on solid ground is all."

"Don't you know, Leila, he's a Jesus freak? He's always trying to convert people," Dwayne chimed in, his tone exaggerated with false friendliness. "Careful, he'll convert you."

"Hey, be nice." Rory smacked Dwayne's shoulder with the back of one hand. "To each their own."

"I don't need to be converted." Leila wasn't sure exactly what they meant, but she wouldn't allow her faith to be questioned. "I know Jesus."

More than Rory and Dwayne did. The thought made her sad.

Colton's expression mirrored her feelings. He stuck his hands in the pockets of his faded jeans and shrugged. "Good for you, Leila. I want everyone to have the chance to know Jesus, that's all. I imagine you do too." He took a step toward Rory and Dwayne. "Y'all are welcome to stop by youth group any Wednesday. You know where Tiffany's house is, right?"

Dwayne snorted, but Rory smacked him again before he could speak. "Thanks for the invite, but with a baby and school and work, my schedule is full up every night, including Wednesdays."

Wednesday nights. Will had told her to ask Jesse where he went on Wednesday nights. Leila glanced back at Colton's car. Jesse sat in the front seat, his expression bleak and distant. "Take Trevor home, please, Rory. I don't feel good about leaving him if you won't promise you'll get him home right away."

"Don't you worry about him. I got my baby." Rory tugged on Trevor, whose little fists gripped Leila's apron straps. The baby squawked and let go, his arms flailing. "Come on, little man, come to Momma. We're going now."

"We are?" Dwayne pulled his Texas Rangers ball cap down over his face and leaned back against the slide. "What if I'm not ready yet?"

"Cowboy up, buddy." Rory kicked his leg with the point of her red boot. "Move it. Sawyer will call Dad and complain for sure."

As soon as she was certain Rory would actually get in the truck and take her son home, Leila started toward Colton's car. Something like shame swept over her. Colton had gone out of his way to help her, and Dwayne had insulted him over something he obviously didn't understand. She should've stood up for him more. "I'm sorry Dwayne talked to you that way."

"It's okay. I'm used to hecklers."

"Why do you do it then?"

He opened the car door for her with a tiny flourish. "Because I have the truth."

Colton had the truth. Did Jesse think he had the truth? Did Leila have the truth? If she did, why didn't she tell Rory, a friend so obviously lost and in need of such a powerful truth?

Leila plopped into the backseat and leaned forward so her words would reach Jesse's ear only. "It's Wednesday night. Where are you going?"

CHAPTER 22

Maybe Gott didn't intend for men to understand women. Or vice versa. Jesse tugged open the car door and bent down to look at Leila. She sat bolt upright, back stiff, in the backseat. Her frown said it all. She didn't have any right to be peeved at him. He hadn't been cavorting in a park with a bunch of Englisch teenagers. Most likely they'd been drinking, knowing that crowd. It struck him as ironic that he would be criticized for the company he kept when his circle of Englisch friends walked the walk when it came to being Christians. They didn't drink or do drugs or have wild parties. They liked Bible studies, softball games, and movie nights. They had paintball parties or went hunting for fun.

"Where are you going?"

Her question reverberated in his ears the entire length of the drive from the park to Tiffany's house. No more than a mile, but it seemed to last an eternity. Colton had made small talk, but Leila didn't bite, and neither did Jesse. The electricity in the air crackled and popped until even Colton looked uncomfortable, and nothing fazed that guy.

Jesse hadn't answered her question because he

couldn't. He didn't know. He could show her this place, he could show her his Wednesday nights, the road he now traversed. No turning back. The choice he had to make. No, it wasn't a choice. Not really. It was a calling that he couldn't ignore.

"What are you looking at?" She stared up at him, her face full of concern. She didn't look mad. She looked sad and confused and nothing like the girl he'd kissed in the hallway at the theater. She looked scared. "What are we doing here?"

"You want to know what I do on Wednesday nights; I'm showing you." He didn't finish the sentence aloud. *I'm trusting you.* "I'm answering your question."

He couldn't keep pretending. If he wanted her in his life, she had to know. She had to decide. She would be the one Plain person, aside from Will, who knew what Jesse faced. She might even understand, if God blessed him to such a great extent. She hadn't moved. Her frown melted into a puzzled look. "Are you sure?"

She knew this was important.

"I want you to know because it explains how I've treated you." He kicked at a scraggly weed sticking up in the crack in the sidewalk. "I know it's confusing. But it's not you. It's me."

"Where are we?"

"This is Tiffany's house."

"You come to Tiffany's house on Wednesday night. Why?"

"Come in and you'll see."

He stepped back. She slid from the seat and slipped past him. Colton pounded up the steps ahead of them.

She followed without looking back. With each step, the strap around Jesse's chest tightened. What if she told Mordecai? What if she told his daed? Was he ready to tell them about this?

Colton held the door for them. "Head into the family room. I'll get Pastor Dave."

His throat dry, tongue stuck to the roof of his mouth, Jesse nodded and tried to swallow as he turned to Leila. He cleared his throat. "This way."

"Who's Pastor Dave?"

"The youth minister from Tiffany and Colton's church."

"Youth minister—"

"Just follow me, okay?"

He led her to the family room where Tiffany and her sisters had shoved back a sofa covered with crocheted blankets and arranged folding chairs in a large circle on a tattered carpet in need of cleaning. Card tables lined one wall under shelves covered with family photos. One table featured sodas, bottled water, cookies, brownies, rice crispy treats, and other snacks that made his stomach rumble despite its queasiness. He hadn't been home for the noon meal, and the corn mush, eggs, and toast he had for breakfast were long gone. They'd loaded another table with flyers about mission trips, brochures, devotionals, and Bibles available for the taking. In one corner, some of the guys tuned electric guitars and checked a portable sound system.

"What is all this?" Leila's voice shrank to a whisper. "Is this some kind of meeting?"

"It's their Wednesday night youth group."

Their youth group. His group. After three months, he could not deny he felt a part of this group. They made him feel at home, not like an outcast. They teased him about his suspenders and his straw hat and his haircut, but they also listened to him and offered kind words of encouragement. They included him in their pranks and asked his opinion about their own quandaries.

They were his friends.

He followed Leila's gaze as it traveled to a cluster of girls sitting cross-legged on the floor making posters. Tiffany looked up, grinned, and waved. She had glitter on her nose and a slash of neon marker above lips bright with pink lipstick. "Look who's here! Glad y'all could make it." She popped up like a jack-in-the-box and padded toward them in feet clad in pink polka-dotted slippers. "You finally had the guts to ask Leila, that's so great. I'm totally psyched!"

"She was at the park and she needed a ride." The words sounded lame in Jesse's ears, like he didn't really want Leila here. He did want her here. Dread tightened in a noose around his throat. "I'm hoping she'll see her way clear to stay for a while."

"I don't know." Spots of red darkened Leila's cheeks. "No offense to you, Tiffany, but I don't think I'm supposed to be here. I don't think Jesse is either."

"You're gonna love it. Oh, there's Samantha. She hasn't been here in forever. Grab a brownie and have a seat. Music starts in five." Tiffany catapulted past them toward the door where a girl, presumably Samantha, stood looking equally as uncertain as Leila did.

Quelling the urge to hurl, Jesse pointed to the first

chair. "Like she said, have a seat. They'll get started any minute."

Leila shook her head and leaned close. "Get started with what?"

"Give them a chance."

"A chance to do what?" Suppressed anger made her blue eyes spark. She looked pretty. Jesse dropped his gaze to the carpet that sparkled with the flotsam and jetsam of glitter from meetings gone by. Leila's voice rose slightly. "This is wrong. It feels wrong."

"Not to me. They sing songs. They talk to each other about Scripture. They pray. And then they go talk to other people about Jesus."

It felt right to him.

"They talk to people about Jesus." Her voice had softened. "To strangers?"

He raised his head and nodded.

Her eyebrows rose and her mouth closed.

"People do that, you know?"

"Have you?"

"No. Not yet. I'm too tongue-tied." He couldn't tell her how sometimes the words burbled up in him and threatened to spill out in a mumble jumble of the sheer joy of knowing God loved him. Even him. Jesus died for him. To save him.

Why, he couldn't imagine. Most days he didn't feel worthy of being a speck of dirt. Then he came to these meetings and he felt awash in love. What Pastor Dave called *agape* love. Brotherly love. He could hold his head up because he was a child of God along with all these other children.

His gaze met Leila's. She cocked her head, her expression quizzical.

"What?"

"You look happy. I've never seen you looking so happy."

"I guess I am." He let his gaze wander to Tiffany, talking Samantha's ear off while trying to foist a brownie on her. Jack and Ricky tuning their guitars. Alison throwing popcorn at poor Luke, on whom she had an obvious crush. They were good kids who liked Jesus and liked talking about Him. How could it be wrong? "I think maybe you could be happy too."

She shook her head. "You think I don't understand what this means? I do understand."

"Just hear them out. For one hour. Just one hour."

After a long moment in which he contemplated spending the rest of his life alone, she sank into the chair and clasped her hands in her lap. "One hour. Then you promise to take me home?"

"Promise."

She clasped her canvas bag in her lap as if someone might steal it. "Okay, but you have to sit with me."

He sank into the chair next to her, sure his legs were about to give way. She hadn't run from the room screaming. "Gladly."

. . .

Leila's hands were slick in her lap. The others clapped and sang at the top of their lungs. What they lacked in musical talent, they made up for in volume. When she'd asked Jesse to bring her, she'd been so sure she could handle it. Jesse's truth. She tried to focus on the lyrics, but Jesse's presence next to her threatened to consume her every thought. The intensity of his desire for her to understand and accept his friends and what they were doing confounded her. In this living room with its shabby couch and recliner and mismatched coffee tables, he looked different. He looked like his friends. He hadn't changed his clothes and he still wore his hat, but he sounded like them when he talked. He had an assurance about him that made him all the more appealing.

For these few moments, he seemed at peace.

In the almost two years she'd been in Bee County, she'd never seen Jesse Glick at peace. In perpetual motion, yes, as if chased by wolves or his own thoughts. Now, in this room, the motion had stopped and a content man sat next to her. He sang with his shoulders thrust back, head held high, smiling. He had a nice baritone and he knew all the words. He tossed her a tentative grin and sang louder.

She sank deeper into the chair, aware of all the eyes watching her, full of curiosity, full of something else. They wanted something from her. They wanted her.

The music died away. Every head bowed. They began to take hands, all around the circle, without hesitation or embarrassment. Girls held hands with boys. Jesse's hand came out. Leila stared at it, then up at him. "It's okay. I promise."

She dashed her palms on her apron and took his offering. His hand felt cool in hers. On the other side, a girl with a diamond stud in her nose and a tattoo of a pink rose on her neck offered a hand. Leila took it. Her fingers were sticky with rice crispy treats.

Leila squeezed her eyes shut and prayed that nothing else would be required of her.

Pastor Dave, who'd turned out to be a mountain of a black man dressed in faded jeans and a white T-shirt that stretched across a broad, muscled chest, had a deep voice with a soft Southern cadence. "Lord, I pray for these young folks, that You would guide them and keep them safe and lead them in Your ways. That Your will be done in their lives. Show them what You would have them do and where You would have them go and what Your plans are for them. Each one of them. Lord, I pray for Jesse, who has decisions to make that will affect his family and his life. It's a rocky road ahead for this young man . . . and for the people he loves . . ."

Leila didn't hear the words after that. Jesse's hand tightened around hers. She tried to jerk away, but he refused to release her. She stood. He followed suit. Everyone looked up, looked at her, at them. "I'm sorry. I'm sorry."

She pulled away from Jesse. He let go, the peace of a few seconds before slipping from his face. She stumbled from the room, through the foyer, and out the front door. The clear, cold night air greeted her. She gulped it down, like a baby starved for her mother's milk.

"Leila. Leila!" Jesse stormed onto the porch and let the screen door slam behind him. "Don't go."

"I'm going home if I have to walk."

"You said you'd give it an hour."

"You didn't tell me you're leaving us. You're leaving

your community." To her horror, tears made her voice crack. She swallowed against them and cleared her throat. "Leaving me."

"I haven't committed."

"But you've talked to Pastor Dave about it."

"I have."

"Why?"

Jesse sank onto the step and patted the spot next to him. "I want to try to explain, but you have to hear me out."

She debated, her head telling her to *go, go, go. Get away*. Her heart demanded she *stay, stay, stay*.

She couldn't drive herself.

Face burning, heart pounding, she plopped down next to him, leaving a gap the size of Caleb between them. "Make it snappy. Mudder will be worried about me."

"Snappy?"

"That's what my boss says at the day care. I have to go home."

"This isn't easy."

"I reckon not. Why would you do this to us?"

To me?

"To know more, to be closer to God, to be able to pray the way I want and talk to people the way I want." He slapped his big hand across his barrel chest. "I feel something here that I don't when I'm at our services. Don't you?"

"I feel . . . different. I feel like I don't belong." She contemplated her hands in her lap, trying to identify feelings that hurled themselves about and then collapsed into a jumbled heap. "I feel far from home."

Too far and getting farther all the time. She stood. "I want to go home. You said you'd take me home."

He stared at her, his dark eyes mournful. "You don't feel it?"

Leila had felt . . . something big and warm and welcoming, but it couldn't matter. If she let it matter, everything would change. Her whole life would change, and in that change came loss. Terrible loss. Her bones ached at the thought. Her skin burned with fever. She shivered. "Come home. Talk to Mordecai. He can help you figure this out. It's not too late."

"I already talked to Phineas."

Phineas might not have his father's way with words, but he had a certain calm to him that Leila had always liked. "And it didn't help?"

"What we believe isn't different. Can't you see?" He slid closer to her and put his hand over hers. His fingers were so strong. The ache subsided. A warmth spread that overcame the chill. He leaned in so his shoulder touched hers. "It's how we practice our faith that's different. I want to shout about Jesus from the rooftops. I think I may be a minister someday."

She wanted to pull away, but somehow she couldn't. Their fingers were entwined, the bond tangible and physical. She could see him standing in front of the room sharing the Word with her family and friends, his family and friends. It could happen, but not because he wanted it to be so, only if God decided. "If you draw the lot."

"I don't believe I have to wait for that. I believe I'm being called."

The ache returned. She peeled her fingers from his. "Gott chose your father when he drew the lot. It could be the same for you. It's up to Gott."

"My father has done God's will all these years. He's done right by his responsibilities. I believe I can do the same. I don't have to wait for some sort of holy slot to open up. Sometimes God speaks to us directly."

"That's so prideful."

"In your way of thinking."

"In our way of thinking. It's yours too. Humility. Obedience. Jesus first, others second, you third."

Jesse captured her hand again and rubbed his fingers over her knuckles. Heat shot up her spine and spread across her neck. She couldn't breathe. *Breathe. In and out.* "I won't try to convince you, even though I know I'm right, because I would never take you from your family. I don't have to save you. We believe the same things. Plain people are godly people. So are these folks. They just want to share the good news of Jesus Christ with people who are lost. Do you understand?"

She closed her eyes and concentrated on the feel of his fingers on hers. She felt at peace when she sat on the bench on Sunday morning with Mudder and Esther and Susan and Deborah and Rebekah and little Hazel. She felt at peace when they sang those long, slow hymns and Leroy spoke the Word. She felt at peace when they said the Lord's Prayer as she had done every day twice a day as long as she could remember.

The feelings she had here and now on this porch with Jesse holding her hand, these feelings were real too. And powerful. They rocked her to the bone. She felt alive. She felt Gott's presence all around her. So close. So inviting. *Gott, forgive me.* How could she want both? "I don't understand anything. Come home and talk to Mordecai. Please."

Jesse's hand dropped and the cold closed in around her. He leaned in until his lips brushed her cheek, soft, soft, so softly. "I will, but not tonight."

"You can't do that. Please don't do that." She backed away, trying to put a physical space between them. It didn't help. The bond forged between them held, as if their hands still touched, as if his lips still warmed her cheek. He didn't play fair. "It's not right."

"I can't help it." He shrugged, his smile bittersweet. "I think about kissing you all the time."

"You want this too." She waved toward the house. "You throw this at me and then ask me to choose you."

"Not just me. Don't just choose me. Choose to believe in what we're doing here. I've watched you. You feel your faith deeply. It's personal to you too. You want to help. You want to share your faith. I can tell." His hands reached for hers. She drew away. He stared at her, his gaze fierce and imploring. "I never meant to put you in this position. I saw you at the park with that guy, and I realized I might not have the chance to tell you the truth and ask you—"

"That guy was a friend of Dwayne's who was concerned about the baby being cold. He was kind. That's all. A kind person."

"Okay, so I overreacted." Jesse clutched his hands together in his lap, his knuckles white. "I'm the kind of person who has strong feelings about a lot of things."

That, they had in common. "About me?"

"About you. About my faith in God. I think you do too."

She'd always felt God's presence in her life, but never more so than when her father died and they'd moved to south Texas to start a new life. Every step of the way He'd held her hand as surely as Daed had when she'd learned to walk as a toddler. But this was something entirely different. The consequences too enormous to contemplate. She would drown in them. "I can't. It's too much."

"At least give it time. Think about it. Listen to what they have to say. Before you turn your back on me and choose another."

"I told you. I only just met the boy at the park. I don't even know him."

"But if it's not him, it'll be Will."

He made it a statement, not a question. Leila closed her eyes, the image of Will's face floating in front of her as he put one hand on her waist and clasped her hand with the other. The dancing had been about this. Will knew about this. He thought he had to compete.

No one had to compete. She had to choose what her life would be. "I should go."

Jesse's Adam's apple bobbed. "Are you sure?"

"You said you'd never take me away from my family."

His gaze dropped to his big hands now limp in his lap. "And I won't." His gaze lifted to her face. "If that's what you choose."

Swallowing hard against hot tears that burned her throat, Leila edged away from him. "How will I get home?"

"I'll take you." Colton stood in the doorway, car keys dangling from his hand. How long had he been there? "Jesse promised you a ride home. We won't abandon you."

So why did she feel so lost?

CHAPTER 23

A propane pole lamp blazed in the front window, signaling to Leila that she must tread carefully in all things. No chance of slipping in unnoticed.

She inched the car door forward until it closed with a soft click. She didn't respond to Jesse's good-bye. She couldn't. She had no words left to say to him. They'd been silent on the ride home from Tiffany's, yet her ears rang with the raucous argument that raged in her head the entire way. She wanted to slap her hands to her ears and block out all sound, all thought, all memory of Jesse's hands and his lips. Everything about him. Pain ripped through her heart at the thought of never feeling his touch again.

What is the right thing, Gott? I'm only a simple woman. How do I know?

No answer floated down to her from on high, no matter how she strained to hear.

She should be thinking about what awaited her in the house and not the way Jesse's gaze sent heat spiraling through her from head to toes. Her hopes that she could postpone any confrontation with Mudder until morning had disappeared when Colton pulled his car onto the dirt road in front of Mordecai's house. Folks were still up. They should be in bed by now. Instead she would have to greet them and explain why she was so late getting home from work. Why she arrived home in Colton's car, Jesse in the front seat.

She pushed open the screen door and let out a gusty sigh. How did she explain her day to Mordecai? Or worse, her mother?

"You're home." Mudder stood in the doorway to the kitchen, her face glowing with a sweaty sheen. She clutched a pile of towels to her chest. "I was about to send Caleb to the Beales' to track you down." She smiled despite the irk in her words.

"What is it?" Leila dropped the cooler and her canvas bag on the braided rug. "Did something happen?"

"The baby's coming."

"The baby? The baby! It's early, isn't it?" Because she'd been gallivanting about in town, she'd almost missed it. The birth of her sister's first child. Leila bolted toward the stairs. A scream echoed from above. "Oh, Deborah, I'm coming."

"She's been at it for hours." Mudder scurried after her, her bare feet close on Leila's heels. "It's about time for her to push."

"Where's Phineas?"

"Out back. I reckon he couldn't stand the screaming."

Leila raced down the hallway, slung open her bedroom door, and barreled through. Deborah lay on the bed, her chest heaving, her face covered with sweat and tears. "Leila, Leila, help me. I have to get this baby out."

Sobs punctuated the words. "I'm trying to be brave, but it feels like it's breaking me in two."

"You're fine, child." Mudder's tone was the calm one Leila remembered from childhood bouts with fever, chicken pox, and influenza. "I've had five babies and it always feels like that toward the end. It means you're almost done."

Leila squeezed between Rebekah, who stood wringing her hands, and Esther, who held a load of dirty towels in her arms. She had the bemused look on her face of a girl who was watching her own future unfold. Unlike Leila, she would soon marry the man she loved, have babies, and settle down in her Plain life as a wife and mother. Leila batted the thought away. This was Deborah's time. Nothing must spoil it.

Susan sat on the far side of the bed, a basin of water and a damp rag in her lap, her face serene. Between Mudder and Susan, the two women had helped deliver dozens of babies into this world. Deborah would be fine. "What can I do to help? Is that water cool?"

Susan smiled up at her. "We're doing fine. Sit with your sister. She could use some company. Rebekah can bring fresh water."

She handed the basin to Rebekah, who scampered toward the door without a word.

"Bring her a glass of water too." Leila scooted onto the bed and grabbed another rag to wipe her sister's face. "I'm so excited for you. Just think, any minute now you'll hold your first bopli in your arms. You and Phineas will be parents. What a blessing."

She was running on at the mouth, but she couldn't

help it. Deborah had what Leila wanted. A man who loved her, married her, and gave her a child. That it hurt to bear that child was a given. It would be worth it.

Deborah chuckled, the sound weak and weary. "It doesn't feel like it right now, but I'm sure you're right. Where have you been, schweschder? I needed you."

Those last three plaintive words shot daggers into Leila's heart. She'd been where she never should have gone. She gallivanted about in Beeville when her sister needed her. Mixing with the Englisch, being a part of their world. Shame burned her cheeks. "It's a long, stupid story. I'll tell you sometime. You'll laugh." Leila glanced up. Mudder and Susan exchanged concerned glances. "No harm done. I'm here now. Let's have us a baby."

Despite those optimistic words, the minutes dragged on. Deborah's screams weakened and turned to whimpers. Phineas appeared in the doorway, his scarred face white and drawn, then disappeared.

Deborah's screams rose again. Leila held one hand while Susan grasped the other. Leila prayed silently as Deborah gathered the last of her waning strength and screamed through another push. The sound of a baby wailing filled the ensuing silence. A plaintive sound. "He took his sweet time getting here, this little one. Has a mind of his own, he does." Mudder made quick work of cutting the cord and wiping down the baby, flailing arms and legs included. She wrapped him in a towel and held him out to Deborah. "He's a little bag of bones, but he won't break."

"A son," Deborah whispered, wonder wending itself around the two words. "A boy."

"Jah. He's breathing good and his skin color is nice and pink. He'll do."

"Get Phineas."

Leila did as Deborah asked. Phineas stood outside the door, head bent, eyes closed. Praying.

"He's here, Phineas, he's here. Your son is here."

Phineas's jaw worked. His lips trembled as he nodded, but he said nothing. Leila wanted to wrap him in a hug, but he'd never accept such a comfort from anyone other than his own fraa. She slipped out of the way and let him enter the room first.

Deborah tilted her precious bundle so her husband could see his son's face. A red, wrinkled face stared back at them, damp black hair spiking around it. The baby's lips puckered; he opened his mouth and wailed once again, this time with greater vigor.

"Hush, hush." Deborah smiled, then kissed his tiny forehead. "He looks like you."

Phineas grunted, a sound that might have been an attempt at a laugh. He kissed his wife and took the baby from her. "I'd like to introduce him to his groossdaadi."

"Do that. I want a word with Leila." Deborah's smile drifted away and she focused on Leila, who tried not to look guilty. She already expected a discussion with Mudder, but Deborah too? Now? At the door, Phineas stopped and turned. "We'll name him Timothy, then."

Mudder made a faint sound, a soft sigh. Deborah nodded. "For Daed."

Leila swiped at her cheeks, hoping they wouldn't see the sudden tears that refused to stay put. "That's a good, strong name."

Mudder hugged Deborah hard, then straightened. "You must be famished. I'll bring you some soup."

"I'll get some clean sheets." Susan followed Mudder to the door.

Deborah eased against the pillow. "Danki, y'all, for everything."

"All in a day's work." A smile blossomed on Mudder's face. "I'm a groossmammi. Who would've thought?"

She bustled from the room, Susan behind her. They were both still smiling. Leila found more tears threatening. She now served as little Timothy's aenti. "We're all grown up, aren't we, schweschder?"

"I don't know about you . . ." Deborah winced and rubbed her belly. She closed her eyes for a second, then opened them. "Come brush out my hair for me? I'm a mess. Where's my kapp?"

Leila picked up the brush from the crate and crawled in bed next to her sister. "Who cares about your hair. How does it feel to be a mudder?"

"Wunderbarr. Unimaginably wonderful." She scooted up so she could lean against the pillows propped on the wall and bent her head forward, letting Leila take out the mangled mess of a braid hanging down her back. "I was in labor all day. When you didn't come home from work, Mudder was worried. She worries about you a lot, much as she tries not to show it."

"I know. It was a mess. Nolan had to work a double shift, so Rory's husband, Dwayne, was to give us a ride home."

"Unless I'm touched in the head after all that labor, I

believe it's still the same distance whether it's Nolan or Dwayne driving. Did he get lost or something?"

"Or something." Leila worked her fingers through a nasty snarl, glad her sister couldn't see her face. "He insisted on going to the park instead of coming home. Some of his friends showed up. They brought alcohol."

"Did you drink?" Deborah's tone was matter of fact. She hadn't done much in the way of running around, but she'd never been one to judge others. "You didn't let him drive you home after that?"

"Nee. I didn't drink and I didn't come home with them."

Deborah swiveled. She grimaced and her hands went to her belly. She breathed, a high, aching sound. "Tell me."

"Now's not the time."

"It'll take my mind off my aches."

Leila told the story with no embellishment. She couldn't see her sister's face, but an occasional clucking sound told her Deborah listened. When she finished, the hair was neat and tidy in its bun, so unlike Leila's own messy life. "Well?"

"Ach." Deborah tucked her kapp over her hair and eased back on the pillows. "My sweet schweschder, the can of worms you've opened."

"I didn't open it. Jesse did."

"Now you know."

"What do you mean?"

"Now you know what Jesse's secret is. You can't pretend ignorance."

"I know."

"That means you have to choose."

Leila plucked at the threadbare sheet. She couldn't tell Deborah—not even Deborah—about the pull she'd felt in Tiffany's living room. The intensity of the worship. The sense that Gott had been there. Right there in the midst of their praise of Him. Near to her. Even her. Little Leila Lantz. So much more of a choice than Deborah could imagine. "I want Jesse to choose me. At least I think I do. There's Will too. He's steady and strong and not taken to flights of fancy."

"It's not just about you."

"I know."

Deborah patted the pillow next to her. Leila snuggled up next to her big sister, aware of the seconds ticking by. Anytime now, Phineas would return and this moment would be lost. This happy time in her sister's life should not be marred by this discussion. "It's okay. Don't worry about it. I know what I have to do."

"Do you?"

"I have to make the right choice."

"Jah."

"That's always been true though."

Deborah closed her eyes, her breathing soft and even. "Jah, but never more than now. You have to decide what you believe, and you have to choose how you want to live."

"You never had any doubts?"

"Nee." Her eyelids fluttered. "Tell Phineas to bring me our baby."

Leila kissed her cheek. Deborah didn't move. "Danki, big schweschder."

She slipped from the bed, careful not to jostle her sister. Rubbing her eyes, shoulders aching with exhaustion, she trudged down the stairs. She'd sleep in Esther's room for the night. The soft, worn cotton of sheets and a pillow called out to her. Tomorrow would be another day. First she needed to eat. Her empty belly rumbled in agreement. It had been too many hours since her PB&J sandwich and oatmeal cookies. Food and then sleep. Choices would have to wait.

Phineas passed her on the stairs, his gaze fixed on the steps as if he feared a wrong step in his new role as daed. She smiled at the fierce concentration on his face. He would be a good daed. She heaved a sigh and started through the front room.

Mordecai stood between her and the kitchen. His grave expression caused her fatigue to flee. Her mother stood behind him, her arms crossed, shoulders bowed. "It's time we have a talk."

"Could we do it in the morning?"

Mordecai shook his craggy head, his beard swaying. "Everyone will sleep better if we do it now."

He turned and disappeared into the kitchen. Leila shuffled after him, inhaling the mouthwatering scent of frying onions. Her stomach growled. Mudder moved between the cabinet and the stove. When she turned, she held a plate piled with fried potatoes and onions, stewed eggplant, and a venison patty with a chunk of sourdough bread on the side. "I reckon you didn't get supper."

Leila accepted the plate and slipped into a chair across from her stepfather. Funny to think of Mordecai that way. Their relationship was so new, yet he held so much authority over her. "I didn't, but it won't happen again. It's not what you think. Nolan had to work a double shift—"

"We think you working in town was a mistake." Mordecai spread his long fingers in wide fans over the rough pine table that separated them. "It's become more and more clear that you're drifting into ways that aren't ours."

"Nee. I'm not."

"Where were you tonight?"

"At the park in town." She blurted out the words without considering her story. They were true enough. Was she willing to lie for Jesse about the rest of her evening? Even if it was a lie of omission? She swallowed against bile that burned the back of her throat. "Dwayne was supposed to bring us home, but he wanted to stop at the park first. Rory was . . . distracted. I didn't want to leave the baby unattended."

Telling Mordecai about her forced visit to the park because of Rory's teenage husband would only reinforce her stepfather's opinion that she'd been led astray, but she couldn't bring herself to share her experience with the youth group. Everything would change. So much was at stake. For Jesse. For her. Even for other girls in the district who might set their sights on a job in Beeville to help their families survive here. Rebekah and Hazel who would come after her.

Mordecai tugged at his beard. His gaze shifted to where Mudder stood, hands in a tub of soapy water, her expression filled with concern. "How did you get home then?"

"A friend of Jesse's gave me a ride."

"Jesse was there." Mordecai's thick eyebrows bunched as his forehead wrinkled. "What was he doing there?"

"He was with a friend who drove by the park. They stopped when they saw me."

"And he brought you home."

"Jah."

"Gut. That's gut."

It was the truth. She let her gaze sink to her hands, bunched in fists on the table. Not telling the whole truth protected not only Jesse, but herself. Jesse's involvement with this youth group was already causing her trouble. Her involvement. She had gone willingly into that room. But she hadn't known what lay ahead. Now she did. Lying was a sin. Not telling the whole truth was a sin of omission.

She couldn't tell the whole truth. She didn't know it yet. Choices remained to be made.

Gott, forgive me. Help me understand these feelings. She had been touched by what she saw. The depth of their fervor, the joy in their beaming faces. She could admit it, now that she was away from Jesse's prying eyes. Something in her had embraced their expression of their faith, loud and noisy and exuberant. Faith so alive, she could almost touch it. No wonder they wanted to tell people about it.

Would she give up her family to experience that feeling all the time? Nee. Nee? Although at this moment in time, she would give much to escape the paralyzing examination of Mordecai's eyes. It was as if he read the very words written by God on her soul. She willed herself not to squirm.

"You're not to get in a car with this Dwayne again. If Nolan can't bring you home, use the phone at the day care to call the store."

Not a problem. "I understand."

"You'll let her go back to work then?" Mudder squeezed her hands together in front of her as if in supplication. "But we—"

"She's not to blame for Nolan's inability to give her a ride." Mordecai tapped his fingers on the table in a restless beat. "She showed good judgment in not leaving the baby alone with young folks who were drinking. She was brought home by a friend of Jesse's."

The goodwill in Mordecai's voice made Leila's face burn. He had faith in her. He trusted her to tell the truth and do the right thing. She wanted to do that so badly, but she couldn't reveal Jesse's secret to the deacon. He would have to take her revelation to the bishop. Jesse's father. She now understood Will's dilemma and the pain it caused him. To be caught between right and wrong on behalf of a friend and cousin. For her, a man for whom she had feelings. Strong feelings.

"Will came by the house this evening."

Leila started. Mudder had many attributes, but reading the minds of her kinner was not one of them. Thanks be to Gott. Her mother's voice held a soft, pleading note, whether for her or for Mordecai, Leila couldn't decide.

"What did he say?" She took a breath. "I mean, what did he want?"

"He *said* he came to tell us Andrew is firing up

the cement mixer tomorrow to help Jacob finish the slab for his milk storage house. Wanted to know if I was headed out to help." Mordecai tugged his glasses from his nose and polished them with his shirtsleeve. He yawned. "I am. While we have the mixer going, we'll work on the honey storage house and make some sidewalks up by the store. Make a day of it. Time for sleep."

He rose and stretched his arms over his head. "Eat your supper. You'll sleep better. Tomorrow is another day, Gott willing."

She picked up her fork. Mudder set a glass of water by her plate, wiped her hands on her apron, and then squeezed Leila's shoulder.

"Mudder?"

"Don't forget your prayers." Mudder trudged to the door. Her tone was soft, sad. "Gott sees and Gott knows the whole truth. Not just the bits and pieces we choose to share."

"I know."

"Whatever went on tonight, He knows. Ask Him for guidance. Trust in His will for you." She disappeared through the doorway.

God's will. Leila forced herself to eat the food in front of her because she couldn't bear to waste it, but the venison and sourdough bread tasted of nothing. Her mouth was so dry she had to gulp water to force the food down. Finally she dropped her fork on her plate, rose, and carried it to the sink. Her stomach roiled as she stared down at the tub of soapy water. She balanced on the edge of an abyss, teetering on the edge of everything she'd ever known and a world so fathomless it seemed a bottomless pit.

Any second, she would fall.

CHAPTER 24

All those illuminated numbers on the dash meant something. Aware of Colton's waning patience, Jesse stared at them. Despite the cool early December air wafting through the open window, his palms were hot and slick on the wheel. His dry mouth made it hard to swallow. He forced himself to put one hand on the round knob of the gearshift and look through the dust, bird droppings, and splattered insects on the windshield of Mr. Wise's ancient Ford pickup truck.

The dirt road on the Wise ranch wound its way as far as the eye could see across flat, brown fields barren of vegetation in winter. A good place to learn to drive. No one he could hit and nothing he could damage within miles. And no one to see him do this thing, which by all accounts a Plain man should not do. "Do you really think I'm ready for this? I mean, what's the hurry?"

"The hurry is I can't keep hauling you all over the place." Colton slurped from a sixteen-ounce Big Red bottle and then settled it into a plastic cup holder dangling from the passenger side door. "If you're gonna help us by leading meetings and doing hospital visits and such, you have to learn to drive. It's time to put up or shut up."

The hint of sarcasm in Colton's voice told Jesse they weren't simply talking about driving. Colton had made it clear he wanted Jesse to dive headfirst into this new life, holding back nothing, not looking back. Colton understood the price Jesse would pay, but he believed their mission to be worth it. Jesse agreed, but that didn't make it easy.

Not with Leila still out there. He'd seen something in her face that night at youth group. She'd felt it. She wanted it. She simply wasn't ready to admit it. Not yet. That hope kept him going.

Or maybe he saw what he wanted to see.

"Earth to Jesse." Colton tapped the dashboard in double time. "Now would be good, dude."

"I don't have a car, so what does it matter if I can drive?" To own a car. To drive. Those things meant freedom to travel in a way not dependent on anyone else. Freedom and independence. Not words often used in the Plain vocabulary. "It's not like I can afford to buy one. I don't even have a license."

"One thing at a time, my friend. License is next on my list. My dad raised four boys. We have half a dozen old junk cars on the ranch. That's how we all learned to drive." Colton waved a hand at the dusty interior of the truck with its ripped upholstery and Hawaiian dancer bobblehead on the dashboard. "Logan learned in this very vehicle last year. We fix them up and drive them. That way if we have an accident—which my dad says all teenage boys will do—it's no big loss. Plus you learn to repair cars. Very important skill for guys to have. Girls like it. You can drive this one or one of the others, it doesn't matter. Next we'll teach you how to change the oil and replace the battery. All the basics."

He sounded genuinely happy about the situation, as if he were passing on to Jesse a family tradition important to him. Not a tradition Jesse had ever expected to share. If his family could see him now. His daed. Leila. They would never understand. He didn't really understand himself.

Jesse studied the gears on the tiny diagram on the knob. 1, 2, 3, 4, 5, R. PUSH IN THE CLUTCH WITH YOUR LEFT FOOT, HIT THE GAS WITH THE RIGHT, AND SHIFT—ALL AT THE SAME TIME. Who had that kind of coordination? How could he watch the road and manage all this shifting stuff too? Buggies were so much easier. Horses did all the work. "Why does it have to be a standard?"

"'Cuz my dad always says a guy needs to know how to drive a stick first. If you can do that, you can drive anything. Farm equipment, pickups, sports cars. Besides, girls like a guy who can drive a stick." Colton leaned against the door and stuck his elbow on the frame of the open window. For a guy about to put his life in Jesse's hands, he looked mighty relaxed. "We're not getting any younger, buddy. Let's do it. Stop stalling. Start her up."

Groaning, Jesse wiggled the stick to make sure it was in Neutral and turned the key in the ignition. The old truck rumbled to life, its engine sounding smooth and silky despite its rusting hulk of an exterior. The smell of exhaust wafted through the windows. A thrill ran through him so acute the hair on his arms bristled. He inhaled. He was driving.

Jesse Glick was driving.

What if Leila could see him now? What would she think? She danced with Will. Would she let Jesse take her for a ride?

"Push in the clutch and the gas at the same time as you go from Neutral to First. Gently. Smoothly." Colton's voice was soft and patient. "Relax, just take it slow, real slow."

Jesse shoved the stick in First. Gears screeched in a horrible grinding noise. The truck jerked. The engine died.

Or not.

"It's okay, it's okay." Colton slapped a hand over his mouth, but it didn't muffle his chuckle. "Everybody does that at first. It takes some coordination."

"No kidding."

It took twenty minutes and a dozen or more attempts, but Jesse got the hang of it. He was determined to do it, if for no other reason than to show Colton he could. If every Wise brother could do it, every Englisch man could do it, Jesse Glick could drive a stick. Somewhere in the second half hour, they made it to the end of the dirt road, much to Jesse's surprise. He stopped at the intersection where dirt and gravel met asphalt.

"Go on, you know you want to." Colton pointed toward the west. "Hit the highway. Let her rip. Get some speed up."

"Are you kidding? The speed limit is like sixty-five out there."

"That's the great thing about a standard. Once you get in gear, if you maintain your speed, you're good. You don't have to downshift until you're ready to slow down."

"I don't have a license."

"You think anybody out here is checking?"

Driving a truck on the highway. He'd watched them sail by for so many years, leaving him and his horse eating dirt, plodding along, five miles an hour. Jesse looked left. He looked right. He slapped the turn signal on. "Here we go."

"Attaboy!"

Jesse jabbed the gas, worked the gears, and made it onto the highway in a wide turn that wasn't half bad. Air rushed through the open windows, bringing with it the smell of winter and damp earth. He inhaled and tried to relax. Thirty, forty, fifty, sixty. They were sailing down the highway. He was driving. Never in his life had he imagined such a feeling. He had control of this one little piece of his life. For these few seconds.

"Feels good, doesn't it?" Colton sucked down his Big Red. "Nothing better than being your own ride."

"It does feel good." He could admit it to Colton. His friend understood about these things. "I don't know exactly why, but it's good."

"It's a guy thing. Every guy wants to drive a truck."

"Not every guy."

They came up over an incline and rounded a deep bend in the highway. A second later an enormous SUV blotted out the road ahead. It blocked the entire lane. Its crumpled front end faced Jesse head-on. A massive truck with welding equipment hanging off its mangled sides blocked the opposite lane.

Beyond it were more cars, smaller, more crumpled. Jesse didn't have time to count them. His foot went from the gas to the brake.

"Easy, easy!" Colton hollered as he fumbled the Big Red bottle. It tumbled down his front, soaking his white T-shirt. "Easy!"

Tires screamed, the brakes squealed. Jesse tried to control the skid, but the truck seemed to have a mind of its own now. Its front end missed the SUV by a hair-breadth. He twisted the wheel and avoided some kind of smaller car turned so it faced the wrong way on the road. The truck bucked and shimmied. Tires screeched, brakes ground. The smell of burnt rubber filled the cab. They careened across the oncoming lane, slammed into the ditch, bounced up the embankment, and smashed into the posts of a barbed-wire fence.

Finally, they stopped moving.

It might have taken all of fifteen seconds to reach this blessed resting place, but it seemed hours had passed. Jesse panted. His lungs couldn't seem to suck in air. Blood pounded in his ears. Black dots floated in his peripheral vision. His legs and arms shook inexplicably. His brain searched the far extremities of his body. No pain except for the bruising hold of the seat belt across his chest.

His hands still grasped the wheel. He couldn't release the white-knuckled grip of his fingers, hard as he tried. He managed to turn his head toward Colton. His friend had both hands wrapped around his seat belt as if will-ing it to hold him in place. "You okay?"

"Yeah, but those folks aren't." His breathing ragged, Colton flipped off his seat belt and shoved open the door. "Looks like it just happened. Let's go."

Spurred by the urgency in his friend's voice, Jesse did the same. He hurled himself from the truck, surprised to find his legs still worked. He darted across the field and onto the highway. A lady stumbled toward him, blood trickling from a cut on her forehead under bleached-blonde bangs. "My girls, my twins, they're hurt. Help us, please help us."

A man hoisted himself from the welding truck's open door and trotted toward the woman. "You better sit down, ma'am, before you fall down. That was a nasty head-on."

The woman's legs collapsed and she crumpled to the ground, hands covering her face.

"I've got her." The man waved Jesse on. "Check on the others."

Jesse kept moving toward the Tahoe. A tiny blonde girl stared back at him from the backseat. Her face crumpled and she began to whimper. The other girl's eyes were closed, her mouth slack. "Colton, they're little girls. They're hurt."

Colton already had his cell phone to his ear. "Help's on the way. Just talk to them. Keep talking to them."

"Hi, I'm Jesse. It'll be fine. Help is coming." He squeezed his head into the opening, avoiding shattered glass. The girls were dressed in matching jean jackets and blue corduroy pants. They were still belted in. "What's your name? What's your sister's name?"

The girl's whimpering subsided. "I'm Hannah. That's Hilary. She won't wake up."

"We're gonna help Hilary. Don't you worry." The prayers welled up in his head, silent entreaty to the Great Physician. Sirens began to scream in the distance. *Thank You, Jesus.* "Where were you headed?"

"Into town to buy Christmas presents for Daddy." Hannah's voice quavered. "We're gonna get him a new charcoal grill. He burned out the bottom of the old one. Mommy likes it when he grills. Then she doesn't have to cook."

"You'll still have plenty of time."

"Hold my hand?"

Hannah's small hand crept toward Jesse's on the window frame. He stuck his out to meet hers. It was clammy. "Help's on the way."

The quiet of the countryside disappeared into a cacophony of ambulances and fire trucks. An EMT jumped from the first ambulance. Jesse squeezed Hannah's hand one last time and let the man do his job, starting with Hilary, who stirred and mumbled when the EMT touched her face with a purple-gloved hand.

Jesse took a breath, sure he'd been holding it for days. *Thank You, Jesus, thank You.*

He eased back and turned around. Seven cars in all. A chain reaction of some kind. He lurched around in a bad dream. If only it were a bad dream. One minute he cruised along the highway, driving a truck, and the next he was confronted with carnage on the road. Little girls hurt and bleeding.

What did that mean?

Colton trotted toward him. The Big Red soaking his shirt made him look bloody. They stood together on the edge of the road, watching the emergency responders assess injuries, prioritize, and transport the injured. Hilary and Hannah went first to the medical center in Beeville. Minutes later the *whop-whop* of the Halo-Flight helicopter blades filled the air. It landed right on the highway, scattering dust and debris. Its presence only served to add to the surreal nature of the afternoon.

"They're transporting the couple from the Neon. They're hurt bad. They'll go to Corpus." Colton fingered his cell phone as if itching to call someone. "The one little girl's injuries are minor. The other one, they need to check her out more. She might have a head injury. The mom needs stitches and she has two broken wrists—air bags, you know."

"Driving was a bad idea."

"You didn't have an accident."

"No, I ran into one."

"And you handled it just fine."

"I wrecked your truck."

Together they turned to survey the pickup. From a distance it looked fine, but the front end was wedged against the fence. Colton stalked through the weeds. "Hardly a scratch. I bet it will start right up."

"The keys are in it."

"You need to do it."

"I don't think so."

"Come on, I'm not asking you to drive anywhere. Just start her up. It's like getting back on a horse after you're thrown."

Only one of them had actually experienced being thrown from a horse, and that was Jesse. The pain of his bruised behind would never be forgotten. "Easy for you to say."

"Y'all the ones who reported this?" A tall state trooper with skin the color of licorice strode toward them, a clipboard in one hand. "I'm looking for witnesses."

"I think a bunch of folks in the cars reported it." Colton leaned against the side of the truck. "We didn't really see anything. The accident had already happened when we drove up on the scene."

The trooper's gaze flitted to Jesse. He seemed to study his attire. Jesse fought the urge to fidget. What if the guy wanted to know who was driving? "You see anything?"

"No. We came around the bend and there they were. He drove off the road to avoid them."

We. He.

The trooper made notes, his pen making a scratching noise on the paper. "I'll need your names and contact information."

Colton recited his number. "You can reach Jesse here through me. His family doesn't have a phone."

The trooper's eyebrows did push-ups, but he didn't comment. "Do you need a tow?"

"Naw, I'll call my dad if we need help."

"Thanks for getting involved. Folks don't always want to do that anymore."

"We do. We're all about getting involved." Colton's gaze encompassed Jesse and the trooper. "That's what life is all about, getting involved."

After the trooper moved away, Jesse brushed past Colton and got in the truck. His friend was right. He'd spent a lot of time standing on the sidelines. Helping people felt good. It gave life meaning. He needed to remember that.

Colton plopped into the seat next to him. "Big Red will never come out of the seat. But in this truck, who cares?"

Jesse turned the key. The engine rumbled. Then it died. And refused to be coaxed into starting again. He blew out air and settled against the seat, his damp shirt stuck to his back. "Now what?"

"Now I call my dad. He'll have my uncle bring his tow truck out. They're at an auction this afternoon, so it'll take him a bit to get here." Colton scrounged around in the space behind the seat and pulled out a small cooler. "But that's okay. I got food."

"How can you eat at a time like this?"

"You can't?"

His friend was right. Jesse was always hungry.

Colton made the call. It didn't sound as if his dad was too upset about the situation. Jesse had met the man a time or two, and he had an easygoing way about him that matched his lumbering size and genial grin. "He says it'll be about an hour. We'll eat and take a nap, how about that?"

The fade of the adrenaline had left Jesse weary beyond measure. "Sure."

Colton rummaged in the cooler and brought out two sandwiches. He handed one to Jesse, said a quick blessing, and then began unwrapping the other one. "Do you know the story in Genesis where Jacob wrestles all night with the Angel of God?"

Here we go. Jesse picked at the wrapper on his sandwich and nodded. "Sure. Who doesn't?"

"Lots of folks in this world, which is why we do what we do, but that's not where I'm going at the moment."

Jesse couldn't wait to find out where Colton was going now. He kept that sarcastic thought to himself. The guy knew his Bible inside and out and had no fear when it came to approaching strangers with the best news possible. Whatever Colton had to say, he said out of a love for Jesus and because he cared about Jesse. Why, Jesse didn't really understand.

"Watching you talk to Leila the other night reminded me of that story."

The bite of ham-and-cheese sandwich in Jesse's mouth lost all flavor in that moment when his mind's eye ran through the images. The anger and the tears and the confusion and the sadness, sometimes one after another, and then mixed together as Leila tried to understand what he was saying. "All I did was make her feel bad and put her in a terrible position of having to either rat me out or lie to her family and my family. I don't feel good about what I did to Leila."

"Jacob didn't want to give it up and give God control of his life. He was fighting Him every step of the way. The Angel of God wrestled with him all night and then finally touched his hip and made it come out of the socket."

Jesse knew the story as well as he knew the story of Adam and Eve or Noah and the ark or Jonah and the great fish. "What does that have to do with me?"

"Give in. God could have caused that hip problem right at the beginning, but He didn't. He wanted Jacob to relent on his own. Instead he wasted a whole night fighting God's will. Let God have control over your life. You're either in or out. You can't keep sitting on the fence."

"I'm not sitting on the fence. I'm all in." Even as he said those words, Jesse knew he hadn't demonstrated to anyone, not Colton, not Leila, not God, that he truly was committed. He'd wavered. It was time to take a stand. "I've been working through my faith and figuring out how to make this change without hurting people. But I will make it."

"I understand that. I never had to make the choices you have to make. That's not lost on me." Colton contemplated his sandwich, took a bite, chewed, and swallowed. "I respect you for doing what you're doing. But you can't make the decision based on your feelings for Leila. If she doesn't have the same calling, you have to come without her."

Jesse shoved the remainder of his sandwich into the plastic bag. He rubbed at his face with the back of his hand, trying to hide the emotions that battered him. He cleared his throat. "I'm just—"

"Crazy about her, I know." Colton tugged a bottle of water from the cooler and twisted off the cap. "That's tougher than I can begin to imagine. I'm blessed to have a girlfriend who's on the same page with me. It's a God-thing that Tiffany and I found each other so early on. So I can't claim to know how you feel about any of this. Leaving your family or Leila. But you're making it worse by prolonging the agony. Make a decision and then make a clean break."

"Did I have to learn how to drive a stick to do that?"

"I guess it's all connected in my mind—wrestling with a stick shift, wresting with an Angel of God, wrestling with your conscience, wrestling with a decision that will change your entire life." Colton squeezed the plastic bag from his sandwich into a ball. It blossomed out again. "Jacob was a new man when it was over. God gave him a new name. He started a new life. You can do that too."

A new man. A new name. A new life. Jesse wanted those things. He wanted them badly. But he also wanted Leila. Whether he could have both was up to God. God's will. "You're right, but I still have to figure some things out, so give me time."

"I hear you, dude. I'll try not to be so obnoxious about it." Colton pulled a bag of Oreos from the cooler and held it out. "Here. Cookies make everything better."

"I think that's peanut butter."

"You do love Leila, don't you?"

Jesse took two cookies, then thought better of it and went back for three more. Even that wouldn't be enough. "Yeah, I do."

"Then don't give up on her."

"It's not fair to her."

"Dude, if you're the man God has chosen for her, then you need to do everything in your power to make her see that." Colton pulled a cookie apart and licked the white frosting in the middle. A look of pure bliss spread across his face. "Don't you see? You could be the love of her life *and* help her have a closer relationship with God. It's a win-win."

"She has a close relationship with God. She's a believer. If she chooses me, chooses us, she loses her family and the only life she's ever known. Not a win-win."

"Nobody said it would be easy." Colton tossed Jesse the bag of cookies. "Somehow I don't see you living your life much different than you do now. A simple, plain life. A good life. One you can share with a good woman. It's a God-thing, dude. If you really believe in what we're doing, you can't do anything else. You have to try. For her sake and yours."

"How can you claim to be so sure of what God's plan is?"

"It's all in the Good Book."

"We—my folks—live by the same Good Book."

"People like to pick and choose the parts of the Book they want to live by. Sometimes they ignore other parts because it's more comfortable or easier or whatever."

Jesse dropped the bag of cookies and shoved open his door. He needed to think. He needed space. "That's not the case with my folks. There's nothing comfortable or easy about our lives."

"I know, I know. I'm not judging. Believe me. I have nothing but respect for the way your folks live their lives. I'm just saying it's not for you. You're called to something else. It's possible Leila is too. Maybe that's why the two of you feel such a pull toward each other."

"If this is you not being obnoxious, we're in trouble." Jesse rubbed his face with the back of his sleeve. It smelled of asphalt and sweat. He hopped from the truck and looked back at Colton. "I'm gonna walk up to the road and wait for your uncle."

"Sorry, dude, I've only got one setting, I guess. Full tilt. Think about what I said, will ya?"

How could Jesse think about anything else? He started toward the road. Colton's voice carried through the open window. "Tomorrow we go to DPS so you can take your driver's test. Get a haircut. You want to look good for the photo on your license, don't you?"

Jesse closed his eyes against the pale, lackluster sun. A haircut. A driver's license. For every action, there was a reaction. Little pieces of his old self chipping off and falling by the wayside until a new man was born.

A man his family wouldn't recognize. But God would. God knew what was in his heart. The desire to tell the world about the love of Jesus and the promise of salvation.

He couldn't cover his ears and block out the voice calling him.

He didn't want to ignore it.

Gott, I'm yours. I surrender all to You.

Now could I talk to You about Leila?

CHAPTER 25

Shivering in a cool, early-morning breeze, Will hopped from the buggy and tied the reins to a fence post at the Glick corral. The mid-December sun shone bright, but the purpose of his visit took the edge off his natural inclination to be buoyed by the light. If Jesse had noticed his arrival, he didn't show it. He had his hands full with a Morgan intent on breaking free of its halter. The horse whinnied, tossed its head, and tried to nip at his own belly. Jesse hung on to the lead with both hands and urged the horse to walk, his tone gentle and cajoling.

Will had seen this behavior before. He felt for the animal and for the Glicks. Colic could be a deadly thing in a horse. He climbed over the fence and dropped into the corral, his weight causing puffs of dust to billow around his scuffed boots.

"Hey."

Jesse looked up, his expression dark and distracted. "Hey."

"Walking him?"

"Jah, but it's been fifteen minutes. Daed said no more than fifteen, twenty at the most. We don't want to wear him out if he's got it bad."

"Colic?"

"Worse, I think. Daed talked to the vet this morning and we gave him some Milk of Magnesia. It didn't help. Looks to be twisted gut."

The worst kind of news. "Vet's been out?"

Jesse shook his head. "Daed talked to him on the phone. We thought we could doctor him ourselves, but it isn't getting better so he went back to the store to call the vet to come out—"

The horse reared up and bucked, hooves flying. The reins whipped from Jesse's hand. He stumbled back, dropped to his knees, then scrambled sideways. The horse careened around the corral as if trying to escape his own pain.

Will threw himself out of the way, rolled, and came up against the fence, the breeze on his face telling him how close he'd come to getting a hoof in the face.

"Grab him, grab him!" Jesse yelled. "Don't let him roll."

Rolling, the horse's first instinct, could exacerbate a twisted gut. Will shot after the animal and scooped up the trailing reins. "Whoa, whoa, hold on, Sugar, come on, boy, slow down."

A series of hard tugs brought the horse under control, but sweat lathered his flanks. His lips curled as he tossed his long, lean neck and whinnied again and again.

"It's okay, boy, it's okay. Easy does it."

Jesse edged closer and snatched the reins from Will. They were both sweating despite a nippy wind that spoke of winter and December finally arriving.

"What are you doing here?" Jesse panted. "You didn't come to see about a horse."

Will leaned over and planted his hands on his dirty pants, trying to catch his breath. He didn't take his gaze from the horse. In his current condition, the animal could bolt again and again until the pain became too much and he sank to the ground, or by some miracle, the medicine took hold and the blockage dissolved. Will tried to gather his thoughts as Jesse smoothed his hands over the horse's back, whispering sweet nothings to the animal.

They'd been friends as long as Will could remember. More than cousins. More like brothers. He couldn't be sure how they'd arrived at this moment. But this would be the moment. He was determined. He wanted to do more than hold Leila's hand and dance with her. He wanted to be the one standing in front of the district one day, promising a lifetime of commitment. Jesse couldn't have it both ways. Living with one boot in this world, one boot in that one.

Right now, he looked the picture of a Plain man, soothing a sick horse and praying that it was enough. That they didn't lose an animal vital to their survival and costly to replace. A deceiving picture, indeed.

Will inhaled and exhaled. The smell of dirt, manure, and straw filled the air, familiar and calming. "Did you go to your youth group thing this week?"

"Jah."

Jesse's tone said he didn't want to talk about it. Will ignored it. "And have you decided what you'll do?"

"I'm working on it." Jesse smoothed his hand over the

horse's nose, his touch gentle. The animal's head dipped and he whinnied, long and low. "Come on, Sugar, come on. You're needed around here, boy."

"Vet will be here soon." Will straightened and heaved another breath. They needed calm as much for the horse as for themselves. "He can give him that mineral-oil treatment and something for the pain. He'll make it."

Jesse wrapped his fingers in the silky hair of the horse's mane. His head dropped until his forehead rested against the mammoth animal's sweaty neck. "If it's more than colic, if it's a twisted gut, he'll need surgery."

This wasn't Will's first go-round with severe colic. The horse would have a fifty-fifty chance of surviving surgery, and where would the money come from? "Cross that bridge when we come to it."

"I could do without the judgment. Daed says we're not to judge others."

The flip-flop of topics didn't surprise Will. "I'm not judging. I'm worried for you."

Jesse raised his head. His face was gray with fatigue, and smudges darkened the skin under his eyes like fresh bruises. "You're worried for Leila."

"I don't deny that." Will tugged the reins from his cousin's hand. "But you're my family and I see you drifting—nee, running—in a direction that takes you far from us. I don't understand it."

"Come to a few meetings and I promise you will. These folks are the real thing. Their faith and devotion are real."

"You'd try to suck me in too?" Will shook his head,

baffled by his cousin's inability to see the consequences of his actions or more, his inability to stop himself from going down this road. What hold did these people have on him that was stronger than the faith and community with which he'd grown up? How could he contemplate a road that would shame his entire family? "I feel like we've lost you. You're not Jesse anymore."

"I'm not the Jesse I used to be. That's true." Jesse faced Will, his expression lighter. He smiled for the first time. "This is a good thing. I'm closer to Jesus than I've ever been before."

"And you won't be close to Jesus if you're baptized and worshipping with your community?" It seemed as if they were speaking different languages. "I don't understand. We worship every other Sunday. Leroy does a good job with the sermons. What more do you need?"

"I need to talk about it, study it, share it."

"So it's about you?"

"Nee. It's about making sure everyone gets the good news."

"The good news?"

"That Jesus loves them."

"And it's your job to tell them?"

The horse bobbed his head and swiveled it, his bared teeth yellow against his dark mane. He strained and nipped at his belly. Jesse tugged at the reins. "Nee, nee, Sugar, you'll only hurt yourself."

Could he not hear his own words? "Jesse—"

"Spreading the good news is my job and your job and everyone's who knows about God's saving grace."

Will stood, boots planted in the dirt, staring. He

had no words for this argument. He only knew what was in his heart. A sense of loss. Sadness. An ache. The man standing before him was a stranger, not the cousin and best friend who had shared every good memory in Will's entire life. The first time fishing. The first time hunting deer. The first swim in the Gulf. Rumspringa. That boy-turned-man had disappeared down a path Will couldn't see, let alone follow. "And your parents?"

"They don't know yet."

"There's no changing your mind?"

Jesse's sigh mingled with the horse's snorts of pain. "I pray every night for a way to stay. That God will soften hearts and open ears to my words."

"Your words. Do you know how prideful that sounds?"

"It's not pride."

"And Leila?"

"She says she can't do it."

Relief washed over Will. He wouldn't lose them both. "Then I ask you not to stand in my way."

"Leila's a grown woman. Her choice will be her choice, not mine or yours." Jesse's voice quavered. "I may have lost the skirmish, but not the war."

"Are you talking about us or her faith?"

"Both. I told her I wouldn't try to convince her, knowing it would mean she would lose her family, her life here." He turned and faced Will. "But then I prayed on it and talked to Colton and I realized I was wrong. Her faith in God's saving grace through Jesus Christ is the only thing she needs in order to find eternal salvation, whether it's here or with me."

Will refused to debate religion with his cousin. Even if he could. He didn't have the fancy words used by Jesse's Englisch friends. "Here she has her family, her community."

"I know." Jesse's jaw worked. "I know what coming with me would mean for her. The loss. But also the gain of a community of believers who read the Bible, study it, talk about it, draw closer to God in every way."

"You want to have your cake and eat it too. You'll tear her away from her family in the name of Gott so you won't have to go on in your new life alone." Will took a step back, then another. An enormous lump formed in his throat. He was losing this battle, losing his best friend. Words seemed to have no effect. Perhaps because he couldn't find the right words in the midst of his own morass of emotion and fear. He was failing Jesse. He must not fail Leila too. "It's selfish and you know it."

"I'm not tearing anyone away. It will be her decision."

Influenced by her feelings—feelings Will recognized—for Jesse. "Stay away from her."

"I can't."

"You won't, you mean."

"It's between her and me."

Will stared at him. Jesse stared back. The impasse festered in the scant few feet between them. Everything had been said.

The sound of an engine rumbling broke the silence. Will tore his gaze from a man he didn't know anymore. A stranger walking in his cousin's boots. Jesse swiveled. A familiar, dusty green SUV bounced on the dirt road, gravel spitting behind it. The vet.

"I'll go and let you tend to the horse." Will brushed past Jesse without looking at him. He didn't dare or he would do or say something he shouldn't. "I hope Sugar makes it."

"Will!"

One syllable full of a million emotions.

Will kept walking.

"Come to a youth group meeting. You'll see. You'll understand."

He whirled. "You'd try to convert me too? Have you no shame?"

"I have only . . ." Jesse's voice was low and so full of emotion it hurt Will's ears. Like gravel scraping skin. "I care about what happens to you."

Plain men didn't talk of such things, but Will understood the inclination. His heart felt as if Sugar had stomped on it. "If you cared about any of us, you'd come to the baptism classes in January and forget this nonsense."

Jesse's face whitened. The dark bruises under his eyes deepened. "I can't. Not if it means keeping my mouth shut about things I know are important."

A door slamming told Will the vet would soon approach. One last-ditch effort. "We'll be baptized in time for Easter and the gmay. It could be you, me, and Leila up there, answering the questions, feeling that water on our heads."

Jesse's Adam's apple bobbed. His jaw worked. "I'll keep praying."

"You do that." Will turned and opened the corral gate for Dr. Martinez, who strode toward them, a huge leather bag in one hand, his gaze already fixed on Sugar. "So will I. For healing for you and for the horse."

"I don't need healing."

Jesse's voice chased Will from the corral and up into the buggy. He sounded so sure of himself.

Will found himself sure of nothing.

CHAPTER 26

Stepping with care so as not to spill her cup of hot black tea, Leila squeezed between the coffee shop tables, thankful for the warmth of the heavy mug in her hands. It was only mid-December, but already they were experiencing unusually cold winter weather for south Texas. She didn't mind. Crisp, cold air served as a nice change from the hot humidity of the long summers in Bee County. She set the cup on the square Formica-topped table for two by the long window framed by red-checked curtains on either side.

She liked to watch the sporadic traffic go by in downtown Beeville while she ate her lunch. She always chose a small table so as not to take up space for customers buying lunch. Marie Diaz, the coffee shop owner, allowed her to eat her peanut-butter-and-jam sandwich in here, even though she never bought more than a tea or an occasional soda when she could afford it. She had one hour for lunch, and she tried to get out of the day care and away from her sweet babies so she'd have plenty of patience for them during the long afternoon that would follow.

Inhaling the mouthwatering scent of Marie's cinnamon rolls, Leila pulled her waxed-paper-wrapped sandwich from the mini cooler and contemplated the plastic container of cold macaroni and cheese. She should be content with her lunch, made with loving hands by family. For some reason, even Mudder's gingersnaps couldn't cheer her up today. Two weeks had gone by since her discussion with Jesse on the front porch of Tiffany's house and not a word from him. He hadn't come by to talk to Mordecai. He hadn't shone a flashlight in her window and asked her to come away with him.

Not that she wanted him to do that. She wrestled with that thought. Sometimes when she lay in bed at night and stared at the ceiling, with Rebekah's soft snores tickling her ears, she did want it. She could admit it in the dark of night. But in broad daylight, sun shining, Hazel giggling at the table, the smell of okra gumbo wafting through the air, Caleb and Esther arguing over the last biscuit, nee, she couldn't imagine another life for herself.

She couldn't have it both ways.

She had to choose. But that had always been the case. One day soon she would stand before her community and be baptized. Or she would walk away from this life. She'd been given a choice, just as Jesse had.

Just as Will had. More choices. She hadn't seen hide nor hair of Will either. One minute he was dancing her around an open field, the next he'd made himself scarce. He came by the house when she wasn't there but couldn't find his way to the door when she was. The story of her life.

"Hey, it's you."

She jumped and hot tea splattered on her hand. "Ouch!"

Tom Fletcher towered over her, his face lighted with a smile that brought out dimples in both cheeks. He wore a fleece-lined leather jacket and faded blue jeans and the usual Texas Rangers ball cap. Not working today. So why was Kaitlin back at the day care instead of with him? Leila stifled the question. He paid for a full week whether or not his child attended every day.

He held a tray laden with a wrapped sandwich of some kind, a bag of chips, one of Marie's slices of chocolate meringue pie, and a large glass of milk. "Sorry, didn't mean to startle you."

"Just daydreaming." Determined not to stare at his handsome face, she settled the mug on the table and dabbed at her hand with a napkin. "It's not your fault I was in never-never land."

"I'm surprised they let you out of your room. Who's watching my baby girl?"

"Don't worry, Shelby has her." Why wasn't he watching her? "It's only for an hour and she's had her bottle, so she's probably down for a nap anyway."

"I was just kidding. I know you have to eat like the next person." He glanced around the coffee shop. Despite the fact that it was lunchtime, a few tables were still open. His gaze landed back on her. "Mind if I join you? I have a couple of questions you might be able to help me with."

The heat on her face had nothing to do with her tea. Leila let her gaze drop to the sandwich in her hand. Lunch with an Englisch man. What would Mudder say? Or Mordecai? Tom was the father of one of her scholars, so to speak. If she were a teacher. She was a babysitter. They were in a public place, many folks around. What harm could there be? Mordecai and Mudder didn't want her around Dwayne and his friends. Tom was different.

"It's okay. If it takes you that long to think of an excuse not to let me sit down, I should move on." Tom balanced his tray on a thick book that looked like something he'd use if he were in school. "I have some studying to do anyway."

"Nee, nee, I didn't mean to be impolite—"

"You're not. If you want to eat alone, I totally understand. You spend all day with crying babies."

"They don't always cry. Just this morning, Kaitlin giggled."

He set the book on the third chair at her table, settled the tray on it, and slapped his ball cap on top of the book. "She doesn't giggle much around me. Her aunt and her cousins can make her laugh though."

Leila set her cooler on the floor and made room for Tom's food. "Try a little squeeze on those thunder thighs. She's ticklish."

"She is." He looked delighted. Then the smile faded. "So was her mother."

"And you're not?" Leila kept her tone light, teasing. "Not even your feet?"

He grinned. "I suppose so."

"Try it. Her laugh is so sweet."

He unwrapped his sandwich—pastrami on rye from the looks of it—and took a bite. She did the same and they chewed in companionable silence for a few seconds.

"You're not working today?"

He shook his head and tapped the mammoth textbook. "I'm studying. I want to be a physician's assistant."

Leila didn't know for sure what that was, but it sounded important. "You have to have a lot more schooling for that?"

"Yep. But it would mean I could do a lot more for sick or hurt people, not just pick them up in an ambulance and turn them over to someone at the ER."

"Do you have to work a lot if you're a physician's assistant?"

He shrugged as he licked a spot of mustard from his thumb. "I work a lot now. Fortunately my sister takes Kaitlin when I work night shifts. She's got three older boys, so she's happy to have a little girl now and again. Working any job in the medical field means odd hours, nights, weekends."

"So why do you want to do it more?"

"Because I help people." His gaze didn't meet hers. "And it keeps me occupied."

And away from his baby daughter. Tom was running from his responsibility. He feared not doing a good job, so he was shirking the duties altogether. "Kaitlin needs her daddy too."

"I know that." He frowned. "Like I said, I have family to help out."

She could understand that. Plain families raised their children as families. "What were your questions?"

He wiped his mouth with a paper napkin and laid the sandwich on his paper plate. "She isn't crawling yet. Shouldn't she be crawling? The book I read said six months."

"She just turned six months, and boy howdy, is she ready to crawl."

"How can you tell?"

"Do you lay her on a blanket on the floor at night?"

"Yeah, sure."

"Does she stay in one place?"

"No. She rolls around from one corner to the other and does this silly bucking thing like she's trying to look behind her by throwing her head back."

"She's a wiggle worm through and through, that girl." Leila couldn't help it. She grinned. "If you put her on her tummy, she does this thing with her legs like she's revving up to start moving. All of this stuff is the start of crawling. She's so close, she's almost there."

"That's what Sam said, but I wondered if the baby was confused or something. She can't seem to get it."

"She will. Who's Sam?" Not that it was any of Leila's business. She was glad Tom had a man friend to whom he could talk.

"My partner." He took another bite, his expression thoughtful. He chewed and swallowed. "I guess I should start baby proofing."

"What do you mean?"

"You know, put plugs in the sockets, locks on the cabinet doors, and such."

Leila nodded. Plain folks didn't have sockets to worry about, and mostly the older children kept an eye on the younger ones to keep them out of trouble. "Probably a good idea."

"How old are you?"

Startled by the question, she dropped her sandwich on the waxed paper and wiped peanut butter from her fingers on the napkin she'd brought from home. "I'm nineteen. Why?"

"Diane and I were nineteen when we got married. My folks said we were too young, but we were in love and we wanted to be together. I thought we were doing the right thing. Getting married all proper and such."

How did a person know if love would last? That's what he was asking. Leila didn't know the answer. How she wished she did. "You were."

"I don't know. Divorce isn't proper."

"Nee, it's not."

"Don't sugarcoat it." His smile took the sting from the words. "Not my choice. I never thought I'd be divorced at twenty-five."

"I know."

"You're the expert. Come over and baby proof the house for me."

"I'm no expert. We don't have sockets."

"'Course you don't." His nose wrinkled. He had a nice nose. "But you work in a day care."

"And then I go home to my family."

"You have a boyfriend?"

The bite of cookie in her mouth turned to sand. She didn't know how to answer that question. Jesse or Will? Did either qualify as a boyfriend?

Tom held up one big hand. "It's none of my business. Sorry."

"I don't know."

"How could you not know?"

"Two men have courted me. Sort of."

"Two? That's progressive."

"That's not how it is. Neither has . . . staked a claim."

"You Amish women aren't much for feminism." He chuckled, a deep, rich sound, and held out a fork. "Help me eat this pie. No way I'll be able to finish it by myself."

"I have a cookie." The stutter in her voice sent more heat waves through her. Sharing a piece of pie on the same plate with the same fork. It was something a couple would do. "But thank you."

"I'm not trying to embarrass you." He dropped the fork on the plate with a sharp ping. "The truth is . . . I'm just lonely."

For a man such as this one—tall, broad shouldered, pleasing to the eye, with a job and a child and family—to say such a thing to her, it made her heart seize up. She inhaled but no relief came. "I'm sorry."

"Not your fault. I shouldn't have said it. It's just that you're easy to talk to." He shoved the plate away, pie untouched, and leaned back in his chair. "They keep saying I should read to Kaitlin. She just wants to grab the book and chew on it. She tears the pages. Is it all that important?"

"It helps them learn words and it's something you do together." Back on solid ground, Leila breathed again. "Get the heavy cardboard books. Then she can't tear the pages. If she gets slobber or spit-up on them, you just wipe them off."

"She does plenty of that. I mean the spit-up and slobber. It's everywhere."

"I reckon she's teething. I felt a couple of buds on her gums this morning when she was fussy after her nap."

"Teething already. Right." He scratched his head, looking perplexed. "How's a guy supposed to keep track of all this?"

"You'll get the hang of it." He had no choice.

He picked up a toothpick and rolled it between his fingers. "Anyone ever tell you you're pretty?"

She squirmed in her chair. Not a soul. Plain folks didn't set much store by looks. "No." The word came out a whisper.

"Even prettier when your face gets pink like that." He grinned, teeth white and even. "I didn't mean to embarrass you. A guy just doesn't meet a lot of women like you. So without adornment and artifice."

She would have to look up those words in the dictionary. Neither got used much at her house. Unable to think of a thing to say, she nodded.

"So do you know which guy you'll choose?"

She watched his long fingers work the toothpick. No calluses there. No scars. Hands that did inside work. Healing hands. "I don't know."

She must've whispered again because he leaned forward, full lips parted, as if straining to hear. "What?"

"I don't know."

He picked up the book on the chair. "You're fortunate to have choices. I keep thinking Kaitlin needs a mother. I'm not equipped for the job. But the idea of getting out there and trying again . . . that scares me. And where does a guy with a baby and a full-time job and studies meet a woman? It's not like I have time or the inclination for bars."

"Have you tried asking someone out from your church?"

He opened the book, then shut it, his fingers smoothing the cover. "My church . . . I haven't been to church since me and Diane split. I guess I feel like God let me down. He let me marry a woman who left the first chance she got."

"He didn't choose your wife for you. You did."

"Thanks for pointing that out."

"Sorry. We believe in taking everything to God. He has a plan for us. His will be done."

She'd heard those words hundreds of times. Now she spoke them to another. She believed them, heart and soul, even as she said them to this troubled, sad, lonely man in need of succor that a simple woman such as herself could not provide. How was that so different from what Jesse wanted to do? A bite of cookie lodged in her throat and she coughed and choked.

"You okay?" Tom rose and smacked her on the back with a big hand, nearly knocking her from her chair. He didn't know his own strength. "Breathe, breathe!"

She coughed again and gasped. "I'm fine, I'm fine."

From someone who wasn't sure of anything anymore.

CHAPTER 27

Surely she knew better than to do such a thing.

Jesse slammed to a stop in the middle of the sidewalk underneath the flickering neon sign that read MARIE'S COFFEE SHOP. Leila sat at a table by the window, big as you please, where everyone who passed by could see her talking and smiling with an Englisch man. The man was tall, dressed in jeans and a leather jacket. He was smooth shaven. He leaned forward as if hanging on Leila's every word.

Someone bumped Jesse from behind, knocking him forward a step. An elderly man, dressed in a long wool overcoat far too heavy for south Texas's mild winters, stumbled back and shook his cane, his grizzled face red. "Watch it, buddy—you don't own the sidewalk."

"Sorry, sorry." Jesse sidestepped the man and allowed him to pass. "I'm sorry."

Still muttering, the old man hobbled on, the cane clacking in a brisk staccato against the cement, the scent of mothballs and spearmint mouthwash wafting behind him.

Jesse pressed himself up against the brick exterior of the squat one-story building and then hazarded a peek inside. If anyone saw him, they'd think he'd lost his mind. Like a spy or something. A spy in suspenders, work boots that had seen better days, and a straw hat. The man's face looked familiar. A second passed as Jesse grappled with memories. The EMT from the accident. That was it. How did Leila know an EMT?

Hurt mixed with anger raced through Jesse like a stampede of javelinas. What was she doing in public with yet another Englischer? This one was no boy like the one in the park. He was a man. Letting her work at the day care had been a mistake. He would tell his daed and Mordecai. He drew a painful breath, his heart thumping in his chest, and closed his eyes against the bright afternoon sun that took the December nip from the air. What a hypocrite he was. He'd been the one to take her to the movies. He'd been the one to kiss her on her first date in her entire life. He'd been the one to confuse her with his waffling, his inability to pick a world and stay in it. What was she to think?

And who was he to judge her? He was doing something far worse in the eyes of their community. He didn't just share meals with Englischers; he worshipped with them. Something he planned to continue to do. Something he wanted her to do with him.

And she knew it. Yet she said nothing.

Gott, forgive me. Help me. I don't know how to do this.

He had no right to interfere. His heart might be

clenched in painful hurt, but his brain shook a finger at him, reminding him. He had no right.

"Hey, Jesse. What are you doing?"

He opened his eyes to find Matthew Plank leaning out the window of a rusty, faded-blue minivan with a series of long aluminum ladders strapped to a rack on top. A vinyl sign stuck to the side read PLANK HOME IMPROVEMENT. Underneath was a rough sketch of a pile of wooden planks with a hammer on top. "Nothing, I'm doing nothing."

Matthew slapped his hand on the passenger door. "You look a little peaked. Are you sick or something? Do you need a ride?"

"Nee. Nee." Jesse straightened and swallowed the bile in the back of his throat. He coughed. "I'm just, I mean, I have to go . . ."

Matthew's gaze bobbed toward the coffee shop, encompassing the window and the occupants at the table so unaware of passersby. "Ah."

"Nee."

"Get in. We're headed over to the Corn House for a quick bite before we get back to work. Come on, join us." Matthew jerked his head toward the driver. His brother Angus, four years younger, twenty pounds heavier, and whiskerless, had both hands on the wheel. "Angus here is a good driver. He's been practicing. He even has his license now. Come on."

Jesse chose not to share with Matthew that not only did he know how to drive, but he had taken his test and received his license earlier in the month. He hadn't used it yet, but it was only a matter of time. "I need a part for the generator. I just came in for it. Mr. Cramer's meeting me at the hardware store later this afternoon to give me a ride back."

"We'll get you there. I promise." Matthew grinned. "Hop in."

Something about Matthew's grin invited Jesse to leave this quagmire behind. Even if only for an hour. Ignoring the voice in his head that said he would soon drown in the quicksand of his own making, he tugged open the sliding door and hauled himself into the back of the van where tepid warm air from the heater grazed his face. Rubbing his cold hands together, he settled back in a seat that featured coffee and grease-stained upholstery.

The interior of the van smelled of an acrid mix of varnish, paint thinner, grease, and man sweat. Next to him was a box of doorknobs and other assorted hardware. He swiveled his head and encountered an assortment of tools and wood stacked in the back. The last row of seats had been removed to make more room for buckets, paintbrushes, and a folded stepladder.

"My company on wheels." Matthew seemed to read his mind. "I don't have a garage so I keep everything in the van, ready to roll."

"Makes sense."

Something about the van felt homey. Jesse settled into the seat and tried to leave behind the miry pit that was his quandary over Leila. A few minutes later they pulled into a spot in front of Jesse's favorite drive-by restaurant. The Corn House sold roasted corn, nachos, Fritos pies, flaming hot Cheetos covered with cheese, and pickles. Nothing good for a person, in other words. The best kind of restaurant.

"What'll it be? It's on me." Matthew already had his billfold out. "I'm all about the Fritos pie myself."

"Roasted corn with chili and lime would be good, but I'll pay for mine." Jesse removed his straw hat and dug behind the thin band inside it that held his tiny savings, trying to remember how much money he had. It wasn't much, but enough to cover his own lunch. "I wouldn't mind a Fritos pie too."

Matthew waved away the money. "My treat. I've been wanting to talk to you for a while."

Everyone seemed to want a piece of him these days: Colton, Will, Matthew. His appetite waned. *Peace, Gott, all I want is peace.*

How to get there?

A few minutes later the van filled with the aroma of roasted corn. Jesse's mouth watered. It had been a long time since breakfast. He took the white paper sack Matthew offered and sank his teeth into the hot corn. Juice ran down his chin. He sopped it up with a paper napkin, ignoring Matthew's grin.

"We're headed to the old Driscoll place. We're restoring both the interior and the exterior." His voice full of undisguised enthusiasm, Matthew scooted around in his seat so he half faced Jesse. "It's a sweet Southern Colonial with big columns in the front. It was built in the original Beeville home district around the mid–eighteen hundreds."

Jesse nodded and tried to look interested. Most of the words didn't mean much to him. Matthew didn't seem to mind. "We have to rebuild the columns in front. They're basically shells wrapped around six-by-six beams. Once they're repaired, we'll put them back in place, just like the originals. It's slow going, but we're getting there. Ain't that right, Angus?"

Angus's shaggy-haired head bobbed. "We're getting there."

Staring out the window at the businesses and then houses that flashed by, Jesse finished his corn, ignored the greasy melted butter on his fingers, and started on the Fritos pie. Angus made a turn onto Jackson Street and then Washington. In minutes they pulled into a drive behind a house that faced Washington. Scaffolding adorned the columns across the front.

"We're here." Matthew balled up his paper sack and threw it into the pile on the floor near Jesse's feet. "You interested in a job by any chance?"

"I have a job at my daed's store."

"Jah, but I can pay you. Restoring old houses pays a decent wage." He chuckled. "Good thing. Ruth is expecting again."

Matthew had left the old ways behind in every sense. No Plain man would make such an announcement. Jesse squirmed in his seat.

"Jah, it's soon after the twins, but God is good. We are blessed."

"Jah."

"So who's the girl?"

"The girl?"

"At Miss Marie's."

"I have to get back."

"You have time. Tell me why you were gawking at a Plain girl sitting in Miss Marie's with some guy."

Jesse shrugged. "I didn't mean to gawk."

"Sure you did. If I hadn't come along, I reckon you'd have gone in there and said something to her. Who is she? I don't recognize her. Must be new since I left."

"She's just a girl. I'm sort of courting her." Only not. "I mean, I took her to the movies once."

"Once?" Matthew's thick black eyebrows rose and fell. "Then you realized you were in a bit of a pickle over staying or going?"

"I already knew that. It was a mistake. Taking her."

Matthew ran his hand through hair already sticking up all over the place. "You gotta go for it." Exactly what Colton said. "So you *are* leaving?"

Since that moment after the crash when he'd bent over little Hilary and Hannah, he had known. God called him to do this. No going back. The questions that remained involved his heart and the girl who'd stolen it. "Yes, but I'm still figuring some things out."

"Like the girl?"

"Jah."

"Does she have a strong faith?"

"Jah."

"Then neither of you has anything to lose and you have so much to gain."

He was worse than Colton. "I have to go."

Matthew tugged a toolbox from the foot well. "You have time. I want you to see the work we're doing. You'd be good at it."

"How do you know?"

"Plain men work hard." Matthew shoved open his door. "My brothers Phillip and Solomon are coming down from Ohio."

"To visit?"

"Nee. Me and Angus have been talking to them about what we're doing. They're thinking about joining us."

"Joining you in the business."

"The business and our way of life."

Even long distance, Matthew could be convincing. "You'd do that to your parents?"

"I'm not doing it to them. I wish they would see the light too. We could all fellowship together. We could start our own worship services."

"You'd have taken four sons from them, if you include yourself."

"They still have Jacob and Silas. Those two will never leave. Jacob drew the lot. He's a deacon now."

"Why are you telling me this?"

"I want you to know you have a place to come, if you decide to do what you're thinking about doing."

Jesse studied the naked beams, waiting to be covered again. They still supported the weight of the porch roof, but they had no beauty. Function, but nothing to shroud their ugliness. The families in his district, including his own, didn't paint their houses or gussy them up in any way. They lived a bare-bones existence and they didn't mind. They didn't care about the junkyard by the Combination Store. They didn't care about the rusty siding on the houses. External beauty didn't matter.

Were his feelings for Leila about the way she looked?

Or a deeper beauty? In her Plain dress, her apron, and her kapp, she still looked beautiful to him. Her lips felt beautiful when he kissed them. If he went to work for Matthew, he likely wouldn't be allowed to see her again.

Ever.

His heart contracted in a painful hiccup. He couldn't stay for her. Yet he didn't want to live without her.

Matthew hopped from his seat. A minute later the van door slid open. "Feel like slinging a hammer for a few minutes?"

Maybe he could pound out his frustration. Jesse swallowed and nodded, unable to form the words.

Matthew paused, hand on the door. "I've been where you are. I know this isn't easy. It shouldn't be easy. Our faith is honed in the fire. God is with you always."

"Isn't He with our families also?"

"He is. And He will carry them through this. Do what you have to do. He will ease their pain, just as He bears yours."

"And Leila?"

"The decision is hers." Matthew handed him a hammer. "But that doesn't mean you shouldn't make your case."

"I've tried."

"Try again. Keep trying."

He was right. "I need to go back to the coffee shop."

"Not right this minute. Choose the time and place well. Take her for a buggy ride."

Jesse took the hammer Matthew offered him and hauled himself from the van. He landed on solid ground for the first time in months.

CHAPTER 28

The thud of a horse's hooves on the dirt road outside her window brought Leila straight up out of bed. She hadn't been able to sleep or slept fitfully, her dreams full of strange uneasiness, since the night of little Timothy's birth. She slid back the curtain and peered out, careful to keep out of sight in her nightgown. A buggy, battery-operated lights flashing and bobbing when the buggy hit ruts in the road, approached.

She closed her eyes. She had to choose. That's what she'd told Deborah. Every night since that conversation with her sister, she'd lain in bed, trying to piece together the quilt of thoughts that would cover her with a peaceful solution.

Always it led her to a place where she felt at cross-purposes with Gott. He knew her name before she was born. He knew how many hairs were on her head. He provided for her just as He provided for the sparrows. Why could she not simply trust that He had a plan? When the time came, she would make the choice He'd planned for her all along.

The way her family worshipped, it was right and good in God's eyes. She believed that. So why had she felt this deep welling of blessedness as she sat next to Jesse in Tiffany's living room? As if God had taken her hand and led her to this place Himself.

Why did she feel completed every time Jesse put his hand on hers?

How could she love her family so much and yet feel so convicted by Jesse's words?

They were stuck at cross-purposes when they were both trying to get to the same place. *What would Gott say about that?* Surely their puny human brains could no more fathom Gott's greater plan than a ladybug or a hummingbird could.

She leaned from the window, staring down. Butch didn't bark. Maybe he only barked at cars. Buggies meant friends. She squinted, trying to see beyond the bright lights to what the darkness held beyond them. The person who hopped from the buggy was tall. Too tall for Jesse.

Will.

She heaved a breath. The memory of his arm around her waist and the gentle way he held her as they danced on Thanksgiving Day sparred with the darker, intense memories of sitting on Tiffany's porch, her shoulder brushing against Jesse's. Of Jesse's kiss.

Light blinded her. It bobbed and skittered away. "Will?" She kept her voice low, hoping not to wake Rebekah and Hazel.

"Jah."

"What are you doing here?"

"What do you think? Come down here."

"Did you come to warn me off someone or something?"

"I came to ask you to take a ride with me." His tone made the words a challenge. "It's a nice night. I have blankets in the buggy if you think it's too cool."

"I'm not dancing anymore. Ever." She couldn't allow herself to be confused by the comfort she found in having his arms around her. "No more boom box."

"I didn't even bring the thing. The batteries are dead."

"Wait there."

Fingers shaking, all thumbs, she scrambled into her clothes. She fumbled in the dark, bumped the crate, and stubbed her toe on the bedpost. Rebekah stirred and muttered in her sleep. "Shush, shush, you'll wake Hazel," Leila whispered. "Go back to sleep."

"Stop talking." Rebekah groaned and rolled over, arm thrown over her little sister. The rest of her words were lost in a mumble laced with sleep.

Leila took another minute to smooth her hair and slap on her kapp. She tiptoed down the stairs, shoes in her hands. At the door, she stopped and listened. Nothing except a house settling and creaking in the night wind. *Gott, help me make the right decision. Heart and head hand in hand.*

On the porch, Will squatted next to Butch, one hand on the dog's back, the other holding the flashlight, creating skittish blobs of light on the floor beneath his boots. He straightened, slipped down the steps, and turned. "Let me help you up."

Knowing full well she didn't need his help, Leila took his hand. His fingers were warm, the skin rough. Gaze on the buggy step, she hauled herself up and forced herself to let go. Her hand wanted to stay wrapped in his. She sighed.

"Why the sigh?" He slid onto the seat next to her and picked up the reins. "Is my company that onerous to you?"

"Nee. Confusing, that's all."

Will didn't answer. The buggy jolted forward, headlights blending with the light of a half-moon to cast elongated shadows on the pitted road. He slapped the reins and the horse picked up his pace. Maybe she had offended him with her honesty. One thing she knew for certain, the relationship between a man and his wife had to be based on honesty. She was confused. How could she have all these feelings for Jesse and yet enjoy Will's company?

Because he made her feel safe. She had to give up nothing to be with him. He was steady and true to their faith. With Will, she could have everything she'd ever wanted. The life her mudder and daed expected her to live.

With Jesse? The abyss opened at her feet and left her breathless with a fearful anticipation. She couldn't see the future with Jesse, only what it didn't hold: her parents, Deborah, Rebekah, Hazel, Caleb, her new nephew.

She saw a gaping hole where her family had once been.

She shivered.

"You're cold. I should've brought more blankets."

Will transferred the reins to one hand and used the other to pull the fleece blanket up around her chest. He turned the buggy onto the road—more of a path than a road—that led to the back side of Mordecai's property. Where the apiaries dotted the landscape during the day. The bees were down for the winter.

Leila tried to relax. She inhaled cool, fresh air that stung her nose and her lungs. White puffs clouded the air with each breath she took. Stars hung crystal clear in the night sky. "It feels good. We spend so much time being hot and sweaty around here. I miss winter."

"I've never experienced a real, cold winter with snow."

So they would talk about the weather again. As they had done before dancing. Will was no conversationalist, but then, neither was she.

"You should visit Tennessee at Christmas one year." Images of Daed throwing snowballs at her, missing, and knocking an arm off the snowman they'd all made together assailed Leila. She hadn't thought of that in a long time. Warm memories despite the cold of that day. "You can have fun playing in the snow and then go inside for cocoa and s'mores."

"We have fun here too."

"Once in a blue moon."

"Often enough."

"Did you come out here to argue with me?"

"Nee. Daed has decided to move the family back to Tennessee."

So Will wouldn't be visiting Tennessee at Christmas. He'd be living there, a thousand miles away. She swallowed the sudden knot that threatened to choke her. "When?"

"After the first of the year."

"So you'll experience winter. The snow and the cocoa and the s'mores."

He jerked on the reins and brought the buggy to a sudden halt. "That's all you have to say?"

"What do you want me to say?"

"That you have a horse in this race."

Leila shoved the blanket away, suddenly warm. "Do I?" It was a stupid question. Of course she did. It wasn't fair to Will to imply otherwise. "I mean, I don't know what to think. You run hot and cold. You show up and then you don't. Do I have a horse in this race?"

Will hopped from the buggy and stormed down the middle of the road, arms flapping. "You tell me."

"You dance with me and then run away." Leila sprang down on her side and marched after him. "You're the one who's been wishy-washy. I have no idea what you think."

"I think it's wrong to horn in on a cousin's girl." He faced her, his white teeth glinting in the moonlight. "I think it's wrong for a girl to kiss one man and dance with another."

Leila slapped her hands on her hips. "Maybe a girl wouldn't do that if someone would speak up and make his intentions clear."

"I just did."

They glared at each other. Leila refused to let her gaze drop. Will's jaw worked. His hands went to his hips in an unconscious imitation of her pose. He sniffed, whirled, and marched away.

"Will Glick, get back here."

He kept walking.

"Fine."

He turned and marched straight at her. He kept coming, not stopping. The look on his face made Leila's fingers flutter to her cheeks. His big hands engulfed hers, drawing them away from her face with that same gentle touch he'd used to wrap her against him in a dance. His face hovered over hers. "I'm here now."

Leila closed her eyes and leaned into him. His fingers left her hands and made their way to her neck, cupping her face so she couldn't move. She stopped breathing.

He let go and she plummeted back to earth.

She opened her eyes. Will towered over her, glowering, his breathing harsh. "I'm here. I may not . . . show how I feel the way some men do, but I'm here."

"I know you are." Did she feel relief or disappointment that he'd stopped short when she'd been so sure he would take one more step forward in this strange dance they did? He was here and being with him cost her nothing. Except Jesse. Jesse. What did it say about her that he crowded her thoughts at this very moment? "I'm . . . I'm . . ."

"You're what?" Will crossed his arms. "You have to make a choice."

Perhaps the choice had already been made for her. *Gott, forgive me.* "I know. I know I do."

"I choose you."

Her heart did that jerky thing again. If he left, the choice was made for her. The coward's way out. She wasn't a coward. "You're not going to Tennessee then?"

"This isn't about whether I'm going and you know it.

This is about what you'll do with all this." He flung his arm toward her and then back so his hand rested on his chest. "With you and me."

She cleared her throat. The pounding of her heart made it hard to think. She didn't want this power to hurt him. *Gott, take this cup from me.* "It's just that I'm...I can't...I mean, I have to figure out something."

His hands went back to his hips. "Jesse?"

"Jesse."

"Do what you have to do." He brushed past her. "Time to go home."

She couldn't tell him about the Wednesday night group. Or the way she'd felt when she suggested Tom go back to church to assuage his loneliness. This wasn't only about Jesse. Leila followed Will to the buggy on shaky legs. "Nothing has been decided yet."

"And if he chooses the district, it'll be because he doesn't want to lose you. He gets you."

"Those are two separate things."

"You need to stay away from him before you get sucked in too."

How could she tell him it was very possible his admonition came too late? She caught his sleeve and tugged. He turned. His expression wasn't the anger she expected. He looked fearful—for her. She wanted to wipe that look away. "I'm strong in my beliefs."

Which was at the root of everything. For Jesse and for her.

"So is Jesse. That's how he got sucked in."

"He was looking for something, or it wouldn't have happened." She accepted Will's offer of a hand and tottered into the buggy. Grateful to be seated, she searched for words to ease his concern. "Give me time."

He settled into the seat next to her. A pulse beat in his jaw. "You have unfinished business. Finish it." He snapped the reins and the buggy jolted forward. "I'll be here one way or another. I'm not going anywhere."

The words hung in the air like a promise. He'd asked for none in return. A gift.

They made the ride back to Mordecai's in silence. Leila kept reliving the look on Will's face when he bent over her. Such determination. Such intent. Such a struggle to abstain.

Such love.

She searched her heart. Did she feel the same? Her hands shook and her legs felt like wet noodles. It was one thing to react to a man's touch. Another to take his heart and give hers in return. Jesse's face hovered in her mind's eye. She couldn't be certain she still possessed her heart to give. Her feelings for Jesse, as muddled as they were, traveled far beyond the kiss they'd shared so long ago in that movie theater.

"You have company."

Will's voice startled her from the painful consideration of her own inability to separate the two. A figure did indeed huddle on the front step. Leila peered through the darkness, unable to make out a face. A baby's wail pierced the dark serenity of the night.

Trevor. Rory, with Trevor wailing on her lap, sat on Mordecai's front porch. No ride home in sight.

CHAPTER 29

Between the crying baby and the crying mommy, the noisy waterworks filled the dark night. Leila pushed aside Butch, who seemed intent on providing some sort of doggy comfort to Rory or investigating the contents of the diaper bag, she couldn't be sure which. Leila shoved aside a pile of stuff that turned out to be two duffel bags, a folded baby stroller, and an overflowing diaper bag. She sank onto the porch step next to Rory and tugged Trevor from her friend's arms. To her surprise, Will had jumped from the buggy right behind her and stood nearby, a comforting presence.

"Hush, baby, hush, hush," she cooed to Trevor as she inhaled his familiar scent of baby wipes and diaper-rash ointment. "You'll wake the whole house."

The sound of the baby's cries receded, only to be replaced by sniffles that emanated from his mother. "What's the matter?" Leila snuggled Trevor against her chest with one hand and patted Rory's shoulder with the other. "Did something happen?"

Silly question. Of course something happened.

Rory laid her head in her arms and sobbed.

"What can I do to help?" Leila rubbed the girl's back. "Do you need a ride home? Will and I can take you."

"Daddy kicked me out." The words were muffled against the girl's arms. "He called Dwayne and told him to come fetch his wife. He stuffed the baby's Pack 'n Play into its bag and set it out on the front porch."

That didn't sound like Nolan. "Did you argue with him?"

The girl raised her head. Tears soaked her face and her eyes were rimmed with red. "I don't know what I'm going to do." Her lower lip quivered and a fresh batch of tears rolled down her cheeks. "I'm pregnant again."

Lord, have mercy.

Leila glanced at Will. Eyebrows raised, he shrugged. A person didn't have words for such a thing. To have kinner was to be blessed in every circumstance. Rory and Dwayne were man and wife. Still, Leila could see why Nolan would be upset, considering he supported his daughter and grandson, while the husband and father did neither. Still, to throw out his grandson . . . he must be heartsick. "And what does Dwayne say?"

"He says it's too soon. He says it's my fault." Rory's voice rose to a shriek. "He says he can't support me and Trevor, let alone another baby."

Rory wailed. Trevor joined in. A regular concert. Any minute Mudder or Mordecai would be at the door to see what the ruckus was all about.

"Hush, hush, both of you." Leila tucked Trevor's pacifier in his mouth and began to rock. "How did you get here?"

"Dwayne got mad and I started yelling and he was

yelling and the baby was crying so I told him to let me out of the car."

Rory swiped at her face with her jacket sleeve. "At first he said no, but then I yelled at him that he wasn't my boss or my keeper or nothing like that. I could raise our babies by myself just fine. To dump me by the side of the road. We'd be just fine."

"But he wouldn't do that," Will interjected. "No man worth his salt would."

"He brought me here instead." A sound like crickets chirping burst from the cell phone in her hand. She flashed it at Leila. "He's been texting me every five seconds, but I'm not answering."

Leila tugged Trevor's blanket up around his face. The *slurp-slurp* of the pacifier had stopped. He slept. She rose. "You'd best come on in. It's cold and it's late."

"I didn't mean to invite myself to a sleepover. I tried calling my friends from school, but everyone's asleep." Rory sounded relieved despite her words. "I'll get one of them to pick me up first thing in the morning. Pam or Alison can give you a ride to work when they come for me."

"Let's see what the morning brings."

"Nothing will be different in the morning." Rory stumbled to her feet. "I have a Spanish test just like always."

Leila opened the screen door and waited for Rory to go in. Will scooped up the bags and strode through the door behind her. "You don't have to do that."

He paused inside the door. "You'd best have a word with your mudder right quick." He settled the bags on the floor and held out his arms. "Give me the baby while you let your folks know they have company."

Mordecai's house. His guests. She eased the sleeping baby into Will's arms. He corralled the child against his chest. He looked as at ease with this task as he had carrying the bags. She hesitated. He looked up from the bundle in his arms. "What?"

"Nothing."

"Then go. Rory looks tuckered out and this baby needs a bed."

"We have a cradle. We'll put him in it so we don't have to set up the Pack 'n Play right now. Rory can have my spot in the bed. I have a sleeping bag."

"I can't put you out of your bed." Rory pointed to the couch. "I'll sleep here."

Not where Mordecai and the boys would pass by in the morning. "I'll be right back."

Leila paused at the closed door that led to Mordecai and Mudder's bedroom. She put her hand on the doorknob, then let it drop. She raised it again to knock. Before she could, the door opened and Mudder peered out. "What's the matter?" Her voice was the barest whisper. "Are you sick?"

"How did you know I was out here?"

"You knocked."

"Nee, I didn't."

"A mudder knows when her child needs her."

"It's Rory. She's here with the baby."

Mudder disappeared from sight. Leila lingered in the hall, not sure what to do next. Was Mudder telling Mordecai? A few seconds later Mudder returned, her hair covered by her kapp. Her nightclothes replaced by a dress. She squeezed through the door and shut it behind her. "Is Rory all right? Is the baby sick?"

"Nee."

Leila waited for her mother to notice that she was already fully dressed, but Mudder brushed past her and trotted on bare feet toward the front room. "She'd best spend the night then. It's too late for her to be gallivanting around the countryside with a baby."

"Mudder."

Her mother paused and looked back. "What is it, child?"

"Her father kicked her out because she's expecting again. He said her husband should take care of her."

"As well he should. Where is this husband?"

"They argued—"

"We'll worry about it in the morning."

Mudder trudged ahead of Leila into the front room. Will had turned on the kerosene lamp and taken up a spot next to the dark fireplace. He'd given the baby to Rory, who huddled in a rocking chair, her sleeping son on her lap, her face wet, head down in the flickering light.

Mudder didn't hesitate. "Will, you'd best get on home now. It's late."

He made his way toward the door without speaking. At the last second, he turned and nodded at Leila. She managed a quick nod back, knowing Mudder missed nothing. He pulled the door closed behind him with a gentle tug that made no sound.

Mudder bustled across the room. "Leila, put the

cradle in your room. Rory's a tiny thing; she'll squeeze in next to Esther. It's time everyone was in bed."

Leila started toward the closet that held the cradle, blankets, quilts, and towels. Outside, an engine raced. A horn shrieked again and again. The sound of splintering wood filled the air, along with ferocious barking and a horse's whinny. Rory bolted from the chair. "Dwayne—he's come back for me."

Trevor wiggled in her arms and began to wail as his mother dashed for the front door. With a fierce frown, Mudder marched after the girl. Leila slid in behind them.

Will's voice rose above the rumble of the engine, Butch's barking, and the shrieking horn. "Stop honking! You almost hit me. You hit the buggy. You could've killed my horse."

"Butch, hush, hush!" Leila squeezed past her mother and raced down the steps. "Are you all right, Will?"

The honking ceased. Butch sat down on the porch, but his jagged teeth remained bared in a snarl.

The buggy lay crumpled against the porch, back wheels bent and broken, one side crushed under the bumper of Dwayne's pickup truck, which looked none the worse for wear. Will slapped his hat against his leg as if removing dust and debris. "I am, but the buggy is destroyed."

"What is going on here?" Mordecai shoved through the screen door and slammed to a halt on the porch. Leila had never seen him angry before, but at this moment, he looked peeved. "A man deserves a decent night's sleep."

"That's what you get for not having porch lights." Dwayne staggered from the truck. The word *porch* came out *pooch*. "I come for my woman." He stumbled and fell flat on his face.

CHAPTER 30

A fall like that had to hurt, but surely the man had it coming. Will squatted next to Dwayne, who sprawled nose down on the ground. He grabbed one arm and shook it. Dwayne didn't move. His head lolled to one side. The smell of alcohol and tobacco wafted from the inert body, making Will long for a clothespin to clip on his nose.

All the commotion had awakened everyone in Mordecai's house. The girls were crowded at the windows, and Mordecai's sons milled on the porch with Leila's brother. It was like a Sunday service in the middle of the night.

"I take it this is your husband." Will glanced toward Rory, who bounced Trevor against her chest and sobbed, tiny, breathless sobs. She nodded and hiccupped as she dropped to her knees next to Dwayne. "I reckon he's in no shape to drive you anywhere."

"Is he all right?" She patted the man's dirty, stubbled cheek. "Dwayne, wake up, babe, wake up, honey."

"From the smell of him, he's drunker than a skunk. He's passed out, that's all."

"How do you know he's not hurt? He just wrecked his truck."

"No, he wrecked my buggy." Will forced himself to keep his voice level. This girl cared for the man on the ground, that was obvious. "That big pickup truck broke it like it was a toothpick. It didn't hurt the truck or him, you can be certain of that."

"It's my fault. I'm so sorry for this. I'm sorry for your buggy. I'll pay for it. I'll find a way, I promise." Tears trailed down Rory's face. Her nose was bright red and running, yet she still managed to look pretty. "I shouldn't have told my dad tonight. I should've waited. We could've done it together."

"Don't worry about the buggy." Will saw no point in rubbing salt in the poor girl's wounds. "Sometimes it just takes people awhile to adjust to new things, I reckon."

"Daddy was so mad. I never seen him so mad." She took a shuddering breath. "Not since I told him about Trevor and me and Dwayne getting married."

"But he got over it the first time." Will couldn't keep his gaze from Leila. What did she think of him giving advice to an Englisch girl about family matters? He couldn't mend things with Jesse or with her. Instead he'd come within a hairbreadth of kissing her. And she knew it. Even thinking about it only muddied the waters more. She stared back at him, eyes wide and unblinking. "Things will work out in the end. They always do."

"Everybody, back in bed. All y'all." Mordecai waved at Esther and Rebekah and shook a finger at his boys.

Everyone melted back into the house as quick as they'd appeared. Mordecai stomped down the steps and halted next to Leila, who had one hand on Rory's shoulder. "We'll drag him out to the barn. Let him sleep it off." He jerked his head toward the buggy, his beard bobbing. "Will, you might as well bed down for the night out there as well. We'll see what we can do with this mess come first light."

"I'm obliged." He straightened. Exhaustion weighed on him like stones on his shoulders. He'd like nothing more than to lay his head down and sleep. The expression on Leila's face told him nothing. Would she be aggravated or embarrassed if he stayed? "But I can take the horse and get myself home if you'll loan me a saddle. Mudder and Daed will wonder where I am come morning."

"True enough. Help me with this boy and I'll rustle you up a saddle."

Will hooked an arm under Dwayne's armpit and Mordecai did the same. Together, they heaved him from the ground. He mumbled something unintelligible, but his head drooped, eyes still closed.

"Wait, wait." Rory rose, her sleeping baby's legs flopping against her. "Dwayne, honey, wake up, baby, wake up."

"He won't wake up." Mordecai kept moving. Will followed his lead. "You'd best get some sleep. He'll be crabbier than a cougar in a cage in the morning."

Rory trailed after them. "He'll be sorry, you'll see. He's a good guy. He really is."

"Go on in the house. Leila will help you get situated."

Will waited until the women were in the house, then snorted. "A good guy? Driving so drunk he ran into my buggy. If I'd been in it, I'd be the one on the ground."

"But you weren't. Gott is good."

Indeed. They half dragged, half carried Dwayne into the barn, too focused on the task to say any more. Inside, they lowered him onto a pile of hay in the first un-occupied stall. Breathing hard, Will brushed his hands together and turned away.

"Long night." Mordecai grabbed a rake and began to fluff more hay into the pile. "Sure you don't want to stay?"

"I'd better get home."

"Because of Leila?"

Will froze, one hand on a saddle that lay across the wooden posts that separated Dwayne's new bedroom from the horse next door. "Come again?"

"That's the only reason I can think for you to be here at this hour."

That Mordecai would speak so openly of this sur-prised Will. "What are you getting at?"

"A man hears things."

"I know I do."

"Abigail's girls have had a rough row to hoe."

"They have."

"You know what you're doing?"

Will snorted. "Does anyone when it comes to this stuff?"

"Can I give you a word of advice?"

"Might as well."

"Pray about it. Put Gott at the center of your life, and everything else will follow."

"Is that what happened with Abigail?"

Dwayne emitted a snore loud enough to wake the horses. Mordecai shut the gate to the stall and headed for the barn door. "It took twelve years for Gott to bless me with another fraa after He took the first one home, but I always figured if it was meant to be, it would come in His time. Lots of folks tried to get me to marry sooner, but it never felt right."

"Until Abigail."

"Until Abigail."

"And you had no doubts?"

"I didn't say that. She came here to marry another man. I had doubts."

Leila might not have been joined to Jesse by the banns, but he had courted her. Will fell in step next to Mordecai, breathing in the cold night air. "She was intended for another. How could you even approach her knowing that?"

"Circumstances brought us together again and again, until it couldn't be denied. She couldn't deny it. I didn't want to deny it." Mordecai brought his big hands to his face and blew as he rubbed them together. "Cold tonight. Wouldn't a little snow be nice?"

Now that was dreaming. Will slipped a blanket onto his horse's back and then heaved the saddle over it. "The whole thing has me a little discombobulated."

"Trust in Gott." Mordecai patted the horse's long neck. "Then trust your heart. When it comes to Leila and when it comes to Jesse."

Will's heart slammed in his chest. His throat ached with the effort not to pour the story out to this man who had been a fixture in his life for as long as he could remember. "I don't know . . . I mean . . ."

"Don't say anything. Just listen." Mordecai cinched the saddle snug under the horse's belly and stepped back. "I ain't blind. Neither is Leroy. The time will come when choices will have to be made. Very soon. We're praying each one of you makes the right choice."

He gestured toward the pile of wood that had been the Glicks' best buggy. "Come over in the morning and we'll see if we can salvage that thing."

"Bright and early."

Mordecai looked back and grinned. "I imagine we could make quite a ruckus in the morning long about sunrise. Roust a guy off his pile of hay."

For the first time all evening, Will had the urge to smile. "Sounds about right."

"Abigail makes a fine pancake. Kaffi too."

"Crack of dawn then."

Will waited until Mordecai was inside and the light in the front room was extinguished. Then he mounted the horse and turned him toward the road and home.

The undercurrents of his conversation with Leila's stepfather most likely would carry him home, but he no longer feared drowning in them. Mordecai was a wise man. Pray. Make God the center of his world. Everything else would come after that.

. . .

Leila rolled over and covered her head with her arm, wanting to block out that rustling sound. As tired as she was, she couldn't sleep. Every time she closed her eyes, Will's face hovered over her as he bent toward her. Heat rolled through her. She'd been so sure he would kiss her, but then he didn't. Thank Gott, he hadn't. It would only muddy the waters further. So why did she keep thinking about the look on his face as he leaned in?

Even the thin sheet seemed too hot and heavy. She tossed it back. The box springs creaked and the mattress rose and fell around her. She rolled back over, raised her head, and opened her eyes to the black of night. She rubbed them with her fists and tried to focus on the figure tiptoeing away from the bed.

Rory slipping away in feet clad in thick, woolly socks.

"Where are you going?" Leila didn't need Rory traipsing around the house at night. Mordecai had the ears of a hound dog. "You need to get some sleep."

Rory glanced back and put a finger to her lips. She shook her head and kept moving.

Sighing, Leila pushed herself from the bed and followed. In the hallway Rory sped up as if pursued by a pack of javelinas. Leila wrapped her housecoat tighter and scurried after her. "Rory, wait, where are you going? It's the middle of the night."

"I need to talk to Dwayne."

"Dwayne is sleeping it off."

Rory stopped. Her head dropped and her shoulders began to shake. She slapped her hands to her face.

"It's okay, it's okay." Leila sped up so she could lay an arm around her friend and squeeze her shoulders. "You need to get some sleep. Everything will look better in the morning."

"How can it? I mean, seriously, how can things get better?" Rory shook free and marched toward the front room. "My dad's furious with me. My husband thinks the way to solve our problems is to get drunk, and I'm a high school kid with a baby and another one on the way. What was I thinking?"

Her wail was enough to wake everyone in the house. Leila grabbed her arm and tugged her toward the kitchen. "Come on. You need a cup of chamomile tea to settle you down. You're expecting. You need to stay calm for your baby."

Rory wailed louder.

"Hush, hush, everyone just got back to sleep. We don't want to wake them again."

"I can't believe I'm having another baby. I just did this."

Leila couldn't answer that one. Not without asking questions that would embarrass both of them. "You've done a good job with Trevor. You'll be a good momma to this new baby."

"I'm so tired all the time." Rory plopped onto a chair and laid her head on the table. "I throw up my breakfast every morning and sometimes lunch too."

"That will pass." So Leila had heard. She put the tea-kettle on the propane stove and turned up the flame. "You have some time to figure things out. Tomorrow you can go say you're sorry to your dad."

"He was so mad. So mad." Rory straightened and ran her fingers through hair already wild from repeated rakings. "And he has a right to be."

That admission was an important one. "Tell him

that. Tell him you're sorry you're putting them through this again. An apology goes a long way."

"You're so lucky." Rory looked around the kitchen. "You have a big family and you all do everything together. You have three sisters and a mother and y'all go to church together and have meals together."

"You don't go to church?" Leila had never dared ask the question before. It wasn't any of her business. They didn't judge other folks' ways of worshipping. Which made her think of Jesse. He'd think her a bad friend for never talking to Rory about her beliefs. "I don't mean to stick my nose where it doesn't belong."

"We went to church when my mom was alive. Every Sunday." Rory's eyes shone and her whole body perked up. "We went to Sunday school and to church picnics and the fall festival and the chili cook-off and the Easter egg hunt."

Leila poured hot water over the tea bags in two big mugs. She carried them to the table and took a seat. This was a conversation friends had where they could see each other's expressions and know what their hearts said. "And when your momma died, everything changed?"

"Totally." Rory spooned enough honey into her cup to sweeten a pitcher of tea. "Daddy barely went out of the house for weeks, except to work. People kept coming by, bringing food and checking on us. He told every single one of them we were fine."

"But you weren't."

"We weren't fine. We aren't fine now."

Letting the fragrance of chamomile, like sweet flowers,

envelop her, Leila sipped her tea. It burned her throat all the way to her stomach. Maybe it would burn away the terrible ache that throbbed in her chest. She, too, remembered the days and weeks and months after her father's death. A smile fixed on her face, Mudder went about her business as if nothing had changed. She tilled the land and planted the garden and fixed the meals and sewed clothes until late in the night, never once shedding a tear in front of her children.

"We weren't fine either, when my father died."

"I thought you Amish folks believed in God's will and God's plan and that people's days are numbered on this earth."

A touch of sarcasm permeated Rory's words, but Leila understood where it had come from. Sometimes a thing happened that was so inconceivable, it was impossible to imagine God meant for it to happen.

Sacrilegious. That's what Mordecai would say. He lost his wife in a horrible van accident that left his son scarred for life. Yet he didn't shake his fist at the sky.

But that didn't mean he hadn't wanted to do it.

"We do." Leila reached across the table and squeezed Rory's hand. "But we're only human. There's a hole in my heart where my daed should be. Gott will fill it up. I know He will. Seek Him out and He will do the same for you. You only have to ask."

Rory laid her head on the table and sobbed. "I want my mom."

Every fiber in Leila's being screamed to join her. "I know you do." She brushed the girl's hair from her face and stroked her head. "It'll get better, I promise."

"When? I need her now. I can't do this by myself anymore."

"You're not alone. You have Gott and your daed and me and Dwayne. I pray for you every day and I know my mudder does and I imagine your daed does too."

The crying subsided and Rory raised her head. "You pray for me?"

"Yes."

"Do you pray Dwayne and I work it out? Or that I come to my senses and realize he's never gonna be a good father? That's what my dad prays, I imagine."

"I pray Gott's will be done in your life, that Dwayne grows up sooner rather than later, and that Trevor will be loved and cared for by both his parents. That you and Dwayne bring Trevor up in a godly home."

Rory smiled through her tears. "You're a good friend."

Surprise blossomed in Leila. She had talked about God to Rory and it had worked. Her friend needed God in her life, and if Leila were truly a good friend, she would help her find Him.

No wonder Jesse felt called. It felt good.

CHAPTER 31

Traffic this early in the morning could only mean one thing. The familiar rumble of a truck engine sent Leila scrambling from the breakfast table, through the front room, and out the door, her cup of kaffi still in her hand. Nolan Beale had come. And early, at that.

She'd dragged herself from bed at dawn to send Caleb to the store to call Mr. Carson to take her to work and Rory to school. Late-night crisis or not, they all had obligations to fulfill in the early-morning light. The money would come from her meager savings, but she had no choice. She couldn't miss work and Rory had to go to school.

Nolan pulled the truck in next to the pile of boards and hardware that had been the Glicks' buggy and turned off the engine. For a second Leila thought he would stay in the truck. After a bit of hesitation he opened the door and emerged, his head covered by a thick wool cap and his coat buttoned up to his neck. He ducked his head against the brisk breeze. Butch sniffed at his hand once, twice, and then settled back at his post on the porch. The dog knew a good man when he saw him.

"What happened here?" Nolan motioned toward the buggy remnants. "Looks bad."

"No one was hurt. Thanks to Gott." She leaned on the railing and stared at the broken wheels piled one on top of the other. Mordecai, Andrew, and Will were on their way to the store to talk to Leroy. He was the best at building buggies. If anyone could restore it, he could. "It got hit by a truck."

Dwayne's truck, which no longer sat in their front yard. Apparently he'd left without trying to talk to Rory. Too ashamed? Too hungover? He hadn't even looked in on his son. She couldn't fathom such an attitude in a father. Still, Nolan already thought poorly of his son-in-law. She hated to heap coals on the boy's head.

"I was looking for Rory." He cleared his throat. "I went by her . . . Dwayne's house. His mother said she hadn't been there. In fact, she hadn't seen Dwayne either. I couldn't think of another place, unless they did something stupid like run off. I'm hoping they didn't run off . . ."

"They didn't run off." Leila shut the door behind her to keep the cold from permeating the house. "Rory's here. She's still getting dressed."

"I can wait."

Leila peered past him to the back of the truck's extended cab. "Where's Sawyer?"

"I dropped him off with my sister. She'll make sure he gets to school on time."

It must all be so confusing for the little boy. "Why don't you come in for a cup of kaffi?"

"I don't want to trouble anyone."

"It's no trouble." Leila held open the door. "Kaffi's hot and so are the pancakes."

Nolan peeled off the wool cap and squashed it in oversized hands. "I ate breakfast."

Leila doubted that, but she kept her mouth closed as she led him into the house and to the table where the women were still cleaning up from breakfast. Mudder looked from Leila to Nolan, then wiped her hands on her apron. "I'll fetch Rory. Esther, you finish up the dishes. Leila, get Nolan some kaffi."

She bustled out and Leila did as she was told. Nolan shifted from one foot to the other, then plopped into a chair that creaked under his large frame.

Hoping the scent of coffee and fresh-made biscuits would soothe the man in some small way, Leila poured him a big mug of coffee and set it in front of him. "Milk? Sugar?"

"No, thanks." He took a sip and his expression eased for a second. "Good coffee. Hits the spot. This is the coldest December we've had in a while."

Men always took refuge in talking about the weather.

"Hot kaffi on a cold day is truly a blessing." She refilled her own cup and returned the pot to its pot holder. "Help yourself to a biscuit. They're hot, too, and we have molasses."

"Y'all must think I'm the worst kind of father."

Leila let the silence after those abrupt words linger for a beat or two, trying to summon a response. "We don't think any such thing. We don't judge people. We have enough planks in our own eyes."

"I surely love that girl, but she's driving me to the edge of the cliff." Nolan grabbed a napkin from the table and swiped at his face. "Without her mother to guide her, she's lost."

"She has you." Leila plopped two biscuits on a plate and set them in front of Nolan. She shoved a saucer of butter and a jar of honey toward him. "Rory loves you and she cares what you think. She's made her share of mistakes, but I reckon we all do."

"Those mistakes don't end with another child to raise and to care for and to teach right from wrong." Nolan twisted a napkin in knots, ignoring the biscuits. "I don't begrudge her the food or the money it takes to raise a baby. It's the responsibility. Without her mother, I'm . . . I've messed this up with Rory. How much better will I do with my grandchildren?"

"They say practice makes perfect." Leila eased into the chair across from him. "I'm just a girl, but it seems to me a father's love goes a long way toward raising a child right."

Nolan's Adam's apple bobbed, but he managed a halfhearted smile. "You've met Dwayne. Tell me you think he can be a father to those children."

"He's the one who ran into our friend's buggy and squashed it." Leila couldn't help herself. Nolan already knew what he was up against. "He was upset. I think he came to apologize to Rory."

"But he got drunk first." Nolan broke off a piece of the biscuit and popped it in his mouth without the benefit of the butter or honey. "I love that girl more than life itself, but when it comes to him, she doesn't have the sense God gave a gnat. He's a kid; he's not cut out to be a father."

"He will be. Give him time. Teach him what he needs to know."

"That's a tall order."

"I reckon you'd best get started so he'll do a better job with the next one."

"Daddy?" Rory stood in the doorway, Trevor on her hip. "I'm so glad you came." She shot across the room, Trevor crowing as he bounced on her hip. "I'm sorry. I'm sorry. I'm so sorry."

Nolan stood and held out his arms. Rory barreled into him so hard, he took a step back and knocked into his chair. "Easy, girl, easy."

"I didn't mean the ugly things I said. You're the best dad ever." The flow of tears had returned once again. "I don't know how you put up with me."

"You're my kid." He wrapped her in a hug that included Trevor, who squealed and shrieked something that sounded a lot like "Poppy." "And this is my grandson."

"Take me back?"

"We have to talk about some things. It can't be like it's been."

"I know, I know. I'll tell Dwayne we're done."

Nolan peeled her arms from his waist and took a step back. "Dwayne's your husband. He's Trevor's father. He has to man up and take responsibility. We'll have a conversation when everyone has calmed down a little."

"Daddy? That's the first time you've ever called Dwayne by his name."

Or admitted that his daughter was married to the man. Leila hid her smile. Indeed, a big day for Nolan Beale and Rory Chapman.

Change was possible. Anything was possible.

CHAPTER 32

Every dollar counted. Especially when they came in two, three, or four at a time. Jesse collected the four dollar bills, two quarters, and two dimes Thelma Doolittle laid on the glass-top counter and slid them into the open cash register drawer. The coins were sticky as if the lady had been eating some of the honey she'd just purchased. The smell of her perfume, like an overgrown row of rosebushes, permeated the store. Ignoring the temptation to hold his breath, he smacked the drawer shut and glanced out the store window. The sun had dropped in the west. This day would soon be over and he still hadn't done what he came to do.

"You don't have any okra?" Thelma's white-haired head tilted over a body shaped like an oversized pear as she surveyed the store crowded with all manner of homemade soaps, candles, jars of honey and jams, books on raising bees, saddles, rocking chairs, quilts, and piles of stuff that could only be described as junk—until someone bought it and declared it treasure. "No produce at all?"

"Too soon for the greenhouse crops, and the fall crops are all gone."

She sighed, a long, drawn-out, gusty sigh that made her triple chin quiver. "It's only December and I'm ready for spring and fresh produce." She picked up her jar and waddled to the door, her cane clacking on the cement floor and her ankle-length, purple-flowered dress rustling around her. "I'll be back Friday. Tell Mordecai I want some of those candles they make from beeswax for Christmas presents."

By Friday, he would be gone. After the conversation he planned to have with Daed, he'd most likely be gone today. The kaffi he'd drunk earlier turned his stomach sour. "I'll tell him."

Thelma put her hand on the doorknob, the rings on all four fingers clinking against the metal, but the door opened before she could turn it. Daed stood on the other side. They exchanged greetings, and Daed held the door wide for her, then trudged in, his craggy face dour. "I took a look at the buggy Will smashed up at Mordecai's. It's nearly beyond repair."

"Will didn't smash it up. A drunk ran into it." Jesse picked up a damp rag and swiped at the fingerprints on the glass. Not that he cared much. It gave him something to do. "Besides, I've seen you do more with less."

"No need to call the boy names."

"Calling him what he is."

"What's got you in such a mood today?"

Jesse's heart did push-ups against his rib cage, making it hard to breathe. The air in the store seemed to dissipate through the cracks in the windows. His shirt stuck to his chest and arms, damp with sweat. "I wanted to have a word with you."

"What's stopping you then?"

God, help me. God, forgive me. "I took a job in town a few days ago. I start there full time on Monday."

Daed stopped mopping his face with a faded gray bandanna. "You have a job here."

"After I tell you what I'm about to tell you, I won't have a job here anymore."

The lines around Daed's mouth and eyes deepened. Furrows grew across his forehead. He stomped to the door and flipped the lock. When he turned, he looked so much like Groossdaadi, an ache blossomed in Jesse's throat.

"Best get it over with then." His icy tone told Jesse his father had switched from daed to bishop in the flick of the wrist that locked the door. "Gott willing, we'll have customers at the door anytime now."

"I took a job with Matthew Plank, working as a carpenter and gopher in his home-repair and renovation business."

All expression slid from his daed's face. He took two steps toward shelves laden with candles made from beeswax. "Matthew and Angus are shunned. You can't work with them. You shouldn't even be talking to them."

"I visited their home a few weeks ago, and earlier this week I helped them shore up some columns on an old house on Washington Street. I also learned to drive and got my driver's license."

"Why would you do this?" The anguish of a father seeped through the frigid demand of a bishop. "You know better. Your mudder and I taught you better."

"I had to have a place to go."

"I don't understand." The father again. "You have a home and a family. Baptism classes start right after the first of the year."

"I won't be there."

Daed picked up a jar of honey, wiped the lid with his bandanna as if removing dust, then straightened the rows of jars that had no need of such care. "If you're not ready now, there'll be another class this summer."

"I'm trying to tell you something."

"Doing a poor job of it, far as I can tell."

Jesse's heart hammered in a painful staccato of emotions he couldn't begin to explain or even understand himself. "I've been going to a youth group in town. We study the Bible and do outreach at the Dairy Queen. We make hospital visits and pray for folks."

Daed's Adam's apple bobbed. "You understand the Ordnung."

"I do."

"You know that once you're baptized these are not activities in which you'll partake."

"Which is why I won't be baptized in the Amish faith."

The bishop's facade cracked and Jesse got a glimpse of a father's pain. It raced like lightning through his own body, a physical pain more real than any he'd ever experienced. The sheer force of it jolted his heart. It might stop beating altogether. "Daed, I'm sorry to cause you pain. I never intended to do that. I love Gott and I've been saved by Jesus Christ. I want others to know and to be saved too."

"What have they done to you?" Daed's booming voice had been reduced to a quivering whisper. "That you would be so arrogant as to think you can guarantee your salvation or anyone else's. Do you think you're Gott? Do you know better than He what His plan is for each of His wretched children on this earth?"

"Nee. But I know what the Bible says."

"You would leave your family and your community for these people?"

"I don't want to. I could keep living at home and working in the store if you let me. I haven't been baptized." Searching for some hint that he could hope, Jesse slipped closer to his father. He stood toe-to-toe and dared to look him in the eye. "I would go into town for church and Bible study. I wouldn't share it with the others."

"You would share this *word* with strangers but contain yourself from telling your brothers and sisters and cousins and friends?" The bishop was back, along with his booming voice. "You know even as you say those words you'll never be able to keep such a promise. You've been infected with the grandiose idea that it's up to *you* to tell everyone about Jesus. It's your job; it's about you. I won't make an exception for you because you're my son. I can't and I won't."

Jesse swallowed a lump in his throat the size of the state of Texas. "I'm not trying to be proud or arrogant. I only know what I read in the Bible and what my pastor tells me."

"You've been to another church?"

"Jah."

Daed backed away, his face contorted as if he'd just seen a terrible monster. "You should leave. Now."

"Daed—"

"You've made your choice." He made a swishing motion with his arms. His voice rose. "Get out. Go on."

"I don't understand. We worship the same God. We have the same Savior."

"We don't go around proclaiming to the world that we know more than they do." Daed stomped around the counter to put a physical barrier between them. "We keep ourselves apart from the world. We shine the light of Christ by our humble, obedient example."

"It's not enough."

"You would judge me and your mudder and the rest of your family?" The words rolled and thundered now like those of the preacher Daed was. "Your arrogance and your pride will be your downfall."

"I don't mean to—"

"Don't go back home." Daed jerked his head toward the back room that housed the district's only telephone. "Call your friends to pick you up. I'll have Mr. Carson bring you your clothes tomorrow."

The pain spiraled through Jesse, so great he clasped both hands to his chest. He might be having a heart attack. "I can't say good-bye to Mudder?"

"I'll break the news to her." Icy cold replaced rolling thunder. "Go."

"I want to tell her—"

"I won't have you poisoning the others."

"It's not poison."

"Go."

Jesse stumbled into the back room. He leaned against the wall, his legs weak, hands and arms shaking. He bent over and tried to catch breath taken by the ferocity of his father's reaction. *Gott, I didn't mean to hurt him. Gott, please forgive me. Gott, help him forgive me. Help him to see what I see.*

He slid to the floor and put his head on his knees, concentrating on breathing. *In and out. In and out.*

After a few minutes, a blessed numbness took hold. He hoisted himself to his feet and picked up the phone. His hand hovered over the buttons. In the aching silence, a hoarse sob, quickly muffled, sounded from the other side of the wall.

Swallowing his own sobs, he punched in Colton's number with fierce jabs that made his finger hurt.

His new life was about to begin.

CHAPTER 33

Sleep at last. The baby cradled against her chest, Leila eased from the rocking chair and slipped over to the closest crib. Duncan had needed a nap because he hadn't slept earlier when the others were having their afternoon nap. His fussiness made it hard to keep the others happy. It had been that kind of day. Thankfully it was almost over. While most of her babies went down on their own, this little boy liked to be rocked to sleep. No doubt thanks to parents who now regretted his inability to sleep on his own because they rocked him when he was only a wee thing. Swaddling had helped. She laid him on his side and made sure his pacifier was secure in his mouth.

She sighed and rubbed her aching lower back. A quick drink of water and she'd begin sanitizing the diaper pails and changing tables before the parents started arriving for pickup. She snagged her water bottle and went to the window to check the weather. Lifting the red-and-white-checked curtain, she peered out. Dark and overcast. It suited her mood. Which seemed a bit selfish of her. One of the other teachers had mentioned the possibility of freezing rain, maybe even snow, in the late afternoon or evening.

All the guests for Adam and Esther's wedding would be arriving in the next few days. Driving all the way from Missouri and Tennessee, a few from Ohio. They didn't need bad weather or treacherous road conditions. And she needed to get home to help Susan and Mudder with the baking and cleaning and flurry of activity a wedding always brought.

"Where is she?"

Startled, the water bottle slipped from her hand and bounced on the thin carpet, its contents spilling and darkening the red, blue, and green balloon patterns. She faced Dwayne. "What are you doing here? You all agreed to meet at the house this weekend to talk, with your parents."

His face dark with a five o'clock shadow and his eyes red rimmed, Dwayne stood in the doorway. He held a bedraggled bunch of daisies in one hand and a heart-shaped box of assorted Whitman's chocolates in the other. His rumpled white T-shirt was tucked in on one side of his faded blue jeans, but not the other. "I need to talk to her now."

"She's helping with the babies. She's working." Leila squatted and sopped up the water with a towel. "You might want to wait until the end of her shift to talk to her so you don't get her in trouble. Didn't she tell you to give her some time?"

"It's been a week. She isn't answering my calls or my texts. Her dad will come to pick her up and I won't get a word in edgewise." His voice rose as he moved from the doorway and stood over her. His hands fisted and unfisted. "I just want to talk to her."

"Keep your voice down. The babies are sleeping." Leila straightened and tossed the towel into an over-flowing dirty-clothes basket. She eyed the door. She couldn't leave the babies. Maybe Miss Daisy would hear the commotion and come in. "She needs time. You need to give her time. Pray about it. Talk to Gott about it."

The look Dwayne gave her was a cross between blank and confused. Maybe he was like Rory, a child whose family had fallen away from faith as times got hard. "You and Rory are married. It's Gott's will for you to be together. You have to figure out how to take care of her and your babies. That will help."

"What do you know about guy-girl stuff? You ain't married. I ain't seen you with anybody but that guy who picked you up at the park."

"Jesse."

"Yeah, and he's been running around town with Tiffany and Colton and those other Jesus freaks."

"They're not freaks. They want to share Gott's love with people. That's something special."

As soon as the words were out of her mouth, Leila knew she truly felt that way.

"Then how come you don't hang out with them?"

Because she would have to give up all the same things Jesse had. "We live our lives a little differently."

"I heard Jesse's living in town now with those Planks—the ones who work on houses. They still wear the weird clothes but drive cars and all."

Jesse, living in town. The word had spread quickly

through their small community when Jesse broke his news to Leroy and he'd been asked to leave. She'd thought—maybe hoped—she would run into him in town, but so far she'd seen neither hide nor hair of him. She swallowed against the ache in her throat. "I have to stay with my family, where I belong."

"You're gonna be an old maid."

If her heart continued to tell her Jesse was the one, then yes, she might very well be. She would work in the day care forever. Or take over teaching at the school for Susan someday. She could love her scholars. "Maybe."

"I know you think I'm a bad person." Dwayne swiped at his face with the sleeve of a thin denim jacket, not much good against the kind of cold this day had brought. "She just caught me off guard, that's all. We didn't plan to have another one, at least not so soon."

They didn't plan at all. Not with Trevor. Not now.

"I don't think you're a bad person." Not all grown up, maybe, and not ready to be a father for sure. "I don't pass judgment."

"I'm going to do right by her. That's what I'm gonna tell her dad when we meet." He sounded as if he was trying to convince himself. "I promise you that. I'm gonna get a better job. No more wrestling. No more partying. Then we can get a place of our own."

"You don't have to promise me anything. It's between you and Rory."

"And Nolan. Don't forget Nolan."

He sounded so bitter. And so young. No older than Caleb. He was probably better prepared to be a husband and father, and he was only eleven.

"Leila, Leila, they're talking about the prison on the radio." Rory scurried into the room, then slammed to a halt. She panted, fear and hurt and uncertainty mingled on a face wet with tears. "What are you doing here?"

"What's going on at the prison?" Dwayne dropped the candy and flowers at her feet and caught at her hand with his. She jerked away. "Is your dad okay?"

"You killed a buggy."

"I didn't mean to. I was drunk."

"You're not even old enough to drink."

"I was drowning my sorrows. I'm sorry." He dropped to his knees and picked up the flowers, holding them out to her. "These are for you, babe. I'm so sorry. I want you. I want our baby. I want to make a family. Please, please take me back."

"Oh baby, so am I." Rory sank to her knees and buried her face in his chest. "I'm sorry. I'm sorry. I just don't know how we're gonna make it. I feel sick all the time. I cry all the time. Trevor keeps me up at night. I'm so tired."

"I'll take care of you. I promise. I promise."

The two huddled together, arms entwined, heads bowed. They could've been praying, if Leila didn't know better. They were so lost, so very lost. What had she done to help them find their way? What kind of friend was she?

Sniffing and wiping away tears, Rory raised her head. "We have to get to the prison. I need to find out if Daddy is all right. Some prisoners got into a fight or something. Shots were fired." She burrowed closer to Dwayne. "My dad's not answering his cell phone."

As if on cue, the sound of a country-western song blared. Rory's phone. "Answer that before you wake the babies."

Rory tugged it from the pocket of her day-care smock and answered. Lines formed across her forehead. Her free hand went to her mouth. She turned her back on them and began to pace, her responses consisting mostly of "I know, I know, I heard, yeah, I know, oh no, oh no."

"What is it? What are they saying?" Dwayne followed after her like an anxious puppy who needed to go outside. "Is it your dad? Is he okay?"

"Shush, shush, will you!" Rory rubbed her forehead with her free hand. "Not you, I'm talking to my husband." She waited some more. "I will. You too. Call me if you hear anything."

The phone dropped to her chest and she gazed at Leila, her face white and scared. "That was my friend Pam. Her dad works at the prison too. She says word has it there was an inmate uprising. Big fights. The guards had to go in and break it up."

"Is your dad all right?"

"I don't know. She says everyone is trying to call over there, but they're not getting an answer. The phones are overloaded. The injured are being taken to the hospital." She whirled and ran to the door, then stopped to look back. "We have to go to the hospital. You have to come with me, Leila, come with me, please."

Leila looked at the clock on the wall. Fifteen minutes to end of shift. Miss Daisy would have to cover her room. Rory was only an aide. Her room had a teacher. "I'll ask."

"I'll do it. Get your stuff. Hurry and get Trevor for me."

Leila did as she was told. Twenty minutes later they were at the hospital. Dwayne led the way through a crowded parking lot and swinging emergency room doors into a large room filled with padded chairs arranged in long rows so those who waited could see a big-screen TV that blared the nightly news. One hand clasped in Rory's, Dwayne threaded his way between a mother with a screaming child and a cluster of men in prison guard uniforms. Teary-eyed women and worried men and children clutching stuffed animals milled around, creating an obstacle course between them and the check-in desk.

Rory tried to stop to talk to the prison guards, but Dwayne tugged her forward. They strode toward the counter. Leila followed behind, a sleeping Trevor cuddled against her chest. A prayer bobbed in her head. *Let him be all right, Lord; let him be all right, please, Lord.*

"Nolan Beale, do you have a Nolan Beale here?"

"We're really, really busy right now." The nurse peered at them over blue-rimmed glasses perched on the end of her long, skinny nose. Her short, blonde hair spiked on her head as if she'd run her hands through it repeatedly. "We'll get to you as soon as we can."

"We're looking for my daddy, Nolan Beale." Rory's voice quavered. "Is he here?"

"Is this related to the incident at the prison?"

"Yes, he works at the prison."

"Did they call to tell you he'd been transported here?"

"No, ma'am."

"Then he's probably not here."

"Could you look, please? Please, just look."

The nurse sighed and ran her hands through her hair, creating more wild spikes. She pushed her glasses up her nose with one finger. She studied the computer screen for a few minutes. "Nope. Don't see that name."

"Are you sure?" Rory broke free from Dwayne's grip and slapped both hands on the counter as if she might hurl herself over it. "Look again."

"He hasn't been triaged, and he hasn't been admitted. I looked." The nurse turned back to a stack of files teetering dangerously near the edge of her desk. "Maybe you got lucky. Maybe he wasn't in the cell block that had the meltdown."

Rory slapped both hands to her face. Tears seeped between her fingers and ran down the backs of her hands. She bent over, her back heaving.

Leila held Trevor out to Dwayne. The look on his face told her he didn't know which was worse—corralling a crying girl or being responsible for a sleeping baby. After a few seconds' hesitation, he took Trevor. Leila turned to Rory. "It's okay. Let's sit down for a minute. He could be on his way here, or he could be getting ready to call you any second."

"Or he's unconscious or he's dead or he's being held hostage by some vicious killer inmates." Rory sank into a chair and sobbed. "All I ever do is give him grief. I make his life miserable and now I might never get to tell him I love him and I appreciate him."

"You're getting way ahead of yourself." Leila rubbed her shoulder in an awkward pattern. She tried to brush away the thought of the prisoner who had escaped the previous summer and held Phineas and Deborah hostage for a few short hours. They had escaped unscathed, but Deborah's expression when she told the story said it all. The man had been angry and desperate, a scary combination. "The prison authorities will call the families. They'll make statements as soon as they get everything under control."

Somehow that didn't seem helpful.

"We would be happy to pray for your father."

Leila closed her eyes, then opened them. No doubt about it. Jesse approached, Colton and Tiffany on his heels. He had some sort of pamphlet in his hands that he kept smoothing with his fingers. He wore gray pants and a white shirt and a jacket that looked like a hand-me-down from a bigger person. It made him look as if he'd shrunk. His gaze caught hers. For one second, he couldn't hide it. He was glad to see her. Then the spark died and a neutral look spread over his face, the kind one would give a new neighbor or a stranger passing on the street.

He squatted in front of Rory. "We've been talking to the other guards—the ones who weren't hurt. They say everything is under control at the prison. Things are still getting sorted out, but no one is in danger now."

Rory shook off Leila's hand and leaned toward the man in front of her. "Do they know anything about my dad? Do they know if he's hurt?"

Jesse glanced back at his friends. "We'll ask around." Colton jerked his head toward two guards deep in conversation next to the admissions counter. One had his arm in a sling and a thick white bandage on his left cheek.

Jesse took Rory's hands in his and bowed his head. He began to pray in a soft, earnest voice Leila had never heard before.

She bowed her head and squeezed her eyes shut, all the while feeling as if she were being disloyal to someone or something, she couldn't be sure what or whom.

"Lord, we ask You to put Your arms around Nolan Beale. Protect him, keep him safe. Calm the prisoners and the guards at the prison. Let Your peace and grace and serenity wash over them. Bring Nolan home safely to his daughter and his son. In Jesus' name we pray. Amen."

Leila managed a whispered amen. When she opened her eyes, Jesse's gaze bored into hers. He stood and backed away. "I'll see if Tiffany or Colton found out anything."

Leila squeezed Rory's arm and stood. "I'll be right back."

She couldn't help herself. She followed him across the room. No doubt he knew she followed, but he didn't stop until he got to the double doors that led to the parking lot.

"Jesse, wait."

He glanced back. "Not here. Outside."

She followed him into the parking lot. Darkness had fallen, but the lights that bathed the lot shone brightly on the cars, reflecting on glass and chrome wheel covers. Nothing could hide the emotion on Jesse's face. Leila crossed her arms, suddenly cold. "Why are you and Tiffany and Colton here? Was someone in your group hurt?"

"We heard what happened and we came to pray for the injured. We came to pray for the guards and the prisoners. Some of our youth group members have folks who work over there. Most of Beeville does."

Leila stared at his face. She found herself memorizing the way his brown eyes devoured her, the way his dark curls hung low on his forehead, the way his full lips parted when he breathed. What would he say if he knew Will had declared his feelings for her? Would Jesse care? The awkward silence stretched. His gaze dropped to the asphalt. "I guess you heard."

"You know how the grapevine is."

"I never meant to hurt you."

"You didn't." Not much. She forced her gaze to her hands clasped in front of her, fearful he would see the truth in her eyes. "I can't believe you'll never be at church again or the singings or at the store. We won't celebrate the holidays together or see each other at . . . weddings."

"You shouldn't even be talking to me."

"You're not shunned. You weren't baptized."

"Splitting hairs."

"I know." She swallowed the lump in her throat and looked around. Several empty benches lined the sidewalk that ran along the outside of the building. "Sit with me?"

"Sure." He smiled. Leila's heart ricocheted around her rib cage in a painful *rat-a-tat-tat*. *No fair. Don't smile that smile.* "Anything for you."

She sank onto the cement bench. Its cold seeped through her skirt. She shivered. Jesse sat next to her, close. Leila fought the urge to lean into him and feel his warmth. "I was wondering if you could do something for me."

"Like I said, anything."

"It's Rory." She recounted the story of Rory's mother's death and the loss of her church life. "Dwayne seems so lost too. He drinks and he parties and he doesn't seem to know how to be a husband or a father."

"What do you want me to do?"

She touched the pamphlet in his hand, her fingers precariously close to his. His fingers stretched. She could almost feel the caress. "Do this thing that you do. Invite them to your youth group. They may be married and have a baby, but they're the right age for your group."

"I can do that. Pastor David works with a lot of teen parents." Enthusiasm buoyed his words. He looked happy for a few seconds, as if he'd found his place. "He teaches them that God forgives every sin. He loves their babies and wants them to be brought up knowing Him. He knew their names before they were born. He knows how many hairs they have on their heads."

Pain twisted in Leila's chest. They knew the same scriptures. Their beliefs bound them together more than they tore them apart. It was obvious to her. But not to people like Mudder.

Jesse stopped. His face reddened. "Sorry, I know you don't have to be convinced. I get carried away. Colton says all newbies do."

She did have her faith, but she'd never seen or felt

the exuberance that billowed from Jesse when he talked about his. She tried to focus on the matter at hand, but a curious warmth curled itself around her heart. She wanted what Jesse had. *Focus. It's not about you.* "Trevor has never been to church."

Jesse slapped the pamphlet against his knee in a one-two-three rhythm, his expression thoughtful. "Nolan needs to go back to church too. The whole family does."

"If you get Rory and Dwayne involved, I'm thinking Nolan will follow. He has the foundation; he's just been lost since his fraa died."

Jesse's gaze skipped from her eyes to her mouth and back. She breathed, reliving for one second the moment in which he leaned down and kissed her at the movie theater. He smiled as if he could read her thoughts. He looked away. "Why are you doing this?"

"I care about what happens to them. I want Trevor to have two happy, Gott-loving parents who raise him up as Gott's child."

A wailing siren drowned his response at first. She leaned toward him. He returned the favor. His breath smelled like peppermint gum, the way it had in the theater. She imagined its warmth on her cheek. "I couldn't hear you." Her voice sounded odd in her ears, as if she'd run a long race. "What did you say?"

"And you think what I do will help them with that?"

His gaze captured her and held her, telling her how important her answer was to him. "I do."

Jesse breathed, a half sigh, then laughed so quietly she almost didn't hear it. "What about you? Can I help you?"

"I have Gott in my life."

The sirens grew closer and closer. Jesse's hand lifted and he brushed a tendril of hair from her face. Her heart stopped beating, then exploded in a rapid-fire beat that left her breathless. "I know you do, but don't you ever yearn for more?"

She broke away from his gaze, the movement so painful the soles of her feet ached, and stood. "Help them. Please."

"We'll reach out to them, but they have to come halfway." Jesse gazed up at her, his face full of conflicting emotions. "Everyone does."

"I'll push from my end. You pull from the other."

He stood, his body so close she could smell his soapy scent and see the faint dusting of freckles on his nose. "We'll make a good team."

Leila fought to breathe. A good team. A good couple. Good parents. So many things that could never be. "Only in this."

"Nee."

"You should forget the *Deutsch*. You don't need it now."

"It's part of who I am."

"Not anymore." She started toward the building, her feet stumbling over themselves. They didn't want to go. They wanted to stay with Jesse.

"Leila."

She looked back.

He chewed on his lip, his eyes wet with unshed tears. "Have you seen my mother?"

Naomi had looked old and tired when Leila last saw

her. Coming to church knowing what everyone was thinking about her son must've been a hard row to hoe. No one passed judgment, but having a son not join the church made every Plain parent feel shame. "At church this past Sunday."

"Did she seem . . . well?"

"She seemed content to let Gott be in charge."

His lips contorted in a half smile. "Right. Tell Will I said hi."

"I can't."

"Tell them I miss them, all of them."

"Come home then."

"I can't."

"Is it worth it?"

He held up the stash of pamphlets. "Every life saved for Christ is one more person who doesn't have to live all of eternity in the absence of God."

"And you personally have to do this?"

"Faith is personal. Salvation is personal."

Because Jesse made it personal. He looked so sure of himself standing there, his head held high. So willing to give up everything for what he believed. What would she give up to save a friend from eternal damnation? She nodded. "Good-bye, Jesse."

His response was lost in the whoop of a siren and the roar of an engine approaching fast. An ambulance whipped through the parking lot and shimmied to a stop under the awning that led to the ER. An EMT—Tom Fletcher—jumped from the passenger side and raced around to the back. He flung the doors open as his partner, an angular woman with blonde hair tied back in a long braid, rounded the other side. Together, the two of them manhandled a gurney to the ground.

The man on the gurney sat up. "I don't need to be lying down. I'm fine. I keep telling you I'm fine."

"Nolan!" Leila dashed from the sidewalk across the parking lot, waving a hand. "Nolan, you're okay. Rory is inside. She's desperate to know if you're all right."

He didn't look all right. Dried blood stained the front of his uniform and caked his upper lip and chin. Bruises darkened both eyes. His nose appeared to have been flattened. When he talked, he revealed a black gaping hole where one of his top front teeth had been only days earlier.

"I'm fine. I keep telling them that."

"Hey, Leila." Tom jerked his head toward the woman with the braid. "Meet my partner, Sam. Mr. Beale will be fine once a doctor takes a look at him and gets some X-rays and some stitches and a few things like that. He can do the whole macho routine after we get him fixed up."

Sam was a woman. A pretty woman. A strong woman who handled the gurney with assurance. Leila didn't have time to consider all the ramifications of this discovery. Light-headed with relief for Rory, Sawyer, and Trevor, she chuckled, the sound hysterical in her ears.

Tom grinned and shoved open the door so he and his partner could wrestle the gurney into the ER. Sam nodded at her, her face full of curiosity.

Leila nodded back, then turned to Jesse. He crossed both arms over his chest and stared at the doors that settled shut behind the gurney.

"What?"

"Does Will know about your Englisch boyfriend?"

"He's not my boyfriend."

"I saw the two of you together at the café the other day. He had his hands on your shoulder."

"I choked on a cookie."

Jesse looked as if he might choke on something else. He inhaled and then shrugged. "None of my business."

"That's right."

"You can court an outsider, but not me?"

"I'm not courting him, and you left, not me."

"I didn't have a choice."

"I'm not courting anyone."

He ducked his head and studied the cement under a pair of black sneakers that looked brand new. "Not even Will?"

She hesitated. She didn't know the answer to that question. "Like you said, none of your business."

"Right."

She whirled and flounced into the ER, leaving him standing in the cold.

Where he belonged. So why was she the one shivering and bereft?

CHAPTER 34

Esther and Adam's wedding went off without a hitch. Leila breathed a sigh of relief as she surveyed tables filled with dirty dishes. The weather had cleared up just long enough for friends and family from out of state to make the long trip for a second time in six weeks. They had at least two more rounds of guests to feed, and then she could slip away to some corner to rub her aching feet and head. As much as she loved Esther, watching her stepsister marry Jesse's brother—who looked so much like Jesse—had been like wading barefoot through a thicket of cacti.

Determined to be happy for them, she stacked dirty plates, picked them up, and started toward the kitchen. Jesse's mother, Naomi, stood in her path. "Congratulations, mother of the groom." Leila forced a smile. She could see Jesse in the woman's dark eyes and the shape of her mouth. "You must be happy to see your oldest hitched."

Naomi nodded, but the smile on her face slipped. Leila tried to recollect if the sharp lines around the woman's mouth and eyes had been there the last time they talked. "Let me help you with those dishes."

"Nee, nee, I've got it."

Despite Leila's protestations, Naomi pulled four plates from the top of the stack with a determined air. She trotted into the kitchen ahead of Leila and deposited them in the only space left on the prep table. "I have to ask you a question." Naomi glanced around at the eight or nine women engaged in every imaginable task, from cutting cakes to pulling a golden-yellow macaroni-and-cheese casserole from the oven to slicing a ham that had been a gift from one of the Englisch families who shopped at the store. "Outside."

Leila set her plates on top of the others and wiped her hands on a dish towel as she followed the other woman out back. Two dozen or more children engaged in a game of kickball in the field that separated the house from the corral and barn. They'd dumped their coats on the ground, and their faces were red with exertion and the cold north wind that whipped their skin. They shouted and screamed with laughter. Leila longed to be so carefree. She patted her damp face with the towel and inhaled the smell of winter, decaying leaves, and damp air.

"I know it's Gott's will, but it seems so sad to me that all my kinner couldn't be here for my firstborn's wedding." Naomi's voice started out strong but tapered off in a quaver. "Adam wanted Jesse by his side for this. He was supposed to be his witness."

"I know. I'm sure Jesse would've liked to have been here."

True, but Jesse answered to a higher calling now. He believed that, and Leila had come to believe it as well. He felt it so strongly he had given up everyone and everything in his life. Including her. It had to be a calling.

"Have you seen him?" Naomi whispered despite the fact that no one stood within earshot.

Leila watched as Caleb sent the ball sailing across the yard. It bonked the boy in left field in the head. He let out a yelp and did a little dance before chasing the ball all the way to the corral fence. This was Naomi. She had a right to know. She asked in private because she didn't want to get Leila in trouble. "Jah."

"How is he?"

Leila faced the woman who had given life to Jesse Glick and then been left behind when he chose to go his own way. "He's good."

"Where is he staying? How is he living?"

The things a mother would worry about. Not like Leroy, who probably lay awake at night thinking about Jesse's sins of pride and disobedience that might earn him eternal damnation.

"He's staying with Angus Plank, I think. He works with him and Matthew now. He spends a lot of time with his Englisch friends though. Did he ever talk to you about them?"

Naomi shook her head. Her fingers plucked at the strings of her kapp. "Not a word. He never said a word. I had no idea he'd been drawn into this . . . this . . . whatever it is."

"Did Leroy tell you what Jesse wants to do?"

"He said he's fallen in with some religious group in town."

"Jesse loves the Lord and he wants to be a preacher himself."

"I don't understand how this happened."

Shouldn't a mother be proud her child was so committed to God he wanted to spend his life telling others about Him? This paradox puzzled Leila without end. She couldn't make sense of any of it. Leroy's admonition that they should obey the Ordnung and their parents in all things didn't help. She'd always done both. Never had she seen a cost in doing so as she did now.

The lost, sad look in Naomi's eyes surely matched her own. "I'm sorry." In an impulse born in the moment, she embraced the other woman. "I'm so very sorry."

"It's not your fault, child." Naomi pulled away. Tears trickled down her thin cheeks. "We have to believe Gott has a purpose in all of this."

Leila wanted to believe that. "Jesse said to tell you he loves you and he misses you."

Naomi put a hand to her quivering lips. The tears streamed now. "I'm sorry. I don't know why I'm acting like this."

"It's okay."

The screen door opened and Mudder stuck her head out. "There you are. Esther says to tell you to get in there. She's saved a seat at the table for you."

Saved a seat. The pairing off had begun. "I'm helping in the kitchen. There's still so much serving to be done and dishes to wash."

Mudder came out onto the porch. Her smile fled as she looked from Leila to Naomi and back. "Nee, you should go. This is a celebration. You don't want to miss the fun."

The steel underlying the words told Leila her mother had assessed the situation and found it wanting. She surely knew Naomi had asked about Jesse. Mudder had been kind but firm. No contact with Jesse would be tolerated. He might not be shunned, but his choices could only lead to problems for Leila. Time to look forward and move on.

Leila wiped her hands on the towel again. "No, I don't want to miss the fun."

As she let the door shut behind her, she heard Mudder offer Naomi a cup of tea. Leave it to Mudder to find her own way to offer comfort. A way that didn't involve violating the Ordnung. Leila smoothed the hair around her kapp and marched into the front room. The benches were full, but Esther had indeed saved a spot on the girls' side at the bench closest to the tables where Esther and Adam sat at the *eck*.

After filling a plate with roast, stuffing, sweet potatoes, and corn, she slid into the spot before perusing her companions. Directly across from her sat Will. He sopped up gravy with a bread crust and lifted it to his mouth. His gaze met hers and his hand hovered in the air. He tossed the bread on his plate. A frown spread across his face. "I was beginning to wonder if you were going to partake in the celebration. Esther said she was expecting you. That's why she left a seat open."

Leila leaned back to look around her cousin Frannie so she could shoot Esther a scowl. Esther grinned right back and jerked her head as if to say *go on*.

Everyone wanted her to go on, to get over Jesse. How she wished she could. She straightened. "I had to help in the kitchen."

"Tons of womenfolk doing that. This is where you belong . . . for now." He glanced at his companions. They were busy talking to their counterparts across the table. Tapping his fork on the table in a nervous rhythm, he leaned forward. "Can we talk later?"

"I don't know."

"I'm sorry . . . about the other day." His voice dropped to a growl. "I shouldn't have been so hard on you."

He paused as if waiting for her to jump in. Leila wanted to leap up and pound on the table. Instead she patted her lips with her napkin and counted to ten. Twice. "I'm not judging you. Or Jesse. Neither should you."

She knew which one she should choose. Her head had made that very clear. Her heart, on the other hand, disagreed. *Sorry, Will.*

He pasted on a smile, but his eyes told her he knew. He knew she longed for another. Yet he kept trying. There was something to be said for that. She needed to move on and Will sat right there in front of her, offering her a way. It made sense. It was logical. If only her heart would listen to her head.

"Let's go for a walk later, talk."

"I have to help clean up."

"Later tonight then? I'll come by in the buggy."

"Tonight I'll be too tired."

"I'll give you a few days." He wouldn't give up. He deserved something for that. Something she couldn't give him. He offered her a hesitant smile. "Have some wedding cake. I'll share mine."

He cut a huge chunk of white cake with chocolate frosting in two equal pieces, then smiled as he handed it over. His hand shook. He surely imagined that some-day they would be eating their own cake seated at the eck, the single women and men nearby.

Leila accepted his offering and ate it, bite after bite, without tasting it. Will's dream most likely would never materialize unless God worked a miracle on her heart, but then her dream would die instead.

If she were a better person, she'd put Will's dream before hers.

CHAPTER 35

Evangelism could happen anywhere. Even during wrestling matches. Unbuttoning his overcoat as he went, Jesse squeezed past two girls, dressed in skimpy cheerleading outfits, who were screaming what he assumed was the name of one of the wrestlers on the mat. He spotted Rory on the second row of the bleachers, her red plaid coat lying in her lap, a bag of unshelled peanuts on top of it. He eased into the open seat next to her and waited for the cheering to die down. He'd never been in the high school gym before. It smelled of teenage boy sweat, dust, and rubber.

What would it have been like if he'd been born in a different family, a different faith? He might be in college, playing baseball, or in the army. Big ifs. It didn't matter. Gott had given him this path on this day. To help Leila's friend. To help Trevor and his unborn brother or sister. Jesse had told Leila he would help and he would, even if it felt as if a knife twisted in his heart every time he thought of her.

She'd asked him to do something for her that her family and her bishop would not have her do. That meant she understood how important it was. She wanted someone to step out in faith and help save a friend. That was all he wanted to do with his life. How could she not understand that? How could they not do it together?

If he did this for Rory, if he succeeded, maybe Leila would see. Maybe she would come to him willingly.

And pay a terrible price if she did. Did he really want her to suffer the loneliness and isolation he felt when he went home to his little bedroom in Angus's narrow trailer every night? He missed his mudder's apple pie. He missed his sister's goofy jokes and his brother's tall tales. He missed the sound of the frogs and the cicadas, even the smell of horse manure, silly as that sounded. He missed the clutter and junk of the Combination Store and his father's crotchety critiques of his work.

He missed his life.

He swallowed against the hollow feeling in the pit of his stomach. It was worth it. He had no doubt of that. Colton's words curled themselves around his heart, giving him warmth against the cold. Jesus called His first disciples to leave their fishing nets, their livelihood, their families, and their homes. To be fishers of men.

He'd given all that up for the very reason that he sat on this hard, uncomfortable bleacher. To help people like Rory. In the time that he had been shadowing Colton, he'd learned a few things. First, evangelism couldn't be rushed. Jumping right in made people uncomfortable and scared them off.

"Be patient. Be prepared. Have the answers to the questions they'll ask. Don't let the hecklers rattle you. You have the truth."

You have the truth.

He settled back on the bleacher and studied the match. He had a basic understanding of wrestling, but not much more. Roughhousing with friends was one thing, but the idea of rolling around in shorts with another guy in front of a screaming crowd made him cringe.

Finally Rory glanced at him, away, and then back again. "What are you doing here?"

"Checking out the wrestling match."

She giggled and tossed back her dark curls. "Thinking about going out for the team?"

"Naw, I'm too old for that stuff."

"I'm sorry Dwayne was rude to your friend Colton the other day at the park. Tell him Dwayne didn't mean it. He just doesn't know how to act sometimes."

"Don't worry about it. Nothing fazes Colton." It was the truth as far as Jesse could tell. His friend took everything to the Lord and left it there. He always walked with a spring in his step and a smile on his face. "How's your dad?"

"Right as rain. His nose is crooked and he has an appointment for a bunch of dental work. He snores when he takes a nap on the couch." She chuckled, her joy in knowing her father's problems were minor shining in her face. "The bruises are fading. He's still wearing the back brace and his ribs hurt, but he doesn't complain. He's lucky he didn't get shanked."

"Has he gone back to work?"

"Nope. Doctor won't let him. He's chomping at the bit, but he's building a play set with swings and a fort for Trevor. It's keeping him busy."

"Good for him. You're blessed to have him as a dad and granddad."

"Yep, I am."

"Is that Dwayne out there on the mat?"

She nodded, pride obvious on her face as she studied the two grunting wrestlers, their faces red, arms locked around each other's necks. "It's Dwayne's last match. He's not going out for wrestling anymore, so Dad told me I could watch him one more time. After this, he'll be working every afternoon and Saturdays at the feed store."

"Is he winning?"

"Yep. Of course. He could be all-state if he stayed on the team, but he knows getting more hours at his job is the most important thing, with the baby coming and all." She held out her bag of peanuts. "Want some? They're the only thing staying down right now. I think it's the salt. Did you actually come here to see me?"

Jesse waved away the bag. "No, thanks, but yeah, I did."

"That's good, because I meant to find you somehow and thank you for praying for me and my dad the other day at the hospital. Nobody's done that for me in a while." She ducked her head. "It was nice."

"You're welcome. We're still praying for you and your dad. Every day."

"Why?"

"Because it seems like you need it."

She plucked at loose peanut shells on her jacket, flicking them to the gym's wooden floor. Her face had turned radish red. "How did you know I was here?"

An easier topic for her. Jesse shrugged. "I stopped by the day care and asked."

"You stopped by the day care?" She pumped her fist, causing some of the peanuts to go flying. She settled the bag on top of her coat. "Did you see Leila? I bet you did. When are you going to quit messing around and ask her out again?"

The crowd's roar halted the conversation for a few seconds. Jesse couldn't be sure, but he thought Dwayne had made a good move. He had the other guy on the mat now. "I can't ask her out. I have to leave her alone."

"You have the guts to bail on your family so you can save the world, but you're too 'fraidy cat to ask a girl out?"

"It's not that simple."

"I know, Leila told me all about it."

"I'm not here to talk about me and Leila—"

"She told me all about it and she cried the whole time."

"She cried?" His gut roiled. Leila cried. His mother cried. His sisters cried. Even his daed had shed tears. But he never thought Leila would cry for him. "Tell her I said I'm sorry."

Rory's face colored a pretty pink. "Well, you know Leila. She hides how she feels, but she wanted to cry. I saw tears in her eyes—"

"Tell her anyway."

"You tell her."

"Look, I came here to invite you and Dwayne—"

"I know, she told me about that too. You're inviting us to the youth group."

She had promised to push if he would pull. Leila kept her promises. "We're hanging out at Tiffany's tomorrow night. There'll be pizza and after group, we're watching a movie. The girls picked the movie this time, so it'll be something you'll like. Dwayne, probably not so much. Popcorn and sodas, the works."

"Sounds cool."

"It does?"

"Dwayne won't be excited, but he promised my dad to be good to me, so what I want, he wants. He knows we only have a sliver of a chance of making this work."

"Stick with this group and you'll have a whole lot better chance."

"Talk to Leila."

"I can't."

She shot up, raised both hands in the air, and screamed. Peanuts went flying. Her coat landed somewhere below the bleachers.

Apparently Dwayne had done something good. Jesse hauled himself to his feet, watching as the referee held Dwayne's arm up and announced him as the winner of the match. The guy grinned from ear to ear, his tank top soaked, chest heaving with exertion. He looked so happy.

His last hurrah.

Rory elbowed Jesse. "People who love each other will give up a lot. There's no prom for me, no cheerleading, no volleyball, none of that kid stuff. Love is grown up."

Who was teaching whom now? "I know."

"Give Leila a chance. Maybe she's willing to give up something for you."

She hopped from the bleachers and ran out to meet Dwayne on the gym floor. She wrapped her arms around her husband, sweat and all.

Jesse stood rooted to the spot, unable to look away. He'd come to teach Rory about God's love, but Leila's friend might know more about the man-woman kind of love than he did.

She might be right. That thought sent a bolt of sheer energy through him.

It felt like hope.

CHAPTER 36

Winter made lovely decorations on the day-care windows. Leila rubbed the glass with her sleeve. Condensation clouded her view of the play area. She breathed on the window and rubbed again. Darkness had settled in early tonight with the cloud cover. Rays from the streetlights bounced off a shiny metal tricycle left in the yard. Someone should've put it in the storage unit. The thought drifted away. Her eyes didn't deceive her. Pellets of white ice dotted the ground. They pinged against the glass in a steady barrage. "We have ice."

Talking to herself again. Not exactly. She had a roomful of babies as an audience. Unfortunately, they weren't old enough to keep up their end of the conversation. She turned with a sigh. This was the last day of work before the day care closed and gave everyone a four-day weekend for the Christmas holiday. She loved her babies, but lately she'd longed to stay in bed in the morning. Morning, noon, and night.

Rory claimed she was depressed, but Leila was fairly certain Plain girls weren't allowed to be depressed. Rory had attended her first youth group on Wednesday, and she'd felt it necessary to give Leila an update on Jesse.

How he looked. How he sang. To whom he spoke. Even how much he ate. Apparently, a lot.

Leila sighed again, this time even more loudly, and picked up the diaper pail. No point in crying over spilled milk. At least that's what Mudder would say.

"No youth group tonight." As if thinking of her could make her appear, Rory stuck her head in the door. "Just got a text from Tiffany. The roads are iced over. They want everyone to stay home and be safe. Phooey. That means no Jesse sightings for you. Sorry about that."

"You know you're not helping by reminding me of him." Leila sounded as whiney as Hazel when she had to go to bed before she was ready. She tried to tame her irritation. "He's not in my life anymore. I'm happy he's moved on."

"Moved on?" Rory snorted and shook her index finger in a snooty little dance. "Moved on? He asked me twenty questions. With this hangdog expression like he's trying to hide it, but it's killing him."

"Really, hush up about it already, will you?" She shouldn't be taking this out on Rory, but her friend was the only person in the world to whom she could talk about this particular thorn in her side. "Sorry, I'm sorry."

"Don't be. I get it. You're having a bad day today." Rory's fingers were flying over her cell phone keyboard as she spoke. "Want me to buy you a donut to sweeten you up?"

"I'm not having a bad day, I'm just . . . I don't know." Simply sad. That's what she was. Sad. She missed Jesse. Which was ridiculous. She hadn't spent that much time with him. "You'd better go help Shelby. It's almost time for parents to come in."

"Uh-oh."

Leila didn't like any comments from Rory that began with *uh-oh*. "What's the matter?"

"Dad says the roads are so bad, he might not be able to get over here. He's saying a lot of parents might be late picking up their kids."

"What are we going to do? Stay all night?"

"We might have to do that." Miss Daisy bustled into the room, her brown corduroy pants making a rubbing sound as her thunderous thighs worked. Spit-up decorated her green-and-red cable-knit sweater and her bun of white hair half fell down as usual. "I'm making the rounds, letting the teachers know. You may have to stay late tonight, until parents can get here. Some of the roads are closed. You know Texas. The slightest bit of precipitation and they go hog wild, closing highways and whatnot."

Leila didn't know. Her first winter in Texas had been mild after some severe storms in the fall, including the spin-offs from a coastal hurricane. So mild she hadn't been sure it actually happened. This year, they'd had a few storms and occasional cold fronts so far, but nothing she'd call winter. "I don't mind staying at all."

She got paid by the hour and she could use the extra money, truth be told.

"Good girl. Rory, stop lollygagging about and help Shelby."

"Yes, ma'am." Rory turned to go, then turned back. "Dad's definitely not getting through. He's staying at the prison overnight. Dwayne's at the house with Sawyer so he's no good. We're stuck."

"Don't worry, I have cocoa, canned soup, and Ramen noodles in the break room." Miss Daisy made these three items sound like a feast. She headed for the door. "And lots of Girl Scout cookies in the freezer. As long as the electricity doesn't go out, we're fine."

The words were barely out of her mouth when the room went dark. Rory shrieked and then giggled. Leila grabbed the changing table, waiting for her eyes to adjust. "What on earth would cause that? It's not like it's storming out."

"The electric lines around here don't know what to do with the extra weight of ice."

"I guess we'll make do." Leila groped on the shelf over the changing table until her hand connected with the cool metal of the large flashlight with which each room in the day care was equipped. "The babies should sleep well in the darkness. I'd better make sure they're all covered and get extra blankets. I reckon it's going to cool off in here if the electricity doesn't come back right away."

"I'll get out the lanterns. Rory, come with me. You can help me distribute them."

They left her alone in the dark with her sleeping babies. Thank Gott babies could sleep through anything. A wail from the far corner immediately followed that thought. Kaitlin. Careful to keep the flashlight aimed at the floor, Leila made her way over to the crib that held Tom's daughter. "Hey, baby girl, you're fine, you're fine." She lifted the chunky-monkey girl into her arms. "Are you wet? I reckon you're wet. A wet diaper is cold on a day like this."

She waited a few seconds for her eyes to adjust to the darkness, then moved to the changing table.

"She definitely doesn't like having a wet bottom." Tom's voice floated in the darkness. A stomping noise told her he was clearing the snow from his boots on the rug. "Sorry, I didn't mean to scare you."

"You didn't. How did you get here?" Leila made quick work of changing the diaper. She didn't want poor Kaitlin to get a chill. Too bad they didn't have a wood-burning stove. A fire would do nicely about now. "I thought all the roads were closed."

"They are, but I'm in an ambulance made to travel in all kinds of weather on all kinds of roads."

"Are you still working?"

"Yes, but my chief said my partner and I could come check on my baby girl and take her to my sister's and then get back to the station. Everyone will stay on duty while this weather lasts."

Leila glanced past Tom, looking for his partner. Curiosity about the person he'd only referenced once or twice overcame her. *Mind your own business.* "In this weather, there's bound to be lots of accidents."

"Most folks are smart enough to stay indoors. There's always a few who think they can drive in anything. Those are the ones we have to scrape off the road."

The stark image sent a chill through Leila. That's exactly what they'd had to do with her brother-in-law, Phineas. Not because of weather, but because of a careless driver. Phineas had survived, but he would carry the marks of that accident with him for the rest of his life.

The woman who had been with Tom at the hospital trotted into the room. She wore her hair in the same long braid as that day. She wore the same blue, fleece-lined coat as Tom did, matching blue pants, and thick-soled work boots. "I saw the lights went out. Thought I'd better come in and see if I could do anything to help." She had the twang of East Texas in a voice unusually husky for a woman.

"My partner, Sam." Tom made quick work of the introductions. "Short for Samantha."

"We don't need anything in the way of help." Leila wiped her hands on her apron and hoisted Kaitlin onto her hip. "Unless you have a wood-burning stove in the back of that ambulance."

Shaking her head, Samantha held out her arms. To Leila's surprise, Kaitlin did the same. She knew Tom's partner and apparently liked her. Leila handed over the baby. Samantha cooed and hugged and kissed like a grandma who hadn't seen her baby in a month of Sundays.

"I guess you like babies."

"She's always threatening to steal Kaitlin away and keep her for a few days." Tom's tone held an undertone of surprise, as if he couldn't believe someone would want to do that. "I told her she has no idea what she's in for."

"Hey, I have nieces and nephews and three younger brothers." Sam tickled Kaitlin's neck and the baby crowed with laughter. "I know what I'm doing. Don't I, Kaitlin, don't I?"

Her chubby cheeks dimpled, the baby snuggled against the woman's chest. "See, she agrees with me."

Leila surveyed the two, laughing and chattering over Kaitlin like parents would. The thought struck her full force. Tom and Samantha could be more than partners. She studied the woman. She had similar interests to Tom or she wouldn't be an EMT. She was passable when it came to looks, not that Leila really knew what to judge her by.

Most importantly, she loved babies.

No, most importantly, did she love God? Leila picked up the flashlight and did a quick count on her babies. "Looks like Kaitlin has become attached to you, Samantha."

Tom chuckled. It was nice to hear him laugh. "What baby wouldn't? She loves to lie on the floor and watch *Sesame Street*, she does a mean patty-cake, patty-cake, and she never gets tired of peek-a-boo-I-see-you."

Someone else had gotten attached to Sam. Leila smiled to herself. Duncan stirred and stretched, his rosebud lips turning down in a frown. She pulled his favorite fuzzy blanket up around his neck. "Shhh, shhhh."

He stilled. She turned to her visitors, considering how to go about this. How would Jesse do it? Go slow, that's what he would say. "So do y'all ever do anything together besides work and watch *Sesame Street*?"

Tom stopped with the tickling that had Kaitlin wiggling all over Sam's chest. "What do you mean?"

"Do you . . . do anything for fun?"

"Sure."

"I mean . . . together."

"Your friend is matchmaking." Leila couldn't see Sam's expression in the dark, but she heard something in her voice. Some embarrassment, maybe, but also something else—possibly hope. "She's just being silly."

"You could go to church together." Leila hopped in before Tom could say anything. "That's always a good start. Kaitlin should go to church, and if you're taking her, you might as well go yourself."

"What is this? Fix Tom Day?"

Tom didn't sound mad, nor did he sound as if he would take Leila's advice. She apparently didn't have Jesse's knack for this. "No, no, I'm just saying. Christmas is right around the corner, and what better time to start going to church than on the day we celebrate the birth of Jesus."

"She's right." Sam lifted Kaitlin in the air, up and down, up and down, eliciting a stream of giggles. "Don't spit up on me, girl. I love Christmas services. You should come with me to church on Christmas Eve, Tom."

"We'll see." He scooped up Kaitlin's diaper bag and handed his partner the baby's coat. "Wrap her up good in her blanket and put her hat on. She doesn't have enough hair to keep her head from getting cold. I'll get the ambulance warmed up."

He strode from the room without saying good-bye. Changing the subject? Running away?

Samantha did as she was told, but she continued to talk to Kaitlin, promising her a visit to church for baby

Jesus' birthday. She bundled the baby from head to toe, then turned to Leila. "Thanks."

"For what?"

"I don't know. Getting the ball rolling." She swung her braid over her shoulder out of reach of Kaitlin's chunky fists. "I've been trying to figure out a way for a while, but I didn't want to seem too forward. I have to work with the guy. If it doesn't work out, it'll be very uncomfortable."

"So make it work."

"Easier said than done."

"Have faith."

"I do. That's why the suggestion we start with church is a wise one. You're a wise woman." Sam wrapped her arms around Kaitlin and headed for the door. In the hallway, she turned back. "I'm sorry we can't give you a ride home. I hate to see you stuck here."

"I can't leave until all the babies are picked up anyway." She crossed the room and stood in the doorway so she could see Sam's retreat down the hall. "I'll be praying for you and Tom."

The words came out of their own volition. She'd never said such a thing in her life. *Gott, where did that come from?*

"I'll take all the prayers I can get," Sam called back. "Keep 'em coming and I'll keep you posted."

"You do that."

Leila went back to her babies. She'd done it again. With Rory and now with Tom and Samantha. She wanted people to be happy. She wanted the babies for whom she cared to grow up in God-fearing, God-loving homes. Each and every one of them. So whose job was it to make sure that happened?

It seemed God was giving her the answer to that question loud and clear.

CHAPTER 37

Leila inhaled the scent of cinnamon wafting from the candle on the table. It mingled with the aroma of the star-shaped chocolate cookies baking in the oven. The kitchen smelled like Christmas. Just thinking of the children's Christmas Eve play earlier at the school made her smile. Caleb had done a fine job singing carols, a grin splitting his dimpled cheeks. He looked so much like Daed. Leila loved this time of year.

Usually.

So why did she feel so blue? Sighing, she opened the oven door and retrieved the cookie sheet. The heat bit through the ancient pot holder, singeing her thumb. She slapped the pan on the counter and sucked on her thumb. "Ouch."

"Considering what a joyous time of year this is, you sure are a sourpuss." Rebekah strolled into the kitchen, baby Timothy snuggled against her chest. The girl must like to live dangerously, as no burp rag resided between the baby and her dress. "You're supposed to use a pot holder."

"I did and I'm not a sourpuss."

"You were a million miles away during the play

tonight." Rebekah snatched a cookie from an earlier, cooled batch. "You'd better hope Mudder was too busy trying to keep Hazel from running up front to notice."

"I can't wait until Hazel is old enough to go to school. She's so ready." Leila tugged Timothy from her sister's arms. The baby cooed and sputtered, his tiny fists sparring with the air. "She was trying to read one of Caleb's bug books yesterday."

"Don't change the subject." Rebekah grabbed another cookie and plopped into a chair at the table. "You love Christmas. What's the matter?"

"Nothing."

"Leila!"

Leila eased onto a chair across the pine table. She held Timothy close to her heart, inhaling the scent of baby. She rubbed the soft silk on his head. He was like a newborn puppy, all bones in a wrinkled sack. "I do love babies."

Rebekah cocked her head and frowned. "Everyone loves babies. You'll have your own. It's only a matter of time if Will Glick has his way."

Timothy fussed. Leila forced herself to ease her grip on him. "Shush, baby, shush." She ducked her head, hoping her sister couldn't see her expression. "I know. I'm just not sure . . ."

"Not sure he's the one? What's not to like?" Rebekah began to extend her fingers on one hand as if counting off. "He's a hard worker, he's handsome, he's tall, he's smart. He likes you, and that in itself is something from where I sit."

"None of that has to do with anything when it

comes to love. That's something you'll learn one day."
Deborah stood in the doorway. "There he is. I was
missing my boy."

Leila turned so Deborah could see Timothy's contented face. The baby's eyes closed and his tiny body
relaxed against her. "You should know. Will was interested in you first."

"At the time all the boys had an interest in all of
us. We were new." Deborah headed toward the counter and the spread of four kinds of Christmas cookies,
gingerbread, banana bread, and cranberry bread. She'd
lost most of the baby weight already. Her apron and her
kapp were clean, neat, and wrinkle free. How she did
that with a newborn fascinated Leila. "They were curious. Will only wanted to get to know me to find out if
there might be something there. He wasn't the least bit
heartbroken when I chose another."

Maybe not, but it surely hurt his pride. The way he'd
slouched on the bench the day of the wedding said as
much. "Do you think it's different with me? I mean, his
feelings are different?"

Deborah began to move the latest batch of cookies
from the pan to a plate. "That's between him and you
to figure out."

"I want cookies." Hazel trotted into the room in bare
feet. It didn't matter the temperature. The girl preferred
not to wear shoes. Pretty soon all of the Lantz womenfolk would be gathered in the kitchen. "And milk."

"There's no milk, but a cookie you shall have."
Deborah handed it to the little girl with a flourish. "Be
sure to brush your teeth before you go to bed, which

you shall do very soon or you'll be too tired to open presents in the morning."

"Nee. I'm not tired." Hazel's face lit up in a grin. She was a miniature Deborah. "I made baby something special."

"No telling or it won't be a surprise." Rebekah patted her lap and Hazel crawled onto it, managing to break the cookie in three places. "Five more minutes, then it's prayers and bed."

A sense of something akin to peace washed over Leila. These three girls, her sisters, they would be fine—better than fine—no matter what happened. Startled by the thought, she straightened. Timothy fussed in his sleep. She patted his rump and rocked. Nothing would happen.

Nothing.

"What's a matter?" Rebekah peered at her. "You look like you're about to cry."

"I'm not crying."

"What's the matter?" Deborah turned from the counter to stare at her. "Are you sick?"

"I'm fine."

"She's a sourpuss." Rebekah pointed a finger at Leila. "Either that, or she has a secret she doesn't want us to know."

"Am not and no, I don't."

"Then what?"

"I love you, my schweschders."

Three mouths dropped open. Eyebrows popped up. Everyone froze for a scant second. Then Rebekah half rose from her seat, her arm around Hazel's middle.

Deborah marched over to the table and slapped a hand on Leila's forehead. "You don't have a fever. What is wrong? Are you sick? Tell me now."

"Nothing." Leila shrugged away from her touch. "Nothing. I just . . . Things are changing, that's all, and I know more changes are coming. And I know we don't have any control over any of it."

"Change is gut and Gott has control." Deborah eased Timothy from Leila's arms. "Coming here was the best thing that ever happened to me, even though I didn't think so at the time. I met Phineas. I thought he was annoying and irritating and mean. Then I didn't. And now we have Timothy. Gott is gut."

No doubt about that, but change could also be hard. It could be brutal. "He is."

How could Leila tell them every bone in her body, every sinew, every muscle, spoke to her of a change coming that they wouldn't like? Not at all. It would be painful and sorrow would abound. She knew it in her heart and nothing she did could change the way she felt.

This time of year centered on hope and joy and new beginnings.

The ache in her chest said her new beginning would also be the end of nights like this, sitting in the kitchen eating warm cookies and holding baby nephews. "I'm just tired, that's all."

Deborah didn't look convinced, but she straightened and smoothed the blanket around her bundle of baby.

"It's Christmas Eve." Rebekah scooted Hazel from her lap. "Time for bed. We have presents to open tomorrow and visiting to do."

To Leila's surprise, Rebekah paused at her chair, then wrapped her arms around Leila in a quick, tight hug. "Merry Christmas, Leila."

"Merry Christmas." It took every ounce of resolve she could muster to keep the quiver from her voice. "See you in the morning."

Deborah stopped in the doorway. "Aren't you coming to bed?"

"I'll be there in a minute."

"See you in the morning."

"See you in the morning."

Everything would look different in the morning. Good or bad.

CHAPTER 38

Jesse tossed pebbles at the second-story window. His pitching arm needed work. The first one missed. The second and third made contact with the glass in a *ping, ping* that he could barely hear from the ground. He peered up at Leila's bedroom window, hoping Rebekah or Hazel wouldn't be the one to wake up. And that Butch was out on some nighttime patrol. Or a nocturnal hunt. The dog didn't like him much. *Come on, Leila, come on.*

"What are you doing?"

He dropped the flashlight, even as he realized that the woman he sought stood before him. "Looking for you. I thought you were in there."

Leila pulled the door shut behind her and adjusted the shawl tight around her shoulders. She had the look of someone awakened suddenly from a deep sleep. Her blonde hair was mussed around a kapp tugged on haphazardly. She looked beautiful. "I heard the engine. I couldn't imagine who would be coming out here at this time of night."

"It's not that late. Y'all just go to bed early because there's nothing else to do." That was unfair. Until a few weeks ago, he'd done the same thing his whole life. He squatted and picked up the flashlight. "I wanted to take you somewhere."

She took a step back. "You can't."

"It's Christmas Eve, the night before we celebrate the most important event in the history of the world. The birth of our Lord Jesus Christ." His voice shook. He took a breath to calm himself. This was so important. For him. And for her. He had to make her see. "Please come with me. As a favor to me, if nothing else."

"Like you said, it's Christmas Eve. Tomorrow we'll celebrate the birth of our Lord Jesus Christ." Her voice didn't shake at all. Her cheeks reddened in the cold and her breath came in white puffs. "And then we'll visit with family. That's important to us. Family."

"Please. You won't be sorry. You won't want to miss this."

"Miss what?"

"Come with me."

Emotions warred on her face. Longing. He was sure he saw longing. And uncertainty. "Please."

She swiveled and looked behind her. "Is that a van?"

Even though he had his driver's license now, he wasn't ready to drive on his own, especially on icy roads. And Matthew didn't seem interested in risking his company van, however old and decrepit, on a newbie driver. Smart man. "Matthew's van. Angus is driving."

"You came out here in Matthew's company van driven by his brother?"

"I did. It's the only transportation I could find on such short notice." Colton wanted to spend his Christmas

Eve with Tiffany. Jesse understood that. He wanted it. With Leila. "Everyone's at the Holly Jolly Christmas celebration."

"Is that what you want me to see?" She frowned, but nothing she did made her any less pretty. "I don't care about lights and parades and Santa Claus."

"Stop arguing with me and put on your shoes."

Leila gave a most unfeminine snort and did as he directed. A few minutes later they were squeezed into the middle seat of the van. Leila wiggled and tucked her hands under her arms. "You don't want to sit up front with Angus? He's not like our driver or something."

"Nee. I want to sit next to you." He paused, trying to get control of his emotions. "I mean, the heater doesn't work very well and it'll be cold back here."

"I don't mind acting like the chauffeur. I'm good at it. I see nothing. I hear nothing." Angus shot her a wide grin in the rearview mirror. "Y'all snuggle up and keep warm."

"There will be no snuggling." As if to make her point, Leila scooted to the far end of the seat and made herself small in the corner, her head against the window. "Or anything of that nature."

Jesse heaved a sigh and tried to relax. The hard part was over. She'd agreed to come. Once she saw what she needed to see, she'd be convinced. Who wouldn't be? "How's everyone in your family?"

"Everyone's gut. My family is fine." This time her voice did quiver ever so slightly. "Esther's wedding was very nice. Everyone came. Folks asked about you."

She faltered and turned to stare out the window.

The moon splashed light on the barren trees along the road and her face. She looked so sad. Jesse didn't want her to be sad. She had to see what he saw. So much joy. So much promise. A future secure. She glanced his way and their gazes held for a second. More unfettered emotion. Confusion. Hurt. Uncertainty. Longing. He was sure of it. She had missed him.

He forced his gaze back to the countryside. Tree limbs dipped and swayed in a northern wind that seeped into the cracks and crevices of the old van. Jesse shivered. He reached under the seat and pulled out an old blanket Matthew used to cover furniture at work sites. "Here, it's cold, cover up."

"Why are you doing this?" She slid closer, her voice a mere whisper. "I can't see how it's ever going to work between us."

"You'll see. It will." He shook the blanket out and covered their laps. He sneezed. "Sorry."

"A little dust doesn't hurt a person." She tucked the blanket around her legs and grasped it, her hands so tight her fingers went white. "I can't stand this. I've missed you so much. Okay, there, I said it. I missed you."

Her face reddened and she glanced toward the back of Angus's head. He leaned over and flipped on the radio with one hand, the other still on the wheel. "Jingle Bells" blared.

Jesse scooted close to her. "Me too."

"What will we do?"

"We'll figure it out."

"I don't see how. I don't know how I could bear a future without my family."

"You have to be willing to see a different future for yourself."

She lowered her head, her eyes closed. Her hand crept out and took his. Her skin was so soft. "I've prayed and prayed and prayed."

"I spent months doing the same thing before I knew what to do." He smoothed the soft hollow between her thumb and forefinger with his own calloused thumb. "I wore holes in the knees of my pants."

"And you received the answer you wanted?"

"It's not possible for us to get the answer we want." He hated to state the obvious. She tried to pull her hand away. He held on tight. "We can't live our lives the way we believe God wants us to and be together with our families."

"So you're not only asking me to choose you, you're asking me to choose a different life of faith?"

"Jah."

"You don't ask much."

The words held a certain bitterness, but also acceptance. Jesse was sure of it. He asked a great deal of her, but God asked for more. Much more. He rubbed his hands over hers, trying to create warmth. She stared at him, blue eyes luminous with tears. Jesse brought her hands to his lips and kissed her fingers one by one. She sighed, a long, ragged sigh. "Don't say anything," he whispered. "Just wait."

She nodded and leaned back against the seat as if worn out. Jesse held on to her hand for dear life.

• • •

Will had exhausted his supply of pebbles. Either Leila slept deeply or she simply ignored him. He studied the ground, searching for something else he could heave at the second-story window that wouldn't break the glass. *Come on, Leila, come on.*

Nothing. He set his package in the sparse brown grass that lined the house under the windows, debating whether to leave. He didn't want to embarrass Leila or her sisters. He'd waited too long and now she was asleep. His family would pass Christmas Day at his Uncle Leroy's, so it was doubtful he would see Leila tomorrow. His daed reckoned it would help take the sting out of Jesse's absence to have the rest of the family close. The first year would be the hardest. Time would ease the pain.

Sighing, he turned to go. Mordecai's dog, Butch, trotted across the yard toward him, his grizzled snoot wide in a grin. Will dropped to one knee and patted his back. "Where have you been? You should've been here, standing guard. That's your job, you know."

Butch woofed and nuzzled Will's chest. He leaned in and wrapped an arm around the animal. He smelled of wet earth and something else . . . manure possibly. The warmth of his fur felt good in the cold night air, but nothing could warm the icy feeling that had descended on Will's heart. He'd been so sure he could convince her. "What am I to do? Tell me that, Butch."

A soft whimper emanated from deep in the dog's throat.

"I know, that's how I feel too."

"Talking to a dog, are you?"

Will looked up. Rebekah stared down at him, her face one big frown. She stepped onto the porch and slid the door closed behind her with infinite care. "What are you doing here? Besides throwing rocks at the window and trying to wake up everyone in the house."

"They were pebbles." Will gave Butch a last pat, picked up the package, and straightened. "Sorry, I didn't mean to wake you. I was looking for Leila."

"It's like a bus station around here." Rebekah pulled her shawl tighter around her slim body. "Leila's okay and all, but I never imagined this tug-of-war over her."

"If you're talking about Jesse, there's no tug-of-war. That's done."

Rebekah's expression softened. "Is that package for Leila?"

He nodded, feeling even more foolish than usual.

"I'm sorry."

"For what?"

Rebekah sighed, her face full of a sad compassion that could only mean one thing. "She's not here."

"What do you mean she's not here?"

"She left about twenty minutes ago."

Someone new courted her already? Will racked his brain trying to think who among his friends would do such a thing. Nee. No one. "With who?"

"I didn't see him, but I heard an engine running so I looked out the window. I saw an old beige-colored van."

Matthew's van. "Jesse? And you let her go?"

His heart slammed against his rib cage. *Too late.* *Too late*, it pounded out in a painful, aching rhythm. Leila had made her choice. Not only had she chosen

Jesse, but she'd chosen how she would spend the rest of her life.

Without Will in it.

All those dreams that bumped into each other and filled his mind in the wakeful moments before sleep dissipated like chimney smoke in a cold wind. No future spent with Leila turning a house into a home and filling it with kinner. No Christmases by the fireplace or having fish fries at the lake or wading in the Gulf. The future gaped, a black, empty void.

"She was already gone." The full moon cast a brilliant light on Rebekah's face, adding a glow to the tears that brightened her eyes. "Her heart's been gone a long time. The rest of her caught up tonight, I reckon." Her voice quavered. "She was acting strangely earlier, in the kitchen. I think she was saying good-bye. I don't think she's coming back. I'm sorry."

"It's not your fault." To Will's chagrin his own voice quavered, matching hers. "She made her choice. I so hoped it would be otherwise."

"You're not to blame either."

A spurt of energy shot through him. It wasn't over. He still had time. Until Leila took vows, he had time. He couldn't give in now, at the ultimate moment. "I'm going after her."

"How? In a buggy? By the time you drive into Beeville, whatever they're doing will be done."

"It doesn't matter. I'll hitch a ride. I have to try."

"Gott bless you."

Some strange impulse made him grab her hand and squeeze. "Danki."

"My mudder doesn't know yet. I don't want to be the one to tell her." She stared down at him, her face so like Leila's, etched with pain. "Bring my schweschder back. Please. So I don't have to tell her."

That was the plan.

CHAPTER 39

Leila didn't know where to look first. Despite the hour, Main Street in Beeville swarmed with people strolling on the sidewalk. Carolers sang in the Depot Pavilion, and Santa posed for photos with little ones after hearing their wishes. Some people drank hot chocolate in front of A Box of Chocolate candy store on Washington Street. All the stores were open and business bustling. She'd never been in town during the Christmas season. The twinkling, multicolored lights decorated storefronts and trees and dangled from electric pole to electric pole, giving the entire town a festive, happy atmosphere that made her smile—almost.

She still didn't know what she was doing in Beeville at night with Jesse. The warmth she felt had nothing to do with the blanket he'd spread over their knees. It had to do with the arm he slid around her shoulder about halfway into town and the way he kept giving her these sidelong glances. She should move away, but she didn't. Because of the cold, that's what she kept telling herself. The cold.

He hadn't said much after that painful conversation at the beginning, but now he leaned forward and looked out the window. "It's really pretty, isn't it?"

"Jah, but it's not what Christmas is about."

"I know that, but they put so much into making these days special in honor of the birth of Jesus. That can't be wrong."

"I'm not saying it's wrong. I'm saying it's unnecessary. Jesus doesn't need sparkling lights and Santas."

"Ah, now who's the authority on what Jesus needs?" His grin softened the criticism. "These celebrations draw people's attention to the meaning of the season."

"Nee, they get people into stores to buy things." That acute observation came from the front seat. Angus chuckled. "It's economics, not religion."

"I know." Jesse threw off the blanket. "But that's not why I brought Leila into town."

He shouldn't talk about her as if she weren't seated right there next to him. "Then why?"

"We're here."

The van jolted to a stop. Leila peered out the window. A small, white, wood-frame church with one stained-glass window shaped like an octagon graced a corner lot. A spotlight in the yard shone on a nativity scene with a life-sized Mary and Joseph separated by a manger complete with a baby Jesus swaddled in a bright-red blanket. "You brought me to a church service?"

"Not just any church service. Come on."

She'd come this far. Leila took the hand Jesse proffered and followed him up the sidewalk to the double doors of the church. They flew open and Colton stuck his head out. "There you are. We thought you were going to miss it. Get in here."

"Miss what?"

"You'll see." Jesse hustled inside, tugging her along with him.

Dozens of rows of padded chairs filled a long, rectangular room. A dark green carpet softened their footsteps and a big white screen filled the back wall. Boughs of pine needles decorated the altar, lined on each side by huge, brilliant poinsettias in red and pink. The scent of the pine needles mingled with ladies' perfume and men's aftershave in a piquant medley.

Almost all of the chairs were full on this Christmas Eve. Leila recognized some of the faces. Marie from the bakery, Miss Daisy from the day care. Samantha and Tom with Kaitlin sitting in the woman's lap. Samantha smiled as she whispered something to Tom. Her blonde hair hung loose and long down her back. She was pretty and Tom looked happy.

And there, Nolan. Rory's dad. He'd come back to church. What wonderful news. Jesse's handiwork. Did that make Samantha and Tom her handiwork? Nee. God's handiwork.

Her gaze roved back to the front and the altar. There stood Rory, wearing a red corduroy dress, which had to be a first, and black cowboy boots. Dwayne looked sharp in a blue suit and a skinny tie, his hair slicked back. They both looked so grown up. Dwayne held Trevor, who wore a suit that matched his daddy's.

"Trevor is being baptized—"

"Shush." Jesse slid into an open seat half toward the

front and motioned for her to take the one next to him. He leaned close and whispered in her ear. "Not baptism. Dedication. Rory and Dwayne are just beginning to figure out what they believe and how to be parents. They still have a long way to go. This is a good first step. Trevor will decide about baptism when he is old enough to understand what it means."

Leila nodded. She couldn't keep from smiling. Rory and Dwayne might not have all the answers yet, but they understood how important it was to find them. For themselves and for Trevor. No wonder Nolan looked so pleased. And Rory radiated happiness. Trevor crowed and she laughed. Grinning, Dwayne shushed him and smoothed his son's locks into place with long fingers.

The pastor posed the question, did they plan to raise their son in the ways of God? They answered yes.

"Will you teach him and train him in God's Word?"

"Yep."

Dwayne's resounding response brought a few chuckles and smiles from the congregation.

"Will you discipline him in godly ways and pray earnestly for him?"

Again with the hearty affirmative response. Rory brushed away tears with a bright-green hankie.

Pastor Walt picked up a brown leather-bound Bible from the podium and began to read:

And she made a vow, saying, "Lord Almighty, if you will only look on your servant's misery and remember me, and not forget your servant but give her a son, then I will give him to the Lord for

*all the days of his life, and no razor will ever be
used on his head."*

"When God answered Hannah's prayer by giving her a son, she remembered her vow:

*"As surely as you live, I am the woman who stood
here beside you praying to the LORD. I prayed for
this child, and the LORD has granted me what I
asked of him. So now I give him to the LORD. For
his whole life he will be given over to the LORD."
And he worshiped the LORD there.*

The pastor took Trevor from Dwayne's arms. The
boy went willingly, arms out, chubby cheeks dimpled
in a grin. "It will be the responsibility of every person
in this room to help these young parents raise this child
up right. You are his church family. Take this responsibility as seriously as you've ever taken anything in
your life."

Leila ducked her head and leaned closer to Jesse.
"You did this?"

"God did this. I just took my cue from you and
offered an invitation."

"I'm so happy for them. So happy for Trevor."

"Me too." Jesse slid his hand over hers. "You understand you played a role in this. In what's happening
right now."

"I didn't do anything."

"You reached out to them. You invited them in."

"Nee."

"Jah."

Pastor Walt began to pray aloud.

Leila closed her eyes and lifted her own prayer for Trevor, Dwayne, Rory, and their unborn baby as the words of the minister rumbled over her. The prayer ended and a group of teenagers shuffled to the front of the sanctuary and picked up their guitars. Seconds later the notes of "Away in a Manger" floated in the air. The congregation stood, their voices mingling as they sang the familiar words. The notes died away. Chatter filled the air. People hugged and shrugged on coats, conversations filled with plans for celebrating and food and gifts yet to be exchanged.

It was a world different from Leila's, yet the same. She had played a small part in this evening. She'd been blessed to witness it.

"Thank you," she whispered to Jesse, "for bringing me. I'm honored to be here for this."

His face etched with trepidation, Jesse took her hand and squeezed. He leaned down until his breath warmed her cheek. He cleared his throat. "Stay with me. Love me. Marry me." His voice was hoarse and ragged. "Join me in this adventure. There are so many Rorys and Trevors out there. Walk this walk with me."

Her heart hammering against her rib cage, Leila stared at his face, so filled with longing and hope. Surely the entire room could hear her heart pound. Her world shrank until it became this room, and then this man. Only him. No other. She forced herself to break from his gaze. No one seemed to notice their little drama. They were busy congratulating Rory and Dwayne.

The happiness on Rory's face lighted the room, brilliant and all encompassing. Her baby boy crawled toward the beautiful, bright poinsettias. His chubby face scrunched up in a grin. "Ma Ma Ma Ma." Was he talking or simply babbling? "Da Da Da."

Momma and Daddy?

Dwayne strode after the child, scooped him up, and held him high in the air. Trevor giggled, a sound that made Leila want to giggle with him in the sheer happiness of it all.

"We can have that. Someday." Jesse's grip on her hand tightened. "Please. Say yes."

Her entire body trembled. Joy, like musical notes, cascaded through her. She could no more say no than she could live without breathing. When the lump in her throat eased, she locked gazes with Jesse. "Jah."

"Did you say yes?" Jesse's voice rose. He threw his arms around her so hard, the breath left her body. "You just said yes, didn't you?"

"I did. I said yes." His hug eased and she could breathe again. "Do you want me to take it back?"

"No, no, no." Jesse stuck both hands in the air, palms wide. "Woo-hoo! Hey, folks, she said yes, she said yes. We're getting married!"

Silence descended on the crowd. Colton stopped in the middle of donning his coat. Tiffany's hand, poised to knot a scarf around her neck, halted. Everyone stared. Then Rory screeched and fist bumped Dwayne. "I knew it. I knew it. Woot!"

Whoops filled the air, followed by applause that grew and expanded, the sound bouncing off the walls amid a chorus of congratulations. Folks began to file by, many people Leila had never met, to offer their best wishes. Each man shook her hand. The women hugged her. They offered help with the wedding and future evenings of child care. As if they'd known her their entire lives.

Jesse introduced the pastor to her simply as Walter. When he smiled, his craggy face lit up. "Come see me. We'll want to do some talking before you exchange your vows."

"We will." The words came out in a whisper.

"I know it must be a bit overwhelming." He squeezed her hand and nodded, his expression so kind Leila wanted to hug him. "Bless you, young lady. If you have any questions about anything, you can find me right here most days. See you soon."

Leila barely had time to offer her thanks before Colton and Tiffany were upon her. They offered high fives. "I knew the minute I laid eyes on you that you were the one for Jesse," Tiffany said, her expression smug. "I just wish Colton would hurry up and pop the question to me. He's been carrying around a ring for like two months."

How Tiffany knew this, Leila had no idea. "He'll ask when the time is right."

Tiffany waggled three fingers in the air and veered toward the door. "Reception at my house. Hot chocolate and cookies. Come on over."

Where else could she go now that she'd said yes? Yes to a new life without any thought as to where she would live until she and Jesse could properly wed. Not at home. Then where?

Rory hugged them both. "I'll be providing you with lots of marital advice, not to worry." She gave Leila an extra squeeze. "And I'll be there to step in when your family doesn't. You can always stay with me until the big day."

"Thank you. You're a good friend."

"Not as good as you are." Rory scooped up Trevor. "See you at the reception."

Leila swallowed her tears. She wouldn't think about that right now. She'd give herself a few minutes of joyful anticipation before venturing into that dark place of consequence and regret. Hand in hand, she and Jesse left the church. The streetlights cast a harsh glow on the cars that lined the curb, including the van. A figure leaned against it.

Jesse's hand tightened on hers. "Will's here."

CHAPTER 40

Leila breathed, all the earlier anticipation and relieved joy washing away in a recriminating flood of guilt tinged with sadness but no regret. Will leaned against the Planks' van, parked haphazardly at the curb in front of the church. His arms were crossed over a package held close to his chest. His head tilted down so his hat covered his face. He looked cold and lonely.

"Let me talk to him alone." Leila tugged her hand from Jesse's. "He deserves to hear it from me. Me alone."

"Leila—"

"Just give me a minute. Please."

Jesse melted back into the crowd, leaving her to go to Will on feet that wanted to run away but instead plodded forward. "What are you doing here? Did you follow me here?"

"That's your question?" He lifted his head and straightened, his features pale, his cheeks dark and hollow in the glare of the streetlights. "You're attending a church service in town on Christmas Eve and you want to know how I found you? Fine, I'll tell you. Rebekah told me you left in the Planks' van. I put two and two together."

"How did you get here?"

"I hitchhiked. It was faster than a buggy."

They never hitchhiked. A cardinal rule in a prison community. "I'm sorry. I'm truly sorry."

"I had to deliver my Christmas present." He held out the package wrapped in plain brown paper. Leila found she couldn't raise her hand to take it. He shook his head and gave an exasperated sigh. "Go on. Take it."

"You shouldn't have."

"You need this gift. You need to study it."

She forced her arms to obey her commands. The package was solid and heavy in her hands.

"Open it."

"Now? Here?"

"Open it."

The command in his voice startled her. He sounded like his Uncle Leroy. "You don't have to yell at me."

"I'm not yelling." His voice subsided. "I'm not yelling. Please open it."

She ripped the paper off with shaking fingers. The Holy Bible. In English and in German. Its heft made her arms ache. "Danki."

"Maybe you'll learn something there. Maybe it will help you figure out some things."

"Is that what you've been doing?"

"Jah." He rubbed his hands together and blew on them, his breath steaming in the cold night. "So far it hasn't helped, but I keep trying."

"We all keep trying."

"You've made your choice, then?"

"I have." She hugged his gift to her chest. Her heart ached with the pain she couldn't stop from causing him. "It almost seems as if it was made for me. A long time ago."

"You danced with me. You walked with me."

She would never forget those moments. She would treasure them, even as she treasured the memories of her childhood back in Tennessee with Deborah and Rebekah and Daed and the others. She would miss them beyond measure. "I tried so hard. I wanted it to be you."

Having Will as a husband would be easy. It would be simple. Plain. And she could have her family near her for the rest of her life. Yet here she stood, promised to another.

"I know you did." Will studied his boots. He cleared his throat. "It shouldn't be so hard, I reckon."

"That's what I'm thinking." She tugged her shawl tight around her shoulders against a brisk northern wind, but it wasn't the night air that made her tremble with cold. "I never intended for any of this to happen, but it did."

"You'll lose everything."

It would look that way to Will and to the entire community. "I'll gain everything."

"You sound like Jesse." Bitterness rasped in his voice. "You've drunk the same cup of pride and arrogance."

"Something happened tonight. Something special. I helped make it happen. I know I can make a difference in people's lives. I want that."

"Your absence from your home will make a difference in your family's life. From now until the day they die."

If he'd driven the arrow into her chest with his bare hands, it couldn't have hurt more. "I know."

He met her gaze. Tears glistened on his cheeks. She raised a hand. His head jerked back. "Your mother has been through a lot."

They all had. "I know, and it breaks my heart to hurt her this way."

"And this is more important? He's more important?"

"The two together are." She struggled with words that wouldn't wound him more. "You're a good man—"

"Don't." He held up his hand. "Don't try to make me feel better. That's not your place. I'll be fine. I forgive you."

She had no doubt he meant it. He would say the words until they were true. As would every member of her family. They would forgive, the fundamental building block of their faith. If God could forgive their every sin, how could they not forgive those who sinned against them? "Danki. That means so much to me. I never meant for any of this to happen."

"It doesn't have to happen. It's not too late. My family has already started packing. They'll be leaving right after the new year, but I'm staying. One way or another." He shoved his hat down on his forehead. "I waited here because I wanted to give you one more chance to make the right choice. To stay with your family and your community who loves you. To choose me. To be with me. If you change your mind, I'll be there if you ever need me."

"I appreciate everything you're saying. I wish I could feel about you the way you feel about me, but I love another."

"Enough to give up everything?"

"Enough to see that I have everything to gain."

"Then I'll go."

"I'll talk to Leroy tomorrow."

"Nee. You'd best stay in town from now on. I'll tell your mudder and Mordecai. And Leroy."

The cold intensified. A shiver ran through her. The skin on her hands felt brittle. Her bones might break and she would shatter into a heap on the hard ground. "I want to say good-bye to my family."

"For now, it's best you write to them. They deserve to hear from you. Whatever happens beyond that is up to Onkel Leroy. And remember, you can always, always come home. We will always take you back. Never forget that." Will's hand came up as if he would touch her. But he didn't. "You know what Onkel Leroy would say? He would say you weren't in Gott's plan for me. Who am I to think I know better than Gott?"

She willed the lump in her throat to ease enough to assure him. "He does have a plan for you. You'll see."

His smile held no malice or bitterness. "I will. You can count on that."

Leila couldn't be sure if those words were for her or for himself. He ambled away, his stride somehow off kilter as if he was too exhausted to walk a straight line. She couldn't bear it. "Let Colton give you a ride home. Please. It's not safe to hitchhike, especially this time of night."

Will turned, lifting the collar of his jacket around his neck as he did. "Colton Wise is how this whole thing started. Better I should walk over to the Stop and Shop and use the phone. Abe Cramer stays up all night watching movies and doing crossword puzzles. He'll give me a ride."

Ignoring the first icy drops of sleet that splattered her face, she watched him walk away, his shadow bobbing in the streetlights, until he disappeared from sight, taking with him a life that had become a distant memory in a few scant moments.

A sob burbled up inside of her, but she refused to let a single tear fall. She closed her eyes. *Gott, be with him. Guide and protect him. Give him a gut fraa to love and cherish, who will bear him kinner and give him the comfort and care he deserves. Ease Mudder's pain. Ease my family's pain. Help me find a way so they aren't punished by my decision. Gott, I pray.*

Fingers squeezed her shoulder. She turned. Jesse stood behind her, his face full of worry and a caring so acute it warmed her from her frozen nose to her icy toes. She managed a watery smile. "He's gone."

Jesse took the Bible from her hands and smoothed his long fingers over the leather cover. "A parting gift. Nice. He's a good man, my cousin Will is."

Jesse had lost so much. Yet here he stood, confident of their future together. Leila breathed a silent prayer of thanksgiving. Having Jesse as her partner in this life would encompass an adventure with ups and downs and bumps along the way, but it would also mean a life filled with love. Jesse's love. God's love. "He said I can't go back home now. I don't have anywhere to stay. Tonight, I mean. Rory said I could stay with her if . . . I don't know if she meant—"

"Don't worry. You'll stay with Tiffany tonight and we'll work the rest out tomorrow. She loves having slumber parties."

A slumber party with an Englisch girl she barely knew. The shifting landscape made Leila dizzy. "This is it, then. I'm really doing this?"

"We'll figure it out together."

"I hope so, because you just told the whole world we're getting married."

"Not the whole world. Just a few good people."

Jesse slipped his arms around her waist and drew her close. The feel of his breath on her neck sent heat rushing through her. She raised her face to his. He felt so solid, an immovable object even as everything—time, the world, the questions without answers—rushed around her, threatening to crush her in an avalanche of change. She could cling to this man, knowing he himself clung to God. They had their Rock and their salvation.

His lips sought hers in a sweet, lingering kiss that reminded her of sunshine and the smell of hay and bright-yellow sunflowers. He tasted like mint and his five o'clock shadow tickled her cheeks. When she thought she would die from lack of breath, he released her. The wondering, incredulous look on his face sent her back for more. She couldn't seem to slake her thirst for him.

"Hey, you two lovebirds, you're gonna freeze to death." Pastor Walt's deep, genial voice floated from the porch where he locked the front door with an oversized key. "Go home."

Leila giggled and pulled away from Jesse. From the look on his face, he was thinking the same thing she was. They didn't have to worry about where they would spend the rest of their days. They were already home.

EPILOGUE

Ties served no purpose other than to aggravate a man. Jesse took a deep breath and exhaled. The butterflies in his stomach continued their kamikaze diving routine. His palms were sweaty and the collar of his white cotton shirt strangled him. One of the things he definitely didn't like about not being Plain anymore: the tie. From figuring out what color to buy to getting the knot right.

Another deep breath. Then another. He leaned into Leila, who peered out a narrow opening in the doorway that led to the sanctuary. Her body, heavy with child, made it hard for him to see anything. "Who's out there? Anybody?"

She giggled, the soft sound like musical notes that always managed to make him feel at peace. She'd never looked prettier than today in her soft blue dress, her hair pulled back in a neat bun, her cheeks pink from the heat, baby weight, and excitement. "Are you kidding? Rory and her family are taking up an entire row. Everybody wants to hear your first sermon."

Not everyone.

Leila put her arm around his waist and squeezed.

Her sweet scent of Dove soap wafted around him, easing the sting of that thought. "You know what I mean."

"I do." He smoothed back his unruly hair without effect. Nobody came to see what he looked like. Only to hear what he said. "It's not a sermon. I'm not preaching. I'm sharing a message."

"Whatever you call it, you'll be fine. Let God guide you and you can't go wrong."

"I guess I'd better get out there."

Leila planted a kiss on his cheek, her lips soft and warm on his skin. "I'll be right up front. Rory saved me a seat."

He grabbed her hand before she could slip through the door. "Are you sure this is what you want? You haven't changed your mind?"

"You're thinking about that right now?"

"I can't help it. This is an irrevocable step on a path I've chosen."

"Nee, this is irrevocable." She smoothed her hands over her belly. "We committed to each other and to this family, you and I. We are family. Those people out there are our family."

A bittersweet smile slipped across her face. "Do I wish our baby would know your mudder and mine, your daed and Mordecai? I do. But that's not within our control. I believe we're following the path God laid out for us. Don't you?"

"I do." The words echoed in his head, reminding him of his vows before her and God. "But I will keep praying for reconciliation."

"Me too." She smiled. "And I'll pray you don't stutter

or lose your place in your sermon. I mean, your message. Now quit procrastinating and get out there!"

"My prayer companion."

"Always." She had spent the previous evening praying with him for God's will for his first message as an associate lay pastor filling in for Pastor Walter, who was taking a much-needed vacation. "They're family. Their hearts are open to your message."

Leila was a wise woman for her age. Jesse had learned that in the year since they'd married. Pastor Walt had done the honors, with Matthew and Colton serving as his best men while Rory had stood with Leila. It wasn't a Plain ceremony, but it came close. No flowers or music, just vows taken in God's house followed by a small reception at Colton's. No honeymoon trip, just unpacking their sparse belongings in a one-bedroom duplex down the street from Matthew's trailer park.

It served as one of the best days of his life. With so many more to come. Studying together every night for their high school diploma equivalency tests. Leila grilling him with questions for tests after he started classes at Coastal Bend College. Good memories with more to come.

Like the day he came home to find her waiting for him with news that fairly burst from her lips. They were having a baby. They'd begun their lives together with almost nothing to their names. Even now, with both of them working, they scraped by to pay rent and utilities and put food on the table. He'd never been happier. How they would make ends meet with a new baby, only God knew. But He did know. Jesse had faith in that.

Today was the next step. At least it would be if he could get his feet to cooperate. He forced himself to stride through the door and across the seemingly endless expanse of threadbare carpet to the front, where he stood before four dozen rows of straight-back chairs with brown padded seats, one aisle down the middle, six chairs on each side. Every chair was full. The smell of candles burning and a bouquet of floral scents born of a dozen or more ladies' perfumes filled the air. He fought the urge to sneeze. The tiny sanctuary went silent when he stepped behind the pulpit and laid his Bible on it.

"Welcome. Please rise for the singing of the first hymn." He nodded to Jack and Ricky. The two boys strummed their guitars and the sweet notes of "Blessed Be His Name" filled the room, mingling with the voices of the congregation. The singing spiraled toward the heavens in a beautiful act of worship made all the more awesome by the flat notes and occasional misspoken lyrics despite the words projected on a big screen behind Jesse.

Every note lifted him up. Every note reminded him God used him as a vessel. God filled him up and waited for the words to spill out and cover others in His grace and His glory.

The notes died away and Jesse lifted his gaze to the congregation before him, with their expectant expressions and their freshly scrubbed faces and Sunday-go-to-meeting outfits. Rory smiled up at him, her arms wrapped around her chubby baby daughter, Sophia, who slept—thankfully. The girl had some powerful lungs.

Trevor wiggled in his seat and Rory elbowed him, her gaze never leaving Jesse's face.

Jesse cleared his throat. "The lesson today comes from Isaiah—"

"Oh, oh, oh no!" Leila stood, then sank back onto her chair. She bent forward, her hands rubbing her swollen belly. "I'm so sorry, I'm sorry."

She stood again. "I'm sorry, everyone, but I think I'm going to have to steal your associate pastor away."

Jesse froze, his message notes still in his hand. "Why? What's . . . ?"

"It's time."

Her meaning sank in. "It's time. It's time!"

The notes fell to the floor. He stumbled across the room and grabbed her arm. "Sorry, folks. I'll get back to you on Isaiah. We're having a baby."

Everyone stood and clapped. Cheers echoed around him. Shouts of joy and encouragement. Their church family cheered them on as they rushed down the aisle to the double doors.

"I'll pull my van from the parking lot to the front curb," Matthew shouted as he trotted ahead of them. "We can pick up her bag later."

This body of Christ had become his family. This baby would have a church full of family.

"We're right behind you," Rory called. "I can't wait to see that new baby."

"I'll finish out the service," Colton promised. "Don't worry about a thing."

Jesse wasn't worried. God's promise. God's timing. God's grace.

"If it's a girl, I think we should name her Grace." He helped Leila down the two steps in front of the church and guided her along the sidewalk. Panting, she paused and gasped. He wrapped his arm around her, worried she might sink to the ground. "Are you okay?"

"Fine. This baby is in a hurry to get here, that's all." She started moving again. "And if it's a boy?"

"Emmanuel."

"God is with us?" She smiled through her pain. "He is, isn't He?"

"Always."

"And I will always be with you." She stretched up and kissed him. "That's a promise."

He kissed her right back, his hands moving to her face. He cupped her cheeks and stared at her eyes, bright with tears and expectation and joy. "I love you."

"I love you too."

"No regrets."

"No regrets."

"Now let's get moving before we have this baby in Matthew Plank's company van."

Together, they hurried to meet their future.

DISCUSSION QUESTIONS

1. What do you think of Will's decision to honor the promise he made to Jesse not to tell his secret, even to Leila, even though he knew Leila might end up getting hurt?

2. Most Amish districts don't allow Sunday school or Bible study groups. How do you feel about their assertion that individual interpretation of the Scriptures leads to division and confusion in a church?

3. The Amish believe in keeping themselves apart from the world. Do you think Leila's decisions were affected by the time she spent at the movies, working at the day care, and in Rory's company? Had she stayed at home, do you think her ultimate decision would have been different? Why?

4. Matthew and his wife were shunned because they chose to leave the Amish church after baptism. The Amish see this as a form of tough love designed to help bring the wayward member back to their ways. How would you feel about not being able to talk to a family member or being shunned yourself? Is this practice in conflict with the Amish belief in forgiveness?

5. How do you feel about Jesse's decision to leave his family so he can answer his calling to be a minister? Have you ever been called to give up something important in your life in order to serve God?

6. Mainstream media often portrays teenagers today as self-absorbed, lazy, and not interested in service. Can you cite examples in your life of teenagers who do what Tiffany and Colton do?

7. Is it possible to mingle in society and maintain your godly principles? Do you find it hard sometimes not to fall into worldly ways even though you know it's not what God wants? How do you fight that temptation?

8. Is there room for both kinds of men—Will and Jesse—in the body of Christ? The one who shows by example and the one who is the fisher of men? Can they work together toward the same end of winning the lost and making disciples?

ACKNOWLEDGMENTS

The Bishop's Son was not an easy book to write for many reasons. I know not everyone will agree with the premise or the conclusions drawn, but I hope everyone will see the need to stand together as Christians who may live our faith a little differently but who all worship the same one, true God. It's not for us to judge, but to love our neighbors as we love ourselves. My thanks to my editor, Becky Monds, for her thoughtful insight and feedback, for her encouragement and enthusiasm. As always, I'm thankful to my agent, Mary Sue Seymour for pushing me down this road even when she had to drag me kicking and screaming. I'm deeply appreciative of Zondervan and HarperCollins Christian Publishing for taking a chance on something a little different with the Amish of Bee County series and standing by it. As always, I can't believe how blessed I am: to the love of my life, Tim Irvin, thank you for putting up with me, for taking care of me, for helping me put one foot in front of the other when that simple act seemed impossible. Love to my kids, Erin and Nicholas, and their special someones. I thank God for the blessing of grandkids who delight and remind us of innocent joy and enthusiasm for simple things—love you Carson and Brooklyn. Thank you to my Lord and Savior for making all of this possible. Let us each in our own way go about winning the lost and making disciples so that no one has to live without the glorious, redeeming light of His love.

Read more Kelly Irvin in the Every Amish Season series!

ABOUT THE AUTHOR

Kelly Irvin is the bestselling author of the Every Amish Season and Amish of Bee County series. *The Beekeeper's Son* received a starred review from *Publishers Weekly*, who called it a "beautifully woven masterpiece." The two-time Carol Award finalist is a former newspaper reporter and retired public relations professional. Kelly lives in Texas with her husband, photographer Tim Irvin. They have two children, three grandchildren, and two cats. In her spare time, she likes to read books by her favorite authors.

Visit her online at KellyIrvin.com
Instagram: kelly_irvin
Facebook: Kelly.Irvin.Author
Twitter: @Kelly_S_Irvin